Wilbur Smith was born in Central Africa in 1933. He was educated at Michaelhouse and Rhodes University.

He became a full-time writer in 1964 after the successful publication of *When the Lion Feeds*, and has since written thirty novels, all meticulously researched on his numerous expeditions worldwide. His books are now translated into twenty-six different languages.

He owns a farm and game reserve and has an abiding concern for the peoples and wildlife of his native continent, an interest strongly reflected in his novels.

Also by Wilbur Smith

THE COURTNEYS

When the Lion Feeds
The Sound of Thunder
A Sparrow Falls
Birds of Prey
Monsoon
Blue Horizon

THE COURTNEYS OF AFRICA

The Burning Shore
Power of the Sword
Rage
A Time to Die
Golden Fox

THE BALLANTYNE NOVELS

A Falcon Flies
Men of Men
The Angels Weep
The Leopard Hunts in Darkness

Also

The Dark of the Sun
Shout at the Devil
Gold Mine
The Diamond Hunters
The Sunbird
Eagle in the Sky
The Eye of the Tiger
Cry Wolf
Hungry as the Sea
Wild Justice
Elephant Song
River God
The Seventh Scroll
Warlock

WILBUR SMITH

POWER OF THE SWORD
&
THE
DIAMOND
HUNTERS

PAN BOOKS

Power of the Sword first published 1986 by William Heinemann.
First published in paperback 1987 by Pan Books.
The Diamond Hunters first published 1971 by William Heinemann.
First published in paperback 1973 by Pan Books.

This omnibus first published 2006 by Pan Books
an imprint of Pan Macmillan Ltd
Pan Macmillan, 20 New Wharf Road, London N1 9RR
Basingstoke and Oxford
Associated companies throughout the world
www.panmacmillan.com

ISBN-13: 978-0-330-44679-2
ISBN-10: 0-330-44679-7

1 3 5 7 9 8 6 4 2

A CIP catalogue record for this book is available from
the British Library.

Typeset by SetSystems Ltd, Saffron Walden, Essex
Printed and bound in Great Britain by
Mackays of Chatham plc, Chatham, Kent

POWER OF THE SWORD

I dedicate this book
to my wife, Danielle

'If I would have given way to an
arbitrary way, for to have all
Laws chang'd according to the Power
of the Sword, I needed not to have
come here.'

King Charles I of England.
Speech on the scaffold, 30 January
1649.

The fog smothered the ocean, muting all colour and sound. It undulated and seethed as the first eddy of the morning breeze washed in towards the land. The trawler lay in the fog three miles offshore on the edge of the current line, where the vast upwellings from the oceanic depths, rich in life-bringing plankton, met the gentle inshore waters in a line of darker green.

Lothar De La Rey stood in the wheelhouse and leaned on the spoked wooden wheel as he peered out into the fog. He loved these quiet charged minutes of waiting in the dawn. He could feel the electric tingle starting in his blood, the lust of the huntsman that had sustained him countless times before, an addiction as powerful as opium or strong spirits.

Casting back in his mind he remembered that soft pink dawn creeping stealthily over the Magersfontein Hills as he lay against the parapets of the trenches and waited for the lines of Highland infantry to come in out of the darkness, to march with kilts swinging and bonnet ribbons fluttering onto their waiting Mausers, and his skin prickled with gooseflesh at the memory.

There had been a hundred other dawns since then, waiting like this to go out against great game – shaggy maned Kalahari lion, scabby old buffalo with heads of armoured horn, sagacious grey elephant with wrinkled hides and precious teeth of long ivory, but now the game was smaller than any other and yet in its multitudes as vast as the ocean from which it came.

His train of thought was interrupted as the boy came down the open deck from the galley. He was barefoot and

1

his legs were long and brown and strong. He was almost as tall as a grown man, so he was forced to stoop through the wheelhouse door balancing a steaming tin mug of coffee in each hand.

'Sugar?' Lothar asked.

'Four spoons, Pa.' The boy grinned back at him.

The fog had condensed in dew droplets on his long eyelashes, and he blinked them away like a sleepy cat. Though his curling blond head was bleached to streaks of platinum by the sun, his eyebrows and lashes were dense and black; they framed and emphasized his amber-coloured eyes.

'Wild fish today.' Lothar crossed the fingers of his right hand in his trouser pocket to ward off the ill luck of having said it aloud. 'We need it,' he thought. 'To survive we need good wild fish.'

Five years previously he had succumbed once more to the call of the hunter's horn, to the lure of the chase and the wilds. He had sold out the prosperous road and railway construction company which he had painstakingly built up, taken everything he could borrow and gambled it all.

He had known the limitless treasures that the cold green waters of the Benguela Current hid. He had glimpsed them first during those chaotic final days of the Great War when he was making his last stand against the hated English and their traitorous puppet Jan Smuts at the head of his army of the Union of South Africa.

From a secret supply base among the tall desert dunes that flanked the South Atlantic, Lothar had refuelled and armed the German U-boats that were scourging the British mercantile fleets, and while he waited out those dreary days at the edge of the ocean for the submarines to come, he had seen the very ocean moved by its own limitless bounty. It was there merely for the taking, and in the years that followed that ignoble peace at Versailles he made his plans while he laboured in the dust and the heat, blasting and cleaving the mountain passes or driving his roads straight across the shimmering plains. He had saved and planned and schemed for this taking.

The boats he had found in Portugal, sardine trawlers, neglected and rotten. There he had found Da Silva also, old and wise in the ways of the sea. Between them they had repaired and re-equipped the four ancient trawlers and then with skeleton crews had sailed them southwards down the length of the African continent.

The canning factory he had found in California, sited there to exploit the tuna shoals by a company which had overestimated their abundance and underestimated the costs of catching these elusive unpredictable 'chicken of the sea'. Lothar had purchased the factory for a small fraction of its original cost and shipped it out to Africa in its entirety. He had re-erected it on the compacted desert sands alongside the ruined and abandoned whaling station which had given the desolate bay its name of Walvis Bay.

For the first three seasons he and old Da Silva had found wild fish, and they had reaped the endless shoals until Lothar had paid off the loans that had fettered him. He had immediately ordered new boats to replace the decrepit Portuguese trawlers which had reached the end of their useful lives, and in so doing had plunged himself more deeply into debt than he had been at the outset of the venture.

Then the fish had gone. For no reason that they could divine, the huge shoals of pilchards had disappeared, only tiny scattered pockets remaining. While they searched futilely, running out to sea a hundred miles and more, scouring the long desert coastline far beyond economic range from the canning factory, the months marched past remorselessly, each one bringing a note for accrued interest that Lothar could not meet, and the running costs of factory and boats piled up so that he had to plead and beg for further loans.

Two years with no fish. Then dramatically, just when Lothar knew himself beaten, there had been some subtle shift in the ocean current or a change in the prevailing wind and the fish had returned, good wild fish, rising thick as new grass in each dawn.

'Let it last,' Lothar prayed silently, as he stared out into the fog. 'Please God, let it last.' Another three months, that was all he needed, just another three short months and he would pay it off and be free again.

'She's lifting,' the boy said, and Lothar blinked and shook his head slightly, returning from his memories.

The fog was opening like a theatre curtain, and the scene it revealed was melodramatic and stagey, seemingly too riotously coloured to be natural as the dawn fumed and glowed like a display of fireworks, orange and gold and green where it sparkled on the ocean, turning the twisting columns of fog the colour of blood and roses so that the very waters seemed to burn with unearthly fires. The silence enhanced the magical show, a silence heavy and lucid as crystal so that it seemed they had been struck deaf, as though all their other senses had been taken from them and concentrated in their vision as they stared in wonder.

Then the sun struck through, a brilliant beam of solid golden light through the roof of the fogbank. It played across the surface, so that the current line was starkly lit. The inshore water was smudged with cloudy blue, as calm and smooth as oil. The line where it met the upwelling of the true oceanic current was straight and sharp as the edge of a knifeblade, and beyond it the surface was dark and ruffled as green velvet stroked against the pile.

'*Daar spring hy!*' Da Silva yelled from the foredeck, pointed out to the line of dark water 'There he jumps!'

As the low sun struck the water a single fish jumped. It was just a little longer than a man's hand, a tiny sliver of burnished silver.

'Start up!' Lothar's voice was husky with excitement,

and the boy flung his mug onto the chart-table, the last few drops of coffee splashing, and dived down the ladderway to the engine-room below.

Lothar flipped on the switches and set the throttle as below him the boy stooped to the crankhandle.

'Swing it!' Lothar shouted down and the boy braced himself and heaved against the compression of all four cylinders. He was not quite thirteen years old but already he was almost as strong as a man, and there was bulging muscle in his back as he worked.

'Now!' Lothar closed the valves, and the engine, still warm from the run out from the harbour, fired and caught and roared. There was a belch of oily black smoke from the exhaust port in the side of the hull and then she settled to a regular beat.

The boy scrambled up the ladder and shot out onto the deck, racing up into the bows beside Da Silva.

Lothar swung the bows over and they ran down on the current line. The fog blew away, and they saw the other boats. They, too, had been lying quietly in the fogbank, waiting for the first rays of the sun, but now they were running down eagerly on the current line, their wakes cutting long rippling Vs across the placid surface and the bow waves creaming and flashing in the new sunlight. Along each rail the crews craned out to peer ahead, and the jabber of their excited voices carried above the beat of the engines.

From the glassed wheelhouse Lothar had an all-round view over the working areas of the fifty-foot trawler and he made one final check of the preparations. The long net was laid out down the starboard rail, the corkline coiled into meticulous spirals. The dry weight of the net was seven and a half tons, wet it would weigh many times heavier. It was five hundred feet long and in the water hung down from the cork floats like a gauzy curtain seventy feet deep. It had cost Lothar over five thousand pounds, more money than an ordinary fisherman would earn in twenty years of unremitting toil, and each of his other three boats was so equipped. From the stern, secured by a heavy painter, each trawler towed its 'bucky', an eighteen-foot-long clinker-built dinghy.

With one long hard glance, Lothar satisfied himself that all was ready for the throw, and then looked ahead just as another fish jumped. This time it was so close that he could see the dark lateral lines along its gleaming flank, and the colour difference – ethereal green above the line and hard gleaming silver below. Then it plopped back, leaving a dark dimple on the surface.

As though it was a signal, instantly the ocean came alive. The waters turned dark as though suddenly shaded by heavy cloud, but this could was from below, rising up from the depths, and the waters roiled as though a monster moved beneath them.

'Wild fish!' screamed Da Silva, turning his weathered and creased brown face back over his shoulder towards Lothar, and at the same time spreading his arms to take in the sweep of ocean which moved with fish.

A mile wide and so deep that its far edge was hidden in the lingering fogbanks, a single dark shoal lay before them. In all the years as a hunter, Lothar had never seen such an accumulation of life, such a multitude of a single species. Beside this the locusts that could curtain and block off the African noon sun and the flocks of tiny quelea birds whose combined weight broke the boughs from the great trees on which they roosted, were insignificant. Even the crews of the racing trawlers fell silent and stared in awe as the shoal broke the surface and the waters turned white and sparkled like a snow bank; countless millions of tiny scaly bodies caught the sunlight as they were lifted clear of the water by the press of an infinity of their own kind beneath them.

Da Silva was the first to rouse himself. He turned and

...an back down the deck, quick and agile as a youth, pausing only at the door of the wheelhouse. 'Maria, Mother of God, grant we still have a net when this day ends.'

It was a poignant warning and then the old man ran to the stern and scrambled over the gunwale into the trailing dinghy while at his example the rest of the crew roused themselves and hurried to their stations.

'Manfred!' Lothar called his son, and the boy who had stood mesmerized in the bows bobbed his head obediently and ran back to his father.

'Take the wheel.' It was an enormous responsibility for one so young, but Manfred had proved himself so many times before that Lothar felt no misgiving as he ducked out of the wheelhouse. In the bows he signalled without looking over his shoulder and he felt the deck cant beneath his feet as Manfred spun the wheel, following his father's signal to begin a wide circle around the shoal.

'So much fish,' Lothar whispered. As his eyes estimated distance and wind and current, old Da Silva's warning was in the forefront of his calculations: the trawler and its net could handle 150 tons of these nimble silver pilchards, with skill and luck perhaps 200 tons.

Before him lay a shoal of millions of tons of fish. An injudicious throw could fill the net with ten or twenty thousand tons whose weight and momentum could rip the mesh to tatters, might even tear the entire net loose, snapping the main cork line or pulling the bollards from the deck and dragging it down into the depths. Worse still, if the lines and bollards held, the trawler might be pulled over by the weight and capsize. Lothar might lose not only a valuable net but the boat and the lives of his crew and his son as well.

Involuntarily he glanced over his shoulder and Manfred grinned at him through the window of the wheelhouse, his face alight with excitement. With his dark amber eyes glowing and white teeth flashing, he was an image of his mother and Lothar felt a bitter pang before he turned back to work.

Those few moments of inattention had nearly undone Lothar. The trawler was rushing down on the shoal, within moments it would drive over the mass of fish and they would sound; the entire shoal, moving in that mysterious unison as though it were a single organism, would vanish back into the ocean depths. Sharply he signalled the turn away, and the boy responded instantly. The trawler spun on its heel and they bore down the edge of the shoal, keeping fifty feet off, waiting for the opportunity.

Another quick glance around showed Lothar that his other skippers were warily backing off also, daunted by the sheer mass of pilchards they were circling. Swart Hendrick glared across at him, a huge black bull of a man with his bald head shining like a cannonball in the early sunlight. Companion of war and a hundred desperate endeavours, like Lothar he had readily made the transition from land to sea and now was as skilled a fisherman as once he had been a hunter of ivory and of men. Lothar flashed him the underhand cut-out signal for 'caution' and 'danger' and Swart Hendrick laughed soundlessly and waved an acknowledgement.

Gracefully as dancers, the four boats weaved and pirouetted around the massive shoal as the last shreds of the fog dissolved and blew away on the light breeze. The sun cleared the horizon and the distant dunes of the desert glowed like bronze fresh from the forge, a dramatic backdrop to the developing hunt.

Still the massed fish held its compact formation, and Lothar was becoming desperate. They had been on the surface for over an hour now and that was longer than usual. At any moment they might sound and vanish, and not one of his boats had thrown a net. They were thwarted by abundance, beggars in the presence of limitless treasure, and Lothar felt a recklessness rising in him. He had waited too long already.

'Throw, and be damned!' he thought, and signalled Manfred in closer, narrowing his eyes against the glare as they turned into the sun.

Before he could commit himself to folly, he heard Da Silva whistle, and when he looked back the Portuguese was standing on the thwart of the dinghy and gesticulating wildly. Behind them the shoal was beginning to bulge. The solid circular mass was altering shape. Out of it grew a tentacle, a pimple, no, it was more the shape of a head on a thin neck as part of the shoal detached itself from the main body. This was what they had been waiting for.

'Manfred!' Lothar yelled and windmilled his right arm. The boy spun the wheel, and she came around and they went tearing back, aiming the bows at the neck of the shoal like the blade of an executioner's axe.

'Slow down!' Lothar flapped his hand and the trawler checked. Gently she nosed up to the narrow neck of the shoal. The water was so clear that Lothar could see the individual fish, each encapsuled in its rainbow of prismed sunlight, and beneath the dark green bulk of the rest of the shoal as dense as an iceberg.

Delicately Lothar and Manfred eased the trawler's bows into the living mass, the propeller barely turning so as not to alarm it and force it to sound. The narrow neck split before the bows, and the small pocket of fish that was the bulge detached itself. Like a sheepdog with its flock, Lothar worked them clear, backing and turning and easing ahead as Manfred followed his hand signals.

'Still too much!' Lothar muttered to himself. They had separated a minute portion of the shoal from the main body, but Lothar estimated it was still well over a thousand tons – even more depending on the depth of fish beneath that he could only guess at.

It was a risk, a high risk. From the corner of his eye he

9

could see Da Silva agitatedly signalling caution, and now he whistled, squeaking with agitation. The old man was afraid of this much fish and Lothar grinned; his yellow eyes narrowed and glittered like polished topaz as he signalled Manfred up to throwing speed and deliberately turned his back on the old man.

At five knots he checked Manfred and brought him around in a tight turn, forcing the pocket of fish to bunch up in the centre of the circle, and then as they came around the second time and the trawler passed downwind of the shoal, Lothar spun to face the stern and cupped both hands to his mouth.

'*Los!*' he bellowed. 'Throw her loose!'

The black Herero crewman standing on the stern flipped the slippery knot that held the painter of the dinghy and threw it overboard. The little wooden dinghy, with Da Silva clinging to the gunwale and still howling protests, fell away behind them, bobbing in their wake, and it pulled the end of the heavy brown net over the side with it.

As the trawler steamed in its circle about the shoal, the coarse brown mesh rasped and hissed out over the wooden rail, the cork line uncoiled like a python and streamed over-side, an umbilical cord between the trawler and the dinghy. Coming around across the wind, the line of corks, evenly spaced as beads on a string, formed a circle around the dense dark shoal and now the dinghy with Da Silva slumped in resignation was dead ahead.

Manfred balanced the wheel against the drag of the great net, making minute adjustments as he laid the trawler alongside the rocking dinghy and shut the throttle as they touched lightly. Now the net was closed, hemming in the shoal, and Da Silva scrambled up the side of the trawler with the ends of the heavy three-inch manila lines over his shoulder.

'You'll lose your net,' he howled at Lothar. 'Only a crazy man would close the purse on this shoal – they'll run away with your net. St Anthony and the blessed St Mark are my witnesses—' But under Lothar's terse direction the Herero crewmen were already into the routine of net recovery. Two of them lifted the main cork line off Da Silva's shoulders and made it fast, while another was helping Lothar lead the purse line to the main winch.

'It's my net, and my fish,' Lothar grunted at him as he started the winch with a clattering roar. 'Get the bucky hooked on!'

The net was hanging seventy feet deep into the clear green water, but the bottom was open. The first and urgent task was to close it before the shoal discovered this escape. Crouched over the winch, the muscles in his bare arms knotting and bunching beneath the tanned brown skin, Lothar was swinging his shoulders rhythmically as he brought the purse line in hand over hand around the revolving drum of the winch. The purse line running through the steel rings around the bottom of the net was closing the mouth like the drawstring of a monstrous tobacco pouch.

In the wheelhouse Manfred was using delicate touches of forward and reverse to manoeuvre the stern of the trawler away from the net and prevent it fouling the propeller, while old Da Silva had worked the dinghy out to the far side of the cork line and hooked onto it to provide extra buoyancy for the critical moment when the oversized shoal realized that it was trapped and began to panic. Working swiftly, Lothar hauled in the heavy purse line until at last the bunch of steel rings came in glistening and streaming over the side. The net was closed, the shoal was in the bag.

With sweat running down his cheeks and soaking his shirt, Lothar leaned against the gunwale so winded that he could not speak. His long silver-white hair, heavy with sweat, streamed down over his forehead and into his eyes as he gesticulated to Da Silva.

The cork line was laid out in a neat circle on the gentle undulating swells of the cold green Benguela Current, with the bucky hooked onto the side farthest from the trawler. But as Lothar watched it, gasping and heaving for breath, the circle of bobbing corks changed shape, elongating swiftly as the shoal felt the net for the first time and in a concerted rush pushed against it. Then the thrust was reversed as the shoal turned and rushed back, dragging the net and the dinghy with it as though it were a scrap of floating seaweed.

The power of the shoal was as irresistible as Leviathan.

'By God, we've got even more than I reckoned,' Lothar panted. Then, rousing himself, he flicked the wet blond hair from his eyes and ran to the wheelhouse.

The shoal was surging back and forth in the net, tossing the dinghy about lightly on the churning waters, and Lothar felt the deck of the trawler list sharply under him as the mass of fish dragged abruptly on the heavy lines.

'Da Silva was right. They are going crazy,' he whispered, and reached for the handle of the foghorn. He blew three sharp ringing blasts, the request for assistance, and as he ran back onto the deck he saw the other three trawlers turn and race towards him. None of them had as yet plucked up the courage to throw their own nets at the huge shoal.

'Hurry! Damn you, hurry!' Lothar snarled ineffectually at them, and then at his crew, 'All hands to dry up!'

His crew hesitated, hanging back, reluctant to handle that net.

'Move, you black bastards!' Lothar bellowed at them, setting the example by leaping to the gunwale. They had to compress the shoal, pack the tiny fish so closely as to rob them of their strength.

The net was coarse and sharp as barbed wire, but they bent to it in a row, using the roll of the hull in the low swell to work the net in by hand, recovering a few feet with each concerted heave.

Then the shoal surged again, and all the net they had won was ripped from their hands. One of the Herero crew was too slow to let it go and the fingers of his right hand were caught in the coarse mesh. The flesh was stripped off his fingers like a glove, leaving bare white bone and raw flesh. He screamed and clutched the maimed hand to his chest, trying to staunch the spurt of bright blood. It sprayed into his own face and ran down the sweat-polished black skin of his chest and belly and soaked into his breeches.

'Manfred!' Lothar yelled. 'See to him!' and he switched all his attention back to the net. The shoal was sounding, dragging one end of the cork line below the surface, and a small part of the shoal escaped over the top, spreading like dark green smoke across the bright waters.

'Good riddance,' Lothar muttered, but the vast bulk of the shoal was still trapped and the cork line bobbed to the surface. Again the shoal surged downwards, and this time the heavy fifty-foot trawler listed over dangerously so that the crew clutched for handholds, their faces turning ashy grey beneath their dark skin.

Across the circle of cork line the dinghy was dragged over sharply, and it did not have the buoyancy to resist. Green water poured in over the gunwale, swamping it.

'Jump!' Lothar yelled at the old man. 'Get clear of the net!' They both understood the danger.

The previous season one of their crew had fallen into the net. The fish had immediately pushed against him in unison, driving him below the surface, fighting against the resistance of his body in their efforts to escape.

When, hours later, they had at last recovered the corpse from the bottom of the net, they had found that the fish had been forced by their own efforts and the enormous pressures in the depths of the trapped shoal into all the man's body openings. They had thrust down his open mouth into his belly; they had been driven like silver daggers into the eye-sockets, displacing the eyeballs and entering the brain. They had even burst through the threadbare stuff of his breeches and penetrated his anus so that his belly and bowels were stuffed with dead fish and he was bloated like a grotesque balloon. It was a sight none of them would ever forget.

'Get clear of the net!' Lothar screamed again and Da Silva threw himself over the far side of the sinking dinghy just as it was dragged beneath the surface. He splashed frantically as his heavy seaboots began to drag him under.

However, Swart Hendrick was there to rescue him. He laid his trawler neatly alongside the bulging cork line, and two of his crew hauled Da Silva up the side while the others crowded the rail and under Swart Hendrick's direction hooked onto the far side of the net.

'If only the net holds,' Lothar grunted, for the two other trawlers had come up now and fastened onto the cork line. The four big boats formed a circle around the captive shoal and, working in a frenzy, the crewmen stooped over the net and started to 'dry up'.

Foot by foot they hauled up the net, twelve men on each trawler, even Manfred taking his place at his father's shoulder. They grunted and heaved and sweated, fresh blood on their torn hands when the shoal surged and burning agony in their backs and bellies, but slowly, an inch at a time, they subdued the huge shoal, until at last it was 'dried up', and the upper fish were flapping helplessly high and dry on the compacted mass of their fellows, who were drowning and dying in the crush.

'Dip them out!' Lothar shouted, and on each of the trawlers the three dip-men pulled the long-handled dip-nets from the racks over the top of the wheelhouses and dragged them down the deck.

The dip-nets were the same shape as a butterfly-net, or those little hand nets with which children catch shrimps and crabs in rock pools at the seaside. The handles of these nets, however, were thirty feet long and the net purse could

14

scoop up a ton of living fish at a time. At three points around the steel ring that formed the mouth of the net were attached manila lines; these were spliced to the heavier winch line by which the dip-net was lifted and lowered. The foot of the net could be opened or closed by a purse line through a set of smaller rings, exactly the same arrangement as the closure of the great main net.

While the dip-net was manhandled into position, Lothar and Manfred were knocking the covers off the hatch of the hold. Then they hurried to their positions, Lothar on the winch and Manfred holding the end of the purse line of the dip-net. With a squeal and clatter Lothar winched the dip-net high onto the derrick above their heads while the three men on the long handle swung the net outboard over the trapped and struggling shoal. Manfred jerked hard on the purse line, closing the bottom of the dip-net.

Lothar slammed the winch gear into reverse and with another squeal of the pulley block the heavy head of the net dropped into the silver mass of fish. The three dip-men leaned all their weight on the handle, forcing the net deeply into the living porridge of pilchards.

'Coming up!' Lothar yelled and changed the winch into forward gear. The net was dragged upwards through the shoal and burst out filled with a ton of quivering, flapping pilchards. With Manfred grimly hanging onto the purse line, the full net was swung inboard over the gaping hatch of the hold.

'Let go!' Lothar shouted at his son, and Manfred released the purse line. The bottom of the net opened and a ton of pilchards showered down into the open hold. The tiny scales had been rubbed from the bodies of the fish by this rough treatment and now they swirled down over the men on the deck like snowflakes, sparkling in the sunlight with pretty shades of pink and rose and gold.

As the net emptied, Manfred jerked the purse line closed and the dip-men swung the handle outboard, the winch

15

squealed into reverse and the net dropped into the shoal for the whole sequence to be repeated. On each of the other three trawlers the dip-men and winch driver also were hard at work, and every few seconds another ton load of fish, seawater and clouds of translucent scales streaming from it, was swung over the waiting hatches and poured into them.

It was heartbreaking, back-straining work, monotonous and repetitive, and each time the net swung overhead the crew were drenched with icy seawater and covered with scales. As the dip-men faltered with exhaustion, the skippers changed them without breaking the rhythm of swing and lift and drop, spelling the men working on the main net with those on the handle of the dip-net, although Lothar remained at the winch, tall and alert and indefatigable, his white-blond hair, thick with glittering fish scales, shining in the sunlight like a beacon fire.

'Silver threepennies.' He grinned to himself, as the fish showered into the holds on all four of his trawlers. 'Shiny threepenny bits, not fish. We will take in a deckload of tickeys today.' 'Tickey' was the slang for a threepenny coin.

'Deckload!' he bellowed across the diminishing circle of the main net to where Swart Hendrick worked at his own winch, stripped to the waist and glistening like polished ebony.

'Deckload!' he bellowed back at Lothar, revelling in the physical effort which allowed him to flaunt his superior strength in the faces of his crew. Already the holds of the trawlers were brimming full, each of them had over a hundred and fifty tons aboard, and now they were going to deckload.

Again it was a risk. Once loaded, the boats could not be lightened again until they reached harbour and were pumped out into the factory. Deckloading would burden each hull with another hundred tons of dead weight, far over the safe limit. If the weather turned, if the wind switched into the north-west, then the giant sea that would build up rapidly would hammer the overloaded trawlers into the cold green depths.

'The weather will hold,' Lothar assured himself as he toiled at the winch. He was on the crest of a wave; nothing could stop him now. He had taken one fearsome risk and it had paid him with nearly a thousand tons of fish, four deck-loads of fish, worth fifty pounds a ton in profits. Fifty thousand pounds in a single throw. The greatest stroke of fortune of his life. He could have lost his net or his boat or his life – instead he had paid off his debts with one throw of the net.

'By God,' he whispered, as he slaved at the winch, 'nothing can go wrong now, nothing can touch me now. I'm free and clear.'

So with the holds full they began to deckload the trawlers, filling them to the tops of the gunwales with a silver swamp of fish into which the crew sank waist-deep as they dried the net and swung the long handle of the dip.

Over the four trawlers hovered a dense white cloud of seabirds, adding their voracious squawking and screeching to the cacophony of the winches, diving into the purse of the net to gorge themselves until they could eat no more, could not even fly but drifted away on the current, bloated and uncomfortable, feathers started and throats straining to keep down the contents of their swollen crops. At the bows and stern of each trawler stood a man with a sharpened boathook, with which he stabbed and hacked at the big sharks that thrashed at the surface in their efforts to reach the mass of trapped fish. Their razor-sharp triangular fangs could cut through even the tough mesh of the net.

While the birds and sharks gorged, the hulls of the trawlers sank lower and still lower into the water, until at last a little after the sun had nooned even Lothar had to call enough. There was no room for another load; each time they swung one aboard it merely slithered over the side to feed the circling sharks.

Lothar switched off the winch. There was probably another hundred tons of fish still floating in the main net, most of them drowned and crushed. 'Empty the net,' he ordered. 'Let them go! Get the net on board.'

The four trawlers, each of them so low in the water that seawater washed in through the scuppers at each roll, and their speed reduced to an ungainly waddling motion like a string of heavily pregnant ducks, turned towards the land in line astern with Lothar leading them.

Behind them they left an area of almost half a square mile of the ocean carpeted with dead fish, floating silver belly up, as thick as autumn leaves on the forest floor. On top of them drifted thousands of satiated seagulls and beneath them the big sharks swirled and feasted still.

The exhausted crews dragged themselves through the quicksands of still quivering kicking fish that glutted the deck to the forecastle companionway. Below deck they threw themselves still soaked with fish-slime and seawater onto their cramped bunks.

In the wheelhouse Lothar drank two mugs of hot coffee then checked the chronometer above his head.

'Four hours' run back to the factory,' he said. 'Just time for our lessons.'

'Oh, Pa!' the boy pleaded. 'Not today, today is special. Do we have to learn today?'

There was no school at Walvis Bay. The nearest was the German School at Swakopmund, thirty kilometres away. Lother had been both father and mother to the boy from the very day of his birth. He had taken him wet and bloody from the childbed. His mother had never even laid eyes upon him. That had been part of their unnatural bargain. He had reared the boy alone, unaided except for the milk that the brown Nama wetnurses had provided. They had grown so close that Lothar could not bear to be parted from him for a single day. He had even taken over his education rather than send him away.

'No day is that special,' he told Manfred. 'Every day we learn. Muscles don't make a man strong.' He tapped his head. 'This is what makes a man strong. Get the books!'

Manfred rolled his eyes at Da Silva for sympathy but he knew better than to argue further.

'Take the wheel.' Lothar handed over to the old boatman and went to sit beside his son at the small chart-table. 'Not arithmetic.' He shook his head. 'It's English today.'

'I hate English!' Manfred declared vehemently. 'I hate English and I hate the English.'

Lothar nodded. 'Yes,' he agreed. 'The English are our enemies. They have always been and always will be our enemies. That is why we have to arm ourselves with their weapons. That is why we learn the language – so when the time comes we will be able to use it in the battle against them.'

He spoke in English for the first time that day. Manfred started to reply in Afrikaans, the South African Dutch patois that had only obtained recognition as a separate language and been adopted as an official language of the Union of South Africa in 1918, over a year before Manfred was born. Lothar held up his hand to stop him.

'English,' he admonished. 'Speak English only.'

For an hour they worked together, reading aloud from the King James version of the Bible and from a two-month-old copy of the *Cape Times*, and then Lothar set him a page of dictation. The labour in this unfamiliar language made Manfred fidget and frown and nibble his pencil, until at last he could contain himself no longer.

'Tell me about Grandpa, and the oath!' he wheedled his father.

Lothar grinned. 'You're a cunning little monkey, aren't you. Anything to get out of work.'

'Please, Pa—'

19

'I've told you a hundred times.'

'Tell me again. It's a special day.'

Lothar glanced out of the wheelhouse window at the precious silver cargo. The boy was right, it was a very special day. Today he was free and clear of debt, after five long hard years.

'All right.' He nodded. 'I'll tell you again, but in English.' And Manfred shut his exercise book with an enthusiastic snap and leaned across the table, his amber eyes glowing with anticipation.

The story of the great rebellion had been repeated so often that Manfred had it by heart and he corrected any discrepancy or departure from the original, or called his father back if he left out any of the details.

'Well then,' Lothar started, 'when the treacherous English King George V declared war on Kaiser Whilhelm of Germany in 1914, your grandpa and I knew our duty. We kissed your grandmother goodbye—'

'What colour was my grandmother's hair?' Manfred demanded.

'Your grandmother was a beautiful German noblewoman, and her hair was the colour of ripe wheat in the sunlight.'

'Just like mine,' Manfred prompted him.

'Just like yours,' Lothar smiled. 'And Grandpa and I rode out on our warhorses to join old General Maritz and his six hundred heroes on the banks of the Orange river where he was about to go out against old *Slim* Jannie Smuts.' *Slim* was the Afrikaans word for tricky or treacherous, and Manfred nodded avidly.

'Go on, Pa, go on!'

When Lothar reached the description of the first battle in which Jannie Smuts' troops had smashed the rebellion with machine-guns and artillery, the boy's eyes clouded with sorrow.

'But you fought like demons, didn't you, Pa?'

'We fought like madmen, but there were too many of them and they were armed with great cannons and machine-guns. Then your grandpa was hit in the stomach and I put him up on my horse and carried him off the battlefield.' Fat tears glistened in the boy's eyes now as Lothar ended.

'When at last he was dying your grandfather took the old black Bible from the saddle bag on which his head was pillowed, and he made me swear an oath upon the book.'

'I know the oath,' Manfred cut in. 'Let me tell it!'

'What was the oath?' Lothar nodded agreement.

'Grandpa said: "Promise me, my son, with your hand upon the book, promise me that the war with the English will never end."'

'Yes,' Lothar nodded again. 'That was the oath, the solemn oath I made to my father as he lay dying.' He reached out and took the boy's hand and squeezed it hard.

Old Da Silva broke the mood; he coughed and hawked and spat through the wheelhouse window.

'You should be ashamed – filling the child's head with hatred and death,' he said, and Lothar stood up abruptly.

'Guard your mouth, old man,' he warned. 'This is no business of yours.'

'Thank the Holy Virgin,' Da Silva grumbled, 'for that is devil's business indeed.'

Lothar scowled and turned away from him. 'Manfred, that's enough for today. Put the books away.'

He swung out of the wheelhouse and scrambled up onto the roof. As he settled comfortably against the coaming, he took a long black cheroot from his top pocket and bit off the tip. He spat the stub overside and patted his pockets for the matches. The boy stuck his head over the edge of the coaming, hesitated shyly and when his father did not send him away – sometimes he was moody and withdrawn and wanted to be alone – Manfred crept up and sat beside him.

Lothar cupped his hands around the flare of the match and sucked the cheroot smoke down deeply into his lungs and then he held up the match and let the wind extinguish it. He flicked it overboard, and let his arm fall casually over his son's shoulders.

The boy shivered with delight, physical display of affection from his father was so rare, and he pressed closer to him and sat still as he could, barely breathing so as not to disturb or spoil the moment.

The little fleet ran in towards the land, and turned the sharp northern horn of the bay. The seabirds were returning with them, squadrons of yellow-throated gannets in long regular lines skimming low over the cloudy green waters, and the lowering sun gilded them and burned upon the tall bronze dunes that rose like a mountain range behind the tiny insignificant cluster of buildings that stood at the edge of the bay.

'I hope Willem has had enough sense to fire up the boilers,' Lothar murmured. 'We have enough work here to keep the factory busy all night and all tomorrow.'

'We'll never be able to can all this fish,' the boy whispered.

'No, we will have to turn most of it to fish oil and fish meal—' Lothar broke off and stared across the bay. Manfred felt his body stiffen and then, to the boy's dismay, he lifted his arm off his son's shoulders and shaded his eyes.

'The bloody fool,' he growled. With his hunter's vision he had picked out the distant stack of the factory boiler-house. It was smokeless. 'What the hell is he playing at?' Lothar leapt to his feet and balanced easily against the trawler's motion. 'He has let the boilers go cold. It will take five or six hours to refire them and our fish will begin to spoil. Damn him, damn him to hell!' Raging still, Lothar dropped down to the wheelhouse. As he yanked the foghorn to alert the factory, he snapped, 'With the money from the fish I'm going to buy one of Marconi's new-fangled shortwave radio machines so we can talk to the factory while we are at sea; then this sort of thing won't happen.'

He broke off again and stared. 'What the hell is going on!' He snatched the binoculars from the bin next to the control panel and focused them. They were close enough now to see the small crowd at the main doors of the factory. The cutters and packers in their rubber aprons and boots. They should have been at their places in the factory.

'There is Willem.' The factory manager was standing on the end of the long wooden unloading jetty that thrust out into the still waters of the bay on its heavy teak pilings. 'What the hell is he playing at – the boilers cold and everybody hanging about outside?' There were two strangers with Willem, standing one on each side of him. They were dressed in dark civilian suits and they had that self-important, puffed-up look of petty officialdom that Lothar knew and dreaded.

'Tax collectors or other civil servants,' Lothar whispered, and his anger cooled and was replaced with unease. No minion of the government had ever brought him good news.

'Trouble,' he guessed. 'Just now when I have a thousand tons of fish to cook and can—'

Then he noticed the motor cars. They had been screened by the factory building until Da Silva made the turn into the main channel that would bring the trawler up to the off-loading jetty. There were two cars. One was a battered old 'T' model Ford, but the other, even though covered with a pale coating of fine desert dust, was a much grander machine – and Lothar felt his heart trip and his breathing alter.

There could not be two similar vehicles in the whole of Africa. It was an elephantine Daimler, painted daffodil yellow. The last time he had seen it, it had been parked outside the offices of the Courtney Mining and Finance Company in the Main Street of Windhoek.

Lothar had been on his way to discuss an extension of his loans from the company. He had stood on the opposite side of the wide dusty unpaved street and watched as she came down the broad marble steps, flanked by two of her obsequious employees in dark suits and high celluloid collars; one of them had opened the door of the magnificent yellow machine for her and bowed her into the driver's seat while the other had run to take the crank handle. Scorning a chauffeur, she had driven off herself, not even glancing in Lothar's direction, and left him pale and trembling with the conflicting emotions that the mere sight of her had evoked. That had been almost a year before.

Now he roused himself as Da Silva laid the heavily burdened trawler alongside the jetty. They were so low in the water that Manfred had to toss the bow mooring-line up to one of the men on the jetty above him.

'Lothar, these men – they want to speak to you.' Willem called down. He was sweating nervously as he jerked a thumb at the man who flanked him.

'Are you Mr Lothar De La Rey?' the smaller of the two strangers demanded, pushing his dusty fedora hat onto the back of his head and mopping the pale line of skin that was exposed beneath the brim.

'That's right.' Lothar glared up at at him with his clenched fists upon his hips. 'And who the hell are you?'

'Are you the owner of the South West African Canning and Fishing Company?'

'Ja!' Lothar answered him in Afrikaans. 'I am the owner – and what of it?'

'I am the sheriff of the court in Windhoek, and I have here a writ of attachment over all the assets of the company.' The sheriff brandished the document he held.

'They've closed the factory,' Willem called down to Lothar miserably, his moustaches quivering. 'They made me draw the fires on my boilers.'

'You can't do that!' Lothar snarled, and his eyes slitted

24

yellow and fierce as those of an angry leopard. 'I've got a thousand tons of fish to process.'

'Are these the four trawlers registered in the company's name?' the sheriff went on, unperturbed by the outburst, but he unbuttoned his dark jacket and pulled it back as he placed both hands on his hips. A heavy Webley service revolver hung on a leather holster from his belt. He turned his head to watch the other trawlers mooring at their berths on each side of the jetty, then without waiting for Lothar to answer he went on placidly, 'My assistant will place the court seals on them and their cargoes. I must warn you that it will be a criminal offence to remove either the boats or their cargoes.'

'You can't do this to me!' Lothar swarmed up the ladder onto the jetty. His tone was no longer belligerent. 'I have to get my fish processed. Don't you understand? They'll be stinking to the heavens by tomorrow morning—'

'They are not your fish.' The sheriff shook his head. 'They belong to the Courtney Mining and Finance Company.' He gestured to his assistant impatiently. 'Get on with it, man.' And he began to turn away.

'She's here,' Lothar called after him, and the sheriff turned back to face him again.

'She's here,' Lothar repeated. 'That's her car. She has come herself, hasn't she?'

The sheriff dropped his eyes and shrugged, but Willem gobbled a reply.

'Yes, she's here – she's waiting in my office.'

Lothar turned away from the group and strode down the jetty, his heavy oilskin breeches rustling and his fists still bunched as though he were going into a fight.

The agitated crowd of factory hands was waiting for him at the head of the jetty.

'What is happening, *Baas*?' they pleaded. 'They won't let us work. What must we do, *Ou Baas*?'

'Wait!' Lothar ordered them brusquely. 'I will fix this.'

25

'Will we get our pay, *Baas*? We've got children—'

'You'll be paid,' Lothar snapped, 'I promise you that.' It was a promise he could not keep, not until he had sold his fish, and he pushed his way through them and strode around the corner of the factory towards the manager's office.

The Daimler was parked outside the door, and a boy leaned against the front mudguard of the big yellow machine. It was obvious that he was disgruntled and bored. He was perhaps a year older than Manfred but an inch or so shorter and his body was slimmer and neater. He wore a white shirt that had wilted a little in the heat, and his fashionable Oxford bags of grey flannel were dusty and too modish for a boy of his age, but there was an unstudied grace about him, and he was beautiful as a girl, with flawless skin and dark indigo eyes.

Lothar came up short at the sight of him, and before he could stop himself, he said, 'Shasa!'

The boy straightened up quickly and flicked the lock of dark hair off his forehead.

'How do you know my name?' he asked, and despite his tone the dark blue eyes sparkled with interest as he studied Lothar with a level, almost adult self-assurance.

There were a hundred answers Lothar could have given, and they crowded to his lips: 'Once, many years ago, I saved you and your mother from death in the desert . . . I helped wean you, and carried you on the pommel of my saddle when you were a baby . . . I loved you, almost as much as once I loved your mother . . . You are Manfred's brother – you are half brother to my own son. I'd recognize you anywhere, even after all this time.'

But instead he said, 'Shasa is the Bushman word for "Good Water", the most precious substance in the Bushman world.'

'That's right.' Shasa Courtney nodded. The man

interested him. There was a restrained violence and cruelty in him, an impression of untapped strength, and his eyes were strangely light coloured, almost yellow like those of a cat. 'You're right. It's a Bushman name, but my Christian name is Michel. That's French. My mother is French.'

'Where is she?' Lothar demanded, and Shasa glanced at the office door.

'She doesn't want to be disturbed,' he warned, but Lothar De La Rey stepped past him, so closely that Shasa could smell the fish slime on his oilskins and see the small white fish scales stuck to his tanned skin.

'You'd best knock—' Shasa dropped his voice, but Lothar ignored him and flung the door of the office open so that it crashed back on its hinges. He stood in the open door and Shasa could see past him. His mother rose from the straight-backed chair by the window and faced the door.

She was slim as a girl, and the yellow crêpe-de-chine of her dress was draped over her small fashionably flattened breasts and was gathered in a narrow girdle low around her hips. Her narrow-brimmed cloche hat was pulled down, covering the dense dark bush of her hair, and her eyes were huge and almost black.

She looked very young, not much older than her son, until she raised her chin and showed the hard, determined line of her jaw and the corners of her eyes lifted also and those honey-coloured lights burned in their dark depths. Then she was formidable as any man Lothar had ever met.

They stared at each other, assessing the changes that the years had wrought since their last meeting.

'How old is she?' Lothar wondered, and then immediately remembered. 'She was born an hour after midnight on the first day of the century. She is as old as the twentieth century – that's why she was named Centaine. So she's thirty-one years old, and she still looks nineteen, as young as the day I found her, bleeding and dying in the desert with the wounds of lion claws deep in her sweet young flesh.'

'He has aged,' Centaine thought. 'Those silver streaks in the blond, those lines around the mouth and eyes. He'll be over forty now, and he has suffered – but not enough. I am glad I didn't kill him, I'm glad my bullet missed his heart. It would have been too quick. Now he is in my power and he'll begin to learn the true—'

Suddenly, against her will and inclination, she remembered the feel of his golden body over hers, naked and smooth and hard, and her loins clenched and then dissolved so she could feel their hot soft flooding, as hot as the blood that mounted to her cheeks and as hot as her anger against herself and her inability to master that animal corner of her emotions. In all other things she had trained herself like an athlete, but always that unruly streak of sensuality was just beyond her control.

She looked beyond the man in the doorway, and she saw Shasa standing out in the sunlight, her beautiful child, watching her curiously, and she was ashamed and angry to have been caught in that naked and unguarded moment when she was certain that her basest feelings had been on open display.

'Close the door,' she ordered, and her voice was husky and level. 'Come in and close the door.' She turned away and stared out of the window, bringing herself under complete control once more before turning back to face the man she had set herself to destroy.

The door closed and Shasa suffered an acute pang of disappointment. He sensed that something vitally important was taking place. That blond stranger with the cat-yellow eyes who knew his name and its derivation stirred something in him, something dangerous and exciting. Then his mother's reaction, that sudden high colour coming up her throat into her cheeks and something in her eyes that he had never seen before – not guilt, surely? Then uncertainty, which was totally uncharacteristic. She had never been uncertain of anything in the world that Shasa knew of. He wanted desperately to know what was taking place behind that closed door. The walls of the building were of corrugated galvanized iron sheeting.

'If you want to know something, go and find out.' It was one of his mother's adages, and his only compunction was that she might catch him at it as he crossed to the side wall of the office, stepping lightly so that the gravel would not crunch under his feet, and laid his ear against the sun-heated corrugated metal.

Though he strained, he could only hear the murmur of voices. Even when the blond stranger spoke sharply, he could not catch the words, while his mother's voice was low and husky and inaudible.

'The window,' he thought, and moved quickly to the corner. As he stepped around it, intent on eavesdropping at the open window, he was suddenly the subject of attention of fifty pairs of eyes. The factory manager and his idle workers were still clustered at the main doors, and they fell silent and turned their full attention upon him as he appeared round the corner.

Shasa tossed his head and veered away from the window. They were all still watching him and he thrust his hands into the pockets of his Oxford bags and, with an elaborate show of nonchalance, sauntered down towards the long wooden jetty as though this had been his intention all along. Whatever was going on in the office now was beyond him, unless he could wheedle it out of his mother later, and he didn't think there was much hope of that. Then suddenly he noticed the four squat wooden trawlers moored alongside the jetty, each lying low in the water under the glittering silver cargo they carried, and his disappointment was a little mollified. Here was something to break the monotony of his hot dreary desert afternoon and his step quickened as he went onto the timbers of the jetty. Boats always fascinated him.

This was new and exciting. He had never seen so many fish, there must be tons of them. He came level with the first boat. It was grubby and ugly, with streaks of human excrement down the sides where the crew had squatted on the gunwale, and it stank of bilges and fuel oil and unwashed humanity living in confined quarters. It had not even been graced with a name: there were only the registration and licence numbers painted on the wave-battered bows.

'A boat should have a name,' Shasa thought. 'It's insulting and unlucky not to give it a name.' His own twenty-five-foot yacht that his mother had given him for his thirteenth birthday was named *The Midas Touch*, a name that his mother had suggested.

Shasa wrinkled his nose at the smell of the trawler, disgusted and saddened by her disgracefully neglected condition.

'If this is what Mater drove all the way from Windhoek for—' He did not finish the thought for a boy stepped around the far side of the tall angular wheelhouse.

He wore patched shorts of canvas duck, his legs were brown and muscled and he balanced easily on the hatch coaming on bare feet.

As they became aware of each other both boys bridled and stiffened, like dogs meeting unexpectedly; silently they scrutinized each other.

30

'A dandy, a fancy boy,' Manfred thought. He had seen one or two like him on their infrequent visits to the resort town of Swakopmund up the coast. Rich men's children dressed in ridiculous stiff clothing, walking dutifully behind their parents with that infuriating supercilious expression upon their faces. 'Look at his hair, all shiny with brilliantine, and he stinks like a bunch of flowers.'

'One of the poor white Afrikaners,' Shasa recognized his type. 'A *bywoner*, a squatter's kid.' His mother had forbidden him to play with them, but he had found that some of them were jolly good fun. Their attraction was of course enhanced by his mother's prohibition. One of the sons of the machine-shop foreman at the mine imitated bird calls in such an amazingly lifelike manner that he could actually call the birds down from the trees, and he had shown Shasa how to adjust the carburettor and ignition on the old Ford which his mother allowed him to use, even though he was too young to have a driver's licence. While the same boy's elder sister, a year older than Shasa, had shown him something even more remarkable when they had shared a few forbidden moments together behind the pumphouse at the mine. She had even allowed him to touch it and it had been warm and soft and furry as a newborn kitten cuddling up there under her short cotton skirt, a most remarkable experience which he intended to repeat at the very next opportunity.

This boy looked interesting also, and perhaps he could show Shasa over the trawler's engine-room. Shasa glanced back at the factory. His mother was not watching and he was prepared to be magnanimous.

'Hello.' He made a lordly gesture and smiled carefully. His grandfather, Sir Garrick Courtney, the most important male person in his existence, was always admonishing him. 'By birth you have a specially exalted position in society. This gives you not only benefit and privilege, but a duty also. A true gentleman treats those beneath his station, black or white, old or young, man or woman, with consideration and courtesy.'

'My name is Courtney,' Shasa told him. 'Shasa Courtney. My grandfather is Sir Garrick Courtney and my mother is Mrs Centaine de Thiry Courtney.' He waited for the deference that those names usually commanded, and when it was not evident, he went on rather lamely, 'What's your name?'

'My name is Manfred,' the other boy replied in Afrikaans and arched those dense black eyebrows over the amber eyes. They were so much darker than his streaked blond hair that they looked as though they had been painted on. 'Manfred De La Rey, and my grandfather and my great-uncle and my father were De La Rey also and they shot the shit out of the English every time they met them.'

Shasa blushed at this unexpected attack and was on the point of turning away when he saw that there was an old man leaning in the window of the wheelhouse, watching them, and two coloured crewmen had come up from the trawler's forecastle. He could not retreat.

'We English won the war and in 1914 we beat the hell out of the rebels,' he snapped.

'We!' Manfred repeated, and turned to his audience. 'This little gentleman with perfume on his hair won the war.' The crewmen chuckled encouragement. 'Smell him, his name should be Lily – Lily the perfumed soldier.' Manfred turned back to him, and for the first time Shasa realized that he was taller by a good inch and his arms were alarmingly thick and brown. 'So you are English, are you, Lily? Then you must live in London, is that right, sweet Lily?'

Shasa had not expected a poor white boy to be so articulate, nor his wit to be so acerbic. Usually he was in control of any discussion.

'Of course I'm English,' he affirmed furiously, and was

seeking a final retort to end the exchange and allow him to retire in good order from a situation over which he was swiftly losing control.

'Then you must live in London,' Manfred persisted.

'I live in Cape Town.'

'Hah!' Manfred turned to his growing audience. Swart Hendrick had come across the jetty from his own trawler, and all the crew were up from the forecastle. 'That's why they are called *Soutpiel*,' Manfred announced.

There was an outburst of delighted guffaws at the coarse expression. Manfred would never have used it if his father had been present. The translation was 'Salt Prick' and Shasa flushed and instinctively bunched his fists at the insult.

'A *Soutpiel* has one foot in London and the other in Cape Town,' Manfred explained with relish, 'and his willy-wagger dangling in the middle of the salty old Atlantic Ocean.'

'You'll take that back!' Anger had robbed Shasa of a more telling rejoinder. He had never been spoken to in this fashion by one of his inferiors.

'Take it back – you mean like you pull back your salty foreskin? When you play with it? Is that what you mean?' Manfred asked. The applause had made him reckless, and he had moved closer, directly under the boy on the jetty.

Shasa launched himself without warning, and Manfred had not anticipated that so soon. He had expected to trade a few more insults before they were both sufficiently worked up to attack each other.

Shasa dropped six feet and hit him with the full weight of his body and his outrage. The wind was driven out of Manfred's lungs in a whoosh as, locked together, they went flying backwards into the morass of dead fish.

They rolled over and with a shock Shasa felt the other boy's strength. His arms were hard as timber balks and his fingers felt like iron butcher's hooks as he clawed for Shasa's face. Only surprise and Manfred's winded lungs saved him from immediate humiliation, and almost too late he remembered the admonitions of Jock Murphy, his boxing instructor.

'Don't let a bigger man force you to fight close. Fight him off. Keep him at arm's length.'

Manfred was clawing at his face, trying to get an arm around him in a half Nelson, and they were floundering into the cold slippery mass of fish. Shasa brought up his right knee and, as Manfred reared up over him, he drove it into his chest. Manfred gasped and reeled back, but then as Shasa tried to roll away, he lunged forward again for the head lock. Shasa ducked his head and with his right hand forced Manfred's elbow up to break the grip, then as Jock had taught him, he twisted out against the opening he had created. He was helped by the fish slime that coated his neck and Manfred's arm like oil, and the instant he was free he threw a punch with his left hand.

Jock had drilled him endlessly on the short straight left. 'The most important punch you'll ever use.'

It wasn't one of Shasa's best, but it caught the other boy in the eye with sufficient force to snap his head back and distract him just long enough to let Shasa get onto his feet and back away.

By now the jetty above them was crowded with coloured trawlermen in rubber boots and blue rollneck jerseys. They were roaring with delight and excitement, egging on the two boys as though they were game cocks.

Blinking the tears out of his swelling eye, Manfred went after Shasa, but the fish clinging to his legs hampered him, and that left shot out again. There was no warning; it came straight and hard and unexpectedly, stinging his injured eye so that he shouted with anger and groped wildly for the lighter boy.

Shasa ducked under his arm and fired the left again, just the way Jock had taught him.

'Never telegraph it by moving the shoulders or the head,' he could almost hear Jock's voice, 'just shoot it – with the arm alone.'

He caught Manfred in the mouth, and immediately there was blood as Manfred's lip was crushed onto his own teeth. The sight of his adversary's blood elated Shasa and the concerted bellow of the crowd evoked a primeval response deep within him. He used the left again, cracking it into the pink swollen eye.

'When you mark him, then keep hitting the same spot.' Jock's voice in his head, and Manfred shouted again, but this time he could hear the pain as well as the rage in the sound.

'It's working,' Shasa exulted. But at that moment he ran backwards into the wheelhouse and Manfred, realizing his opponent was cornered, rushed at him through the slimy fish, spreading both arms wide, grinning triumphantly, his mouth full of blood from his cut lip and his teeth dyed bright pink.

In panic Shasa dropped his shoulders, braced himself for an instant against the wheelhouse timbers and then shot forward, butting the top of his head into Manfred's stomach.

Once again Manfred wheezed as the air was forced up his throat, and for a few confused seconds they writhed together in the mess of pilchards, with Manfred gurgling for breath and unable to get a hold on his opponent's slippery limbs. Then Shasa wriggled away and half crawled, half swam to the foot of the wooden ladder of the jetty and dragged himself onto it.

The crowd was laughing and booing derisively as he fled, and Manfred clawed angrily after him, spitting blood and fish slime out of his injured mouth, his chest heaving violently to refill his lungs.

Shasa was halfway up the ladder when Manfred reached up and grabbed his ankle, pulling both his feet off the rungs. Shasa was stretched out by the heavier boy's weight like a victim on the rack, clinging with desperate strength to the top of the ladder, and the faces of the coloured fishermen were only inches from his as they leaned over the jetty and howled for his blood, favouring their own.

With his free leg Shasa kicked backwards, and his heel caught Manfred in his swollen eye. He yelled and let go, and Shasa scrambled up onto the jetty and looked around him wildly. His fighting ardour had cooled and he was trembling.

His escape down the jetty was open and he longed to take it. But the men around him were laughing and jeering and pride shackled him. He glanced around and, with a surge of dismay that was so strong that it almost physically nauseated him, he saw that Manfred had reached the top of the ladder.

Shasa was not quite sure how he had got himself into this fight, or what was the point at issue, and miserably he wished he could extricate himself. That was impossible, his entire breeding and training precluded it. He tried to stop himself trembling as he turned back to face Manfred again.

The bigger boy was trembling also, but not with fear. His face was swollen and dark red with killing rage, and he was making an unconscious hissing sound through his bloody lips. His damaged eye was turning purplish mauve and puffing into a narrow slit.

'Kill him, *kleinbasie*,' screamed the coloured trawlermen. 'Murder him, little boss.' And their taunts rallied Shasa. He took a deep steadying breath and lifted his fists in the classic boxer's stance, left foot leading and his hands held high in front of his face.

'Keep moving,' he heard Jock's advice again, and he went up on his toes and danced.

'Look at him!' the crowd hooted. 'He thinks he is Jack Dempsey! He wants to dance with you, Manie. Show him the Walvis Bay Waltz!'

However, Manfred was daunted by the desperate determination in those dark blue eyes and by the clenched white
knuckles of Shasa's left hand. He began to circle him,
hissing threats.

'I'm going to rip your arm off and stick it down your
throat. I'm going to make your teeth march out of your
backside like soldiers.'

Shasa blinked but kept his guard up, turning slowly to
face Manfred as he circled. Though both of them were
soaked and glistening with fish slime and their hair was
thick with the gelatinous stuff and speckled with loose
scales, there was nothing ludicrous nor childlike about
them. It was a good fight and promised to become even
better, and the audience gradually fell silent. Their eyes
glittered like those of a wolf pack and they craned forward
expectantly to watch the ill-matched pair.

Manfred feinted left and then charged and rushed from
the side. He was very fast, despite his size and the heaviness
of his legs and shoulders. He carried his shining blond head
low and the black curved eyebrows emphasized the ferocity
of his scowl.

In front of him Shasa seemed almost girlishly fragile. His
arms were slim and pale, and his legs under the sodden grey
flannel seemed too long and thin, but he moved well on
them. He dodged Manfred's charge and as he pulled away,
his left arm shot out again, and Manfred's teeth clicked
audibly at the punch and his head was flicked back as he
was brought up on his heels.

The crowd growled, '*Vat hom*, Manie, get him!' and
Manfred rushed in again, throwing a powerful round-house
punch at Shasa's pale petal-smooth face.

Shasa ducked under it and, in the instant that Manfred
was screwed off balance by his own momentum, stabbed his
left fist unexpectedly and painfully into the purple, puffed-
up eye. Manfred clasped his hand over the eye and snarled
at him. 'Fight properly, you cheating *Soutie*.'

'Ja!' a voice called from the crowd. 'Stop running away. Stand and fight like a man.'

At the same time Manfred changed his tactics. Instead of feinting and weaving, he came straight at Shasa, and kept on coming, swinging with both hands in a terrifying mechanical sequence of blows. Shasa fell back frantically, ducking and swaying and dodging, at first stabbing out with his left hand as Manfred followed him relentlessly, cutting the swollen skin that had begun to bag under his eye, hitting him in the mouth again and then again until his lips were distorted and lumpy. But it was as though Manfred was inured to the sting of these blows now and he did not alter the rhythm of punches nor slacken his attack.

His brown fists, hardened by work at the winch and net, flipped Shasa's hair as he ducked or hissed past his face as he ran backwards. Then one caught him a glancing blow on the temple and Shasa stopped aiming his own counter-punches and struggled merely to stay clear of those swinging fists, for his legs started to turn numb and heavy under him.

Manfred was tireless, pressing him relentlessly, and despair combined with exhaustion to slow Shasa's legs. A fist crashed into his ribs, and he grunted and staggered and saw the other fist coming at his face. He could not avoid it, his feet seemed planted in buckets of treacle and he grabbed at Manfred's arm and hung on grimly. That was exactly what Manfred had been trying to force him to do, and he whipped his other arm around Shasa's neck.

'Now, I've got you,' he mumbled through swollen bloody lips, as he forced Shasa to double over, his head pinned under Manfred's left arm. Manfred lifted his right hand high and swung it in a brutal upper-cut.

Shasa sensed rather than saw the fist coming, and twisted so violently that he felt as though his neck had snapped. But he managed to take the blow on the top of his forehead rather than in his unprotected face. The shock of it was driven like an iron spike from the top of his skull down his spine. He knew he could not take another blow like that.

Through his starring vision he realized that he had tottered to the edge of the jetty, and he used the last vestiges of his strength to drive them both towards the very edge. Manfred had not been expecting him to push in that direction and was braced the wrong way. He could not resist as they went flying over and fell back onto the trawler's fish-laden deck six feet below.

Shasa was pinned beneath Manfred's body, still caught in the headlock, and instantly he sank into the quicksand of silver pilchards. Manfred tried to swing another punch at his face, but it slogged into the soft layer of fish that was spreading over Shasa's head. He abandoned the effort and merely leaned his full weight on Shasa's neck, forcing his head deeper and still deeper below the surface.

Shasa started to drown. He tried to scream but a dead pilchard slid into his open mouth and its head jammed in his throat. He kicked and lashed out with both hands and writhed with all his remaining strength, but remorselessly his head was thrust downward. The fish lodged in his throat choked him. The darkness filled his head with a sound like the wind, blotting out the murderous chorus from the jetty above, and his struggles became less urgent until he was flopping and flapping his limbs loosely.

'I'm going to die,' he thought with a kind of detached wonder. 'I'm drowning—' and the thought faded with his consciousness.

'You have come here to destroy me,' Lothar De La Rey accused her with his back against the closed door. 'You have come all this way to watch it happen, and to gloat on it.'

'You flatter yourself,' Centaine answered him disdainfully. 'I have not that much interest in you personally. I have come to protect my considerable investment. I have come for fifty thousand pounds plus accrued interest.'

'If that was true you wouldn't stop me running my catch through the plant. I've got a thousand tons out there – by sunset tomorrow evening I could turn it into fifty thousand pounds.'

Impatiently Centaine lifted her hand to stop him. The skin of the hand was tanned a creamy coffee colour in contrast to the silver white diamond as long as the top joint of the tapered forefinger that she pointed at him.

'You are living in a dream world,' she told him. 'Your fish is worth nothing. Nobody wants it – not at any price, certainly not fifty thousand.'

'It's worth all of that – fish meal and canned goods—'

Again she gestured him to silence. 'The warehouses of the world are filled with unwanted goods. Don't you understand that? Don't you read a newspaper? Don't you listen to the wireless out here in the desert? It's worthless – not even worth the cost of processing it.'

'That's not possible.' He was angry and stubborn. 'Of course I've heard about the stock market, but people have still got to eat.'

'I've thought many things about you,' she had not raised her voice, she was speaking as though to a child, 'but I have never thought you stupid. Try to understand that something has happened out there in the world that has never happened before. The commerce of the world has died; the factories of the world are closing; the streets of all the major cities are filled with the legions of the unemployed.'

'You are using this as an excuse for what you are doing. You are conducting a vendetta against me.' He came towards her. His lips were icy pale against the dark mahogany tan. 'You are hounding me for some fancied offence committed long ago. You are punishing me.'

'The offence was real.' She stepped back from his advance, but she held his gaze and her voice though low-pitched was bleak and hard. 'It was monstrous and cruel and unforgivable, but there is no punishment I could deal out to you which would fit that crime. If there is a God, he will demand retribution.'

'The child,' he started. 'The child you bore me in the wilderness—' For the first time he penetrated the armour of her composure.

'You'll not mention your bastard to me.' She clasped one hand with the other to prevent them trembling. 'That was our bargain.'

'He's our son. You cannot avoid that fact. Are you content to destroy him also?'

'He's your son,' she denied. 'I have no part of him. He does not affect me or my decision. Your factory is insolvent, hopelessly, irredeemably insolvent. I cannot expect to recover my investment, I can only hope to retrieve a part.'

Through the open window there came the sound of men's voices, even at a distance they sounded excited and lustful, baying like hounds as they take the scent. Neither of them glanced in that direction; all their attention was concentrated on each other.

'Give me a chance, Centaine.' He heard the pleading timbre in his own voice and it disgusted him. He had never begged before, not with anybody, not once in his life, but now he could not bear the prospect of having to begin all over again. It would not be the first time. Twice before he had been rendered destitute, stripped of everything but pride and courage and determination by war and the fortunes of war. Always it had been the same enemy, the

British and their aspirations of empire. Each time he had started again from the beginning and laboriously rebuilt his fortune.

This time the prospect appalled him. To be struck down by the mother of his child, the woman he had loved – and, God forgive him, the woman he loved still against all probabilities. He felt the exhaustion of his spirit and his body. He was forty-six years old; he no longer had a young man's store of energy on which to draw, and he thought he glimpsed a softening in her eyes as though she was moved by his plea, wavering at the point of relenting.

'Give me a week – just one week, Centaine, that's all I ask,' he abased himself, and immediately realized that he had misread her.

She did not alter her expression, but in her eyes he could see that what he had mistaken for compassion was instead the shine of deep satisfaction. He was where she had wanted him all these years.

'I have told you never to use my Christian name,' she said. 'I told you that when I first learned that you had murdered two people whom I loved as dearly as I have ever loved anyone. I tell you that again.'

'A week. Just one week.'

'I have already given you two years.'

Now she turned her head towards the window, no longer able to ignore the sound of harsh voices, like the blood roar of a bullfight heard at a distance.

'Another week will only get you deeper into my debt and force heavier loss on me.' She shook her head, but he was staring out the window and now her voice sharpened. 'What is happening down there on the jetty?' She leaned her hands on the sill and peered down the beach.

He stepped up beside her. There was a dense knot of humanity halfway down the jetty, and from the factory all the idle packers were running down to join it.

'Shasa!' Centaine cried with an intuitive surge of maternal concern. 'Where's Shasa?' Lothar vaulted lightly over the sill and raced for the jetty, overhauling the stragglers and then shouldering his way through the circle of yelling, howling trawlermen just as the two boys teetered on the edge of the jetty.

'Manfred!' he roared. 'Stop that! Let him go!'

His son had the lighter boy in a vicious headlock, and he was swinging overhand punches at his trapped head. Lothar heard one crack against the bone of Shasa's skull.

'You fool!' Lothar started towards them. They had not heard his voice above the din of the crowd, and Lothar felt a slide of dread, a real concern for the child and a realization of what Centaine's reaction would be if he were injured.

'Leave him!' Before he could reach the wildly struggling pair, they reeled backwards and tumbled over the edge of the jetty. 'Oh my God!' He heard them hit the deck of the trawler below, and by the time he reached the side and looked down they were half buried in the deckload of glittering pilchards.

Lothar tried to reach the ladder head, impeded by the press of coloured trawlermen who crowded forward to the edge so as not to miss a moment of the contest. He struck out with both fists, clearing his way, shoving his men aside, and then clambered down to the deck of the trawler.

Manfred was lying on top of the other boy, forcing his head and shoulders beneath the mass of pilchards. His own face was contorted with rage, and lumped and discoloured with bruises. He was mouthing incoherent threats through blood-smeared and puffed lips, and Shasa was no longer struggling. His head and shoulders had disappeared but his trunk and his legs twitched and shuddered in the spontaneous nerveless movements of a man shot through the head.

Lothar seized his son by the shoulders and tried to drag him off. It was like trying to separate a pair of mastiffs and he had to use all his strength. He lifted Manfred bodily and threw him against the wheelhouse with a force that knocked the belligerence out of him and then grabbed Shasa's legs and pulled him out of the engulfing quicksilver of dead pilchards. He came slithering free, wet and slippery. His eyes were open and rolled back into his skull exposing the whites.

'You've killed him,' Lothar snarled at his son, and the furious tide of blood receded from Manfred's face leaving him white and shivering with shock.

'I didn't mean it, Pa. I didn't—'

There was a dead fish jammed into Shasa's slack mouth, choking him, and fish slime bubbled out of his nostrils.

'You fool, you little fool!' Lothar thrust his finger into the corners of the child's slack mouth and prised the pilchard out.

'I'm sorry, Pa. I didn't mean it,' Manfred whispered.

'If you've killed him, you've committed a terrible offence in the sight of God.' Lothar lifted Shasa's limp body in his arms. 'You'll have killed your own—' He did not say the fateful word, but bit down hard on it and turned to the ladder.

'I haven't killed him,' Manfred pleaded for assurance. 'He's not dead. It will be all right, won't it, Pa?'

'No.' Lothar shook his head grimly. 'It won't be all right – not ever.' Carrying the unconscious boy, he climbed up onto the jetty.

The crowd opened silently for Lothar. Like Manfred, they were appalled and guilty, unable to meet his eyes as he shouldered past them.

'Swart Hendrick,' Lothar called over their heads to the tall black man. 'You should have known better. You should have stopped them.'

Lothar strode away up the jetty, and none of them followed him.

Halfway up the beach path to the factory Centaine

Courtney waited for him. Lothar stopped in front of her with the boy hanging limply in his arms.

'He's dead,' Centaine whispered hopelessly.

'No,' Lothar denied with passion. It was too horrible to think about, and as though in response Shasa moaned and vomited from the corner of his mouth.

'Quickly.' Centaine stepped forward. 'Turn him over your shoulder before he chokes on his own vomit.'

With Shasa hanging limply over his shoulder like a haversack, Lothar ran the last few yards to the office and Centaine swept the desktop clear.

'Lay him here,' she ordered, but Shasa was struggling weakly and trying to sit up. Centaine supported his shoulders and wiped his mouth and nostrils with the fine cloth of her sleeve.

'It was your bastard.' She glared across the desk at Lothar. 'He did this to my son, didn't he?' And she saw the confirmation in his face before he looked away.

Shasa coughed and brought up another trickle of fish slime and yellow vomitus, and immediately he was stronger. His eyes focused and his breathing eased.

'Get out of here.' Centaine leaned protectively over Shasa's body. 'I'll see you both in hell – you and your bastard. Now get out of my sight.'

The track from Walvis Bay ran through the convoluted valleys of the great orange dunes, thirty kilometres to the railhead at Swakopmund. The dunes towered three and four hundred feet on either side. Mountains of sand with knife-edge crests and smooth slip faces, they trapped the desert heat in the canyons between them.

The track was merely a set of deep ruts in the sand,

marked on each side by the sparkling glass of broken beer bottles. No traveller took this thirsty road without adequate supplies for the journey. At intervals the tracks had been obliterated by the efforts of other drivers, unskilled in the art of desert travel, to extract their vehicles from the clinging sands, leaving gaping traps for those who followed.

Centaine drove hard and fast, never allowing her engine revolutions to drop, keeping her momentum even through the churned-up areas and holes where the other vehicles had bogged down, directing the big yellow car with deft little touches of the wheel so that the tyres ran straight and the sand did not pile and block them.

She held the wheel in a racing driver's grip, leaning back against the leather seat with straight arms ready for the kick of the wheel, watching the tracks far ahead and anticipating each contingency long before she reached it, sometimes snapping down through the gears and swinging out of the ruts to cut her own way around a bad stretch. She scorned even the elementary precaution of travelling with a pair of black servants in the back seat to push the Daimler out of a sand trap. Shasa had never known his mother to bog down, not even on the worst sections of the track out to the mine.

He sat up beside her on the front seat. He wore a suit of old but freshly laundered canvas overalls from the stores of the canning factory. His soiled clothing stinking of fish and speckled with vomit was in the boot of the Daimler.

His mother hadn't spoken since they had driven away from the factory. Shasa glanced surreptitiously at her, dreading her pent-up wrath, not wanting to draw attention to himself, yet despite himself unable to keep his eyes from her face.

She had removed the cloche hat and her thick dark cap of hair, cut fashionably into a short Eton crop, rippled in the wind and shone like washed anthracite.

'Who started it?' she asked, without taking her eyes from the road.

Shasa thought about it. 'I'm not sure. I hit him first, but—' he paused. His throat was still painful.

'Yes?' she demanded.

'It was as though it was arranged. We looked at each other and we knew we were going to fight.' She said nothing and he finished lamely. 'He called me a name.'

'What name?'

'I can't tell you. It's rude.'

'I asked what name?' Her voice was level and low, but he recognized that husky warning quality.

'He called me a *Soutpiel*,' he replied hastily. He dropped his voice and looked away in shame at the dreadful insult, so he did not see Centaine struggle to stifle the smile and turn her head slightly to hide the sparkle of amusement in her eyes.

'I told you it was rude,' he apologized.

'So you hit him – and he's younger than you.'

He had not known that he was the elder, but he was not surprised that she knew it. She knew everything.

'He may be younger, but he's a big Afrikaner ox, at least two inches taller than I am,' he defended himself quickly.

She wanted to ask Shasa what her other son looked like. Was he blond and handsome as his father had been? What colour were his eyes? Instead she said, 'And so he thrashed you.'

'I nearly won.' Shasa protested stoutly. 'I closed his eyes and I bloodied him nicely. I nearly won.'

'Nearly isn't good enough,' she said. 'In our family we don't nearly win – we simply win.'

He fidgeted uncomfortably and coughed to relieve the pain in his injured throat.

'You can't win, not when someone is bigger and stronger than you,' he whispered miserably.

'Then you don't fight him with your fists,' she told him. 'You don't rush in and let him stick a dead fish down your throat.' He blushed painfully at the humiliation. 'You wait your chance, and you fight him with your own weapons and on your own terms. You only fight when you are sure you can win.'

He considered that carefully, examining it from every angle. 'That's what you did to his father, didn't you?' he asked softly, and she was startled by his perception so that she stared at him and the Daimler bumped out of the ruts.

Quickly she caught and controlled the machine, and then she nodded. 'Yes. That's what I did. You see, we are Courtneys. We don't have to fight with our fists. We fight with power and money and influence. Nobody can beat us on our own ground.'

He was silent again, digesting it carefully, and at last he smiled. He was so beautiful when he smiled, even more beautiful than his father had been, that she felt her heart squeezed by her love.

'I'll remember that,' he said. 'Next time I meet him, I'll remember what you said.'

Neither of them doubted for a moment that the two boys would meet again – and that when they did, they would continue the conflict that had begun that day.

The breeze was onshore and the stink of rotting fish was so strong that it coated the back of Lothar De La Rey's throat and sickened him to the gut.

The four trawlers still lay at their berths but their cargoes were no longer glittering silver. The fish had packed down and the top layer of pilchards had dried out in the sun and turned a dark, dirty grey, crawling with metallic green flies as big as wasps. The fish in the holds had squashed under their own weight, and the bilge pumps were pouring out steady streams of stinking brown blood and fish oil that discoloured the waters of the bay in a spreading cloud.

All day Lothar had sat at the window of the factory office while his coloured trawlermen and packers lined up to be paid. Lothar had sold his old Packard truck and the few sticks of furniture from the corrugated shack in which he and Manfred lived. These were the only assets that did not belong to the company and had not been attached. The second-hand dealer had come across from Swakopmund within hours, smelling disaster the way the vultures do, and he had paid Lothar a fraction of their real value.

'There is a depression going on, Mr De La Rey, everybody is selling, nobody is buying. I'll lose money, believe me.'

With the cash that Lothar had buried under the sandy floor of the shack there was enough to pay his people two shillings on each pound that he owed them for back wages. He did not have to pay them, of course, it was the company's responsibility – but that did not occur to him, they were his people.

'I'm sorry,' he repeated to each one of them as they came to the pay window. 'That's all there is.' And he avoided their eyes.

When it was all gone, and the last of his coloured people had wandered away in disconsolate little groups, Lothar locked the office door and handed the key to the deputy sheriff.

Then he and the boy had gone down to the jetty for the last time and sat together with their legs dangling over the end. The stink of dead fish was as heavy as their mood.

'I don't understand, Pa.' Manfred spoke through his distorted mouth with the crusty red scab on the upper lip. 'We caught good fish. We should be rich. What happened, Pa?'

'We were cheated,' Lothar said quietly. Until that moment there had been anger, no bitterness – just a feeling

49

of numbness. Twice before he had been struck by a bullet. The .303 Lee Enfield bullet on the road to Omaruru when they were opposing Smuts' invasion of German South West Africa, and then much later the Luger bullet fired by the boy's mother. He touched his chest at the memory, and felt the rubbery puckered pit of the scar through the thin cotton of his khaki shirt.

It was the same thing, first the shock and the numbness and then only much later the pain and the anger. Now the anger came at him in black waves, and he did not try to resist. Rather he revelled in it, it helped to assuage the memory of abasing himself, pleading for time from the woman with the taunting smile in her dark eyes.

'Can't we stop them, Pa?' the boy asked, and neither of them had to define that 'them'. They knew their enemy. They had grown to know them in three wars; in 1881 the first Boer War, then again in the Great Boer War of 1899 when Victoria called her khaki multitudes from across the oceans to crush them, and then in 1914 when the British puppet Jannie Smuts had carried out the orders of his imperial masters.

Lothar shook his head, unable to answer, choked by the strength of his anger.

'There must be a way,' the boy insisted. 'We are strong.' He recalled the feeling of Shasa's body slowly weakening in his grip and he flexed his hands involuntarily. 'It's ours, Pa. This is our land. God gave it to us – it says so in the Bible.' Like so many before him, the Afrikaner had interpreted that book in his own way. He saw his people as the children of Israel, and Southern Africa as the promised land flowing with milk and honey.

Lothar was silent and Manfred took his sleeve. 'God did give it to us, didn't he, Pa?'

'Yes.' Lothar nodded heavily.

'Then they've stolen it from us: the land, the diamonds, and the gold and everything – and now they have taken our boats and our fish. There must be a way to stop them, to win back what belongs to us.'

'It's not as easy as that.' Lothar hesitated how to explain it to the child. Did he truly understand it himself, how it had happened? They were squatters in the land that their fathers had wrested from the savages and the wilderness at the point of their long muzzle-loading guns.

'When you grow up you'll understand, Manie,' he said.

'When I grow up I'll find a way to beat them.' Manfred said it so forcefully that the scab on his lip cracked open and a droplet like a tiny ruby glowed upon it. 'I'll find a way to get it back from them. You'll see if I don't, Pa.'

'Well, my son, perhaps you will.' Lothar placed his arm around the boy's shoulders.

'Remember Grandpa's oath, Pa? I'll always remember. The war against the English will never end.'

They sat together until the sun touched the waters of the bay and turned them to molten copper, and then in the darkness they went up the jetty, out of the stench of decaying fish and along the edge of the dunes.

As they approached the shack there was smoke rising from the chimney and when they entered the lean-to kitchen, there was a fire on the open hearth. Swart Hendrick looked up from it.

'The Jew has taken the table and the chairs,' he said. 'But I hid the pots and the mugs.'

They sat on the floor and ate straight from the pot, a porridge of maize meal flavoured with salty wind-dried fish. Nobody spoke until they had finished.

'You didn't have to stay.' Lothar broke the silence and Hendrick shrugged.

'I bought coffee and tobacco at the store. The money you paid me was just enough.'

'There is no more,' Lothar said. 'It is all gone.'

'It's all been gone before.' Hendrick lit his pipe with a twig from the fire. 'We have been broke many times before.'

'This time it is different,' Lothar said. 'This time there is no ivory to hunt or—' He broke off as his anger choked him again, and Hendrick poured more coffee into the tin mugs.

'It is strange,' Hendrick said. 'When we found her, she was dressed in skins. Now she comes in her big yellow car,' he shook his head and chuckled, 'and we are the ones in rags.'

'It was you and I that saved her,' Lothar agreed. 'More than that, we found her diamonds for her, and dug them from the ground.'

'Now she is rich,' Hendrick said, 'and she comes to take what we have also. She shouldn't have done that.' He shook his great black head. 'No, she shouldn't have done that.'

Lothar straightened up slowly. Hendrick saw his expression and leaned forward eagerly, and the boy stirred and smiled for the first time.

'Yes.' Hendrick began to grin. 'What is it? Ivory is finished – it's all been hunted out long ago.'

'No, not ivory. This time it will be diamonds,' Lothar replied.

'Diamonds?' Hendrick rocked back on his heels. 'What diamonds?'

'What diamonds?' Lothar smiled at him, and his yellow eyes glowed. 'Why, the diamonds we found for her, of course.'

'Her diamonds?' Hendrick stared at him. 'The diamonds from the H'ani Mine?'

'How much money have you got?' Lothar demanded and Hendrick's eyes shifted. 'I know you well,' Lothar went on impatiently and seized his shoulder. 'You've always got a little bit salted away. How much?'

'Not much.' Hendrick tried to rise but Lothar held him down.

'You have earned well this last season. I know exactly how much I have paid you.'

'Fifty pounds,' grunted Hendrick.

'No.' Lothar shook his head. 'You've got more than that.'

'Perhaps a little more.' Hendrick resigned himself.

'You have got a hundred pounds,' Lothar said definitely. 'That's how much we will need. Give it to me. You know you will get it back many times over. You always have, and you always will.'

The track was steep and rocky and the party straggled up it in the early sunlight. They had left the yellow Daimler at the bottom of the mountain on the banks of the Liesbeek stream and begun the climb in the ghostly grey light of pre-dawn.

In the lead were two old men in disreputable clothing, scuffed velskoen on their feet and sweatstained shapeless straw hats on their heads. They were both so lean as to appear half starved, skinny but sprightly, their skin darkened and creased by long exposure to the elements, so that a casual observer might have thought them a couple of old hoboes – and there were enough of that type on the roads and byways in these days of the great Depression.

The casual observer would have been in error. The taller of the two old men limped slightly on an artificial leg and was a Knight Commander of the Order of the British Empire, a holder of the highest award for valour that the Empire could offer, the Victoria Cross, and he was also one of the most eminent military historians of the age, a man so rich and careless of worldly wealth that he seldom bothered to count his fortune.

'Old Garry,' his companion addressed him, rather than

as Sir Garrick Courtney. 'That is the biggest problem we have to deal with, old Garry.' He was explaining in his high, almost girlish voice, rolling his Rs in that extraordinary fashion that was known as the 'Malmesbury bray'. 'Our people are deserting the land and flocking to the cities. The farms are dying, and there is no work for them in the cities.' His voice was unwinded although they had climbed 2,000 feet up the sheer turreted side of Table Mountain without a pause, maintaining the pace that had outdistanced all the younger members of the party.

'It's a recipe for disaster,' Sir Garrick agreed. 'They are poor on the farms, but when they leave them they starve in the cities. Starving men are dangerous men, *Ou Baas*. History teaches us that.'

The man he called 'old master' was smaller in stature, though he carried himself straighter. He had merry blue eyes under the drooping brim of his Panama hat and a grey goatee beard that waggled as he spoke. Unlike Garry, he was not rich; he owned only a small farm on the high frost-browned veld of the Transvaal, and he was as careless of his debts as Garry was of his fortune, but the world was his paddock and had heaped honours upon him. He had been awarded honorary doctorates by fifteen of the world's leading universities, Oxford and Cambridge and Columbia amongst them. He was the freeman of ten cities, London and Edinburgh and the rest. He had been a general in the Boer forces and now he was general in the army of the British Empire, a Privy Councillor, a Companion of Honour, a King's Counsel, a bencher of the Middle Temple and a Fellow of the Royal Society. His chest was not wide enough for all the stars and ribbons he was entitled to wear. He was without question the cleverest, wisest, most charismatic and influential man that South Africa had ever produced. It was almost as though his spirit was too big to be contained by terrestrial borders, as though he were a true citizen of the wide world. This was the one chink in his armour, and his enemies had sent their poison-tipped arrows through it. 'His heart is across the sea, not with you,' and it had brought down his government of the South African Party of which he had been prime minister, minister of defence and of native affairs. Now he was leader of the opposition. However, he was a man who thought of himself as a botanist by preference and a soldier and politician by necessity.

'We should wait for the others to catch up.' General Jan Smuts paused on a lichen-covered rocky platform and leaned on his staff. The two of them peered back down the slope.

A hundred paces below them a woman plodded grimly up the path; the outline of her thighs through her heavy calico skirts were thick and powerful as the haunches of a brood mare, and her bare arms were as muscled as those of a wrestler.

'My little dove,' Sir Garry murmured fondly as he watched his bride. After fourteen long years of courtship she had only acceded to his suit six months before.

'Do hurry, Anna,' the boy behind her on the narrow path entreated. 'It will be noon before we reach the top and I'm dying for breakfast.' Shasa was as tall as she was, though half her bulk.

'Go ahead if you are in such a big hurry,' she growled at him. The thick solar topee was pulled low over her red, round face. Her features were as folded as those of a friendly bulldog. 'Though why anybody should want to reach the top of this cursed mountain—'

'I'll give you a shove,' Shasa offered, and placed both hands on Lady Courtney's massive round buttocks. 'Heave ho! And up she rises!'

'Stop that, you wicked boy,' Anna gasped as she scrambled to adjust to her sudden rapid ascent, 'or I'll break this stick over your backside. Oh! Stop now. That's enough.'

Until she had become Lady Courtney, she had been

plain Anna, Shasa's nurse and his mother's beloved maid. Her meteoric rise up the social ladder had in no way altered their relationship.

They arrived gasping and protesting and laughing on the ledge. 'Here she is, Grandpater! Special delivery!' Shasa grinned at Garry Courtney, who separated them firmly and fondly. The beautiful boy and the homely red-faced woman were the most precious of all his treasures, his wife and his only grandson.

'Anna, my sweeting, you mustn't tax the boy's strength so,' he warned her with a straight face, and she struck him on the arm half playfully and half in exasperation.

'I should be seeing to the lunch rather than gallivanting around on this mountain.' Her accent was still thick Flemish, and she relapsed thankfully into Afrikaans as she turned to General Smuts. 'How much further is it, *Ou Baas?*'

'Not far, Lady Courtney, not far at all. Ah! Here are the others. I was beginning to worry about them.'

Centaine and her companions emerged from the edge of the forest further down the slope. She wore a loose white skirt that left her legs bare from the knees and a white straw hat decorated with artificial cherries. When they caught up with the leaders, Centaine smiled at General Smuts. 'I'm winded, *Ou Baas*. May I lean on you for the last lap?' And though she was barely glowing with exertion he gallantly offered her his arm and they were first to reach the crest.

These annual picnics on Table Mountain were the traditional family way of celebrating Sir Garrick Courtney's birthday, and his old friend General Smuts made a point of never missing the occasion.

On the crest they all spread out to sit in the grass and catch their breath. Centaine and the old general were a little apart from the others. Below them lay the whole sweep of the Constantia Valley, patchworked with vine-yards in full green summer livery. Scattered amongst them the Dutch gables of the great châteaux glowed like pearls in the low rays of the sun and the smoky mountains of the Muizenberg and Kabonkelberg formed a solid amphitheatre of grey rock, hemming in the valley to the south while in the north the far mountains of the Hottentots Holland were a rampart that cut off the Cape of Good Hope from the continental shield of the African Continent. Directly ahead, wedged between the mountains, the waters of False Bay were ruffling and flecking at the rising importunity of the south-easter. It was so beautiful that they were silenced for many minutes.

General Smuts spoke first. 'So, Centaine, my dear, what did you want to talk about?'

'You are a mind-reader, *Ou Baas*.' She laughed ruefully. 'How do you know these things?'

'These days, when a pretty girl takes me aside, I can be sure it's business and not pleasure.' He twinkled at her.

'You are one of the most attractive men I've ever met—'

'Ah ha! Such a compliment! It must be serious.'

Her change of expression confirmed it. 'It's Shasa,' she said simply.

'No problem there – or I miss my guess.'

She took a single-paged document from her skirt pocket and handed it to him. It was a school report. The embossed crest was a bishop's mitre, the emblem of the country's most exclusive public school.

The general glanced at it. She knew how swiftly he could read even a complicated legal document, so when he handed it back to her almost immediately she was not put out. He would have it all, even down to the headmaster's summation on the last line: 'Michel Shasa is a credit to himself and to Bishops.'

General Smuts smiled at her. 'You must be very proud of him.'

'He is my entire life.'

'I know,' he said, 'and that is not always wise. A child soon becomes a man, and when he leaves he will take your life with him. However, in what way can I help you, my dear?'

'He is bright and personable and he has a way with people, even those much older than himself,' she replied. 'I would like to have a seat for him in Parliament, to begin with.'

The general removed the Panama hat from his head and smoothed back his sparkling silver hair with the palm of his hand. 'I do think he should finish his schooling before he enters Parliament, don't you, my dear!' he chuckled.

'That's it. That is exactly what I want to know from you, *Ou Baas*. Should Shasa go home to Oxford or Cambridge, or will that count against him later when he goes to the electorate? Should he rather attend one of the local universities – and if so, should it be Stellenbosch or the University of Cape Town?'

'I will think about it, Centaine, and I will give you my advice when it is time to make the final decision. But in the meantime may I be bold enough to warn you of something else, a state of mind which could prejudice your plans for the young man.'

'Please, *Ou Baas*,' she begged. 'A word of yours is worth—' she did not have to find a comparison, for the general went on softly.

'That word "home" – it is a fatal one. Shasa must decide where his true home is, and if it is across the sea, then he must not count on my assistance.'

'How foolish of me.' He saw that she was truly angry with herself. Her cheeks darkened and her lips hardened. *Soutpiel*. She remembered that jeer. One foot in London, the other in Cape Town. It was no longer amusing.

'It won't happen again,' she said, and she laid her hand on his arm to impress him with her sincerity. 'So you will help him?'

'Can we have breakfast now, Mater?' Shasa called across.

'All right, put the basket on the bank of the stream over there.' She turned back to the old man. 'Can I count on you?'

'I am in opposition, Centaine—'

'You won't be for long. The country must come to its senses at the next election.'

'You must realize I cannot promise you anything now.' He was choosing his words carefully. 'He is still a child. However, I will be watching him. If he fulfils this early promise, if he meets my standards, then he will have all my support. God knows how we need good men.'

She sighed with pleasure and relief, and he went on more easily. 'Sean Courtney was an able minister in my government.'

Centaine started at the name. It brought back so many memories, so much intense pleasure, and deep sorrow, so many dark and secret things. But the old man appeared not to have noticed her consternation as he went on. 'He was also a dear and trusted friend. I would like to have another Courtney in my government, someone to trust, a good friend, perhaps one day another Courtney in my cabinet.'

He stood and helped her to her feet. 'I'm as hungry as Shasa, and the smell of food is too good to resist.'

Yet when the food was offered, the general ate most frugally, while the rest of them, led by Shasa, attacked the food with ravenous appetites sharpened by the climb. Sir Garry carved from the cold cuts of lamb and pork and the turkey, and Anna dished out slices of the pies, Melton Mowbray, ham and egg, minced fruit and cubes of pigs' trotter embedded in delicious clear gelatine.

'One thing is certain,' Cyril Slaine, one of Centaine's general managers, declared with relief. 'The basket will be a sight lighter on the way down.'

'And now,' the general roused them from where they sprawled, satiated, on the bank of the tiny burbling stream, 'and now for the main business of the day.'

'Come on everybody.' Centaine was the first on her feet in a swirl of skirts, gay as a girl. 'Cyril, leave the basket here. We'll pick it up on the way back.'

They skirted the very edge of the grey cliff, with the world spread below them, until the general suddenly darted off to the left and scrambled over rock and through flowering heather and protea bush, disturbing the sugar birds that were sipping from the blooms. They rose in the air, flirting their long tail feathers and flashing their bright yellow belly patches with indignation at the intrusion.

Only Shasa could keep up with the general, and when the rest of the party caught the pair of them again, they were standing on the lip of a narrow rocky glen with bright green swamp grass carpeting the bottom.

'Here we are, and the first one to find a disa wins a sixpence,' General Smuts offered.

Shasa dashed away down the steep side of the glen, and before they were halfway down he was yelling excitedly.

'I've found one! The sixpence is mine!'

They straggled down from the rough rim and at the edge of the swampy ground formed a hushed and attentive circle around the graceful lily-stemmed orchid.

The general went down on one knee before it like a worshipper. 'It is indeed a blue disa, one of the rarest flowers on our earth.' The blossoms that adorned the stem were a marvellous cerulean blue, shaped like dragon's heads, their gaping throats lined with imperial purple and butter yellow. 'They only grow here on Table Mountain, nowhere else in the world.'

He looked up at Shasa. 'Would you like to do the honours for your grandfather this year, young man?'

Shasa stepped forward importantly to pick the wild orchid and hand it to Sir Garry. This little ceremony of the blue disa was part of the traditional birthday ceremony and they all laughed and applauded the presentation.

Watching her son proudly, Centaine's mind went back to the day of his birth, to the day the old Bushman had named him Shasa, 'Good Water', and had danced for him in the sacred valley deep in the Kalahari. She remembered the birth song that the old man had composed and sung, the Bushman language clicking and rustling in her head again, so well remembered, so well loved:

> His arrows will fly to the stars
> And when men speak his name
> It will be heard as far —

the old Bushman had sung,

> And he will find good water,
> Wherever he travels, he will find good water.

She saw again in her mind, the old long-dead Bushman's face, impossibly wrinkled and yet glowing that marvellous apricot colour, like amber or mellowed meerschaum, and she whispered deep in her throat, using the Bushman tongue.

'Let it be so, old grandfather. Let it be so.'

On the return journey the Daimler was only just large enough to accommodate all of them, with Anna sitting on Sir Garry's lap and submerging him beneath her abundance.

As Centaine drove down the twisting road through the forest of tall blue gum trees, Shasa leaned over the seat from behind her and encouraged her to greater speed. 'Come on, Mater, you've still got the hand brake on!'

Sitting beside Centaine, the general clutched his hat and stared fixedly at the speedometer. 'That can't be right. It feels more like one hundred miles an hour.'

Centaine swung the Daimler between the elaborately gabled white main gates of the estate. The pediment above, depicting a party of dancing nymphs bearing bunches of grapes, had been designed by the famous sculptor Anton Anreith. The name of the estate was blazoned in raised letters above the sculpture:

WELTEVREDEN 1790

'Well Satisfied' was the translation from the Dutch, and Centaine had purchased it from the illustrious Cloete family exactly one year after she had pegged the claims to the H'ani Mine. Since then she had lavished money and care and love upon it.

She slowed the Daimler almost to walking pace. 'I don't want dust blowing over the grapes,' she explained to General Smuts, and her face reflected such deep content as she looked out on the neatly pruned rows of trellised vines that he thought how the estate had been aptly named.

The coloured labourers straightened up from the vines and waved as they passed. Shasa leaned from the window and shouted the names of his favourites and they grinned with huge gratification at being singled out.

The road, lined with mature oaks, led up through two hundred acres of vines to the château. The lawns around the great house were bright green Kikuyu grass. General Smuts had brought shoots of the grass back from his East African campaign in 1917 and it had flourished all over the country. In the centre of the lawn stood the tall tower of the slave bell, still used to toll the beginning and end of the day's labours. Beyond it rose the glacial white walls and massive Anreith gables of Weltevreden under its thatched roof.

Already the house servants were hurrying out to fuss around them as they spilled out of the big yellow machine.

'Lunch will be at one-thirty,' Centaine told them briskly. '*Ou Baas*, I know Sir Garry wants to read his latest chapter to you. Cyril and I have a full morning's work ahead,' she broke off. 'Shasa, where do you think you are off to?'

The boy had sidled to the end of the stoep and was within an ace of escaping. Now he turned back with a sigh. 'Jock and I were going to work out the new pony.' The new polo pony had been Cyril's Christmas present to Shasa.

'Madame Claire will be waiting for you,' Centaine pointed out. 'We agreed that your mathematics needed attention, didn't we?'

'Oh Mater, it's holiday time—'

'Every day you spend idly, there is someone out there working. And when he meets you he is going to whip you hollow.'

'Yes, Mater.' Shasa had heard that prediction many times before, and he looked to his grandfather for support.

'Oh, I'm sure your mother will allow you a few hours to yourself after your maths tuition,' he came in dutifully. 'As you pointed out, it is officially holiday time.' He looked hopefully at Centaine.

'Might I also enter a plea on my young client's behalf?' General Smuts backed him, and Centaine capitulated with a laugh.

'You have such distinguished champions, but you will work with Madame Claire until elevenses.'

Shasa thrust his hands into his pockets and with slumped shoulders went to find his tutor. Anna disappeared into the house to chivy the servants and Garry led General Smuts away to discuss his new manuscript.

'All right.' Centaine jerked her head at Cyril. 'Let's get to work.' He followed her through the double teak front doors down the long *voorkamer*, her heels clicking on the black and white marble floors, to her study at the far end.

Her male secretaries were waiting for her. Centaine could not abide the continual presence of other females. Her secretaries were both handsome young men. The study was filled with flowers. Every day the vases were refilled from the gardens of Weltevreden. Today it was blue hydrangeas and yellow roses.

She seated herself at the long Louis XIV table she used as a desk. The legs were in richly ornate ormolu and the top was expansive enough to hold the memorabilia she had assembled.

There were a dozen photographs of Shasa's father in separate silver frames covering his life from schoolboy to dashing young airman in the RFC. The last photograph depicted him with the other pilots of his squadron standing in front of their single-seater scout planes. Hands thrust into his pockets, cap on the back of his head, Michael Courtney grinned at her, seemingly as certain of his immortality as he had been on the day that he died in the pyre of his burning aircraft. As she settled into her leather wingbacked chair, she touched the photograph, rearranging it slightly. The maid could never get it exactly right.

'I've read through the contract,' she told Cyril as he took the chair facing her. 'There are just two clauses I am not happy with. The first is clause twenty-six.' He turned to it obediently, and with her secretaries standing attentively on each side of her chair she began the day's work.

Always it was the mine which occupied Centaine first.

64

The H'ani Mine was the source, the spring from which it all flowed, and as she worked she felt her soul yearning towards the vastness of the Kalahari, towards those mystic blue hills and the secret valley which had concealed the treasures of the H'ani for countless aeons before she had stumbled upon them, dressed in skins and a last tattered remnant of cloth, great with the child in her womb and living like an animal of the desert herself.

The desert had captured part of her soul, and she felt joyous anticipation rising in her. 'Tomorrow,' she thought, 'tomorrow Shasa and I will be going back.' The lush vineyards of the Constantia Valley and the chateau of Weltevreden filled with beautiful things were part of her also, but when they cloyed she had to go back to the desert and have her soul burned clean and bright once more by the white Kalahari sun. As she signed the last of the documents and handed them to her senior secretary for witnessing and sealing, she stood and crossed to the open french doors.

Down in the paddock beyond the old slave quarters Shasa, released from his mathematics, was schooling his pony under Jock Murphy's critical eye.

It was a big horse; the limitation on size had recently been dropped by the International Polo Association, but he moved well. Shasa turned him neatly at the end of the paddock and brought him back at a full gallop. Jock tossed a ball to his nearside and Shasa leaned out to take it on his backhand. He had a firm seat and a strong arm for one so young. He swung in a good full arc and the crisp click of the bamboo-root ball carried to where Centaine stood and she saw the white flash of its trajectory in the sunlight.

Shasa reined the pony down and swung him back. As he passed again Jock Murphy tossed another ball to his offside forehand. Shasa topped the shot and it bounced away sloppily.

'Shame on you, Master Shasa,' Jock called. 'You are chopping again. Let the head of your stick take your shot through.'

Jock Murphy was one of Centaine's finds. He was a stocky, muscular man with a short neck and perfectly bald head. He had done everything: Royal Marines, professional boxer, opium runner, master at arms to an Indian maharajah, race-horse trainer, bouncer in a Mayfair gambling club and now he was Shasa's physical instructor. He was a champion shot with rifle, shotgun and pistol, a ten-goal polo player, deadly on the snooker table. He had killed a man in the ring, ridden in the Grand National, and he treated Shasa like his own son.

Once in every three months or so he went on the whisky and turned into a devil incarnate. Then Centaine would send someone down to the police station to pay the damages and bail Jock out. He would stand in front of her desk, his Derby hat held in front of his chest, shaky and hungover, his bald head shiny with shame, and apologize humbly.

'It won't happen again, missus. I don't know what came over me. Give me another chance, missus, I won't let you down.'

It was useful to know a man's weakness: a leash to hold him and a lever to move him.

There was no work for them in Windhoek. When they arrived, having walked and begged lifts on trucks and wagons all the way from the coast, they moved into the hobo encampment near the railway tracks on the outskirts of the town.

By tacit agreement the hundred or so down-and-outers and drifters and out-of-workers were allowed to camp here with their families, but the local police kept a wary eye on them. The huts were of tarpaper and old corrugated iron sheets and rough thatch and in front of each squatted dejected clusters of men and women. Only the children, dusty and skinny and sun-browned, were noisy and almost defiantly rambunctious. The encampment smelled of wood smoke and the shallow pit latrines.

Somebody had erected a crudely lettered sign facing the railway tracks: 'Vaal Hartz? Hell No!' Anyone who applied for unemployment benefits was immediately sent by the government labour department to work on the huge Vaal Hartz river irrigation project for two shillings a day. Rumours of the conditions in the labour camps there had filtered back, and in the Transvaal there had been riots when the police had attempted forcibly to transport men to the scheme.

All the better spots in the encampment were already occupied, so they camped under a small camelthorn bush and hung scraps of tarpaper in the branches for shade. Swart Hendrick was squatting beside the fire, slowly trickling handfuls of white maize meal into a soot-blackened billy of boiling water. He looked up as Lothar came back from another unsuccessful job hunt in the town. When Lothar shook his head, Hendrick returned to his cookery.

'Where is Manfred?'

Hendrick pointed with his chin at another shack near by. A dozen or so ragged men were sitting in a fascinated knot listening to a tall bearded man in their midst. He had the intense expression and fanatically dark eyes of a zealot.

'Mal Willem,' Hendrick muttered. 'Crazy William,' and Lothar grunted as he searched for Manfred and then recognized his son's shining blond head amongst the others.

Satisfied that the boy was safe, Lothar took his pipe from his top pocket, blew through it and then filled it with Magaliesberg shag. The pipe stank, and the black tobacco was rank and harsh, but cheap. He longed for a cheroot as he lit the pipe with a twig from the fire. It tasted disgusting, but he felt the soothing effect almost immediately and he tossed the tobacco pouch to Hendrick and leaned back against the trunk of the thorn tree.

'What did *you* find out?'

Hendrick had spent most of the night and morning in the coloured shanty town across the other side of Windhoek. If you want to know a man's intimate secrets, ask the servants who wait at his table and make his bed.

'I found out that you can't get a drink on credit – and the Windhoek maids don't do it for love alone.' He grinned.

Lothar spat tobacco juice and glanced across at his son. It worried him a little that the boy avoided the camp urchins of his own age and sat with the men. Yet the men seemed to accept him.

'What else?' he asked Hendrick.

'The man is called Fourie. He has been working at the mine for ten years. He comes in with four or five trucks every week and goes back loaded with stores.' For a minute Hendrick concentrated on mixing the maize porridge, applying exactly the right heat from the fire.

'Go on.'

'Then, on the first Monday of every month, he comes in one small truck, the four other drivers with him riding in the back, all of them armed with shotguns and pistols. They go directly to the Standard Bank in Main Street. The manager and his staff come to the side door. Fourie and one of his drivers carry a small iron box from the truck into the bank. Afterwards Fourie and his men go down to the corner bar and drink until closing time. In the morning they go back to the mine.'

'Once a month,' Lothar whispered. 'They bring in a whole month's production at one time.' Then he looked up at Hendrick. 'You said the corner bar?' And when the big black man nodded, 'I'll need at least ten shillings.'

'What for?' Hendrick was immediately suspicious.

'One of us has to buy the barman a drink and they don't

serve blacks at the corner bar.' Lothar smiled maliciously, then raised his voice. 'Manfred!'

The boy had been so mesmerized by the speaker that he had not noticed his father's return. He scrambled to his feet guiltily.

Hendrick dumped a lump of fluffy white maize porridge into the lid of the billy and poured *maas*, thick soured milk, over it before he handed it to Manfred where he squatted crosslegged beside his father.

'Did you know that it's all a plot by the Jewish owners of the gold mines in Johannesburg, Papa?' Manfred asked, his eyes shining like a religious convert's.

'What is?' Lothar grunted.

'The Depression.' Manfred used the word importantly, for he had just learned it. 'It's been arranged by the Jews and the English so that they will have all the men they want to work for them for nothing on their mines and in their factories.'

'Is that so?' Lothar smiled as he spooned up the *maas* and maize meal. 'And did the Jews and the English arrange the drought as well?' His hatred of the English did not extend beyond the borders of reason, though it could not have been more intense had the English indeed engineered the drought that had turned so many of his people's farms into sandy wastelands, the topsoil blown away on the wind, and the livestock into desiccated mummies embalmed in their own plank-hard skins.

'It's so, Papa!' Manfred cried. '*Oom* Willem explained it to us.' He pulled a rolled sheet of newsprint from his back pocket and spread it across his knee. 'Just look at this!'

The newspaper was *Die Vaderland*, an Afrikaans-language publication, 'The Fatherland', and the cartoon that Manfred was pointing out with a forefinger that trembled with indignation was in its typical style: 'Look what the Jews are doing to us!'

The main character in the cartoon was 'Hoggenheimer',

one of *Die Vaderland*'s creations, depicted as a gross creature in frock coat and spats, a huge diamond sparkling in his cravat, diamond rings on the fingers of both his hands, a top hat over his dark Semitic curls, a thick drooping lower lip and a great hooked beak of a nose the tip of which almost touched his chin. His pockets were stuffed with five-pound notes and he brandished a long whip as he drove a loaded wagon towards distant steel headgear towers labelled 'gold mines'. In the traces of the wagon were human beings instead of trek-oxen. Lines of men and women, skeletal and starving, with huge tortured eyes as they toiled onwards under Hoggenheimer's whip. The women wore the traditional *voortrekker* bonnets, and the men slouch hats, and so that there could be no mistake, the artist had labelled them *Die Afrikaner Volk*, 'the Afrikaans people', and the caption to the cartoon was 'The New Great Trek'.

Lothar chuckled and handed the news-sheet back to his son. He knew very few Jews, and none who looked like Hoggenheimer. Most of them were as hardworking and ordinary as anyone else, and now were as poor and starving.

'If life were as simple as that . . .' He shook his head.

'It is, Papa! All we have to do is get rid of the Jews, *Oom* Willem explained it.'

Lothar was about to reply when he realized that the smell of their food had attracted three of the camp's children, who were standing at a polite distance watching each spoonful he raised to his mouth. The cartoon was no longer important.

There was one older girl, about twelve years of age. She was blonde, her long braids bleached as silver and fine as the Kalahari grass in winter. She was so thin that her face seemed all bone and eyes, prominent cheekbones and a high straight forehead. Her eyes were the light blue of the desert sky. Her dress was of old flour sacks sewn together, and her feet were bare.

Clinging to her skirts were two smaller children. A boy

with a shaven head and large ears. His skinny brown legs stuck out of his patched khaki shorts. The small girl had a runny nose, and she sucked her thumb as she clung to her elder sister's skirts with the other hand.

Lothar looked away but suddenly the food lost its flavour and he chewed with difficulty. He saw that Hendrick was not looking at the children either. Manfred had not noticed them and was still poring over the news-sheet.

'If we feed them, we'll have every kid in the camp on our backs,' Lothar murmured, and he made a resolution never to eat in public again.

'We've got just enough left for tonight,' Hendrick agreed. 'We cannot share it.'

Lothar raised the spoon to his mouth, and then lowered it. He stared at the food on his tin plate for a moment and then beckoned the eldest girl.

She came forward shyly.

'Take it,' Lothar ordered gruffly.

'Thank you, Uncle,' she whispered. '*Dankie, Oom.*'

She whipped the plate under her skirt, hiding it from other eyes, and then dragged the two little ones away. They disappeared amongst the huts.

The girl returned an hour later. The plate and spoon had been polished until they shone. 'Does *Oom* have a shirt or anything that I can wash for him,' she asked.

Lothar opened his pack and handed over his and Manfred's soiled clothing. She brought the laundry back at sunset, smelling faintly of carbolic soap and neatly folded.

'Sorry, *Oom*, I didn't have a smoothing iron.'

'What is your name?' Manfred asked her suddenly. She glanced around at him, blushed scarlet and looked at the ground.

'Sarah,' she whispered.

71

L othar buttoned the clean shirt. 'Give me the ten shillings,' he ordered.

'We'd have our throats cut if anybody knew that I have that much money,' Hendrick grumbled.

'You are wasting my time.'

'Time is the only thing we have plenty of.'

Including the barman, there were only three men in the corner bar when Lothar pushed through the swing doors.

'Quiet tonight,' Lothar remarked as he ordered a beer, and the barman grunted. He was a nondescript little man with wispy grey hair and steel-framed spectacles.

'Take a drink for yourself,' Lothar offered, and the man's expression changed.

'I'll take a gin, thank you.' He poured from a special bottle that he produced from under the counter. They both knew that the colourless liquid was water and the silver shilling would go directly into the barman's pocket.

'Your health.' He leaned over the counter, prepared to be affable for a shilling and the possibility of another.

They chatted idly, agreeing that times were hard and would get harder, that they needed rain and that the Government was to blame for it all.

'How long have you been in town? I haven't seen you around.'

'One day – one day too long,' Lothar smiled.

'I didn't catch your name.' And when Lothar told him, he showed genuine interest for the first time.

'Hey,' he called down the bar to his other customers. 'Do you know who this is? It's Lothar De La Rey! Don't you remember the reward posters during the war? He is the one that broke the hearts of the *rooinekke*.' 'Red neck' was the derogatory term for the newly arrived Englishman whose neck was inflamed by the sun. 'Man, he blew up the train at Gemsbokfontein.'

So great was their approbation that one of them even

bought him another beer, but prudently limited his largesse to Lothar alone.

'I'm looking for a job,' Lothar told them when they had all become firm friends, and they all laughed.

'I heard there was work out at the H'ani Mine,' Lothar persisted.

'I'd know if there was,' the barman assured him. 'The drivers from the mine come in here every week.'

'Would you give them a good word about me?' Lothar asked.

'I'll do better. You come in Monday and I'll set you up with Gerhard Fourie, the chief driver. He is a good pal of mine. He'll know what's happening out there.'

By the time Lothar left, he was established as a good fellow and a member of the inner clique of the corner bar, and when he returned four nights later he was hailed by the barman.

'Fourie is here,' he told Lothar. 'Down at the end of the bar. I'll introduce you after I've served these others.'

The bar-room was half full this evening, and Lothar was able to study the driver. He was a powerful-looking man of middle age, with a big slack gut from sitting hours each day behind the driving-wheel. He was balding but had grown the hair above his right ear and then plastered it across his pate with brilliantine. His manner was bluff and loud; he and his mates had the well-satisfied air of men who had just performed a difficult task. He didn't look like a man that you could threaten or frighten, but Lothar had not yet finally decided on what approach to make.

The barman beckoned to him. 'Like you to meet a good friend.' They shook hands. The driver turned it into a contest, but Lothar had half-expected that and shortened his grip, taking his fingers rather than his palm so that Fourie could not exert full force. They held each other's eyes until the driver winced and tried to pull his hand away. Lothar let him go.

'Buy you a drink.' Lothar felt easier now – the man was not as tough as he put out, and when the barman told them who Lothar was and related an exaggerated version of some of his exploits during the war, Fourie's manner became almost fawning and obsequious.

'Look here, man.' He drew Lothar aside and lowered his voice. 'Erik tells me you're looking for a job out at the H'ani Mine. Well, you can forget it, and that's straight. They haven't taken on any new men in a year or longer.'

'Yes.' Lothar nodded glumly. 'Since I asked Erik about the job, I've learned the truth about the H'ani Mine. It will be terrible for you all when it happens.'

The driver looked uneasy. 'What are you talking about, man? What truth is this?'

'Why, I thought you'd know.' Lothar seemed amazed by his ignorance. 'They are going to close the mine in August. Shut it down. Pay everybody off.'

'Good Christ, no!' There was fear in Fourie's eyes. 'That's not true – it can't be true.' The man was a coward, gullible, easily impressed and even more easily influenced. Lothar was grimly satisfied.

'I'm sorry, but it's best to know the truth, isn't it?'

'Who told you this?' Fourie was terrified. He drove past the hobo camp down by the railway every week. He had seen the legion of the unemployed.

'I am walking out with one of the women who works for Abraham Abrahams.' He was the attorney who conducted all the business of the H'ani Mine in Windhoek. 'She saw the letters from Mrs Courtney in Cape Town. There is no doubt. The mine is shutting down. They can't sell the diamonds. Nobody is buying diamonds, not even in London and New York.'

'Oh my God! My God!' whispered Fourie. 'What are we going to do? My wife isn't well and we've got the six children. Sweet Jesus, my kids will starve.'

'It's all right for somebody like you. I'll bet you've got a couple of hundred quid saved up. You'll be all right.'

But Fourie shook his head.

'Well, if you haven't got anything saved, you'd best put a few pounds aside before they lay you off in August.'

'How does a man do that? How do I save – with a wife and six kids?' Fourie demanded hopelessly.

'I tell you what.' Lothar took his arm in a friendly concerned grip. 'Let's get out of here. I'll buy a bottle of brandy. Let's go some place where we can talk.'

The sun was up by the time Lothar got back to the camp the following morning. They had emptied the brandy bottle while they talked the night away. The driver was intrigued and tempted by Lothar's proposition but unsure and afraid.

Lothar had to explain and convince him of every single point, particularly of his own safety. 'Nobody will ever be able to point a finger at you. I give you my sacred word on it. You'll be protected even if something goes wrong – and nothing will go wrong.'

Lothar had used all his powers of persuasion, and he was tired now as he trudged through the encampment and squatted down beside Hendrick.

'Coffee?' he asked and belched the taste of old brandy into his mouth.

'Finished.' Hendrick shook his head.

'Where is Manfred?'

Hendrick pointed with his chin. Manfred was sitting under a thorn bush at the far end of the camp. The girl Sarah was beside him, their blond heads almost touching as they pored over a sheet of newsprint. Manfred was writing on the margin of the page with a charcoal stick from the camp fire.

'Manie is teaching her to read and write,' Hendrick explained.

Lothar grunted and rubbed his bloodshot eyes. His head ached from the brandy.

'Well,' he said. 'We've got our man.'

'Ah!' Hendrick grinned. 'Then we will need the horses.'

The private railway coach had once belonged to Cecil Rhodes and the De Beers Diamond Company. Centaine Courtney had purchased it for a fraction of the price that a new carriage would have cost her, a fact that gave her satisfaction. She was still a Frenchwoman and knew the value of a sou and a franc. She had brought out a young designer from Paris to redecorate the carriage in the Art Deco style, which was all the rage, and he had been worth every penny of his fee.

She looked around the saloon, at the uncluttered lines of the furnishings, at the whimsical nude nymphs which supported the bronze light-fittings and the Aubrey Beardsley designs inlaid with exquisite workmanship into the lightwood panelling and she remembered that the designer had struck her at first as being a homosexual, with his long flowing locks, his darkly decadent eyes and the features of a beautiful, bored and cynical faun. Her first estimate had been far wide of the truth, as she had discovered to her delight on the circular bed which he had installed in the coach's main bedroom suite. She smiled at the memory and then checked the smile as she saw that Shasa was watching her.

'You know, Mater, I sometimes think I can see what you are thinking, just by looking into your eyes.' He said these disconcerting things sometimes, and she was sure that he had grown another inch in the last week.

'I certainly hope that you cannot.' She shivered. 'It's cold in here.' The designer had incorporated, at enormous expense, a refrigeration machine which cooled the air in the saloon. 'Do turn that thing off, *chéri*.'

She stood up from her desk and went out through the frosted glass doors onto the balcony of the coach and the hot desert air rushed at her and flattened her skirts across her narrow boyish hips. She lifted her face to the sun and let the wind ruffle her short curly hair.

'What time is it?' she asked with her eyes closed and face uplifted, and Shasa who had followed her out leaned against the balcony rail and consulted his wristwatch.

'We should be crossing the Orange river in the next ten minutes, if the engine driver has kept us on schedule.'

'I never feel as though we are home until I cross the Orange.' Centaine went to lean beside him and slipped her arm through his.

The Orange river drained the western watershed of the southern African continent, rising high in the snowy mountains of Basutoland and running down fourteen hundred miles through grassy veld and wild gorges, at some seasons a clear slow trickle and at other times a thunderous brown flood bringing down the rich chocolate silts so that some called it the Nile of the south. It was the boundary between the Cape of Good Hope and the former German colony of South West Africa.

The locomotive whistled and the coupling jolted as the brakes squealed.

'We are slowing for the bridge.' Shasa leaned out over the balcony, and Centaine bit back the caution that came automatically to her lips.

'Beg your pardon, you can't baby him forever, Missus,' Jock Murphy had advised her. 'He's a man now, and a man's got to take his own chances.'

The tracks curved down towards the river, and they could see the Daimler riding on the flat bed behind the locomotive. It was a new vehicle, Centaine changed them every year. However, it also was yellow, as they all were, but with a black bonnet and black piping around the doors. The train journey to Windhoek saved them the onerous drive across the desert, but there was no line out to the mine.

'There it is!' Shasa called. 'There is the bridge!'

The steelwork seemed feathery and insubstantial as it crossed the half mile of riverbed, leapfrogging across its concrete buttresses. The regular beat of the bogey wheels over the cross ties altered as they ran out onto the span, and the steel girders beneath them rang like an orchestra.

'The river of diamonds,' Centaine murmured as she leaned shoulder to shoulder with Shasa and peered down into the coffee-brown waters that swirled around the piers of the bridge beneath them.

'Where do the diamonds come from?' Shasa asked. He knew the answer, of course, but he liked to hear her tell it to him.

'The river gathers them up, from every little pocket and crevice and pipe along its course. It picks up those that were flung into the air during the volcanic eruptions at the beginning of the continent's existence. For hundreds of millions of years it has been concentrating the diamonds and carrying them down towards the coast.' She glanced sideways at him. 'And why aren't they worn away, like all the other pebbles?'

'Because they are the hardest substance in nature. Nothing wears or scratches a diamond,' he answered promptly.

'Nothing is harder or more beautiful,' she agreed, and held up her right hand before his face so that the huge marquis cut diamond on her forefinger dazzled him. 'You will grow to love them. Everybody who works with them comes to love them.'

'The river,' he reminded her. He loved her voice. The

husky trace of her accent intrigued him. 'Tell me about the river,' he demanded, and listened avidly as she went on.

'Where the river runs into the sea, it has thrown its diamonds up on the beaches. Those beaches are so rich in diamonds that they are the forbidden area, the Spieregebied.'

'Could you fill your pockets with diamonds, just pick them up like fallen fruit in the orchard?'

'It's not as easy as that,' she laughed. 'You could search for twenty years and not find a single stone, but if you knew where to look and had even the most primitive equipment and a great deal of luck—'

'Why can't we go in there, Mater?'

'Because, mon chéri, it is all taken. It belongs to a man named Oppenheimer – Sir Ernest Oppenheimer – and his company called De Beers.'

'One company owns it all. That's not fair!' he protested, and Centaine was delighted to notice the acquisitive sparkle in his eyes for the first time. Without a healthy measure of avarice, he would not be capable of carrying through the plans she was so carefully laying for him. She had to teach him to be greedy – for wealth and for power.

'He owns the Orange river concessions,' she nodded, 'and he owns the Kimberley and Wesselton and Bultfontein and all the other great producing mines, but more, much more than that, he controls the sale of every single stone, even those produced by us, the few little independents—'

'He controls us – he controls the H'ani?' Shasa demanded indignantly, his smooth cheeks flushing.

Centaine nodded. 'We have to offer every diamond we mine to his Central Selling Organization, and he will set a price upon it.'

'And we have to accept his price?'

'No, we don't! But we would be very unwise not to do so.'

'What could he do to us if we refused?'

'Shasa, I have told you often before. Don't fight with somebody stronger than yourself. There aren't many people stronger than us – not in Africa anyway – but Sir Ernest Oppenheimer is one of them.'

'What could he do?' Shasa persisted.

'He could eat us up, my darling, and nothing would give him greater pleasure. Each year we become richer and more attractive to him. He is the one man in the world that we have to be afraid of, especially if we were rash enough to come near this river of his.' She swept a gesture across the wide river.

Although it had been named Orange by its Dutch discoverers for the Stadtholders of the House of Orange, the name could have as readily applied to its startling orange-coloured sandbanks. The bright plumage of the waterfowl clustered upon them were like precious stones set in red gold.

'He owns the river?' Shasa was surprised and perplexed.

'Not legally, but you approach it at your own peril for he protects it and the diamonds it contains with his jealous wrath.'

'So there are diamonds here?'

Eagerly Shasa scanned the banks as though he expected to see them sparkling seductively in the sunlight.

'Dr Twentyman-Jones and I both believe it – and we have isolated some very interesting areas. Two hundred miles upstream is a waterfall that the Bushmen called the Place of the Great Noise, Aughrabies. There the Orange thunders through a narrow rocky chute and falls into the deep, inaccessible gorge below. The gorge should be a treasurehouse of captured diamonds. Then there are other ancient alluvial beds where the river has changed its course.'

They left the river and its narrow strip of greenery and the loco accelerated again as they ran on northwards into the desert. Centaine watched Shasa's face carefully as she went on explaining and lecturing. She would never go on until she reached the point of boredom – at the first sign of inattention, she would stop. She did not have to press. There was all the time necessary for his education, but the one single most important consideration was never to tire him, never to outrun his immature strength or his undeveloped powers of concentration. She must retain his enthusiasm intact and never jade him. This time his interest persisted beyond its usual span, and she recognized it was time for another advance.

'It will have warmed up in the saloon. Let's go in.' She led him to her desk. 'There are some things I want to show you.' She opened the confidential summary of the annual financial reports of the Courtney Mining and Finance Company.

This would be the difficult part, even for her the paperwork was deadly dull, and she saw him immediately daunted by the columns of figures. Mathematics was his only weak subject.

'You enjoy chess, don't you?'

'Yes,' he agreed cautiously.

'This is a game also,' she assured him. 'But a thousand times more fascinating and rewarding, once you understand the rules.' He cheered up visibly – games and rewards Shasa understood.

'Teach me the rules,' he invited.

'Not all at one time. Bit by bit, until you know enough to start playing.'

It was evening before she saw the fatigue in the lines at the corners of his mouth and the white rims to his nostrils, but he was still frowning with concentration.

'That's enough for today.' She closed the thick folder 'What are the golden rules?'

'You must always sell something for more than it cost you.'

She nodded encouragement.

'And you must buy when everybody else is selling, and you must sell when everybody else is buying.'

'Good.' She stood up. 'Now a breath of fresh air before we change for dinner.'

On the balcony of the coach she placed her arm around his shoulders, and she had to reach up to do so. 'When we get to the mine, I want you to work with Dr Twentyman-Jones in the mornings. You may have the afternoons free, but you'll work in the mornings. I want you to get to know the mine and all its workings. Of course, I will pay you.'

'That isn't necessary, Mater.'

'Another golden rule, my darling, never refuse a fair offer.'

Through the night and all the following day they ran on northwards across great spaces bleached by the sun, with blue mountains traced in darker blue against the desert horizons.

'We should get into Windhoek a little after sunset,' Centaine explained. 'But I have arranged for the coach to be shunted on to a quiet spur and we will spend the night aboard and leave for the mine in the morning. Dr Twentyman-Jones and Abraham Abrahams will be dining with us, so we will dress.'

In his shirtsleeves Shasa was standing in front of the long mirror in his compartment, struggling with his black bowtie – he had not yet entirely mastered the art of shaping the butterfly – when he felt the coach slowing and heard the loco blow a long eerie blast.

He felt a prickle of excitement and turned to the open window. They were crossing the shoulder of hills above the town of Windhoek, and the street lights came on even as he watched. The town was the size of one of Cape Town's suburbs and only the few central streets were lit.

The train slowed to a walking pace as they reached the outskirts of the town, and Shasa smelled wood-smoke.

Then he noticed that there was some sort of encampment amongst the thorn trees beside the tracks. He leaned out of the window to see more clearly and stared at the clusters of untidy shanties, wreathed in the blue smoke of campfires and shaded by the deepening dusk. There was a crudely lettered sign facing the tracks and Shasa read it with difficulty: 'Vaal Hartz? Hell No!' It made no sense and he frowned as he noticed two figures standing near the sign, watching the passing train.

The shorter of the two was a girl, barefoot and with a thin shapeless dress over her frail body. She did not interest him and he transferred his attention to the taller, more robust figure beside her. Immediately he straightened in shock and rising indignation. Even in the poor light, he recognized that silver-blond shock of hair and the black eyebrows. They stared at each other expressionlessly, the boy in the white dress shirt and black tie in the lighted window and the boy in dusty khaki. Then the train slid past and hid them from each other.

'Darling—' Shasa turned from the window to face his mother. She was wearing sapphires tonight and a blue dress as filmy and light as woodsmoke. 'You aren't ready yet. We'll be in the station in a minute – and what a mess you have made of your tie. Come here and let me do it for you.'

As she stood in front of him and shaped the bow with dextrous fingers, Shasa struggled to contain and suppress the anger and sense of inadequacy that a mere glimpse of the other boy had aroused in him.

The driver of the locomotive shunted them off the main track onto a private spur beyond the sheds of the railway workshop and uncoupled them beside the concrete ramp where Abraham Abrahams' Ford was already parked, and Abe scampered up on to the balcony the moment the coach came to a stop.

'Centaine, you are more beautiful than ever.' He kissed her hand and then each of her cheeks. He was a little man, just Centaine's height, with a lively expression and quick, alert eyes. His ears were pricked up as though he were listening to a sound that nobody else could hear.

His studs were diamond and onyx, which was flashy, and his dinner jacket was a little too extravagantly cut, but he was one of Centaine's favourite people. He had stood by her when her total wealth had amounted to something less than ten pounds. He had filed the claims for the H'ani Mine and since then conducted most of her legal business and many of her private affairs as well. He was an old and dear friend but, more important, he did not make mistakes in his work. He wouldn't have been here if he did.

'Dear Abe.' She took both his hands and squeezed them. 'How is Rachel?'

'Outstanding,' he assured her. It was his favourite adjective. 'She sends her apologies, but the new baby—'

'Of course.' Centaine nodded, understanding. Abraham knew her preferences for masculine company and seldom brought his wife with him, even when invited to do so.

Centaine turned from her lawyer to the other tall stoop-shouldered figure that was hovering at the gate of the balcony.

'Dr Twentyman-Jones.' She held out her hands.

'Mrs Courtney,' he murmured like an undertaker.

Centaine put on her most radiant smile. It was her own little game, to see if she could inveigle him into the smallest display of pleasure. She lost again. His apparent gloom deepened until he looked like a bloodhound in mourning.

Their relationship went back almost as far as Centaine's with Abraham. He had been a consulting mining engineer with the De Beers Diamond Company, but he had evaluated and opened the H'ani workings for her back in 1919. It had taken almost five years of her most winning persuasion before he had agreed to come to work for the H'ani Mine as Resident Engineer. He was probably the best diamond man in South Africa, which meant the best in the world.

Centaine led the two of them into the saloon and waved the white-jacketed barman aside.

'Abraham, a glass of champagne?' She poured the wine with her own hands. 'And Dr Twentyman-Jones, a little Madeira?'

'You never forget, Mrs Courtney,' he admitted miserably as she carried the glass to him. Between them it was always full titles and surnames, although their friendship had stood all the tests.

'I give you good health, gentlemen.' Centaine saluted them, and when they had drunk she glanced across at the far door.

On cue Shasa came through and Centaine watched critically as he shook hands with each of the men. He conducted himself with just the correct amount of deference for their age, showed no discomfort when Abraham over-effusively embraced him and then returned Twentyman-Jones's greeting with equal solemnity. She gave a small nod of approval and took her seat behind her desk. It was her sign that the niceties had been observed and they could get on to business. The two men quickly perched on the elegant but uncomfortable Art Deco chairs and leaned towards her attentively.

'It has come at last,' Centaine told them. 'They have

cut our quota.' They rocked back in their seats and exchanged a brief glance before turning back to Centaine.

'We have been expecting it for almost a year,' Abraham pointed out.

'Which does not make the actuality any more pleasant,' Centaine told him tartly.

'How much?' Twentyman-Jones asked.

'Forty per cent,' Centaine answered, and he looked as though he might burst into tears while he considered it.

Each of the independent diamond producers was allocated a quota by the Central Selling Organization. The arrangement was informal and probably illegal, but nonetheless rigorously enforced, and none of the independents had ever been foolhardy enough to test the legality of the system or the share of the market they were given.

'Forty per cent!' Abraham burst out. 'That's iniquitous!'

'An accurate observation, dear Abe, but not particularly useful at this stage.' Centaine looked to Twentyman-Jones.

'No change in the categories?' he asked. The quotas were broken down by carat weight into the different types of stones, from dark industrial boart to the finest gem quality, and by size from the tiny crystals of ten points and smaller to the big valuable stones.

'Same percentages,' Centaine agreed, and she slumped in his chair, pulled a notebook from his inside pocket and began a series of quick calculations. Centaine glanced behind her to where Shasa leaned against the panelled bulkhead.

'Do you understand what we are talking about?'

'The quota? Yes, I think so, Mater.'

'If you don't understand, then ask,' she ordered brusquely and turned back to Twentyman-Jones.

'Could you appeal for a ten per cent increase at the top end?' he asked, but she shook her head.

'I have already done so and they turned me down. De Beers in their infinite compassion point out that the biggest drop in demand has been at the top end, at the gem and jewellery level.'

He returned to his notebook, and they listened to his pencil scratching on the paper until he looked up.

'Can we break even?' Centaine asked quietly, and Twentyman-Jones looked as though he might shoot himself rather than reply.

'It will be close,' he whispered, 'and we'll have to fire and cut and hone, but we should be able to pay costs, and perhaps even turn a small profit still, depending upon the floor price that De Beers sets. But the cream will be skimmed off the top, I'm afraid, Mrs Courtney.'

Centaine felt weak and trembly with relief. She took her hands off the desk and placed them in her lap so the others might not notice. She did not speak for a few moments, and then she cleared her throat to make certain her voice did not quaver.

'The effective date for the quota cut is the first of March,' she said. 'That means we can deliver one more full package. You know what to do, Dr Twentyman-Jones.'

'We will fill the package with sweeteners, Mrs Courtney.'

'What is a sweetener, Dr Twentyman-Jones?' Shasa spoke for the first time, and the engineer turned to him seriously.

'When we turn up a number of truly excellent diamonds in one period of production, we reserve some of the best of them, set them aside to include in a future package which might be of inferior quality. We have a reserve of these high quality stones which we will now deliver to the CSO while we still have the opportunity.'

'I understand,' Shasa nodded. 'Thank you, Dr Twentyman-Jones.'

'Pleased to be of service, Master Shasa.'

Centaine stood up. 'We can go in to dinner now,' and the white-jacketed servant opened the sliding doors through into the dining-room where the long table gleamed with silver and crystal and the yellow roses stood tall in their antique celadon vases.

A mile down the railway track from where Centaine's coach stood, two men sat huddled over a smoky campfire watching the maize porridge bubbling in the billy-can and discussing the horses. The entire plan hinged on the horses. They needed at least fifteen, and they had to be strong, desert-hardened animals.

'The man I am thinking of is a good friend,' Lothar said.

'Even the best friend in the world won't lend you fifteen good horses. We can't do it with less than fifteen, and you won't buy them for a hundred pounds.'

Lothar sucked on the stinking clay pipe and it gurgled obscenely. He spat the yellow juice into the fire. 'I'd pay a hundred pounds for a decent cheroot,' he murmured.

'Not my hundred, you won't,' Hendrick contradicted him.

'Leave the horses for now,' Lothar suggested. 'Let's go over the men we need for the relays.'

'The men are easier than the horses.' Hendrick grinned. 'These days you can buy a good man for the price of a meal, and have his wife for the pudding. I have already sent messages to them to meet us at Wild Horse Pan.'

They both glanced up as Manfred came out of the darkness, and when Lothar saw his son's expression he stuffed the notebook into his pocket and stood up quickly.

'Papa, you must come quickly,' Manfred pleaded.

'What is it, Manie?'

'Sarah's mother and the little ones. They are all sick. I told them you would come, Papa.'

Lothar had the reputation of being able to heal humans and animals of all their ills, from gunshot wounds and measles to staggers and distemper.

Sarah's family was living under a tattered sheet of tarpaulin near the centre of the encampment. The woman lay beneath a greasy blanket with the two small children beside her. Though she was probably not older than thirty years, care and punishing labour and poor food had greyed and shrunken her into an old woman. She had lost most of her upper teeth so that her face seemed to have collapsed.

Sarah knelt beside her with a damp rag with which she was trying to wipe her flushed face. The woman rolled her head from side to side and mumbled in delirium.

Lothar knelt on the woman's other side, facing the girl. 'Where is your pa, Sarah? He should be here.'

'He went away to find work on the mines,' she whispered.

'When?'

'Long ago.' And then she went on loyally, 'But he is going to send for us, and we are going to live in a nice house—'

'How long has your ma been sick?'

'Since last night.' Sarah tried again to place the rag on the woman's forehead but she struck it away weakly.

'And the babies?' Lothar studied their swollen faces.

'Since the morning.'

Lothar drew back the blanket and the stench of liquid faeces was thick and choking.

'I tried to clean them,' Sarah whispered defensively, 'but they just dirty themselves again. I don't know what to do.'

Lothar lifted the little girl's soiled dress. Her small pot belly was swollen with malnutrition and her skin was chalky white. An angry crimson rash was blazoned across it.

Involuntarily Lothar jerked his hands away. 'Manfred,' he demanded sharply. 'Have you touched them – any of them?'

'Yes, Pa. I tried to help Sarah clean them.'

'Go to Hendrick,' Lothar ordered. 'Tell him we are leaving immediately. We have to get out of here.'

'What is it, Pa?' Manfred lingered.

'Do as I tell you,' Lothar told him angrily, and when Manfred backed away into the darkness, he returned to the girl.

'Have you been boiling your drinking water?' he asked, and she shook her head.

It was always the same, Lothar thought. Simple country people who had lived far from other human habitation all their lives, drinking at sweet clean springs and defecating carelessly in the open veld. They did not understand the hazards when forced to live in close proximity to others.

'What is it, *Oom?*' Sarah asked softly. 'What is wrong with them?'

'Enteric fever.' Lothar saw that it meant nothing to her. 'Typhoid fever,' he tried again.

'Is it bad?' she asked helplessly, and he could not meet her eyes. He looked again at the two small children. The fever had burned them out, and the diarrhoea had dehydrated them. Already it was too late. With the mother there was perhaps still a chance, but she had been weakened also.

'Yes,' Lothar said. 'It is bad.' The typhoid would be spreading through the encampment like fire in the winter-dry veld. There was already a good chance that Manfred might have been infected, and at the thought he stood up quickly and stepped away from the foulsmelling mattress.

'What must I do?' Sarah pleaded.

'Give them plenty to drink, but make sure the water is boiled.' Lothar backed away. He had seen typhoid in the concentration camps of the English during the war. The death-toll had been more horrible than that of the battle-field. He had to get Manfred away from here.

'Do you have medicine for it, *Oom?*' Sarah followed

him. 'I don't want my ma to die – I don't want my baby sister – if you can give me some medicine—' She was struggling with her tears, bewildered and afraid, turning to him in pathetic trust.

Lothar's only duty was to his own, yet he was torn by the child's little display of courage. He wanted to tell her, 'There is no medicine for them. There is nothing that can be done for them. They are in God's hands now.'

Sarah came after him and took Lothar's hand, tugging desperately at it as she tried to lead him back to the shelter where the woman and the two small children lay dying.

'Help me, *Oom*. Help me to make them better.'

Lothar's skin crawled at the girl's touch. He could imagine the loathsome infection being transferred from her warm soft skin. He had to get away.

'Stay here,' he told her, trying to disguise his revulsion. 'Give them water to drink. I will go to fetch medicine.'

'When will you come back?' She looked up trustingly into his face, and it took all his strength to tell the lie.

'I will come back as soon as I can,' he promised, and gently broke her grip.

'Give them water,' he repeated, and turned away.

'Thank you,' she called after him softly. 'God bless you, you are a kind man, *Oom*.'

Lothar could not reply. He could not even look back. Instead he hurried through the darkened camp. This time, because he was listening for them, he picked up the other little sounds from the huts he passed: the fretful feverish cry of a child, the gasp and moan of a woman in the terrible abdominal cramps of enteric fever, the concerned murmurs of those who tended them.

From one of the tarpaper huts a gaunt dark creature emerged and clutched at his arm. He was not sure whether it was man or woman until she spoke in a cracked almost demented falsetto.

'Are you a doctor? I have to find a doctor.'

Lothar shrugged off the clawed hand and broke into a run.

Swart Hendrick was waiting for him. He had the pack on his shoulder already and was kicking sand over the embers of the campfire. Manfred squatted on one side, beneath the thorn tree.

'Enteric.' Lothar said the dread word. 'It's through the camp already.'

Hendrick froze. Lothar had seen him stand down the charge of a wounded bull elephant, but he was afraid now. Lothar could see it in the way he held his great black head and smell it on him, a strange odour like that of one of the copper-hooded desert cobras when aroused.

'Come on, Manfred. We are getting out.'

'Where are we going, Pa?' Manfred remained squatting.

'Away from here – away from the town and this plague.'

'What about Sarah?' Manfred ducked his head on to his shoulders, a stubborn gesture which Lothar recognized.

'She is nothing to us. There is nothing we can do.'

'She's going to die – like her ma, and the little kids.' Manfred looked up at his father. 'She's going to die, isn't she?'

'Get up on your feet,' Lothar snarled at him. His guilt made him fierce. 'We are going.' He made an authoritative gesture and Hendrick reached down and hauled Manfred to his feet.

'Come, Manie, listen to your Pa.' He followed Lothar, dragging the boy by his arm.

They crossed the railway embankment and Manfred stopped pulling back. Hendrick released him, and he followed obediently. Within the hour they reached the main road, a dusty silver river in the moonlight running down the pass through the hills, and Lothar halted.

'Are we going for the horses now?' Hendrick asked.

'Yes.' Lothar nodded. 'That's the next step.' But his head

turned back in the direction they had come and they were all silent, looking back with him.

'I couldn't take the chance,' Lothar explained. 'I couldn't let Manfred stay near them.' Neither of them answered. 'We have to get on with our preparations – the horses, we have to get the horses—' His voice trailed off.

Suddenly Lothar snatched the pack from Hendrick's shoulder and threw it to the ground. He ripped it open angrily and snatched out the small canvas roll in which he kept his surgical instruments and store of medicines.

'Take Manie,' he ordered Hendrick. 'Wait for me in the gorge of the Gamas river, at the same place we camped on the march from Usakos. You remember it?'

Hendrick nodded. 'How long will it be before you come?'

'As long as it takes them to die,' said Lothar. He stood up and looked at Manfred.

'Do what Hendrick tells you,' he ordered.

'Can't I come with you, Pa?'

Lothar did not bother to reply. He turned and strode back amongst the moonlit thorn trees and they watched him until he disappeared. Then Hendrick dropped to his knees and began re-rolling the pack.

Sarah squatted beside the fire, her skirts pulled up around her skinny brown thighs, slitting her eyes against the smoke as she waited for the soot-blackened billy to boil.

She looked up and saw Lothar standing at the edge of the firelight. She stared at him, and then slowly her pale delicate features seemed to crumple and the tears streamed down her cheeks, glistening in the light of the flames.

'I thought you weren't coming back,' she whispered. 'I thought you had gone.'

Lothar shook his head abruptly, still so angry with his

own weakness that he could not trust himself to speak. Instead he squatted across the fire from her and spread the canvas roll. Its contents were pitifully inadequate. He could draw a rotten tooth, lance a boil or a snakebite, or set a broken limb, but to treat runaway enteric there was almost nothing. He measured a spoonful of a black patent medicine, Chamberlain's Famous Diarrhoea Remedy, into the tin mug and filled it with hot water from the billy.

'Help me,' he ordered Sarah and between them they lifted the youngest child into a sitting position. She was without weight and he could feel every bone in her tiny body, like that of a fledgling taken from the nest. It was hopeless.

'She'll be dead by morning,' he thought, and held the mug to her lips. She did not last that long; she slipped away a few hours before dawn. The moment of death was ill-defined, and Lothar was not certain it was over until he felt for the child's pulse at the carotid and felt the chill of eternity in her wasted flesh.

The little boy lasted until noon and died with as little fuss as his sister. Lothar wrapped them in the same grey, soiled blanket and carried them in his arms to the communal grave that had been already dug at the edge of the camp. They made a small lonely little package on the sandy floor of the square excavation, at the end of the row of larger bodies.

Sarah's mother fought for her life.

'God knows why she should want to go on living,' Lothar thought, 'there isn't much in it for her.' But she moaned and rolled her head and cried out in the delirium of fever. Lothar began to hate her for the stubborn struggle to survive that kept him beside her foul mattress, forced to share in her degradation, to touch her hot fever-racked skin and dribble liquid into her toothless mouth.

At dusk he thought she had won. Her skin cooled and she was quieter. She reached out feebly for Sarah's hand

and tried to speak, staring up at her face as though she recognized her, the words catching and cawing in the back of her throat and thick yellow mucus bubbling in the corners of her lips.

The effort was too much. She closed her eyes and seemed to sleep. Sarah wiped her lips and held on to the thin bony hand with the blue veins swelling under the thin skin.

An hour later the woman sat up suddenly, and said clearly: 'Sarah, where are you, child?' then fell back and fought for a long strangling breath. The breath ended in the middle and her bony chest subsided gradually, and the flesh seemed to droop from her face like warm candlewax.

This time Sarah walked beside him as Lothar carried the woman to the grave site. He laid her at the end of the row of corpses. Then they walked back to the hut.

Sarah stood and watched Lothar roll the canvas pack, and her small white face was desolate. He went half a dozen paces and then turned back. She was quivering like a rejected puppy, but she had not moved.

'All right,' he sighed with resignation. 'Come on, then.' And she scampered to his side.

'I won't be any trouble,' she gabbled, almost hysterical with relief. 'I'll help you. I can cook and sew and wash. I won't be any trouble.'

'What are you going to do with her?' Hendrick asked. 'She can't stay with us. We could never do what we have to do with a child of her age.'

'I could not leave her there,' Lothar defended himself, 'in that death camp.'

'It would have been better for us.' Hendrick shrugged. 'But what do we do now?'

They had left the camp in the bottom of the gorge and climbed to the top of the rocky wall. The children were far below on the sandbank at the edge of the only stagnant green pool in the gorge that still held water.

They squatted side by side, Manfred with his right hand extended as he held the handline. They saw him lean back and strike, then heave the line in hand over hand. Sarah jumped up and her excited shrieks carried up to where they sat. They watched Manfred swing the kicking slippery black catfish out of the green water. It squirmed on the sand, glistening with wetness.

'I will decide what to do with her,' Lothar assured him, but Hendrick interrupted.

'It better be soon. Every day we waste the waterholes in the north are drying out, and we still don't even have the horses.'

Lothar stuffed his clay pipe with fresh shag and thought about it. Hendrick was right; the girl complicated everything. He had to get rid of her somehow. Suddenly he looked up from the pipe and smiled.

'My cousin,' he said, and Hendrick was puzzled.

'I did not know you had a cousin.'

'Most of them perished in the camps, but Trudi survived.'

'Where is she, this beloved cousin of yours?'

'She lives on our road to the north. We'll waste no time in dumping the brat with her.'

'I don't want to go,' Sarah whispered miserably. 'I don't know your aunt. I want to stay here with you.'

'Hush,' Manfred cautioned her. 'You'll wake Pa and Henny.' He pressed closer to her and touched her lips to quieten her. The fire had died down and the moon had set.

Only the desert stars lit them, big as candles against the black velvet curtain of the sky.

Sarah's voice was so small now that he could barely make out the words, though her lips were inches from his ear. 'You are the only friend I have ever had,' she said, 'and who will teach me to read and write?'

Manfred felt an enormous weight of responsibility conferred upon him by her words. His feelings for her to this moment had been ambivalent. Like her he had never had friends of his own age, never attended a school, never lived in a town. His only teacher had been his father. He had lived all his life with grown men; his father and Hendrick and the rough hard men of the road camps and trawler fleet. There had been no woman to caress or gentle him.

She had been his first female companion, though her weakness and silliness irritated him. He had to wait for her to catch up when they climbed the hills and she wept when he beat a squirming catfish to death or wrung the neck of a fat feathered brown francolin taken in one of his noose snares. However, she could make him laugh and he enjoyed her voice when she sang, thin but sweet and melodious. Then again although her adulation was sometimes cloying and excessive, he experienced an unaccountable sense of wellbeing when she was with him. She was quick to learn and in the few days they had been together she already had the alphabet by heart and the multiplication tables from two to ten.

It would have been much better if she had been a boy, but then there was something else. The smell of her skin and the softness of her intrigued him. Her hair was so fine and silky. Sometimes he would touch it as though by accident and she would freeze and keep very still under his fingers, so that he was embarrassed and dropped his hand self-consciously.

Occasionally she would brush against him like an

affectionate cat and the strange pleasure this gave him was out of all proportion to the brief contact; and when they slept under the same blanket, he would awake in the night and listen to her breathing and her hair tickled his face.

The road to Okahandja was long and hard and dusty. They had been on it for five days now. They travelled only in the early morning and late evening. In the noonday the men would rest up in the shade, and the two children could sneak away to talk and set snares or go over Sarah's lessons. They did not play games of make-believe as other children of their age might have done. Their lives were too close to harsh reality. And now a new threat had been thrust upon them: the threat of separation which grew more menacing with each mile of road that fell behind them. Manfred could not find the words of comfort for her. His own sense of coming loss was aggravated by her declaration of friendship. She snuggled against him under the single blanket and the heat that emanated from her thin frail body was startling. Awkwardly he slipped an arm around her thin shoulders and her hair was soft against his cheek.

'I'll come back for you.' He had not meant to say that. He had not even thought it before that moment.

'Promise me.' She twisted so that her lips were by his ear. 'Promise me you will come back to fetch me.'

'I promise I will come back to you,' he repeated solemnly, appalled at what he was doing. He had no control over his future, could never be certain of honouring a promise like that.

'When?' She fastened on it eagerly.

'We have something to do.' Manfred did not know the details of what his father and Henny were planning. He only understood that it was arduous and somehow dangerous. 'Something important. No, I can't tell you about it. But, when it is over, we will come back for you.'

It seemed to satisfy her. She sighed, and he felt the

tension go out of her limbs. Her whole body softened with sleepiness, and her voice drifted into a low murmur.

'You are my friend, aren't you, Manie?'

'Yes. I'm your friend.'

'My best friend?'

'Yes, your best friend.'

She sighed again and fell asleep. He stroked her hair, so soft and fluffy under his hand, and he was assailed by the melancholy of impending loss. He felt that he would weep, but that was a girlish thing and he would not let it happen.

The following evening they trudged ankle-deep in the floury white dust up another fold in the vast undulating plain, and when the children caught up with Lothar at the crest, he pointed wordlessly ahead.

The cluster of iron roofs of the little frontier town of Okahandja shone in the lowering sunlight like mirrors, and in their midst was the single spire of a church. Also clad in corrugated iron, it barely topped the trees which grew around it.

'We'll be there after dark.' Lothar eased his pack to his other shoulder and looked down at the girl. Her fine hair was plastered with dust and sweat to her forehead and cheeks, and her untidy sunstreaked blond pigtails stuck out behind her ears like horns. The sun had burned her so dark that were it not for the fair hair she might have been a Nama child. She was dressed as simply and her bare feet were white with floury dust.

Lothar had considered and then rejected the idea of buying her a new dress and shoes at one of the little general-dealer's stores along the road. The expense might have been worthwhile, for if the child were rejected by his cousin – He did not follow the thought further. He would clean her up a little at the borehole that supplied the town's water.

'The lady you will be staying with is *Mevrou* Trudi Bierman. She is a very kind religious lady.'

Lothar had little in common with his cousin. They had not met in thirteen years. 'She is married to the dominie of the Dutch Reformed Church here at Okahandja. He is also a fine God-fearing man. They have children your age. You will be very happy with them.'

'Will he teach me to read like Manie does?'

'Of course he will.' Lothar was prepared to give any assurance to rid himself of the child. 'He teaches his own children and you will be like one of them.'

'Why can't Manie stay with me?'

'Manie has to come with me.'

'Please, can't I come with you too?'

'No, you cannot. You'll stay here – and I don't want to go over that again.'

At the reservoir of the borehole pump Sarah bathed the dust from her legs and arms and dampened her hair before re-plaiting her pigtails.

'I'm ready,' she told Lothar at last, and her lips trembled while he looked her over critically. She was a grubby little urchin, a burden upon them, but somehow a fondness for her had crept in upon him. He could not help but admire her spirit and her courage. Suddenly he found himself wondering if there was no other way than abandoning the child and it took an effort to thrust the idea aside and steel himself to what must be done.

'Come on then.' He took her hand and turned to Manfred. 'You wait here with Henny.'

'Please let me come with you, Pa,' Manfred begged. 'Just as far as the gate. Just to say goodbye to Sarah.'

Lothar wavered and then agreed gruffly. 'All right, but keep your mouth shut and remember your manners.'

He led them down the narrow sanitary lane at the rear of the row of cottages until they came to the back gate of a larger house beside the church and obviously attached to it. There was no mistaking that it was the pastory. There was a light burning in the back room, the fierce white light of a Petromax lamp, and the bugs and moths were drumming against the wire screening that covered the back door.

The sound of voices raised in a dolorous religious chant carried to them as they opened the gate and went up the kitchen path. When they reached the screen door they could see in the lighted kitchen beyond a family seated at a long deal table, singing together.

Lothar knocked on the door and the hymn trailed away. From the head of the table a man rose and came towards the door. He was dressed in a black suit that bagged at the knees and elbows but was stretched tightly across his broad shoulders. His hair was thick and long, hanging in a greying mane to his shoulders and sprinkling the dark cloth with a flurry of dandruff.

'Who is it?' he demanded, in a voice trained to boom out from the pulpit. He flung open the screen door and peered out into the dark. He had a broad intelligent forehead with the arrowhead of a sharp widow's peak emphasizing its depth, and his eyes were deep-set and fierce as those of a prophet from the Old Testament.

'You!' He recognized Lothar, but made no attempt to greet him further. Instead he looked back over his shoulder. '*Mevrou*, it is your godless cousin come in from the wilderness like Cain!'

The fair-headed woman rose from the foot of the table, hushing the children and signalling them to remain in their seats. She was almost as tall as her husband, in her forties and well fleshed, with a rosy complexion and braids piled on top of her head in the Germanic fashion. She folded her thick creamy-skinned arms across her bulky shapeless bosom.

'What do you want with us, Lothar De La Rey?' she demanded. 'This is the God-fearing home of Christian folk; we want nothing of your wanton ways and wild behaviour.' She broke off as she noticed the children and stared at them with interest.

'Hello, Trudi.' Lothar drew Sarah forward into the light. 'It has been many years. You look well and happy.'

'I am happy in God's love,' his cousin agreed. 'But you know I have seldom been well.' She assumed an expression of suffering and Lothar went on quickly.

'I am giving you another chance of Christian service.' He pushed Sarah forward. 'This poor little orphan – she is alone. She needs a home. You could take her in, Trudi, and God will love you for it.'

'Is it another of your—' His cousin glanced back into the kitchen at the interested faces of her own two daughters, and then lowered her voice and hissed at him, 'Another of your bastards?'

'Her family died in the typhoid epidemic.'

It was a mistake. He saw her recoil from the girl. 'That was weeks ago. She is free of the disease.'

Trudi relaxed a little and Lothar went on quickly. 'I cannot care for her. We are travelling, and she needs a woman.'

'We have too many mouths already—' she began, but her husband interrupted her.

'Come here, child,' he boomed and Lothar shoved Sarah towards him. 'What is your name?'

'Sarah Bester, *Oom*.'

'So you are of the *Volk*?' the tall dominie demanded. 'One of the true Afrikaner blood?'

Sarah nodded uncertainly.

'And your dead mother and father were wed in the Reformed Church?' She nodded again. 'And you believe in the Lord God of Israel?'

'Yes, *Oom*. My mother taught me,' Sarah whispered.

'Then we cannot turn the child away,' he told his wife. 'Bring her in, woman. God will provide. God always provides for his chosen people.'

Trudi Bierman sighed theatrically and reached for Sarah's arm. 'So thin, and filthy as a Nama piccaninny.'

'And you, Lothar De La Rey,' the dominie pointed a finger at him. 'Has not the merciful Lord yet shown you the error of your ways, and placed your feet on the path of righteousness?'

'Not yet, dear cousin.' Lothar backed away from the door, his relief undisguised.

The dominie's attention flicked to the boy standing in the shadows behind Lothar. 'Who is this?'

'My son, Manfred.' Lothar placed a protective arm over the boy's shoulder, and the dominie came closer and stooped to study his face closely. His great dark beard bristled and his eyes were wild and fanatical, but Manfred stared directly into them, and saw them change. They warmed and lightened with the sparkle of good humour and compassion.

'Do I frighten you, *Jong?*' His voice mellowed, and Manfred shook his head.

'No, *Oomie* – or not too much anyway.'

The dominie chuckled. 'Who teaches you your Bible, *Jong?*' He used the expression meaning 'young' or 'young man'.

'My father, *Oom.*'

'Then God have mercy on your soul.' He stood up and thrust his beard out at Lothar.

'I would you had left the boy, rather than the girl,' he told him, and Lothar tightened his grip on Manfred's shoulder. 'He is a likely looking lad, and we need good men in the service of God and the *Volk.*'

'He is well taken care of.' Lothar could not conceal his agitation, but the dominie dropped his compelling gaze back to Manfred.

'I think, *Jong,* that you and I are destined by Almighty God to meet again. When your father drowns or is eaten by a lion or hanged by the English, or in some other fashion punished by the Lord God of Israel, then come back here. Do you hear me, *Jong?* I need you, the *Volk* need you, and

God needs you! My name is Tromp Bierman, the Trumpet of the Lord. Come back to this house!'

Manfred nodded. 'I will come back to see Sarah. I promised her.'

As he said it the girl's courage broke and she sobbed and tried to pull free from Trudi's grip.

'Stop that, child.' Trudi Bierman shook her irritably. 'Stop blubbering.' Sarah gulped and swallowed the next sob.

Lothar turned Manfred away from the door. 'The child is hard-working and willing, cousin. You will not regret this charity,' he called over his shoulder.

'That we shall see,' his cousin muttered dubiously, and Lothar started back down the path.

'Remember the Lord's word, Lothar De La Rey,' the Trumpet of the Lord bugled after them. 'I am the Way and the Light. Whosoever believeth in me—'

Manfred twisted in his father's grip and looked back. The tall gaunt figure of the dominie almost filled the kitchen doorway, but at the level of his waist Sarah's small face peered around him – in the light of the Petromax it was white as bone china and glistened with her tears.

F our men were waiting for them at the rendezvous. During the desperate years when they had fought together in guerilla commando, it had been necessary for every man to know the reassembly points. When cut up and separated in the running battles against the Union troops, they had scattered away into the veld and days later come together at one of the safe places.

There was always water at these assembly points, a seep in the rocky crevice of a hillside, a Bushman well or a dry riverbed where they could dig for the precious stuff. The assembly points were always sited with an all-round view so that a following enemy could never take them by surprise. In addition, there was always grazing nearby for the horses and shelter for the men, and they had laid down caches of supplies at these places.

The rendezvous that Lothar had chosen for this meeting had an additional advantage. It was in the hills only a few miles north of the homestead of a prosperous German cattle-rancher, a good friend of Lothar's family, a sympathizer who could be relied upon to tolerate their presence on his lands.

Lothar entered the hills along the dried watercourse that twisted through them like a maimed puffadder. He walked in the open so that the waiting men could see him from afar, and they were still two miles from the rendezvous when a tiny figure appeared on the rocky crest ahead of them, windmilling his arms in welcome. He was quickly joined by the other three and then they came running down the rough hillside to meet Lothar's party in the riverbed.

Leading them was 'Vark Jan', or 'Pig John', the old Khoisan warrior with his yellow wrinkled features that bespoke his mixed lineage of Nama and Bergdama and, so he boasted, of even the true Bushman. Allegedly, his grandmother had been a Bushman slave captured by the Boers in one of the last great slave raids of the previous century. But then he was a famous liar and opinion was divided as to the truth of this claim. He was followed closely by Klein Boy, Swart Hendrick's bastard son by a Herero mother.

He came directly to his father and greeted him with the traditional deferential clapping of hands. He was as tall and as powerfully built as Hendrick himself, but with the finer features and slanted eyes of his mother, and his skin was not as dark. Like wild honey it changed colour as the sunlight played upon it. These two had worked on the trawlers at Walvis Bay, and Hendrick had sent them ahead to find the other men they needed and bring them to the rendezvous.

Lothar turned to these men now. It was twelve years since last he had seen them. He remembered them as wild fighting men – his hunting dogs, he had called them with affection and total lack of trust. For like wild dogs they would have turned and savaged him at the first sign of weakness.

Now he greeted them by their old *noms de guerre*: 'Legs', the Ovambo with legs like a stork and 'Buffalo', who carried his head hunched on his thick neck like that animal. They clasped hands, then wrists and then hands again in the ritual greeting of the band reserved for special occasions, as after long separation or a successful foray, and Lothar studied them and saw how twelve years and easy living had altered them. They were fat and soft and middle-aged but, he consoled himself, the tasks he had for them were not demanding.

'So!' He grinned at them. 'We have pulled you off the fat bellies of your wives, and away from your beer-pots.' And they roared with laughter.

'We came the same minute that Klein Boy and Pig John spoke your name to us,' they assured him.

'Of course, you came only because of the love and loyalty you bear me—' Lothar's sarcasm was biting, 'the way the vulture and the jackal come for love of the dead, not of the feast.'

They roared again. How they had missed the whip of his tongue.

'Pig John did mention gold,' the Buffalo admitted, between sobs of laughter. 'And Klein Boy whispered that there might be fighting again.'

'It is sad, but a man of my age can pleasure his wives only once or twice a day, but he can fight and enjoy old companions and plunder day and night without end – and the loyalty we bear you is wide as the Kalahari,' Stork Legs said, and they hooted with laughter and beat each other upon the back.

Still rumbling with occasional laughter, the group left the riverbed and climbed up to the old rendezvous point. It was a low overhanging shelf of rock, the roof blackened with the soot of countless campfires and the rear wall decorated with the ochre-coloured designs and drawings of the little yellow Bushmen who, before them, had used this shelter down the ages. From the entrance of the shelter there was a sweeping view out across the shimmering plains. It would be almost impossible to approach the hilltop undetected.

The four firstcomers had already opened the cache. It had been hidden in a cleft of rock further down the side of the hill, and the entrance closed with boulders and plastered over with clay from the riverbank. The contents had survived the years better than Lothar had expected. Of course, the canned food and the ammunition cases had all been sealed, while the Mauser rifles were packed in thick yellow grease and wrapped in greasepaper. They were in perfect condition. Even most of the spare saddlery and clothing had been preserved by the desert's dry air.

They feasted on fried bully beef and toasted ship's biscuit, food they had once hated for its monotony but now was delicious and evocative of countless other meals, back in those desperate days rendered attractive by the passage of the years.

After they had eaten they picked over the saddlery and boots and clothing, rejecting those items damaged by insects and rodents or dried out like parchment, cannibalizing and re-stitching and polishing with dubbin until they had equipment and arms for all of them.

While they worked Lothar considered that there were dozens of these caches, scattered through the wilderness, while in the north at the secret coastal base from which he had refuelled and re-equipped the German U-boats there must still be thousands of pounds' worth of stores. Until now it had never occurred to him to raid them for his own account – somehow they had always been in patriotic trust.

He felt the prickle of temptation: 'Perhaps if I chartered a boat at Walvis and sailed up the coast—' But then with a sudden chill he remembered that he would never see Walvis Bay or this land again. There would be no return after they had done what they were setting out to do.

He jumped to his feet and strode to the entrance of the rock shelter. As he stared out across the dun and heatshot plain with its dotted camel-thorn trees, he felt a premonition of terrible suffering and unhappiness.

'Could I ever be happy elsewhere?' he wondered. 'Away from this harsh and beautiful land?' His resolve wavered. He turned and saw Manfred watching him with a troubled frown. 'Can I make this decision for my son?' He stared back at the boy. 'Can I condemn him to the life of an exile?'

He thrust the doubts aside with an effort, shaking them off with a shudder like a horse driving the stinging flies from its hide, and called Manfred to him. He led him away from the shelter, and when they were out of earshot of the others told him what lay ahead of them, speaking to him as an equal.

'All we have worked for has been stolen from us, Manie, not in the sight of the law but in the sight of God and natural justice. The Bible gives us redress against those who have deceived or cheated us – an eye for an eye, a tooth for a tooth. We will take back what has been stolen from us. But, Manie, the English law will look upon us as criminals. We will have to fly, to run and hide, and they will hunt us like wild animals. We will survive only by our courage and our wits.'

Manfred stirred eagerly, watching his father's face with bright eager eyes. It all sounded romantic and exciting and he was proud of his father's trust in discussing such adult matters with him.

'We will go north. There is good farming land in Tanganyika and Nyasaland and Kenya. Many of our own *Volk* have already gone there. Of course, we will have to change our name, and we can never return here, but we will make a fine new life in a new land.'

'Never come back?' Manfred's expression changed. 'But what about Sarah?'

Lothar ignored the question. 'Perhaps we will buy a beautiful coffee shamba in Nyasaland or on the lower slopes of Kilimanjaro. There are still great herds of wild game upon the plains of Serengeti, and we will hunt and farm.'

Manfred listened dutifully but his expression had dulled. How could he say it? How could he tell his father: 'Pa, I don't want to go to a strange land. I want to stay here.'?

He lay awake long after the others were snoring and the camp-fire had burned down to a red smear of embers, and he thought about Sarah, remembering the pale pixie face smeared with tears and the hot thin little body under the blanket beside him: 'She is the only friend I've ever had.'

He was jerked back to reality by a strange and disturbing sound. It came from the plain below them but it seemed that distance could not take the fierce edge from the din.

His father coughed softly and sat up, letting his blanket fall to his waist. The awful sound came again, rising to an impossible crescendo and then dying away in a series of deep grunts, the death rattle of a strangling monster.

'What is it, Pa?' The hair at the back of Manfred's neck had risen and prickled as though to the touch of a nettle.

'They say even the bravest of men is afraid the first time he hears that sound,' his father told him softly. 'That is the hunting roar of a hungry Kalahari lion, my son.'

In the dawn when they climbed down the hillside and reached the plain, Lothar, who was leading, stopped abruptly and beckoned Manfred to his side.

'You have heard his voice – now here is the track of his feet.' He stooped and touched one of the pad marks, the size of a dinner plate, that was pressed deeply into the soft yellow earth.

'An old *maanhar*, a solitary, old, maned male.' Lothar traced the outline of the spoor. Manfred would see him do that often in the months ahead, always touching the sign as though to draw out its secrets through his fingertips. 'See how his pads are worn smooth, and how he walks with his weight back towards his ankles. He favours his right fore, a cripple. He will find a meal hard to take, perhaps that is why he keeps close to the ranch. Cattle are easier to kill than wild game.'

Lothar reached out and plucked something from the lowest branch of thorns. 'Here, Manie,' he placed a small tuft of coarse red-gold hair in Manfred's palm. 'There is a tress of his mane he left for you.' Then he stood up and stepped over the spoor. He led them on down into the broad saucer of land, watered by a string of natural artesian springs, where the grass grew thick and green and high as their knees, and they passed the first herds of cattle, humpbacked and with dewlaps that almost brushed the earth, their coats shiny in the early sunlight.

The homestead of the ranch stood on the higher ground beyond the wells, in a plantation of exotic date palms imported from Egypt. It was an old colonial German fort, a legacy from the Herero war of 1904 when the whole territory had erupted in rebellion against the excesses of German colonization. Even the Bondelswarts and Namas had joined the Herero tribe and it had taken 20,000 white troops and an expenditure of £60 million to quell the rebellion. Added to the cost, in the final accounting, were the 2,500 German officers and men killed and the 70,000 men, women and children of the Herero people shot, burned and starved to death. This casualty list constituted almost precisely seventy per cent of the entire tribe.

The homestead had originally been a frontier fort, built to hold off the Herero regiments. Its thick whitewashed outer walls were crenellated and even the central tower was furnished with battlements and a flagstaff upon which the German imperial eagle still defiantly flew.

The count saw them from afar, coming down the dusty road past the springs, and sent out a trap to bring them in. He was of Lothar's mother's generation, but still tall and lean and straight. A white duelling scar puckered the corner of his mouth and his manners were old-fashioned and formal. He sent Swart Hendrick to quarters in the servants' wing and then led Lothar and Manfred through to the cool dark central hall where the countess had black bottles of good German beer and jugs of homemade ginger beer already set out for them.

Their clothes were whisked away by the servants while they bathed, and were returned within an hour, laundered and ironed, their boots polished until they gleamed. For dinner there was a baron of tender beef from the estate, running with its own fragrant juices, and marvellous Rhine wines to wash it down. To Manfred's unqualified delight, this was followed by a dozen various tarts and puddings and trifles, while for Lothar the greater treat was the civilized discourse of his host and hostess. It was a deep pleasure to discuss books and music, and to listen to the precise and beautifully enunciated German of his hosts.

When Manfred could eat not another spoonful, and had to use both hands to cover his yawns, one of the Herero servingmaids led him away to his room, and the count poured schnapps for Lothar and brought a box of Havanas for his approval while his wife fussed over the silver coffee pot.

When his cigar was drawing evenly the count told

Lothar: 'I received the letter you sent me from Windhoek, and I was most distressed to hear of your misfortune. Times are very difficult for all of us.' He polished his monocle upon his sleeve before screwing it back into his eye and focusing it upon Lothar again. 'Your sainted mother was a fine lady. There is nothing that I would not do for her son.' He paused and drew upon the Havana, smiled thinly at the flavour and then said, 'However—'

Lothar's spirits dropped at that word, always the harbinger of denial and disappointment.

'However, not two weeks before I received your letter the purchasing officer for the army remount department came out to the ranch and I sold him all our excess animals. I have retained only sufficient for our own needs.'

Though Lothar had seen at least forty fine horses in the herd grazing on the young pasture that grew around the ranch, he merely nodded in understanding.

'Of course, I have a pair of excellent mules – big, strong beasts, that I could let you have at a nominal price – say fifty pounds.'

'The pair?' Lothar asked deferentially.

'Each,' said the count firmly. 'As to the other suggestion in your letter, I make it a firm rule never to lend money to a friend. That way one avoids losing both friend and money.'

Lothar let that slide by, and instead returned to the count's earlier remarks. 'The army remount officer – he has been buying horses from all the estates in the district?'

'I understand he has purchased almost a hundred.' The count showed relief at Lothar's gentlemanly acceptance of his refusal. 'All excellent animals. He was interested only in the best – desert-hardened and salted against the horse-sickness.'

'And he has shipped them south on the railway, I expect?'

'Not yet,' the count shook his head. 'Or he had not

112

done so when last I heard. He is holding them on the pool of the Swakop river on the far side of the town, resting them and letting them build up their strength for the rail journey. I heard that he plans to send them down the line when he has a hundred and fifty altogether.'

They left the fort the following morning after a gargantuan breakfast of sausage and prepared meats and eggs, all three of them riding up on the broad back of the grey mule for which Lothar had finally paid twenty pounds with the head halter thrown in to sweeten the bargain.

'How were the servants' quarters at the fort?' Lothar asked.

'Slave quarters, not servants' quarters,' Hendrick corrected him. 'In them a man could starve to death or, from what I heard, be flogged to death by the count.' Hendrick sighed. 'If it had not been for the generosity and good nature of the youngest of the Herero maids—'

Lothar nudged him sharply in the ribs and shot a warning glance towards Manfred, and Hendrick went on smoothly.

'So do we all escape on one sway-backed ancient mule,' he observed. 'They will never catch us on this gazelle-swift creature.' He slapped the fat rump and the mule maintained its easy swaying gait, its hooves plopping in the dust.

'We are going to use him for hunting,' Lothar told him, and grinned at Hendrick's perplexed frown.

Back at the rock shelter, Lothar worked quickly, making up twelve pack-saddles of ammunition, food and equipment. When they were lashed and loaded, he laid them out at the entrance of the shelter.

'Well,' Hendrick grinned. 'We've got the saddles. All we need are the horses.'

'We should leave a guard here.' Lothar ignored him, 'But we'll need every man with us.'

He gave the money to Pig John, the least untrustworthy of the gang.

'Five pounds is enough to buy a bathtub full of Cape Smoke,' he pointed out, 'and a glassful of it will kill a bull buffalo. But remember this, Pig John, if you are too drunk to stay in the saddle when we ride, I'll not leave you for the police to question. I'll leave you with a bullet in the head. I give you my oath on it.'

Pig John tucked the banknote into the sweatband of his slouch hat. 'Not a drop of it will touch my lips,' he whined ingratiatingly. 'The *baas* knows he can trust me with liquor and women and money.'

It was almost twenty miles back to the town of Oka-handja and Pig John set out immediately to be there well in advance of Lothar's arrival. The rest of the party, with Manfred leading the mule, climbed down the hillside.

There had been no wind since the previous day, so the lion's tracks were still clearly etched and uneroded, even in that loose soil. The hunters, all armed with the new Mausers, and with bandoliers of ammunition belted over their shoulders, spread out in a fan across the lion spoor and went away at a trot.

Manfred had been warned by his father to keep well back, and with the memories of the beast's wild roarings still in his ears, was pleased to amble along at the mule's slow plod. The hunters were out of sight ahead, but they had marked their trail for him with broken branches and blazes on the trunks of the camel-thorn trees so he had no difficulty following.

Within an hour they found the spot at which the old red tom had killed one of the count's heifers. He had stayed on the carcass until he had consumed everything but the head and hooves and larger bones. But even from these he had licked the flesh as proof of his hunger and restricted hunting prowess.

Quickly Lothar and Hendrick cast forward in a circle around the trampled area of the kill and almost immediately cut the outgoing spoor.

'He left not more than a few hours ago,' Lothar estimated, and then as one of the grass stalks trodden down by
the big cat's paws, slowly rose and straightened of its own
accord, he amended his guess. 'Less than half an hour – he
might have heard us coming up.'

'No.' Hendrick touched the spoor with the long peeled
twig he carried. 'He has gone on at a walk. He isn't worried,
he hasn't heard us. He is full of meat and will go now to
the nearest water.'

'He's going south.' Lothar squinted against the sun to
check the run of the spoor. 'Probably heading for the river
and that will take him closer to the town, which suits us
very well.'

He reslung the Mauser on his shoulder and signalled his
men to stay in extended order. They went on up the low
rise of a consolidated dune and before they reached the top
the lion broke, flushing from the cover of a low clump of
scrub directly ahead of them, and went away from them
across the open ground at an extended catlike run. But his
belly, gorged with meat, swung weightily at each stride as
though he were heavily pregnant.

It was long range, but the Mausers whip-cracked all
along the line as they opened up on the running beast.
Dust spurted wide and beyond him. All Lothar's men
except Hendrick were appalling marksmen. He could never
convince them that the speed of the bullet was not directly
proportional to the force with which one pulled the trigger,
or break them of the habit of tightly closing their eyes as
they ejected the bullet from the barrel with all their
strength.

Lothar saw his own first shot kick dust from beneath the
lion's belly. He had misjudged the range, always a problem
over open desert terrain. He worked the bolt of the Mauser
without taking the butt from his shoulder and lifted his aim
until the pip of the foresight rode just above the beast's
shaggy flowing red mane.

The lion checked to the next shot, breaking his stride, swinging his great head around to snap at his flank where it had stung him, and the sound of the jacketed bullet slapping into his flesh carried clearly to the line of hunters. Then the lion flattened once more into his gallop, ears back, growling with pain and outrage as he vanished over the rise.

'He won't go far!' Hendrick waved the line of hunters forward.

The lion is a sprinter. He can only maintain that blazing gallop over a very short distance before he is forced back into a trot. If you press him further, he will usually turn and come back at you.

Lothar, Hendrick and Klein Boy, the strongest and fittest of them, pulled ahead of the line.

'Blood!' Hendrick shouted as they reached the spot where the lion had taken Lothar's bullet. 'Lung blood!' The splashes of crimson were frothy with the wind of the ruptured lungs. They raced along the bloody spoor.

'*Pasop!*' Lothar called as they reached the rise over which the beast had disappeared. 'Look out! He'll be lying in wait for us—' And at the warning the lion charged back at them.

He had been lying in a patch of sansevieria just beyond the crest, flattened against the earth with his ears laid back upon his skull. But the moment Lothar led them over the crest, he launched himself at him from a distance of only fifty feet.

The lion kept low to the ground, with his ears still back so that his forehead was flat and broad as that of an adder and his eyes were a bright implacable yellow. His gingery red mane was fully erect, increasing his bulk until he appeared monstrous, and such a blast of sound came out of those gaping fang-lined jaws that Lothar flinched and was an instant slow on the shot. As the butt of the Mauser touched his shoulder, the lion rose from the ground in front of him, filling all his vision and the blood from his torn lungs blew in a pink cloud and spattered into Lothar's face.

His instinct was to fire as swiftly as possible into the enormous shaggy bulk of the lion as it towered over him on its hindlegs, but he forced himself to shift his aim. A shot in the chest or neck would not stop the beast from killing him, the Mauser bullet was light, designed for men not great game, and that first bullet would have desensitized the lion's nervous system and flooded his system with adrenalin. The brain shot was the only one which would stop him at such close quarters.

Lothar shot him on the point of his muzzle, between the flared pink pits of his nostrils, and the bullet tore up between the cat's eyes, through the butter-yellow brain in its bony casket and out through the back of his skull – but still the lion was driven on by the momentum of its charge. The huge muscular body slammed into Lothar's chest, and the rifle cartwheeled from his hands as he was hurled backwards to hit the earth with his shoulder and the side of his head.

Hendrick dragged him into a sitting position and wiped the sand from his mouth and nostrils with his bare hands, and then the alarm faded from his eyes and he grinned as Lothar struck his hands away weakly.

'You are getting old and slow, *Baas*,' Hendrick laughed.

'Get me up before Manie sees me,' Lothar ordered him, and Hendrick put a shoulder under him and hoisted him.

He swayed on his feet, leaning heavily on Hendrick, holding the side of his head where it had struck but already he was giving orders.

'Klein Boy! Legs! Go back and hold the mule before it smells the lion and bolts with Manie!'

He pulled away from Hendrick and crossed unsteadily to the lion's carcass. It lay on its side and already the flies were gathering on the shattered head. 'We'll need every man and a bit of luck to get him loaded.'

Even though the cat was old and lean and out of condition, scarred by years of hunting in thorn veld and his coat dull and shaggy, yet his belly was crammed with beef and he would weigh four hundred pounds or more. Lothar picked his rifle out of the sand and wiped it down carefully, then he propped it against the carcass and hurried back over the ridge, still limping from the fall and massaging his neck and temple.

The mule with Manfred perched on his back was coming towards him, and Lothar broke into a run.

'Did you get him, Pa?' Manfred yelled excitedly. He had heard the firing.

'Yes.' Lothar yanked him down from the mule's back. 'He's lying just beyond the rise.'

Lothar checked the mule's head halter. It was new and strong, but he clipped an extra length of rope on to the iron chin ring and put two men on each rope. Then carefully he blindfolded the mule with a strip of canvas.

'All right. Let's see how he takes it.' The men on the head halter dragged on it with their concerted weight, but the mule dug in his hooves, mutinying against the blindfold, and would not budge.

Lothar went round behind him, taking care to keep out of the way of his back hooves, and twisted the mule's tail. Still the animal stood like a rock. Lothar leaned over and bit him at the root of the tail, sinking his teeth into the soft tender skin, and the mule let fly with both back hooves in a head-high kick.

Lothar bit him again, and he capitulated and trotted forward towards the ridge, but as he reached it the light breeze shifted and the mule filled both nostrils with the fresh hot smell of lion.

The scent of lion has a remarkable effect on all other animals, domestic or wild, even on exotics from an environment where it is impossible that either they or even their remote ancestors could possibly ever have had contact with a lion.

Lothar's father had always selected his hunting dogs by offering the litter of puppies a green wet lion skin to sniff. Most of the pups would howl with terror and stumble away with their tails tucked up between their hind legs. A very few pups, not more than one in twenty, nearly always bitches, would stand, albeit with every hair on their bodies erect and small growls shaking them from tail to tip of quivering nostrils. These were the dogs he kept.

Now the mule smelt the lion and went berserk. The men on the head ropes were hauled off their feet as it reared and whinnied, and Lothar ducked out from under its lashing hooves. Then it burst into a ponderous gallop and dragged the four handlers, stumbling and falling and shouting, half a mile over thorn scrub and through deep water-worn dongas, before at last it stopped in a cloud of its own dust, sweating and trembling, its flanks heaving with terror.

They dragged him back again, the blindfold firmly in place, but the moment he smelled the carcass again the entire performance was repeated, though this time he only managed a gallop of a few hundred yards before exhaustion and the weight of four men brought him up short.

Twice more they led him back to the dead lion and twice more he bolted, each time for a shorter distance, but finally he stood, trembling in all four legs, and sweating with terror and fatigue as they lifted the carcass onto his back and tried to lash the lion's paws under his chest. That was too much. Another copious flood of nervous sweat drenched the mule's body, and he reared and bucked and kicked until the carcass slid off his back in a heap.

They wore him down, and after an hour of struggling, the mule stood at last, shaking piteously and blowing like a blacksmith's bellows, but with the dead lion securely lashed upon his back.

When Lothar took the lead rope and tugged upon it, the mule stumbled along meekly behind him, following him down towards the bend in the river.

From the top of one of the low wooded kopjes Lothar looked down across the Swakop river to the roofs and the church spire of the village beyond. The Swakop made a wide bend, and in the elbow directly below there were three small green pools hemmed in with yellow sandbanks. The river flowed only in the brief periods after rain.

They were watering the horses at the pools, bringing them down from the stockades of thorn branches on the bank to drink before closing them in for the night. The count had been right, the army buyers had chosen the best. Lothar watched them avariciously through his binoculars. Desert bred, they were powerful animals, full of vigour as they frolicked and milled at the edge of the pool or rolled in the sand with their legs kicking in the air.

Lothar switched his attention to the drovers, and counted five of them, all coloured troopers in casual khaki uniform, and he looked for white officers in vain.

'They could be in camp,' he muttered and focused the glasses on the cluster of brown army tents beyond the horse stockades.

There was a low whistle from behind him, and when he looked over his shoulder, Hendrick was signalling from the foot of the kopje. Lothar slid off the skyline and then scrambled down the slope. The mule, his blood-soaked burden still on his back, was tethered in the shade. He had become almost resigned to it, though every now and again he gave a spontaneous shudder and shifted his weight nervously. The men were lying under the sparse branches of the thorn trees, eating bully out of the cans and Pig John stood up as Lothar reached him.

'You are late,' Lothar accused him, and seizing the front of his leather vest he pulled him close and sniffed his breath.

'Not a drop, Master,' Pig John whined. 'I swear on my sister's virginity.'

'That is a mythical beast.' Lothar released him, and glanced down at the sack at Pig John's feet.

'Twelve bottles. Just like you said.'

Lothar opened the sack and took out a bottle of the notorious Cape Smoke. The neck was sealed with wax and the brandy was a dark poisonous brown when he held it to the light.

'What did you find out in the village?' He returned the bottle to the sack.

'There are seven horse handlers at the camp—'

'I counted five.'

'Seven.' Pig John was definite and Lothar grunted.

'What about the white officers?'

'They rode out towards Otjiwaronga yesterday, to buy more horses.'

'It will be dark in an hour.' Lothar glanced at the sun. 'Take the sack and go to the camp.'

'What shall I tell them?'

'Tell them you are selling – cheap, and then give them a free taste. You are a famous liar, tell them anything.'

'What if they don't drink?'

Lothar laughed at the improbability but didn't bother to answer. 'I will move after moonrise, when it clears the tree-tops. That will give you and your brandy four hours to soften them up.'

The sack clinked as Pig John slung it over his shoulder.

'Remember, Pig John, I want you sober or I'll have you dead – and I mean it.'

'Does Master think I am some kind of animal, that I can't take a drink like a gentleman?' Pig John demanded and drawing himself up marched out of the camp with affronted dignity.

From his look-out Lothar watched Pig John cross the dry sandbanks of the Swakop and trudge up the far side under his sack. At the stockade the guard challenged him and Lothar watched through the glasses as they talked, until at last the coloured trooper set his carbine aside and peered into the neck of the sack that Pig John held open for him.

Even at that distance and in the deepening dusk, Lothar saw the flash of the guard's white teeth as he grinned with delight and turned to call his companions from the tented encampment. Two of them came out in their underclothes, and a long heated discussion ensued with a great deal of gesticulation and shoulder slapping and head shaking, until Pig John cracked the wax seal on one of the bottles and handed it to them. The bottle passed quickly from one to the other, and each of them pointed the base briefly at the sky like a bugler sounding the charge and then gasped and grinned through watering eyes. Finally, Pig John was led like an honoured guest into the encampment, lugging his sack, and disappeared from Lothar's view.

The sun set and night fell and Lothar remained on the ridge. Like a yachtsman he was intensely aware of the strength and direction of the night breeze as it switched erratically. An hour after dark it settled down into a steady warm stream on the back of Lothar's neck.

'Let it hold,' Lothar murmured, and then whistled softly, the cry of a scops owlet. Hendrick came almost at once and Lothar indicated the wind.

'Cross the river well upstream and circle out beyond the camp. Not too close. Then turn back and keep the wind in your face.'

At that moment there was a faint shout from across the

river and they both looked up. The camp-fire in front of the tents had been built up until the flames roared high enough to lick the under branches of the camel-thorn trees and silhouetted against them were the dark figures of the coloured troopers.

'What the hell do you think they are doing?' Lothar wondered. 'Dancing or fighting?'

'By now they don't know themselves,' Hendrick chuckled. They were reeling around the fire, colliding and clinging together, then separating, collapsing in the dust and crawling on their knees, or with enormous effort heaving themselves to their feet only to stand swaying with legs braced apart and then collapse again. One of them was stripped naked, his thin yellow body gleaming with sweat as he pirouetted wildly and then fell into the fire, to be dragged out by the heels by a pair of his companions, all three of them screeching with laughter.

'Time for you to go.' Lothar slapped Hendrick's shoulder. 'Take Manie with you and let him be your horse holder.'

Hendrick started back down the slope but paused as Lothar called softly after him, 'Manie is in your charge. You'll answer for him with your own life.'

Hendrick did not reply but disappeared into the night. Half an hour later Lothar glimpsed them crossing the pale sandbanks of the river, a dark shapeless movement in the starlight, and then they were gone into the scrub beyond.

The horizon lightened and the stars in the east paled before the rising moon, but in the camp across the river the drunken gyrations of the troopers had now descended into swinish inertia. Through the glasses Lothar could make out bodies, scattered haphazard like casualties on the battle-field, and one of them looked very much like Pig John, although Lothar couldn't be certain for he lay face down in the shadow on the far side of the fire.

'If it's him, he's a dead man,' Lothar promised and stood

up. It was time to move at last, for the moon was clear of the horizon, horned and glowing like a horseshoe from the blacksmith's forge.

Lothar picked his way down the slope, and the mule snorted and blew through his nostrils, still standing miserably under his dreadful burden.

'Almost over now.' Lothar stroked his forehead. 'You've done well, old fellow.' He loosed the head halter, adjusted the Mauser slung over his shoulder and led the mule around the side of the kopje and down the bank to the river.

There was no question of a stealthy approach, not with that great pale animal and his swaying load. Lothar unslung the rifle and rammed a cartridge into the breech as they plodded through the sand of the riverbed and he watched the line of trees on the bank ahead, even though he expected no challenge.

The camp-fire had died down, and there was complete silence until they climbed the bank and Lothar heard the stamp of a hoof and the soft fluttering breath of one of the animals in the stockade ahead. The breeze was behind Lothar, steady still, and suddenly there was a shrill unhappy whinny.

'That's it – get a good whiff of it.' Lothar led the mule towards the stockade.

Now there was the trample of hooves and the sound of restless animals as they began to mill and jostle one another. Alarm transmitted by the rank smell of the bleeding lion carcass was spreading infectiously through the herd. A horse whinnied in terror, and immediately others reared in panic. Lothar could see their heads above the thornbush wall of the stockade, manes flying in the moonlight, front hooves lashing out wildly.

Against the windward wall of the stockade Lothar held the mule, and then cut the rope that held the lion to its back. The carcass slid over and hit the ground, the wind from its lungs was driven up the dead throat with a low belching roar and the animals on the far side of the brush wall surged and screamed and began to swirl around the stockade in a living whirlpool of horseflesh.

Lothar stooped and split the lion's belly from the crotch of the back legs to the sternum of the ribs, driving his blade deeply so that it slashed through the bladder and guts, and instantly the stench was thick and rank.

The horse herd was in chaos. He could hear them crashing into the far wall of the stockade as they attempted to escape from the awful scent. Lothar lifted the rifle to his shoulder, aiming only feet over the maddened horses, and emptied the magazine. The shots crashed out in quick succession, the muzzle-flashes lighting the stockade, and the herd in terrified concert burst through the wall of the stockade, pouring through it in a dark river, their manes tossing like foam as they galloped away into the night, heading downwind to where Hendrick waited with his men.

Hurriedly Lothar tethered the mule, and reloading the rifle as he ran, headed for the dying camp-fire. One of the troopers, aroused by the escaping horses even from his drunken stupor, was on his feet, staggering determinedly towards the stockade.

'The horses,' he was screaming. 'Come on you drunken thunders! We have to stop the horses!' He saw Lothar. 'Help me! The horses—'

Lothar lifted the butt of the Mauser under his chin. The trooper's teeth clicked together and he sat down in the sand and then slowly toppled over backwards again. Lothar stepped over him and ran forward.

'Pig John!' he called urgently. 'Where are you?' There was no reply and he went past the fire to the inert figure he had seen from the lookout. He rolled it over with his foot, and Pig John looked up at the moon with sightless eyes and a tranquil smile on his wrinkled yellow face.

'Up!' Lothar kicked him with a full swing of the boot.

Pig John's smile did not waver. He was far past any pain. 'All right, I warned you!'

Lothar worked the Mauser's bolt and flicked over the safety-catch with his thumb. He put the muzzle of the rifle to Pig John's head. If he was handed over to the police alive it would take only a few strokes of the hippo-hide sjambok whip to get Pig John talking. Though he did not know the full details of the plan, he knew enough to ruin their chances and to put Lothar on the wanted list for horse-theft and the destruction of army property. He took up the slack in the trigger of the Mauser.

'It's too good for him,' he thought grimly. 'He should be flogged to death.' But his finger relaxed, and he swore at himself for his own foolishness as he flipped the safety-catch and ran back to fetch the mule.

Even though Pig John was a skinny little man, it took all of Lothar's strength to swing his relaxed rubbery body over the mule's back. He hung there like a piece of laundry on the drying line, arms and legs dangling on opposite sides. Lothar leapt up behind him, whipped the mule into his top gait, a laboured lumbering trot, and steered him directly down the wind.

After a mile Lothar thought he must have missed them, and slowed the mule just as Hendrick stepped out of the moon shadows ahead of him.

'How goes it? How many did you get?' Lothar called anxiously, and Hendrick laughed.

'So many we ran out of halters.'

Once each of his men had captured one of the escaped horses, he had gone up on its bare back and cut off the bunches of fleeing animals, turning them and holding them while Manfred ran in and slipped the halters over their heads.

'Twenty-six!' Lothar exulted as he counted the strings of roped horses. 'We'll be able to pick and choose.' He tempered his own jubilation. 'All right, we'll move out right away. The army will be after us as soon as they can get troops up here.'

He slipped the halter off the mule's head and slapped his rump. 'Thank you, old fellow,' he said. 'You can get on back home.' The mule accepted the offer with alacrity and actually managed to gallop the first hundred yards of his homeward journey.

Each of them picked a horse and mounted bareback with a string of three or four loose horses behind him, and Lothar led them back towards the rock shelter in the hills.

At dawn they paused briefly while Lothar checked over each of the stolen horses. Two had been injured in the mêlée in the stockade and he turned them loose. The others were of such fine quality and condition that he could not choose between them though they had many more than they required.

While they were sorting the horses Pig John regained consciousness and sat up weakly. He muttered prayers to his ancestors and Hottentot gods for a release from his suffering and then vomited a painful gush of vile brandy.

'You and I still have business to settle,' Lothar promised him unsmilingly, then turned to Hendrick. 'We'll take all these horses. We are certain to lose some in the desert.' Then he raised his right arm in the cavalry command: 'Move out!'

They reached the rock shelter a little before noon, but they paused only to load the waiting pack-saddles onto the spare horses and then each of them chose a mount and saddled up. They led the horses down the hill and watered them, allowing them to drink their fill.

'How much of a start do we have?' Hendrick asked.

'The coloured troopers can do nothing without their white officers and it might take them two or three days to get back. They will have to telegraph Windhoek for orders, and then they will have to make up a patrol. I'd say three days at least, more likely four or five.'

'We can go a long way in three days,' Hendrick said with satisfaction.

'Nobody can go further,' Lothar agreed. It was a fact not a boast. The desert was his dominion. Few white men knew it as well as he, and none better.

'Shall we mount up?' Hendrick asked.

'One more chore.' Lothar took the spare leather reins out of his saddle-bag and looped them over his right wrist with the brass buckles hanging to his ankles as he crossed to where Pig John sat miserably in the shade of the riverbank with his face buried in his hands. In his extremity he did not hear Lothar's tread in the soft sand until he stood over him.

'I promised you,' Lothar told him flatly, and shook out the heavy leather thongs.

'Master, I could not help it,' shrieked Pig John and he tried to scramble to his feet.

Lothar swung the thongs and the brass buckles blurred in a bright arc in the sunlight. The blow caught Pig John around the back and the buckles snapped around his ribs and gouged out a groove in his flesh below the armpit.

Pig John howled. 'They forced me. They made me drink—'

The next blow knocked him off his feet. He kept screaming, although now the words were no longer coherent, and the leathers cracked on his yellow skin, the weals rising in thick shiny ridges and turning purple-red as ripe grapeskins. The sharp buckles shredded his shirt as though it had been torn off him by lion's claws, and the sand clotted his blood into wet balls as it dribbled into the riverbed.

He stopped screaming at last and Lothar stood back panting and wiped the wet red leather thongs on a saddle cloth and looked at the faces of his men. The beating had been for them as much as for the man curled at his feet.

They were wild dogs and they understood only strength, respected only cruelty.

Hendrick spoke for them all. 'He was paid a fair price. Shall I finish him?'

'No! Leave a horse for him.' Lothar turned away. 'When he comes round he can follow us, or he can go to hell where he belongs.' He swung up into the saddle of his own mount and avoided his son's stricken eyes as he raised his voice. 'All right – we are moving out.'

He rode with long stirrups in the Boer fashion, slouched down comfortably in the saddle, and Hendrick pushed his mount up on one side of him and Manfred on the other.

Lothar felt elated; the adrenalin of violence was like a drug in his blood still and the open desert lay ahead of him. With the taking of the horses he had crossed the frontier of law – he was an outlaw once again, free of society's restraint, and he felt his spirit towering on high like a hunting falcon.

'By God. I'd almost forgotten what it was like to have a rifle in my hand and a good horse between my legs.'

'We are men once again,' Hendrick agreed, and leaned across to embrace Manfred. 'You too. Your father was your age when he and I first rode out to war. We are going to war again. You are a man as he was.' And Manfred forgot the spectacle he had just witnessed and swelled with pride at being counted in this company. He sat up straight in the saddle and lifted his chin.

Lothar turned his face into the north-east, towards the hinterland where the vast Kalahari brooded, and led them away.

That night while they camped in a deep gorge which shielded the light of their small fire, the sentinel roused them with a low whistle. They rolled out of their blankets, snatched up their rifles and slipped away into the darkness.

The horses stirred and whickered, and then Pig John

rode in out of the darkness and dismounted. He stood wretchedly by the fire, his face swollen and discoloured with bruises like a cur dog expecting to be driven away. The others came out of the shadows and without looking at him or otherwise acknowledging his existence climbed back into their blankets.

'Sleep on the other side of the fire from me,' Lothar told him harshly. 'You stink of brandy.' And Pig John wriggled with relief and gratification that he had been accepted back into the band.

In the dawn they mounted again and rode on into the wide hot emptiness of the desert.

The road out to H'ani Mine was probably one of the most rugged in South West Africa and every time she negotiated it Centaine promised herself: We must really do something about having it repaired. Then Dr Twentyman-Jones would give her an estimate of the cost of resurfacing hundreds of miles of desert track and of erecting bridges over the river courses and consolidating the passes through the hills, and Centaine's good frugal sense would reassert itself.

'After all it only takes three days, and I seldom have to drive it more than three times a year, and it is really quite an adventure.'

The telegraph line that connected the mine to Windhoek had been expensive enough. After an estimate of fifty pounds it had finally cost her a hundred pounds for every single mile and she still felt resentment every time she looked at that endless line of poles strung together with gleaming copper wire that ran beside the track. Apart from the cost, it spoiled the view, detracting from the feeling of wildness and isolation which she so treasured when she was out in the Kalahari.

She remembered with a twinge of nostalgia how they had slept on the ground and carried their water in the first years. Now there were regular stages at each night's stop, thatched rondavels and windmills to raise water from the deep bores, servants living permanently at each station to service the rest houses, providing meals and hot baths and a log fire in the hearth on those crisp frosty nights of the Kalahari winter – even paraffin refrigerators manufacturing heavenly ice for the sundowner whisky in the fierce summer heat. The traffic on the road was heavy, the regular convoy under Gerhard Fourie carrying out fuel and stores had cut deep ruts in the soft earth and churned up the crossings in the dried river-beds, and worst of all the gauge of the tyres of the big Ford trucks was wider than that of the yellow Daimler so that she had to drive with one wheel in the rut and the other bouncing and jolting over the uneven middle ridge.

Added to all this it was high summer and the heat was crushing. The metal of the Daimler's coachwork could raise blisters on the skin, and they were forced to halt regularly when the water in the radiator boiled and blew a singing plume of steam high in the air. The very heavens seemed to quiver with blue fire, and the far desert horizons were washed away by the shimmering glassy whirlpools of heat mirage.

If only they could make a machine small enough to cool the air in the Daimler, she thought, like the one in the railway coach – and then she burst out laughing. *Tiens:* I must be getting soft! She remembered how, with the two old Bushmen who had rescued her, she had travelled on foot through the terrible dune country of the Namib and they had been forced to cover their bodies with a plaster of sand and their own urine to survive the monstrous heat of the desert noons.

'Why are you laughing, Mater?' Shasa demanded.

'Oh, just something that happened long ago, before you were born.'

'Tell me, oh please tell me.' He seemed unaffected by the heat and the dust and the merciless jolting of the chassis. But then why should he be? She smiled at him. This is where he was born. He too is a creature of the desert.

Shasa took her smile for acquiescence. 'Come on, Mater. Tell me the story.'

'*Pourquoi pas*? Why not?' And she told him and watched the shock in his expression.

'Your own pee-pee?' He was aghast.

'That surprises you?' She mocked him. 'Then let me tell you what we did when the water in our ostrich-egg bottles was finished. Old O'wa, the Bushman hunter, killed a gemsbok bull with his poisoned arrow and we took out the first stomach, the rumen, and we squeezed out the liquid from the undigested contents and we drank that. It kept us going just long enough to reach the sip-wells.'

'Mater!'

'That's right, *chéri*, I drink champagne when I can, but I'll drink whatever keeps me alive when I have to.'

She was silent while he considered that, and she glanced at his face and saw the revulsion turn to respect.

'What would you have done, *chéri*, drunk it or died?' she asked, to make sure the lesson was learned.

'I would have drunk,' he answered without hesitation, and then with affectionate pride, 'You know, Mater, you really are a crackerjack.' It was his ultimate accolade.

'Look!' She pointed ahead to where the lion-coloured plain, its far limits lost in the curtains of mirage, seemed to be covered with a gauzy cinnamon-coloured veil of thin smoke.

Centaine pulled the Daimler off the track and they climbed out onto the running-board for a better view.

'Springbok. The first we have seen on this trip.' The beautiful gazelle were moving steadily across the flats, all in the same direction.

'There must be tens of thousands.'

The springbok were elegant little animals with long delicate legs and lyre-shaped horns.

'They are migrating into the north,' Centaine told him. 'There must have been good rains up there, and they are moving to the water.'

Suddenly the nearest gazelles took fright at their presence and began the peculiar alarm display that the Boers called 'pronking'. They arched their backs and bowed their long necks until their muzzles touched their fore hooves, and they bounced on stiff legs, flying high and lightly into the shimmering hot air while from the fold of skin along their backs they flashed a flowing white crest of hair.

This alarm behaviour was infectious and soon thousands of gazelle were bounding across the plain like a flock of birds. Centaine jumped down from the running-board and mimicked them, forking the fingers of one hand over her head as horns and with the fingers of the other showing the crest hair down her back. She did it so skilfully that Shasa hooted with laughter and clapped his hands.

'Bully for you, Mater!' He jumped down and joined her, and they pranced in a circle, until they were weak with laughter and exertion. Then they leaned against the Daimler and clung to each other for support.

'Old O'wa taught me that,' Centaine gasped. 'He could imitate every animal of the veld.'

When they drove on she let Shasa take the wheel, for the crossing of the plain was one of the easier stretches of the journey and he drove well. She lay back in the corner of her seat and after a while Shasa broke the silence.

'When we are alone you are so different.' He searched for the words. 'You are such jolly good fun. I wish we could just be like this forever.'

'Anything you do too long becomes a bore,' she told him gently. 'The trick is to do it all, not just one thing. This is good fun but tomorrow we will be at the mine and

133

there will be another type of excitement for us to experience and after that there will be something else. We'll do it all, and we will wring from each moment the last drop it has to offer.'

Twentyman-Jones had gone ahead to the mine while Centaine stayed on for three days in Windhoek to go over the paperwork with Abraham Abrahams. So he had alerted the servants at the rest houses as he passed through.

When they reached the last stage that evening, the bath water was so hot that even Centaine who enjoyed her bath at the correct temperature for boiling lobster was forced to add cold before she could bear it. The champagne was that marvellous 1928 Krug, pale and chilled to the temperature she preferred, just low enough to frost the bottle, and though there was ice, she would not allow the barbaric habit of standing the bottle in a bucket of it.

'Cold feet, hot head – bad combination for both men and wine,' her father had taught her. As always she drank only a single glass from the bottle and afterwards there was the cold collation that Twentyman-Jones had provided for her and stored in the paraffin refrigerator, fare suitable for this heat and which he knew she enjoyed – rock lobster from the green Benguela Current with rich white flesh curled in their spiny red tails and salad vegetables grown in the cooler highlands of Windhoek, lettuce crackling crisp, tomatoes crimson ripe and pungent onions purple tinted – then, as the final treat, wild truffles gleaned from the surrounding desert by the tame Bushmen who tended the milk herd. She ate them raw and the salty fungus taste was the taste of Kalahari.

They left again in the pitch darkness before dawn, and at sunrise they stopped and brewed coffee on a fire of camel-thorn branches; the grainy red wood burned with an intense blue flame and gave to the coffee a peculiar and delicious aroma. They ate the picnic breakfast that the rest-house cook had provided and washed it down with the smoky coffee and watched the sunrise smearing the sky and desert with bronze and gilding it with gold leaf. As they went on, so the sun rose higher and drained the land of colour, washing it with its silver-white bleach.

'Stop here!' Centaine ordered suddenly, and when they climbed up onto the roof of the Daimler and stared ahead, Shasa was puzzled.

'What is it, Mater?'

'Don't you see it, *chéri?*' She pointed, 'There! Above the horizon.'

'It floated in the sky, indistinct and ethereal.

'It's standing in the sky,' Shasa exclaimed, discerning it at last.

'The mountain that floats in the sky,' Centaine murmured. Each time she saw it like this the wonder of it was still as fresh and enchanting as the first time. 'The place of All Life.' She gave the hills their Bushman name.

As they drove on so the shape of the hills hardened, becoming a sheer rock palisade below which were spread the open mopani forests. In places the cliffs were split and riven with gulleys and gorges. In others they were solid and tall and daubed with bright lichens, sulphur yellow and green and orange.

The H'ani Mine was nestled beneath one of these sheer expanses of rock, and the buildings seemed insignificant and incongruous in this place.

Centaine's brief to Twentyman-Jones had been to make them as unobtrusive as possible, without, of course, affecting the productivity of the workings, but there was a limit to just how far he had been able to follow her instructions. The fenced compounds of the black workers and the weathering grounds for the blue diamondiferous earth were extensive, while the steel tower and elevator of the washing gear stuck up high as the derrick of an oil rig.

However, the worst depredation had been caused by the appetite of the steam boiler, hungry as some infernal Baal for cordwood. The forest along the foot of the hills had been cut down to satisfy it, and the second growth had formed a scraggly unsightly thicket in place of the tall grey-barked timber.

Twentyman-Jones was waiting for them as they climbed out of the dusty Daimler in front of the thatched administration building.

'Good trip, Mrs Courtney?' he asked, lugubrious with pleasure. 'You'll want a rest and clean up, I expect.'

'You know better than that, Dr Twentyman-Jones. Let's get down to work.' Centaine led the way down the wide verandah to her own office. 'Sit beside me,' she ordered Shasa as she took her seat at the stinkwood desk.

They began with the recovery reports, then went on to the cost schedules; and as Shasa struggled to keep up with the quick calling and discussion of figures, he wondered how his mother could change so swiftly from the girl companion who had hopped around in imitation of a springbok only the previous day.

'Shasa, what did we establish was the cost per carat if we average twenty-three carats per load?' She fired the question at Shasa suddenly, and when he muffed it she frowned. 'This isn't the time for dreams.' And she turned her shoulder to him to emphasize the rebuke. 'Very well, Dr Twentyman-Jones, we have avoided the unpleasant long enough. Let us consider what economies we have to institute to meet the quota cut and still keep the H'ani Mine working and turning a profit.'

It was dusk before Centaine broke off and stood up. 'We'll pick it up from there tomorrow.' She stretched like a cat and then led them out onto the wide verandah.

'Shasa will be working for you as we agreed. I think he should begin on the haulage.'

'I was about to suggest it, Ma'am.'

'What time do you want me?' Shasa asked.

'The shift comes on at five am but I expect Master Shasa

136

will want to come on later?' Twentyman-Jones glanced at Centaine. It was, of course, a challenge and a test, and she remained silent, waiting for Shasa to make the decision on his own account. She saw him struggling with himself. He was at that stage of growth when sleep is a drug and rising in the morning a brutal penance.

'I'll be at the main haulage at four-thirty, sir,' he said, and Centaine relaxed and took his arm.

'Then it had best be an early night.'

She turned the Daimler into the avenue of small iron-roofed cottages which housed the white shift bosses and artisans and their families. The orders of society were strictly observed on the H'ani Mine. It was a microcosm of the young nation. The black labourers lived in the fenced and guarded compounds where whitewashed buildings resembled rows of stables. There were separate, more elaborate quarters for the black boss-boys, who were allowed to have their families living with them. The white artisans and shift bosses were housed in the avenues laid out at the foot of the hills, while the management lived up the slopes, each building larger and the lawns around it more extensive the higher it was sited.

As they turned at the end of the avenues there was a girl sitting on the stoep of the last cottage and she stuck her tongue out at Shasa as the Daimler passed. It was almost a year since Shasa had last seen her and nature had wrought wondrous changes in her during that time. Her feet were still bare and dirty to the ankles, and her curls were still wind-tousled and sun-streaked, but the faded cotton of her blouse was now so tight that it constricted her blossoming breasts. They were forced upwards and bulged out over the top in a deep cleavage and Shasa wriggled in the seat as he realized that the twin red-brown coin-shaped marks on the blouse, though they looked like stains, were in fact showing through the thin cloth from beneath.

Her legs had grown longer, her knees were no longer knobbly, and they shaded from coffee brown at the ankles to smooth cream on the inside of her thighs. She sat on the edge of the verandah with her knees apart and her skirts pulled high and rucked up between her legs. As Shasa's gaze dropped, she let her knees fall a little further open. Her nose was snubbed and sprinkled with freckles, and she wrinkled it as she grinned. It was a sly cheeky grin, and her tongue was bright pink between white teeth.

Guiltily Shasa jerked his eyes away and stared ahead through the windshield. But he remembered vividly every last detail of those forbidden minutes behind the pump-house and the heat rose in his cheeks. He could not help glancing at his mother. She was looking ahead at the road and had not noticed. He felt relief until she murmured, 'She is a common little hussy, ogling everything in pants. Her father is one of the men we are retrenching. We'll be rid of her before she causes real trouble for us and herself.'

He should have known she had not missed that brief exchange. She saw everything, he thought, and then he felt the impact of her words. The girl was being sent away, and he was surprised by his feeling of deprivation. It was a physical ache in the floor of his stomach.

'What will happen to them, Mater?' he asked softly. 'I mean, the people we are firing.' While he had listened to his mother and Twentyman-Jones discussing the retrenchments, he had thought of them merely as numbers; but with that glimpse of the girl, they had become flesh and blood. He remembered his adversary the blond boy, and the little girl that he had seen from the window of the railway coach, standing beside the tracks in the hobo camp, and he imagined Annalisa Botha in the place of that strange girl.

'I don't know what will become of them.' His mother's mouth tightened. 'I don't think it is anything that should concern us. This world is a place of harsh reality, and each of us has to face it in his own way. I think we should rather consider what would be the consequences if we did not let them go.'

'We would lose money.'

'That is right, and if we lose money, we have to close down the mine, which would mean that all the others would lose their jobs, not just the few that we have to fire. Then we all suffer. If we did that with everything we own, in the end we would lose everything. We would be like the rest of them. Would you prefer that?'

Suddenly Shasa had a new mental image. Instead of the blond boy standing in the hobo camp, it was himself, barefoot in dusty, tattered khakis, and he could almost feel the night chill through the thin shirt and the rumble of hunger in his guts.

'No!' he said explosively, and then dropped his voice. 'I wouldn't like that.' He shivered at the persistent images her words had invoked. 'Is that going to happen, Mater? Could it happen? Might we also be poor?'

'We could be, *chéri*. It could happen quickly and cruelly if we are not on guard every minute. A fortune is extremely difficult to build but very easy to destroy.'

'Is it going to happen?' he insisted, and he thought about the *Midas Touch*, his yacht, and the polo ponies, and his friends at Bishops, and the vineyards of Weltevreden and he was afraid.

'Nothing is certain.' She reached across and took his hand. 'That's the fun of this game of life, if it was then it wouldn't be worth playing.'

'I wouldn't like to be poor.'

'No!' She said it as vehemently as he had. 'It will not happen, not if we are cunning and bold.'

'What you said about the trade of the world coming to a halt. People no longer able to buy our diamonds . . .' Before those had been merely words, now they were a dreadful possibility.

'We must believe that the wheels will one day begin to turn again, one day soon, and we must play the golden rules. Do you remember them?' She swung the Daimler through the climbing turns up the slope and around the spur of the hills so that the mine buildings disappeared behind the rock wall of the cliff.

'What was the first golden rule, Shasa?' she prompted him.

'Sell when everybody else is buying and buy when everybody else is selling,' he repeated.

'Good. And what is happening now?'

'Everybody is trying to sell.' It dawned upon him and his grin was triumphant.

'He's so beautiful, and he has the sense and the instinct,' she thought as she waited for him to follow the coils of the serpent until he reached its head and discovered the fangs. His expression changed as it happened. He looked at her crestfallen.

'But, Mater, how can we buy if we haven't got the money?'

She pulled to the side of the track and cut the engine. Then turned to him seriously and took both his hands.

'I am going to treat you as a man,' she said. 'What I tell you is our secret, our private business that we share with nobody. Not Grandpater or Anna, or Abraham Abrahams or Twentyman-Jones. It's our thing, yours and mine alone.' He nodded and she drew a deep breath. 'I have a premonition that this catastrophe that has engulfed the world is our pivot, an opportunity that very few are ever offered. For the last few years I have been preparing to exploit it. How did I do that, *chéri?*'

He shook his head, staring at her fascinated.

'I have turned everything, with the exception of the mine and Weltevreden, into cash, and even on those I have borrowed heavily, very heavily.'

'That's why you called all the loans. That's why we went

to Walvis for that fish factory and the trawlers – you wanted the money.'

'Yes, *chéri*, yes,' she encouraged him, unconsciously shaking hands, willing him to see it. And his face lit again.

'You are going to buy!' he exclaimed.

'I have already begun,' she told him. 'I have bought land and mining concessions, fishing concessions and guano concessions, buildings. I have even bought the Alhambra Theatre in Cape Town and the Coliseum in Johannesburg. But most of all I have bought land, and the option to buy more land, tens and hundreds of thousands of acres, *chéri*, at two shillings an acre. Land is the only true store of wealth.'

He could not really grasp it, but he sensed the enormity of what she told him and she saw it in his eyes.

'Now you know our secret,' she laughed. 'If I have guessed right, we will double and redouble our fortune.'

'And if it doesn't change. If the,' he searched for the word, 'if the Depression goes on and on for ever, what then, Mater?'

She pouted and dropped his hands. 'Then, *chéri*, nothing will matter very much, one way or the other.'

She started the Daimler and drove up the last pitch of the road to the bungalow standing alone in its wide lawns, with lights burning in the windows and the servants lined up respectfully on the front verandah in their immaculate white livery to welcome her.

She parked at the bottom of the steps, turned off the engine and turned to him again.

'No, Shasa *chéri*, we are not going to be poor. We are going to be richer, much richer than we ever were before. And then later, through you, my darling, we will have power to go with our wealth. Great fortunes, enormous power. Oh, I have it all planned, so carefully planned!'

er words filled Shasa's head with turbulent thoughts. He could not sleep.

'Great fortune, enormous power.' The words excited and disturbed him. He tried to visualize what they meant and saw himself like a strongman at the circus, in leopardskins and leather wristbands, standing with arms akimbo, huge biceps flexed, upon a pyramid of golden sovereigns, while a congregation in white robes knelt and made obeisance before him.

He ran the images through his head over and over, each time altering some detail, all of them pleasurable but lacking the final touch until he bestowed upon one of his white-robed worshippers a crown of unruly wind-tousled sun-streaked curls. He placed her in the front rank, and she lifted her forehead from the ground and stuck her tongue out at him.

His erection was so quick and hard that it made him gasp, and before he could prevent himself he had slipped his hand under the sheet and prised it out of the fly of his pyjamas.

Jock Murphy had warned him about it. 'It will spoil your eye, Master Shasa. I have seen many a good man with a bat or a polo stick ruined by Mrs Palm and her five daughters.'

But in his fantasy Annalisa was sitting up, her long legs apart, and she was slowly drawing up the skirt of her white robe. The skin of her legs was smooth as butter, and he moaned softly. She was staring at the front of his leopard-skin costume, her tongue whisking lightly over her parted lips, and the white skirt rose higher and higher, and his fist began to jerk rhythmically. He could not prevent it.

Up and up rode the white skirt, never quite reaching the fork of her crotch. Her legs seemed to stretch forever, like the railway tracks across the desert, running on and on and never meeting. He choked and jerked into a sitting position on the feather mattress, doubled over his flying fist, and when it came it was sharp and painful as a bayonet driven up into his intestines, and he cried out and fell back against the pillows.

Annalisa's sly grinning freckled face receded, and the wet front of his pyjamas began to turn icy cold, but he did not have the will to strip them off.

When the servant woke him with a tray of coffee and a dish of hard sweet rusks, he felt dazed and exhausted. It was still dark outside, and he rolled over and pulled the pillows over his head.

'Madam your mother, she says I wait here until you get up,' said the Ovambo servant darkly, and Shasa dragged himself to the bathroom trying to conceal the dry stain on the front of his pyjamas.

One of the grooms had his pony saddled and waiting at the front steps of the bungalow. Shasa took a moment to joke and laugh with the groom and then greet and caress his pony, rubbing foreheads with him and blowing softly into his nostrils.

'You are getting fat, Prester John,' he chided the pony. 'We'll have to work that off you with the polo sticks.'

He swung up into the saddle and took the short cut, following the pipe track around the shoulder of the hill. The pipeline carried the water from the spring around the hills to the mine and the washing gear. He passed the pumphouse and felt a guilty pang at its associations with last night's depravity, but then the dawn lit the plains below the cliffs and he forgot that in the pleasure of watching the veld come alive and greet the sun.

On this side of the hills Centaine had ordered that the forest be left untouched and the mopani was tall and stately. A covey of francolin were dawn-crying in the thicket down the slope, and a grey duiker, returning from the spring, bounded across the track under the pony's nose. Shasa laughed as he shied theatrically.

'Stop that, you old show-off!'

He turned the corner of the cliff and the contrast was

depressing. The desecrated forest, the deforming scar of the workings on the hillside, the graceless square iron buildings and the stark skeletal girders of the washing gear, how ugly they were.

He gave the pony a touch with his heels and they galloped the last mile and reached the main haulage just as Twentyman-Jones' old Ford came up the track from the village with headlights still burning. He checked his watch as he stepped out and looked sad as he saw that Shasa was three minutes ahead of time.

'Have you ever been down the haulage, Master Shasa?'

'No, sir.' He was going to add, 'My Mater has never allowed it,' but somehow that seemed superfluous, and for the first time he felt a twinge of resentment at his mother's all-pervading presence.

Twentyman-Jones led him to the head of the haulage and introduced him to the shift boss.

'Master Shasa will be working with you,' he explained. 'Treat him normally – just like you would treat any other young man who will one day be your managing director,' he instructed. It was impossible to tell by Twentyman-Jones' expression when he was joking, so nobody laughed.

'Get a tin helmet for him,' Twentyman-Jones ordered, and while Shasa adjusted the straps of the helmet he led him to the foot of the sheer cliff.

The incline tunnel had been cut into the base of the cliff, a round aperture into which the steel rail tracks angled downwards at forty-five degrees before disappearing into the dark depths. A string of cocopans stood at the head of the tracks, and Twentyman-Jones led him to the first truck and they climbed into the steel bin. The shift swarmed into the trucks behind them, a dozen white foremen and one hundred and fifty black workers in ragged dusty overalls and helmets of bright unpainted metal, laughing and ragging each other in boisterous horseplay.

The steam winch of the winding gear clattered and

hissed and the string of trucks jerked forward and then, rocking and swaying, ran down the steeply inclined ramp on the narrow-gauge railway tracks. The steel wheels rumbling and clacking over the joints of the track, they dropped down into the dark maw of the tunnel.

Shasa stirred uneasily, stabbed with unreasoning fear at the sudden absolute blackness that engulfed them. However, in the trucks behind him the Ovambo miners were singing, their deep melodious voices echoing in the dark confines of the tunnel, a marvellous chorus raised in an African work chant, and Shasa relaxed and leaned closer to Twentyman-Jones to follow his explanation.

'The incline is forty-five degrees and the capacity of the winding gear is one hundred tons, in mining parlance that is sixty loads of ore. Our target is six hundred loads a shift raised to the surface.'

Shasa was trying to concentrate on the figures; he knew his mother would question him this evening, but the darkness and singing and the rumble of the swaying trucks distracted him. Ahead of him there was a tiny coin of brilliant white light that grew swiftly in size until abruptly they burst out of the far end of the tunnel and involuntarily Shasa gasped with astonishment.

He had studied the diagrams of the pipe and, of course, there were photographs on his mother's desk at Weltervreden but they had not adequately prepared him for its immensity.

It was an almost perfectly round hole in the centre of the hills. It was open to the sky, and the sides of the excavation were vertical and sheer, a circular wall of grey rock like a cockpit. They had entered it through the tunnel that connected the workings to the far side of the hills and the narrow ramp on which they were riding continued down at the same angle of forty-five degrees until it reached the floor of the excavation two hundred feet below them. The drop on either hand was breathtaking. The great rock-lined hole was a mile across, and its sheer walls four hundred feet from the tip to the floor.

Twentyman-Jones was still lecturing him. 'This is a volcanic pipe, a blow hole from the earth's depths up which the molten magma was forced to the surface in the beginning of time. In those temperatures, as hot as the sun, and enormous pressures the diamonds were forged, and they were brought up in the fiery lava.' Shasa stared around him, screwing his head to take in the proportions of the huge excavation as Twentyman-Jones went on, 'Then the pipe was pinched off at depth, and the magma in it cooled and solidified. The upper layer, exposed to air and sun, was oxidized into the classical "yellow ground" of the diamond-iferous formation. We worked down through that for eleven years, and only recently we reached the "blue ground".' He made an expansive gesture that took in the slaty blue rock that formed the floor of the huge pit. 'That is the deeper deposit of the solidified magma, hard as iron and as full of diamonds as currants in a hot cross bun.'

They reached the floor of the workings and climbed down from the truck.

'The operation is fairly straightforward,' Twentyman-Jones went on. 'The new shift comes in at first light and begins work on the previous evening's blast. The broken ground is lashed and loaded into the cocopans and sent up the haulage to the surface. After that they mark out and drill the shot-holes for the next blast and then they set the charges. At dusk we pull out the shift, and the shift boss lights the fuses. After the blast we leave the workings overnight to settle and for the fumes to disperse, then the next morning we begin the whole process over again. There,' he pointed to an area of shattered blue grey rock, 'that's last night's blast. That's where we will begin today.'

Shasa had not expected to be so absorbed by the fascination of this mighty excavation, but his interest grew more intense as the day went on. Not even the heat and the dust daunted him. The heat was trapped between the sheer walls when at noon the sun beat down directly onto the uneven broken floor. The dust was floury, rising from the shattered ore body as the hammer-men swung their ten-pound sledges to crack the larger lumps into manageable pieces. The dust hung in a fog over the lashing teams as they loaded the cocopans, and it coated their faces and their bodies and turned them into ghostly grey albinos.

'We get a bit of miners' phthisis,' Twentyman-Jones admitted. 'The dust gets into their lungs and turns to stone. Ideally we should hose the ore down and keep it wet to lay the dust, but we are short of water. We haven't enough for the washing gear. We certainly can't afford to splash it around. So men die and are crippled, but it takes ten years to build up in the lungs, and we give them, or their widows, a good pension, and the miners' inspector is sympathetic, though his sympathy costs a penny.'

At noon Twentyman-Jones called Shasa across. 'Your mother said you need only work half the shift. I'm going up now. Are you coming?'

'I'd rather not, sir,' Shasa answered diffidently. 'I'd like to watch them charge the holes for the blast.'

Twentyman-Jones shook his head sorrowfully. 'Chip off the old block!' and went away still muttering.

The shift boss allowed Shasa to light the fuses, under his careful supervision. It gave Shasa a sense of importance and power to touch the flaring chesa stick, the igniter, to the bunched tips of the fuses, passing quickly down the line and watching the fire run down the twisted white fuses, turning them sizzling black in the swirl of blue smoke.

He and the shift boss rode up on the haulage to the cry of 'Fire in the hole!' and Shasa lingered at the head of the main haulage until the shots fired and he felt the earth tremble beneath his feet.

Then he saddled Prester John and, dusty, streaked with sweat, bone-tired and happy as he had seldom been in his life, he rode back along the pipe track.

He was not even thinking about her when he reached the pumphouse, but there she was, perched up on top of the silver-painted waterpipe. The shock was such that when Prester John shied under him he almost lost his seat and had to snatch at the pommel.

She had plaited a wreath of wild flowers into her hair and unbuttoned the top of her blouse. In one of the books in the library at Weltevreden there was an illustration of satyrs and nymphs dancing in the forest. The book was kept in the forbidden section to which his mother guarded the key, but Shasa had invested some of his pocket money in a duplicate and lightly clad nymphs were among his favourites of all that treasure house of erotica.

Annalisa was one of these, a wood nymph, only part human, and she slanted her eyes at him slyly and her eye teeth were pointed and very white.

'Hello, Annalisa.' His voice cracked treacherously, and his heart was beating so wildly that he thought it might spring into his throat and choke him.

She smiled but did not reply, instead she caressed her own arm, a slow lingering stroke from her wrist to her bare shoulder. He watched her fingers raising the fine coppery hair on her forearm and his loins swelled.

She leaned forward and placed her forefinger on her lower lip, still grinning slyly, and her bosom changed shape and the opening of her blouse gaped and he saw that the skin in the vee was so white and translucent that the tiny blue veins showed through it.

He kicked out of the stirrups and swung a leg over Prester John's withers in the showy polo player's forward dismount, but the girl whirled to her feet, hoisted her skirts high and, with a flash of creamy thighs, sprang lightly over the pipeline and disappeared into the thick scrub on the hillside beyond.

Shasa raced after her, and found himself struggling through dense undergrowth. It clawed at his face and seized his legs. He heard her giggle once, not far ahead of him, but a rock twisted under his boot and he fell heavily, winding himself. When he pulled himself up and limped after her, she was gone.

A while longer he floundered around in the scrub, his ardour swiftly cooling, and by the time he battled his way back to the pipe track to find that Prester John had taken full advantage of the diversion and decamped, he was bubbling over with anger at himself and the girl.

It was a long tramp back to the bungalow and he hadn't realized how tired he was. It was dark by the time he got home. The pony with empty saddle had raised the alarm and Centaine's concern changed instantly to relieved fury when she saw him.

A week in the heat and dust of the workings and the monotony of the work began to pall, so Twentyman-Jones sent Shasa to work in the winch room of the main haulage. The winch driver was a taciturn, morose man and jealous of his job. He would not allow Shasa to touch the controls of the winch.

'My union doesn't allow it.' He stood his ground stubbornly and after two days Twentyman-Jones moved Shasa to the weathering ground.

Hure the ore was tipped out and spread in the open by gangs of Ovambo labourers, all stripped to the waist and chanting in chorus as they went through the laborious repetitive process of tip and spread under the urgings of their white supervisor and his gang of black boss-boys.

On this weathering ground lay the stockpile of the H'ani Mine, thousands of tons of ore spread out on an area the size of four polo fields. When the blue ground was blasted out of the pipe it was hard as concrete; only gelignite and the ten-pound sledgehammers would break it. But after it had been lying in the sun on the weathering ground for six months it began to break down and crumble until it was chalky and friable and could be reloaded in the cocopans and taken to the mill and the washing gear.

Shasa was placed in charge of a gang of forty labourers, and soon struck up a friendship with the Ovambo boss-boy. Like all the black tribesmen he had two names, his tribal name which he did not divulge to his white employers, and his work name. The Ovambo's work name was Moses. He was fifteen years or so younger than the other boss-boys, and had been selected for his intelligence and initiative. He spoke both English and Afrikaans well, and the respect that the black labourers usually reserved for the grey hair of age he earned from them with his billy club and boot and acid wit.

'If I was a white man,' he told Shasa, 'one day I would have Doctela's job.' 'Doctela' was the Ovambo name for Twentyman-Jones, and Moses went on, 'I might still have it, one day – or if not me, then my son.' Shasa was shocked and then intrigued by such an outrageous notion. He had never before met a black who did not know his place in society. There was a disturbing presence about the tall Ovambo, who looked like one of the drawings of an Egyptian pharaoh from the forbidden section of the Weltevreden library, but that hint of danger made him more intriguing to Shasa.

They usually spent the lunch-hour break together, Shasa helping Moses to perfect his reading and writing in the grubby ruled notebook which was his most prized possession. In return the Ovambo taught Shasa the rudiments of his language, especially the oaths and insults, and the meaning of some of the work chants, most of which were ribald.

'Is baby-making work or pleasure?' was the rhetorical opening question of Shasa's favourite chant, and he joined in the response to the delight of the gang he was supervising: 'It cannot be work or the white man would make us do it for him!'

Shasa was just over fourteen years old. Some of the men he supervised were three times his age, and none of them thought it strange. Instead they responded to his teasing and his sunny smile and his sorry attempts to speak their language. His men were soon spreading five loads to four of the other teams, and they ended the second week as top gang on the grounds.

Shasa was too involved with the work and his new friend to notice the dark looks of the white supervisor, and even when he made a pointed remark about *kafferboeties*, or 'nigger-lovers', Shasa did not take the reference personally.

On the third Saturday, after the men had been paid at noon, he rode down to the boss-boys' cottage at Moses' invitation and spent an hour sitting in the sun on the front doorstep of the cottage drinking sour milk from the calabash that Moses' shy and pretty young wife offered, and helping him read aloud from the copy of Macaulay's *History of England* he had smuggled out of the bungalow and brought down in his saddlebag.

The book was one of his set works at school so Shasa considered himself something of an authority on it, and he was enjoying the unusual role of teacher and instructor until at last Moses closed the book.

'This is very heavy work, Good Water,' he had translated Shasa's name directly into the Ovambo, 'worse than spreading ore in the summer. I will work on it later,' and he went into the single-roomed cottage, placed the book in his locker and came back with a roll of newspaper.

'Let us try this.' He offered the paper to Shasa, who spread it on his lap. It was poor quality yellow newsprint and the ink smudged onto his fingers. The name on the top of the page was *Umlomo Wa Bantu*, and Shasa translated it without difficulty: 'The Mouth of the Black Nations', and he glanced down the columns of print. The articles were mostly in English, though there were a few in the vernacular.

Moses pointed out the editorial, and they started working through it.

'What is the African National Congress?' Shasa was puzzled. 'And who is Jabavu?'

Eagerly the Ovambo began to explain, and Shasa's interest turned to unease as he listened.

'Jabavu is the father of the Bantu, of all the tribes, of all the black people. The African National Congress is the herder who guards our cattle.'

'I don't understand.' Shasa shook his head. He did not like the direction that the discussion was taking, and he began to squirm as Moses quoted:

Your cattle are gone, my people
Go rescue them! Go rescue them!
Leave your breechloader
And turn instead to the pen.
Take paper and ink,
For that will be your shield.
Your rights are going
So take up your pen
Load it with ink
And do battle with the pen.

'That is politics,' Shasa interrupted him. 'Blacks don't take part in politics. That's white men's business.' This was the cornerstone of the South African way of life.

The glow went out of Moses' expression and he lifted the newspaper off Shasa's lap and stood up.

'I will return your book to you when I have read it.' He avoided Shasa's eyes and went back into the cottage.

O n the Monday Twentyman-Jones stopped Shasa at the main gate of the weathering grounds. 'I think you have learned all there is to know about weathering, Master Shasa. It's about time we moved you along to the mill house and washing gear.'

And as they followed the railway tracks up to the main plant, walking beside one of the cocopans which was full of the crumbling weathered ore, Twentyman-Jones remarked: 'It is just as well not to become too familiar with the black labourers, Master Shasa, you will find they tend to take advantage if you do.'

Shasa was puzzled for a moment, then he laughed. 'Oh, you mean Moses. He isn't a labourer, he is a boss-boy, and he is jolly bright, sir.'

'A bit too bright for his own good,' Twentyman-Jones agreed bitterly. 'The bright ones are always the malcontents and trouble-stirrers. Give me an honest dumb nigger every time. Your friend Moses is trying to organize a black mine-workers' union.'

Shasa knew from his grandfather and his mother that Bolsheviks and trade unionists were the most dreaded monsters, intent on tearing down the framework of civilized society. He was appalled to learn that Moses was one of these, but Twentyman-Jones was going on:

'We also suspect that he is at the centre of a nice little IDB operation.'

IDB was the other monster of civilized existence – Illicit Diamond Buying – the trade in stolen diamonds, and Shasa

153

was revolted by the idea that his friend could be both a trade unionist and an illicit dealer.

Yet Twentyman-Jones' next words depressed him. 'I am afraid Mister Moses will head the list of those we will be laying off at the end of the month. He is a dangerous man. We will simply have to get shot of him.'

'They are getting rid of him simply because the two of us are friends.' Shasa saw through it. 'It's because of me.' He was swamped with a sense of guilt, and guilt was followed almost immediately by anger. Quick words leapt to his tongue. He wanted to cry, 'It's not fair!' But before he spoke he looked at Twentyman-Jones and knew intuitively that any defence he attempted of Moses would only seal the boss-boy's fate.

He shrugged. 'You know what is best, sir,' he agreed, and he saw the slight relaxation in the set of the old man's shoulders.

'Mater,' he thought, 'I will talk to Mater,' and then, with intense frustration, 'If only I could do it myself, if only I could say what must be done.' And then it dawned upon him that this was what his mother had meant when she spoke of power. The ability to charge and direct the orders of existence that surrounded him.

'Power,' he whispered to himself. 'One day I will have power. Enormous power.'

The work in the mill house was more exacting and interesting. The friable weathered ore was loaded into the bins and then fed through the hoppers into the rollers which crushed it to the correct consistency for the washing gear. The machinery was massive and powerful, the din almost deafening as the ore tumbled out of the hoppers into the feed chute and was sucked into the spinning steel rollers with a continuous roar. One hundred and fifty tons an hour; it went in one end as chalky lumps the size of ripe watermelons and poured out the far end as gravel and dust.

Annalisa's brother, Stoffel, who had on Shasa's last visit to the H'ani adjusted the timing on his old Ford and who was also the skilled mimic of bird calls, was now an apprentice in the mill house. He was delegated to show Shasa around, and undertook the assignment with gusto and relish.

'You have to be goddamned careful with the mucking settings on the rollers or you crush the bloody diamonds to powder.' Stoffel emphasized his newly acquired manliness and authority with oaths and obscenity.

'Come on, Shasa, I'll show you the grease points. All points have to be grease-gunned at the beginning of every shift.' He crawled under the bank of thundering rollers, shouting into Shasa's ear to make himself heard. 'Last month one of the other apprentices got his mucking arm in the bearing. It pulled it off like a chicken's wing, man. You should have seen the blood.' Ghoulishly he pointed out the dried stains on the concrete floor and galvanized walls. 'Man, I tell you, he squirted blood like a garden hose.'

Stoffel climbed the steel catwalk like a monkey and they looked down on the roller mill tables. 'One of the Ovambo kaffirs fell off here, right smack into the ore bin, there wasn't even a scrap of bone bigger than your finger left of him when he came out the other end of the rollers. Ja, man, it's a bloody dangerous job,' he told Shasa proudly. 'You've got to keep on your mucking toes all the time.'

When the mine hooter blew the lunch hour he led Shasa around to the shady side of the mill house and they perched comfortably on the ventilator housing. Under the sanction of the work place they could associate quite openly, and Shasa felt grown-up and important in his blue workman's overalls as he opened the lunch box that the chef at the bungalow had sent down for him.

'Chicken and tongue sandwiches and jam roly-poly,' he checked the contents. 'Do you want some, Stoffel?'

'No, man. Here comes my sister with my lunch.' And Shasa lost all interest in his own lunch box.

Annalisa was pedalling down the avenue on a black-framed Rudge with the nest of canteens dangling from the handlebars. It was the first time that he had seen her since the meeting at the pumphouse, though he had looked for her each day since then. She had tucked her skirts into her bloomers to keep them clear of the chain. She stood up on the pedals and her legs pumped rhythmically as she came through the gates of the mill house and the wind flattened the thin stuff of her dress against the front of her body. Her breasts were disproportionately large for her slim brown limbs.

Shasa watched her with total fascination. She became aware of him, sitting beside her brother, and her entire bearing changed. She dropped back onto the saddle and squared her shoulders, lifting one hand from the handlebars to try and smooth the windblown tangle of her hair. She braked the Rudge, stepped down off the pedals and propped the machine against the bottom of the ventilator housing.

'What's for lunch, Lisa?' Stoffel Botha demanded.

'Sausage and mash.' She handed the canteens up to him. 'Same as always.'

The sleeves of her dress were cut back and when she lifted her arms Shasa saw the bush of coarse blond hair in her armpits tangled and wet with perspiration and he crossed his legs quickly.

'Sis, man!' Stoffel registered his disgust. 'It's always sausage and mash!'

'Next time I'll ask Ma to cook fillet steak and mushrooms.' She lowered her arms and Shasa realized he was staring but could not stop himself. She pulled the opening at the neck of her blouse closed and he saw a faint flush under the suntanned skin at her throat, but she had not yet looked directly at him.

'Thanks for nothing,' Stoffel dismissed her, but she lingered.

'You can have some of mine,' Shasa offered.

'I'll swop you,' Stoffel offered generously, and Shasa glanced into the canteen and saw the lumpy potato mash swimming in thin greasy gravy.

'I'm not hungry.' He spoke to the girl for the first time. 'Would you like a sandwich, Annalisa?'

She smoothed the skirt over her hips and looked directly at him at last. Her eyes slanted like a wild cat's, and she grinned slyly.

'When I want something from you, Shasa Courtney, I will whistle for it – like this.' She pouted her lips into a rosy cupid's bow and whistled like a snake charmer, at the same time slowly raising her forefinger in an unmistakably obscene gesture.

Stoffel let out a delighted guffaw and punched Shasa's arm. 'Man, she's got the hots for you!'

While Shasa blushed scarlet, and sat speechless with shock, Annalisa turned away deliberately and picked up the bicycle. She went out through the gates standing on the pedals and swinging the Rudge from side to side under her so that her tight round buttocks oscillated with each stroke.

That evening as he turned Prester John onto the pipe track Shasa's pulse started to gallop with anticipation, and as he approached the pumphouse he slowed the pony to a walk, afraid of disappointment, reluctant to turn the corner of the building.

Yet he was still not prepared for the shock when he saw her. She was draped languidly against one of the stanchions of the pipeline, and Shasa was speechless as she came slowly upright and sauntered to the head of his pony without looking up at the rider.

She held the cheek strap of his halter and crooned to the pony. 'What a pretty boy.' The pony blew through his nostrils, and shifted his weight. 'What a lovely soft nose.' She stroked his muzzle with a lingering touch.

'Would you like a little kiss then, my pretty boy.' She pursed her lips, pink and soft and moist, and glanced up at Shasa before she leaned forward and deliberately kissed the pony's muzzle, slipping her arms around his neck. She held the kiss for long seconds and then laid her cheek against the pony's cheek. Beginning to sway, humming softly in her throat and rocking her hips gently, she at last looked up at Shasa with those sly slanting eyes.

He was struggling to find something to say, confused by the rush of his emotions, and she moved slowly to the pony's shoulder and stroked his flank.

'So strong.' Her hand brushed Shasa's thigh lightly, almost unintentionally, and then came back more deliberately and she was no longer looking at his face. He could not cover himself, could not hide his violent reaction to her touch, and suddenly she let out a shocking screech of laughter and stood back with both hands on her hips.

'Are you going to camp out, Shasa Courtney?' she demanded, and he was puzzled and embarrassed. He shook his head dumbly.

'Then what are you putting up a tent for?' She hooted, gazing shamelessly at the front of his breeches and he doubled up awkwardly in the saddle. With a disconcerting change of mood, she seemed to take pity on him and she went back to the pony's head and led him along the track, giving Shasa a chance to recover his composure.

'What did my brother tell you about me?' she asked, without looking round.

'Nothing,' he assured her.

'Don't believe what he says.' She was unconvinced. 'He always tries to make out bad things about me. Did he tell you about Fourie, the driver?' Everybody at the mine knew how Gerhard Fourie's wife had caught the two of them in the cab of his truck after the Christmas party. Fourie's wife was older than Annalisa's mother, but she had blackened both the girl's eyes and torn her only good dress to tatters.

'He didn't tell me anything,' Shasa reiterated stoutly, and then with interest, 'What happened?'

'Nothing,' she said quickly. 'It was all lies.' And then, with another change of direction, 'Would you like me to show you something?'

'Yes, please.' Shasa answered with alacrity. He had an inkling of what it might be.

'Give me an arm.' She came to his stirrup and he leaned down and they hooked elbows. He swung her up and she was light and strong. She sat behind him astride the pony's rump and slid both arms around Shasa's waist.

'Take the path to the left.' She directed him and they rode in silence for ten minutes.

'How old are you?' she asked at last.

'Almost fifteen.' He stretched the truth a little and she said, 'I'll be sixteen in two months.' If there had been any doubts as to who was in charge, this declaration effectively settled it. Shasa deferred to her and she felt it in his carriage. She pressed her breasts to his back as though to emphasize her control and they were big and rubbery hard and burned him through his thin cotton shirt.

'Where are we going?' he asked after another long silence. They had by-passed the bungalow.

'Hush up! I'll show you when we get there.'

The track had narrowed and become rougher. Shasa doubted anybody had passed this way in months, other than the small wild beasts that still lived this close to the mine. Finally it petered out altogether against the base of the cliff, and Annalisa slid down from the pony's back.

'Leave your horse here.'

He tethered the pony and looked around him with interest. He had never been so far along the base of the cliffs. They must be three miles from the bungalow at least.

Below them the scree slope plunged downwards at a steep angle, and the ground was riven with gorges and ravines, all of them choked with rank thorny undergrowth.

'Come on,' Annalisa ordered. 'We haven't got much time. It will be dark soon.' She ducked under a branch and started down the slope.

'Hey!' Shasa cautioned her. 'You can't go down there. You'll hurt yourself.'

'You're scared,' she mocked.

'I am not.' The taunt goaded him onto the rock-strewn slope and they climbed downwards. Once Annalisa paused to pluck a spray of yellow flowers from a thorn bush, then they went on, helping each other over the bad places, crouching under the thorn branches, teetering on the boulders and hopping across the gaps like a pair of rock rabbits until they reached the bottom of the ravine and paused to catch their breath.

Shasa bent backwards from the waist and stared up at the cliff that towered above them, sheer as a fortress wall, but Annalisa tugged his arm to gain his attention.

'It's a secret. You have to swear an oath not to tell anybody, especially not my brother.'

'All right, I swear.'

'You have to do it properly. Lift your right hand and put the other on your heart.' Solemnly she led him through the oath, and then took his hand and drew him to a lichen-covered pile of boulders. 'Kneel down!'

He obeyed, and she carefully pulled aside a leafy branch that screened a niche amongst the boulders. Shasa gasped and pulled back, coming half to his feet. The niche was shaped like a shrine. There was a collection of empty glass jars arranged on the floor but the wild flowers in them had withered and turned brown. Beyond the floral offering a pile of white bones had been carefully arranged in a small pyramid and surmounting this was a human skull, with gaping eye sockets and yellow teeth.

'Who is it?' Shasa whispered, his eyes wide with superstitious awe.

'The witch of the mountain.' Annalisa took his hand. 'I found her bones lying here, and I made this magic place.'

'How do you know she's a witch?' Shasa had a bad attack of the creeps by now, and his whisper shook and cracked.

'She told me so.'

That raised such frightful images that he did not question her further; skulls and bones were creepy enough, voices from beyond were a hundred times worse, and the hairs at the back of his neck and along his arms itched and stood erect. He watched while she changed the withered flowers for the fresh yellow acacia blossom and then sat back on her ankles and took his hand again.

'The witch will grant you one wish,' she whispered, and he thought about it.

'What do you want?' she tugged his hand.

'Can I wish for anything?'

'Yes, anything,' she nodded, watching his face eagerly.

Staring at the bleached skull his awe faded; he was suddenly aware of a new sensation. Something seemed to reach out to him, a sensation of warmth and familiar comfort that he had known before only as an infant when his mother held him to her bosom.

There were still small pieces of dried scalp attached to the dome of the skull, like brown parchment, and tiny peppercorns of black hair, soft furry little balls like those on the head of the tame Bushman who herded the milk cows at the way station on the road from Windhoek.

'Anything?' he repeated. 'I can wish for anything?'

'Yes, anything you want.' Annalisa leaned against his side, and she was soft and warm and her body smelled of fresh sweet young sweat.

Shasa leaned forward and touched the skull on its white bony forehead, and the sense of warmth and comfort was stronger. He was aware of a benign feeling – of love – that was not too strong a word, yes, of love, as though he were being overlooked by someone or something that cared for him very deeply.

'I wish,' he said softly, almost dreamily, 'I wish for enormous power.'

He imagined a prickling sensation in the fingertips that touched the skull, like the discharge of static electricity, and he jerked his hand away sharply.

Annalisa exclaimed in exasperation and pulled her body away from him at the same time. 'That's a silly wish.' She was clearly piqued, and he could not understand why. 'You are a stupid boy, and the witch won't grant a stupid wish like that.'

She flounced to her feet and drew the screening branch over the niche. 'It's late. We must go back.'

Shasa did not want to leave this place, and he lingered.

Annalisa called from up the slope. 'Come on, it will be dark in an hour.'

When he reached the path again she was sitting propped against the rock wall of the cliff facing him.

'I've hurt myself.' She said it like an accusation. They were both flushed and panting from the climb.

'I'm sorry,' he gasped. 'How did you hurt yourself?'

She pulled the hem of her skirt halfway up her thigh. One of the red-tipped wait-a-bit thorns had rowelled her, raising a long red scratch across the smooth buttery skin of her inner thigh. It had barely broken the skin, but a line of blood droplets had welled up, like a necklace of tiny bright rubies. He stared at it as though mesmerized and she sank back against the rock, lifted her knees and spread her thighs, holding the bunch of her skirts into her crotch.

'Put some spit on it,' she ordered.

Obediently he knelt between her feet and wet his forefinger.

'Your finger is dirty,' she admonished him.

'What shall I do then?' He was at a loss.

'With your tongue – put spit on it with your tongue.'

He leaned forward and touched the wound with the tip of his tongue. Her blood had a strange salty metallic taste as he licked it.

She placed one hand on the nape of his neck and stroked the dense dark curl of his hair.

'Yes, like that, clean it,' she murmured. Her fingers twisted into his hair and she held his head, pressing his face to her skin, and then deliberately directed him higher, raising her skirt slowly with her free hand as his mouth travelled upwards.

Then peering between the spread of her thighs, he saw that she was sitting on a piece of her clothing, a scrap of white cloth printed with pink roses, and with a tingle of shock he realized that in the few minutes that she had been alone she must have removed her panties and spread them as a cushion on the soft moss-covered earth. She was naked under the skirt.

Shasa woke with a start and he could not think where he was. The ground was hard under his back and a pebble was digging into his shoulder, there was a weight across his chest making it difficult for him to breathe. He was cold, and it was dark. Prester John stamped and snorted and he saw the pony's head silhouetted against the stars.

Suddenly he remembered. Annalisa's leg was thrown over his and her face was against his throat; she sprawled half across his chest. He pushed her off so violently that she woke with a cry.

'It's dark!' he said stupidly. 'They'll be out looking for us by now!'

He tried to stand but his breeches were around his knees. He remembered vividly the practised way that she had unbuttoned them and worked them over his hips. He yanked them up and fumbled with his fly.

'We've got to get back. My mother—'

Annalisa was on her feet beside him, hopping on one leg as she tried to find the opening of her panties with her bare foot. Shasa looked at the stars. Orion was on the horizon. 'It's after nine o'clock,' he said gloomily.

'You should have stayed awake,' she whined, and put a hand on his shoulder to steady herself. 'My Pa will lather me. He said next time he'd kill me.'

Shasa shrugged off her hand. He wanted to get away from her yet he knew he could not.

'It was your fault.' She stooped and grabbed her panties at the ankles, hoisted them to her waist and then settled her skirts over them. 'I'm going to tell Pa that it was your fault. He'll take the sjambok to me this time. Oh! he'll whop the skin off me.'

Shasa unhitched the pony and his hands were shaking. He could not think clearly, he was still half asleep and groggy. 'I won't let him.' His gallantry was half-hearted and unconvincing. 'I won't let him hurt you.'

It seemed only to infuriate her. 'What can you do? You're only a baby.' The word triggered something else in her mind. 'What will happen if you've given me a baby, hey? It will be a bastard; did you think of that while you were sticking that thing of yours into me?' she demanded waspishly.

Shasa was stung by the unfairness of her accusation. 'You showed me how. I wouldn't have done it if you hadn't.'

'A fat lot of good that's going to do us.' She was weeping now. 'I wish we could just run away.'

The notion held a definite appeal for Shasa, and he discarded it only reluctantly. 'Come on,' he said, and boosted her up onto Prester John's back and then swung up behind her.

They saw the torches of the search parties down on the plain below them as they turned the shoulder of the mountain. There were headlights on the road also, moving slowly, obviously searching the verges, and faintly they heard the shouts of the searchers, calling for them as they moved about in the forest far below.

'My Pa's going to kill me this time. He'll know what we've been doing,' she snuffled and sobbed and her self-pity irritated him. He had long ago given up trying to comfort her.

'How will he know?' he snapped. 'He wasn't there.'

'You don't think you were the first one I've done it with,' she demanded, seeking to injure him. 'I've done it with plenty of others, and Pa has caught me twice. Oh, he'll know all right.'

At the thought of her performing those strangely marvellous tricks of hers with others, Shasa felt a hot rush of jealousy which was gradually cooled by reason.

'Well,' he pointed out. 'If he knows about all the others, it isn't going to do you much good to try to put the blame on me.'

She had trapped herself and she let out another broken-hearted sob, and was still weeping theatrically when they met the search party coming on foot along the pipe track.

S hasa and Annalisa sat on opposite sides of the bungalow's drawing-room, instinctively keeping as far from each other as possible. As they heard the Daimler pull up outside in a flare of headlights and crunch of gravel, Annalisa began to weep again, snuffling and rubbing her eyes to work up a few more tears.

They heard Centaine's quick light tread across the verandah, followed by Twentyman-Jones' more deliberate stork-like steps.

Shasa stood up and held his hands in front of him in the attitude of the penitent as Centaine stopped in the doorway. She was dressed in jodhpurs and riding-boots and a tweed hacking jacket, with a yellow scarf knotted at her throat. She was flushed, and relieved and furious as an avenging angel.

Annalisa saw her face and let out a howl of anguish, only half acting.

'Shut your mouth, girl,' Centaine told her quietly. 'Or I'll see you get good reason to blubber.' She turned to Shasa. 'Are either of you hurt?'

'No, Mater.' He hung his head.

'Prester John?'

'Oh, he's in good fettle.'

'So, that's it then.' She did not have to elaborate. 'Dr Twentyman-Jones, will you take this young lady down to her father? I have no doubt that he will know how to deal with her.' Centaine had spoken briefly to the father only an hour before, big and bald and paunchy with tattoos on his muscled arms, belligerent and red-eyed, reeking of cheap brandy and opening and closing his hairy paws as he mouthed his intentions towards his only daughter.

Twentyman-Jones took the girl by her wrist, pulled her to her feet and led her snivelling towards the door. As he passed Centaine, her expression softened and she touched his arm. 'What ever would I do without you, Dr Twentyman-Jones?' she asked quietly.

'I suspect that you would get along very well on your own, Mrs Courtney, but I'm glad I could help.' He dragged Annalisa from the room and they heard the whirr of the Daimler's engine.

Centaine's expression hardened again and she turned back to Shasa. He fidgeted under her scrutiny.

'You've been disobedient,' she told him. 'I warned you away from that little *poule*.'

'Yes, Mater.'

'She's been with half the men on the mine. We'll have to take you to a doctor when we get back to Windhoek.'

He shuddered and glanced down at himself involuntarily at the thought of a host of disgusting microbes crawling over his most intimate flesh.

'Disobedience is bad enough, but what have you done that is truly unforgivable?' she demanded.

Shasa could think of at least a dozen trespasses without really extending himself.

'You've been stupid,' Centaine said. 'You've been stupid enough to get caught out. That is the worst sin. You've made a laughing stock of yourself with everybody on the mine. How will you ever be able to lead and command when you cheapen yourself like this?'

'I didn't think of that, Mater. I didn't think of anything much. It just all sort of happened.'

'Well, think of it now,' she told him. 'While you are taking a long hot bath with half a bottle of Lysol in it, think hard about it. Goodnight.'

'Goodnight, Mater.' He came to her and after a moment she offered her cheek. 'I'm sorry, Mater.' He kissed her cheek. 'I'm sorry I made you ashamed of me.'

She wanted to throw her arms around him and pull his beautiful beloved head to her and hold him hard and tell him that she would never be ashamed of him.

'Goodnight, Shasa,' she said, standing cool and erect until he left the room and she heard his footsteps drag disconsolately down the passage. Then her shoulders slumped.

'Oh, my darling – oh my baby,' she whispered. Suddenly, for the first time in many years, she felt the need for an opiate. She crossed quickly to the massive stinkwood cabinet and poured cognac from one of the heavy decanters and took a mouthful. The spirit was peppery on her tongue and the fumes brought tears to her eyes. She swallowed it down and set the glass aside.

'That isn't going to help much,' she decided, and crossed to her desk. She sat down in the wingbacked buttoned leather chair and she felt small and frail and vulnerable. For Centaine, it was an alien emotion and it frightened her.

'It's happened,' she whispered. 'He is becoming a man.' Suddenly she hated the girl. 'The dirty little harlot. He isn't ready for that yet. Too early she has let the demon out, the demon of his de Thiry blood.' She was intimate with that same demon, for it had plagued her all her life. That wild passionate de Thiry blood.

'Oh my darling.' She was going to lose some part of him now – had already lost it, she realized. Loneliness came to her like a ravening beast that had lain in ambush for her all these years.

There had only been two men who might have assuaged that loneliness. Shasa's father had died in his frail machine of canvas and wood while she had stood by helplessly and watched him blacken and burn. The other man had placed himself beyond her reach for ever with one brutal senseless act. Michael Courtney and Lothar De La Rey – both dead to her now.

Since then there had been lovers, many lovers, brief transient affairs experienced only at the level of the flesh, a mere antidote for the boil of her blood. None of them had been allowed to pass into that deep place of her soul. But now the beast of loneliness burst through those guarded portals and laid waste her secret places.

'If only there was someone,' she lamented as she had done only once before in her life, when she lay upon the childbed on which she had given birth to Lothar De La Rey's gold-headed bastard. 'If only there was somebody I could love and who would love me in return.'

She leaned forward in the big leather chair and picked up the silver-framed photograph, the photograph that she carried with her wherever she travelled, and studied the face of the young man in the centre of the group of fliers. For the first time she realized that over the years the picture had faded and yellowed and the features of Michael Courtney, Shasa's father, had blurred. She stared at the handsome young face and tried desperately to make the picture clearer and crisper in her own memory, but it seemed to smear and recede even further from her.

'Oh Michel,' she whispered. 'It was all so long ago. Forgive me. Please forgive me. I have tried to be strong and brave. I've tried for your sake and the sake of your son, but—'

She set the frame back upon the desk and crossed to the window. She stared out into the darkness. 'I'm going to lose my baby,' she thought. 'And then one day I will be alone and old and ugly – and I'm afraid.' She found she was shivering, hugging her own arms, but then her reaction was swift and unequivocal.

'There is no time for weakness and self-pity on the journey that you have chosen.' She steeled herself, standing small and erect and alone in the silent darkened house. 'You have to go on. There is no turning back, no faltering, you have to go on to the end.'

'**W**here is Stoffel Botha?' Shasa demanded of the mill house supervisor when the mine hooter blew to signal the beginning of the lunch hour. 'Why isn't he here?'

'Who knows?' The supervisor shrugged. 'I had a note from the main office saying he wasn't coming. They didn't tell me why. Perhaps he has been fired. I don't know. I don't care – he was a cocky little bastard, anyway.' And for the rest of the shift Shasa tried to suppress his feeling of guilt by concentrating on the run of ore through the thundering rollers.

When the final hooter blew, and the cry of *Shahile!* 'It has struck!' was shouted from one gang of black labourers to the next, Shasa mounted Prester John and turned his head towards the avenue of cottages in which Annalisa's family lived. He knew he was risking his mother's wrath, but a defiant sense of chivalry urged him on. He had to find out how much damage and unhappiness he had caused.

However, at the gates of the mill house he was distracted.

Moses, the boss-boy from the weathering grounds, stepped in front of Prester John and took his head.

'I see you, Good Water,' he greeted Shasa in his soft deep voice.

'Oh Moses.' Shasa smiled with pleasure, his other troubles forgotten for the moment. 'I was going to visit you.'

'I have brought your book.' The Ovambo handed the thick copy of *History of England* up to him.

'You couldn't possibly have read it,' Shasa protested. 'Not so soon. It took even me months.'

'I will never read it, Good Water. I am leaving the H'ani Mine. I go with the trucks to Windhoek tomorrow morning.'

'Oh no!' Shasa swung down out of the saddle and

gripped his arm. 'Why do you want to go, Moses?' Shasa feigned ignorance out of a sense of his guilt and complicity.

'It is not for me to want or not to want.' The tall boss-boy shrugged. 'Many men are leaving on the trucks tomorrow. Doctela has chosen them, and the lady your mother has explained the reason and given us a month's wages. A man like me does not ask questions, Good Water.' He smiled, a sad bitter grimace. 'Here is your book.'

'Keep it.' Shasa pushed it back. 'It is my gift to you.'

'Very well, Good Water. I will keep it to remind me of you. Stay in peace.' He turned away.

'Moses—' Shasa called him back and then could find nothing to say. He thrust out his hand impulsively and the Ovambo stepped back from it. A white man and a black man did not shake hands.

'Go in peace,' Shasa insisted, and Moses glanced around almost furtively before he accepted the grip. His skin was strangely cool. Shasa wondered if all black skin was like that.

'We are friends,' Shasa said, prolonging the contact. 'We are, aren't we?'

'I do not know.'

'What do you mean?'

'I do not know if it is possible for us to be friends.' Gently he freed his hand and turned away. He did not look back at Shasa as he skirted the security fence and went down to the compound.

The convoy of heavy trucks ground across the plains, keeping open intervals to avoid the dust thrown up by the preceding vehicle. The dust rose in a feathery spray, high in the still heated air like the yellow smoke from a bush fire burning on a wide front.

Gerhard Fourie, in the lead truck, slumped at the wheel with his belly hanging into his lap; it had forced open the buttons of his shirt, exposing the hairy pit of his navel. Every few seconds he glanced up from the road to the rearview mirror above his head.

The back of the truck was piled with the baggage and furniture of the families, both black and white, that had been laid off from the mine. On top of this load were perched the unfortunate owners. The women had knotted scarves over their hair for the dust; they clutched their young children as the trucks bounced and swayed over the uneven tracks. The elder children had made nests for themselves amongst the baggage.

Fourie reached up and readjusted the mirror slightly, centring the image of the girl behind him. She was wedged between an old tea chest and a shabby suitcase of imitation leather. She had propped a blanket roll behind her back and she was dozing, her streaky blond head nodding and lolling to the truck's motion. One knee was slightly raised, her short skirt rucked up and as she fell asleep so her knee dropped to one side and Fourie caught a glimpse of her underpants, patterned with pink roses, wedged between those smooth young thighs. Then the girl jerked awake and closed her legs and rolled on her side.

Fourie was sweating, not merely from the heat; drops of it glinted in the dark unshaven stubble that covered his jowls. He took the stub of cigarette from between his lips with shaky fingers and inspected it. Saliva had soaked through the ricepaper and stained it with yellow tobacco juice. He flicked it out of the side window and lit another, driving with one hand and watching the mirror, waiting for the girl to move again. He had sampled that young flesh, he knew how sweet and warm and available it was, and he wanted it again with a sickness of desire. He was prepared to take any risk for just another taste of it.

Ahead of him the clump of grey camel-thorn trees swam

out of the heat mirage. He had travelled this road so often that the journey had its landmarks and rituals. He checked his pocket watch and grunted. They were twenty minutes late on this stage. But then the trucks were all overloaded with this throng of newly unemployed and their pathetic possessions.

He pulled the truck off the track beside the trees and climbed stiffly out onto the running-board and shouted: 'All right, everybody. Pinkle pause. Women on the left, men on the right. Anybody who isn't back in ten minutes gets left behind.'

He was the first back to the truck, and he busied himself at the left-hand rear wheel, making a show of checking the valve but watching for the girl.

She came out from amongst the trees, smoothing her skirts. She looked petulant and hot and grubby with floury dust. But when she saw Fourie watching her, she tossed her head and swung her tight little buttocks and ostentatiously ignored him.

'Annalisa,' he whispered, as she raised one bare foot to climb over the tailboard of the truck beside him.

'Your mother's, Gerhard Fourie!' she hissed back at him. 'You just leave me alone, or I'll tell my Pa!'

At any other time she might have responded more amiably, but her thighs and buttocks and the small of her back were still criss-crossed with purple weals from where her father had lambasted her. Temporarily she had lost interest in the male sex.

'I want to talk to you,' Fourie insisted.

'Talk, ha! I know what you want.'

'Meet me outside the camp tonight,' he pleaded.

'Your bollocks in a barrel.' She jumped up into the truck and his stomach turned over as he saw the full length of those slim brown legs.

'Annalisa, I'll give you money.' He was desperate; the sickness was burning him up.

Annalisa paused and looked down at him thoughtfully. His offer was a revelation that opened a chink into a new world of fascinating possibilities. Up to that moment it had never occurred to her that a man might give her money to do something which she enjoyed more than eating or sleeping.

'How much?' she asked with interest.

'A pound,' he offered.

It was a great deal of money, more than she had ever had in her hand at any one time, but her mercenary instinct was aroused, she wanted to see how far this could be taken. So she tossed her head and flounced, watching him out of the corner of her eye.

'Two pounds,' Fourie whispered urgently, and Annalisa's spirits soared. Two whole pounds! She felt bold and pretty and borne along by good fortune. The stripes across her back and legs were fading. She slanted her eyes in that sly knowing expression that maddened him and she saw the sweat start on his chin and his lower lip trembled.

It emboldened her even further, and she drew breath and held it, and then whispered daringly: 'Five pounds!' She ran the tip of her tongue around her lips, shocked by her own courage in naming such an enormous sum. It was almost as much as her father earned in a week.

Fourie blanched and wavered. 'Three,' he blurted, but she sensed how close he was to agreement and she drew back affronted.

'You are a smelly old man.' She filled her voice with scorn and turned away.

'All right! All right!' he capitulated. 'Five pounds.' She grinned at him victoriously. She had discovered and entered a new world of endless riches and pleasure.

She put the tip of her finger in her mouth. 'And if you want that too, it will cost you another pound.' There were no limits to her daring now.

The moon was only days from full and it washed the desert with molten platinum, while the shadows along the ravine walls were leaden blue smudges. The camp sounds carried faintly along the ravine, somebody was chopping firewood, a bucket clanged and the women's voices at the cooking fires were like bird sounds heard from afar. Closer at hand a pair of prowling jackal cried, the odours from the cooking pots exciting them into their wild, wailing, almost agonized chorus.

Fourie squatted against the wall of the ravine and lit a cigarette, watching the ravine along which the girl must come. The flare of the match illuminated his fleshy unshaven features and he was so intent that he was totally unaware of the predatory eyes that watched him out of the blue moon shadows close by. His whole existence centred on the arrival of the girl and already he was breathing with eager little grunts of anticipation.

She was like a wraith in the moonlight, silvery and ethereal, and he heaved himself to his feet and crushed out the cigarette.

'Annalisa!' he called, his voice low and quivering with the need of her.

She stopped just out of reach before him, and when he lunged for her she danced away lightly and laughed with a mocking tinkle.

'Five pounds, *Meneer*,' she reminded him, and drew nearer as he fumbled the crumpled bank notes out of his back pocket. She took them and held them up to the moon. Then, satisfied, tucked them away in her clothing and stepped boldly up to him.

He seized her around the waist and covered her mouth with his wet lips. She broke away at last, laughing breathlessly, and held his wrist as he reached under her skirt.

'Do you want the other pound's worth?'

'It's too much,' he panted. 'I haven't got that much.'

175

'Ten shillings, then,' she offered, and touched the front of his body with a small cunning hand.

'Half a crown,' he gasped. 'That's all I have got.' And she stared at him, still touching him, and saw she could get no more out of him.

'All right, give it to me,' she agreed, and hid the coin before she went down on her knees in front of him as though for his blessing. He placed both hands on her curly sunstreaked head and drew her towards him, bowing his head over her and then closing his eyes.

Something hard was thrust into his ribs from behind with such force that the wind was driven from his lungs and a voice grated in his ear.

'Tell the little bitch to disappear.' The voice was low and dangerous and dreadfully familiar.

The girl leaped to her feet, wiping her mouth on the back of her hand. She stared for an instant over Fourie's shoulder with wide terrified eyes, then whirled and raced up the ravine towards the camp on long flying legs.

Fourie fumbled clumsily with his clothing and turned to face the man who stood behind him with the Mauser rifle pointed at his belly.

'De La Rey!' he blurted.

'Were you expecting somebody else?'

'No! No!' Fourie shook his head wildly. 'It's just – so soon.' Since last they had met Fourie had had time to repent of their bargain. Cowardice had won the long battle over avarice, and because he wanted it so he had convinced himself that Lothar De La Rey's scheme was like so many others that he had dreamed about, merely one of those fantasies with which those for ever doomed to poverty and futile labour consoled themselves.

He had expected, and hoped, never to hear of Lothar De La Rey again. But now he stood before him, tall and deadly with his head shining like a beacon in the moonlight and topaz lights glinting in those leopard eyes.

'Soon?' Lothar asked. 'So soon? It's been weeks, my old and dear friend. It all took longer to arrange than I expected.' Then Lothar's voice hardened as he asked, 'Have you taken the diamond shipment into Windhoek yet?'

'No, not yet—' Fourie broke off, and silently reviled himself. That would have been his escape. He should have said 'Yes! I took it in myself last week.' But it was done, and miserably he hung his head and concentrated on fastening the last buttons of his breeches. Those few words spoken too hastily might yet cost him a lifetime in prison and he was afraid.

'When will the shipment go in?' Lothar placed the muzzle of the Mauser under Fourie's chin and lifted his face to the moon. He wanted to watch the man's eyes. He did not trust him.

'They have delayed it. I don't know how long. I heard some rumour that they have to send in a big package of stones.'

'Why?' Lothar asked softly, and Fourie shrugged.

'I just heard it will be a big package.'

'As I warned you, it's because they are going to close the mine.' Lothar watched his face carefully. He sensed that the man was wavering. He had to steel him. 'It will be the last shipment, and then you will be out of work. Just like those poor bastards you have on your trucks.'

Fourie nodded glumly. 'Yes, they have fired them.'

'It will be you next, old friend. And you told me what a good family man you are, how much you love your family.'

'Ja.'

'Then no more money to feed your children, no money to clothe them, not even a few pounds to pay the little girls for their clever tricks.'

'Man, you mustn't talk like that.'

'You do what we agreed and there will be all the little girls you want, any way you want them.'

'Don't talk like that. It's dirty, man.'

177

'You know the arrangements. You know what to do just as soon as they tell you when the shipment is going in.'

Fourie nodded but Lothar insisted. 'Tell me about it. Repeat it to me.' And he listened while Fourie reluctantly recited his instructions, correcting him once on a detail, and at last smiled with satisfaction.

'Don't let us down, old friend. I do not like to be disappointed.' He leaned close to Fourie and stared into his eyes, then quite suddenly turned and slipped away into the moon shadows.

Fourie shuddered and stumbled away up the ravine towards the camp like a drunkard. He was almost there before he remembered that the girl had his money but had not completed her part of the bargain. He wondered if he could talk her into doing so at the next camp, and then morosely decided that his chances were not very good. Yet somehow it didn't seem so urgent now. The ice that Lothar De La Rey had injected into his blood seemed to have settled in his loins.

They rode through the open forest below the cliffs, and their mood was carefree and gay with anticipation of the days that lay ahead.

Shasa rode Prester John, with the 7mm Mannlicher sporting rifle in the leather scabbard under his left knee. It was a beautiful weapon, the butt and foregrip in choice selected walnut, and the blue steel engraved and inlaid with silver and pure gold: hunting scenes exquisitely rendered and Shasa's name scripted in precious metal. The rifle had been a fourteenth birthday present from his grandfather.

Centaine rode her grey stallion, a magnificent animal. His hide was marbled with black in a lacy pattern across his shoulders and croup, while his mane and muzzle and eye patches were also shiny jet black, in startling contrast to the snowy hide beneath. She called him Nuage, Cloud, after a stallion that her father had given her when she was a girl.

Centaine wore an Australian cattleman's wide-brimmed hat and a kudu-skin gilet over her shirt. There was a yellow silk scarf knotted loosely at her throat, and a sparkle in her eyes.

'Oh, Shasa, I feel like a schoolgirl playing hookey! We've got two whole days to ourselves.'

'Race you to the spring!' he challenged her, but Prester John was no match for Nuage and when they reached the spring Centaine had already dismounted and was holding the stallion's head to prevent him bloating himself with water.

They remounted and rode on deeper into the wilderness of the Kalahari. The further they went from the mine the less had been the intrusion of human presence, and the wild life more abundant and confident.

Centaine had been trained in the ways of the wild by the finest of all instructors, the wild Bushmen of the San, and she had lost none of her skills. It was not only the larger game that engaged her. She pointed out a pair of quaint little bat-eared foxes that Shasa would have missed. They were hunting grasshoppers in the sparse silver grass, pricking their enormous ears as they crept forward in a pantomime of stealth before the heroic leap onto their formidable prey. They laid their tell-tale ears against their fluffy necks and flattened against the earth as the horses passed.

They startled a yellow sand-cat from an ant-bear burrow, and so intent was the big cat on its escape that it ran headlong into the sticky yellow web of a crab spider. The animal's comical efforts to wipe the web from its face with both front paws while at the same time continuing its flight had them both reeling in the saddle.

Once in the middle of the afternoon they spotted a herd of stately gemsbok trotting in single file across the horizon. They held their heads high, the long straight slender horns transformed by distance and the angle of view into the single straight horn of the unicorn. The mirage turned them into strange long-legged monsters and then swallowed them up completely.

As the lowering sun painted the desert with shadow and fresh colour, Centaine picked out another small herd of springbok and pointed out a plump young ram to Shasa. 'We are only half a mile from camp and we need our dinner.'

Eagerly Shasa drew the Mannlicher from its scabbard.

'Cleanly!' she cautioned him. It troubled her a little to see how he enjoyed the chase.

She stayed back and watched him dismount. Using Prester John as a stalking horse, Shasa angled in towards the herd. Prester John understood his role and kept himself between Shasa and the game, even pausing to graze when the springbok became restless, only moving closer when they had settled down again.

At two hundred paces Shasa squatted and braced his elbows on his knees, and Centaine felt a rush of relief as the springbok ram dropped instantly to the shot. She had once seen Lothar De La Rey gut shoot one of the lovely gazelle. The memory still haunted her.

When she rode up she saw that Shasa had hit the animal cleanly behind the shoulder, and the bullet had passed through the heart. She watched critically as Shasa dressed out the game the way Sir Garry had taught him.

'Keep all the offal,' she told him. 'The servants love the tripes.' So he wrapped it in the wet skin and bundled the carcass up onto Prester John's back and tied it behind the saddle.

The camp was at the foot of the hills, below a seep well in the cliff which provided water. The previous day Centaine had sent three servants ahead with the pack horses and the camp was comfortable and secure.

They dined on grilled kebabs of liver, kidneys and heart, larded with laces of fat from the springbok's belly cavity. Then they sat late at the fire, drinking coffee that tasted of wood smoke, talking quietly and watching the moon rise.

In the dawn they rode out, bundled in sheepskin jackets against the chill. They had not gone a mile before Centaine pulled up Nuage's head and leaned far out of the saddle to examine the earth.

'What is it, Mater?' Shasa was always sensitive to every nuance of her moods, and he saw how excited she was.

'Come quickly, *chéri*.' She pointed out the tracks in the soft earth. 'What do you make of these?'

Shasa swung down from the saddle and stooped over the sign.

'Human beings?' He was puzzled. 'But so small. Children?' He looked up at her, and her shining expression gave him the clue.

'Bushmen!' he exclaimed. 'Wild Bushmen.'

'Oh yes,' she laughed. 'A pair of hunters. They are after a giraffe. Look! Their tracks are overlaying those of the quarry.'

'Can we follow them, Mater? Can we?' Now Shasa was as excited as she was.

Centaine agreed. 'Their spoor is only a day old. We can catch them if we hurry.'

Centaine rode on the spoor with Shasa trailing behind her, careful not to spoil the sign. He had never seen her work like this, taking it at a canter over the bad places where even his sharp young eyes could see nothing.

'Look, a Bushman toothbrush.' She pointed to a fresh twig, the end chewed to a brush, that lay discarded beside the spoor and they rode on.

'This is where they first spotted the giraffe.'

'How do you know that?'

'They have strung their bows. There are the marks of the butts.'

The little men had pressed the tips of their bows against the earth to arch them.

'Look, Shasa, now they have begun stalking.'

He could see no change in the spoor and said so.

'Shorter and stealthier paces – weight forward on the toes,' she explained, and then, a few hundred paces farther, 'Here they went down on their bellies, snake-crawling in for the kill. Here they went up on their knees to loose their arrows, and here they leapt to their feet to watch them strike.' Twenty paces farther on she exclaimed, 'See how close they were to the quarry. This is where the giraffe felt the sting of the barbs and started to gallop – look how the hunters followed at a run, waiting for the poison of the arrows to take effect.'

They galloped along the line of the chase until Centaine rose in the stirrups and pointed ahead.

'Vultures!'

Four or five miles ahead the blue of the heavens was dusted with a fine cloud of black specks. The cloud turned in slow vortex, high above the earth.

'Slowly now, *chéri*,' Centaine cautioned him. 'It could be dangerous if we frighten and panic them.'

They brought the horses down to a walk and rode up slowly to the site of the kill.

The giraffe's huge carcass, partly flayed and dismembered, lay on its side. Against the surrounding thorn bushes crude sunshelters of thatch had been erected, and the bushes were festooned with strips of meat and ribbons of entrails set out to dry in the sun, the branches bowed under their weight.

The area was widely trodden by small feet.

'They have brought the women and children to help cut up and carry,' Centaine said.

'Phew! It pongs terribly!' Shasa screwed up his nose. 'Where are they, anyway?'

'Hiding,' Centaine said. 'They saw us coming, probably from five miles away.' She stood up in the stirrups and swept the broad-brimmed hat from her head to show her face more clearly, and she called out in a strange guttural clicking tongue, turning slowly and repeating the message to every quarter of the silent brooding desert that encompassed them.

'It's creepy.' Shasa shivered involuntarily in the bright sunlight. 'Are you sure they are still here?'

'They're watching us. They aren't in a hurry.'

Then a man rose out of the earth so close to them that the stallion shied and nodded his head nervously. The man wore only a loincloth of animal skin. He was a small man, yet perfectly formed, with elegant and graceful limbs built for running. Hard muscle lay flat down his chest and sculpted his naked belly into the same ripples that the ebb tide leaves on a sandy beach.

He held his head proudly, and though he was clean-shaven, it was evident he was in the full flowering of his manhood. His eyes had a Mongolian slant to the corners and his skin glowed with a marvellous amber colour seeming almost translucent in the sunlight.

He lifted his right hand in a greeting and a sign of peace and he called, birdlike and high, 'I see you, Nam Child,' using Centaine's Bushman name, and she cried aloud for joy.

'I see you also, Kwi!'

'Who is with you?' the bushman demanded.

'This is my son, Good Water. As I told you when first we met, he was born in the holy place of your people and O'wa was his adopted grandfather and H'ani was his grandmother.'

Kwi, the Bushman, turned and called out into the empty

desert. 'This is the truth, oh people of the San. This woman is Nam Child, our friend, and the boy is he of the legend. Greet them!'

Out of the seemingly barren earth against which they had hidden rose the little golden people of the San. With Kwi there were twelve of them; two men, Kwi and his brother Fat Kwi, their wives and the naked children. They had hidden with all the art of wild creatures, but now they crowded forward chirruping and clicking and laughing and Centaine swung down from the saddle to meet and embrace them, greeting each of them by name and finally picking up two of the toddlers and holding one on each hip.

'How do you know them so well, Mater?' Shasa wanted to know.

'Kwi and his brother are related to O'wa, your adopted Bushman grandfather. I first met them when you were very small and we were developing the H'ani Mine. These are their hunting grounds.'

They passed the rest of that day with the clan, and when it was time to leave Centaine gave each of the women a handful of brass 7mm cartridges and they shrieked with joy and danced their thanks. The cartridges would be strung with ostrich shell beads into necklaces that would make them the envy of every other San woman they met in their wandering. Shasa gave Kwi his ivory-handled hunting knife and the little man tried the edge with his thumb and grunted with wonder as the skin parted, and he displayed the bloody thumb proudly to each of the women.

'What a weapon I have now.'

Fat Kwi got Centaine's belt, and they left him studying the reflection of his own face in the polished brass buckle.

'If you wish to visit us again,' Kwi called after them, 'we will be at the mongongo tree grove near O'chee Pan until the rains break.'

'They are so happy with so little,' Shasa said, looking back at the tiny dancing figures.

'They are the happiest people in this earth,' Centaine agreed. 'But I wonder for how much longer.'

'Did you truly live like that, Mater?' Shasa asked. 'Like a Bushman? Did you really wear skins and eat roots?'

'So did you, Shasa. Or rather you wore nothing at all just like one of those grubby little scamps.'

He frowned with the effort of memory. 'Sometimes I dream about a dark place, like a cave with water that smoked.'

'That was the thermal spring in which we bathed, and in which I found the first diamond of the H'ani Mine.'

'I would like to visit it again, Mater.'

'That isn't possible.' He saw her mood change. 'The spring was in the centre of the H'ani pipe, in what is now the main excavation of the mine. We dug it out and destroyed the spring.' They rode on in silence for a while. 'It was the holy place of the San – and yet, strangely, they did not seem to resent it when we,' she hesitated over the word and then said it firmly, 'when we desecrated it.'

'I wonder why. I mean if some strange race turned Westminster Abbey into a diamond mine!'

'A long time ago I discussed it with Kwi. He said that the secret place belonged not to them but the spirits and if the spirits had not wanted it so they would not have let it happen. He said the spirits had lived there so long that perhaps they were bored and wished to move on to another home, just like the San do.'

'I still cannot imagine you living like one of the San women, Mater. Not you. I mean it just goes beyond imagination.'

'It was hard,' she said softly. 'It was hard beyond the telling of it, beyond imagination – and yet without that tempering and toughening I would not be what I am now. You see, Shasa, out here in the desert when I had almost reached the breaking point I swore an oath. I swore that I, and my son, would never again be so deprived. I swore that we would never again have to suffer those terrible extremes.'

'But I was not with you then.'

'Oh yes,' she nodded. 'Oh yes, you were. I carried you within me on the Skeleton Coast and through the heat of the dune lands and you were part of that oath when I made it. We are creatures of the desert, my darling, and we will survive and prosper when others fail and fall. Remember that. Remember it well, Shasa, my darling.'

E arly the next morning they left the servants to break camp, load the pack horses and follow them as they turned their horses regretfully in the direction of the H'ani Mine. At noon they rested under a camel-thorn tree, lying against their saddles and lazily watching the drab little weavers above their heads busily adding to their communal nest that was already the size of an untidy haystack. When the heat went out of the sun, they caught the hobbled horses, upsaddled and rode along the base of the hills.

Shasa straightened in the saddle suddenly and shaded his eyes with one hand as he looked up at the hills.

'What is it, *chéri?*'

He had recognized the rocky gorge to which Annalisa had led him.

'Something is worrying you,' Centaine insisted, and Shasa felt a sudden urge to lead his mother up the gorge to the shrine of the witch of the mountain. He was about to speak when he remembered his oath and he stopped, teetering uneasily on the brink of betrayal.

'Don't you want to tell me?' She was watching the struggle on his face.

'Mater doesn't count. She's like me. It's not as though I were telling a stranger,' he justified himself and burst out before his conscience could overtake him. 'There is the skeleton of a Bushman in the gorge up there, Mater. Would you like me to show you?'

Centaine paled under her suntan and stared at him. 'A Bushman?' she whispered. 'How do you know it's a Bushman?'

'The hair is still on the skull – little Bushman peppercorn curls, just like Kwi and his clan.'

'How did you find it?'

'Anna—' he broke off and flushed with guilt.

'The girl showed you?' Centaine helped him.

'Yes.' He nodded and hung his head.

'Can you find it again?' Centaine's colour had returned, and she seemed eager and excited as she leaned across and tugged his sleeve.

'Yes, I think so, I marked the place.' He pointed up the cliffs. 'That notch in the rocks and that cleft shaped like an eye.'

'Show me, Shasa,' she ordered.

'We will have to leave the horses and go up on foot.'

The climb was onerous, the heat in the gorge fierce and the hooked thorns snatched at them as they toiled upwards.

'It must be about here.' Shasa climbed up on one of the tumbled boulders and orientated himself. 'Perhaps just a little more to the left. Look for a pile of rock with a mimosa growing below it. There is a branch covering a small niche. Let's spread out and search.'

They picked their way slowly up the gorge, moving a little apart to cover more ground and keeping in touch with whistles and calls when scrub and rocks separated them.

Centaine did not respond to Shasa's whistle, and he stopped and repeated it, cocking his head for her reply and feeling a prickle of concern in the silence.

'Mater, where are you?'

'Here!' Her voice was faint, wracked with pain or some deep emotion and he scrambled over the rock to reach her.

She stood small and forlorn in the sunlight, holding her hat against the front of her hips. Moisture sparkled on her cheeks. He thought it was sweat, until he saw the soft slow slide of tears down her face.

'Mater?' He moved up behind her and realized that she had found the shrine.

She had drawn the screening branch aside. The small circle of glass jars was still in place, the floral offering brown and withered.

'Annalisa said the skeleton was a witch,' Shasa breathed with superstitious awe as he stared over Centaine's shoulder at the pathetic pile of bones and the small neat white skull that surmounted it.

Centaine shook her head, unable to speak.

'She said the witch guarded the mountain and that she would grant a wish.'

'H'ani.' Centaine choked on the name. 'My beloved old grandmother.'

'Mater!' Shasa seized her shoulders and steadied her as she swayed on her feet. 'How do you know?'

Centaine leaned against his chest for support but did not reply.

'There could be hundreds of Bushman skeletons in the caves and gorges,' he went on lamely, and she shook her head vehemently.

'How can you be certain?'

'It's her.' Centaine's voice was blurred with grief. 'It's H'ani, the chipped canine tooth, the design of ostrich shell beads on her loincloth.' Shasa had not noticed the scrap of dry leather decorated with beads that lay beneath the pile of bones, half buried in dust. 'I don't even need that proof. I know it's her. I just know it.'

'Sit down, Mater.' He lowered her to sit on one of the lichen-covered boulders.

'I'm all right now. It was just such a shock. I've searched for her so often over the years. I knew where she must be.'

She looked around her vaguely. 'O'wa's body must be somewhere close at hand.' She looked up at the cliff that seemed to hang over them like a cathedral roof. 'They were up there trying to escape when he gunned them down. They must have fallen close together.'

'Who shot them, Mater?'

She drew a deep breath, but even then her voice shook as she said his name. 'Lothar. Lothar De La Rey!'

For an hour longer they searched the bottom and sides of the gorge, looking for the second skeleton.

'It's no good.' Centaine gave up at last. 'We will never find him. Let him lie undisturbed, Shasa, as he has all these years.'

They climbed down to the little rock shrine, and as they returned they plucked the wild flowers along the way.

'My first instinct was to gather her remains and give them a decent burial,' Centaine whispered as she knelt in front of the shrine, 'but H'ani wasn't a Christian. These hills were her holy place. She will be at peace here.'

She arranged the flowers with care and then sat back on her heels.

'I'll see that you are never disturbed, my beloved old grandmother, and I will come to visit you again.' She stood up and took Shasa's hand. 'She was the finest, gentlest person I have ever known,' she said softly. 'And I loved her so.' Still hand in hand they went down to where they had tethered the horses.

They did not speak again on the ride home, and the sun had set and the servants were anxious by the time they reached the bungalow.

At breakfast the next morning Centaine was brisk and brittly cheerful, though there were dark bruised smudges beneath her eyes and the lids were puffed from weeping.

'This is our last week before we must return to Cape Town.'

'I wish we could stay here for ever.'

'For ever is a long time. You have school waiting for you, and I have my duties. We will come back here, you know that.' He nodded and she went on. 'I have arranged for you to spend this last week working in the washing plant and sorting rooms. You'll enjoy that. I guarantee it.'

She was right, as usual. The washing plant was a pleasant place. The flow of water over the wiffle boards cooled the air, and after the unremitting thunder of the mill plant it was blessedly quiet. The atmosphere in the long brick room was like the cathedral calm of a holy place, for here the worship of Mammon and Adamant reached its climax.

Shasa watched with fascination as the crushings from the mill plant were carried in on the slowly moving conveyor belt. The oversize rubble had been screened off and returned for another crushing under the spinning rollers. These were the fines. They dropped from the end of the moving belt into the puddling tank, and from there were pushed by the agitating arms of the revolving sweep down the sloping boards of the wiffle table.

The lighter materials floated away and were run off to the waste dump. The heavier gravels, containing the diamonds, were carried on through a series of similar ingenious separating devices until there remained only the concentrates, one thousandth part of the original gravels.

These were washed over the grease drums. The drums revolved slowly, each of them coated with a thick layer of heavy yellow grease. The wet gravel flowed easily over the surface, but the diamonds were dry. One of the diamond's peculiar qualities is its unwettability. Soak it, boil it as long as you wish, but it remains dry. Once the dry surface of the precious stones touched the grease they stuck to it like insects to fly paper.

The grease drums were locked behind heavy bars and a white supervisor sat overlooking each of them, watching them constantly. Shasa peered through the bars for the first time and saw the small miracle occur only a few inches from his nose: a wild diamond captured and tamed like some marvellous creature of the desert. He actually witnessed the moment when it flowed out of the upper bin in a wet porridge of gravel, and he saw it touch the grease and adhere precariously to the slick yellow surface, causing a tiny V-shaped disturbance to the flow like a rock in the ebb of the tide. It moved, seeming to lose its grip in the grease for an instant, and Shasa wanted to thrust out his hand and seize it before it was for ever lost, but the gaps between the steel bars were too narrow. Then the diamond stuck fast and breasted the gentle flood of gravel, sitting up proudly, dry and transparent like a blister on the yellow skin of a gigantic reptile. It left him with a feeling of awe, the same feelings as he had experienced when he witnessed his mare Celeste give birth to her first foal.

He spent the entire morning passing from one to the other of the huge yellow drums and then back again down the line, watching the diamonds sticking on the grease more and more thickly with each hour that passed.

At noon the washroom manager came down the line with his four white assistants, more than were necessary, other than to watch each other and forestall any opportunity for theft. With a broad-bladed spatula they scraped the grease from the drums and collected it in the boiling pot, then meticulously spread each drum with a fresh coating of yellow grease.

In the locked de-greasing room at the far end of the building the manager placed the steel pot on the spirit stove and boiled off the grease until finally he was left with a pot half full of diamonds, and Dr Twentyman-Jones was there to weigh each stone separately and record it in the leather-bound recovery book.

'Of course you will notice, Master Shasa, that none of these stones is smaller than half a carat.'

'Yes, sir.' Shasa had not thought of that. 'What happened to the smaller ones?'

'The grease table is not infallible – indeed the stones must have a certain minimum weight to get them to adhere. The others, even a few large valuable stones, pass across the table.'

He led Shasa back to the washroom and showed him the trough of wet gravel that had survived the journey over the drums. 'We drain all the water and reuse it. Out here water is precious stuff, as you know. Then all the gravel has to be hand picked.' As he spoke two men emerged from the door at the end of the room and each scooped a bucket of gravel from the trough.

Shasa and Twentyman-Jones followed them back through the doorway into a long narrow room well lit with glass skylights and high windows. A single long table ran the length of the room, its top clad in a polished metal sheet.

On each side of the table sat rows of women. They looked up as the two men entered and Shasa recognized the wives and daughters of many of the white workers as well as those of the black boss-boys. The white women sat together nearest the door and, with a decent and proper distance between them, the black women sat separated at the far end of the room.

The bucket boys dumped the damp gravel onto the metal table top and the women transferred their attention back to it. Each had a pair of forceps in one hand and a flat wooden scoop in the other. They drew a little of the gravel towards them, spread it with the scoop and then picked over it swiftly.

'It's a job at which the women excel,' Twentyman-Jones explained as they passed down the line, watching over the stooped shoulders of the women. 'They have the patience and the sharp eyes and the dexterity that men lack.'

Shasa saw that they were picking out tiny opaque stones, some as small as sugar grains, others the size of small green peas, from the duller mass of gravel.

'Those are our bread and butter stones,' Twentyman-Jones remarked. 'They are used in industry. The jewellery grade stones that you saw in the grease room are the strawberry jam and the cream.'

When the mine hooter signalled the end of the day shift, Shasa rode down with Twentyman-Jones in the front seat of his Ford from the washing gear to the office block. On his lap he carried the small locked steel box in which was the day's recovery.

Centaine met them on the verandah of the administration building and led them into her office. 'Well, did you find it interesting?' she asked, and smiled at Shasa's hearty response.

'It was fascinating, Mater, and we got one real beauty. Thirty-six carats – it's a jolly great monster of a diamond!' He set the box on her desk and when Twentyman-Jones unlocked it he showed her the diamond as proudly as if he had mined it with his own hands.

'It's big,' Centaine agreed, 'but the colour isn't particularly good. There, hold it to the light. See, it's as brown as whisky and soda, and even with the naked eye you can see the inclusions and flaws, those little black specks inside the stone and that tear through the middle.'

Shasa looked crestfallen that his stone was so denigrated and she laughed and turned to Twentyman-Jones. 'Let's show him some really good diamonds. Will you open the vault please, Dr Twentyman-Jones?'

Twentyman-Jones pulled out the bunch of keys from the fob pocket of his waistcoat and led Shasa down the passage to the steel grille door at the end. He opened it with his key and relocked it behind them before they went down the stairs to the underground vault. Even from Shasa he screened the lock with his body as he tumbled the combination and then used a second key before the thick green Chubb steel door swung ponderously aside and they went into the strongroom.

'The industrial-grade stones are kept in these canisters.' He touched them as he passed. 'But we keep the high-grade stuff separately.'

He unlocked the smaller steel door set in the rear wall of the vault and selected five numbered brown paper packages from the crowded shelf.

'These are our best stones.' He handed them to Shasa as a mark of his trust, and then they went back again, opening and re-locking each door as they passed through.

Centaine was waiting for them in her office, and when Shasa placed the packages in front of her she opened the first and gently spread the contents on her blotter.

'Golly gee!' Shasa goggled at the array of large stones glittering with a soapy sheen. 'They are gi-normous!'

'Let's ask Dr Twentyman-Jones to give us a dissertation,' Centaine suggested, and hiding his gratification behind a sombre countenance, he picked up one of the gem stones.

'Well, Master Shasa, here is a diamond in its natural crystalline formation, the octahedron of eight faces – count them. Here is another in a more complicated crystalline form, the dodecahedron of twelve faces, while these others are massive and uncrystallized. See how rounded and amorphous they are. Diamonds come in many guises.'

He laid each in Shasa's open palm, and not even his prim monotonous recital could dull the fascination of this shining treasure. 'The diamond has a perfect cleavage, or as we call it "grain", and can be split in all four directions, parallel to the octahedral crystal planes.'

'That's how the cutters cleave a stone before polishing,'

Centaine cut in. 'During your next holidays I will take you to Amsterdam so you can see it done.'

'This rather greasy sheen will disappear when the stones are cut and polished.' Twentyman-Jones took over again, resenting her intrusion. 'Then all their fire will be revealed as their very high refractive power captures the light within and dispersive powers separate it into the spectral colours.'

'How much does this one weigh?'

'Forty-eight carats.' Centaine consulted the recovery book. 'But remember it may lose more than half its weight when it is cut and polished.'

'Then how much will it be worth?'

Centaine glanced at Twentyman-Jones.

'A great deal of money, Master Shasa.' Like the true lover of any beautiful object, gem or painting, horse or statue, he disliked placing a monetary value upon it, so he hedged and returned to his lecture. 'Now I want you to compare the colours of these stones—'

Darkness fell outside the windows, but Centaine switched on the lights and they huddled over the small pile of stones for another hour, meeting question with answer and talking quietly and intently until at last Twentyman-Jones swept the stones back into their packages and stood up.

'"Thou hast been in Eden, the Garden of God,"' he quoted unexpectedly, '"every precious stone was thy covering, the sardius, topaz and diamond ... Thou wast upon the holy mountain of God; thou hast walked up and down in the midst of the stones of fire."' He stopped and looked self-conscious. 'Forgive me. I don't know what got into me.'

'Ezekiel?' Centaine asked, smiling fondly at him.

'Chapter 28, verses thirteen and fourteen.' He nodded, trying not to show how impressed he was by her knowledge. 'I'll put these away now.'

'Dr Twentyman-Jones,' Shasa stopped him. 'You didn't answer my question. How much are these stones worth?'

'Are you referring to the entire package?' He looked uncomfortable. 'Including the industrials and boart still in the strong room?'

'Yes, sir, how much, sir?'

'Well, if De Beers accepts them at the same prices as our last package they will fetch considerably in excess of a million pounds sterling,' he replied sadly.

'A million pounds,' Shasa repeated, but Centaine saw in his expression that such a figure was incomprehensible to him, like the astronomical distances between stars that must be expressed in light years. He will learn, she thought, I will teach him.

'Remember, Shasa, that is not all profit. From that sum we will have to pay all the expenses of the mine over the past months before we can figure a profit. And even from that we have to give the tax collectors their pound of bleeding flesh.'

She stood up behind the desk and then held out her hand to prevent Twentyman-Jones leaving the room as an idea struck her.

'As you know Shasa and I are going in to Windhoek this coming Friday. Shasa has to return to school at the end of next week. I will take the diamonds into the bank with me in the Daimler—'

'Mrs Courtney!' Twentyman-Jones was horrified. 'I couldn't allow that. A million pounds' worth, good Lord alive. It would be criminally irresponsible of me to agree.' He broke off as he saw her expression alter; her mouth settled into that familiar stubborn shape and the lights of battle glinted in her eyes. He knew her so well, like his own daughter, and loved her as much, he realized that he had made the grievous error of challenging and forbidding her. He knew what her reaction must be and he sought desperately to head her off.

'I was thinking only of you, Mrs Courtney. A million pounds of diamonds would attract every scavenger and predator, every robber and footpad for a thousand miles around.'

'It was not my intention to bruit it abroad. I will not broadcast it a thousand miles around,' she said coldly.

'The insurance,' inspiration came to him at last, 'the insurance will not cover losses if the package is not sent in by armed convoy. Can you truly afford to take that chance – a loss of a million pounds of revenue against a few days saved?'

He had hit upon the one argument that might stop her. He saw her thinking about it carefully, a chance of losing a million pounds against a minimal loss of face, and he sighed silently with relief when she shrugged.

'Oh, very well then, Dr Twentyman-Jones, have it your own way.'

Lothar had carved the road to H'ani Mine through the desert with his own hands and sprinkled every mile of it with the sweat of his brow. But that had been twelve years before, and now his memory of it had grown hazy. Still he remembered half a dozen points along the road which might serve his purpose.

From the stage camp where he had intercepted Gerhard Fourie's convoy they followed the rutted tracks south and west in the direction of Windhoek, travelling at night to save them from discovery by unexpected traffic on the road.

On the second morning, just as the sun was rising, Lothar reached one of the points he remembered and found it ideal. Here the road ran parallel to the deep rocky bed of a dry river before looping down through the deep cutting that Lothar had excavated to cross the riverbed and climb out the far side through another cutting.

He dismounted and walked out along the edge of the high bank to study it carefully. They could trap the diamond truck in the gut of the cutting, and block it with rocks rolled down from the top of the bank. There was certain to be water under the sand in the riverbed for the horses while they waited for the truck to show up; they would need to keep in condition for the long hard journey ahead. The riverbed would hide them.

Then again this was the remotest stretch of the road, it would take days for the police officers to be alerted and then to reach the ambush spot. He could certainly expect to establish an early and convincing lead, even if they chose the risky alternative of following him into the hard unrelenting wilderness across which he would retreat.

'This is where we will do it,' he told Swart Hendrick.

They set up their primitive camp in the sheer bank of the riverbed at the point where the telegraph line took the short cut across the loop in the road. The copper wires were strung over the riverbed from a pole on the near bank that was out of sight of the road.

Lothar climbed the pole and clipped on his taps to the main telegraph line, then led his wires down the pole, tacking them to the timber to avoid casual discovery, and then to his listening post in the dug-out that Swart Hendrick had burrowed into the bank of the river.

The waiting was monotonous, and Lothar chafed at being tied to the earphones of the telegraph tap but he could not afford to miss the vital message when it was flashed from the H'ani Mine, the message which would give him the exact departure time of the diamond truck. So during the dreary hot hours of daylight he had to listen to all the mundane traffic of the mine's daily business, and the distant operator's skills on the keyboard were such that they taxed his ability to follow and translate the rapid fire of dots and dashes that echoed in his earphones. He scribbled them into his notebook and afterwards translated the groups and jotted in the words between the lines. This was a private telegraph line and therefore no effort had been made to encode the transmission, the traffic was in the clear.

During the day he was alone in the dugout. Swart Hendrick took Manfred and the horses out into the desert, ostensibly to hunt, but really to school and harden both the boy and the animals for the journey that lay ahead and to keep them out of sight of any traffic on the road.

For Lothar the long monotonous days were full of doubts and foreboding. There was so much that could go wrong, so many details that had to mesh perfectly to ensure success. There were weak links, and Gerhard Fourie was the weakest of these. The whole plan hinged on the man, and he was a coward, a man easily distracted and discouraged.

'Waiting is always the worst time,' Lothar thought, and he remembered the fears that had assailed him on the eve of other battles and desperate endeavours. 'If you could just do it and have done with it, instead of having to sit out these dragging days.'

Suddenly the buzz of the call sign echoed in his earphones and he reached quickly for his notebook. The operator at the H'ani Mine began to transmit and Lothar's pencil danced across the pages as he kept up with him. There was a curt double tap of acknowledgement from the Windhoek station as the message ended, and Lothar let the earphones drop around his neck as he translated the groups:

For Pettifogger Prepare Juno's private coach for inclusion in the Sunday night express mailtrain to Cape Town Stop Juno arriving your end noon Sunday Ends Vingt

Pettifogger was Abraham Abrahams. Centaine must have selected the code name when she was annoyed with him, while *Vingt* was a pun on Twentyman-Jones' name; the French connotation suggested Centaine's influence again,

199

but Lothar wondered who had selected Juno as Centaine Courtney's code name and grimaced at how appropriate it was.

So Centaine was leaving for Cape Town in her private coach. Somehow he felt guilty relief that she would not be close at hand when it happened, as though distance might lessen the shock for her. To reach Windhoek comfortably by noon on Sunday, Centaine must leave the H'ani Mine early on Friday, he calculated quickly; that would bring her to the cutting here on the riverbank on Saturday afternoon. Then he deducted a few hours from his estimate; she drove that Daimler like a demon.

He sat in the hot, stuffy little dugout and suddenly he felt an overwhelming desire to see her again, to have just a glimpse of her as she passed. 'We can use it as a rehearsal for the diamond truck,' he justified himself.

The Daimler came out of the shimmering distances like one of the whirling dust devils of the hot desert noons. Lothar saw the dust column from ten miles or more and signalled Manfred and Swart Hendrick into their positions at the top of the cutting.

They had dug shallow trenches at the key points, scattering the disturbed earth and letting the dry breeze smooth and blend it with the surroundings. Then they had screened the positions with branches of thorn scrub until Lothar was satisfied that they were undetectable from further than a few paces.

The rocks with which they would block both ends of the cutting had been gathered laboriously from the riverbed and poised on the edge of the bank. Lothar had taken great care to make them seem natural, and yet a single slash with a knife across the rope that held the prop under the rock pile would send them tumbling down onto the narrow track at the bottom of the cutting.

This was a rehearsal, so none of them were wearing masks.

Lothar made one last hard scrutiny of the arrangements and then turned back to watch the swiftly approaching column of dust. It was already close enough for him to make out the tiny shape of the vehicle beneath it and hear the faint beat of its engine.

'She shouldn't drive like that,' he thought angrily. 'She'll kill herself.' He broke off and shook his head ruefully. 'I'm acting like a doting husband,' he realized. 'Let her break her damned neck, if that is what she wants.' Yet the idea of her death gave him a painful pang, and he crossed his fingers to turn the chance away. Then he crouched down in his trench and watched her through the screen of thorn branches.

The stately vehicle rocked and bounced over the tracks as it swung onto the loop of the road. The engine beat strengthened as Centaine changed down and then accelerated out of the turn, using power to pull out of the incipient skid as the floury dust clutched at the front wheels. It was done with élan, he thought grudgingly, as she hit the gears again and bore down on the head of the cutting at speed.

'Merciful God, is she going to take it at full bore?' he wondered. But at the last moment she cut the throttle and used the gearbox and the drag of the clinging dust to pull up at the top end of the cutting.

As she opened the door and stepped out onto the running-board with dust billowing around her, she was only twenty paces from where he lay, and he felt his heart banging against the earth. 'Can she still do this to me?' he wondered at himself. 'I should hate her. She has cheated and humiliated me and she has spurned my son and denied him a mother's love, and yet, and yet—' He would not let the words form, and he tried deliberately to harden himself against her.

'She's not beautiful,' he told himself, as he studied her face; but she was much more. She was vital and vibrant, and there was an aura about her. 'Juno,' he recalled the code name, 'the goddess. Powerful and dangerous, mercurial and unpredictable, but endlessly fascinating and infinitely desirable.'

She looked directly towards him for a moment and he felt the strength and resolve flow out of him at the touch of those dark eyes, but she had not seen him and she turned away.

'We will walk down, *chéri*,' she called to the young man who stepped out of the opposite side of the Daimler, 'to see if the crossing is safe.'

Shasa seemed to have grown inches in the short time since Lothar had last seen him. They left the vehicle and went side by side down the track below where Lothar lay.

Manfred was in his trench at the bottom end of the cutting. He also watched the pair come down the track. The woman meant nothing to him. She was his mother but he did not know that and there was no instinctive response within him. She had never given him suck or even held him in her arms. She was a stranger, and he glanced at her without any emotion, then turned all his attention to the youth at her side.

Shasa's good looks offended him. 'He's pretty as a girl,' he thought, trying to scorn him, but he saw the new breadth to his rival's shoulders and fine muscle in his brown arms where he had rolled his sleeves high.

'I would like another bout with you, my friend.' The almost forgotten sting and humiliation of Shasa's left fist hurt again like a fresh wound, and he touched his own face with his fingertips, scowling at the memory. 'Next time I won't let you do your little dance.' And he thought about how hard it had been to touch that pretty face, the way it had swayed and dipped just beyond his reach and he felt the frustration anew.

The couple reached the foot of the cutting below where Manfred lay and stood talking quietly for a while, then Shasa trudged out into the wide riverbed. The roadway through the sand had been corduroyed with branches of acacia, but the wheels of heavy trucks had broken them up. Shasa rearranged them, stamping the jagged ends into the sand.

While he worked Centaine turned back to the Daimler. There was a canvas water bag hanging on the bracket of the spare wheel and she unhooked it, raised it to her lips and took a mouthful. She gargled softly and then spat it into the dust. Then she slipped off the long white dustjacket that protected her clothing and unbuttoned her blouse. She soaked the yellow scarf and wiped the damp cloth down her throat and over her bosom, gasping with pleasure at the coolness on her skin.

Lothar wanted to turn his head away, but he could not; instead he stared at her. She wore nothing under the pale blue cotton blouse. The skin of her bosom was untouched by the sun, pale smooth and pearly as fine bone china. Her breasts were small, without any puckering and sagging, the tips pointed and still clear rose-coloured as those of a girl, not of a woman who had borne two sons. They bounced elastically as she drew the wet scarf over them and she looked down at them as she bathed the gleam of perspiration from them. Lothar moaned softly in his throat at the need of her that rose freshly and strongly from deep within him.

'All set, Mater,' Shasa called as he started back up the track, and quickly Centaine rebuttoned the front of her blouse.

'We've wasted enough time,' she agreed and slipped back behind the wheel of the Daimler. As Shasa slammed his door she gunned the big motor down the track, kicking up sand and splinters of acacia in a spray from the back wheels as she crossed the riverbed and flew up the far bank. The rumble of the engine dwindled into the desert silence and Lothar found he was trembling.

None of them moved for many minutes. It was Swart

203

Hendrick who rose to his feet first. He opened his mouth to speak and then saw the expression on Lothar's face and remained silent. He scrambled down the bank and set off back towards the camp.

Lothar climbed down to the spot where the Daimler had stopped. He stood looking down at the damp earth where she had spat that mouthful of water. Her footprints were narrow and neat in the dust, and he felt a strong urge to stoop and touch them but suddenly Manfred spoke close behind him.

'He is a boxer,' he said, and it took Lothar a moment to realize that he was talking about Shasa. 'He looks a real sissy, but he can fight. You can't hit him.' He put up his fists and shadow-boxed, shuffling and dancing in the dust, imitating Shasa.

'Let's get back to the camp, out of sight,' Lothar said, and Manfred dropped his guard and thrust his hands into his pockets. Neither of them spoke again until they reached the dugout.

'Can you box, Pa?' Manfred asked. 'Can you teach me to box?'

Lothar smiled and shook his head. 'I always found it easier to kick a man between his legs,' he said. 'And then hit him with a bottle or a gun butt.'

'I would like to learn to box,' Manfred said. 'Someday I *will* learn.'

Perhaps the idea had been germinating there all along but suddenly it was a firm declaration. His father smiled indulgently and clapped him on the shoulder.

'Get out the flour bag,' he said. 'And I will teach you to bake soda bread instead.'

'Oh, Abe, you know how much I detest these soirées,' Centaine exclaimed irritably. 'Crowded rooms filled with tobacco smoke, exchanging inanities with strangers.'

'This man could be very valuable to know, Centaine. I will go further than that, he could be the most valuable friend you'll ever make in this territory.'

Centaine pulled a face. Abe was right, of course. The administrator was in fact the governor of the territory with wide executive powers. He was appointed by the Government of the Union of South Africa under the powers of mandate conferred on it by the Treaty of Versailles.

'I expect he is another pompous old bore, just like his predecessor was.'

'I haven't met him,' Abe admitted. 'He only arrived in Windhoek to take up his appointment within the last few days and will not be sworn in until the first of next month, but our new concessions in the Tsumeb area are on his desk at this moment, awaiting his signature.'

He saw her eyes shift and he pressed the advantage. 'Two thousand square miles of exclusive prospecting rights – worth a few hours of boredom?'

But she wouldn't give in that easily, and she counter-attacked. 'We are due to hook onto the express that leaves this evening. Shasa must be back at Bishops on Wednesday morning.' Centaine stood up and paced the saloon of her coach, stopping to rearrange the roses in the vase above her desk so she did not have to look at him as he deflected her thrust.

'The next express leaves Tuesday evening. I have made arrangements for your coach to hook on. Master Shasa can leave on this evening's express, I have hooked a coupé for him. Sir Garry and his wife are still at Weltevreden, they would meet him at Cape Town station. It needs only a telegraph to arrange it.' Abraham smiled across the saloon at Shasa. 'I'm sure, young man, you can make the journey without anyone to hold your hand?'

Abe was a cunning little devil, Centaine conceded, as Shasa rushed indignantly to take up the challenge.

'Of course I can, Mater. You stay here. It's important to meet the new administrator. I can get home on my own. Anna will help me pack for school.'

Centaine threw up her hands. 'If I die of boredom, Abe, let it be on your conscience for as long as you live!'

She had at first planned to wear her full suite of diamonds, but decided against it at the last moment. 'After all, it's only a little provincial reception, with fat farmers' wives and petty civil servants. Besides, I don't want to blind the poor old dear.'

So she settled for a yellow silk evening dress by Coco Chanel. She had worn it before, but in Cape Town, so it was unlikely anybody here had seen it.

'It was expensive enough to bear two airings,' she consoled herself. 'Too good for them, anyway.'

She settled on a pair of solitaire diamond ear studs, not too large to be ostentatious, but around her neck she wore the huge yellow diamond the colour of champagne on a platinum chain. It drew attention to her small pointed breasts; she liked the effect.

Her hair was a worry, as always. It was full of electricity from the dry desert air. She wished Anna was here, for she was the only one who could manage that lustrous unruly bush. In despair she tried to make a virtue of its disorder, deliberately fluffing it out into a halo and holding it up with a velvet band around her forehead.

'That's enough fuss.' She didn't feel like a party at all. Shasa had left on the mail train as Abe had planned and already she was missing him keenly. On top of that she was anxious to get back to Weltevreden herself and resented having to stay over.

Abe called for her an hour after the time stipulated on the invitation card that was embossed with the administrator's coat of arms. During the drive Rachel, Abe's wife, regaled them with an account of her recent domestic triumphs and tragedies, including a detailed report of her youngest offspring's bowel movements.

The administrative building, the Ink Palace, had been designed by the German colonial administration in heavy Gothic imperial style; when Centaine swept a glance around the ballroom, she saw that the company was no better than she had expected. It comprised mainly senior civil servants, heads and deputy heads of departments with their wives, the officers of the local garrison and police force, together with all the town's prominent businessmen and the big land-owners who lived close enough to Windhoek to respond to the invitation.

Amongst them were a number of Centaine's own people, all the managers and under-managers of the Courtney Finance and Mining Company. Abe had provided her with an up-to-date bulletin so that as each came forward diffidently to present their spouses, Centaine was able to make some gracious personal comment which had them glowing and grinning with gratification. Abe stood by to make sure that none of them imposed upon her, and after the appropriate interval gave her the excuse to escape.

'I think we should pay our respects to the new administrator, Mrs Courtney.' He took her arm and led her towards the reception line.

'I have been able to get a few facts about him. He is a Lieutenant-Colonel Blaine Malcomess and commanded a battalion of the Natal Mounted Rifles. He had a good war and ended with a bar to his Military Cross. In private life he is a lawyer, and—'

The police band was belting out a Strauss waltz with zeal and gusto and the dance floor was already crowded. As

207

they came up to the tail of the reception line, Centaine saw with satisfaction that they would be the last to be presented.

Centaine was paying little attention to their host at the head of the line as she moved along on Abe's arm, leaning across him to listen to Rachel on his other arm who was giving her a family recipe for chicken soup but at the same time Centaine was trying to decide just how early she could make her escape.

Abruptly she realized that they had reached the head of the line, the very last to do so, and that the administrator's A.D.C. was announcing them to their host.

'Mr and Mrs Abraham Abrahams and Mrs Centaine de Thiry Courtney.' She looked up at the man who stood before her and involuntarily she dug her fingernails into the soft inside of Abraham Abrahams' elbow with such force that he winced. She did not notice it, for she was staring at Colonel Blaine Malcomess.

He was tall and lean, and he stood well over six feet. His bearing was relaxed without any military stiffness and yet he seemed to be balanced on the balls of his feet as though he could explode into movement at any moment.

'Mrs Courtney,' he offered her his hand, 'I am delighted you were able to come. You were the one person I particularly wanted to meet.' His voice was a clear tenor, with a faint lilt to it that might have been Welsh. An educated and cultivated voice, with modulations which lifted a little electric rash of pleasure on her forearms and at the nape of her neck.

She took his hand. The skin was dry and warm, and she could feel the restrained strength of his fingers as they pressed hers gently. 'He could crush my hand like an egg-shell,' she thought, and the idea gave her a delicious little chill of apprehension. She studied his face.

His features were large, the bones of his jaw and cheek

and forehead seemed weighty and massive as stone. His nose was big with a Roman bridge to it, his brow was beetling and his mouth was big and mobile. He reminded her strongly of a younger more handsome Abraham Lincoln. He isn't yet forty, she estimated, so young for the rank and the job.

Then she realized with a start that she was still holding his hand, and that she had not replied to his greeting. He was leaning over her, studying her as openly and intently as she was him, and Abe and Rachel were looking from one to the other of them with interest and amusement. Centaine had to shake her hand lightly to free it from his grip, and to her horror she felt the hot rush of blood up her throat into her cheeks.

'I'm blushing!' It was something she had not done in years.

'I have been fortunate enough to be associated with your family before this,' Blaine Malcomess told her. His teeth also were large and square and very white. His mouth was wide, even wider when he smiled. A little shakily she smiled back.

'Have you?' She realized that it wasn't the most sparkling conversational gambit, but her wits seemed to have deserted her. She was standing there like a schoolgirl, blushing and gawking at him. His eyes were a most startling shade of green. They distracted her.

'I served under General Sean Courtney in France,' he told her, still smiling. Somebody had cut his hair too short at the temples, it made his large ears stick out. That irritated her – and yet the sticking-out ears made him endearing and appealing.

'He was a fine gentleman,' Blaine Malcomess went on

'Yes, he was,' she replied and upbraided herself, 'Say something witty, something intelligent – he'll think you a clod.'

He was wearing dress uniform, dark blue and gold with a double row of medal ribbons. Since girlhood uniforms had always affected her.

'I heard that you were at General Courtney's head-quarters in Arras for a few weeks in 1917. I was still in the line then; I didn't go on his staff until the end of that year.'

She took a deep breath to steady herself and at last managed to get control again. 'What turbulent days those were, with the universe crashing in ruins about us,' she said, her voice low and husky, her French accent empha-sized a little, and she thought, 'What is this? What's happening to you, Centaine? This is not the way it is supposed to be. Remember Michael and Shasa. Give this man a friendly nod and pass on.'

'It seems that I have performed my duties for the moment,' Blaine Malcomess glanced at his A.D.C. for confirmation and then turned back to Centaine. 'May I have the honour of this waltz, Mrs Courtney?' He offered his arm, and without a moment's hesitation she laid her fingers lightly in the crook of his elbow.

The other dancers veered away, leaving them an open space as they walked out side by side onto the floor. She turned to face Blaine and stepped into the circle of his arm.

He didn't have to move, merely the way he held her told her that he would be a marvellous dancer. Immediately she felt light and dainty and fleet of foot, and she arched her back and leaned out against the circle of his arm while his lower body seemed to meld with hers.

He took her on one spinning whirling circuit of the floor, and when she matched his every move feather light and swift, he began a complicated series of dips and counter-turns, and she followed him without conscious effort, seeming to skim the ground, yet totally under his control, responding to his every whim.

When at last the music ended with a crashing chord and the musicians fell back in their seats sweating and panting,

Centaine felt unreasonable resentment towards them. They had not played long enough. Blaine Malcomess was still holding her in the middle of the floor and they were laughing delightedly at each other while the other dancers formed a ring around them and applauded.

'Unfortunately that seems to be it for the moment,' he said, still making no effort to release her, and his words roused her. There was no longer any excuse for physical contact and she stepped back from him reluctantly and acknowledged the applause with a small curtsey.

'I do think we have earned a glass of champagne.' Blaine signalled one of the white-jacketed waiters and they stood at the edge of the dance floor and sipped the wine and watched each other's eyes avidly as they talked. The exertion had raised a light sheen of sweat on his broad forehead and she could smell it on his body.

They were alone in the centre of the crowded room. With a subtle inclination of her shoulders and head Centaine dissuaded the one or two bolder souls who approached as if to join them, and after that the others stayed back.

The band, refreshed and eager, took their seats on the bandstand once more and this time launched into a foxtrot. Blaine Malcomess did not have to ask. Centaine set her almost untouched champagne on the silver tray that the waiter proffered and lifted her arms as Blaine faced her.

The more sedate rhythm of the foxtrot enabled them to continue talking, and there was so much to talk about. He had known Sean Courtney well, and held him in affection and admiration. Centaine had loved him almost as much as she had loved her own father. They discussed the dreadful circumstances in which Sean Courtney and his wife had been murdered, and their mutual horror and outrage at the deed seemed to draw them still closer together.

Blaine knew the beloved northern provinces around

211

Arras in her native France, and his battalion had held a section of the line near Mort Homme, her home village. He remembered the burnt-out ruins of her family's château.

'We used it as an artillery observation post,' he told her. 'I spent many hours perched up in the north wing.' His description induced a pleasant nostalgia, a fine sadness to heighten her emotions.

He loved horses as she did, and was a twelve-goal polo player.

'Twelve goals!' she exclaimed. 'My son will be most impressed. He has just been rated a four-goal man.'

'How old is your son?'

'Fourteen.'

'Very good for a youngster of that age. I'd like to see him in action.'

'That would be fun,' she agreed, and suddenly she wanted to tell him all about Shasa, but again the music ended and cut her short, and this time he frowned also.

'They are playing very short pieces, aren't they?'

Then she felt him start and he released her waist. Though she kept her hand on his arm, the strange elated mood which had gripped them both shattered, and something dark and intrusive passed like a shadow between them. She was not sure what it was.

'Ah,' he said sombrely. 'I see she has returned. She really wasn't at all well this evening but she always was a plucky one.'

'To whom are you referring?' Centaine asked. His tone had filled her with foreboding and she should have been warned by it, but still the shock of it made her flinch when he said softly:

'My wife.'

Centaine felt quite giddy for a moment, and she only kept her balance with an effort when she let her hand fall from his arm.

212

'I would like you to meet my wife,' he said. 'May I introduce you to her?'

She nodded, unwilling to trust her voice, and when he offered his arm again she hesitated before she took it, and this time laid her fingertips only lightly upon it.

He led her across the floor towards the group at the foot of the main staircase, and as they approached Centaine searched the faces of the women, trying to guess which one it would be. Only two of them were young and none was beautiful, none could compete with her in looks or strength or poise or talent or wealth. She felt a surge of confidence and anticipation replace the momentary confusion and despondency that had thrown her off balance. Without thinking about it she knew she was going into a desperate contest, and she was buoyed up with battle lust and the enormity of the prize at stake. She was eager to identify and assess her adversary and she lifted her chin and set her shoulders as they stopped before the group.

The ranks of men and women opened respectfully, and there she was, looking up at Centaine with lovely tragic eyes. She was younger than Centaine and possessed of a rare and exquisite beauty. She wore her gentle nature and goodness like a shining cloak for all to see, but her sadness was in the smile she gave Centaine as Blaine Malcomess introduced them.

'Mrs Courtney, may I present my wife Isabella?'

'You dance exquisitely, Mrs Courtney. I have been watching you and Blaine with great pleasure,' she said. 'He does so love dancing.'

'Thank you, Mrs Malcomess,' Centaine whispered huskily, while inside she raged. 'Oh, you little bitch. It's not fair. You aren't fighting fair. How can I ever win now? Oh God, how I hate you.'

Isabella Malcomess sat in a wheelchair with her nurse behind her. The ankles of her thin paralysed legs showed under the hem of her evening dress. They were pale and skeletal and her feet seemed fragile and vulnerable in their sequined dancing pumps.

'He'll never leave you.' Centaine felt herself choke on her grief. 'He's that kind of man – he'll never desert a crippled wife!'

C entaine awoke an hour before dawn and lay for a moment wondering at the strange sense of well-being that possessed her. Then she remembered and threw back the sheets, eager for the day to begin. With both bare feet upon the floor she paused, and her eyes instinctively went to the framed photograph of Michael Courtney on the bedside table.

'Michel, I'm sorry,' she whispered. 'I love you. I still love you, I always will, but I can't help this other thing. I didn't want it. I didn't look for it. Please forgive me, my darling. It's been so long and so lonely. I want him, Michel. I want to marry him and have him for myself.' She took up the frame and for a moment held it to her bosom. The she opened the drawer, laid the photograph face down upon her folded lace underwear, and closed the drawer again.

She jumped to her feet and reached for the yellow Chinese silk dressing-gown with the bird of paradise embroidered down the back. Belting it she hurried through to the saloon of the coach and seated herself at her desk to compose the telegraph to Sir Garry in their private code, for the message would be transmitted over the public lines.

Please urgently forward all intelligence on Lieutenant-Colonel Blaine Malcomess, newly appointed administrator of South West Africa. Reply in code. Love Juno.

She rang for her secretary and chafed while she waited for him. He came through in a flannel dressing-gown, owl-eyed and unshaven.

'Get that off right away.' She handed him the flimsy. 'Then get me Abraham Abrahams on the telephone.'

'Centaine, it's six o'clock in the morning,' Abe protested, 'and we didn't get to bed until three o'clock.'

'Three hours is enough sleep for any good lawyer. Abe, I want you to invite Colonel Malcomess and his wife to dine with me in my coach this evening.'

There was a long weighty silence, and the static hissed on the line.

'You and Rachel are invited, of course.' She filled the silence.

'It's much too short notice,' he said carefully, obviously choosing his words with precision. 'The administrator is a busy man. He won't come.'

'Get the invitation to him personally.' Centaine ignored the protest. 'Send your messenger round to his office and see he gets it. Under no circumstances let his wife receive the invitation first.'

'He won't come,' Abe repeated stubbornly. 'At least I hope to God he won't come.'

'What do you mean by that?' she snapped.

'You are playing with fire, Centaine. Not just a little candle flame, but a great raging bush fire.'

She pursed her lips. 'Mind your own business, and I'll mind mine—' she started, and he broke in on her.

' – Kiss your own sweetheart, and I'll kiss mine,' he finished the childhood law for her, and she giggled. He had never heard Centaine Courtney giggle before; it took him by surprise.

'How appropriate, dear Abe.'

She giggled again, and his voice was truly agitated when he told her, 'You pay me an enormous retainer to mind your business for you. Centaine, you set a hundred tongues wagging last night – the whole town will be agog this morning. You are a marked woman, everybody watches you. You just cannot afford to carry on like this.'

'Abe, you and I both know that I can afford to do any damned thing I choose. Send that invitation – please!'

She rested that afternoon. It had been a late night and she was determined to look her best for the evening. Her secretary woke her a little after four o'clock in the afternoon. Abe had received a reply to the invitation. The administrator and his lady would be pleased to dine with her that evening. She smiled triumphantly, then turned to decode the telegram from Sir Garry which had also arrived while she was asleep.

'For Juno stop. Subject's full names Blaine Marsden Malcomess born Johannesburg 28 July 1893.'

'So he is nearly thirty-nine years old,' she exclaimed, 'and he is a Leo. My big growly lion!' She returned eagerly to the cable:

Second son of James Marsden Malcomess lawyer and mining entrepreneur, chairman Consolidated Goldfields and director numerous associated companies, deceased 1922. Subject was educated St John's College Johannesburg and Oriel College Oxford. Academic honours include Rhodes scholarship and Oriel scholarship. Sporting honours include full blue cricket and half blues athletics and polo. Graduated MA (Hons) Oxon 1912. Called to the Bar 1913. Commissioned 2nd-Lieutenant Natal Mounted Rifles 1914. Service in South West Africa Campaign. Mentioned in despatches twice. Promoted Captain 1915. France with BEF 1915. Military Cross August 1915. Promoted Major and Bar to MC 1916. Promoted Lieutenant-Colonel O.C. 3rd Battalion 1917. Staff of General Officer Commanding 6th Division 1918. Versailles Armistice negotiations on staff of

General Smuts. Partner in law firm Stirling & Malcomess from 1919. Member Parliament for Gardens 1924.
Deputy Minister Justice 1926–9. Appointed Administrator South West Africa 11 May 1932. Married Isabella
Tara née Harrison 1918. Two daughters Tara Isabella
and Mathilda Janine.

That came as a further shock to Centaine. She had not
thought about children.

'At least she hasn't given him a son.' The thought was
so cruel that she assuaged the prickle of guilt by calculating
the age of his daughters. 'I expect that they look like their
mother. Horrible little angels that he dotes on,' she decided
bitterly, and read the few comments with which Sir Garry
had ended the long cable.

'Enquiries addressed to *Ou Baas* indicate that subject is
considered a rising force in law and politics. Cabinet rank
a strong probability when SA Party returns to power.'
Centaine smiled fondly at the mention of General Jan
Christian Smuts and then read on:

Wife thrown from horse 1927. Extensive spinal damage.
Prognosis unfavourable. Stop. Father James Marsden left
estate probated £655,000 in equal shares to two sons.
Stop. Subject's present financial circumstances not
ascertained, but estimated as substantial. Stop. Presently
rated 12 goals polo. Captained SA team versus Argen-
tine 1929. Stop. Hope and expect your query businesslike. If not implore you exercise restraint and caution as
consequences highly prejudicial all parties. Stop. Shasa
safely ensconced Bishops. Stop. Anna joins me in
sending all love. Ends. Ovid.

She had selected Sir Garry's codename out of affection and
respect for his craft, but now she threw the telegraph flimsy
down on her desk angrily.

'Why does everybody know what's best for me — except me?' she asked aloud. 'And why isn't Anna here to help me with my hair? I look an absolute fright.' She looked in the mirror over the mantel for confirmation that it was not true. Then she dragged her hair back from her face with both hands while she studied her skin for blemish or wrinkles. She found only the faintest hairlines at the corners of her eyes yet they made her discontent extreme.

'Why is it that all the most attractive men are already married? And why, oh why couldn't that silly little namby-pamby have stuck in the saddle instead of falling on her pretty little backside.'

Centaine had contrived to make a great deal of fuss over Isabella Malcomess' reception and the transfer of her wheelchair from the platform to the balcony of the coach. She had four of the coach attendants and her secretaries standing by to assist.

Blaine Malcomess waved them away irritably, then he stooped over his wife. She slipped both her arms around his neck and he lifted her as though she were as light as a little girl. With their faces almost touching he smiled at her tenderly and then went up the steps onto the balcony as though he were unburdened. Isabella's legs dangled pathetically from under her skirts. They were wasted and lifeless and Centaine experienced an unexpected and unwelcome rush of sympathy for her.

'I don't want to pity her,' she thought fiercely as she followed them into the saloon.

Blaine set her down, without asking Centaine's permission, in the chair that subtly dominated the saloon and was naturally the focus of all attention, the chair that was always and exclusively reserved for Centaine herself. Blaine went down on one knee before his wife and gently arranged her feet, setting them neatly side by side on the silk carpet. Then he smoothed her skirt over her knees. It was obvious that he had done all this countless times before.

Isabella touched his cheek lightly with her fingertips, and smiled down on his head with such trust and adoration that Centaine felt entirely superfluous. Despair overwhelmed her. She could not intervene between these two. Sir Garry and Abe were both right. She had to relinquish him without a struggle, and she felt an almost saintly sense of righteousness.

Then Isabella looked up at Centaine over the head of her kneeling husband. Against the fashion she wore her hair long and straight. It was so fine and silky that it formed a thick sheet, lustrous as watered satin, that flowed down over her bare shoulders. Her hair was the colour of roasted chestnuts, but it flickered with glowing red stars and highlights each time she moved her head. Her face was round as a medieval madonna's, and lit with serenity. Her eyes were brown and starred with rods of gold that fanned out from the luminous black pupils.

Isabella looked at Centaine across the full length of the saloon, then she smiled – a slow complacent possessive smile – and the light in her brown and gold eyes changed. She stared into Centaine's dark wild honey eyes and she challenged her. It was as clear to Centaine as if she had stripped off one of her elbow-length gloves with its embroidered seed pearls and struck Centaine in the mouth with it.

'You silly little thing – you shouldn't have done that!' All Centaine's noble resolutions crumbled before that gaze. 'I was ready to let you keep him, I truly was. But if you want to fight for him – well then, so do I.' And she stared back at Isabella and silently took up her challenge.

The dinner was a resounding success. Centaine had carefully vetted the menu but had not trusted her chef with either the dressing for the rock lobster or the sauce for the

219

roast sirloin and had prepared both of these with her own hands. They drank champagne with the lobster and a marvellous velvety Richebourg with the sirloin.

Abe and Blaine were relieved and delighted that Isabella and Centaine were being so utterly charming and considerate to each other. It was obvious that they would become close friends. Centaine included the crippled girl in almost every remark she made, and was solicitous of Isabella's comfort, herself arranging cushions at her back or feet.

Centaine's stories were self-mocking and entertaining as she made light of how she had survived the dreadful crossing of the dune lands, widowed and pregnant, with only wild Bushmen as companions.

'How brave of you.' Isabella Malcomess got the point of the story. 'I am sure there are very few women who would have had your resourcefulness and strength.'

'Colonel Malcomess, can I prevail on you to carve the roast. Sometimes being a woman alone does have its drawbacks. There are things that only a man does well, wouldn't you agree, Mrs Malcomess?'

Rachel Abrahams sat quietly and apprehensively. She was the only one apart from the two principals who understood what was happening, and her sympathy was all with Isabella Malcomess, for she could imagine her own little nest and nestlings being threatened by a circling predator.

'You have two daughters, Mrs Malcomess?' Centaine asked sweetly. 'Tara and Mathilda Janine, such pretty names.' She let her rival know that she had done her researches thoroughly. 'But you must find it difficult to cope, girls being always much more of a handful than boys?'

Rachel Abrahams, at the end of the table, winced. With a single light flick of the blade Centaine had pointed up Isabella's disability and her failure to provide a son and heir for her husband.

'Oh, I have plenty of time to devote to my domestic

duties,' Isabella assured her, 'not being in trade, as it were. And the girls are such darlings, they are devoted to their father, of course.'

Isabella was a skilled duellist. 'Trade' was a word that made Centaine's aristocratic blood seethe behind her concerned smile, and it was a master stroke to link the girls so securely to Blaine. Centaine had seen his doting expression at mention of them. She turned to him and changed the subject to politics.

'Recently General Smuts was a guest at Weltevreden, my Cape home. He is deeply concerned by the growth of secret militant societies amongst the lower classes of Afrikanerdom. In particular the so-called *Ossewa-Brandwag* and the *Afrikaner Broederbond*, the best translation of which would be the "Nightguard of the Wagon Train" and the "Afrikaner Brotherhood". I also feel they are highly dangerous and prejudicial to the nation's best interests. Do you share this concern, Colonel Malcomess?'

'Indeed, Mrs Courtney, I have made a special study of these phenomena. But I do not think that you are correct in saying these secret societies include the lower classes of Afrikanerdom, quite the opposite. The membership is restricted to pure-blooded Afrikaners in positions of potential or actual influence in politics, government, religion and education. However, I agree with your conclusions. They are dangerous, more dangerous than most people realize, for their ultimate aim is to gain control of every facet of our lives, from the minds of the young to the machinery of justice and government, and to prefer their members above all consideration of merit or worth. In many ways this movement is the counterpart of the rising wave of National Socialism in Germany under Herr Hitler.'

Centaine leaned across the table to enjoy every nuance and inflection of his voice, encouraging him with question or shrewd sharp comment. With that voice, she thought, he could sway me and a million voters. Then she realized that the two of them were behaving as if they were the only ones at the table and she returned quickly to Isabella.

'Would you agree with your husband on that, Mrs Malcomess?' and Blaine laughed indulgently and answered for her.

'I'm afraid my wife finds politics a total bore, don't you, my dear? And I'm not sure that she isn't very perceptive in that belief.' He drew a gold watch from the fob pocket of his dinner jacket.

'It is after midnight. I have enjoyed myself so hugely that we have overstayed our welcome, I'm sure.'

'You are right, darling.' Isabella was relieved and eager to end it. 'Tara has been sickly. She complained of a stomach ache before we left.'

'Tara, the little vixen, always complains of a stomach ache when she knows we are going out,' he chuckled, but they all rose.

'I won't let you go without the solace of a brandy and a cigar,' Centaine demurred. 'Although I refuse to accept the barbaric custom of leaving the men to those pleasures alone while we poor females gather to giggle and talk babies so we will all go through to the saloon together.'

However, as she led them through, her secretary was hovering nervously.

'Yes, what is it?' She was annoyed until she saw that he was holding a telegraph flimsy like a warrant for his own execution.

'From Dr Twentyman-Jones, ma'am, and it's urgent.'

She accepted the flimsy but did not unfold it until she had made sure that her guests had coffee and liqueurs and that both Blaine and Abe were each armed with a Havana. Then she excused herself and slipped through to her bedroom.

For Juno. Strike committee headed by Gerhard Fourie has called out all white employees. Stop. Plant and pit

222

under picket lines and shipment of goods embargoed.
Stop. Strikers demanding reinstatement of all
retrenched white employees and guaranteed job security
for all. Stop. Request your instructions. Ends. Vingt.

Centaine sat down on her bed. The paper in her hand
fluttered. She had never been more angry in her life. It was
treachery, a gross and unforgivable betrayal. It was her
mine, they were her diamonds. She paid their wages, and
hers was the absolute right to hire and fire. 'The shipment
of goods' that Twentyman-Jones referred to was the parcel
of diamonds on which her fortune hinged. Their demands,
if pandered to, would render the H'ani Mine unprofitable.
Who was this Gerhard Fourie, she wondered, and then
remembered he was the chief transport driver.

She went to the door and opened it. Her secretary was
waiting in the corridor.

'Ask Mr Abrahams to come to me.'

When Abe stepped through the door she handed him
the telegraph flimsy.

'They don't have the right to do this to me,' she said
fiercely, and waited impatiently while he read it through.

'Unfortunately, Centaine, they do have the right. Under
the Industrial Conciliation Act of 1924—'

'Don't spout acts at me now, Abe,' she cut him off.
'They are a bunch of bolsheviks biting the hand that feeds
them.'

'Centaine, don't do anything hasty. If we were to—'

'Abe, get the Daimler offloaded from the truck immediately and send Dr Twentyman-Jones a telegraph. Tell him
I'm coming and he is to do nothing, make no concessions
nor promises until I arrive.'

'You'll leave in the morning, of course?'

'I will not,' she snapped. 'I will leave in half an hour
from now, just as soon as my guests have gone and you
have the Daimler detrained.'

'It's one in the morning—' He saw her face and abandoned that line of protest. 'I'll telegraph the staff at the first staging station to expect you.'

'Just tell them to be ready to refuel. I won't be staying over. I'm driving straight through to the mine.' And she went to the door, paused to compose herself and then, smiling easily, went back into the saloon.

'Is something wrong, Mrs Courtney?' The smile had not deceived Blaine Malcomess, and he rose to his feet. 'Is there anything I can do to help you?'

'Oh, just a small nuisance. Trouble out at the mine. I have to go back there right away.'

'Not tonight, surely?'

'Yes, tonight—'

'On your own?' He was troubled, and his concern pleased her. 'It's a long hard journey.'

'I prefer to travel alone.' Then she added with a meaningful intensity, 'Or to chose my travelling companion with great care.' She paused, then went on, 'Some of my employees have called a strike. It's unreasonable and they have no case to justify their action. I'm certain that I can smooth it over. However, sometimes these things get out of hand. There might be violence, or vandalism.'

Quickly Blaine reassured her. 'I can guarantee you full government co-operation. A police detachment could be sent to maintain the peace, if you so wish.'

'Thank you. I would appreciate that. Knowing that I can call upon you is a great relief and comfort.'

'I will arrange it first thing tomorrow,' he said. 'But of course it will take a few days.' Again they were behaving as though they were alone; their voices were low and filled with significance beyond what the words suggested.

'Darling, we should leave Mrs Courtney to prepare for her journey.' Isabella spoke from her chair and he started as though he had forgotten she were there.

'Yes, of course. We will leave at once.'

Centaine went with them down the railway platform to where Blaine's Chevrolet tourer was parked beneath the single streetlight. She walked beside Isabella's wheelchair.

'I did so enjoy meeting you, Mrs Malcomess, and I'd love to meet your girls. Won't you bring them out to Weltevreden when next you are in Cape Town?'

'I don't know when that will be,' Isabella refused politely. 'My husband will be immersed in his new appointment.'

They reached the waiting vehicle and while the chauffeur held the rear door open, Blaine lifted Isabella from the chair and seated her on the leather seat. He closed the door carefully and turned to Centaine. His back was to his wife, and the chauffeur was loading the wheelchair into the boot. They were alone for the time being.

'She is a courageous and wonderful woman,' he said softly as he took Centaine's hand. 'I love her and can never leave her, but I wish—' he broke off and his grip on her fingers was painful.

'Yes,' Centaine answered as softly. 'I also wish—' and she revelled in the pain of his grip. He ended it too soon for her and went around to the opposite side of the Chevrolet, while Centaine stooped to the crippled girl at the open window.

'Please do remember my invitation,' she began, but Isabella thrust her face closer and the serene and beautiful mask cracked so that the terror and the hatred showed through.

'He's mine,' she said. 'And I won't let you have him.' Then she leaned back in her seat and Blaine slid in beside her and took her hand.

The Chevrolet pulled away, the official pennant on the bonnet fluttering, and Centaine stood under the streetlight and stared after it until the headlights faded.

225

L othar De La Rey slept with the earphones of the
telegraph tap on the sheepskin roll beside his head,
so that the first bleep of the transmission woke him
and he snatched up the headset and called to Swart
Hendrick. 'Light the candle, Hennie, they are transmitting.
At this time of night it must be important.'

Yet he was still unprepared for the import of the message
when he scribbled it out in his notebook: 'Strike Committee headed by Gerhard Fourie has called out all white
employees—'

Lothar was stunned by Twentyman-Jones' message.

'Gerhard Fourie. What on earth is that miserable bastard
playing at,' he asked himself aloud, and then leapt up and
went out of the dugout to pace agitatedly in the loose sand
of the riverbed while he attempted to work it out.

'A strike – why would he call a strike now? *Shipment of
goods embargoed*. That has to mean the diamonds. The
strikers are refusing to let the diamonds leave the mine.'
He stopped suddenly and punched his fist into his own
palm. 'That's it. That's what it's all about. He has called
the strike to worm himself out of our bargain. His nerve
has given in, but he knows I will kill him for it. This is his
way out. He isn't going to co-operate. The whole thing has
fallen through.'

He stood out in the riverbed and a dark impotent rage
overwhelmed him.

'All the risks I have taken, all the time and work and
hardship. The theft of the horses, all for nothing, all wasted
because of one yellow-bellied—'

If Fourie had been there he would have shot him down
without compunction.

'*Baas!*' Hendrick yelled urgently. 'Come quickly! The
telegraph!'

Lother sprinted back to the dugout and snatched up the
headset. The operator at the Courtney Mining and Finance
Company in Windhoek was transmitting.

'For Vingt. I am returning with all speed. Stop. Make no concessions nor promises. Stop. See that all loyal employees are armed and protected from intimidation. Stop. Assure them of my gratitude and material appreciation. Stop. Close the company store immediately, no food or supplies to be sold to strikers or their families. Stop. Cut off water reticulation and electricity supply to strikers' cottages. Stop. Inform Strike Committee that police detachment en route. Ends. Juno.'

Despite himself and his rage at Fourie, Lothar threw back his head and laughed with delight and admiration.

'Fourie and his strikers don't realize what they are taking on,' he roared. 'By God, I'd prefer to tickle an angry black mamba with a short stick than get in Centaine Courtney's way right now.' He sobered and thought about it for a while, then he told Hendrick and Manfred quietly:

'I have a feeling that those diamonds will be coming through to Windhoek, strike or no strike. But I don't think Fourie will be driving the truck, in fact I don't give Fourie much chance of driving anything again. So we won't have a nice polite co-operative escort to hand the package over to us as we had planned. But the diamonds will be coming through, and we are going to be here when they do.'

The yellow Daimler passed their position at eleven o'clock the following night. Lothar watched the glow of the headlights gradually harden into solid white beams of light that swept across the plain towards him and then dipped and disappeared into the riverbed only to blaze up into the moonless sky as the Daimler pointed its nose up the cutting and climbed out of the riverbed again. The engine bellowed in low gear on the steep incline and then settled to a high whine as it shot over the top and sped away into the north-east towards the H'ani Mine.

Lothar struck a match and checked his watch. 'Say she left Windhoek an hour after her telegraph last night – that means she has reached here in twenty-two hours' straight driving, over these roads in the dark.' He whistled softly. 'If she keeps going like that, she'll be at the H'ani Mine before noon tomorrow. It doesn't seem possible.'

The blue hills rose out of the heat mirage ahead of Centaine, but this time their magic was unable to captivate her. She had been at the wheel for thirty-two hours with only brief intervals of rest while she refuelled at the staging posts, and once when she had pulled to the side of the road and slept for two hours.

She was tired. The weariness ached in the marrow of her bones, burned her eyes like acid and lay upon her shoulders and crushed her down in the leather seat of the Daimler as though she wore a suit of heavy chain mail. Yet her anger fuelled her, and when she saw the galvanized iron roofs of the mine buildings shining in the sun her weariness dropped away.

She stopped the Daimler and stepped down in the road to stretch and swing her arms, forcing fresh blood into her stiff limbs. Then she twisted the rearview mirror and examined her face in it. Her eyes were bloodshot and red-rimmed with little wet balls of mud and mucus in the corners. Her face was deathly white, powdered with pale dust and drained of blood by her fatigue.

She wet a cloth with cool water from the canvas water bag and cleaned the dust from her skin. Then from her toilet bag she took the bottle of eyewash and little blue eyebath. She bathed her eyes. They were clear and bright again when she checked in the mirror, and she patted her pale cheeks until the blood rouged them. She readjusted the scarf around her head, stripped off the full-length white dust-jacket that protected her clothes and she looked clean and rested and ready for trouble.

There were little groups of women and children gathered

at the corners of the avenues. They watched her sullenly and a little apprehensively as she drove past them on the way to the administration building. She sat straightbacked behind the wheel and looked directly ahead.

As she neared the office, she saw the pickets who had been lolling under the thorn tree outside the gates hastily reorganizing themselves. There were twenty at least, most of the able-bodied white artisans on the mine. They formed a line across the road and linked arms facing her. Their faces were ugly and threatening.

'Nothing goes in! Nothing goes out!' they began to chant as she slowed. She saw that most of them had armed themselves with clubs and pick handles.

Centaine thrust the palm of her hand down on the button and the Daimler's horn squealed like a wounded bull elephant and she drove hard at the centre of the picket line with the accelerator pedal pressed to the floorboards. The men in the centre saw her face behind the windshield and realized that she would run them down. At the last minute they scattered.

One of them yelled, 'We want our jobs!' and swung his pick handle against the rear window. The glass starred and collapsed over the leather seat, but Centaine was through.

She pulled up in front of the verandah just as Twentyman-Jones hurried out of his office struggling with his jacket and necktie.

'We weren't expecting you until tomorrow at the very earliest.'

'Your friends were.' She pointed at the shattered window, and his voice went shrill with indignation.

'They attacked you? That's unforgivable.'

'I agree,' she said. 'And I'm not going to be the one who does the forgiving.'

Twentyman-Jones wore a huge service pistol holstered on his skinny hip. Behind him was little Mr Brantingham, the mine bookkeeper, his head bald as an ostrich egg and

229

much too large for his narrow rounded shoulders. Behind his gold-rimmed pince-nez he was close to tears, but he carried a double-barrelled shotgun in his pudgy white hands.

'You are a brave man,' Centaine told him. 'I won't forget your loyalty.'

She led Twentyman-Jones into her office and sat down thankfully at her desk. 'How many other men are with us?'

'Only the office staff, eight of them. The artisans and mine staff are all out, though I suspect there has been pressure on some of them.'

'Even Rodgers and Maclear?' They were her senior overseers. 'Are they out also?'

'I'm afraid so. Both of them are on the strike committee.'

'With Fourie?'

'The three of them are the ringleaders.'

'I'll see that they never work again,' she said bitterly, and he dropped his eyes and mumbled:

'I think we have to bear in mind that they haven't broken the law. They have the legal right to withhold their labour, and to bargain collectively—'

'Not when I am struggling to keep the mine running. Not when I am trying to ensure that there will be jobs for at least some of them. Not after all I've done for them.'

'I'm afraid they do have that right,' he insisted.

'Whose side are you on, Dr Twentyman-Jones?'

He looked stricken. 'You should never have to ask that question,' he said. 'From the first day we met I've been your man. You know that. I was merely pointing out your legal position.'

Immediately contrite, Centaine stood up and reached for his arm to console him.

'Forgive me. I'm tired and jumpy.' She had stood up too quickly and the blood drained from her head. She turned deathly pale and swayed giddily on her feet. He seized her and steadied her.

230

'When did you last sleep? You have driven from Windhoek without rest.' He led her to the leather sofa and forced her gently down upon it.

'You are going to sleep now, for at least eight hours. I'll have fresh clothes brought down from your bungalow.'

'I must speak to the ringleaders.'

'No.' He shook his head as he drew the curtains. 'Not until you are refreshed and strong again. Otherwise you could make mistakes of judgement.'

She sagged back and pressed her fingers into her closed eyelids. 'You are right – as always.'

'I'll wake you at six this evening, and I'll inform the strike committee that you will interview them at eight. That will give us two hours to plan our strategy.'

The three members of the strike committee filed into Centaine's office, and she stared at them for fully three minutes without speaking. She had deliberately had all the chairs removed, except those in which she and Twentyman-Jones sat. The strikers were forced to stand before her like schoolboys.

'There are over a hundred thousand men out of work in this country at the present time,' she said in a dispassionate voice. 'Any one of whom would go down on his knees for your jobs.'

'That won't bloody work,' said Maclear. He was a nondescript-looking man, of medium height and uncertain age, but Centaine knew he was quick-witted, tenacious and resourceful. She wished he was with her rather than against.

'If you are going to use foul language in front of me, Mr Maclear,' she said, 'you can leave immediately.'

'That won't work either, Mrs Courtney.' He smiled sadly in acknowledgement of her spirit. 'You know our rights, and we know our rights.'

Centaine looked at Rodgers. 'How is your wife, Mr Rodgers?' A year previously she had paid for the woman to travel to Johannesburg for urgent treatment by one of the leading abdominal surgeons in the Union. Rodgers had gone with her on full pay, and all expenses paid.

'She's well, Mrs Courtney,' he said sheepishly.

'What does she think of this nonsense of yours?' He looked down at his feet. 'She's a sensible lady,' Centaine went on. 'I would think she is worrying about her three little ones.'

'We are all together,' Fourie cut in. 'We are all solid, and the women are behind us. You can forget all that—'

'Mr Fourie, please do not interrupt me when I am speaking.'

'Playing the high and mighty lady muck-a-muck around here is going to get you nowhere,' he blustered. 'We've got you and your bloody mine and your bloody diamonds over a barrel. You are the one who has got to do the listening when we speak, and that's the plain fact of the matter.' He grinned cockily and looked to his mates for approbation. The grin concealed his trepidation. On one side he had Lothar De La Rey and his threat. If he could not come up with a good enough excuse for not performing his obligations he knew he was a dead man. He had to aggravate the strike until someone else transported the diamonds and gave him an escape. 'You aren't going to get one single bloody diamond off this property until we say so, lady. We're keeping them here as hostages. We know you've got a really whopping packet sitting there in the strongroom, and that's where it will stay, until you listen to what we have to say.' He was a good enough judge of character to guess what Centaine Courtney's reaction to that threat would be.

Centaine studied his face intently. There was something that did not ring true, something devious and convoluted in his manner. He was being too deliberately aggressive and provocative.

'All right,' she agreed quietly. 'I'll listen. Tell me what you want.'

She sat quietly while Fourie read the list of demands. Her face was impassive, the only signs of her anger that Twentyman-Jones knew so well were the soft flush of blood that stained her throat and the steady rhythmic tap of her foot on the wooden floor.

Fourie reached the end of the reading and there was another long silence. Then he proffered the document.

'This is your copy.'

'Put it on my desk,' she ordered, disdaining to touch it. 'The people that were retrenched from this mine last month were given three months' pay in lieu of notice,' she said. 'Three times more than they were entitled to, you know that. They were all given good letters of reference, you know that also.'

'They are our mates,' Fourie said stubbornly. 'Some of them our family.'

'All right.' She nodded. 'You have made your position clear. You may leave now.' She rose and they looked at one another in consternation.

'Aren't you going to give us an answer?' Maclear asked.

'Eventually,' she nodded.

'When will that be?'

'When I am ready and not before.'

They filed towards the door, but before he reached it, Maclear turned back and faced her defiantly.

'They've closed the company store and cut off the water and electricity to our cottages,' he challenged her.

'On my orders,' she agreed.

'You can't do that.'

'I don't see why not. I own the store, the generator, the pumphouse and the cottages.'

'We've got wives and children to feed.'

'You should have thought about them before you started your strike.'

'We can take what we want, you know. Even your diamonds. You can't stop us.'

'Make me a very happy woman,' she invited. 'Do it. Break into the store and steal the goods from the shelves. Dynamite the strongroom and take my diamonds. Assault my loyal people. Nothing would please me more than to see the three of you in gaol for life – or dancing on the gallows tree.'

As soon as they were alone again, she turned to Twentyman-Jones.

'He is right. The first and only consideration is the diamonds. I have to get them safely into the bank vaults in Windhoek.'

'We can send them in under police escort,' he agreed, but she shook her head.

'It might take five more days for the police to reach here. There is all sorts of red tape before they can move. No, I want those diamonds away from here before dawn. You know the insurance doesn't cover riot and civil disturbance. If something happens to them I will be ruined, Dr Twentyman-Jones. They are my lifeblood. I cannot risk them falling into the hands of these ignorant arrogant brutes.'

'Tell me what you intend.'

'I want you to take the Daimler round to its garage in the rear. Have it refuelled and checked. We will load the diamonds through the back door.' She pointed across her office to the concealed door she used sometimes when she wished to avoid being seen entering or leaving. 'At midnight when the pickets are asleep you will cut the barbed-wire fence directly opposite the garage door.'

'Good.' He was following her intentions. 'That will let us out into the sanitary lane. The pickets are at the main gates on the opposite side of the compound. They haven't posted anyone on the rear side. Once we are clear of the lane it's a straight run out onto the main road to Windhoek, we'll be clear in a matter of seconds.'

'Not we, Dr Twentyman-Jones,' she said, and he stared at her.

'You don't intend going alone?' he asked.

'I have just made the journey alone, swiftly and with not the least sign of trouble. I anticipate no problem with the return. I need you here. You know I cannot leave the mine to Brantingham or one of the clerks. You have to be here to deal with these strikers. Without you they may wreck the plant or sabotage the workings. It would only take a stick or two of dynamite.'

He wiped his face with his open hand, from forehead to chin, in an agony of indecision, torn between two duties: the mine which he had built up from nothing and which was his pride, and the woman who he loved as dearly as a daughter or a wife he had never had. At last he sighed. She was right, it had to be that way.

'Then take one of the men with you,' he pleaded.

'Brantingham, bless him?' she asked, raising her eyebrows, and he threw up both hands as he saw how ridiculous that idea was.

'I'll take the Daimler around to the back,' he said. 'Then I'll get a telegraph through to Abe in Windhoek. He can send out an escort immediately to meet you on the road, that is if the strikers haven't cut the wires yet.'

'Don't send that until I am clear,' Centaine instructed. 'The strikers may just have had enough sense to have put a tap on the line, in fact that is probably why they have not cut it yet.'

Twentyman-Jones nodded. 'Very well. What time do you intend breaking out?'

'Three o'clock tomorrow morning,' she said, without hesitation. It was the hour when human vitality was at its lowest ebb. That was when the strike picket would be least prepared for swift reaction.

'Very well, Mrs Courtney. I will have my cook prepare you a light dinner – and then I suggest you get some rest. I will have everything ready and wake you at two-thirty.'

S he woke the instant he touched her shoulder and sat up.

'Half past two o'clock,' Twentyman-Jones said. 'The Daimler is refuelled and the diamonds loaded. The barbed wire is cut. I have drawn you a bath and there is a selection of fresh clothes from the bungalow.'

'I will be ready in fifteen minutes,' she said.

They stood beside the Daimler in the darkened garage and spoke in whispers. The double doors were open, and there was a crescent moon lighting the yard.

'I have marked the gap in the wire.' Twentyman-Jones pointed and she saw the small white flags drooping from the barbed wire strands fifty yards away.

'The canisters of industrial diamonds are in the boot, but I have put the package of top stones on the passenger seat beside you.' He leaned through the open window and patted the black despatch box. It was the size and shape of a small suitcase, but of japanned steel with a brass lock.

'Good.' Centaine buttoned her dust-jacket and pulled on her soft dogskin driving gauntlets.

'The shotgun is loaded with Number Ten birdshot, so you can fire at anybody who tries to stop you without risk of committing murder. It'll just give them a good sting. But if you mean business, there is a box of buckshot in the glove compartment.'

Centaine slid in behind the wheel and pulled the door closed gently so as not to alert a listener out in the silent night. She placed the double-barrelled shotgun on top of the diamond chest and cocked both hammers.

'There is a basket in the boot, sandwiches and a Thermos of coffee.'

She looked at him out of the side window and said seriously, 'You are my tower.'

'Don't let anything happen to you,' he said. 'A pox on the diamonds, we can dig more of them. You are unique, there's only one of you.' Impulsively he unbuckled the service revolver from around his waist and leaned into the Daimler to push it into the pocket at the back of the driver's seat. 'It's the only insurance I can offer you. Remember there is a cartridge under the hammer,' he said. 'Pray you never need it.' He stepped back and gave her a laconic salute. 'God speed!'

She started the Daimler and the great seven-litre engine rumbled softly. She flipped off the handbrake, switched on the headlights and gunned the Daimler out through the open doors and across the yard, going up through the gears in a deft series of racing changes.

She aimed the mascot on the bonnet between the white markers, roared through the gap in the fence at forty miles an hour, and felt a loose strand of barbed wire scrape down the side of the coachwork. Then she tramped down on the brake and spun the wheel, steering the front wheels onto the dusty lane, meeting the skid and then going flat on the accelerator pedal again. She shot down the lane with the Daimler roaring at full power.

Above the engine she heard faint shouts and saw the dark indistinct figures of a mob of strikers racing down the fence from the main gate to try and intercept her at the corner of the lane. She picked up the shotgun and thrust the double muzzles through the window beside her. In the headlights the faces of the running men were ugly with rage, their mouths dark pits as they shouted at her.

Two of them were swifter than their mates, and they reached the corner of the lane just as the Daimler came level. One of the strikers flung his pick handle and it cartwheeled through the beam of the headlights and clanged off the bonnet.

Centaine depressed the shotgun, aiming for their legs, and fired both barrels, with long spurts of orange flame and blurts of sound. Birdshot lashed their legs and the strikers howled with shock and pain and leapt off the road as Centaine roared past them and turned onto the main road down the slope and out into the desert.

For Pettifogger. Urgent and Imperative. Juno unaccompanied departed this end 3 am instant carrying goods. Stop. Immediately despatch armed escort to intercept her en route. Ends. Vingt.

Lothar De La Rey stared at the message he had copied onto his pad by the guttering flame of the candle.

'Unaccompained,' he whispered. 'Juno unaccompained. Carrying goods. By Christ Almighty, she's coming through alone – with the diamonds.' He calculated swiftly. 'She left the mine at three am. She'll be here an hour or so after noon.'

He left the dugout and climbed the bank. He found a place to sit and lit one of his precious cheroots. He looked at the sky, watching the crescent moon sink into the desert. When the dawn turned the eastern horizon into a peacock's tail of colour, he went down to the camp and blew flame from last night's ashes.

Swart Hendrick came out of the dugout and went to urinate noisily in the sand. He came back to the fire buttoning his breeches, yawning widely and sniffing the coffee in the billy.

'We are changing the plan,' Lothar told him, and Hendrick blinked and became warily attentive.

'Why?'

'The woman is bringing the diamonds through alone. She won't give in easily. I don't want her hurt in any way.'

'I wouldn't—'

'The hell you wouldn't. When you get excited, you shoot,' Lothar cut him off brusquely. 'But that's not the only reason.' He ticked off the others on his fingers. 'First: one woman alone requires only one man. I have time enough to re-rig the ropes to bring down the boulders into the cutting from my position. Two: the woman knows you, it doubles the risk of having us recognized. Three,' he paused, the true reason was that he wanted to be alone with Centaine again. It would be the last time. He would never be coming back this way again. 'Lastly, we will do it this way because I say we will. You will stay here with Manfred and the horses, ready to ride as soon as I have done the job.'

Hendrick shrugged. 'I will help you rig the ropes,' he grunted.

C entaine stopped the Daimler at the head of the cutting and left the engine running as she jumped out onto the running-board and surveyed the crossing.

Her own outward tracks were still clear and sharp and untouched in the soft lemon-coloured dust. There had been no other traffic through the drift since she had passed the night before last. She unhooked the water bag and drank three mouthfuls, and then corked it again and hung it on the spare wheel bracket, climbed back into the cab, slammed the door and let off the handbrake.

She let the Daimler trundle down the incline, swiftly gathering speed, when suddenly there was a rush of earth and rock, a swirling cloud of dust obscured the cutting directly ahead of her and she hit the brake hard.

The bank had collapsed on one side, and had almost filled the cutting with rock and loose earth.

'Merde!' she swore. It would mean a delay while she cleared the rubble or found another place to cross. She snapped the Daimler into reverse and twisted in her seat looking back through the missing rear window that the striker had knocked out, preparing to back up the incline – and she felt the first flutter of alarm against her ribs.

The bank had collapsed behind the Daimler also, sliding down in a soft churned ramp. She was trapped in the cutting, and she leaned out of the open window and looked about her anxiously, coughing in the dust that still billowed around her vehicle.

As it cleared she saw that the road ahead was only partially blocked. On the opposite side to the landslide there was still a narrow gap, not sufficient for the wide track of the Daimler to get through, but there was a spade strapped to the roofrack. A few hours' work in the burning sun should clear the way enough for her to work the Daimler through, but the setback galled her. She reached for the door handle, then a premonition of danger stopped her hand and she looked up the bank beside her.

There was a man standing at the top of the rise, looking down at her. His boots at the level of her eyes were scuffed and white with dust. There were dark sweat patches on his blue shirt. He was a tall man, but he had the lean hard look of a soldier or a hunter. However, it was the rifle that he carried across his hip, pointing down into her face and the mask he wore that terrified her.

The mask was a white flour bag. She could read the red and blue lettering on it: 'Premier Milling Co. Ltd', an innocuous kitchen article endowed with infinite menace by the two eye-holes that had been cut into the cloth. The mask and the rifle told her exactly what to expect.

A whole series of thoughts flashed through her mind as she sat frozen at the wheel staring up at him.

The diamonds are not insured. That was the thought at the forefront of her mind. *The next staging post is forty miles ahead*, was the next thought, and then: *I forgot to reload the shotgun – spent shells in both barrels.*

The man above her spoke, his voice muffled by the mask and obviously disguised.

'Switch off the engine!' He gestured with the rifle to enforce the order. 'Get out!'

She got out and looked around her desperately, her terror gone now, burned away by the need to think and act. Her eyes fastened directly ahead on the narrow gap left between the soft ramp of raw earth where the landslide had poured down in front of her and the steep firm bank on the other side.

'I can get through,' she thought, 'or at least I can try.' And she ducked back into the cab.

'Stop!' The man above her yelled, but she slammed the Daimler into low gear.

The rear wheels spun in the fine yellow dust, throwing it back in twin fountains. The Daimler lurched forward, the tail swaying and skidding, but it gathered speed sharply and Centaine aimed the bonnet at the narrow gap between the bank and the slide of earth and rock.

She heard the man above her shout again, and then a warning rifle shot cracked over the top of the cab but she ignored it and concentrated on taking the Daimler out of the trap.

She rode her offside wheels high up the incline of the bank, and the Daimler reared over on its side almost to the point of capsizing, but its speed was still building up. Centaine was heavily shaken and tossed about so that she had only her grip on the steering wheel to keep her in her seat as the big car canted even further over.

Still the gap was too narrow; her nearside wheels

smashed into the piled earth and rock. The Daimler bucked wildly, throwing its nose high, flying up and forward like a hunter at a fence. Centaine was hurled towards the windshield, but she flung up a hand to brace herself and clung to the wheel with the other.

The Daimler came down again with a rending crash, jerking Centaine back against the padded leather seat. She felt unyielding rock slam up into the Daimler's belly like a boxer taking a heavy body blow, and the back wheels crabbed over the pile of broken earth, the rubber tyres screeching as they sought purchase on the tumbled boulders. Then they caught and flung the Daimler forward again.

It dropped down the far side of the obstacle, and hit hard. Centaine heard something break, the clanging rupture of one of the steering rods and the wheel spun without resistance in her hands. The Daimler had fought its way over the barrier, but it was mortally wounded and out of control. The steering gone and the throttle linkage jammed wide open.

Centaine screamed and clung to the walnut dashboard as it roared down the cutting towards the riverbed, slamming into one bank and then hurling across and crashing into the other, the coachwork banging and ripping and buckling at each impact.

She tried desperately to reach the ignition switch, but the speedometer needle was flicking at the 30 mph notch and she was thrown across the passenger seat. The steel corner of the diamond case gouged her ribs, then she was thrown back the other way.

The door beside her burst open just as the Daimler roared out of the cutting into the riverbed and Centaine was hurled out through it. Instinctively she doubled herself into a ball, as though she were taking a fall from a galloping horse, and she rolled in the soft white sand, head over heels, coming up at last on her knees.

The Daimler was slewing wildly across the riverbed, the engine still roaring, and one of the front wheels, damaged by the rocks of the barrier, flew off, bounding and leaping like a wild creature until it struck the far bank.

The front end of the Daimler dropped and the nose dug into the sand. The engine was still roaring and the huge vehicle somersaulted end over end and came down on its back. The three remaining wheels pointed at the sky, spinning in a blur, the glass in the windows crackling and splintering into diamond chips, the cab buckling and sagging, hot oil pouring out of the slats in the bonnet and soaking into the sand.

Centaine pushed herself up and was running as she regained her feet. The sand clung to her ankles. It was like running in a bath of treacle, and terror had heightened her senses so that time seemed to stand still. It was like one of those terrible dreams in which all her movements were reduced to slow motion.

She dared not look behind her. That menacing masked figure must surely be close. She tensed for the grip of the hand that would seize her at any instant or the slam of a bullet into her back, but she reached the Daimler and dropped on her knees in the sand beside it.

The driver's door had been torn off and she crawled half-way into the aperture. The shotgun was wedged against the steering control but she dragged it clear and ripped open the small door of the glove compartment. The cardboard box of shotgun shells was scarlet with black lettering:

ELEY KYNOCH
12 GAUGE
25 X 330

It broke open under her frantic fingers and the red brass-tipped shells spilled into the sand around her knees.

She pushed across the breech lock of the shotgun with her thumb and broke open the gun. The two empty birdshot cartridges flew out with a crisp click-click of the ejectors – and the gun was snatched out of her hands.

The masked man stood over her. He must have moved like a hunting leopard to come down the bank and across the riverbed so quickly. He flung the empty shotgun out across the sand. It landed fifty feet away, but the impetus of the throw had swung him off balance. Centaine launched herself at him, coming off her knees and driving her whole weight into his chest, just below the raised left arm that he had used to throw the shotgun.

It was unexpected, and he was balanced on one foot. They went over together in the sand. For an instant Centaine was on top of him, and then she wriggled away, came to her feet and floundered back towards the Daimler. The engine was still racing, blue smoke pouring from the engine as the oil drained away from the sump and it overheated.

The pistol! Centaine seized the handle of the rear door and threw her weight against it. Through the window she could see the leather holster and the chequered butt of Twentyman-Jones' service revolver protruding from the seat pocket, but the door was jammed.

She ducked back to the gaping front door and tried to reach it over the back of the driver's seat, but bone-hard fingers dug into her shoulders and she was dragged bodily out of the doorway. Instantly she spun in his grip, and his face was very close to hers. The thin white cotton bag covered his entire head, like the head of a KuKlux Klansman. The eye-holes were dark as the hollow sockets in a skull, but there was a glint of human eyes deep in the shadow and she went for them with her fingernails.

He jerked his head away but her forefinger hooked in the thin cloth and ripped it down to his chin. He seized her wrists and instead of pulling away she hurled herself against him and drove her right knee up into his groin. He twisted violently and caught her knee on the side of his upper thigh. She felt the shock of the blow drive into the rubbery muscle of his leg, but his grip on her wrists tightened as though she had been caught in the jaws of a steel gin trap.

She ducked her head and fastened her teeth into his wrist like a ferret, at the same time kicking and kneeing him in the lower body and shins, raining blows at him, most of them slogging into his hard flesh or bouncing off bone.

He was grunting and trying to control her. Obviously he hadn't expected this type of wild resistance, and the pain in his wrist must have been excruciating. Already the hinges of her jaws were cramping with the force of her bite. She could feel tissue and flesh splitting and tearing between her teeth and his blood welled into her mouth, hot and coppery and salt-tasting.

With his free hand the masked man seized a handful of her thick curly hair and tried to pull her head back. She was breathing through her nose, snuffling like a bulldog and gritting her teeth in with all her strength, and she reached the bone. It grated under her teeth, and the man was tugging and jerking at her head, giving small agonized cries and grunts.

She closed her eyes, expecting him at any moment to slam his fist into the side of her head and break the grip of her teeth, but he was strangely gentle and considerate in his reaction, not attempting to inflict injury or pain, merely trying to pull her off.

She felt something burst in her mouth. She had bitten through an artery in his wrist. Blood pumped against the roof of her palate with hot spurts that threatened to choke and drown her. She let it pour from the corners of her mouth without relaxing her bite. It sprayed from her lips and splattered them both as he jerked her head from side to side. He was moaning with agony now, and at last he used punitive force.

He dug thumb and forefinger into the hinges of her jaw. His fingers were like iron spikes. Pain shot down into her locked jaws and up behind her eyes, and she opened her mouth and flung herself backwards, again taking him by surprise, breaking out of his grip and darting away back towards the Daimler.

This time she thrust her arm over the back of the driver's seat and reached up to the butt of the revolver. It slipped from the greased holster, and while she fumbled with a shaking hand to get a hold on it, the masked man seized her hair from behind and jerked her backwards. The heavy pistol fell through her fingers and clattered against the steel of the inverted cab.

She rounded on him again, snapping at his face with teeth that were still stained pink with his blood. The torn mask flapped over his face, blinding him for an instant and he stumbled and fell holding her in his arms. She was kicking and scratching and slashing at him as he rolled on top of her and pinned her with his full weight, holding her arms spread like a crucifix – and suddenly she stopped struggling and stared up at him.

The flap of his mask hung open and she could see his eyes. Those strange pale topaz-coloured eyes with the long dark lashes, and she gasped.

'Lothar!'

He stiffened with the shock of his name, and they lay, locked like lovers, legs entangled, their lower bodies pressed together, both panting wildly and smeared with his blood, staring at each other wordlessly.

Abruptly he released her and stood up. He pulled the mask off his head and his tousled golden locks fell about his ears and tumbled down his forehead into his eyes as he wrapped the mask tightly around his mutilated wrist. He realized that it was seriously injured, the tendons and bone were exposed and the flesh was mangled and tattered where she had chewed it. Bright scarlet arterial blood soaked through the white cloth immediately and dripped into the sand.

Centaine pulled herself into a sitting position and watched him. The engine of the Daimler had stalled, and there was silence except for their breathing.

'Why are you doing this?' she whispered.

'You know why.' He knotted the cloth with his teeth, and suddenly she flung herself sideways and reached desperately into the cab, her fingers scrabbling again for the pistol. She touched it, but could not get her fingers around the butt before he pulled her away and pushed her over backwards in the sand.

He picked up the pistol and unclipped the lanyard. He would the lanyard around his forearm as a tourniquet and grunted with satisfaction as the seep of blood shrivelled.

'Where are they?' He looked down at her where she lay.

'What are you talking about?'

He stooped and looked into the cab of the Daimler, then pulled out the black japanned despatch box.

'Keys?' he asked.

She stared back at him defiantly and he squatted and placed the box firmly in the sand, then stepped back a pace. He cocked the pistol and fired a single shot. The report was stunning in the desert silence, and Centaine's ear drums buzzed with the memory. The bullet had torn the lock of the despatch box away and a circle of the black paint flaked from the lid leaving the metal beneath shiny and bright.

Lothar pocketed the pistol, and knelt and lifted the lid. The case was filled with small packages, each neatly wrapped in brown paper and sealed with red wax. He picked out one package, favouring his injured hand, and read aloud the inscription in Twentyman-Jones' ornate old-fashioned penmanship:

He tore open the heavy cartridge paper with his teeth and shook out a sprinkle of gems into the palm of his injured hand. In the white sunlight they had that peculiar soapy sheen of uncut diamonds.

'Very pretty,' he murmured and dropped the loose stones into his pocket. He packed the torn parcel back into the despatch case and closed the lid.

'I knew you were a murderer,' she said. 'I never thought you a common thief.'

'You stole my boats and my company. Don't talk to me about thieves.' He tucked the despatch case under his arm and stood up. He went round to the boot of the Daimler and managed to open it a crack, even though the vehicle was inverted, and he checked the contents.

'Good,' he said. 'You've had the sense to bring spare water. Twenty gallons will last you a week, but they'll find you before then. Abrahams is sending out an escort to meet you. I intercepted the instruction from Twentyman-Jones.'

'You swine,' she whispered.

'I will cut the telegraph wires before I leave. As soon as that happens they will realize at both ends that something is wrong. You'll be all right.'

'Oh God, I hate you.'

'Stay with the vehicle. That's the first law of desert survival. Don't go wandering off. They will rescue you in about two days – and I will have two days' start.'

'I thought I hated you before, but now I know the real meaning of the word.'

'I could have taught it to you,' he said quietly, as he picked the abandoned shotgun out of the sand. 'I came to know it well – over the years that I was rearing your son. Then again when you came back into my life only to tear down everything I ever dreamed about and worked for.' He swung the shotgun like an axe against one of the boulders. The butt shattered but he went on until it was bent and battered and useless. He dropped it.

Then he slung the Mauser over his shoulder and transferred the despatch case to his other hand. He held the injured hand in its blood-wet wrapping against his chest. Clearly the pain was fierce; he had paled under his deep bronze tan and there was a catch in his voice as he went on.

'I tried not to hurt you – if you hadn't struggled—' he broke off. 'We will not meet again, ever. Goodbye, Centaine.'

'We will meet again,' she contradicted him. 'You know me well enough, you must realize that I will not rest until I have full retribution for this day's work.'

He nodded. 'I know you will try.' He turned away.

'Lothar!' she called sharply, and then softened her voice when he turned back. 'I'll make you a bargain – your company and your boats free of all debt for my diamonds.'

'A bad bargain.' He smiled sadly. 'By now the plant and boats are worth nothing, while your diamonds—'

'Plus fifty thousand pounds and my promise not to report this affair to the police.' She tried to keep the edge of desperation out of her voice.

'Last time it was I who was begging – do you recall? No, Centaine, even if I wanted, I could not go back now. I have burned my bridges.' He thought about the horses, but could not tell her. 'No bargain, Centaine. Now I must go.'

'Half the diamonds – leave half, Lothar.'

'Why?'

'For the love we once shared.'

He laughed bitterly. 'You will have to give me a better reason than that.'

'All right. If you take them you will destroy me, Lothar. I cannot survive their loss. Already I am finely drawn. I will be utterly ruined.'

'As I was when you took my boats.' He turned and trudged through the sand to the bank, and she stood up.

'Lothar De La Rey!' she shouted after him. 'You refused my offer – then take my oath instead. I swear, and I call on God and all his saints to witness, I swear that I will never rest again until you swing by the neck from the gallows.'

He did not look back, but she saw him flinch his head at the threat. Then cradling his injured wrist and burdened by the rifle and the despatch case, he climbed the high bank and was gone.

She sank down on the sand and a wave of reaction swept over her. She found she was shaking wildly and uncontrollably. Despondency and humiliation and despair came at her in waves like a storm surf battering an unresisting beach, sweeping over it then sucking back and gathering and rushing forward again. She found she was weeping, thick, slow tears dissolving the clots of his drying blood from her lips and chin, and her tears disgusted her as much as the taste of blood at the back of her throat.

Disgust gave her the strength and resolution to pull herself to her feet and cross to the Daimler. Miraculously the water bag was still on its bracket. She washed away the blood and the tears. She gargled the taste of his blood from her mouth and spat it pink into the sand and she thought of following him.

He had taken the revolver and the shotgun was a battered and twisted piece of steel.

'Not yet—' she whispered, 'but very soon. I have given you my oath on it, Lothar De La Rey.'

Instead she went to the boot of the inverted Daimler. She had to scoop away the sand with her hands before she could get it fully open. She took out the two ten-gallon cans of water and the canisters of industrial diamonds, carried them to the shade of the bank and buried them in the sand to hide them and to keep the water as cool as possible.

Then she returned to the Daimler and impatiently unpacked the other survival equipment that she always carried, suddenly deadly afraid that the telegraph tap had been offloaded or forgotten – but it was there in the tool box with the wheel jack and spanners.

She lugged the reel of wire and the haversack containing the tap as she followed Lothar's tracks up the bank and found where he had tethered his horse.

'He said he was going to cut the telegraph—' She shaded her eyes and peered along the river course. 'He should have guessed I would have carried a tap with me. He isn't going to get his two days' start.'

She picked out the line of telegraph poles cutting across the road loop and the bend of the river. The tracks of Lothar's horse followed the bank, and she broke into a run and trotted along them.

She saw the break in the wires from two hundred yards off. The severed copper wires dangled to earth in two lazy inverted parabolas and she quickened her pace. When she reached the spot where the telegraph line crossed the river and looked down the bank she immediately recognized the remnants of Lothar's camp. Sand had been hastily kicked over the fire, but the embers still smouldered.

She dropped the coil of wire and the haversack and scrambled down the bank. She found the dugout and realized that more than one man had been living here for some considerable time. There were three mattresses of cut grass.

'Three.' She puzzled over it for a few moments, and then worked it out. 'He has his bastard with him.' She still couldn't bring herself to think of Manfred as her son. 'And the other one will be Swart Hendrick. He and Lothar are inseparable.'

She ducked from the dugout and stood for a moment undecided. It would take time to rig the tap to the severed wires, and it was vitally important to find out which way

Lothar had ridden if she was to set the pursuit on him before he got clear.

She made her decision. 'I'll rig the telegraph after I know which way to send them.'

It was unlikely he would head east into the Kalahari. There was nothing out there.

'He'll head back towards Windhoek,' she guessed, and she made her first cast in that direction. The area around the camp was thickly trodden with spoor of horse and men. They had been here for at least two weeks, she judged. Only her Bushman training enabled her to make sense of the tangled tracks.

'They didn't go out that way,' she decided at last. 'Then they must have headed south for Gobabis and the Orange river.'

She made her next cast in that direction, circling the southern perimeter of the camp, and when she found no spoor fresher than the previous day, she looked to the north.

'Surely not.' She was confused. 'There is nothing out there before the Okavango river and Portuguese territory – the horses will never make it across the wastes of Bushmanland.'

Nevertheless she made her next cast across that northern segment and almost immediately cut the outgoing spoor, fresh and cleanly printed in the soft earth.

'Three riders each leading a spare horse, not an hour ago. Lothar must be taking the northern route after all. He is crazy – or he has worked out something.' She followed the fresh spoor for a mile, to make certain that he had not doubled or backtracked. The spoor ran straight and un-wavering into the shimmering heat mists of the northern wastes, and she shivered as she remembered what it was like out there.

'He must be crazy,' she whispered. 'But I know he isn't. He's going for the Angola border. That's his old base from the ivory-poaching days. If he reaches the river we'll never see him again. He has friends over there, the Portuguese traders who bought his ivory. This time Lothar will have a million pounds of diamonds in his pocket and the wide world to choose from. I have to catch him before he gets across.'

Her spirits quailed at the enormity of the idea and she felt despondency come at her again. 'He has prepared this carefully – everything is in his favour. We'll never catch him.' She fought off the beast of despair. 'Yes, we will. We have to. I have to outwit and beat him. I simply have to, just to survive.'

She whirled and ran back to the abandoned camp.

The severed telegraph wires drooped to earth and she gathered the ends and clipped the bridging wires from the coil to them, drawing them just taut enough to keep them clear of the earth.

She put her tap into the circuit and screwed the terminals to the pack of dry-cell batteries. The batteries had been renewed before she left Windhoek. They should still be full of life. For a dreadful moment her mind went blank and she could not remember a single letter of the Morse code, then it returned with a rush and she hammered quickly on the brass key.

'Juno for Vingt. Acknowledge.'

For long seconds there was only echoing silence in her headphones, then the startling beep of the reply:

'Vingt for Juno. Go ahead.'

She tried to pick the short word and terse abridged phrase as she told Twentyman-Jones of the robbery and gave her position, then went on:

'Negotiate stand-off with strikers as recovery of goods mutually essential. Stop. Take truck to northern tip of O'chee Pan and locate Bushman encampment in mongongo forest. Stop. Bushleader named Kwi. Stop. Tell Kwi "Nam Child *kaleya*". Repeat "Nam Child *Kaleya*"' – and she gave thanks that the word *kaleya* bore phonetic rendition into the Roman alphabet and required neither the complicated tonals nor the clicks of the Bushman language. *Kaleya* was the distress call, the cry for help that no clan member could ignore. 'Bring Kwi with you,' she went on and continued with her further instructions; and when she signed off Twentyman-Jones acknowledged and then sent:

'Are you safe and unharmed. Query. Vingt.'

'Affirmative. Ends. Juno.'

She mopped the sweat off her face with the yellow silk scarf. She was sitting in the direct rays of the sun. Then she flexed her fingers and bent once more to the keyboard and tapped out the call sign of her operator in the offices of Courtney Mining and Finance Company in Windhoek.

The acknowledgement was prompt. Obviously the operator had been following her transmission to Twentyman-Jones, but she asked:

'Have you copied previous?'

'Affirmative,' he tapped back.

'Relay previous to Administrator Colonel Blaine Malcomess plus following for Malcomess. Quote: Request co-operation in capture of culprits and recovery of stolen goods. Stop. Do you have report on large number stolen horses or purchase of horses by one Lothar De La Rey within last three months. Respond soonest. Ends. Juno.'

The distant operator acknowledged and then continued:

'Pettifogger for Juno.' Abe must have been summoned to the telegraph office the minute they received their first transmission. 'Greatly concerned for your safety. Stop. Remain your present position. Stop.'

And Centaine exclaimed irritably, 'I sucked that egg long ago, Abe.' But she copied the rest of it.

'Armed escort left Windhoek 5 am instant. Stop. Should reach you early tomorrow. Stop. Stand by for Malcomess. Ends. Pettifogger.'

The wires were long enough to allow her to move the

keyboard into the strip of shade below the bank and while she waited she gave all her concentration to the task ahead.

Certain facts were apparent and the first of these was that they were never going to catch Lothar De La Rey in a stern chase. He had too long a lead, and he was going into country over which he had travelled and hunted for half his life. He knew it better than any living white man, better than even she did, but not better than little Kwi.

'We have to work out his route and cut him off, and we will have to use horses. Trucks will be useless over that terrain. Lothar knows that, he is banking on that. He will choose a route that trucks can never follow.'

She closed her eyes and visualized a map of the northern territory, that vast forbidding sweep of desert called Bushmanland.

She only knew of surface water at two points, one the place she always thought of as Elephant Pan, and the other a deep seep below a hillock of shale. They were secret Bushman places, both of which old O'wa, her adopted grandfather, had shown her fifteen years before. She wondered if she could find either water-hole again, but she was certain that Lothar knew them and could ride directly to them. He probably knew of other water-holes that she did not.

The beep of the telegraph disturbed her and she reached for it eagerly.

'Malcomess for Juno. Police report theft of 26 horses from military remount depot Okahandja 3rd of last month. Stop. Only two animals recovered. Stop. State your further requirements.'

'I was right! Lothar has set up staging posts across the desert,' she exclaimed, and she closed her eyes and tried to visualize a map of the northern territory, estimating distances and times. At last she opened her eyes again, and bent to the telegraph key.

'Convinced fugitives attempting to reach Okavango

river direct. Stop. Assemble small mobile force of desert-trained men with spare horses. Stop. Rendezvous Kalkrand Mission Station soonest. Stop. I will join you with Bushman trackers.'

T wentyman-Jones reached her before the escort from Windhoek. O'chee Pan was on his direct route, only a few miles from the road. The company truck came rumbling over the plain and Centaine ran down the tracks to meet it, waving both hands above her head and laughing wildly with relief. She had changed into breeches and ridingboots from her luggage in the Daimler.

Twentyman-Jones jumped down from the cab and came to her in a long-legged lolloping run. He caught her and held her to his chest.

'Thank God,' he muttered fervently. 'Thank God you are safe.'

It was the first time ever that he had embraced her and he was immediately embarrassed. He released her and stepped back scowling to cover it.

'Did you get Kwi?' she demanded.

'In the truck.'

Centaine ran to the truck. Kwi and Fat Kwi were crouched in the back, clearly both of them terrified by the experience. They looked like little wild animals in a cage, their dark eyes huge and swimming.

'Nam Child!' shrieked Kwi, and both of·them rushed to her for comfort, twittering and clicking with relief and joy. She hugged them like frightened children, murmuring assurance and endearments.

'I will be with you now. There is nothing to fear. These are good men and I will not leave you. Think what stories you will be able to tell the clan when you return. You will be famous amongst all the San, your names will be spoken through all the Kalahari.' And they giggled merrily at the notion, childlike, their fears all forgotten.

'I will be even more famous than Fat Kwi,' Kwi boasted, 'for I am older and fleeter and cleverer than he is,' and Fat Kwi bridled.

'You will both be famous.' Hastily Centaine averted the brewing dispute. 'For we are going to track evil men who have done me great harm. You will follow them and lead me to them, and afterwards I will give you such gifts as you have seen only in your dreams and all men will say that there were never before two hunters and trackers such as Kwi and his brother Fat Kwi. But now we must hurry before the evil ones escape us.'

She ran back to Twentyman-Jones and the little San stayed close at her heels like faithful dogs.

'De La Rey left the industrials. I've buried them in the riverbed.' She stopped with surprise when she recognized the two other men with Twentyman-Jones. The driver was Gerhard Fourie and his companion was Maclear, one of the other members of the strike committee. Both of them looked sheepish as Maclear spoke for them.

'Right pleased we all are to see you safe and well, Mrs Courtney. Wasn't a man at the mine who wasn't worried sick about you.'

'Thank you, Mr Maclear.'

'Anything we can do, we'll do. We are in this together, Mrs Courtney.'

'That's right, Mr Maclear. No diamonds, no wages. Will you please help me recover the industrials that the thieves left and then we will head for Kalkrand. Have you got enough fuel to get us there, Mr Fourie?'

'I'll have you there by morning, Mrs Courtney,' the driver promised. Kalkrand was the end of the line. The track went no further.

The road that Fourie took to bring them to Kalkrand was a wide circle, avoiding the bad land of central

Bushmanland. It headed north and west and then back to the east, so they would be 150 miles north of the point where Lothar had intercepted Centaine but 70 miles farther west when they reached Kalkrand. Their net gain on Lothar would be barely 80 miles, even less if he had taken a more easterly route towards the Okavango river. Of course it was also possible that Centaine's guess was wrong and that he had escaped in some other direction. She wouldn't let herself even think about that possibility.

'There has been other traffic on this road within the last few hours,' she told Twentyman-Jones as she peered ahead through the windscreen. 'It looks like two other trucks. Do you think it could be the police detachment that Colonel Malcomess is sending?'

'If it is, then the man is a marvel to have got them away so quickly.'

'Of course they would have followed the main road north to Okahandja before turning off in this direction.' Centaine wanted so badly for it to be so, but Twentyman-Jones shook his head dubiously.

'More likely a supply convoy for the mission station. My bet is that we will have to hang around the mission station waiting for the police and the horses to arrive.'

The galvanized roofs of the mission station appeared out of the morning haze ahead of them. It was a desolate spot below a low ridge of red shale probably chosen for the subterranean water supply. A pair of gaunt windmills stood like crowned sentinels over the boreholes that supplied the station.

'German Dominican fathers,' Twentyman-Jones told Centaine as they bumped over the last mile. 'They serve the nomadic Ovahimba tribes of this area.'

'Look!' Centaine interrupted him eagerly. 'There are the trucks parked next to the church, and horses watering at the windmill. And there, look! A uniformed trooper. It's them! They are waiting for us. Colonel Malcomess was as good as his promise.'

Fourie pulled up alongside the two sand-coloured police trucks and Centaine jumped down and shouted at the police trooper as he ran to meet them from the watering troughs below the windmill.

'Hello, Constable, who is in charge here—' and then she broke off and stared as a tall figure appeared on the verandah of the stone-walled building beside the little church.

He wore khaki gaberdine riding breeches and polished brown boots, and he was shrugging on a field officer's tunic over his shirt and suspenders, as he ran lightly down the steps and came towards her.

'Colonel Malcomess. I never expected you to be here in person.'

'You asked for full co-operation, Mrs Courtney.' He offered his hand and static electricity flashed a blue spark between their finger-tips. Centaine laughed and jerked her hand away. Then, when he still held his hand towards her, she took it again. His grip was firm and dry and reassuring.

'You aren't going into the desert with us, are you? You have your duties as administrator.'

'If I don't go, then you don't either.' He smiled. 'I have received strict instructions from both the prime minister, General Hertzog, and from the leader of the opposition, General Smuts, that I am not to let you out of my personal charge. Apparently, madam, you have a reputation for headstrong action. The two old gentlemen are very perturbed.'

'I have to go,' she broke in. 'Nobody else can handle the Bushman trackers. Without them the robbers will get clean away.'

He inclined his head in agreement. 'I am sure the

intention of the two worthy generals is that neither of us go, but I chose to interpret their orders rather as instruction that both of us should.' And suddenly he grinned like a naughty schoolboy about to play truant. 'You are stuck with me, I'm afraid.'

She thought of being with him out in the desert, far from his wife. For a moment she forgot Lothar De La Rey and the diamonds, and suddenly she realized that they were still holding hands and that everybody was watching them. She dropped his hand and asked briskly:

'When can we leave?'

In reply he turned and bellowed, 'Upsaddle! Upsaddle! We ride immediately!'

While the troopers ran to the horses, he turned back to her, businesslike and competent.

'And now, Mrs Courtney, will you be good enough to let me know your intentions – and where the hell we are going?'

She laughed. 'Do you have a map?'

'This way.' He led her into the mission office and quickly introduced her to the two German Dominican fathers who ran the station. Then he leant over his large-scale map spread on the desk.

'Show me what you have in mind,' he invited, and she stood beside him, not quite touching him.

'The robbery took place here.' She touched the spot with her fore-finger. 'I followed the tracks in this direction. He is heading for Portuguese territory. I am absolutely sure of that. But he has to go three hundred miles to reach it.'

'So what you have done is circled out ahead of him,' he nodded, 'and now you want to ride eastwards into the desert and cut him off. But it's a big piece of country. Needle in a haystack, don't you think?'

'Water,' she said. 'He has left his spare horses at water. I'm sure of that.'

'The horses stolen from the army? Yes, I understand, but there is no water out there.'

'There is,' she told him. 'It's not marked on the map but he knows where it is. My bushmen know where it is. We will intercept him at one of the water-holes, or we will cut his spoor there if he has beaten us to it.'

He straightened up and rolled the map. 'Do you think that possible?'

'That he has got ahead of us?' Centaine asked. 'You have to remember he is a hard man, and this desert is his home paddock. Never underestimate him, Colonel. That would be a serious mistake.'

'I have examined the man's record.' He stuffed his map into the leather case and then placed on his head a khaki solar helmet of thick cork with a sweeping rim that protected his neck. It covered his ears and increased his already impressive height. 'He is a dangerous man. He once had a price of ten thousand pounds on his head. I don't expect this to be easy.'

A police sergeant appeared in the doorway behind him. 'All ready, Colonel.'

'Do you have Mrs Courtney's mount saddled?'

'Yes, sir!' The sergeant was lean and brown and muscular, with thick drooping moustaches, and Centaine approved the choice. Blaine Malcomess saw her scrutiny.

'This is Sergeant Hansmeyer. He and I are old companions from Smuts' campaign.'

'How do you do, Mrs Courtney. Heard all about you, ma'am,' the sergeant saluted her.

'Glad to have you with us, Sergeant.'

Quickly they shook hands with the Dominican fathers and went out into the sunlight. Centaine went to the big strong bay gelding Blaine had allocated to her and adjusted her stirrup leathers.

'Mount up!' Blaine Malcomess ordered, and while the

sergeant and his four troopers swung up into the saddle, Centaine turned quickly to Twentyman-Jones.

'I wish I was coming with you, Mrs Courtney,' he said. 'Twenty years ago nothing would have stopped me.'

She smiled. 'Hold thumbs for us. If we don't get those diamonds back you'll probably be working for De Beers again and I'll be doing needlework in the poorhouse.'

'Rot the swine who did this to you,' he said. 'Bring him back in chains.'

Centaine went up onto the gelding's back and he felt good and steady under her. She kneed him up beside Blaine's horse.

'You can slip your hunting dogs, Mrs Courtney.' He smiled at her.

'Take us to the water, Kwi,' she called, and the two little Bushmen, their bows and quivers of poisoned arrows on their naked backs, turned to face the east. Their small heads covered with peppercorns of dark wool bobbing, their tight round buttocks bulging out from their brief loincloths and neat childlike feet flying, they went away. They were born to run, and the horses extended into a trot to hold them in sight.

Centaine and Blaine rode side by side at the head of the column. The sergeant and his four troopers followed in single file, each of them trailing two spare horses on lead reins. The spare horses carried water, twenty gallons in big felt-covered round bottles, three days' supply if they used it with care, for men and animals were desert-hardened.

Centaine and Blaine rode in silence, though every once in a while she glanced at him out of the corner of her eye. Impressive on his feet, Blaine was imperial in the saddle. Mounted he had become a centaur, part of the horse beneath him, and she saw now how he had earned his international reputation as a polo player.

Watching him she found herself correcting little flaws in her own carriage and seat on the horse, bad habits which she had drifted into over the years, until she looked as good as he did in the saddle. She felt she could ride for ever across this desert she loved with this man at her side.

They crossed the ridge of weathered shale and Blaine spoke for the first time. 'You were right. We would never have got the trucks across there. It had to be on horseback.'

'We haven't hit the calcrete yet, and then there is the sand. We'd be forever digging out the wheels,' she agreed.

The miles drifted back behind them. The Bushmen bobbed ahead of them, never wavering but running straight and certain towards their distant goal. Every hour Blaine halted the column and let the horses blow while he dismounted and went back to talk quietly to his men, getting to know them, checking the panniers on the spare horses, making certain that they were not galling, taking precautions to avert fatigue and injury before they arose. Then when the five minutes was up he ordered them forward again at the trot.

They rode until it was fully dark before he halted them; then he supervised the issue of water and made sure the horses were rubbed down and knee-haltered before he came to the small fire at which Centaine sat. She had completed her own chores, seeing the Bushmen fed and settled for the night, and now she was preparing the meal for Blaine and herself. She handed him the mess tin as he squatted opposite her.

'I regret, sir, that the pheasant and caviar is off the menu. However, I can heartily recommend the bully beef stew.'

'Strange how good it tastes when you eat it like this.' He ate with honest appetite, then scrubbed the empty plate with dry sand and handed it back to her. He lit a cheroot with a twig from the fire. 'And how good a cheroot tastes with a trace of woodsmoke.'

She tidied and packed for a quick start in the morning and then came back to the fire and hesitated as she reached her seat opposite him. He moved over on the saddle cloth on which he was sitting, leaving half of it free, and without a word she crossed to it and sat with her legs curled up under her. Only inches separated them.

'It's so beautiful,' she murmured, looking up at the night sky. 'The stars are so close. I feel I could reach up and pluck them, and wear them around my neck like a garland of wild flowers.'

'Poor stars,' he said softly. 'They would pale into insignificance.'

She turned her head and smiled at him, letting the compliment lie between them, savouring it for a moment before she lifted her face to the sky again. 'That is my personal star.' She pointed out Acrux in the Great Cross. Michael had chosen it for her. Michael – she felt a sting of guilt at his memory, but it was not so sharp now.

'Which is your star?' she asked.

'Should I have one?'

'Oh, yes,' she nodded. 'It's absolutely essential.' She paused, then went on almost shyly, 'Would you let me choose one for you?'

'I would be honoured.' He wasn't mocking her, he was serious as she was.

'There.' She swivelled towards the north, where the path of the Zodiac was blazed across the sky. 'That star there, Regulus, in the constellation of the Lion, your birth sign. I choose that and I give it to you, Blaine.' She used his given name at last.

'And I accept it most gratefully. Every time I see it from now on, I will think of you, Centaine.'

It was a love token, given and accepted, both of them understood that and they were silenced by the significance of the moment.

'How did you know that my birth sign was Leo?' he asked at last.

'I found out,' she answered guilelessly. 'I thought it was necessary to know. You were born on 28 July 1893.'

'And you,' he replied, 'were born on the first day of the new century. You were named for that. I found out. I also thought it necessary to know.'

They were riding long before it was light the next morning, eastwards again with the Bushmen their harbingers.

The sun rose and its heat crushed down upon them, drying the sweat upon the horses' flanks into white salt crystals. The troopers rode hunched down as though under a heavy burden. The sun swung through its zenith and slid down into the west. Their shadows stretched out on the earth ahead of them and colour returned to the desert, shades of ochre and peachy rose and burnt amber.

Ahead of them Kwi stopped suddenly and snuffled the dry flinty air with his flattened nostrils. Fat Kwi imitated him, like a pair of gundogs scenting the pheasant.

'What are they doing?' Blaine asked, as they reined up behind. Before she could answer, Kwi let out a piping cry and then went away at a full run, Fat Kwi streaking after him.

'Water.' Centaine stood in the stirrups. 'They have smelled the water.'

'Are you serious?' he stared at her.

'I couldn't believe it the first time,' she laughed. 'O'wa could smell it from five miles. Come on, I'll prove it to you.' She urged the gelding into a canter.

Ahead of them a low irregularity in the terrain appeared out of the dusty haze, a hillock of purple shale, bare of all vegetation except for a strange antediluvian tree on its summit, a kokerboom with bark like a reptile's skin.

Centaine felt a pang of memory and nostalgia. She recognized the place. She had last been here with the two little yellow people she had loved, and Shasa heavy in her womb.

Before they reached the hillock, Kwi and Fat Kwi broke their run and stopped, side by side, to examine the earth at their feet. They were chattering excitedly when Centaine rode up, and she translated for Blaine, her tongue tripping with her own excitement.

'We have cut the spoor. It's De La Rey, no doubt about it. Three riders coming up from the south heading for the fountain. They have abandoned their used-up horses, and they're riding hard, pushing their mounts to the limit. The horses are floundering already. De La Rey has judged it finely.'

Centaine could barely contain her relief. She had guessed right. Lothar was heading for the Portuguese border after all. He and the diamonds were not far ahead of them.

'How long, Kwi?' she demanded anxiously, springing down to examine the spoor for herself.

'This morning, Nam Child,' the little Bushman told her, pointing to the sky, showing where the sun had stood when Lothar passed.

'Just after dawn. We are eight hours or so behind them,' she told Blaine.

'That's a lot to make up.' He looked serious. 'Every minute we can save will count from now on. Troop forward!'

When they were half a mile from the hillock with its kokerboom crest, Centaine told Blaine, 'There have been other horses grazing around here. A large troop of them over many weeks. Their sign is everywhere. It was just as we guessed, De La Rey has had one of his men herding them here. We should find further evidence of that at the waterhole.' She broke off and peered ahead. There were three dark amorphous heaps lying at the base of the hill.

'What are they?' Blaine was as puzzled as she was. Only when they rode up did they realize what they were.

'Dead horses!' Centaine exclaimed. 'De La Rey must have shot his used-up horses.'

'No.' Blaine had dismounted to examine the carcasses. 'No bullet holes.'

Centaine looked around. She saw the primitive stockade in which the fresh horses had been kept awaiting Lothar's arrival and the small thatched hut where the man left to tend them had lived.

'Kwi,' she called to the Bushman. 'Find the spoor going away from here. Fat Kwi, search the camp. Look for anything which will tell us more about these evil men that we are chasing.' Then she urged her gelding towards the fountain head.

It lay beneath the hillock. Subterranean water had been trapped between strata of the impervious purple shale and brought to the surface here. The hooves of wild game and the bare feet of San people who had drunk here over the millennia had worn down the shale banks. The water lay fifteen feet down in the bottom of a steep conical depression.

On the side nearest the hillock a layer of shale overhung the pool like the roof of a verandah, shading the water from direct rays of the sun, cooling it and protecting it from rapid evaporation. It was a tiny clear pool, not much larger than a bath tub, fed constantly by the upwelling from the earth. From experience, Centaine knew that it was brackish with dissolved minerals and salts, and strongly tainted with the droppings and urine of the birds and animals that drank from the spring.

The pool itself held her attention for only a second, and then she stiffened in the saddle and her hand flew to her mouth, an instinctive expression of her horror as she stared at the crude manmade structure that had been erected on the bank at the edge of the pool.

A thick branch of camel-thorn had been peeled of its bark and planted in the hard earth as a signpost. At its base rocks had been piled in a pyramid to support it, and on its summit an empty half-gallon can had been placed like a helmet. Below the can a plank was nailed to the post, and on it were burned black charred words, probably written with the tip of a ramrod heated in the fire:

THIS WELL IS POISONED

The empty can was bright red with a black skull and crossbones device and below that the dreaded title:

ARSENIC

Blaine had come up beside her and they were both so silent that Centaine imagined she could hear the shale beneath them ticking softly like a cooling oven, then Blaine spoke:

'The dead horses,' he said, 'that accounts for it. The dirty bastard.' His voice crackled with outrage. He pulled his horse around and galloped across to join the troop. Centaine heard him calling, 'Sergeant. Check the water that is left. The well is poisoned,' and Sergeant Hansmeyer whistled softly.

'Well, that's the end of the chase. We will be lucky to get back to Kalkrand again.'

Centaine found she was trembling with anger and frustration. 'He is going to get clean away,' she told herself. 'He has won on the first trick.'

The gelding smelled the water and tried to get down the bank. She forced him away with her knees, slapping him across the neck with the loose end of the reins. She tethered him at the end of the horse line and measured a ration of oats and mash into his nose bag.

Blaine came to her. 'I'm sorry, Centaine,' he said quietly. 'We'll have to turn back. To go on without water is suicide.'

'I know.'

'It's a pretty filthy trick.' He shook his head. 'Poisoning a water-hole that supports so much desert life. The destruction will be horrible. I have only seen it done once before. When we were on the march up from Walvis in 1915—' he broke off as little Kwi came trotting up to them chattering excitedly. 'What does he say?' Blaine asked.

'One of the men we are following is sick,' Centaine answered quickly. 'Kwi has found these bandages.'

Kwi had a double handful of stained and soiled cloth which he offered to Centaine.

'Put them down, Kwi,' she ordered sharply. She could smell the pus and corruption on the bundle. Obediently Kwi set it down at her feet, and Blaine drew the bayonet from its scabbard on his belt to spread the strips of cloth on the sand.

'The mask!' Centaine exclaimed, as she recognized the flour sack that Lothar had worn over his head. It was stiff with dried blood and yellow pus, as were the strips torn from a khaki shirt.

'The sick man lay down while the other changed the saddles to the new horses, and then they had to lift him to his feet and help him to mount.' Kwi had read all this from the spoor.

'I bit him,' Centaine said softly. 'While we were struggling I sank my teeth into his wrist. I felt the bone. It was a very deep wound I gave him.'

'A human bite is almost as dangerous as a snake bite,' Blaine nodded. 'Untreated it will nearly always turn to blood-poisoning. De La Rey is a sick man, and his arm must be a mess, judging by these.' He touched the reeking bandages with the toe of his riding-boot. 'We would have had him. In his condition, we would almost certainly have caught him before he reached the Okavango river. If only we had enough water to go on.' He turned away, unwilling to watch her unhappiness, and he spoke sharply to Sergeant

Hansmeyer. 'Half water rations from now on, Sergeant. We will start back to the mission at nightfall. Travel in the cool of the night.'

Centaine could not stand still. She whirled and strode back towards the water-hole, and stood at the top of the bank staring at the notice board with its fatal message.

'How could you do it, Lothar?' she whispered. 'You are a hard and desperate man, but this is a dreadful thing—'

She went slowly down the steep bank and squatted at the edge of the water. She reached out and touched the water with her fingertip. It was cold, cold as death, she thought, and wiped the finger carefully on the leg of her breeches as she stared into the pool.

She thought about Blaine's remark, 'I have only seen it done once before. When we were on the march up from Walvis in 1915,' and suddenly a forgotten conversation sprang up from deep in her mind where it had lain buried all these years. She remembered Lothar De La Rey's face in the firelight, his eyes haunted as he confessed to her.

'We had to do it, or at least at the time I thought we did. The Union forces were pressing us so hard. If I had guessed at the consequences—' He had broken off and stared into the fire. She had loved him so dearly then. She had been his woman. Though she did not yet know it, she already had his child in her womb, and she had reached out and taken his hand to comfort him.

'It doesn't matter,' she had whispered, but he had turned a tragic face to her.

'It does matter, Centaine,' he had told her. 'It was the foulest thing I have ever done. I returned to the water-hole a month later like a murderer. I could smell it from a mile or more. The dead were everywhere, zebra and gemsbok, jackals and little desert foxes, birds, even the vultures that had feasted on the rotting carcasses. So much death. It was something that I will remember on the day I die, the one thing in my life of which I am truly ashamed, something I will have to answer for.'

Centaine straightened up slowly. She felt her rage and disappointment slowly snuffed out by a rising tide of excitement. She touched the water again and watched the circle of ripples spread out across the limpid surface.

'He meant it,' she spoke aloud. 'He was truly ashamed. He could never have done the same thing again.' She shivered with dread as she decided what she was going to do, and to bolster her courage she went on in a voice that shook slightly, 'It's a bluff. The notice is a bluff. It must be—' then she broke off as she remembered the three dead horses. 'He put them down. They were finished, and he used poison on them as part of the bluff. Probably gave it to them in a bucket, but not the water-hole. He wouldn't have done that twice.'

Slowly she took the hat from her head and used the wide brim to skim the floating layer of dust and rubbish from the surface of the pool. Then she scooped a hatful of the clear cool water, holding it in both hands, steeling herself to do it. She took a deep breath and touched the water with her lips.

'Centaine!' Blaine roared in shock and rage as he bounded down the bank and snatched the hat out of her hands. The water splashed over her legs soaking her breeches. He seized her by the arms and jerked her to her feet. His face was swollen and dark, his eyes blazing with anger as he shouted in her face. 'Have you gone stark staring mad, woman?'

He was shaking her brutally, his fingers digging into the flesh of her upper arms.

'Blaine, you are hurting me.'

'Hurting you? I could willingly thrash you, you crazy—'

'Blaine, it's a bluff, I'm sure of it.' She was frightened of him. His rage was a terrible thing to watch. 'Blaine. Please! Please listen to me.'

She saw the change in his eyes as he regained control. 'Oh God,' he said, 'I thought—'

'You are hurting me,' she repeated stupidly, and he released her.

'I'm sorry.' He was panting as though he had run a marathon. 'Don't do that to me again, woman – next time I don't know what I will do.'

'Blaine! Listen to me. It's a bluff. He didn't poison the water. I would stake my life on it.'

'You almost did,' he growled at her, but he was listening now. 'How did you reach that conclusion?' He leaned closer to her, interested and ready to be convinced.

'I knew him once. Knew him well. I heard him make an oath. It was he who poisoned the water-hole you talked about, back in 1915. He admitted it, but he swore that he would never be able to do it again. He described the carnage at the water-hole, and he swore an oath.'

'The dead horses lying out there,' Blaine demanded, 'how do you explain them?'

'All right. He poisoned them. He would have to have destroyed them anyway. They were broken; he couldn't leave them for the lions.'

He strode to the edge of the water and stared down into it.

'You were going to take that chance—' he broke off and shuddered, then turned from the water and called sharply.

'Sergeant Hansmeyer!'

'Sir.' The sergeant hurried across from the horse lines.

'Sergeant, bring the lame mare to me,' and Hansmeyer went to the lines and led the animal back. She was favouring her right fore and they would have to leave her anyway.

'Let her drink!' Blaine ordered.

'Sir?' Hansmeyer looked puzzled, and then when he realized Blaine's intention, he became alarmed. 'From the spring? It's poisoned, sir.'

'That's what we are going to find out,' Blaine told him grimly. 'Let her drink!'

Eagerly the black mare scrambled down the bank and bent her long neck to the pool.

She sucked up the water in great gulps. It sloshed and gurgled into her belly, and she seemed to swell before their eyes.

'I didn't think to use one of the horses,' Centaine whispered. 'Oh, it will be terrible if I have guessed wrongly.'

Hansmeyer let the mare drink until she was satiated, and then Blaine ordered, 'Take her back to the lines.'

He checked his wristwatch. 'We'll give her an hour,' he decided, and took Centaine's hand. He led her to the shade thrown by the overhang of the bank and they sat together.

'You say you knew him?' he asked at last. 'How well did you know him?'

'He worked for me – years ago. He did the first development work at the mine. He is an engineer, you know.'

'Yes. I know he is an engineer. It's in his file.' He was silent. 'You must have got to know him very well for him to admit something like that to you? It's a very intimate thing, a man's guilt.'

She did not reply. 'What can I tell him?' she thought. 'That I was Lothar De La Rey's mistress? That I loved him and bore him a son?'

Suddenly Blaine chuckled. 'Jealousy is really one of the most unlovely emotions, isn't it? I withdraw the question. It was impertinent. Forgive me.'

She laid her hand on his arm and smiled at him gratefully.

'That doesn't mean I have forgiven you for the fright you gave me,' he told her with mock severity. 'I could still quite happily turn you over my knee.'

The thought of it gave her a funny little perverse twinge of excitement. His rage had frightened her and that excited her also. He had not shaved since they had left the mission.

His new beard was thick and dark as the pelt of an otter, except there was a single silver hair in it. It grew at the corner of his mouth, shining like a star in the night.

'What are you staring at?' he asked.

'I was wondering if your beard would scratch – if you decided to kiss me instead of spanking me.'

She saw him struggling like a drowning man in a rip tide of temptation. She imagined the fears and the doubts and the anguish of wanting that boiled behind those green eyes, and she waited, her face turned up to him, neither pulling back nor thrusting forward, waiting for him to accept the inevitability of it.

When he took her mouth it was fiercely, almost roughly, as though he was angry with his own inability to resist, and angry with her for leading him into this dangerous wilderness of infidelity. He sucked all the strength out of her body so that she went limp in his arms, only the grip of her own arms around his neck matched his and her mouth was deep and wet and soft and open for him to probe.

He broke away from her at last and sprang to his feet. He stood over her, looking down at her. 'May God have pity on us,' he whispered, and strode away up the bank, leaving her alone with her joy and disquiet and guilt and with the raging flame he had kindled in her belly.

Sergeant Hansmeyer summoned her at last. He came to the pool and stood at the top of the bank.

'Colonel Malcomess is asking for you, Missus.'

She followed him back to the horse lines, and she felt strangely detached from reality. Her feet seemed not to touch the earth and everything was dreamlike and far away.

Blaine stood with the lame mare, holding her head and stroking her neck. She made little fluttering sounds in her nostrils and nibbled at the front of his tunic. Blaine looked over her head as Centaine came up on the mare's other side. They stared at each other.

'No turning back,' he said softly, and she accepted the ambiguity of his words. 'We go forward – together.'

'Yes, Blaine,' she agreed meekly.

'And to hell with the consequences,' he said harshly.

A second longer they held each other's eyes, and then Blaine lifted his voice. 'Sergeant, water all the horses and fill the bottles. We have nine hours to make up on the chase.'

They kept going through the night. The little Bushmen stayed on the spoor with only the stars and a sliver of moon to light it for them, and when the sun rose the tracks were still strung out ahead of them, each filled with purple shadow by the acutely slanted rays.

Now there were four riders in the fleeing band, for the horse herder from the fountain had joined them and they were leading a spare horse each.

An hour after dawn, they found where the fugitives had camped the previous night. Lothar had abandoned two of his horses here; they had broken down from the brutal treatment, hard riding in these severe conditions. They stood beside the remains of the camp fire which Lothar had smothered with sand. Kwi brushed away the sand and knelt to blow on the ashes, a tiny flame sprang up under his breath and he grinned like a pixie.

'We have made up five or six hours on them while they slept,' Blaine murmured, and looked at Centaine. She straightened up immediately from her weary slump but she was pale and light-headed with fatigue.

'He's using up his horses like a prodigal,' she said, and they both looked at the two animals that Lothar had abandoned. They stood with heads hanging, muzzles almost touching the ground, a pair of chestnut mares, one with a white blazed forehead and the other with white socks. Both of them moved only with pain and difficulty, and their tongues were black and swollen, protruding from the sides of their mouths.

'He did not waste water on them,' Blaine agreed. 'Poor devils.'

'You will have to put them down,' Centaine said.

'That's why he left them, Centaine,' he said gently.

'I don't understand.'

'The shots,' he explained. 'He'll be listening for gun-fire—'

'Oh Blaine! What are we going to do? We can't leave them.'

'Make coffee and breakfast. We are all played out – horses and men. We must rest for a few hours before we go on.' He swung down from the saddle and untied his blanket roll. 'In the meantime I will take care of the cripples.'

He shook out his sheepskin underblanket as he walked across to the first mare. He stopped in front of her and unbuckled the flap of his holster. He drew his service pistol and wrapped the sheepskin over his right hand that held the pistol.

The mare dropped instantly to the muted thud of the pistol, and kicked spasmodically before relaxing into still-ness. Centaine looked away, busying herself with measuring coffee into the billy as Blaine walked heavily across to the blazed chestnut mare.

There was a tiny movement of air, not truly a sound, light as the flirt of a sunbird's wing, but both Swart Hendrick and Lothar De La Rey lifted their heads and pulled up their mounts. Lothar raised his hand for silence and they waited, holding their breath.

It came again, another spit of distant muted gunfire, and Lothar and Hendrick glanced at each other.

'The arsenic trick did not work,' grunted the big black Ovambo. 'You should have really poisoned the water, not pretended,' and Lothar shook his head wearily.

'She must be riding like a she-devil. They are only four hours behind us, less if they push their horses. I never believed she could come on so quickly.'

'You cannot be sure that it is her,' Hendrick told him.

'It's her.' Lothar showed no trace of doubt. 'She promised me she would come.' His voice was hoarse, his lips cracked and flaky with dry skin. His eyes were bloodshot, gummed with yellow mucus thick as clotted cream and deeply underscored with bruised purple smudges. His beard was parti-coloured, gold and ginger and white.

His arm was wrapped in bandage to the elbow, the yellow discharge had seeped through the cloth. He had looped a cartridge belt around his neck as a sling, and the arm was supported partly by the belt and partly by the black japanned despatch case strapped to the pommel of his saddle.

He turned to look back across the plain with its sparse covering of scrub and camel-thorn, but the movement brought on another wave of giddiness and he swayed and snatched at the despatch case to prevent himself falling.

'Pa!' Manfred grabbed his good arm, his face contorted with concern. 'Pa! Are you all right?'

Lothar closed his eyes before he could answer. 'All right,' he croaked. He could feel the infection swelling and distorting the flesh of his hand and forearm. The skin felt thin and stretched to the point of bursting like an overripe plum, and the heat of the poison flowed with his blood. He could feel it throbbing painfully in the glands below his armpit and from there spreading out through his whole body, squeezing the sweat out through his skin, burning his eyes and pounding in his temples, shimmering a desert mirage in his brain.

'Go on,' he whispered. 'Got to go on,' and Hendrick

picked up the lead rein with which he was guiding Lothar's horse.

'Wait!' blurted Lothar, rocking in the saddle. 'How far to the next water?'

'We'll be there before noon tomorrow.'

Lothar was trying to concentrate but the fever filled his head with steam and heat.

'The horse irons. It's time for the horse irons.'

Hendrick nodded. They had carried the horse irons from the cache in the hills. They weighed seventy pounds, a heavy burden for one of the lead horses. It was time to be rid of some of that weight now.

'We'll give her a bait to lead her onto them,' Lothar croaked.

The short rest, the hasty meal and even the strong, hot, oversweetened coffee seemed only to have increased Centaine's fatigue.

'I will not let him see it,' she told herself firmly. 'I'll not give in until they do.' But her skin felt so dry that it might tear like paper and the glare ached in her eyes, filling her skull with pain.

She glanced sideways at Blaine. He sat straight and tall in the saddle, invincible and indefatigable, but he turned his head and his eyes softened as he looked at her.

'We'll break for a drink in ten minutes,' he told her softly.

'I'm all right,' she protested.

'We are all tired,' he said. 'There is no shame in admitting it.' He broke off and shaded his eyes, peering ahead.

'What is it?' she demanded.

'I'm not sure.' He lifted the binoculars that hung on his chest and focused them on the dark blob far ahead that had caught his attention. 'I still can't recognize what it is.' He passed the glasses to her and Centaine stared through them.

'Blaine!' she exclaimed. 'The diamonds! It's the diamond case! They have dropped the diamonds.'

Her fatigue fell away from her like a discarded cape and before he could stop her she put her heels into her gelding's flanks and urged him into a gallop, overtaking the Bushmen. The two spare horses were forced to follow her, straining on their lead reins, the water bottles bouncing wildly on their backs.

'Centaine!' Blaine shouted, and spurred his mount after her, trying to catch her.

Sergeant Hansmeyer had been drooping in the saddle, but he roused himself instantly as the two leaders galloped away.

'Troop, forward!' he shouted, and the whole party was tearing ahead.

Suddenly Centaine's gelding screamed with agony and reared under her. She was almost thrown from the saddle, but recovered her balance with a fine feat of horsemanship, and then the spare horses were whinnying and kicking and lashing out in agony. Blaine tried to turn out, but he was too late and his mount broke down under him, his spare horses shrieking and bucking on their leads.

'Halt!' he screamed, turning desperately to try and stop Sergeant Hansmeyer's charge, signalling him with both arms. 'Halt! Troop, halt!' The Sergeant reacted swiftly, swinging his mount to block the troopers who followed him, and they came up short in a tangle of milling, tramping horses, the dust swirling over them in a fine mist.

Centaine sprang down from the saddle and checked her gelding's front legs, they were both sound and she lifted a rear hoof and stared in disbelief. A burr of rusted iron was stuck to the frog of the gelding's hoof and dark blood was already pouring from the wound it had inflicted, mingling into a muddy paste with the fine desert dust.

Gingerly Centaine took hold of the metal rose and tried to pull it away, but it was buried deeply and the gelding trembled with the pain. She tugged and twisted, carefully avoiding the protruding spikes, and at last the horrible thing came free in her hand, wet with the gelding's blood. She straightened and looked across at Blaine. He also had been busy with his own mount's feet and held two of the bloody irons in his hands.

'Horse irons,' Blaine told her. 'I haven't seen the cruel damned things since the war.' They were crudely forged, shaped like the ubiquitous devil thorns of the African veld, four pointed stars aligned so that one point was always standing upright. Three inches of sharp iron that would cripple man or beast, or would slash the tyres of a following vehicle.

Centaine looked around and saw that the earth all around where she stood was strewn with the wicked spikes. Dust had been lightly brushed over them to conceal them from casual observation but had in no way reduced their effectiveness.

Quickly she stooped again to the task of ridding all three of her horses of the spikes. The gelding had picked them up in both rear hooves and the spare horses had three and two hooves damaged. She plucked the iron spikes from their flesh and hurled them away angrily.

Sergeant Hansmeyer had dismounted his troopers and they came up to assist her and Blaine, stepping cautiously for the spikes would readily penetrate the soles of their boots. They cleared a narrow corridor through which the horses could be led back to safe ground, but all six of them had been brutally maimed. They hobbled slowly and painfully, reluctant to touch the earth with their damaged hooves.

'Six of them,' Blaine whispered bitterly. 'Wait until I get my hands on that bastard.' He drew the .303 rifle from the scabbard on his saddle and ordered Hansmeyer, 'Put our saddles onto two of your spare horses. Top up all the water bottles from those on the crippled horses. Have two of your troopers mark a path around the area of the horse irons. Move it quickly! We can't waste a minute.'

Centaine left them and went forward, cautiously circling around the booby-trapped patch of earth. She reached the black japanned despatch case which had deceived her and picked it up. The lid flapped open, the lock smashed by Lothar's bullet, and she turned the case upside down. It was empty. She let it drop and looked back.

Blaine's men had worked swiftly. Their saddles had been transferred to undamaged horses. They had chosen a black gelding for her and Sergeant Hansmeyer was leading it. The whole troop was circling out in single file, leaning out of the saddle to check for any more horse irons in their path. She knew that from now on they would not be able to relax for a moment, for she knew that Lothar would not have laid all his spikes. They would find more along the spoor.

Hansmeyer came up beside her. 'We are ready to go, ma'am.' He handed her the reins to the fresh horse and she mounted, then they all looked back.

Blaine stood with the Lee Enfield rifle on his hip, and with his back turned to them faced the line of six crippled horses. He seemed to be praying, or perhaps he was merely steeling himself, but his head was bowed.

He lifted it slowly and threw the butt of the rifle to his shoulder. He fired without lowering the rifle, his right hand flicking the bolt back and forth, and the shots crashing out in rapid succession, blending into a long-drawn-out drum-roll of sound. The horses fell on top of one another, in a twitching, jerking pile. He turned away then, and even at that distance Centaine glimpsed his expression.

She found she was weeping. The tears poured down her

face, and she could not stop them. Blaine rode up beside her. He glanced at her, and when he saw her tears, he stared straight ahead, letting her get over it.

'We have lost nearly an hour,' he said. 'Troop forward!'

Twice more before nightfall the Bushman stopped the column and they had to pick their way cautiously around a scattering of the wicked spikes. Each time it cost them precious minutes.

'We are losing ground,' Blaine estimated. 'They heard the rifle shots and they are alerted. They know they have got fresh horses waiting somewhere ahead. They are pushing harder – much harder than we dare.'

T he country changed with dramatic suddenness as they emerged from the wastes of Bushmanland into the gently wooded more benevolent Kavango area.

Along the undulating ridges of the ancient compacted dunes grew tall trees, combretum the lovely bush willow, and albizia with its fine feathery foliage, and stands of young mopani between them. The shallow valleys were covered with fine desert grasses whose silver and pink seed heads brushed their stirrup irons as they rode through.

The water was not far below the surface here and all Nature seemed to respond to its presence. For the first time since leaving the mission at Kalkrand, they saw large game, zebra and redgolden impala, and they knew that the waterhole for which they were riding could be only a few miles ahead for these animals would drink daily.

It was not too soon for all the horses were used up and weak, struggling onwards beneath the weight of their riders. A few inches remained in the water bottles, seeming to mock their thirst with hollow gurgles at each pace.

Lothar De La Rey could not remain in the saddle unaided. Swart Hendrick rode on one side of him and his bastard son Klein Boy on the other. They supported him when sudden bouts of delirium overcame him and he laughed and ranted and would have slipped from the saddle and tumbled to earth. Manfred trailed behind them, watching his father anxiously, but too exhausted and thirsty to assist him.

They struggled up another rise in the endless succession of consolidated dunes, and Swart Hendrick stood in the stirrups and peered down into the gentle basin ahead of them, barely daring to hope that they had been able to ride directly to their destination through the trackless land where every vista mirrored the previous one and the one that followed. All they had to steer by was the sun and the instinct of the desert creature.

Then his spirits soared, for ahead of them there were the tall grey mopani trunks nurtured into giants by the water over which they stood and the four great umbrella acacia exactly as they had been imprinted in his memory. Between their trunks Hendrick caught the soft sheen of standing water.

The horses managed a last jolting trot down the slope and through the trees, and then out over the bare clay that surrounded the shrunken puddle of water in the centre.

The water was the colour of *café au lait*, not ten paces across at the widest point nor deeper than a man's knee. Around it the hoofprints and pad marks of dozens of various types of wild animals – from the tiny multiple V scratches of quail and francolin to the huge round prints of a bull elephant the size of dustbin lids – had been sculpted into the black clay and then baked by the sun as hard as concrete.

Hendrick and Klein Boy drove their mounts into the centre of the pool and then flung themselves face down into the lukewarm muddy water, snorting and gasping and laughing wildly as they scooped it into their mouths.

Manfred helped his father to dismount at the edge, and

then ran to scoop a hatful and bring it to Lothar where he had collapsed into a sitting position, supporting himself on his own knees.

Lothar drank greedily, choking and coughing as the water went down the wrong way. His face was flushed and swollen, his eyes fever-bright and the poison in his blood burning him up.

Swart Hendrick waded to the side, his boots squelching and water pouring from his sodden clothing, still grinning – until a thought struck him and he stopped. The grin was gone from his thick black lips and he glared about him.

'Nobody here,' he grunted. 'Buffalo and Legs – where are they?' He broke into a run, spraying water at each pace as he headed for the primitive hut that stood in the shade of the nearest umbrella acacia.

It was empty and derelict. The charcoal of the camp-fire was scattered widely; the freshest signs were days – no, weeks old. He raged through the forest, and at last came back to Lothar. Between them Klein Boy and Manfred had helped Lothar into the shade and he lay back against the trunk of the acacia.

'They've deserted.' Lothar anticipated Hendrick's report. 'I should have known. Ten horses, worth fifty pounds each. It was too much temptation.' The rest and the water seemed to have strengthened him; he was lucid again.

'They must have run away within days of us leaving them.' Hendrick sank down beside him. 'Surely they have taken the horses and sold them to the Portuguese, then gone home to their wives.'

'Promise me that when you see them again you will kill them slowly, Hendrick, very slowly.'

'I dream of how I will do it,' Hendrick whispered. 'First I will make them eat their own manhoods, I will cut them off with a blunt knife and I will feed them to them in small pieces.'

They were both silent, staring at the small group of their

four horses which stood at the pool's edge. Their bellies were distended with water but their heads were hanging pathetically, noses almost touching the baked clay.

'Seventy miles to the river, seventy miles at least.' Lothar broke the silence, and he began to unwrap the filthy rags that covered his arm.

The swelling was grotesque. His hand was the size and shape of a ripe melon. The fingers stuck stiffly out of the blue ball of flesh. The swelling carried up the forearm to the elbow, trebling the girth of his lower limb, and the skin had burst open and clear lymph leaked out of the tears. The bite wounds were deep, slimy, yellow pits, the edges flared open like the petals of a flower, and the smell of infection was sweet and thick as oil in Lothar's own nostrils and throat, disgusting him.

Above the elbow the swelling was not so intense, but there were livid scarlet lines beneath the skin running right up to Lothar's shoulder. He reached up and gently explored the swollen glands in his armpit. They were hard as musket balls buried in his flesh.

'Gangrene,' he told himself, and he realized now that the carbolic acid solution with which he had originally cleansed the bite wounds had aggravated the condition. 'Too strong,' he muttered. 'Too strong solution.' It had destroyed the capillary vessels around the wound, preparing the way for the gangrene that had followed. 'The hand should come off.' He faced the fact at last, and for a moment he even considered attempting the operation himself. He imagined starting at the elbow joint and cutting –

'I can't do it,' he decided. 'I can't even think of it. I have to go on as far as the gangrene will let me, for Manie's sake.' He looked up at the boy.

'I need bandages.' He tried to make his voice firm and reassuring, but it came out as a raven's croak, and the boy started and tore his eyes from the ravaged limb.

Lothar dusted the suppurating wounds with carbolic crystals – all that he had – and bound them up with strips of blanket. They had used up all their extra clothing for bandages.

'How far is she behind us, Henny?' he asked, as he knotted the bandage.

'We have won time,' Hendrick guessed. 'They must be saving their horses. But look at ours.'

One of the animals had lain down at the edge of the water, the sign of capitulation.

'Five or six hours behind us.' And it was seventy miles to the river, with no guarantee that the pursuers would honour the border and not pursue them across. Lothar did not have to voice those doubts; they were all too aware of them.

'Manfred,' he whispered. 'Bring the diamonds.' The boy placed the canvas haversack beside Lothar and he unpacked it carefully.

There were twenty-eight of the small brown cartridge paper packages with their red wax seals. Lothar separated them into four piles, seven packages in each.

'Equal shares,' he said. 'We cannot value each package, so we will cut them four ways and give the youngest first pick.' He looked across at Hendrick. 'Agreed?'

Swart Hendrick understood that the sharing of the booty was at last an admission that not all of them were going to reach the river. Hendrick lowered his eyes from Lothar's face. He and this golden-haired, white-skinned devil had been together since the far-off time of their youth. He had never considered what held them together. He felt a deep, unwavering antagonism and distrust towards all white men except this one. They had dared so much, seen so much, shared so much. He did not think of it as love or as friendship. Yet the thought of the parting which lay just ahead filled him with a devastating despair, as though a little death awaited him.

'Agreed,' he said, in that deep resonant tone, like the chime of a bass bell, and he looked up at the white boy. The man and the boy were one unit in Hendrick's mind. What he felt for the father was also for the son.

'Choose, Manie,' he ordered.

'I don't know.' Manfred put both hands behind his back, reluctant to touch one of the piles.

'Do it,' snapped his father, and obediently he reached out and touched the nearest pile.

'Pick them up,' Lothar ordered, and then looked at the black youth. 'Choose, Klein Boy.'

There were two piles left, and Lothar grinned through cracked lips. 'How old are you, Henny?'

'As old as the burned mountain, as young as the first flower of spring,' the Ovambo said, and they both laughed.

'If I had a diamond for every time we have laughed together,' Hendrick thought, 'I would be the richest man in the world.' And it required an effort to keep the smile on his face. 'You must be younger than I am,' he spoke aloud. 'For I have always had to care for you like a nursemaid. Choose!'

Lothar shoved his chosen pile across to Manfred. 'Put it in the haversack,' he told him, and Manfred packed their share of the booty into the canvas bag and strapped it closed while the two black men filled the pockets of their tunics with their packages.

'Now fill the water bottles. It's only seventy miles to the river,' Lothar said.

When they were ready to leave Hendrick stooped to help Lothar to his feet, but he struck Hendrick's hands away irritably and used the trunk of the acacia to push himself upright.

One of the horses could not rise and they left it lying at the water's edge. Another broke down within the first mile, but the other two limped on gamely. Neither of them could any longer support the full weight of a man, but one carried the water bottles and Lothar used the other as a crutch. He staggered along beside it with his good arm draped over its neck.

The other three men took it in turns to lead the horses, and they trudged on determinedly northwards. Sometimes Lothar laughed without reason and sang in a strong, clear voice, carrying the tune so beautifully that Manfred felt a buoyant rush of relief. But then the singing quavered and his voice broke and cracked. He shouted and raved and pleaded with the fever phantoms that crowded about him, and Manfred ran back to him and circled his waist with a helping arm and Lothar quieted down.

'You are a good boy, Manie,' he whispered. 'You've always been a good boy. We are going to have a wonderful life from now on. A fine school for you, you will become a young gentleman – we'll go to Berlin together, the opera—'

'Oh, Papa, don't talk. Save your strength, Papa.' And Lothar subsided once more into an oppressive silence, toiling on mechanically with his boots dragging and scuffing, and only the labouring horse and his son's strong young arm preventing him from crashing face forward onto the hot Kalahari sands.

Far ahead of them the first of the granite kopjes showed above the sparse heat-blighted forest. It was round as a pearl and the smooth rock glowed silver grey in the sunlight.

Centaine stopped her horse on the crest of the rise and looked down into the basin of land beyond. She recognized the tall trees from the top branches of which, many years before, she had glimpsed her first wild African elephant, and a little of the childlike wonder of that moment had remained with her over all that time.

Then she saw the water, and all else was forgotten. It was not easy to control the horses once they had smelled it. She had heard of desert travellers dying of thirst at the water-hole when they allowed their cattle and horses to rush ahead and trample the water into thick mud. But Blaine and his sergeant were experienced men and controlled them firmly.

As soon as the horses had been watered and picketed, Centaine pulled off her boots and waded fully dressed into the pool, ducking under the surface to soak her clothing and her hair and revelling at the chill of the muddy water.

At the far end of the pool Blaine had stripped to his breeches and was knee-deep, scooping water over his head. Centaine studied him surreptitiously. It was the first time she had seen him bare-chested, and his body hair was thick and dark and springing, sparkling with water droplets. There was a small black mole below the nipple of his right breast, which for no good reason intrigued her, otherwise his body was without blemish; his skin had the sheen of polished marble, like the Michelangelo statue of David, and his muscles were flat and hard-looking. The sun had stained a dark brown V below his throat and his arms were brown up to the distinct lines that his shirtsleeves had left; beyond that his skin was the pale ivory that she found so attractive that she had to look away from it.

As she came up to him he hurriedly pulled on his shirt again, and the water soaked through it in darker patches. His modesty made her smile.

'De La Rey found no spare horses here,' she told him, and he looked puzzled.

'Are you sure?'

'Kwi says that there were two men waiting here with many horses but that they left many days ago. He cannot count beyond the ten fingers on his hand, it was longer than that. Yes, I am sure Lothar De La Rey found no fresh horses.'

Blaine smoothed his wet hair straight back with both hands. 'Then my guess is that something has gone wrong with his plans. He would never have used up his horses like that unless he was expecting to find remounts.'

'Kwi says they have gone ahead on foot. They are leading their remaining horses, and the horses are obviously too weak to carry a man.' She broke off as Kwi called shrilly from the edge of the forest and she and Blaine hurried over to join him.

'They are desperate,' Blaine said, as they saw the pile of abandoned equipment beneath the acacia tree. 'Saddles and canned food, blankets and billy cans.' He turned over the pile with his feet. 'They've even dumped ammunition – and, yes, by God, the last of those damned horse irons.' The small wooden case lay on its side with the last few pounds of the vicious iron spikes spilling from it. 'They have stripped down, and they are making one last desperate run to reach the river.'

'Look here, Blaine,' Centaine called to him, and he went to her and examined the small pile of soiled bandages that lay at her feet.

'His condition is worsening,' Centaine murmured, but strangely there was no gloating in her voice, no triumph in her eyes. 'I think he is a dying man, Blaine.'

Unaccountably he felt the need to commiserate with her, to console her. 'If we can get him to a doctor—' he broke off, the impulse was ludicrous. They were hunting a vicious criminal who, Blaine knew, would not hesitate to shoot him down at the first opportunity.

'Sergeant Hansmeyer,' he called harshly. 'See the men fed and the horses watered again before we leave in an hour.' He turned back to Centaine and saw with relief that she had rallied.

'An hour is not enough – let's see we use every minute of it.'

They sat together in the shade. Neither of them had eaten much; the heat and their fatigue had destroyed their appetite. Blaine took a cheroot from his leather case and then changed his mind. He slipped it back into the case and dropped the case into the pocket of his tunic.

'When I first met you I thought that you were brilliant and adamant and beautiful as one of your own diamonds,' he said.

'And now?' she asked.

'I have seen you weep for maimed horses, and I have sensed in you a deep compassion for a man who has done you cruel injury,' he replied. 'When we left Kalkrand I was in love with you. I suppose I was in love with you from the first hour I met you. I couldn't help that, but now I also like you and respect you.'

'Is that a different thing from love?'

'It is a very different thing from *being* in love,' he affirmed, and they were silent for a while before she tried to explain.

'Blaine, I have been alone for a long time with a small child to protect and to plan for. When I came to this land as a girl, I served a hard, unrelenting apprenticeship in this desert. I learned that there was nobody I could rely upon but myself, no way to survive but through my own strength and determination. That hasn't altered. I still have nobody but myself on whom I can rely. Isn't that so, Blaine?'

'I wish it were not.' He did not attempt to avoid her gaze but looked back at her candidly. 'I wish—'

He broke off and she finished the statement for him. 'But, you have Isabella and your girls.'

He nodded. 'Yes, they cannot fend for themselves.'

'And I can – isn't that right, Blaine?'

'Don't be bitter with me, please. I did not seek this. I have never made you any promises.'

'I'm sorry.' She was immediately contrite. 'You are right.

You have never promised me anything.' She glanced at her watch. 'Our little hour is up,' she said, and rose in a single lithe movement to her feet.

'I shall just have to go on being strong and hard,' she said. 'But never tax me with it again, please Blaine. Never again.'

They had been forced to abandon five of their own horses since leaving the water-hole of the elephant, and Blaine was alternating between walking and riding in an attempt to save the remaining animals. They rode for half an hour and then dismounted and led for the next half hour.

Only the Bushmen were unaffected by the thirst and fatigue and heat, and they chafed at the halting and torturous pace they were forced to adopt.

'The only consolation is that De La Rey is doing even worse than we are.' From the spoor they could read that the fugitives, reduced to a single horse between them, were making even slower progress. 'And it's still thirty miles or more to the river.' Blaine checked his watch. 'Time to walk again, I'm afraid.'

Centaine groaned softly as she swung down from the saddle. She ached in every muscle, and the tendons of her hamstrings and calves felt like twisted wire strands.

They trudged forward and every pace required a conscious effort. Centaine's tongue filled her mouth, thick and leathery, and the mucous membrane of her throat and nostrils was swollen and painful so that it was difficult to breathe. She tried to collect her saliva and hold it in her mouth, but it was gummy and sour, serving only to make her thirst more poignant.

She had forgotten what it was like to be truly thirsty, and the soft sloshing sound of the water bottles on the saddle of the horse she was leading became a torment. She could think of nothing but when they would next be allowed to drink. She kept glancing at her wrist-watch, convincing herself that it had stopped, that she had forgotten to wind it, that at any moment Blaine would lift his arm to halt the column and they could unscrew the stoppers on the water bottles.

Nobody spoke from choice. All orders were terse and monosyllabic, every word an effort.

'I won't be the first to give in,' Centaine decided grimly, and then she was alarmed that the thought had even occurred to her. 'Nobody will give in. We have to catch them before the river and the river is not far ahead.'

She found she was focusing only on the earth at her feet, losing interest in her surroundings, and she knew that was a dangerous sign, the first small surrender. She forced herself to look up. Blaine was ahead of her. She had fallen back in those few paces, and she made a huge effort and dragged her horse forward until she was side by side with him again. Immediately she felt heartened, she had won another victory over her body's frailty.

Blaine smiled at her, but she saw that it had cost him an effort also. 'Those kopjes are not marked on the map,' he said.

She had not noticed them, but now she looked up and a mile ahead saw their smooth bald granite heads raised above the forest. She had never been this far north; it was new territory for her.

'I don't think this country has ever been surveyed,' she whispered, and then cleared her throat and spoke more clearly. 'Only the river itself has been mapped.'

'We will drink when we reach the foot of the nearest hill,' he promised her.

'A carrot for the donkey,' she murmured, and he grinned.

'Think about the river. That is a garden full of carrots.' And they relapsed into silence; the Bushmen led them directly towards the hills. At the base of the granite cone they found the last of Lothar De La Rey's horses.

It lay on its side, but it lifted its head as they walked up to it. Blaine's mare whickered softly, and the downed animal tried to reply but the effort was too much. It dropped its head flat against the earth and its short hampered breathing raised tiny wisps of dust that swirled around its nostrils. The Bushmen circled the dying animal and then conferred excitedly. Kwi ran a short way towards the grey side of the kopje and looked up.

They all followed his example, staring up the steep rounded expanse of granite. It was two or three hundred feet high. The surface was not as smooth as it had appeared at a distance. There were deep cracks, some lateral, others running vertically from the foot to the summit, and the granite was flaking away in the 'onion peel' effect caused by heat expansion and contraction. This left small sharp-edged steps which would give footholds and make it possible for a man to reach the top, though it would be an exposed and potentially dangerous climb.

On the summit a cluster of perfectly round boulders, each the size of a large dwelling house, formed a symmetrical crown. The whole was one of those natural compositions so artful and contrived that it seemed to have been conceived and executed by human engineers. Centaine was strongly reminded of the dolmens which she had visited as a child in France, or of one of those ancient Mayan temples in the South American jungles which she had seen illustrated.

Blaine had left her side and led his mount towards the foot of the granite cliff, and something on the crest of the kopje caught Centaine's eye. It was a flicker of movement in the shadow beneath one of the crowning boulders on the summit, and she shouted a warning.

'Blaine, be careful! On the top—' He was standing at his horse's head with the reins over his shoulder, staring upwards. But before he could respond to her warning there was a thud as though a sack of wheat had been dropped on a stone floor. Centaine did not recognize the sound as a high-velocity bullet striking living flesh until Blaine's horse staggered, its front legs collapsed and it dropped heavily, dragging Blaine with it.

Centaine was stunned until she heard the whiplash crack of the Mauser from the summit of the kopje and she realized that the bullet had reached them before the sound.

All around her the troopers were shouting and wrestling with their panicking horses, and Centaine spun and vaulted for the saddle of her own mount. With one hand on the pommel and without touching the stirrup irons she was up, dragging the horse's head around.

'Blaine, I'm coming,' she screamed. He had scrambled to his feet beside the carcass of his horse, and she rode for him. 'Grab my stirrup,' she called, and the Mausers up on the hill were cracking bullets amongst them. She saw Sergeant Hansmeyer's horse shot dead beneath him and he was pitched headlong from the saddle.

Blaine ran to meet her and seized her dangling stirrup. She turned the horse and heeled him into a full gallop, pumping the reins, heading back for the sparse cover of the mopani two hundred yards behind them.

Blaine was swinging on the stirrup leather, his feet skimming the ground, making giant strides as he kept level with her.

'Are you all right?' she yelled.

'Keep going!' His voice strained at the effort and she looked back under her arm. The gunfire still crackled and snapped around them. One of the troopers turned back to help Sergeant Hansmeyer, but as he reached him a bullet hit his horse in the head and it crashed over and flung the trooper sprawling to earth.

'They are picking off the horses!' Centaine cried, as she realized that hers was the only animal still unscathed. All the others were down, killed with a single shot in the head for each of them. It was superb marksmanship, for the men on the summit were firing downhill at a range of one hundred and fifty paces or more.

Ahead of her Centaine saw a shallow ravine that she had not noticed before. There was a tangle of fallen dead mopani branches upon the nearest bank, a natural palisade, and she rode for it, forcing her winded horse down the bank in a scrambling leap and then immediately springing down and seizing his head to control him.

Blaine had been dragged off his feet and had rolled down the bank, but he pulled himself up. 'I walked into that ambush like a greenhorn,' he snarled, angry at himself. 'Too bloody tired to think straight.' He jerked the rifle out of the scabbard on Centaine's saddle and climbed quickly to the lip of the bank.

Ahead of him the dead horses lay below the steep smooth slope of the kopje, and Sergeant Hansmeyer and his troopers were dodging and jinking as they sprinted back for the cover of the ravine. Mauser-fire crackled, kicking up spouts of yellow dust about their feet, and they winced and ducked at the implosion of air in their eardrums as passing shot whipped about their heads.

Magically the Bushmen had disappeared, like little brown leprechauns, at the first shot. Centaine knew they would not see them again. Already they were on their way back to join their clan at O'chee Pan.

Blaine pushed up the rear sight of the Lee Enfield to four hundred yards and aimed for the crest of the kopje, where a feather of drifting blue gunsmoke betrayed the hidden gunmen. He fired as fast as he could work the bolt, spraying bullets to cover the fleeing troopers, watching white chips of granite burst from the skyline of the kopje as the raking fire withered away. He snatched a clip of ammunition from his bandolier and pressed the brass cartridges into the open breech of the hot rifle, slammed the bolt shut and flung the weapon to his shoulder, and poured fire up at the marksmen on the crest of the kopje.

One by one Hansmeyer and his troopers reached the ravine and tumbled into it, sweating and panting wildly. With grim satisfaction Blaine noticed that each of them had carried his rifle with him, and they wore their bandoliers strapped across their chests, seventy-five rounds a man.

'They shot the horses in the head but never touched a man.'

Hansmeyer's breathing whistled in his throat as he struggled with the words.

'They never fired a shot near me,' Centaine blurted. Lothar must have taken great care not to endanger her. She realized with a tremor just how easily he could have put a bullet into the back of her skull as she fled.

Blaine was reloading the Lee Enfield, but he looked up and smiled humourlessly. 'The fellow is no idiot. He knows that he has shot his bolt, and he is not looking to add murder to the long list of the charges against him.' He looked at Hansmeyer. 'How many men on the kopje?' he demanded.

'I don't know,' Hansmeyer answered. 'But there is more than one. The rate of fire was too much for one man, and I heard shots overlapping.'

'All right, let's find out how many there are.' Blaine beckoned Centaine and Hansmeyer up beside him and explained.

Centaine took his binoculars and moved down the ravine until she was well out on the flank and below a dense tuft of grass which grew on the lip of the ravine. She used the tuft as a screen and raised her head until she could make out the summit of the kopje. She focused the binoculars and called, 'Ready!'

Blaine had his helmet on the ramrod of his rifle, and he lifted it and Hansmeyer fired two shots into the air to draw the attention of the marksmen on the kopje.

Almost immediately the answering fusillade crackled from the hilltop. More than one shot fired simultaneously, and dust kicked off the lip of the ravine inches from the khaki helmet while ricochet howled away over the mopani trees.

'Two or three,' Hansmeyer called.

'Three,' Centaine confirmed, lowering the binoculars as she ducked down. 'I saw three heads.'

'Good.' Blaine nodded. 'We've got them then, just a matter of time.'

'Blaine.' Centaine loosened the strap of her water bottle from the saddle. 'That's all we have got.' She shook the bottle, and it was less than a quarter full. They all stared at it, and involuntarily Blaine licked his lips.

'We will be able to recover the other bottles, just as soon as it's dark,' he assured them, and then briskly, 'Sergeant, take two troopers with you, try and work your way around the other side of the kopje. Make sure nobody leaves by the back door.'

L othar De La Rey sat propped against one of the huge round granite boulders at the top of the kopje. He sat in the shade, with the Mauser across his lap. He was bare-headed and his long golden hair blew softly across his forehead.

He stared out towards the south, across the plain and the scattered mopani forest, in the direction from which the relentless pursuit would come. The climb up the sheer granite wall had taxed him severely and he was not yet recovered from it.

'Leave me one water bottle,' he ordered and Hendrick placed it beside him.

'I have filled it from those,' Hendrick indicated the pile

of discarded, empty water bottles. 'And we have a full bottle to see us as far as the river.'

'Good.' Lothar nodded and checked the other equipment that was laid out beside him on the granite slab.

There were four hand grenades – the old 'potato masher' type with a wooden handle. They had lain in the cache with the horse irons and other equipment for almost twenty years and he could not rely upon them.

Klein Boy had left his rifle and his bandolier of Mauser ammunition with the grenades. So Lothar had two rifles and 150 rounds – more than enough, if the grenades worked. If they didn't it wouldn't matter anyway.

'All right,' Lothar said quietly. 'I have everything I need. You can go.'

Hendrick turned his cannonball of a head to peer into the south. They were on a grandstand, high above the world, and the sweep of their horizon was twenty miles or more, but there was as yet no sign of the pursuit.

Hendrick started to rise to his feet, and then paused. He squinted into the heat haze and the glare. 'Dust!' he said. It was still five miles away, a pale haze above the trees.

'Yes.' Lothar had seen it minutes before. 'It could be a herd of zebra, or a willy willy, but I wouldn't bet my share of the loot on it. Move out now.'

Hendrick did not obey immediately. He stared into the white man's sapphire-yellow eyes.

Hendrick had not argued nor protested when Lothar had explained what they must do. It was right, it was logical. They had always left their wounded, often with just a pistol at hand, for when the pain or the hyenas closed in. And yet, this time Hendrick felt the need to say something, but there were no words that could match the enormity of the moment. He knew he was leaving a part of his own life upon this sunblasted rock.

'I will look after the boy,' he said simply, and Lothar nodded.

'I want to talk to Manie.' He licked his dry, cracked lips and shivered briefly with the heat of the poison in his blood. 'Wait for him at the bottom. It will take only a minute.'

'Come.' Hendrick jerked his head, and Klein Boy stood up beside him. Together they moved with the swiftness of hunting panthers to the cliff, and Klein Boy slipped over the edge. Hendrick paused and looked back. He raised his right hand.

'Stay in peace,' he said simply.

'Go in peace, old friend,' Lothar murmured. He had never called him friend before and Hendrick flinched at the word. Then he turned his head so Lothar could not see his eyes, and a moment later he was gone.

Lothar stared after him for long seconds, then shook himself lightly, driving back the self-pity and the sickly sentiment and the fever mists which threatened to close in and unman him completely.

'Manfred,' he said, and the boy started. He had been sitting as close as he dared to his father, watching his face, hanging on every word, every gesture he made.

'Pa,' he whispered. 'I don't want to go. I don't want to leave you. I don't want to be without you.'

Lothar made an impatient gesture, hardening his features to hide this softness in him. 'You will do as I tell you.'

'Pa—'

'You have never let me down before, Manie. I have been proud of you. Don't spoil it for me now. Don't let me find out that my son is a coward—'

'I'm not a coward!'

'Then you will do what you have to do,' he said harshly, and before Manfred could protest again he ordered, 'Bring me the haversack.'

Lothar placed the bag between his feet and with his

300

good hand unbuckled the flap. He took one of the packages from it and tore open the heavy brown paper with his teeth. He spilled the stones into a small pile on the granite beside him and then spread them. He picked out ten of the biggest and whitest gems.

'Take off your jacket,' he ordered, and when Manfred handed the garment to him Lothar pierced a tiny hole in the lining with his clasp knife.

'These stones will be worth thousands of pounds. Enough to see you full grown and educated,' he said, as he stuffed them one at a time into the lining of the jacket with his forefinger.

'But these others – there are too many, too heavy, too bulky to hide. Dangerous for you to carry them with you, a death warrant.' He pushed himself to his feet with an effort. 'Come!'

He led Manfred amongst the cluster of huge boulders, bracing himself against the rock to keep himself from falling while Manfred supported him from the other side.

'Here!' He grunted and lowered himself to his knees, Manfred squatting down beside him. At their feet the granite cap was cracked through as though split with a chisel. At the top the crack was only as wide as two handspans, but it was deep, they could not see the bottom of it though they peered down thirty feet or more. The crack narrowed gradually as it descended and the depths of it were lost in shadow.

Lothar dangled the haversack of diamonds over the aperture. 'Mark this place well,' he whispered. 'Look back often when you go northwards so that you will remember this hill. The stones will be waiting for you when you need them.'

Lothar opened his fingers and the haversack dropped into the crack. They heard the canvas scraping against the sides of the granite cleft as it fell, and then silence as it jammed deep down in the narrow throat of the crack.

Side by side they peered down, and they could just make out the lighter colour and the contrasting texture of the canvas thirty feet down, but it would escape even the concentrated scrutiny of anyone who did not know exactly where to look for it.

'That is my legacy to you, Manie,' Lothar whispered, and crawled back from the aperture. 'All right, Hendrick is waiting for you. It is time for you to go. Go quickly now.'

He wanted to embrace his son for the last time, to kiss his eyes and his lips and press him to his heart, but he knew it would undo them both. If they clung to each other now, they could never bring themselves to part.

'Go!' he ordered, and Manfred sobbed and flung himself at his father.

'I want to stay with you,' he cried.

Lothar caught his wrist and held him at arm's length.

'Do you want me to be ashamed?' he snarled. 'Is that how you want me to remember you, snivelling like a girl?'

'Pa, don't send me away, please. Let me stay.'

Lothar drew back, released his grip on Manfred's wrist and immediately whipped his open palm across his face and then swung back with his knuckles. The double slap knocked Manfred onto his haunches, leaving livid red blotches on his pale cheeks, and a tiny serpent of bright blood crawled from his nostril down over his upper lip. He stared at Lothar with shocked and incredulous eyes.

'Get out of here,' Lothar hissed at him, summoning all his courage and resolve to make his voice scornful and his expression savage. 'I won't have a blubbering little ninny hanging around my neck. Get out of here before I take the strap to you!'

Manfred scrambled to his feet and backed away, still staring with horrified disbelief at his father.

'Go on! Get away!' Lothar's expression never wavered, and his voice was angry and disdainful and unrelenting. 'Get out of here!'

Manfred turned and stumbled to the edge of the cliff. There he turned once more and held out his hands. 'Pa! Please don't—'

'Go, damn you. Go!' The boy scrambled over the edge, and the sounds of his clumsy descent dwindled into silence.

Only then Lothar let his shoulders droop, and he sobbed once, then suddenly he was weeping silently, his whole body shaking.

'It's the fever,' he told himself. 'The fever has weakened me.' But the image of his son's face, golden and beautiful and destroyed with grief, still filled his mind and he felt something tearing in his chest, an unbearable physical pain. 'Forgive me, my son,' he whispered through his tears. 'There was no other way to save you. Forgive me, I beg you.'

Lothar must have relapsed into unconsciousness, for he awoke with a start and could not remember where he was or how he had got there. Then the smell of his arm, sick and disgusting, brought it back to him, and he crawled to the edge of the cliff and looked out towards the south. He saw his pursuers then for the first time, and even at the distance of a mile or more he recognized the two wraithlike little figures that danced ahead of the column of horsemen.

'Bushmen,' he whispered. Now he understood how they had come so swiftly. 'She has put her tame Bushmen onto me.' He realized then that there had never been any chance of throwing them off the spoor; all that time Lothar had used in covering their sign and in anti-tracking subterfuges had been wasted. The Bushmen had followed them with barely a check over the worst going and most treacherous tracking terrain.

Then he looked beyond the trackers and counted the

number of men coming against him. 'Seven,' he whispered, and his eyes narrowed as he tried to pick out a smaller feminine figure amongst them, but they were dismounted leading their horses and the intervening mopani obscured his vision.

He transferred all his attention from the approaching horsemen to his own preparations. His only concern now was to delay the pursuit as long as possible, and to convince the pursuers that all of his band were still together here upon the summit. Every hour he could win for them would give Hendrick and Manie just that much more chance of escape.

It was slow and awkward working with one hand, but he jammed Klein Boy's rifle into a niche of the granite with the muzzle pointing down towards the plain. He looped a strap from one of the water bottles over the trigger and led the other end to his chosen shooting stance in the shadows, protected by a flare of the granite ledge.

He had to pause for a minute to rest, for his vision was starring and breaking up into patches of blackness, and his legs felt too weak to support his weight. He peeped over the edge and the horsemen were much closer, on the point of emerging from the mopani forest into the open ground. Now he recognized Centaine, slim and boyish in her riding-breeches, and he could even make out the bright yellow speck of the scarf around her throat.

Despite the fever heat and the darkness in his head, despite his desperate circumstances, he still found a bitter-sweet admiration for her. 'By God, she never gives up,' he muttered. 'She'll follow me over the other side to the frontiers of hell.'

He crawled to the pile of discarded water bottles and dragging them after him, arranged them in three separate piles along the lip of the ledge, and he knotted the leather straps together so that he could agitate all the piles simultaneously with a single twitch of the strap in his hand.

'Nothing else I can do,' he whispered, 'except shoot straight.' But his head was throbbing and his vision danced with the hot mirage of his fever. Thirst was an agony in his throat and his body was a furnace.

He unscrewed the stopper on the water bottle and drank, carefully controlling himself, sipping and holding it in his mouth before swallowing. Immediately he felt better, and his vision firmed. He closed the water bottle and placed it beside him with the spare ammunition clips. Then he folded his jacket into a cushion on the lip of granite in front of him and laid the Mauser on top of it. The pursuers had reached the foot of the kopje and were clustered about his abandoned horse.

Lothar held up his good hand in front of his eyes with fingers extended. There was no tremor, it was steady as the rock on which he lay and he cuddled the butt of the Mauser in under his chin.

'The horses,' he reminded himself. 'They can't follow Manie without horses—' and he drew a long breath, held it, and shot Blaine Malcomess' chestnut mare in the centre of the white blaze.

As the echoes of the shot still bounced from the cliffs of the surrounding hills, Lothar flicked the bolt of the Mauser and fired again, but this time he jerked the strap attached to the other rifle and the report of the two shots overlapped. The double report would deceive even an experienced soldier into believing there was more than one man on the summit.

Strangely, in this moment of deadly endeavour, the fever had receded. Lothar's vision was bright and clear, the sights of the Mauser starkly outlined against each target and his gun hand steady and precise as he swung the rifle from one horse to the next and sent each one crashing to earth with a head shot. Now they were all down except one: Centaine's mount.

He picked Centaine up in the field of his gunsight. She

was galloping back towards the mopani, lying flat over her horse's neck, her elbows pumping, a man hanging from her stirrup, and Lothar lifted his forefinger from the curve of the trigger. It was an instinctive reaction; he could not bring himself to send a bullet anywhere near her.

Instead he swung the barrel away from her. The riders of the downed horses, all four of them, were straggling away towards the mopani. Their thin cries of panic carried to the summit. They were easy marks; he could have knocked them down with a single bullet for each, but instead he made it a game to see how close he could come without touching one of them. They ducked and cavorted as the Mauser fire whipped around them. It was comical, hilarious. He was laughing as he worked the bolt, and suddenly he heard the wild hysterical quality of his laughter ringing hollowly in his own skull and he bit it off. 'I'm losing my head,' he thought. 'Got to last it out.'

The last of the running men disappeared into the forest and he found himself shaking and sweating with reaction.

'Got to be ready,' he encouraged himself. 'Got to think. Can't stop now. Can't let go.'

He crawled to the second rifle and reloaded it, then rolled back to his shooting stance in the shadow of the summit boulders.

'Now they are going to try and mark me,' he guessed. 'They'll draw fire and watch for—'

He saw the helmet being offered invitingly above the lip of the ravine at the edge of the forest and grinned. That was a hoary old trick; even the red-necked pommy soldiers had learned not to fall for it as far back as the opening years of the Boer War. It was almost insulting that they should try to entice him with it now.

'All right then!' he taunted them. 'We'll see who foxes who!'

He fired both rifles simultaneously, and a moment later jerked the straps attached to the piles of empty water bottles. At that range the movement of the round felt-covered bottles would show against the skyline just like the heads of hidden riflemen.

'Now they will send men to circle the hill,' he guessed, and watched for movement amongst the trees on his flanks, the Mauser ready, blinking his eyes rapidly to clear them.

'Five hours until dark,' he told himself. 'Hendrick and Manie will be at the river by dawn tomorrow. Got to hold them until then.'

He saw a flash of movement out on the right flank: men crouching and running forward in short bursts, outflanking the kopje, and he aimed for the trunks over their heads. Mauser fire whiplashed and bark exploded from the mopani, leaving wet white wounds on the standing timber.

'Keep your heads down, *myne heeren!*'

Lothar was laughing again, hysterical, delirious cackles. He forced himself to stop it, and immediately the image of Manie's face appeared before him, the beautiful topaz eyes swimming with tears and the flash of blood on his upper lip.

'My son,' he lamented. 'Oh God, how will I live without you!'

Even then he would not accept that he was dying, but blackness filled his skull and his head dropped forward onto the filthy pus-stained bandage that swaddled his arm. The stench of his own decaying flesh became part of the delirious nightmares which continued to torment him even in unconsciousness.

He came back to reality gradually, and he was aware that the sunlight had mellowed and the terrible heat had passed. There was a tiny breeze fanning the hilltop and he panted for the cooler air, sucking it gratefully into his lungs. Then he became aware of his thirst and his hand shook as he reached for the water bottle; it required an enormous effort to remove the stopper and lift it to his lips. One gulp and the bottle slipped from his grip and precious water splashed the front of his shirt and glugged from the bottle, pooling on the rock, evaporating almost immediately. He had lost fully a pint before he could retrieve the bottle and the loss made him want to weep. Carefully he screwed the stopper closed, then lifted his head and listened.

There were men on the hill. He heard the distinct crunch of a steel-shod boot biting into a granite foothold and he reached for one of the 'potato masher' grenades. With the Mauser over his shoulder he crawled back from the edge and used the rock to pull himself to his feet. He could not stand unassisted, and he had to lean his way around the boulder. He crept forward cautiously with the grenade ready.

The summit was clear; they must still be climbing the cliff. He held his breath and listened with all his being. He heard it again, close at hand, the scrape and slide of cloth against granite and a sharp involuntary inhalation of breath, a gasp of effort as somebody missed and then retrieved a foothold just below the summit.

'They are coming up from behind,' he told himself as though explaining to a backward child. Every thought required an effort. 'Seven-second delay on the fuse of the grenade.' He stared down at the clumsy weapon that he held by its wooden handle. 'Too long. They are very close.'

He lifted the grenade and tried to pull the firing-pin. It had corroded and was firmly stuck. He grunted and heaved at it and the pin came away. He heard the primer click and he began to count.

'A thousand and one, a thousand and two—' And at the fifth second he stooped and rolled the grenade over the edge. Out of sight, but close by, someone shouted an urgent warning.

'Christ! It's a grenade!' And Lothar laughed wildly.

'Eat it, you jackals of the English!' He heard them sliding and slipping as they tried to escape and he braced himself for the explosion, but instead he heard only the clatter and rattle of the grenade as it bounced and dropped down the slope.

'Misfire!' He stopped laughing. 'Oh damn it to hell.'

Then abruptly, but belatedly, the grenade exploded, far down the cliff. A crash of sound followed by the rattle and whine of shrapnel on the rock, and a man cried out.

Lothar fell to his knees and crawled to the edge. He looked over. There were three khaki-uniformed men on the cliff, sliding and scrambling downwards. He propped the Mauser on the lip and fired rapidly. His bullets left lead smears on the rock close beside the terrified troopers. They dropped the last few feet and started back towards the trees. One of them was hurt, hit by shrapnel; his companions supported him on each side and dragged him away.

Lothar lay exhausted by the effort for almost an hour before he could drag himself back to the south side of the summit. He looked down at the dead horses lying in the sun. Already their bellies were swelling, but the water bottles were still strapped to their saddles. 'The water is the magnet,' he whispered. 'By now they will be really thirsty. They will come for the water next.'

At first he thought the darkness was only in his mind again, but when he rolled his head and looked into the west he saw the last orange flash of the sunset in the sky. Before his eyes it faded and the sudden African night was upon them.

He lay and listened for them to try to reach the water, and he wondered as he had so often before at the mystic sounds of the African night, the gentle muted orchestra of insect and bird, the piping of the hunting bats flitting around the dome of rock and out on the plain the plaintive yip of jackal and the occasional outlandish grunting bark of the nocturnal honey badger. Lothar had to try to discount these distractions and listen for manmade sounds in the darkness directly below the cliff.

It was only the clink of a stirrup iron that alerted him,

and he tossed the grenade with a full swing of his arm out over the abyss. The heavy crump of the explosion blew a puff of air into his face, and by the sudden flare of flame he saw far below the dark figures standing over the dead horse. He made out two of them, though he could not be certain there were not others, and he tossed the second grenade.

In the brief burst of orange light he saw them racing back towards the trees; they ran so lightly that they could not have been burdened by water bottles.

'Sweat it out,' he taunted them, but he had only the one remaining grenade. He held it to his chest as though it were some rare treasure. 'Must be ready when they come again. Can't let them get the water.' He was talking aloud, and he knew it was a sign of his delirium. Every time he felt the swimming dizziness he lifted his head and tried to focus on the stars.

'Got to hold out,' he told himself seriously. 'If I can only keep them here until noon tomorrow.' He tried to make the calculations of time and distance but it was too much for him. 'Must be eight hours since Hendrick and Manie left. They will keep going all night. They haven't got me to hold them back. They can make the river before dawn. If only I can hold them another eight hours they will get clear away—' But the weariness and the fever overwhelmed him and he cradled his forehead in the curve of his elbow.

'Lothar!' It was his imagination, he knew that, but then his name was called again. 'Lothar!' And he lifted his head and shivered with the cold of the night and the memories that her voice summoned up.

He opened his mouth and then closed it. He would not reply, would give nothing away. But he listened avidly for Centaine Courtney to call again.

'Lothar, we have a wounded man.' He judged that she was at the edge of the forest. He could imagine her, determined and brave, that small firm chin lifted, those dark eyes.

310

'Why do I still love you?' he whispered.

'We must have water for him.' Strange how clearly her voice carried. He could pick out the inflection of her French accent and somehow he found that touching. It brought tears to his eyes.

'Lothar! I am coming out to fetch the water.'

Her voice was closer, stronger – clearly she had left the shelter of the trees.

'I'm alone, Lothar.' She must be halfway across the open ground.

'Go back!' He tried to shout, but it was a mumble. 'I warned you. I have to do it.' He fumbled for the grenade. 'Can't let you take the water – for Manie's sake. I have to do it.'

He hooked his finger through the firing ring of the grenade.

'I have reached the first horse,' she called. 'I am taking the bottle. Just one bottle, Lothar.'

She was in his power. She was standing at the foot of the cliff. It wouldn't need a long throw. All he had to do was roll the grenade over the edge and it would fly out like a toboggan along the curve of the cliff and land at her feet.

He imagined the flash of the explosion, that sweet flesh that had cradled his, and harboured his son, torn and rent by razor-edged shrapnel. He thought how much he hated her – and realized that he loved her as much, and the tears in his eyes blinded him.

'I'm going back now, Lothar. I have one bottle,' she called, and he heard in her voice gratitude and an acknowledgement of the bond between them that no deed, no passage of time could sever. She spoke again, dropping her voice so it reached him as a faint whisper.

'May God forgive you, Lothar De La Rey.' And then no more.

Those gentle words wounded him as deeply as any he had ever heard from her. There was a finality to them that he found unbearable, and he dropped his head onto his arm to smother the cry of despair which rose in his throat, and the darkness rustled in his head like the wings of a black vulture as he felt himself falling, falling, falling.

'This one is dead,' Blaine Malcomess said quietly, standing over the prostrate figure. They had climbed the cliff at two places in the darkness; then in the dawn they had carried the summit in a concerted rush only to find it undefended. 'Where are the others?'

Sergeant Hansmeyer hurried out of the shadowy cluster of boulders. 'There is no one else on the hill, sir. They must have got clean away.'

'Blaine!' Centaine called urgently. 'Where are you? What is happening?' He had insisted that she remain at the foot of the kopje until they had captured the summit. He had not yet signalled her to come up, but here she was, only a minute behind their attack.

'Over here,' he snapped. And then, as she ran towards him, 'You disobeyed an order, madam.'

She ignored the accusation. 'Where are they?' She broke off as she saw the body. 'Oh God, it's Lothar.' She went down beside him.

'So this is De La Rey. Well, he's dead, I'm afraid,' Blaine told her.

'Where are the others?' Centaine looked up at him anxiously. She had been both dreading and anticipating finding Lothar's bastard; she still tried to avoid using the boy's name, even to herself.

'Not here.' Blaine shook his head. 'Given us the slip. De La Rey fooled us and put up a good rearguard delay. They have got clear away. They'll be across the river by now.'

Manfred. Centaine capitulated and thought of him by

name. Manfred, my son. And her disappointment and sense of loss was so strong that it shocked her. She had wanted him to be there. To see him at last. She looked down at his father, and other emotions, long buried and suppressed, rose in her.

Lothar lay with his face cradled in the crook of his elbow. The other arm, bound up in strips of stained blanket, was outflung. She touched his neck below the ear, feeling for the carotid artery, and exclaimed immediately she felt the fever heat of his skin.

'He's still alive.'

'Are you sure?' Blaine squatted beside her. Between them they rolled Lothar onto his back, and they saw the grenade lying under him.

'You were right,' Blaine said softly. 'He did have another grenade. He could have killed you last night.'

Centaine shivered as she stared down at Lothar's face. He was no longer beautiful and golden and brave. The fever had ruined him, his features had collapsed like those of a corpse and he was shrunken and grey.

'He is badly dehydrated,' she said. 'Is there water left in that bottle?' While Blaine dribbled water into his mouth, Centaine unwrapped the festering rags from his arm.

'Blood poisoning.' She recognized the livid lines beneath the skin and the stench of his rotting flesh. 'That arm will have to come off.' Though her voice was steady and business-like, she was appalled at the damage she had wrought. It seemed impossible that a single bite could have caused that. Her teeth were one of her good features and she was proud of them, always kept them clean and white and cared for. That arm looked as though it had been savaged by one of the carrion eaters, by a hyena or a leopard.

'There is a Portuguese Roman Catholic mission at Cuangar on the river,' Blaine said. 'But he'll be lucky if we can get him there alive. With all but one of the horses

313

dead, we'll all be lucky to make it as far as the river ourselves.' He stood up. 'Sergeant, send one of your men to fetch the first-aid kit and then have the rest of them search every inch of this hilltop. A million pounds' worth of diamonds are missing.'

Hansmeyer saluted and hurried away, rapping out orders at his troopers.

Blaine sank down beside Centaine. 'While we are waiting for the medical kit, I suppose we had better search his clothing and equipment in the off-chance that he kept any of the stolen diamonds with him.'

'It's an off-chance all right,' Centaine agreed with bitter resignation. 'The diamonds are almost certainly with his son and that big black Ovambo ruffian of his. And without our Bushmen trackers—' She shrugged.

Blaine spread Lothar's dusty stained tunic on the rock and began examining the seams, while Centaine bathed Lothar's injured arm and then bound it up with clean white bandages from the medical kit.

'Nothing, sir.' Hansmeyer reported back. 'We've gone over every inch of this rock, every nook and cranny.'

'Very well, Sergeant. Now we have to get this beggar off the kopje without letting him fall and break his neck.'

'Not that he doesn't deserve it.'

Blaine grinned. 'He does deserve it. But we don't want to do the hangman out of his five guineas, do we now, Sergeant?'

They were ready to move out within the hour. Lothar De La Rey was strapped into a drag litter of mopani saplings behind their single remaining horse, and the wounded trooper, the grenade shrapnel still in his back and shoulder, rode up in Centaine's saddle.

Centaine lingered on at the foot of the kopje after the column had started northwards towards the river once more, and Blaine came back to stand beside her.

He took her hand and she sighed and leaned lightly

against his shoulder. 'Oh, Blaine, for me so much has ended here in this Godforsaken wilderness, on this sun-blasted lump of rock.'

'I think I can understand how much the loss of the diamonds means.'

'Do you, Blaine? I don't think so. I don't think even I can take it in yet. Everything has changed – even my hatred for Lothar—'

'There is still a chance we will recover the stones.'

'No, Blaine. You and I both know there is no chance. The diamonds are gone.'

He did not attempt to deny it, did not offer false comfort.

'I have lost it all, everything I ever worked for – for me and my son. It's all gone.'

'I didn't realize—' he broke off and looked down at her with pity and deep concern. 'I understood it would be a hard blow, but everything? Is it that bad?'

'Yes, Blaine,' she said simply. 'Everything. Not all at once, of course, but now the whole edifice will start to crumble and I will struggle to shore it up. I will borrow and beg and plead for time, but the foundation is gone from under me. A million pounds, Blaine, it's an enormous sum of money. I will stave off the inevitable for a few months, a year perhaps, but it will go faster and faster, like a house of cards, and at the end it will come crashing down around me.'

'Centaine, I am not a poor man,' he began. 'I could help you—' She reached up and laid her forefinger on his lips.

'There is one thing I would ask from you,' she whispered. 'Not money – but in the days ahead, I will need some comfort. Not often, just when it gets very bad.'

'I will be there whenever you need me, Centaine. I promise you that. You have only to call.'

'Oh, Blaine.' She turned to him. 'If only!'

'Yes, Centaine – if only.' And he took her in his arms. There was no guilt nor fear, even the terrible threat of ruin and destitution that hung over her seemed to recede when she was in his arms.

'I wouldn't even mind being poor again, if only I had you beside me always,' she whispered, and he could not reply. In desperation he bowed his head over her and stopped her lips with his mouth.

The Portuguese priest doctor at Cuangar Mission took off Lothar De La Rey's arm two inches below the elbow. He operated by the bright flat white light of the Petromax lantern, and Centaine stood at his side, sweating behind the surgical mask, responding to the doctor's requests in French, trying to prevent herself freezing in horror at the rasping of the bone saw and the suffocating stench of chloroform and gangrene that filled the daub and thatch hut that served as an operating theatre. When it was over, she slipped away to the earthpit lavatory and vomited up her revulsion and pity. Alone in the mission hut that had been allocated to her, under the billowing ghostly mosquito net, she could still taste it in the back of her throat. The gangrene smell seemed to have impregnated her skin and lingered in her hair. She prayed that she might never smell it again, nor ever be forced to live through another hour as harrowing as watching the man she had once loved shorn of a limb, turned into a cripple before her eyes.

The prayer was in vain, for at noon the following day the priest doctor murmured regretfully, '*Désolé, mais j'ai manqué l'infection. Il faut couper encore une fois* – I am sorry, but I have missed the infection. It is necessary to cut again.'

The second time, because she now knew what to expect, seemed even worse than the first. She had to press her fingernails into the palms of her hands to prevent herself fainting as the priest took up the gleaming silver saw and

316

cut through the exposed bone of Lothar's humerus only inches below the great joint of the shoulder. For three days afterwards Lothar lay in a pale coma, seeming already to have passed the division between life and death.

'I cannot say.' The priest shrugged away her anxious plea for reassurance. 'It is up to the good Lord now.'

Then on the evening of the third day when she entered his hut, the sapphire-yellow eyes swivelled towards her in their deep coloured sockets, and she saw recognition flare for an instant before Lothar's eyelids dropped down over them.

However, it was two days more before the priest allowed Blaine Malcomess to enter the hut. Blaine cautioned Lothar and placed him under formal arrest.

'My sergeant will have complete charge of you until you are passed fit to travel by Father Paula. At that time you will be brought by boat downriver to the border post at Runtu under strict guard, and from there by road to Windhoek where you will stand your trial.'

Lothar lay against the bolster, pale and skeletal thin. His stump, wrapped in a turban of gauze bandage, the end stained yellow with iodine, looked like a penguin's wing. He stared at Blaine expressionlessly.

'Now, De La Rey, you don't need me to tell you that you will be a lucky man to escape the gallows. But you will give yourself a fighting chance of leniency if you tell us where you have hidden the diamonds, or what you have done with them.'

He waited for almost a minute, and it was difficult not to be ruffled by that flat yellow stare with which Lothar regarded him.

'Do you understand what I'm trying to tell you, De La Rey?' he broke the silence, and Lothar rolled his head away, stared out of the paneless window of the hut down towards the riverbank.

'I think you know that I am administrator of the

territory. I have power to review your sentence; my recommendation for clemency would almost certainly be acceded to by the minister of justice. Don't be a fool, man. Give up the diamonds. They are no use to you where you are going, and I will guarantee you your life in return.'

Lothar closed his eyes.

'Very well, De La Rey. We understand each other then. Don't expect any mercy from me.' He called Sergeant Hansmeyer into the hut. 'Sergeant, the prisoner has no privileges, none at all. He will be under guard day and night, twenty-four hours a day, until you hand him over to the appropriate authority in Windhoek. You will be directly responsible to me. You understand?'

'Yes, sir.' Hansmeyer drew himself to attention.

'Look after him, Hansmeyer. I want this one. I want him badly.'

Blaine strode out of the hut, down to where Centaine sat alone under the open-sided thatched *setengi* on the riverbank. He dropped into the camp chair beside hers and lit a cheroot. He inhaled the smoke, held it a moment and then blew it out forcefully and angrily.

'The man is intransigent,' he said. 'I offered him my personal guarantee of leniency in exchange for your diamonds. He didn't even deign to reply. I don't have the authority to offer him a free pardon but, believe me, if I did I wouldn't hesitate. As it is there is nothing more I can do.' He drew on the cheroot again and glared out across the wide green river. 'I swear he will pay for what he has done to you – pay in full measure.'

'Blaine.' She laid her hand lightly on his muscular brown forearm. 'Spite is too petty an emotion for a man of your stature.'

He glanced sideways and, despite his rancour, he smiled. 'Don't credit me with too much nobility, madam. I am many things, but not a saint.'

He looked boyish when he grinned like that, except that

318

his green eyes took on a wicked slant and his ears stuck out at the most endearing angle.

'Oh la, sir, it might be amusing to test the limits of your nobility and sanctity – one day.'

He chuckled with delight. 'What a shameless but interesting proposal.' And then he became serious again. 'Centaine, you know that I should never have come on this expedition. At this moment my duties are being sadly neglected, and I will certainly have incurred the justified wrath of my superiors in Pretoria. I must get back to my office just as soon as I can. I have arranged with Father Paulus for canoes and paddlers to take us downriver to the border post at Runtu. I hope we will be able to requisition a police truck from there. Hansmeyer and his troopers will stay on to guard De La Rey and bring him in as soon as he is fit enough to travel.'

Centaine nodded. 'Yes, I also have to get back and start picking up the pieces, papering over the cracks.'

'We can leave first light tomorrow.'

'Blaine, I would like to speak to Lothar – to De La Rey, before we leave.' When he hesitated, she went on persuasively: 'A few minutes alone with him, please Blaine. It's important to me.'

Centaine paused in the doorway of the hut while her eyes adjusted to the gloom.

Lothar was sitting up, bare to the waist, a cheap trade blanket spread over his legs. His body was thin and pale; the infection had burned the flesh off his bones and his ribs were a gaunt rack.

'Sergeant Hansmeyer, will you leave us alone for a minute?' Centaine asked, and she stood aside.

As he passed her, Hansmeyer said quietly, 'I'll be within call, Mrs Courtney.'

In the silence that followed, Centaine and Lothar stared at each other, and it was she who gave in and spoke first.

'If you set out to ruin me, then you have succeeded,' she said, and he wriggled the stub of his missing arm, a gesture which was at once both pathetic and obscene.

'Who has ruined whom, Centaine?' he asked, and she dropped her eyes.

'Won't you give me back at least a part of what you have stolen from me?' she asked. 'For the sake of what we shared once long ago?'

He did not reply, but instead lifted his hand and touched the ancient puckered scar on his chest. She winced, for it was she who had fired that shot from the Luger pistol at the time of her disillusion and revulsion.

'The boy has the diamonds, hasn't he?' she asked. 'Your—' she was about to say, 'Your bastard?' but she changed it: 'Your son?'

Lothar remained silent and she went on impulsively: 'Manfred, our son.'

'I never thought I'd hear you say that.' He could not disguise the pleasure in his tone. 'Will you remember he is our son, conceived in love, when you are tempted to destroy him also?'

'Why should you think I would do that?'

'I know you, Centaine,' he said.

'No.' She shook her head vehemently. 'You do not know me.'

'If he stands in your way, you will destroy him,' he said, flatly.

'Do you truly believe that?' She stared at him. 'Do you really believe that I am so ruthless, so vindictive, that I would take my revenge on my own son?'

'You have never acknowledged him as that.'

'I have now. You have heard me do it more than once in the last few minutes.'

'Are you promising me that you will not harm him?'

'I do not have to promise you, Lothar De La Rey. I am merely saying it. I will not harm Manfred.'

'And naturally you expect something from me in return,' he demanded, leaning forward. He was breathing with difficulty, sweating with the effort of fighting off his physical weakness. His sweat had a rank and sour smell in the gloomy confines of the hut.

'Would you offer me anything in return?' she asked quietly.

'No,' he said. 'Nothing!' And he sank back against the bolster, exhausted but defiant. 'Now let me hear you withdraw your promise.'

'I made no promise,' she said quietly. 'But, I repeat, Manfred, our son, is safe from me. I will never deliberately do anything to harm him. I do not give you the same assurance, however.'

She turned and called. 'Thank you, Sergeant, we have finished our business.' And she stooped to leave.

'Centaine—' he cried weakly, and he wanted to tell her, 'Your diamonds are in the cleft on the summit of the hill.' But when she turned back he bit down on the words and said only, 'Goodbye, Centaine. It is finished at last.'

The Okavango is one of Africa's most beautiful rivers. It rises in the highlands of the Angolan plateau above 4,000 feet and flows south and east, a wide deep torrent of green water that it seems must reach the ocean, so swift and determined is its flow. However, it is a landlocked river, debouching first into the mis-named Okavango Swamps, a vast area of lucid lagoons and papyrus banks, studded with islets on which graceful ivory nut palms and great wild figs stand tall. Beyond that the river emerges again but shrivelled and weakened as it enters the desolation of the Kalahari Desert and disappears for ever beneath those eternal sands.

This section of the river that Centaine and Blaine set out upon was that above the swamps where the river was at its grandest. Their craft was a native *mukoro*, a dugout canoe fashioned from a single treetrunk over twenty feet long, rounded but not perfectly straight.

'The owl and the pussy cat put to sea in a beautiful banana-shaped boat,' quoth Blaine, and Centaine laughed a little apprehensively until she saw how masterfully their paddlers handled the misshapen craft.

They were two amiable coal-black giants of the river tribe. They had the balance of gymnasts and their bodies were forged and hardened to Grecian perfection by a lifetime of wielding their paddles and their long punting poles. They stood at the stern and bows, singing their melodious work chant and trimming their narrow unstable craft with a relaxed, almost instinctive ease.

Amidships Blaine and Centaine lolled on cushions of rawhide stuffed with the fluffy heads of the papyrus reeds. The narrow beam forced them to sit in tandem, with Blaine in the lead, his Lee Enfield rifle across his lap ready to discourage the close approach of any of the numerous hippopotami which infested the river. 'The most dangerous animal in Africa by far,' he told Centaine.

'What about lions and elephants and poisonous snakes?' she challenged.

'The old hippo gets two humans for every one killed by all the other species put together.'

This was Centaine's first venture into these parts. She was a creature of the desert, unacquainted with the river or the swamps, unfamiliar with the boundless life they supported. Blaine, on the other hand, knew the river well. He had first been ordered here when serving with General

322

Smuts' expeditionary force in 1915 and had since returned often to hunt and study the wildlife of the region. He seemed to recognize every animal and bird and plant, and he had a hundred stories, both true and apocryphal, with which to amuse her.

The mood of the river changed constantly; at places it narrowed and raced through rock-lined gaps and the long canoe flew like a lance upon it. The paddlers directed it past outcrops of fanged rock upon which the current humped up and split, and with delicate touches of the paddles took them through the creaming whirlpools beyond and into the next flying stretch where the surface was moulded like green Venetian glass into standing waves by its own speed and momentum. Centaine whooped breathlessly, half in terror and half in exhilaration, like a child on a roller coaster. Then they emerged onto broad shallow stretches, the flow broken by islands and sandbanks and bordered by wide flood plains on which grazed herds of wild buffalo, massive indolent-seeming beasts, black as hell and crusted with dried mud, great bossed horns drooping mournfully over their trumpet-shaped ears, standing belly-deep in the flood plains, lifting their black drooling muzzles in comical curiosity to watch them pass.

'Oh Blaine! What are those? I've never seen them before.'

'Lechwe. This is as far south as you will find them.'

There were vast herds of these robust water antelope with coarse wiry red coats, the rams standing as tall as a man's chest and carrying long gracefully recurved horns. The hornless ewes were fluffy as children's toys. So dense were the herds that when they fled from the human presence they churned the water until it sounded like the thunderous passage of a steam locomotive heard at a distance.

On nearly every tall tree along the river's banks were posted pairs of fish eagles, their white heads shining in the sunlight. They threw back their heads, belling out their throats to chant their weird yelping call as the *mukoro* glided past.

On the white sandbanks the long saurian shapes of the crocodiles were silhouetted, ugly and evil as they lifted themselves on their stubby deformed legs and waddled swiftly to the water's edge, then slipping away below the surface, only the twin knobs of their scaly eyebrows still showing.

In the shallows clusters of smooth rounded boulders, dark grey edged with baby pink, caught Centaine's attention, but she did not recognize them until Blaine warned:

'Watch them!' and the paddlers sheered off as one of the huge boulders moved, raising a head the size of a beer keg, gaping red, the mighty jaws lined with tusks of yellow ivory, and it bellowed at them with the deep sardonical laughter of a demented god.

Blaine shifted the rifle slightly. 'Don't be taken in by that jovial haw haw haw – he isn't really amused,' he told Centaine as he worked the bolt and pushed a cartridge into the breech.

As he spoke the bull hippo charged at them through the shallows, breaking the water into white foam with his elephantine bounds, blaring his hoarse menacing laughter, his jaws gaping, clashing the long curved yellow ivories whose razor edges could scythe the thick fibrous papyrus stems, or crush in the frail sides of a *mukoro*, or cut a swimming man into two pieces with equal ease.

The *mukoro* drove forward under the long powerful thrusts of the two oarsmen, but the hippopotamus gained on them rapidly and Blaine sprang to his feet, balancing in the unstable craft. He lifted the rifle to his shoulder and fired so rapidly that the reports blended together, and Centaine flinched at the whiplash of gunfire over her head and looked back, expecting to see the bullets strike on the great fleshy grey head and blood spurt from between those glassy pinkshot little eyes. But Blaine had aimed inches over the beast's forehead. The bristly ears twitched and fluttered like sunbirds' wings to the shock of passing shot, and the bull broke his charge and came up short, just his head showing above the surface, blinking rapidly with comical astonishment. The *mukoro* pulled swiftly away, and the bull submerged in a huge swirl of green water as if to cover his embarrassment at his own ineffectual performance.

'Are you all right, Centaine?' Blaine lowered the rifle.

'That was a little frosty.' She tried to keep her voice level with only partial success.

'Not as bad as it seemed – sound and fury, not too much of the deadly intent.' He smiled at her.

'I'm glad you didn't kill him.'

'Not much point in turning the old boy into four tons of rotting carrion and making twenty widows of his fat wives.'

'Is that why he chased us – protecting his females?'

'Probably, but you can never tell with wild animals. Perhaps one of his cows is calving, or he has unpleasant memories of human hunters, or perhaps he just felt plain bolshy today.'

His coolness in crisis had impressed her almost as much as his humanity in sparing the threatening beast.

'Only schoolgirls worship their heroes,' she reminded herself firmly as the canoe sped onwards, and then found herself studying the breadth of Blaine's shoulders and the way he held his head upon them. His dark hair was cut short down the back of his neck, and his neck was strong but not bulled, pleasingly proportioned and smooth, only his ears were too large, and the tips were pink where the sunlight seemed to shine through them. She felt an almost irresistible urge to lean forward and kiss the soft skin just behind where they jutted out, but she controlled herself with a giggle.

325

He turned and demanded with a smile, 'What's so funny?'

'A girl always feels weak and giggly after Prince Charming saves her from a fire-breathing dragon.'

'Mythical creatures, dragons.'

'Don't scoff,' she chided him. 'Anything is possible here, even dragons and princes. This is never-never land. Santa Claus and the good fairy are waiting just around the next bend.'

'You are just a little bit crazy, do you know that?'

'Yes, I know that,' she nodded. 'And I think I should warn you, it's both contagious and infectious.'

'Your warning comes too late.' He shook his head sadly. 'I think I've caught it already.'

'Good,' she said, and giving in to her whim, she leaned forward and kissed that soft spot behind his ear.

He shivered theatrically. 'Now look what you've done.' He turned again and showed her the gooseflesh standing in little pimples on his forearms. 'You must promise never to do that again. It's too dangerous.'

'Like you, I never make promises.' She saw the quick shadow of regret and guilt in his eyes and cursed herself for alluding to his lack of commitment to her and thereby spoiling the mood.

'Oh, Blaine, look at those birds. Surely they aren't real are they? It proves me right, this is never-never land.' She tried to retrieve the mood.

They were drifting past a high sheer bank of red clay bright as a blood orange that was perforated by thousands of perfectly round apertures, and a living swirling cloud of marvellously coloured birds hung over the bank, darting in and out of the myriad entrances to their nesting burrows.

'Carmine bee-eaters,' Blaine told her, sharing her wonder at the glory of the flashing darts of flaming pink and turquoise blue, with their long delicately streaming tail feathers and pointed wingtips sharp as stilettos. 'They are so unearthly, I am beginning to believe you,' he said. 'Perhaps we have indeed passed through the mirror.'

They spoke little after that, but somehow their silences seemed to bring them even closer. They only touched once more when Centaine laid her hand, palm open, along the side of his neck, and for a moment he covered her hand with his own, a gentle fleeting exchange.

Then Blaine spoke briefly to the leading oarsman.

'What is it, Blaine?' she asked.

'I told him to find a good place to camp for the night.'

'Isn't it still very early?' She glanced at the sun.

'Yes.' He turned and smiled at her, almost sheepishly. 'But then I'm trying for the record trip between Cuangar and Runtu.'

'The record?'

'Slowest journey ever.'

Blaine chose one of the large islands. The white sandbar folded upon itself to form a secret lagoon, clear and green and screened by tall waving papyrus. While the two paddlers piled driftwood for the fire and cut papyrus fronds to thatch night shelters for them, Blaine picked up his rifle.

'Where are you going?' Centaine asked.

'See if I can get a buck for dinner.'

'Oh, Blaine, please don't kill anything, not today. Not this special day.'

'Aren't you tired of bully beef?'

'Please,' she insisted and he set his rifle aside with a smile and a rueful shake of his head and went to make sure that the huts were ready and the mosquito nets rigged over each separate bed. Satisfied, Blaine dismissed the paddlers and they climbed into the *mukoro*.

'Where are they off to?' Centaine demanded as they poled out into the current.

'I told them to camp on the mainland,' Blaine answered,

and they each looked away, suddenly awkward and shy and intensely aware of their isolation as they stared after the departing canoe.

Centaine turned and walked back to the camp. She knelt beside her saddle bags, which were her only luggage, and without looking up told him, 'I haven't bathed since last night. I'm going to swim in the lagoon.' She had a bar of yellow soap in her hand.

'Do you have a last message for the folks back home?'

'What do you mean?'

'This is the Okavango river, Centaine. The crocodiles here gobble little girls as hors d'oeuvres.'

'You could stand guard with the rifle—'

'Delighted to oblige.'

' – and with your eyes closed!'

'Rather defeats the object, doesn't it?'

He scouted the edge of the lagoon and found shallow water below an outcropping of black water-polished rock where the bottom was white sand and an approaching crocodile would show clearly, and he sat on the highest pinnacle of rock with the Lee Enfield loaded and the safety-catch off.

'You are on your honour not to peek,' she warned, standing on the beach below him, and he concentrated on a flock of spur-wing geese flogging their heavy wings as they passed across the lowering sun, but acutely aware of the rustle of her falling clothing.

He heard the water ripple, and her little gasp and then, 'All right, now you can watch for crocodiles.'

She was sitting on the sandy bottom, just her head above the surface, her back towards him and her hair scraped up and tied on top of her head.

'It's heavenly, so cool and refreshing.' She smiled over her shoulder, and he could see the gleam of her white flesh through the green water and he thought he might not be able to bear the pain of his wanting. He knew that she was deliberately provoking him, but he could neither resist her nor steel himself against her wiles.

Isabella Malcomess had been thrown from her horse almost five years previously, and since then they had not known each other as man and woman. They had attempted it only once, but he could not bear to think about the agony and humiliation they had both suffered at their failure.

He had a healthy lusty body and a huge appetite for living. It had taken all his strength and determination to discipline himself to this unnatural monastic existence. He had succeeded at last, so that he was now unprepared for the savage escape of all those fettered desires and instincts.

'Eyes closed again,' she called gaily. 'I'm going to stand and work up some suds.'

He was unable to reply; he only just contained the groan that came up his throat, and he stared down fixedly at the rifle in his lap.

Centaine screamed on a wild rising note of terror. 'Blaine!'

He was on his feet in that instant. Centaine was standing thigh deep, the green water just lapping the deep cleft of her small round buttocks, the naked swell of her hips narrowing into a tiny waist. Her exquisitely sculpted back and shoulders were stiff with horror.

The crocodile was coming in from deep water with slashing sweeps of its long cockscombed tail, a bow wave spreading back from its hideous armoured snout in a sharp arrowhead of ripples. The reptile was almost as long as the *mukoro*, twenty feet from its nose to the tip of its crested tail.

'Run, Centaine, run!' he bellowed, and she whirled and floundered back towards him. But the reptile was moving as swiftly as a horse at full gallop, the water breaking into a roiling wake behind it, and Centaine was blocking Blaine's aim, running directly back towards him.

Blaine sprang down from the rock and waded knee-deep into the water to meet her, his rifle held at high port across his chest.

'Down!' he shouted at her. 'Fall flat!' And she responded instantly, diving forward at full length, and he fired over her back, a snap shot for the huge reptile was almost upon her.

The bullet cracked against the armoured scales of its hideous skull. The crocodile arched its back, exploding out of the water, drenching Blaine and covering Centaine in a breaking wave of foam. It stood on its massive tail, its dwarfed forelegs clawing desperately, its creamy belly chequered with symmetrical patterns of scales, the long angular snout pointed to the sky, and with a bellow it collapsed over backwards.

Blaine dragged Centaine to her feet and with one arm around her backed towards the beach, pointing the rifle like a pistol with his free hand. The crocodile was in monstrous convulsions, its primitive brain damaged by the bullet. It rolled and thrashed in uncontrolled erratic circles, snapping its jaws so that the jagged yellow teeth clashed like a steel gate slamming in a high wind.

Blaine thrust Centaine behind him and with both hands lifted the rifle. His bullets rang against the scaly head, tearing away chunks of flesh and bone, and the reptile's tail fluttered and lashed weakly. It dived over the edge of the shallow sandbank into the dark green beyond, came up in one last swirl and then was gone.

Centaine was shaking with terror, her teeth chattering so she could hardly speak. 'Horrible, oh what an awful monster!' and she threw herself against his chest, and clung to him. 'Oh Blaine, I was terrified.' Her face was pressed to his chest so that her voice was blurred.

'It's all right now.' He tried to calm her. 'Easy, my darling, it's all over. It's gone.' He propped the rifle against the rocks and enfolded her in his arms.

He was stroking her and soothing her, at first without passion, as he would have gentled one of his own daughters when she woke from a nightmare screaming for him; then he became acutely aware of the silkiness of her bare wet skin under his hands. He could feel every plane of her back, the smooth curves of muscle on each side of her spine, and he could not prevent himself tracing with his fingertips the ridge of her spine. It felt like a string of polished beads beneath her skin; he followed it down until it disappeared into the divide of her small hard bottom.

She was quiet now, only breathing in little choking gasps, but at his touch she curled her spine like a cat, inclining her pelvis towards him, and he seized one of her buttocks in each hand and pulled her to him. She did not resist, but her whole body thrust forward to meet his. 'Blaine.' She said his name and lifted her face.

He kissed her savagely, with the anger of a man of honour who knows he can no longer keep his vows, and they locked together breathing each other's breath, their tongues twisting together, kneading, pressing, so deep that they threatened to choke each other with their fervour.

She pulled away. 'Now,' she stammered. 'It has to be now,' and he lifted her in his arms like a child and ran with her, back through the clinging white sand to the thatched shelter, and he fell onto his knees beside the mattress of papyrus fronds and lowered her gently onto the blanket that covered it.

'I want to look at you,' he blurted, pulling back onto his haunches, but she squirmed up and reached for him.

'Later – I can't wait – please, Blaine. Oh God, do it now.' She was tearing at the buttons on his shirt front, clumsy with haste, desperate with haste.

He ripped off his sodden shirt and threw it away, and

331

she was kissing him again, smothering his mouth, while both of them fumbled with his belt buckle, getting in each other's way, wildly laughing and gasping, bumping their noses together, bruising their lips between their teeth.

'Oh God, hurry – Blaine.'

He tore away from her and hopped on one leg as he tried to rid himself of his wet clinging breeches. He looked awkward and ungainly and he almost toppled over into the soft white sand in his haste. And she laughed wildly, breathlessly – he was so funny and beautiful and ridiculous and she wanted him so, and if he took a second longer something inside her would burst and she knew she would die.

'Oh please, Blaine – quickly come to me.'

Then at last he was naked as she was and as he came over her she seized his shoulder with one hand and fell backwards, pulling him with her, spreading her knees and lifting them high, with the other hand groping for him, finding him and guiding him.

'Oh Blaine, you're so – oh yes, like that, I can't – I want to scream.'

'Scream!' He encouraged her as he plunged and rocked and thrust above her. 'There is no one to hear you. Scream for both of us!'

And she opened her mouth wide and gave vent to all her loneliness and wanting and incredulous joy in a rising crescendo that he joined at the end, roaring wildly with her in the most complete and devastating moment of her existence.

Afterwards she wept silently against his bare chest and he was puzzled and compassionate and concerned.

'I was too rough – forgive me! I did not mean to hurt you.'

She shook her head and gulped back her tears. 'No, you never hurt me, it was the most beautiful—'

'Then why do you cry?'

'Because everything that is good seems so fleeting, the more wonderful it is, the sooner it is past, while the wretched vile times seem to last for ever.'

'Don't think like that, my little one.'

'I don't know how I will go on living without you. It was hell before, but this will only make it a thousand times worse.'

'I don't know where I will find the strength to walk away from you,' he whispered in agreement. 'It will be the hardest thing I ever have to do in my life.'

'How much longer do we have?'

'Another day – then we will be at Rundu.'

'When I was a little girl my father gave me a brooch of amber with an insect embedded in it. I wish we could preserve this moment like that, capture it eternally in the precious amber of our love.'

Their parting was a gradual process, not a merciful guillotine stroke, but over the following days a slow intrusion of events and people that prised them apart so that they must suffer the smallest tear, each new wrench, in all its detailed agony.

From the morning they reached the border post at Rundu and went ashore to meet the police sergeant who was in command, they seemed constantly to be with strangers, always on their guard so that every glance that passed between them, every word or stolen caress, made them more dreadfully aware of impending separation. Only when the dusty police truck carried them down the last hills into Windhoek was the torturous process completed.

The world awaited them: Isabella, lovely and tragic in her wheelchair, and her daughters bubbling with laughter, mischievous and enchanting as elves, competing for Blaine's embraces; the superintendent of police and the territorial secretary and droves of petty officials and reporters and photographers; Twentyman-Jones and Abe Abrahams, Sir Garry and Lady Courtney, who had hurried up from their estate at Ladyburg the moment they heard of the robbery, and piles of messages of concern and congratulation, telegrams from the prime minister and from the *Ou Baas*, General Smuts, and from a hundred friends and business associates.

Yet Centaine felt detached from the hubbub. She watched it all through a screen of gossamer which muted sound and shape and gave it a dreamlike quality as though half of her was far away, drifting upon a beautiful green river, making love in the warm soft night while the mosquitoes whined outside the protective net, walking hand in hand with the man she loved, a tall strong gentle man with soft green eyes, the hands of a pianist and lovely sticky-out ears.

From her railway coach she telephoned Shasa and tried to sound enthusiastic about the fact that he was now the captain of his cricket eleven and about his mathematics marks which had at last taken an upward turn.

'I don't know when I will be back at Weltevreden, *chéri*. I have so many things to see to. We never recovered the diamonds, I'm afraid. There will have to be talks with the bank and I'll have to make new arrangements. No, of course not, silly boy! Of course we aren't poor, not yet, but a million pounds is a lot of money to lose, and then there will be the trial. Yes, he is an awful man, Shasa – but I don't know if they will hang him. Good Lord, no! They won't let us watch—'

Twice that first day of their separation she telephoned the residency in the forlorn hope that Blaine would answer, but it was a woman, either a secretary or Isabella, and each time she hung up without speaking.

They met again at the administrator's office the next day. Blaine had called a press conference and there was a crowd of journalists and photographers packed into the ante-chamber. Once again Isabella was there in her wheel-chair, with Blaine attentive and dutiful and unbearably handsome behind her. It took all Centaine's acting ability to shake hands in a friendly fashion, and then to joke lightly with the members of the press, even posing with Blaine for the photographs, and at no time to allow herself to moon at him. But afterwards as she drove herself back to the offices of the Courtney Mining and Finance Company, she had to pull off into a side road and sit quietly for a while to compose herself. There had been no opportunity for a single private exchange with Blaine.

Abe was waiting for her the moment she walked in through the front doors and he followed her up the stairs and into her office. 'Centaine, you are late. They have been waiting in the boardroom for almost an hour. I can't say with any great display of patience either.'

'Let them wait!' she told him with bravado she did not feel. 'They had better get accustomed to it.' The bank was her single largest creditor.

'The loss of the stones has frightened ten different shades of yellow out of them, Centaine.'

The bank directors had been demanding this meeting since the minute they heard she had arrived back in town.

'Where is Dr Twentyman-Jones?'

'He is in there with them, pouring oil on the troubled waters.' Abe laid a thick folder in front of her. 'Here are the schedules of the interest repayments.'

She glanced at them. She already knew them by heart. She could recite dates and amounts and rates. She had already prepared her strategy in detail but it was all dreamy and unreal, like a children's game.

'Anything new that I should know about before we go into the lions' den?' she asked.

'A long cable from Lloyd's of London. They have repudiated the claim. No armed escort.'

Centaine nodded. 'We expected that. Will we take them to court? What do you advise?'

'I am taking silk's opinion on that, but my own feeling is that it will be a waste of time and money.'

'Anything else?'

'De Beers,' he said. 'A message from Sir Ernest Oppenheimer himself.'

'Sniffing around already, is he?' She sighed, trying to make herself care, but she thought of Blaine instead. She saw him bending over the wheelchair. She pushed the image from her mind and concentrated on what Abe was telling her.

'Sir Ernest is coming up from Kimberley. He will be arriving in Windhoek on Thursday.'

'By some lucky chance,' she smiled cynically.

'He requests a meeting at your earliest convenience.'

'He has a nose like a hyena and the eyesight of a vulture,' Centaine said. 'He can smell blood and pick out a dying animal from a hundred leagues.'

'He is after the H'ani Mine, Centaine. He has been lusting after the H'ani for thirteen years.'

'They are all after the H'ani, Abe. The bank, Sir Ernest, all the predators. By God, they'll have to fight me for it.'

They stood up and Abe asked, 'Are you ready?'

Centaine glanced at herself in the mirror over the mantel, touched her hair, wet her lips with the tip of her tongue, and suddenly it all clicked into crisp focus again. She was going into battle, her mind cleared, her wits sharpened and she smiled a bright, confident, patronizing smile at herself. She was ready again.

'Let's go!' she said, and as they marched into the long boardroom with its stinkwood table and the six huge magically lyrical Pierneef murals of the desert places decorating the walls, she lifted her chin and her eyes sparkled with assumed confidence.

'Do forgive me, gentlemen,' she cried lightly, attacking

immediately with the full force of her personality and sexual allure and watching them wilt before it, 'but I assure you that you now have me, and my full attention, for as long as you want me.'

Deep inside her there was still that empty aching place which Blaine had filled for a few fleeting moments, but it was buttressed and fortified, she was impregnable once again, and as she took the leather upholstered chair at the head of the table she recited silently to herself like a mantra: 'The H'ani belongs to me – no one shall take it from me.'

Manfred De La Rey moved as swiftly through the darkness as the two grown men who led him northwards. The humiliation and pain of his father's dismissal had invoked within him a new defiance and steely determination. His father had called him a blubbering ninny.

'But I am a man now,' he told himself, striding onwards after the dark figure of Swart Hendrick. 'I will never cry again. I am a man, and I will prove it every day I live. I will prove it to you, Pa. If you are watching over me still, you will never have to be ashamed of me again.'

Then he thought of his father alone and dying upon the hilltop, and his grief was overwhelming. Despite his resolution, his tears rose to swamp him and it took all his strength and his will to thrust them down.

'I am a man now.' He fixed his mind upon it, and indeed he stood as tall as a man, almost as tall as Hendrick, and his long legs thrust him forward tirelessly. 'I will make you proud of me, Papa. I swear it. I swear it before God.'

He neither slackened his pace nor uttered a single complaint throughout that long night, and the sun was clear of the treetops when they reached the river.

As soon as they had drunk Hendrick had them up again and moving northwards. They travelled in a series of loops, swinging away from the river during the day, hiding out in the dry mopani, and then turning back to slake their thirst and follow the riverbank all the hours of darkness.

It was twelve of these nights of hard marching before Hendrick judged them clear of any pursuit.

'When will we cross the river, Hennie?' Manfred asked.

'Never,' Swart Hendrick told him.

'But it was my father's plan to cross to the Portuguese, to Alves De Santos the ivory trader, and then to travel to Luanda.'

'That was your father's plan,' Hendrick agreed. 'But your father is not with us. There is no place for a strange black man in the north. The Portuguese are even harder than the Germans or the English or the Boers. They will cheat us out of our diamonds, and beat us like dogs and send us to work on their labour gangs. No, Manie, we are going back – back to Ovamboland and our brothers of the tribe, where everyone is a friend and we can live like men and not animals.'

'The police will find us,' Manie argued.

'No man saw us. Your father made certain of that.'

'But they know you were my father's friend. They will come for you.'

Hendrick grinned. 'In Ovamboland my name is not Hendrick, and a thousand witnesses will swear I was always in my kraal and knew no white robber. To the white police all black men look the same, and I have a brother, a clever brother, who will know how and where to sell our diamonds for us. With these stones I can buy two hundred fine cattle and ten fat wives. No, Manie, we are going home.'

'And what will happen to me, Hendrick? I cannot go with you to the kraals of the Ovambo.'

'There is a place and a plan for you.' Hendrick placed

his arm around the white boy's shoulders, a paternal gesture. 'Your father has entrusted you to me. You do not have to fear. I will see you safe before I leave you.'

'When you go, Hendrick, I will be alone. I will have nothing.' And the black man could not answer him. He dropped his arm and spoke brusquely. 'It is time to march again; a long, hard road lies ahead of us.'

They left the river that night and turned back towards the south-west, skirting the terrible wastes of Bushmanland, keeping to the gentler, better watered lands, striking a more leisurely pace but still avoiding all habitation or human contact until, on the twentieth day after leaving Lothar De La Rey on his fatal hilltop, they followed a wooded ridge through well-pastured country and at last in the dusk looked down on a sprawling Ovambo village.

The conical huts of thatch were built in haphazard clusters of four or five, each surrounded by an enclosure of woven grass matting, and these were grouped around the big central cattle kraal with its palisade of poles set into the earth. The smell of woodsmoke drifted up to them on pale blue wisps, and it mingled with the ammoniacal scent of cattle dung and the floury smell of maize cakes baking on the coals. The cries of children's laughter and the voices of the women were melodious as wild bird calls. They picked out the gaudy flashes of the skirts of bright trade cotton as the women came up in single file from the water-hole with brimming clay pots balanced gracefully upon their heads.

However, they made no move to approach the village. Instead they lay concealed upon the ridge, watching for strangers or any sign of the unusual, even the smallest hint of danger, Hendrick and Klein Boy quietly discussing each movement they spotted, each sound that carried up from the village until Manfred grew impatient.

'Why are we waiting, Hennie?'

'Only the stupid young gemsbok rushes eagerly into the pitfall,' Hendrick grunted. 'We will go down when we are certain.'

In the middle of the afternoon a small black urchin drove a herd of goats up the slope. He was stark naked except for the slingshot hanging around his neck, and Hendrick whistled softly.

The child started and stared at their hiding-place fearfully. Then, when Hendrick whistled again, he crept towards them cautiously. Suddenly he crinkled into a grin too big and white for his grubby face and he rushed straight at Hendrick.

Hendrick laughed and lifted him onto his hip, and the child gabbled at him in ecstatic excitement.

'This is my son,' Hendrick told Manie, and then he questioned the child and listened to his piping replies with attention.

'There are no strangers in the village,' he grunted. 'The police were here, asking for me, but they have gone.'

Still carrying the child, he led them down the hill towards the largest of the clusters of huts, and he stooped through the opening in the matting fence. The yard was bare and swept, the circle of huts facing inwards. There were four women working in a group, all of them wearing only loincloths of coloured trade cotton; they rocked on the balls of their feet, singing softly in chorus, stamping and crushing the raw dried maize in tall wooden mortars, their bare breasts jerking and quivering with each stroke of the long poles they wielded as pestles in time to their chant.

One of the women shrieked when she saw Hendrick and rushed to him. She was an ancient crone, wrinkled and toothless, her pate covered with pure white wool. She dropped on her knees and hugged Hendrick's thick powerful legs, crooning with happiness.

'My mother,' said Hendrick, and lifted her to her feet.

Then they were surrounded by a swarm of delighted chattering women, but after a few minutes Hendrick quieted them and shooed them away.

'You are lucky, Manie,' he grunted, with a sparkle in his eyes. 'You will be allowed only one wife.'

At the entrance to the farthest hut the only man in the kraal sat on a low carved stool. He had kept completely aloof from the screeching excitement, and now Hendrick crossed to him. He was much younger than Hendrick, with paler, almost honey-coloured skin. However, his muscle had been forged and tempered by hard physical labour, and there was a confidence about him, that of a man who has striven and succeeded. He had also an air of grace, and fine intelligent features with a Nilotic cast like those of a young pharaoh. Surprisingly he held a thick battered book in his lap, a copy of Macaulay's *History of England*.

He greeted Hendrick with calm reserve, but their mutual affection was apparent to the white boy watching them.

'This is my clever young brother; same father, but different mothers. He speaks Afrikaans and much better English than even I do, and he reads books. His English name is Moses.'

'I see you, Moses.' Manie felt awkward under the penetrating scrutiny of those dark eyes.

'I see you, little white boy.'

'Do not call me "boy",' Manie said hotly. 'I am not a "boy".'

The men exchanged glances and smiled. 'Moses is a boss-boy on the H'ani Diamond Mine,' Hendrick explained in placatory fashion, but the tall Ovambo shook his head and replied in the vernacular.

'No longer, Big Brother. I was sacked over a month ago. So I sit here in the sun drinking beer and reading and thinking, performing all those onerous tasks which are a man's duty.' They laughed together, and Moses clapped his hands and called to the women imperiously.

'Bring beer – do you not see how my brother thirsts?'

For Hendrick it was good to divest himself of his western European clothing and dress again in the comfortable loincloth, to let himself drift back into the pace of village life. It was good to savour the tart effervescent sorghum beer, thick as gruel and cool in the clay pots, and to talk quietly of cattle and game, of crops and rain, of acquaintances and friends and relatives, of deaths and births and matings. It was a long leisurely time before they came circumspectly to the pressing issues which had to be discussed.

'Yes,' Moses nodded. 'The police were here. Two dogs of the white men in Windhoek who should be ashamed to have betrayed their own tribe. They were not dressed in uniform, but still they had the stink of police upon them. They stayed many days, asking questions about a man called Swart Hendrick – smiling and friendly at first, then angry and threatening. They beat a few of the women, your mother—' He saw Hendrick stiffen and his jaw clench and went on quickly, 'She is old but tough. She has been beaten before; our father was a strict man. Despite the blows, she did not know Swart Hendrick, nobody knew Swart Hendrick, and the police dogs went away.'

'They will return,' said Hendrick, and his half-brother nodded.

'Yes. The white men never forget. Five years, ten years. They hanged a man in Pretoria for killing a man twenty-five years before. They will return.'

They drank in turn from the pot of beer, sipping with relish and then passing the black pot from hand to hand.

'So there was talk of a great robbery of diamonds on the road from the H'ani, and they mentioned the name of the white devil with whom you have always ridden and fought, with whom you went out on the big green to catch fish. They say that you were with him at the taking of the

342

diamonds, and that they will hang you on a rope when they find you.'

Hendrick chuckled and counterattacked. 'I also have heard stories of a fellow who is neither unknown nor unrelated to me. I have heard he is well versed in the disposal of stolen diamonds. That all the stones taken from the H'ani Mine pass through his hands.'

'Now who could have told you such vile lies?' Moses smiled faintly, and Hendrick gestured to Klein Boy. He brought a rawhide bag from its hiding place and placed it in front of his father. Hendrick opened the flap and, one at a time, lifted out the small packages of brown cartridge paper and laid them on the hard bare earth of the yard – fourteen in a row.

His brother took up the first package and with his sheath knife split the wax seal. 'This is the mark of the H'ani Mine,' he remarked, and carefully unfolded the paper. His expression did not change as he examined the contents. He placed the package aside and opened the next. He did not speak until he had opened all fourteen, and studied them. Then he said softly, 'Death. There is death here. A hundred deaths, a thousand deaths.'

'Can you sell them for us?' Hendrick asked, and Moses shook his head.

'I have never seen such stones, so many together. To try to sell these all at once would bring disaster and death upon us all. I must think upon this, but in the meantime we dare not keep these deadly stones in the kraal.'

The next morning in the dawn the three of them – Hendrick and Moses and Klein Boy – left the village together and climbed to the crest of the ridge where they found the leadwood tree that Hendrick remembered from the days when he roamed here as a naked herdboy. There was a hollow in the trunk, thirty feet above the ground, which had been the nesting hole of a pair of eagle owls.

While the others stood guard, Klein Boy climbed to the nesting hole, carrying the rawhide bag.

It was many days more before Moses gave his carefully considered summation.

'My brother, you and I are no longer of this life or this place. Already I have seen the first restlessness in you. I have seen you look out to the horizon with the expression of a man who longs to breast them. This life, so sweet at first, palls swiftly. The taste of beer goes flat on the tongue, and a man thinks of the brave things he has done, and the braver things which wait for him still somewhere out there.'

Hendrick smiled. 'You are a man of many skills, my brother, even that of looking into a man's head and reading his secret thoughts.'

'We cannot stay here. The death stones are too dangerous to keep here, too dangerous to sell.'

Hendrick nodded. 'I am listening,' he said.

'There are things which I have to do. Things which I believe are in my destiny, and of which I have never spoken, not even to you.'

'Speak of them now.'

'I speak of the art which the white men call politics and from which we as black men are excluded.'

Hendrick made a dismissive scornful gesture. 'You read too many books. There is no profit or reward in that business. Leave it to the white men.'

'You are wrong, my brother. In that art lie treasures which make your little white stones seem paltry. No, do not scoff.'

Hendrick opened his mouth and then closed it slowly. He had not truly thought about this before, but the young man facing him had a powerful presence, a quivering intensity which stirred and excited him although he did not understand fully the implication of his words.

344

'My brother, I have decided. We will leave here. It is too small for us.'

Hendrick nodded. The thought did not disturb him. He had been a nomad all his life, and he was ready to move on again.

'Not only this kraal, my brother. We will leave this land.'

'Leave this land!' Hendrick started up and then sank back on his stool.

'We have to do this. This land is too small for us and the stones.'

'Where will we go?'

His brother held up his hand. 'We will discuss that soon, but first you must rid us of this white child you have brought amongst us. He is even more dangerous than the stones. He will bring the white police down upon us even more swiftly. When you have done that, my brother, we will be ready to go on to do what we have to do.'

Swart Hendrick was a man of great strength, both physical and mental. He feared very little, would attempt anything and suffer much for what he wanted, but always he had followed someone else. Always there had been a man even fiercer and more fearless than he to lead him.

'We will do as you say, my brother,' he agreed, and he knew instinctively that he had found someone to replace the man he had left to die upon a rock in the desert.

'I will wait here until the sun rises tomorrow,' Swart Hendrick told the white boy. 'If you do not return by then, I will know you are safe.'

'Will I see you again, Hennie?' Manie asked wistfully, and Hendrick hesitated on the brink of empty promise.

'I think that our feet will be on different paths from now on, Manie.' He reached out and placed a hand on Manfred's shoulder. 'But I shall think of you often – and, who knows, one day the paths may come together again.' He squeezed the boy's shoulder and he noticed that it was sheathed in muscle, like that of a man full grown. 'Go in peace, and be a man like your father was.'

He pushed Manfred away lightly, but the white boy lingered. 'Hendrick,' he whispered, 'there are many things I want to say to you – but I do not have the words.'

'Go,' Hendrick said. 'We both know. It does not have to be spoken of. Go, Manie.'

Manfred picked up his pack and blanket roll and stepped out of the undergrowth onto the dusty rutted road. He started down towards the village, towards the spire of the church which he recognized somehow as a symbol of a new existence, that at once both beckoned and repelled him.

At the bend in the road he looked back. There was no sign of the big Ovambo, and he turned and trudged down the main street towards the church at the far end.

Without conscious decision he turned from the main street down a side opening and approached the pastory along the sanitary lane as he had done on the last visit with his father. The narrow lane was hedged with fleshy moroto plants, and he whiffed the sanitary buckets behind the little sliding doors of the outhouses that backed onto the lane. He hesitated at the back gate of the pastory and then lifted the latch and started at a snail's pace up the long pathway.

Halfway along the path he was stopped by a bellow, and he stared about him apprehensively. There was another roar and a loud voice lifted in exhortation or acrimonious argument. It came from a ramshackle building at the bottom of the yard, a large woodshed perhaps.

Manfred sidled down towards the shed and peered around the jamb of the door. The interior was dark but as his eyes adjusted Manfred saw that it was a toolroom, with an anvil and forge at one end and tools hanging on the walls. The earthen floor was bare and in the centre of it knelt Tromp Bierman, the trumpet of God.

He was wearing dark suit trousers and a white shirt with the white tie of his office. His suit jacket hung on a pair of blacksmith's tongs above the anvil. Tromp Bierman's bushy beard was pointed to the roof and his eyes were closed, his arms lifted in an attitude of surrender or supplication; but his tone was far from submissive.

'Oh Lord God of Israel, I call upon you most urgently to give answer to your servant's prayers for guidance in this matter. How can I perform your will if I do not know what it is? I am only a humble instrument, I dare not take this decision alone. Look down, oh Lord God, have pity on my ignorance and stupidity and make known your intentions—'

Tromp broke off suddenly and opened his eyes. The great shaggy leonine head turned, and the eyes, like those of an Old Testament prophet, burned into Manfred's soul.

Hastily Manfred snatched the shapeless sweatstained hat from his head and held it with both hands to his chest.

'I have come back, *Oom*,' he said. 'Just like you said I must.'

Tromp stared at him ferociously. He saw a sturdy lad, broad-shouldered and with powerful shapely limbs, a head of dusty golden curls and contrasting eyebrows black as coal dust over strange topaz-coloured eyes. He tried to see beyond the pale surface of those eyes and was aware of an aura of determination and lucid intelligence that surrounded the youth.

'Come here,' he ordered, and Manfred dropped his pack and went to him. Tromp seized him by the hand and dragged him down.

'Kneel, *Jong*, get down on your knees and give thanks to your Maker. Praise the Lord God of your fathers that he has heard my supplications on your behalf.'

Dutifully Manfred closed his eyes and clasped his hand.

'Oh Lord, forgive your servant's importunity in bringing to your notice such other trivial matters, when in fact you were occupied with more dire affairs. We thank you for delivering into our care this young person, whom we shall temper and hone into a sword. A mighty blade that shall strike down the Philistine, a weapon that shall be wielded to your glory, in the just and righteous cause of your chosen people, the Afrikaner *Volk*.' He prodded Manfred with a forefinger like a pruning shear.

'Amen!' Manfred gasped at the pain.

'We will glorify and praise you all the days of our life, O Lord, and we beg of you to bestow upon this chosen son of our people the fortitude and the determination—'

The prayer, punctuated by Manfred's fervent 'Amens' lasted until Manfred's knees ached and he was dizzy with fatigue and hunger. Then suddenly Tromp hauled him to his feet and marched him up the path to the kitchen door.

'*Mevrou*,' the trumpet of God sounded. 'Where are you, woman?'

Trudi Bierman rushed breathlessly into the kitchen at the summons and then stopped aghast, staring at the boy in ragged, filthy clothing.

'My kitchen,' she wailed. 'My beautiful clean kitchen. I have just waxed the floor.'

'The Lord God has sent this *Jong* to us,' Tromp intoned. 'We will take him into our home. He will eat at our table, he will be as one of our own.'

'But he is filthy as a kaffir.'

'Then wash him, woman, wash him.'

At that moment a girl slipped timidly through the doorway behind the matronly figure of Trudi Bierman and then stiffened like a frightened fawn as she saw Manfred.

Manfred barely recognized Sarah. She had filled out, firm well-scrubbed flesh covered her elbows, which had so recently been bony lumps on sticklike arms. Her once pale cheeks were apple pink, the eyes that had been lacklustre were clear and bright, her blond hair, brushed until it shone, was plaited into twin pigtails and pinned on top of her head, and she wore long modest but spotless skirts to her ankles.

She let out a cry and rushed at Manfred with arms outstretched, but Trudi Bierman seized her from behind and shook her soundly.

'You lazy wicked girl. I left you to finish your sums. Back you go this instant.' She pushed her roughly from the room and turned back to Manfred, her arms folded and her mouth pursed.

'You are disgusting,' she told him. 'Your hair is long as a girl's. Those clothes—' Her expression hardened even more fearsomely. 'And we are Christian folk in this house. We'll have none of your father's godless wild ways, do you understand?'

'I'm hungry, Aunt Trudi.'

'You'll eat when everybody else eats, and not before you are clean.' She looked at her husband. '*Menheer*, will you show the boy how to build a fire in the hotwater geyser?'

She stood in the doorway of the tiny bathroom and remorselessly supervised his ablutions, brushing aside all his attempts at modesty and his protests at the temperature of the water, and when he faltered, taking the bar of blue mottled soap herself and scrubbing his most tender and intimate creases and folds.

Then with only a skimpy towel about his waist she led him by the ear down the back steps and sat him on a fruit box. She armed herself with a pair of sheep shears and Manfred's blond hair fell about his shoulders like wheat before the scythe. When he ran his hand over his scalp it was stubbly and bristly and the back of his neck and the skin behind his ears felt cool and draughty.

Trudi Bierman gathered up his discarded clothing with a pantomime of distaste and opened the furnace of the

349

geyser. Manfred was only just in time to rescue his jacket, and when she saw his expression as he backed away from her, holding the garment behind his back and surreptitiously fingering the small lumps in the lining, she shrugged.

'Very well – perhaps with a wash and a few patches. In the meantime I'll find you some of the dominie's old things.'

Trudi Bierman took Manfred's appetite as a personal challenge to her kitchen and her culinary skills. She kept heaping his plate even before he had finished, standing over him with a ladle in one hand and the handle of the stewpot in the other. When at last he fell back satiated, she went to fetch the milk tart from the pantry with a victorious gleam in her eye.

As strangers in the family, Manfred and Sarah were allocated the lowliest seats in the centre of the table, the two plump, pudding-faced, blond Bierman daughters sitting above them.

Sarah picked at her food so lightly that she earned Trudi Bierman's ire. 'I didn't cook good food for you to fiddle with, young lady. You'll sit here as long as it takes you to clean your place, spinach and all – even if that takes all night.' And Sarah chewed mechanically, never taking her eyes from Manfred's face.

It was the first time that Manfred had paid for a meal with two graces, before and after, and each of them seemed interminable. He was nodding and swaying in his chair when Tromp Bierman startled him fully awake with an 'Amen' like a salvo of artillery.

The pastory was already groaning at the seams with Sarah and the Bierman offspring. There was no place for Manfred, so he was allocated a corner of the toolshed at the bottom of the yard. Aunt Trudi had turned a packing case on end to act as a cupboard for his few cast-off items of clothing and there was an iron bed with a hard lumpy coir mattress and a faded old curtain hung on a string to screen his sleeping corner.

'Don't waste the candle,' Aunt Trudi cautioned him from the doorway of the toolshed. 'You will only get a new one on the first day of each month. We are thrifty folk here. None of your father's extravagances, thank you!'

Manfred pulled the thin grey blanket over his head to protect his naked scalp from the chill. It was the first time in his life that he had had a bed and room of his own and he revelled in the sensation, sniffing the aroma of axle grease and paraffin and the dead coals in the forge as he fell asleep.

He woke to a light touch on his cheek and cried out; confused images rushed out of the darkness to terrify him. He had dreamed of his father's hand, reeking of gangrene, that had reached across from the far side of the grave and he struggled up from under the blanket.

'Manie, Manie. It's me.' Sarah's voice was as terrified as his own cry had been. She was silhouetted by the moonlight through the single uncurtained window, thin and shivering in a white nightdress, her hair brushed out and hanging to her shoulders in a silvery cloud.

'What are you doing here?' he mumbled. 'You mustn't come here. You must go. If they find you here they will—' he broke off. He was not sure what the consequences would be, but he knew instinctively that they would be severe. This strange but pleasant new sense of security and belonging would be shattered.

'I've been so unhappy.' He could tell by her voice that she was crying. 'Ever since you went away. The girls are so cruel – they call me *vuilgoed*, "trash". They tease me because I can't read and do sums the way they can and because I speak funny. I've cried every night since you went away.'

Manfred's heart went out to her, and despite his nervousness at being discovered, he reached out for her and drew her down onto the bed. 'I'm here now. I'll look after you, Sarie,' he whispered. 'I won't let them tease you any more.'

She sobbed against his neck, and he told her sternly, 'I don't want any more crying, Sarie. You aren't a baby any more. You must be brave.'

'I was crying because I was happy,' she sniffed.

'No more crying – not even when you are happy,' he ordered. 'Do you understand?' And she nodded furiously, and made a little choking sound as she brought her tears under control.

'I've thought about you every day,' she whispered. 'I prayed to God to bring you back like you promised. Can I get into bed with you, Manie? I'm cold.'

'No,' he said firmly. 'You must go back, before they catch you here.'

'Just for a moment,' she pleaded and before he could protest she had wriggled around, lifted the blanket and slipped under the corner.

She wrapped herself around him. The nightdress was thin and worn, her body cold and shivery, and he could not bring himself to chase her out.

'Five minutes,' he muttered. 'Then you have to go.'

Swiftly the heat flowed back into her small body, and her hair was soft against his face and smelt good, like the fur of an unweaned kitten, milky and warm. She made him feel old and important, and he stroked her hair with a paternal proprietary feeling.

'Do you think God answers our prayers?' she asked softly. 'I prayed the hardest I know how, and here you are, just like I asked.' She was silent a moment. 'But it took a long time and a lot of prayers.'

'I don't know about prayers,' he admitted. 'My pa never prayed much. He never taught me how.'

'Well, you better get used to it now,' she warned him. 'In this house, everybody prays all the time.'

When she at last crept out of the toolshed back to the

big house, she left a warm patch on the mattress, and a warmer place in his heart.

I t was still dark when Manfred was roused by a blast from the Trumpet of God in person.

'Ten seconds and then you get a bucket of cold water, *Jong*.' And Uncle Tromp led him, shivering and covered in goosebumps, to the trough beside the stables.

'Cold water is the best cure for the sins of the young flesh, *Jong*,' Uncle Tromp told him with relish. 'You will muck out the stables and curry the pony before breakfast, do you hear?'

The day was a dizzying succession of labour and prayer, the household chores sandwiched between long sessions of school work and even longer sessions on their knees, while either Uncle Tromp or Aunt Trudi exhorted God to step up their performance or visit them with all kinds of retribution.

Yet by the end of the first week Manfred had subtly but permanently rearranged the pecking order amongst the younger members of the household. He had quelled the Bierman girls' first furtive but concerted attempts at mockery with a steady implacable stare from his yellow eyes, and they retreated in twittering consternation.

Over the school books it was different. His cousins were all dedicated scholars, with the benefit of a lifetime of enforced study. As Manfred grimly applied himself to the tome on German grammar and Melckes' *Mathematics for Secondary Schools*, their smug self-satisfied smiles at his floundering replies to Aunt Trudi's catechism were all the incentive he needed.

'I'll show them,' he promised himself, and he was so committed to the task of catching and overhauling his cousins that it was days before he became aware of how the

Bierman girls were victimizing little Sarah. Their cruelty was refined and secretive; a jibe, a name, a mocking face; calculated exclusion from their games and laughter; sabotage of her domestic chores, a soot stain on garments Sarah had just ironed, rumpled linen on a bed she had just made, grease marks on dishes she had washed; and vicious grins when Sarah was chastised for laziness and negligence by Aunt Trudi, who was only too pleased to perform this godly duty with the back of a hairbrush.

Manfred caught each of the Bierman girls alone. Held them by the pigtails and looked into their eyes from a range of a few inches while he spoke in a soft measured voice that hissed with passion and ended ' – and don't run and tell tales to your mother, either'. Their deliberate cruelty ended with dramatic suddenness, and under Manfred's protection Sarah was left severely alone.

At the end of that first week, after the fifth church service of a long, tedious Sunday, one of the cousins appeared in the doorway of the toolshed where Manfred was stretched on his bed with his German grammar.

'My pa wants to see you in his study.' And the messenger wrung one hand in a parody of looming disaster.

Manfred soused his short-cropped hair under the tap and tried to brush it flat in the splinter of mirror wedged above his bed. It immediately sprang up again in damp spikes and he gave up the effort and hurried to answer the summons.

He had never been allowed into the front rooms of the pastory. They were sacrosanct, and of these the dominie's study was the holy of holies. He knew from warnings, repeated by his cousins with morbid relish, that a summons to this room was always associated with punishment and pain. He trembled on the threshold, knowing that Sarah's nightly visits to the toolshed had been discovered, and he started wildly at the bellow that answered his timid knock, then pushed the door open slowly and stepped inside.

Uncle Tromp stood behind the sombre stinkwood desk,

leaning on clenched fists that were placed in the centre of the blotter. 'Come in, *Jong*. Shut the door. Don't just stand there!' he roared and dropped heavily into his chair.

Manfred stood before him, trying to form the words of repentance and atonement, but before he could utter them, Uncle Tromp spoke again.

'Well, *Jong*, I have had reports of you from your aunt.' His tone was at odds with his ferocious expression. 'She tells me that your education has been sadly neglected, but that you are willing and seem to be applying yourself.' Manfred sagged with relief so intense that he had difficulty following the long exhortation that followed. 'We are the underdogs, *Jong*. We are the victims of oppression and Milnerism.' Manfred knew about Lord Milner from his father; the notorious English governor and opponent of Afrikanderdom under whose decree all children who spoke the Afrikaans language in school were forced to wear a dunce's cap with the legend 'I am a donkey – I spoke Dutch' inscribed upon it. 'There is only one way that we can overcome our enemies, *Jong*. We have to become cleverer and stronger and more ruthless than they are.'

The Trumpet of God became so absorbed by his own words, that he lifted his gaze to the elaborate patterns of the fancy plastered ceiling and his eyes glazed over with a mixture of religious and political fanaticism, leaving Manfred free to glance around him furtively at the over-furnished room.

Bookshelves covered three walls, all of them stacked with religious and serious tomes. John Calvin and the authors of the Presbyterian form of church government predominated, though there were works of history and philosophy, law and biography, dictionaries and encyclopaedia and shelves of hymns and collected sermons in High Dutch, German and English.

The fourth wall, directly behind Uncle Tromp's desk, carried a gallery of photographs, stern ancestors in Sunday finery in the top row and then, below them, devout congregations or learned members of synod, all featuring amongst them the unmistakable likeness of Tromp Bierman – a gradually maturing and ageing succession of Tromps, from clean-shaven and bright-eyed youth to bearded leonine maturity in the front row.

Then, quite incongruously and startlingly, a framed and yellowing photograph, the largest of them all and situated in the most prominent position, depicting a young man stripped to the waist, wearing full-length tights, and about his middle a magnificent belt, gleaming with engraved silver buckles and medallions.

The man in the photograph was Tromp Bierman aged no more than twenty-five, cleanshaven, his hair parted in the middle and plastered flat with brilliantine, his powerful body marvellously muscled, his clenched fists held before him, crouching in the classic stance of the pugilist. A small table in front of him held a treasure of glittering cups and sporting trophies. The young man smiled out of the photograph, strikingly handsome, and in Manfred's eyes, impossibly dashing and romantic.

'You are a boxer,' he blurted out, unable to contain his wonder and admiration, and the Trumpet of God was cut off in mid-blast. The great shaggy head lowered, the eyes blinking as they readjusted to reality and then swivelling to follow Manfred's gaze.

'Not just a boxer,' said Uncle Tromp. 'But a champion. Light heavyweight champion of the Union of South Africa.' He looked back and saw the expression on Manfred's face, and his own expression warmed and melted with remembrance and gratification.

'Did you win all those cups – and that belt?'

'I surely did, *Jong*. I smote the Philistines hip and thigh. I struck them down in their multitudes.'

'Did you only fight Philistines, Uncle Tromp?'

'They were all Philistines, *Jong*. As soon as they stepped

into the ring with me they became Philistines and I fell upon them without mercy, like the hammer and the sword of the Almighty.' Tromp Bierman lifted his clenched fists in front of him and shot out a swift tattoo of punches, firing them across the desk, stopping each blow only inches from Manfred's nose.

'I made my living with these fists, Jong. All comers at ten pounds a time. I fought Mike Williams and put him down in the sixth, the great Mike Williams himself.' He grunted as he weaved and boxed in his chair 'Ha! Ha! Left! Right! Left! I even thrashed the black Jephta, and I took the title from Jack Lalor in 1916. I can still hear the cheers now as Lalor hit the canvas. Sweet, my Jong, so very sweet—' he broke off, and replaced his hands in his lap, his expression becoming dignified and stern once again. 'Then your Aunt Trudi and the Lord God of Israel called me from the ring to more important work.' And the gleam of battle lust faded regretfully from Uncle Tromp's eyes.

'Boxing and being champion – that would be the most important thing for me,' Manfred breathed, and Tromp's gaze focused thoughtfully upon him. He looked him over carefully from the top of his cropped head to his large but well-proportioned feet in battered velskoen.

'You want to learn to fight?' He dropped his voice, and glanced at the door, a conspiratorial gesture.

Manfred could not answer; his throat was closed with excitement, but he nodded vigorously and Uncle Tromp went on in his normal piercing tones.

'Your Aunt Trudi doesn't approve of brawling. Quite right too! Fisticuffs are for hooligans. Put the thought from your mind, Jong. Think on higher planes.' He shook his head so vigorously that his beard was disarranged, it took that effort to dislodge the notion from his own head, and he combed his beard with his fingers as he went on.

'To return to what I was saying. Your aunt and I think it best that you drop the name De La Rey for the time

357

being. You shall adopt the name Bierman until the notoriety of your father's trial fades. There has already been too much mention of that name in the newspapers, those organs of Lucifer. Your aunt is quite right in not allowing them into this house. There will be a great hoo-ha once the trial of your father begins in Windhoek next month. It could bring shame and disgrace on you and this family.'

'My father's trial?' Manfred stared at him without comprehension. 'But my father is dead.'

'Dead? Is that what you thought?' Tromp stood up and came around the desk. 'Forgive me, *Jong*.' He placed both his huge hands on Manfred's shoulders. 'I have caused you unnecessary suffering by not speaking of this earlier. Your father is not dead. He has been captured by the police, and he will stand trial for his life at the Supreme Court in Windhoek on the twentieth of next month.'

He steadied Manfred as the boy reeled at the impact of the words and then went on with a gentle rumble. 'Now you understand why we want you to change your name, *Jong*.'

Sarah had hurried through her ironing and sneaked out of the house. She was perched now on top of the woodpile with her knees drawn up under her chin, hugging her legs with both arms as she watched Manfred at work. She loved to watch him with the axe. It was a long two-handed axe, with a red-painted head and a bright edge to the blade. Manie sharpened it on the whetstone until he could shave the fine gold hair off the back of his hand with it.

He had taken off his shirt and given it to her to hold. His chest and back were all shiny with sweat. She liked the way he smelled when he sweated, like newly baked bread, or like a sun-warm fig just picked from the tree.

Manfred laid another log in the cradle and stood back. He spat on the palms of his hands. He always did that and she involuntarily worked up a ball of spit in her own mouth in sympathy. Then he hefted the long axe and she tensed herself.

'Five times table,' he ordered, and swung the axe in a long looping blow. It hummed faintly over his head as he brought it down. The bright blade buried itself in the log with a clunk and at the same instant Manie gave a sharp explosive grunt of effort.

'Five ones are five,' she recited in time to the swinging axe.

'Five twos are ten.' Manie grunted and a white wedge of wood flew as high as his head.

'Five threes are fifteen.' The axe head spun a bright circle in the yellow light of the lowering sun, and Sarah chanted shrilly as the wood chips pelted down like hail.

The log dropped from the cradle in two pieces just as Sarah cried, 'Five tens are fifty.' Manie stepped back and leaned on the axe handle, and grinned at her.

'Very good, Sarie, not a single mistake.'

She preened with pleasure – and then stared over his shoulder, her expression suddenly stricken and guilty. She leapt down from the woodpile and in a swirl of skirts scampered back up the path to the house.

Manie turned quickly. Uncle Tromp was leaning against the corner of the toolshed watching him.

'I'm sorry, Uncle Tromp.' He ducked his head. 'I know she shouldn't be here, but I just can't send her away.'

Uncle Tromp pushed himself away from the wall and came slowly to where Manfred stood. He moved like a great bear with long arms dangling, and he circled Manfred slowly, examining him with a small distracted frown creasing his forehead.

Manfred squirmed self-consciously, and Uncle Tromp prodded his gut with a large painful finger.

'How old are you, *Jong?*'

Manfred told him and Uncle Tromp nodded. 'Three years to full growth. You'll class light-heavy, I'd say, unless you make a spurt at the end and go full heavyweight.'

Manfred felt his skin prickle at the unfamiliar but somehow tremendously exciting terms, and Uncle Tromp left him and went to the woodpile. Deliberately he stripped off the dark jacket of his suit and folded it neatly. He laid it on the woodpile and then unknotted his white minister's tie and laid that meticulously on top of his jacket. He came back to Manfred rolling up the sleeves of his white shirt.

'So you want to be a boxer?' he asked, and Manfred nodded, unable to speak.

'Put the axe away.' Manfred buried the blade in the chopping stump and faced his uncle again. Uncle Tromp held up his open right hand, palm towards Manfred.

'Hit it!' he said. Manfred clenched his fist and made a tentative round-arm swing.

'You aren't knitting socks, *Jong*, you aren't kneading bread. What are you, a man or a kitchen maid? Hit it, man. Hit it! That's better, don't swing it around the back of your head, shoot it out! Harder! Harder! That's more like it. Now your left, that's it! Left! Right! Left!'

Uncle Tromp was holding up both hands now, swaying and dancing in front of him, and Manfred followed him eagerly, socking alternate fists into the big open palms.

'All right.' Tromp dropped his hands. 'Now hit me. Hit me in the face. Go on, hard as you can. Right on the button. Let's see you knock me on my back.'

Manfred dropped his hands and stepped back.

'I can't do that, Uncle Tromp,' he protested.

'Can't do what, *Jong?* What can't you do?'

'I couldn't hit you. It wouldn't be right. It wouldn't be respectful.'

'So we are talking respect now, not boxing. We are

360

talking powder puffs and ladies' gloves, are we?' Uncle Tromp roared. 'I thought you wanted to fight. I thought you wanted to be a man and now I find a snot-nosed whining baby.' He changed his voice to a cracked falsetto. 'It wouldn't be right, Uncle Tromp, it wouldn't be respectful,' he mimicked.

Suddenly his right hand shot out and the open palm cracked against Manfred's cheek, a stinging slap that left the scarlet imprint of fingers on his skin.

'You're not respectful, *Jong*. You're yellow. That's what you are, a yellow-bellied whimpering little boy. You're not a man! You'll never be a fighter!'

The other huge paw blurred with speed, coming so fast and unexpectedly that Manfred barely saw it. The pain of the blow filled his eyes with tears.

'We'll have to find a skirt for you, girlie, a yellow skirt.'

Uncle Tromp was watching him carefully, watching his eyes, praying silently for it to happen as he poured withering contempt on the sturdy youth who retreated, bewildered and uncertain. He followed and struck again, cutting Manfred's lower lip, splitting the soft skin against his teeth, leaving a smear of blood down his chin.

'Come on!' he exhorted silently, behind the jeering flood of insults. 'Come on, please, come on!'

Then with a great explosion of joy that filled his chest to bursting, he saw it happen. Manfred dropped his chin, and his eyes changed. Suddenly they glowed with a cold yellow light, implacable as the stare of a lion in the moment before it launches its charge, and the youth came at him.

Though he had been waiting for it, expecting it, praying for it, still the speed and savagery of the attack caught Uncle Tromp off-balance. Only the old fighter's instinct saved him, and he deflected that first murderous assault, sensing the power in the fists that grazed his temple and ruffled his beard as they passed, and for the first few desperate seconds there was no time for thought. All his wits and attention were needed to stay on his feet and keep the cold, ferocious animal he had created at bay.

Then experience and ringcraft, long forgotten, reasserted themselves, and he ducked and dodged and danced easily just beyond the boy's reach, deflecting the wild punches, watching objectively as though he sat in a ringside seat, assessing with rising delight the way in which the untutored youth used either fist with equal power and dexterity.

'A natural two-handed puncher! He doesn't favour his right, and he gets his shoulders behind every punch without being taught how,' he exulted.

Then he looked again at the eyes and felt a chill of awe at what he had loosed upon the world.

'He's a killer.' He recognized it. 'He has the instinct of the leopard who kills for the taste of blood and the simple joy of it. He no longer sees me. He sees only the prey before him.'

That knowledge had distracted him. He caught a right-hander on his upper arm and it jarred the teeth in his jaws and the bones of his ankles. He knew it would bruise him from the shoulder to the elbow, and his breath burned in his throat. His legs were turning to lead. He could feel his heart drumming against his ribs. Twenty-two years since he had been in the ring; twenty-two years of Trudi's cooking and his most vigorous exercise undertaken either at his desk or in the pulpit, while the youth before him was like a machine, boring in remorselessly, both fists swinging, those yellow eyes fixed upon him in a murderous myopic stare.

Uncle Tromp gathered himself, waited for the opening as Manfred swung right-handed, and then he counter-punched with his left, always his best, the same blow that had dropped black Jephta in the third, and it went in with that beautiful little click of bone against bone.

Manfred dropped to his knees, stunned, the killing

362

yellow light fading from his eyes to be replaced by a dull bemused look, as though awakening from a trance.

'That's it, *Jong*.' The Trumpet of God's fine note was reduced to a breathy gasp. 'Down on your knees and give thanks to your Maker.' Uncle Tromp lowered his bulk beside Manfred and placed a thick arm around his shoulders. He raised his face and his unsteady voice to heaven. 'Almighty God, we give You thanks for the strong body with which You have endowed Your young servant. We give You thanks also for his natural left – while realizing that it will need a lot of hard work – and we humbly beseech You to look favourably upon our efforts to instil in him even the rudiments of footwork. His right hand is a blessing directly from You, for which we will always be eternally grateful, though he will have to learn not to telegraph it five days in advance of the punch.'

Manfred was still shaking his head and rubbing his jaw, but he responded to the probing thumb in his ribs with a fervent 'Amen.'

'We will begin roadwork immediately, O Lord, while we set up a ring in the toolshed in which to learn the ropes, and we humbly beseech Your blessing on our enterprise and Your co-operation in keeping it from coming to the notice of Your servant's partner in holy matrimony, Trudi Bierman.'

Most afternoons, under the pretext of visiting one of his parishioners, Uncle Tromp would put the pony in the trap and drive out of the front gate with a flourish, waving to his wife on the front stoep. Manfred would be waiting at the clump of camel-thorn trees beside the main Windhoek road, already barefoot and stripped to khaki shorts, and he would trot out and fall in beside the trap as Uncle Tromp shook the fat pony into a canter.

'Five miles today, *Jong* – down to the river bridge and back, and we'll do it a bit faster than yesterday.'

The gloves that Uncle Tromp had smuggled down from the trunk in the loft were cracked with age, but they patched them with woodglue and the first time he laced them onto Manfred's hands he watched while the lad lifted them to his nose and sniffed them.

'The smell of leather and sweat and blood, *Jong*. Fill your nostrils with it. You'll live with it from now on.'

Manfred punched the tattered old gloves together, and for a moment that flat yellow light glowed in his eyes again, then he grinned.

'They feel good,' he said.

'Nothing feels better,' Uncle Tromp agreed, and led him to the heavy canvas kitbag filled with river sand that hung from the rafters in the corner of the toolshed.

'To begin with I want to see that left hand do some work. It's like a wild horse; we have to break it and train it, teach it not to waste strength and effort. It has to learn to do our bidding, not flap around in the air.'

They built the ring together, quarter-full size for the toolshed would take no more, and they sank the corner poles deep in the earthen floor and cemented them in. Then they stretched a sheet of canvas over the floor. The canvas and the cement had been commandeered from one of Uncle Tromp's wealthy parishioners, 'For the glory of God and the *Volk*,' an appeal that could not be lightly dismissed.

Sarah, sworn to secrecy by the most solemn and dreadful oath that Manfred and Uncle Tromp could concoct between them, was allowed to watch the ringwork, even though she was a thoroughly partisan audience and cheered shrilly and shamelessly for the younger participant.

After two of these sessions, which left Uncle Tromp

unmarked but blowing like a steam engine, he shook his head ruefully. 'It's no use, *Jong*, either we have to find you another sparring partner, or I'll have to start training again myself.'

Thereafter the pony was left tethered in the camel-thorn clump and Uncle Tromp grunted and gasped beside Manfred on the long runs, while the sweat fell from his beard like the first rains of summer.

However, his protuberant gut shrivelled miraculously, and soon from under the layers of soft fat that covered his shoulders and chest the outline of hard muscle reappeared. Gradually they stepped up the rounds from two to four minutes with Sarah, elected official timekeeper, measuring each round with Uncle Tromp's cheap silver pocket watch which made up for its dubious accuracy by its size.

It was almost a month before Uncle Tromp could say to himself, though he would never have dreamed of saying it to Manfred, 'He is starting to look like a boxer now.' Instead he said: 'Now I want speed. I want you to be fast as a mamba – brave as a ratel.'

The mamba was the most dreaded of all Africa's serpents. It could grow as thick as a man's wrist and reach twenty feet in length. Its venom could inflict death on a fully grown man in four minutes, an excruciating death. The mamba was so swift that it could overhaul a galloping horse, and the strike was so swift as to cheat the eye.

'Fast as a mamba – brave as a ratel,' Uncle Tromp repeated, as he would a hundred, a thousand times in the years ahead.

The ratel was the African honey badger, a small animal with a loose but thick tough skin that could defy the bite of a mastiff or the fangs of a leopard, a massive flattened skull from which the heaviest club bounced harmlessly, and the heart of a lion, the courage of a giant. Normally mild and forbearing, it would fearlessly attack the largest adversary the instant that it was provoked. Legend had it that the ratel possessed an instinct for the groin and that it would rush in and rip the testicles out of any male animal, man or bull buffalo or lion, who threatened it.

'I've got something to show you, *Jong*.' Uncle Tromp led Manfred to the big wooden chest against the back wall of the toolshed and opened the lid. 'It's for you. I ordered it by mail order from Cape Town. It arrived on the train yesterday.'

He placed the tangle of leather and rubber in Manfred's arms.

'What is it, Uncle Tromp?'

'Come, I'll show you.'

Within minutes Uncle Tromp had rigged the complicated contraption.

'Well, what do you think, *Jong*?' He stood back, beaming hugely through his beard.

'It's the best present anyone has ever given me, Uncle Tromp. But what is it?'

'You call yourself a boxer and you don't know a speed bag when you see one!'

'A speed bag! It must have cost a lot of money.'

'It did, *Jong*, but don't tell your Aunt Trudi.'

'What do we do with it?'

'This is what we do!' cried Uncle Tromp, and he started the bag rattling against the frame in a rapid staccato rhythm, using both fists, taking the ball on the bounce, keeping it going unerringly until at last he stepped back panting.

'Speed, *Jong*, fast as a mamba.'

Faced with Uncle Tromp's generosity and enthusiasm, Manfred had to gather all his courage to speak the words that had been burning his tongue all these weeks.

He waited until the last possible moment of the last possible day before blurting out, 'I have to go away, Uncle Tromp,' and he watched in agony the disappointment and

366

disbelief flood over the craggy bearded face that he had come so swiftly and naturally to love.

'Go away? You want to leave my house?' Uncle Tromp stopped short in the dust of the Windhoek road and wiped the sweat from his face with the threadbare towel draped around his neck. 'Why, *Jong*, why?'

'My pa,' Manfred answered. 'My pa's trial starts in three days' time. I have to be there, Uncle Tromp. I have to go, but I will come back. I swear I will come back, just as soon as I can.'

Uncle Tromp turned from him and began to run again, pounding down the long straight road, the dust puffing from under his bearlike feet at each pace, and Manfred sprinted up beside him. Neither of them spoke again until they reached the clump of trees where the pony trap was hitched.

Oom Tromp climbed up into the driver's seat and picked up the reins. He looked down at Manfred standing beside the front wheel.

'I wish, *Jong*, that I had a son of my own to show me such loyalty,' he rumbled softly, and shook the pony into a trot.

The following evening, long after dinner and the evening prayers, Manfred lay on his bed, the candle on the shelf above his head carefully screened so that not a glimmer could alert Aunt Trudi to his extravagance. He was reading Goethe, his father's favourite author. It wasn't easy. His German had improved vastly. On two days a week Aunt Trudi insisted that no other language was spoken in the household, and she initiated erudite discussion at the dinner-table in which all members of the family were expected – nay, forced, to participate. Still Goethe wasn't a romp, and Manfred was concentrating so fiercely on his convoluted use of verbs that he didn't know Uncle Tromp was in the room until his shadow fell across the bed and the book was lifted from his hand.

'You will ruin your eyes, *Jong*.'

Manfred sat up quickly and swung his legs off the bed while Uncle Tromp sank down beside him.

For a few moments the old man leafed through the book. Then he spoke without looking up. 'Rautenbach is going in to Windhoek tomorrow in his T-model Ford. He is taking in a hundred turkeys to market, but he will have room for you on the back. You'll have to put up with flying feathers and turkey shit, but it's cheaper than the train.'

'Thank you, Uncle Tromp.'

'There is an old widow in town, devout and decent – also a very good cook. She'll take you in. I've written to her.' He drew a sheet of his notepaper from his pocket and placed it in Manfred's lap. The single sheet was folded and sealed with a blob of red wax, a back country minister's stipend could not encompass the luxury of envelopes.

'Thank you, Uncle Tromp.' Manfred could think of nothing else to say. He wanted to fling his arms round that thick bearlike neck and lay his cheek against the coarse grey-shot beard, but he controlled himself.

'There may be other expenses,' Uncle Tromp gruffed. 'I don't know how you will get back here. Anyway—' He groped in his pocket, seized Manfred's wrist with the other hand, and pressed something into his open palm.

Manfred looked down at the two bright half-crown coins in his hand and shook his head slowly.

'Uncle Tromp—'

'Say nothing, *Jong* – especially not to your Aunt Trudi.' Uncle Tromp began to stand, but Manfred caught his sleeve.

'Uncle Tromp. I can pay you back – for this and all the other things.'

'I know you will, *Jong*. You will pay me back a thousand times, in pride and joy one day.'

'No, no, not one day. I can pay you back now.'

Manfred sprang eagerly from the bed and ran to the

upended packing case standing on four bricks that was his wardrobe. He knelt and thrust his arm into the space below the box and brought out a yellow tobacco bag. He hurried back to where Uncle Tromp sat on the iron bed, pulling open the drawstring of the small pouch, his hands shaking with excitement and eagerness to please.

'Here, Uncle Tromp, open your hand.'

Smiling indulgently Uncle Tromp held out his huge paw, the back of it covered with coarse black curls, the fingers thick as good farmer's sausages.

'What have you here, *Jong?*' he demanded jovially, and then the smile froze as Manfred spilled a cascade of glittering stones into his hand.

'Diamonds, Uncle Tromp,' Manfred whispered. 'Enough to make you a rich man. Enough to buy you anything you need.'

'Where did you get these, *Jong?*' Uncle Tromp's voice was calm and dispassionate. 'How did you come by these?'

'My pa – my father. He put them into the lining of my jacket. He said they were for me, to pay for my education and my upbringing, to pay for all the things that he wanted to do for me but had never been able.'

'So!' said Uncle Tromp softly. 'It is all true then, all of what the newspapers say. It isn't just English lies. Your father is a brigand and a robber.' The huge hand clenched into a fist over the glittering treasure. 'And you were with him, *Jong*. You must have been there when he did these terrible things that they accuse him of, that they will try and condemn him for. Were you with him, *Jong?* Answer me!' His voice was rising like a storm wind, and now he let out a bellow. 'Did you commit this great evil with him, *Jong?*' The other hand shot out and seized the front of Manfred's shirt. He pulled Manfred's face to within inches of his own jutting beard. 'Confess to me, *Jong*. Tell it all to me, every last scrap of evil. Were you with him when your father attacked this Englishwoman and robbed her?'

369

'No! No!' Manfred shook his head wildly. 'It's not true. My father wouldn't do a thing like that. They were our diamonds. He explained it to me. He went to get back what was rightfully ours.'

'Were you with him when he did this thing, *Jong*? Tell me the truth,' Uncle Tromp interrupted him with another roar. 'Tell me, were you with him?'

'No, Uncle Tromp. He went alone. And when he came back he was hurt. His hand – his wrist—'

'Thank you, Lord!' Uncle Tromp looked upwards with relief. 'Forgive him for he knew not what he did, O Lord. He was led into sin by an evil man.'

'My father isn't evil,' Manfred protested. 'He was cheated out of what was truly his.'

'Silence, *Jong*.' *Oom* Tromp rose to his full height, splendid and awesome as a biblical prophet. 'Your words are an offence in the sight of God. You will make retribution here and now.'

He dragged Manfred across the toolroom and pushed him in front of the black iron anvil.

'Thou shalt not steal. That is the very word of God.' He placed one of the diamonds in the centre of the anvil. 'These stones are the ill-begotten fruits of a terrible evil.' He reached to the rack beside him and brought down a four pound sledgehammer. 'They must be destroyed.' He thrust the hammer into Manfred's hands.

'Pray for forgiveness, *Jong*. Beg the Lord for his charity and forgiveness – and strike!'

Manfred stood with the hammer in his hands, holding it at high port across his chest, staring at the diamond on the anvil.

'Strike, *Jong*! Break that cursed thing or be for ever cursed by it,' roared Uncle Tromp. 'Strike, in the name of God. Rid yourself of the guilt and the shame.'

Slowly Manfred raised the hammer on high and then paused. He turned and looked at the fierce old man.

'Strike swiftly,' roared Uncle Tromp. 'Now!' And Manfred swung, the same fluid, looping, overhead blow with which he chopped wood, and he grunted with effort as the head of the hammer rang on the anvil.

Manfred lifted the hammer slowly. The diamond was crushed to white powder, finer than sugar, but still the vestiges of its fire and beauty remained as each minute crystal caught and magnified the candlelight; and when Uncle Tromp brushed the diamond dust from the anvil top with his open hand it fell in a luminous rainbow cloud to the earthen floor.

Uncle Tromp laid another fiery stone upon the anvil, a fortune such as few men could amass in ten years of unremitting labour, and stood back.

'Strike!' he cried, and the hammer hissed as it turned in the air, and the anvil rang like a great gong. The precious dust was brushed aside and another stone laid in its place.

'Strike!' roared the Trumpet of God, and Manfred worked with the hammer, grunting and sobbing in his throat with each fateful blow until at last Uncle Tromp cried:

'Praised be the name of the Lord. It is done!' And he fell on his knees, dragging Manfred down with him, and side by side they knelt before the anvil as though it were an altar and the white diamond dust coated their knees as they prayed.

'Oh Lord Jesus, look upon this act of penance with favour. Thou who gave up Thy life for our redemption, forgive Thy young servant whose ignorance and childishness has led him into grievous sin.'

It was after midnight and the candle was guttering in a puddle of its own wax before Uncle Tromp rose from his knees and pulled Manfred up with him.

'Go to your bed now, *Jong*. We have done all we can to save your soul for the time being.'

He watched while Manfred undressed and slipped under

the grey blanket. Then he asked quietly: 'If I forbade you to go to Windhoek in the morning, would you obey me?'

'My father,' whispered Manfred.

'Answer me, *Jong*, would you obey me?'

'I don't know, Uncle Tromp, but I don't think I could. My pa—'

'You have so much to repent already. It would not do to add the sin of disobedience to your load. Therefore, I place no such restriction upon you. You must do what loyalty and your conscience dictate. But for your own sake and mine, when you reach Windhoek, use the name of Bierman not De La Rey, *Jong*, do you hear me?'

'Judgement today! I make a rule never to predict the outcome of any piece of legislation or judicial process,' Abe Abrahams announced from his chair facing Centaine Courtney's desk. 'However, today I break my own rule. I predict that the man will get the rope. No question about it.'

'How can you be that certain, Abe?' Centaine asked quietly, and Abe looked at her with covert admiration for a moment before replying. She was wearing a simple low-waisted dress which could justify its expense only by its exquisite cut and the fineness of the silk jersey material. It showed off her fashionable small bosom and boyishly slim hips as she stood against the french windows. The bright white African sunlight behind her formed a nimbus about her head, and it took an effort to look away from her and to concentrate on the burning cheroot which he held up to enumerate his points.

'Firstly, the small matter of guilt. Nobody, not even the defence, has made any serious attempt to suggest anything other than he is guilty as all hell. Guilty in intention and execution, guilty of planning it in detail and carrying it out as planned, guilty of all manner of aggravating circumstances, including attacking and robbing a military remount depot, firing on the police and wounding one of them with a grenade. The defence has as good as admitted their only hope will be to pull some arcane technical rabbit from the legal hat to impress His Lordship, a hope which so far has not materialized.'

Centaine sighed. She had spent two days in the witness stand. Though she had remained calm and unshakable in the face of the most rigorous and aggressive cross-examination, she was exhausted by it, and haunted by a sense of culpability, of having driven Lothar to that desperate criminal folly, and now guilty of heading the pack that was pulling him down and would soon rend him with all the vindictiveness that the law allowed.

'Secondly,' Abe waved the cheroot, 'the man's record. During the war he was a traitor and a rebel with a price on his head, a desperado with a long string of violent crimes to his discredit.'

'He was pardoned for his wartime crimes,' Centaine pointed out. 'A full pardon signed by the prime minister and the minister of justice.'

'Still, they will count against him.' Abe wagged his head knowingly. 'Even the pardon will make it worse for him: biting the hand of mercy, flouting the dignity of the law. The judge won't like that, believe me.'

Abe inspected the end of the cheroot. It was burning evenly with a firm inch of grey ash and he nodded approvingly. 'Thirdly,' he went on, 'the man has shown no remorse, not a jot nor a shred of it. He has refused to tell anybody what he did with the filthy loot.'

He broke off as he saw Centaine's distress at the mention of the missing diamonds, and continued hurriedly: 'Fourthly, the emotional aspects of the crime, attacking a lady of the highest standing in the community.' He grinned suddenly. 'A helpless female so unable to defend herself that she bit his arm off.'. She frowned and he became serious again. 'Your own courage and integrity will count heavily against him, your dignity in the witness box. You have seen the newspapers: Joan of Arc and Florence Nightingale in one person, the veiled suggestion that his attack upon you might have been more dastardly and beastly than modesty will allow you to tell. The judge will want to reward you with the man's head on a platter.'

She looked at her wristwatch. 'The court will reconvene in forty minutes. We should go up the hill.'

Abe stood up immediately. 'I love to watch the law in operation, the dignified and measured pace of it, the trappings and ritual of it, the slow grinding of evidence, the sorting of the chaff from the wheat—'

'Not now, Abe,' she stopped him as she adjusted her hat in the mirror above the mantel, draping the black veil over one eye, setting the small brim at an elegant angle and then picking up her crocodile-skin handbag and tucking it under her arm. 'Without any further oratory from you, let's just go and see this awful thing through.'

They drove up the hill in Abe's Ford. The press was waiting for them in front of the courthouse, thrusting their cameras into the open window of the Ford and blinding Centaine with bursting flash bulbs. She shielded her eyes with her handbag but the moment she stepped out of the automobile they were around her in a pack, yelling their questions.

'What will you feel if they hang him?'

'What about the diamonds? Can your company survive without them, Mrs Courtney?'

'Do you think they'll do a deal for the diamonds?'

'What are your feelings?'

Abe ran interference for her, barging his way through the crowd, dragging her by the wrist into the comparative quiet of the courthouse.

'Wait here for me, Abe,' she ordered, and slipped away

down the passageway, weaving through the crowd that was waiting for the doors of the main courtroom to open. Heads turned to watch her and a buzz of comment followed her down the passage, but she ignored it and turned the corner towards the ladies' toilets. The office set aside for the defence was directly opposite the ladies' room and Centaine glanced around to make sure she was unobserved, then turned to that door, tapped upon it sharply, pushed it open and stepped inside. She shut the door behind her and, as the defence counsel looked up, she said: 'Excuse this intrusion, gentlemen, but I must speak to you.'

Abe was still waiting where she had left him when Centaine returned only minutes later.

'Colonel Malcomess is here,' he told her, and all her other preoccupations were forgotten for the moment.

'Where is he?' she demanded eagerly. She had not seen Blaine since the second day of the trial when he had given his evidence in that ringing tenor lilt that raised the fine hair on the back of Centaine's neck, evidence that was all the more damning for its balanced unemotional presentation. The defence had tried to trip him on his description of the shooting of the horses and the grenade attack, but had swiftly sensed that he would provide little for their comfort and let him leave the stand after a few futile minutes of cross-examination. Since then Centaine had looked for him unavailingly each day.

'Where is he?' she repeated.

'He has gone in already,' Abe replied, and Centaine saw that while she had been away the ushers had opened the double doors to the main courtroom.

'Charlie is holding seats for us. No need to join the scrum,' Abe took her arm and eased her through the moving crowd. The ushers recognized her and helped clear the aisle for her to reach the seats in the third row that Abe's assistant was holding for them.

Centaine was covertly searching through the bustle for

Blaine's tall form, and she started when the press of bodies opened for a moment and she saw him on the opposite side of the aisle. He was searching also and saw her a moment later; his reaction was as sharp as hers had been. They stared at each other from a few yards that seemed to Centaine to be an abyss wide as an ocean; neither of them smiled as they held each other's eyes. Then the crowd in the aisle intervened once again, and she lost sight of him. She sank down in the seat beside Abe and made a little show of searching in her handbag to give herself time to recover her composure.

'Here he is,' Abe exclaimed, and for a moment she thought he was referring to Blaine. Then she saw that the warders were bringing Lothar De La Rey through from the cells.

Although she had seen him in the dock for every one of the last five days, she was still not hardened to the change in him. Today he wore a faded blue workman's shirt and dark slacks. The clothes seemed too large for him, and one sleeve was pinned up loosely over his stump. He shuffled like an old man and one of the warders had to help him up the steps into the dock.

His hair was completely white now, even his thick dark eyebrows were laced with silver. He was impossibly thin and his skin had a greyish lifeless look; it hung in little loose folds under his jaw and on his scrawny neck. His tan had faded to the yellowish colour of old putty.

As he sank onto the bench in the dock, he lifted his head and searched the gallery of the court. There was a pathetic anxiety in his expression as he ran his eyes swiftly over the packed benches. Then Centaine saw the little flare of joy in his eyes and his masked smile as he found what he was seeking. She had watched this scene enacted every morning for five days, and she twisted in her seat and looked up at the gallery behind her. But from where she sat the angle was wrong. She could not see who or what had attracted Lothar's attention.

'Silence in court,' the usher called and there was a shuffling and scrabbling as the body of the court came to its feet and Judge Hawthorne led his two assessors to their seats. He was a silver-haired little man with a benign expression and lively sparkling eyes behind his pince-nez. He looked more like a schoolmaster than the hanging judge that Abe said he was.

Neither he nor his assessors wore wigs or the colourful robes of the English courts. Roman Dutch law was more sombre in its trappings. They wore simple black gowns and white swallow-tailed neckties, and the three of them conferred quietly, inclining their heads together while the body of the court settled down and the coughing and throat-clearing and foot-shuffling abated. Then Judge Hawthorne looked up and went through the formality of convening the court and the charge sheet was read once again.

Now an expectant hush fell over the courtroom. The reporters leaned forward with their notebooks poised; even the barristers in the front row of benches were silenced and stilled. Lothar was expressionless but deathly pale as he watched the judge's face.

Judge Hawthorne was concentrating on his notes, heightening the tension with subtle showmanship until it was barely supportable. Then he looked up brightly and launched without preliminaries into the delivery of his summation and judgement.

First he detailed each of the charges, beginning with the most serious: three counts of attempted murder, two of assault with intent to inflict grievous bodily harm, one of armed robbery. There were twenty-six charges in all and it took almost twenty minutes for the judge to cover each of them.

'The prosecution has presented all these charges in an orderly and convincing manner.'

The red-faced prosecutor preened at the compliment and Centaine felt an unreasonable irritation at this petty vanity.

'This court was particularly impressed with the evidence of the main prosecution witnesses. His Excellency the Administrator's testimony was a great help to me and my assessors. We were most fortunate in having a witness of this calibre to relate the details of the pursuit and arrest of the accused, from which arise some of the most serious charges in this case.' The judge looked up from his notes directly at Blaine Malcomess. 'I wish to record the most favourable impression that Colonel Malcomess made upon this court, and we have accepted his evidence without reservation.'

From where she was sitting Centaine could see the back of Blaine's head. The tips of his large ears turned pink as the judge looked at him, and Centaine felt a rush of tenderness as she noticed. His embarrassment was somehow endearing and touching.

Then the judge looked at her.

'The other prosecution witness who conducted herself impeccably and whose evidence was unimpeachable, was Mrs Centaine Courtney. The court is fully aware of the great hardship with which Mrs Courtney has been inflicted and the courage which she has displayed, not only in this courtroom. Once again, we were most fortunate to have the benefit of her evidence in assisting us to reach our verdict.'

While the judge was speaking, Lothar De La Rey turned his head and looked at Centaine steadily. Those pale accusing eyes disconcerted her and she dropped her own gaze to the handbag in her lap to avoid them.

'In contrast, the defence was able to call only one witness, and that was the accused himself. After due consideration, we are of the opinion that much of the accused's evidence was unacceptable. The witness's attitude was at all times hostile and unco-operative. In particular we reject the witness's assertion that the offences were committed singlehanded, and that he had no accomplices in their commission. Here the evidence of Colonel Malcomess, of Mrs Courtney and of the police troopers is unequivocal and collaborative.'

Lothar De La Rey turned his head slowly in the judge's direction once more and stared at him with that flat, hostile expression which had so antagonized Judge Hawthorne over the five long days of the trial, and the judge returned his gaze levelly as he went on.

'Thus we have considered all the facts and the evidence presented to us and are unanimous in our verdict. On all twenty-six charges we find the accused, Lothar De La Rey, guilty as charged.'

Lothar neither flinched nor blinked, but there was a concerted gasp from the body of the court, followed immediately by a buzz of comment. Three of the reporters leapt up and scampered from the courtroom, and Abe nodded smugly beside Centaine.

'I told you, the rope,' he murmured. 'He will swing, for sure.' The ushers were attempting to restore order. The judge came to their assistance.

He rapped his gavel sharply and raised his voice. 'I will not hesitate to have this court cleared—' he warned, and once again a hush settled over the courtroom.

'Before passing sentence, I will listen to any submissions in mitigation that the defence may wish to put to the bench.' Judge Hawthorne inclined his head towards the young barrister charged with the defence, who immediately rose to his feet.

Lothar De La Rey was destitute and unable to afford his own defence. Mr Reginald Osmond had been appointed by the court to defend him. Despite his youth and inexperience – it was his first defence on a capital charge – Osmond had thus far acquitted himself as well as could have been expected, given the hopeless circumstances of his client's case. His cross-examination had been spirited and nimble, if ineffectual, and he had not allowed the prosecution to make any gratuitous gains.

'If it please my lord, I should like to call a witness to give evidence in mitigation.'

'Come now, Mr Osmond, surely you don't intend to introduce a witness at this stage? Do you have precedents for this?' The judge frowned.

'I respectfully commend your lordship to the matter of the Crown versus Van der Spuy 1923 and to the Crown versus Alexander 1914.'

The judge conferred for a few moments with his assessors and then looked up with a stagy sigh of exasperation. 'Very well, Mr Osmond. I am going to allow you your witness.'

'Thank you, my lord.' Mr Osmond was so overcome with his own success that he stuttered a little as he blurted eagerly: 'I call Mrs Centaine de Thiry Courtney to the stand.'

This time there was a stunned silence. Even Judge Hawthorne fell back in his tall carved chair before a buzz of surprise and delight and anticipation swept through the court. The press were standing to get a view of Centaine as she rose and from the gallery a voice called: 'Put the noose around the bastard's neck, luv!'

Judge Hawthorne recovered swiftly and his eyes flashed behind his pince-nez as he glared up at the gallery, trying to identify the wag.

'I will not tolerate a further outburst. There are severe penalties for contempt of court,' he snapped, and even the journalists sat down again hurriedly and, chastened, applied themselves to their notepads.

The usher handed Centaine into the witness stand and then swore her in while every man in the room, including

380

those on the bench, watched, most of them in open admiration, but a few, including Blaine and Abraham Abrahams, with puzzlement and perturbation.

Mr Osmond stood to open his examination, his voice pitched low with nervous respect.

'Mrs Courtney, will you please tell the court how long you have known the accused—' he corrected himself hurriedly, for now Lothar De La Rey was no longer merely accused, he had been convicted, ' – the prisoner.'

'I have known Lothar De La Rey for nearly fourteen years.' Centaine looked across the room at the stooped grey figure in the dock.

'Would you be good enough to describe, in your own words, the circumstances of your first meeting.'

'It was in 1919. I was lost in the desert. I had been a castaway on the Skeleton Coast after the sinking of the *Protea Castle*. For a year and a half I had been wandering in the Kalahari desert with a small group of San Bushmen.' All of them knew the story. At the time it had been a sensation, but now Centaine's narrative, related in her French accent, brought it all vividly to life.

She conjured up the desolation and misery, the fearful hardships and loneliness that she had endured, and the room was deathly quiet. Even Judge Hawthorne was hunched down in his chair, supporting his chin on his clenched fist, absolutely still as he listened. They were all with her as she struggled through the clinging sand of the Kalahari, dressed in the skins of wild animals, her infant son on her hip, following the tracks of a horse, a shod horse, the first sign of civilized man that she had encountered in all those desperate months.

They chilled with her and shared her despair as the African night fell across the desert and her chances of succour receded; they willed her onwards, through the darkness, seeking the glow of a camp-fire far ahead, then started in horror as she described the sinister shape, dark with menace, that suddenly confronted her, and flinched as though they also had heard the roar of a hungry lion close at hand.

Her audience gasped and stirred as she described her fight for her life and the life of her infant; the way the circling lion drove her up into the highest branches of a tall mopani and then climbed up towards her like a cat after a sparrow. Centaine described the sound of its hot panting breath in the darkness and at last the shooting agony as the long yellow claws hooked into the flesh of her leg and she was drawn inexorably from her perch.

She could not go on, and Mr Osmond prompted her gently. 'Was it at this stage that Lothar De La Rey intervened?'

Centaine roused herself. 'I'm sorry. It all came back to me—'

'Please, Mrs Courtney, do not tax yourself.' Judge Hawthorne rushed to her aid. 'I will recess the court if you need time—'

'No, no, my lord. You are very kind, but that won't be necessary.' She squared her shoulders and faced them again. 'Yes, that was when Lothar De La Rey came up. He had been camped close at hand, and was alerted by the roars of the animal. He shot the lion dead while it was in the act of savaging me.'

'He saved your life, Mrs Courtney.'

'He saved me from a dreadful death, and he saved my child with me.'

Mr Osmond bowed his head in silence, letting the court savour the full drama of the moment, then he asked gently: 'What happened after that, madam?'

'I was concussed by my fall from the tree; the wound in my leg mortified. I was unconscious for many days, unable to care for myself or my son.'

'What was the prisoner's reaction to this?'

'He cared for me. He dressed my wounds. Tended every need of mine and of my child.'

'He saved your life a second time?'

'Yes.' She nodded. 'He saved me once again.'

'Now, Mrs Courtney. The years passed. You became a wealthy lady, a millionairess?'

Centaine was silent, and Osmond went on. 'Then one day three years ago the prisoner approached you for financial assistance for his fishing and canning enterprise. Is that correct?'

'He approached my company, Courtney Mining and Finance, for a loan,' she said, and Osmond led her through the series of events up to the time that she had closed down Lothar's canning factory.

'So, Mrs Courtney, would you say that Lothar De La Rey had reason to believe that he had been unfairly treated, if not deliberately ruined by your action?'

Centaine hesitated. 'My actions were at all times based on sound business principles. However, I would readily concede that from Lothar De La Rey's standpoint, it could have seemed that my actions were deliberate.'

'At the time, did he accuse you of attempting to destroy him?'

She looked down at her hands and whispered something.

'I am sorry, Mrs Courtney. I must ask you to repeat that.'

And she flared at him, her voice cracking with strain. 'Yes, damn it. He said that I was doing it to destroy him.'

'Mr Osmond!' The judge sat up straight, his expression severe. 'I must insist that you treat your witness in a more considerate fashion.' He sank back in his seat, clearly moved by Centaine's recital, and then raised his voice again. 'I will recess the court for fifteen minutes to allow Mrs Courtney time to recover herself.'

When they reconvened, Centaine entered the witness stand again and sat quietly while the formalities were completed and Mr Osmond prepared to continue his examination.

From the third row Blaine Malcomess smiled at her encouragingly, and she knew that if she did not look away from him every single person in the courtroom would be aware of her feelings. She forced herself to break contact with his eyes and instead looked up at the gallery above his head.

It was an idle glance. She had forgotten the way in which Lothar De La Rey searched the gallery each morning, but now she was seeing it from the same angle as he did from the dock. And suddenly her eyes flicked to the furthest corner of the gallery, drawn irresistibly by another set of eyes, by the intensity of a glowering gaze that was fastened upon her, and she started and then swayed in her seat, giddy with shock, for she had stared once again into Lothar's eyes: Lothar's eyes as they had been when first she met him, yellow as topaz, fierce and bright, with dark brows arched over them – young eyes, unforgettable, unforgotten eyes. But the eyes were not set in Lothar's face, for Lothar sat across the courtroom from her, bowed and broken and grey. This face was young, strong and full of hatred, and she knew, she knew with a mother's sure instinct. She had never seen her younger son – at her insistence, he had been taken away, wet from the womb, at the very moment of birth, and she had turned her head away so as not to see his squirming naked body. But now she knew him, and it was as though the very core of her existence, the womb which had contained him, ached at this glimpse of his face, and she had to cover her mouth to prevent herself crying out with the pain of it.

'Mrs Courtney! Mrs Courtney!' The judge was calling her, his tone quickening with alarm, and she forced herself to turn her head towards him.

'Are you all right, Mrs Courtney? Are you feeling well enough to continue?'

'Thank you, my lord, I am quite well.' Her voice seemed to come from a great distance, and it took all her willpower not to look back at the youth in the gallery – at her son, Manfred.

'Very well, Mr Osmond. You may proceed.'

It required an enormous effort of will for Centaine to concentrate on the questions as Osmond led her once more over the robbery and the struggle in the dry riverbed.

'So then, Mrs Courtney, he did not lay a finger upon you until you attempted to reach the shotgun?'

'No. He did not touch me until then.'

'You have already told us that you had the shotgun in your hand and were attempting to reload the weapon.'

'That is correct.'

'Would you have used the weapon if you had succeeded in reloading it?'

'Yes.'

'Can you tell us, Mrs Courtney, would you have shot to kill?'

'I object, my lord!' The prosecutor sprang angrily to his feet. 'That question is hypothetical.'

'Mrs Courtney, you do not have to answer that question, if you do not choose,' Judge Hawthorne told her.

'I will answer.' Centaine said clearly, 'Yes, I would have killed him.'

'Do you think the prisoner knew that?'

'My lord, I object. The witness cannot possibly know.'

Before the judge could rule, Centaine said clearly, 'He knew me, he knew me well. He knew I would kill him if I had the chance.'

The pent-up emotion of the courtroom exploded in ghoulish relish and it was almost a minute before quiet could be restored. In the confusion Centaine looked up at the corner of the high gallery again. It had taken all her self-control not to do so before.

The corner seat was empty. Manfred had gone, and she

felt confused by his desertion. Osmond was questioning her again, and she turned to him vaguely.

'I'm sorry. Will you repeat that, please?'

'I asked, Mrs Courtney, if the prisoner's assault on you, as you stood there with the shotgun in your hands intent on killing him—'

'My lord, I object. The witness was intent only on defending herself and her property,' the prosecutor howled.

'You'll have to rephrase that question, Mr Osmond.'

'Very well, my lord. Mrs Courtney, was the force that the prisoner used against you inconsistent with that needed to disarm you?'

'I'm sorry.' Centaine could not concentrate. She wanted to search the gallery again. 'I don't understand the question.'

'Did the prisoner use more force than that necessary to disarm you and prevent you shooting him?'

'No. He simply pulled the shotgun away from me.'

'And later when you had bitten his wrist. When you had buried your teeth in his flesh, inflicting a wound that later would result in the amputation of his arm, did he strike you or inflict any other injury upon you in retaliation?'

'No.'

'The pain must have been intense, and yet he did not use undue force upon you?'

'No.' She shook her head. 'He was—' Centaine searched for the word, ' – he was strangely considerate, almost gentle.'

'I see. And before he left you, did the prisoner make sure that you had sufficient water for survival? And did he give you advice concerning your well-being?'

'He checked that I had sufficient spare water, and he advised me to stay with the wrecked vehicle until I was rescued.'

'Now, Mrs Courtney,' Osmond hesitated delicately. 'There has been speculation in the press that the prisoner might have made some form of indecent assault—'

Centaine interrupted him furiously. 'That suggestion is repugnant and totally false.'

'Thank you, madam. I have only one more question. You knew the prisoner well. You accompanied him while he was hunting to provide meat for you and your child once he had rescued you. You saw him shoot?'

'I did.'

'In your opinion, if the prisoner had wanted to kill you or Colonel Malcomess, or any of the police officers pursuing him, could he have done so?'

'Lothar De La Rey is one of the finest marksmen I have ever known. He could have killed all of us on more than one occasion.'

'I have no further questions, my lord.'

Judge Hawthorne wrote at length on the notepad before him and then tapped his pencil thoughtfully upon the desk for another few seconds before he looked up at the prosecutor.

'Do you wish to cross-examine the witness?'

The prosecutor came to his feet scowling sulkily. 'I have no further questions for Mrs Courtney.'

He sat down again, folded his arms and stared angrily at the revolving punkah fan on the ceiling.

'Mrs Courtney, the court is grateful to you for your further evidence. You may now return to your seat.'

Centaine was so intent on searching the gallery for her son that she tripped on the steps at the foot of the tiers of benches and both Blaine and Abe jumped up to help her. Abe reached her first and Blaine sank back into his seat as Abe led Centaine to hers.

'Abe,' she whispered urgently. 'There was a lad in the gallery while I was giving evidence. Blond, around thirteen years old, though he looks more like seventeen. His name is Manfred – Manfred De La Rey. Find him. I want to speak to him.'

'Now?' Abe looked surprised.

'Right now.'

'The submission in mitigation. I'll miss it.'

'Go!' she snapped. 'Find him.' And Abe jumped up, bowed to the bench and hurried out of the courtroom just as Mr Reginald Osmond rose to his feet once again.

Osmond spoke with passion and sincerity, using Centaine's evidence to full advantage, repeating her exact words: '"He saved me from a dreadful death, and he saved my child with me."' Osmond paused significantly and then went on. 'The prisoner believed that he deserved the gratitude and generosity of Mrs Courtney. He placed himself in her power by borrowing money from her, and he came to believe – mistakenly, but genuinely – that his trust in her had been betrayed.' His eloquent plea for mercy went on for almost half an hour, but Centaine found herself thinking of Manfred rather than the plight of his father. The look which the boy had levelled at her from the gallery troubled her deeply. The hatred in it had been a palpable thing and it resuscitated her sense of guilt, a guilt which she believed she had buried so many years before.

'He will be alone now. He will need help,' she thought. 'I have to find him. I have to try and make it up to him in some way.'

She realized then why she had so steadfastly denied the boy over all these years, why she had thought of him only as 'Lothar's bastard', why she had gone to extreme lengths to avoid any contact with him. Her instinct had been correct. Just a single glimpse of his face and all the defences which she had built up so carefully came tumbling down, all the natural feelings of a mother which she had buried so deeply were revived to overwhelm her.

388

'Find him for me, Abe,' she whispered, and then realized that Reginald Osmond had completed his submission with a final plea: 'Lothar De La Rey felt that he had been grievously wronged. As a result, he committed a series of crimes which were abhorrent and indefensible. However, my lord, many of his actions prove that he was a decent and compassionate man, caught up in stormy emotions and events too powerful for him to resist. His sentence must be severe. Society demands that much. But I appeal to your lordship to show a little of the same Christian compassion that Mrs Courtney has displayed here today, and to refrain from visiting upon this hapless man, who has already lost one of his limbs, the extreme penalty of the law.'

He sat down in a silence that lasted for many long seconds, until Judge Hawthorne looked up from the reverie into which he had sunk.

'Thank you, Mr Osmond. This court will recess and reconvene at two o'clock this afternoon, at which time we will impose sentence.'

Centaine hurried from the courtroom, searching eagerly for Abe or for another glimpse of her son. She found Abe on the front steps of the courthouse, in deep conversation with one of the police guards. But he broke off and came to her immediately.

'Did you find him?' she demanded anxiously.

'I'm sorry, Centaine. No sign of anyone of that description.'

'I want the boy found and brought to me, Abe. Use as many men as you need. I don't care what it costs. Search the town. Do everything possible to find him. He must be staying somewhere.'

'All right, Centaine. I'll get on to it right away. You say his name is Manfred De La Rey – then he will be related to the prisoner?'

'His son,' she said.

'I see.' Abe looked at her thoughtfully. 'May I ask why you want him so desperately, Centaine? And what you are going to do with him when you find him?'

'No, you may not ask. Just find him.'

'Why do I want him?' she repeated Abe's question to herself wonderingly. 'Why do I want him after all these years?' And the answer was simple and self-evident. 'Because he is my son.

'And what will I do with him if I find him? He is poisoned against me. He hates me. I saw that in his eyes. He does not know who I really am. I saw that also. So what will I do when I meet him face to face,' and she answered herself as simply: 'I don't know, I just do not know.'

'The maximum penalty provided by law for the first three offences on the prisoner's charge sheet is death by hanging,' said Judge Hawthorne. 'The prisoner has been found guilty of these and the further offences with which he has been charged. In the normal course of events this court would have had no hesitation in inflicting that supreme penalty upon him. However, we have been given pause by the extraordinary evidence of an extraordinary lady. The submissions made voluntarily by Mrs Centaine de Thiry Courtney are all the more remarkable for the fact that she has suffered most grievously at the prisoner's hands – physically, emotionally and materially – and also for the fact that her admissions might be construed by small-minded and mean persons as invidious to Mrs Courtney herself.

'In twenty-three years' service on the bench I have never been privileged to witness such a noble and magnanimous performance in any courtroom, and our own deliberations must, by necessity, be tempered by Mrs Courtney's example.' Judge Hawthorne bowed slightly towards where Centaine sat, then took the pince-nez from his nose and looked at Lothar De La Rey.

'The prisoner will rise,' he said.

'Lothar De La Rey, you have been found guilty of all the various charges brought against you by the Crown, and for purpose of sentence, these will be taken as one. It is, therefore, the sentence of this court that you be imprisoned at hard labour for the rest of your natural life.'

For the first time since the beginning of the trial, Lothar De La Rey showed emotion. He recoiled from the judge's words. His face began to work, his lips trembling, one eyelid twitched uncontrollably, and he lifted his remaining hand, palm up, in appeal towards the dark-robed figure on the bench.

'Kill me, rather.' A wild heart-cry. 'Hang me rather than lock me up like an animal—'

The warders hurried to him, seized him from either side and led him shaking and calling out piteously from the dock, while a hush of sympathy held the whole room. Even the judge was affected, his features set and grim as he stood up and slowly led his assessors from the room. Centaine remained sitting, staring at the empty dock as the subdued crowd filed out of the double doors like mourners leaving a funeral.

'Kill me, rather!' She knew that plea would stay with her for the rest of her life. She bowed her head and covered her eyes with her hands. In the eye of her mind she saw Lothar as he had been when she first met him, hard and lean as one of the red Kalahari lions, with pale eyes that looked to far horizons shaded blue by distance, a creature of those great spaces washed with white sunlight. And she thought of him now, locked in a tiny cell, deprived for the rest of his life of the sun and the desert wind.

'Oh Lothar,' she cried in the depths of her soul. 'How

could something once so good and beautiful have ended like this? We have destroyed each other, and destroyed also the child that we conceived in that fine noon of our love.'

She opened her eyes again. The courtroom had emptied and she thought she was alone until she sensed a presence near her and she turned quickly and Blaine Malcomess was there.

'Now I know how right it was to love you,' he said softly. He stood behind her, his head bowed over her, and she looked up at him and felt the terrible regret and sorrow begin to lift.

Blaine took her hand that lay along the back of the bench and held it between both of his. 'I have been struggling with myself all these last days since we parted, trying to find the strength never to see you again. I almost succeeded. But you changed it all by what you did today. Honour and duty and all those other things no longer mean anything to me when I look at you now. You are part of me. I have to be with you.'

'When?'

'As soon as possible,' he said.

'Blaine, in my short life I have done so much damage to others, inflicted so much cruelty and pain. No more. I also cannot live without you, but nothing else must be destroyed by our love. I want all of you, but I will accept less – to protect your family.'

'It will be hard, perhaps impossible,' he warned her softly. 'But I accept your conditions. We must not inflict pain on others. Yet I want you so much—'

'I know,' she whispered, and stood up to face him. 'Hold me, Blaine, just for a moment.'

Abe Abrahams was searching for Centaine through the empty passages of the courthouse. He reached the double doors of the courtroom and pushed one leaf open quietly.

Centaine and Blaine Malcomess stood in the aisle between the tiers of oak benches. They were in each other's arms, oblivious to anything around them, and he stared for a moment without comprehension, then softly closed the door again and stood guard before it, wracked by fear and happiness for her.

'You deserve love,' he whispered. 'Pray God, this man can give it to you.'

'Eden must have been like this,' Centaine thought. 'And Eve must have felt the way I do today.'

She drove slower than her usual frantic pace. Although her heart cried out for haste, she denied it to make the anticipation keener.

'I have been without sight of him for five whole months,' she whispered. 'Five minutes longer will only make it sweeter when at last I am in his arms again.'

Despite Blaine's assurances and best intentions, the conditions that Centaine had placed upon them had prevailed. They had not been alone together since those stolen moments in the empty courtroom. During most of that time they had been separated by hundreds of miles, Blaine shackled by his duties in Windhoek, Centaine at Weltevreden, fighting desperately day and night for the survival of her financial empire which was now in its death throes, stricken by the loss of the diamond shipment, no part of which had ever been recovered. In her mind she compared it to the hunting arrow of O'wa, the little yellow Bushman: a tiny reed, frail and feather-light, but tipped with virulent poison which not the greatest game of the African veld could withstand. It weakened and slowly paralysed the quarry, which first reeled and swayed on its feet, then dropped and lay panting, unable to rise, waiting for the cold lead of death to seep through the great veins and arteries or for the swift mercy stroke of the hunter.

'That is where I am now, down and paralysed, while the hunters close in on me.'

All these months she had fought with all her heart and all her strength, but now she was tired – tired to every last fibre of muscle and mind, sick tired to her bones. She looked up at the rearview mirror above her head and hardly recognized the image that stared back at her with stricken eyes, dark with the heavy mascara of fatigue and despair. Her cheekbones seemed to gleam through the pale skin, and there were chiselled lines of exhaustion at the corners of her mouth.

'But today I will set despair aside. I won't think about it again, not for a minute. Instead I will think of Blaine and this magical display that nature has laid out for me.'

She had left Weltevreden at dawn and was now one hundred and twenty miles north of Cape Town, driving through the vast treeless plains of Namaqualand, heading down to where the green Benguela current caressed Africa's rocky western shores, but she was not yet in sight of the ocean.

The rains had come late this year, delaying the spring explosion of growth, so that although it was only weeks before Christmas, the veld was ablaze with its royal show of colour. For most of the year these plains were dun and windswept, sparsely populated and uninviting. But now the undulating expanses were clothed in an unbroken mantel so bright and vividly coloured that it confused and tricked the eye. Wild blooms of fifty different varieties and as many hues covered the earth in banks and flocks and stands, massed together with their own kind so that they resembled a divine patchwork quilt, so bright that they seemed to burn with an incandescent light that was reflected from the very heavens and the eye ached with so much colour.

Closer at hand the earthen road, rough and winding, was the only reference point in this splendid chaos, and even it was soon obliterated by flowers. The twin tracks were separated by a dense growth of wild blooms that filled the middle ridge between them and swept the underside of the old Ford with a soft rushing sound like the water of a mountain stream as Centaine drove slowly up another gentle undulation and stopped abruptly at the top. She switched off the engine.

The ocean lay before her, its green expanse flecked with brilliant white and lapped by this other ocean of blazing blooms. Through the open window the sea wind ruffled Centaine's hair and caused the fields of wild flowers to nod and sway in unison, keeping time to the swells of ocean beyond.

She felt the care and terrible strain of those last months recede in the face of so much vibrant beauty, and she laughed spontaneously at the joy of it and shaded her eyes from the glare of orange and red and sulphur-yellow flower banks and searched the seashore eagerly.

'It's a shack,' Blaine had warned her in his last letter. 'Two rooms and no running water, an earth latrine and an open hearth. But I have spent my holidays there since a child and I love it. I have shared it with nobody else since my father's death. I go there alone whenever I can. You will be the first.' And he had drawn a map of the road to it.

She picked it out immediately, standing on the edge of the ocean, perched upon the horn of rock where the shallow bay turned. The thatched roof had blackened with age but the thick adobe walls were whitewashed as bright as the foam that curled out on the green sea, and a wisp of smoke smeared towards her from the chimney.

Beyond the building she saw movement and picked out a tiny human shape on the rocks at the edge of the sea, and suddenly she was desperate with haste.

The engine would not fire, though she cranked the starter until the battery faltered.

'*Merde!* And *double merde!*' It was an old vehicle, used and abused by one of her under-managers on the estate until she had commandeered it to replace the ruined Daimler, and now its failure was an unwelcome reminder of her financial straits, so different from when she had driven a new daffodil-yellow Daimler every year.

She let off the handbrake and let the Ford trundle down the slope, gathering speed until she jumped the clutch and the engine started with a shudder and roar of blue smoke and she flew down the hill and parked behind the white-washed shack.

She ran out onto the black rocks above the water and the swaying beds of black-stemmed kelp that danced to the scend of the sea, and she waved and shouted, her voice puny on the wind and the rumble of the ocean but he looked up and saw her and came at a run, jumping from rock to slippery wet rock.

He wore only a pair of khaki shorts, and he carried a bunch of live rock lobsters in one hand. His hair had grown since last she had seen him. It was damp and curly with sea salt, and he was laughing, his mouth open and his big teeth flashing whitely and he had grown a moustache. She wasn't sure whether she liked that, but the thought was lost in the tumult of her own emotions and she ran to meet him and flung herself against his bare chest.

'Oh Blaine,' she sobbed. 'Oh God, how I've missed you.' Then she lifted her mouth to him. His face was wet with seaspray and it was salty on his lips. His moustache prickled. She had been right first time, she didn't like it – but then he lifted her high and was running with her towards the shack, and she held him tightly with both arms around his neck, bouncing in his arms, jolted by his long strides, and laughing breathlessly with her own fierce need of him.

B laine sat on a three-legged stool in front of the open hearth on which a fire of milkwood burned and perfumed the air with its fragrant incense. Centaine stood before him, working up a lather in the china shaving mug with his badger-hair brush, while Blaine complained.

'It took five months to grow – and I was so proud of it.' He twirled the ends of his moustache for the last time. 'It's so dashing, don't you think?'

'No,' said Centaine firmly. 'I do not. I'd prefer to be kissed by a porcupine.' She bent over him and lathered both sides of his upper lip with a thick foam, and then stood back and surveyed her handiwork with a critical eye.

Perched on the stool Blaine was still stark naked from their love-making, and suddenly Centaine grinned wickedly. Before he could fathom her intentions or move to protect himself, she had stepped forward again and daubed his most intimate extremity with a white blob of lather from the brush.

He looked down at himself, appalled. 'Him too?' he demanded.

'That would be cutting off my nose to spite my own face,' she giggled. 'Or something like that.' Then she put her head on one side and gave her considered opinion. 'The little devil looks a lot better with a moustache than you do.'

'Careful with that adjective "little",' he admonished her, and reached for his towel. 'Come along, old fellow, you don't have to put up with this disrespect.' He wrapped the towel around his waist and Centaine nodded.

'That's better. Now I can concentrate on the job without distraction,' and she took up the cut-throat razor that lay ready on the table-top and stropped it on the leather with quick practised strokes.

'Where did you learn that? I am beginning to feel jealous.'

'My papa,' she explained. 'I always trimmed his moustaches. Now hold still!'

She took the tip of his large nose between thumb and forefinger and lifted it.

'For what we are about to receive—' Blaine's voice was muffled by her grip on his nose. He closed his eyes and winced as the steel rustled over his upper lip, and a few moments later Centaine stepped back and wiped the lather and hair from the blade, laid the razor aside and came back to dry his upper lip and then stroke the smooth skin with her fingertip.

'It looks better; it feels better,' she told him. 'But there is still the final test.' And she kissed him.

'Hmmm!' She murmured her approval, and then still without breaking the kiss she wriggled round and sat on his lap.

It went on for a long time until she broke away and looked down. The towel had slipped. 'I say, here comes the little moustached devil again, obviously spoiling for trouble.' She reached down and gently wiped away the last traces of lather from the tip.

'You see! Even he looks a lot better cleanshaven.'

Blaine stood up with her in his arms. 'I think it is time, woman, that you learned the hard way that you can get away with just so much and then we must establish who is the boss around here.' And he carried her to the bunk against the far wall.

Much later they sat side by side cross-legged on the bunk with a single brightly coloured Basuto blanket draped over their bare shoulders, leaning together and watching the fire shadows flicker along the rough plastered walls, listening to the wind off the ocean soughing around the eaves of the thatched roof in the darkness outside, cupping their hands around steaming mugs of fish soup.

'One of my specialities,' Blaine had boasted, and it was thick with chunks of fresh galjoen fish and lobster that he had caught that day. 'Wonderful powers of rejuvenation for those suffering from over-exertion.'

Blaine recharged the mugs twice, for they were both ravenous, and then Centaine went to the fire, her naked body gleaming in the ruddy glow of the firelight, to bring him a smouldering twig to light his cheroot. When it was burning evenly, she climbed under the blanket again and snuggled against him.

'Did you ever find that young boy you were looking for?' he asked lazily. 'Abe Abrahams came to me for help, you know.'

He was unaware how the question had affected her, for she controlled the reflex stiffening of her body and simply shook her head. 'No. He disappeared.'

'He was Lothar De La Rey's son. I deduced that.'

'Yes,' she agreed. 'I was worried about him. He must have been deserted and alone after his father's sentence.'

'I'll keep looking for him,' Blaine promised. 'And let you know if anything comes up.' He stroked her hair. 'You are a kind person,' he murmured. 'There was no reason why you should concern yourself with the boy.'

They were silent again, but reference to the outside world had broken the spell and started a trail of thought that was unpleasant but had to be followed to the end.

'How is Isabella?' she asked, and felt the muscles of his chest tighten and swell beneath her cheek, but he inhaled a puff from the cheroot before he answered.

'Her condition is deteriorating. Atrophy of the nerves of her lower body. Ulceration. She has been in Groote Schuur hospital since Monday. The ulcers at the base of her spine will not heal.'

'I'm sorry, Blaine.'

'That is how I have managed to get away these few days. The girls are with their grandmother.'

'That makes me feel awful.'

'I would feel worse if I couldn't see you,' he replied.

'Blaine, we must keep to our resolution. We must never hurt her or the girls.'

He was silent again, then abruptly he flicked the stub of the cheroot across the room into the fire. 'It looks as though she will have to go to England. There is a surgeon at Guy's Hospital who has performed miracles.'

'When?' Her heart felt like a cannonball in her chest, suffocating her with its weight.

'Before Christmas. It depends on the tests they are doing now.'

'You will have to go with her, of course.'

'That would mean resigning as administrator and damaging my chances—' he broke off; he had never discussed his ambitions with her.

'Your chances of a place in a future cabinet and possibly one day the premiership,' she finished for him.

He stirred, taking her face between his hands and turning it gently so he could look into her eyes. 'You knew?' he asked, and Centaine nodded.

'Do you think that cruel of me?' he asked. 'That I could let Isabella go on her own, for my selfish ambitions?'

'No,' she said seriously. 'I know about ambition.'

'I offered,' he said, while unquiet shadows clouded the green of his eyes. 'Isabella would not accept it. She insisted that I stay here.' He laid her head back against his chest and stroked the hair back from her temple. 'She is an extraordinary person – such courage. The pain is almost unceasing now. She cannot sleep without laudanum, and always more pain and more laudanum.'

'It makes me feel so guilty, Blaine, but no matter what, I am glad for the opportunity to be with you. I am taking nothing from her.'

But that was not true, and she knew it. She lay awake long after he was asleep. She lay with her ear pressed to his chest and listened to his heart and the slow filling and emptying of his lungs.

When she woke he was dressed in the old pair of khaki shorts and taking down a bamboo fishing rod with an old Scarborough reel from the rack on the wall above the hearth. 'Breakfast in twenty minutes,' he promised, leaving her cuddled down in the bunk, but he was back before then carrying a gleaming gunmetal and silver fish almost as long as his arm. He arranged it on a grid over the embers and then came to her and pulled the blanket off.

'Swim!' he grinned sadistically, and she screamed.

'You are crazy. It's freezing! I'll die of pneumonia.' She protested as wildly all the way down to the deep rock-lined pool in which he dunked her.

The water was clear as air and so cold that when they clambered out their bodies glowed bright pink all over and her nipples were standing out as hard and dark as ripe olives. But the icy water had honed their appetites and they sprinkled lemon juice on the hot succulent white flesh of the Galjoen and wolfed it down with chunks of brown bread and salty yellow farm butter.

Satiated at last they sat back and Blaine looked at her. She wore only one of his navy blue roll-necked fisherman's jerseys but the hem reached almost to her knees. She had piled her damp unruly tangle of hair on top of her head and tied it there with a yellow ribbon.

'We could go for a walk,' he suggested. 'Or—'

She thought about that for a few seconds and then decided. 'I rather think I'll settle for the "or".'

'Your wish, madam, is my command,' he replied courteously, and stood over her to lift the heavy jersey off over her head.

In the middle of the morning he lay flat on his back on the bunk while Centaine was propped on an elbow above him, tickling his lips and closed eyelids with a feather that she had plucked from the seam of one of the pillows.

'Blaine,' she said softly. 'I am selling Weltevreden.'

He opened his eyes, caught her wrist and sat up quickly. 'Selling?' he demanded. 'Why?'

'I have to,' she answered simply. 'The estate, the house and everything in it.'

'But why, my darling? I know how much it means to you. Why sell it?'

'Yes, Weltevreden means a great deal to me,' she agreed. 'But the H'ani Mine means more. If I sell the estate, there is just a chance, a very small chance, that I will be able to save the mine.'

'I didn't know,' he said gently. 'I had no idea things were that bad.'

'How could you know, my love?' She caressed his face. 'Nobody else does.'

'But I don't understand. The H'ani Mine – surely it is making profits sufficient—'

'No, Blaine. Nobody is buying diamonds nowadays. Nobody is buying anything any more. This depression, this terrible depression! Our quota has been slashed. The prices we are being paid for our stones are less than half of what they were five years ago. The H'ani Mine is not quite breaking even. It is losing a small amount every month. But if I can hold on until the economy of the world turns around—' she broke off. 'The only chance I have of doing that is by selling Weltevreden. That is all I have left to sell. That way I might be able to hold on until the middle of next year, and surely this terrible depression must be over by then!'

'Yes, of course it will!' he agreed readily, and then after a pause, 'I have some money, Centaine—'

She laid her fingers on his lips, smiled sadly and shook her head.

He lifted her hand away from his mouth and insisted, 'If you love me then you must let me help you.'

'Our bargain, Blaine,' she reminded him. 'Nobody else must be hurt. That money belongs to Isabella and the girls.'

'It belongs to me,' he said. 'And if I choose—'

'Blaine! Blaine!' she stopped him. 'A million pounds might save me now – a million pounds! Do you have that much? Any lesser amount would be wasted, simply disappear into the bottomless pit of my debts.'

He shook his head slowly. 'So much?' Then he admitted regretfully, 'No. I don't have a third part of that, Centaine.'

'Then we will not speak of it again,' she told him firmly. 'Now show me how to catch crayfish for dinner. I don't want to talk of anything unpleasant for the rest of our time together. There will be plenty of time for ugliness when I get home.'

On their last afternoon they climbed the slope behind the shack, wading hand in hand through the bright banks of wild blooms. The pollen painted their legs the colour of saffron and the bees rose in noisy swarms as they disturbed them, then resettled as they passed on.

'Look, Blaine, see how every flower turns its head to follow the sun as it moves across the sky. I am like one of them, and you are my sun, my love.'

They wandered along the slope, and Blaine plucked the choicest blooms and plaited them into a crown. He placed it on her head. 'I crown you Queen of my heart,' he intoned, and though he smiled when he said it, his eyes were serious.

They made love lying on the mattress of wild flowers, crushing the stems and leaves beneath them, enveloped in the herby aroma of their juices and the perfume of their blooms, and afterwards Centaine asked him as she lay in his arms, 'Do you know what I'm going to do?'

'Tell me,' he invited, his voice drowsy from their loving.

'I'm going to give them something to talk about,' she said. 'A year from now they may say, "Centaine Courtney went out," but they'll have to add, "but she went out in style."'

'What do you propose?'

403

'Instead of the usual Christmas high jinks, I'm going to throw a bash to end all bashes! Open house at Weltevreden for a week, champagne and dancing every night.'

'It will also throw the creditors off the scent for a while longer,' he grinned at her. 'But I don't suppose you had thought of that, had you? You devious little vixen.'

'That's not the only reason. It will give us an excuse to be together in public. You will be there, won't you?'

'That depends.' He was serious again, and they both knew it depended on Isabella, but he did not say it. 'I'd have to find a pretty good excuse.'

'I'll give you an excuse,' she said excitedly. 'I'll make it a polo week – a twenty-goal tournament. I'll invite teams from all over the country, all the top players. You are the national captain. You could not reasonably refuse, could you?'

'I don't see how,' he agreed. 'Talk about devious!' And he shook his head in admiration.

'It will give you a chance to meet Shasa. I told you he had been pestering me ever since he heard that I knew you.'

'That I'd enjoy.'

'You will have to put up with a bit of hero-worship.'

'You could invite a few junior teams,' Blaine suggested. 'Give them a tournament of their own. I'd like to watch your son ride.'

'Oh, Blaine! What a wonderful idea!' She clapped her hands excitedly. 'My poor darling. It will probably be Shasa's last chance to ride his own ponies. Of course, I will have to sell them when I sell Weltevreden.' The shadows were in her eyes again for a moment, but then she rallied and her eyes sparkled. 'But as I said, we'll go out in style.'

Shasa's team, the Weltevreden Invitation, under 16 years, had won through to the final round of the junior league, mostly by virtue of their handicap allowance. Shasa was the only plus player. Of the other three members of the team, two were scratch handicaps and the third was a minus one.

However, they had finally come up against the Natal Juniors, four of the top youngsters, all of them two- and three-goal players except their captain. Max Theunissen had only made the age limit by a few months. He was rated five goals, the best in Africa for his age, with height and weight in the saddle, a good eye and a powerful wrist. He used all these advantages to the full, adopting a hard driving style of play.

Shasa was the next best rated player in the country, at four goals, but he lacked the older boy's weight and strength. Max was backed by his strong team-mates, and all Shasa's skill and determination were not sufficient to prevent his team crumbling under the onslaught, leaving Shasa virtually unaided to try and stem the rout.

In five chukkas Max had pounded in nine goals against Shasa's best efforts in defence, wiping out the Weltevreden team's handicap start, so that on handicap the teams were all square as they came in to change ponies for the last chukka.

Shasa flung himself out of the saddle, his face flushed with exertion and frustration and anger and shouted at his chief groom. 'Abel, you didn't tighten the girth properly.'

The coloured groom bobbed his head nervously. 'You checked it, Master Shasa.'

'Don't answer back, man.' But he wasn't even looking at Abel. He was glaring across the field at the Natal pony lines where Max Theunissen was surrounded by a cluster of his admirers. 'I'll ride Tiger Shark for this chukka,' he shouted at Abel over his shoulder.

'You said Plum Pudding,' Abel protested.

'And now I say Tiger Shark. Change the saddles and check the bandages on his forelegs.'

Plum Pudding was a small pony, getting a little on in years – and round in the middle – but still with an uncanny instinct to judge the run of the ball and set Shasa up for the shot. The two of them had developed a marvellous rapport. However, as befitted his advancing years, Plum Pudding was becoming cautious. He no longer enjoyed a heavy ride off and flinched from putting his plump shoulder to that of another pony at full gallop. Shasa had seen that at the other lines Max Theunissen had called for his black stallion, Nemesis. On this pony he had terrorized the junior league over the past four days, riding so cunningly close to foul play that the umpires had difficulty bringing him to book; he had succeeded in frightening most of the young lighter riders off the line even when they had the right of way, and riding off those who had the courage to stand up to him with such sadistic vigour that there had been two or three close calls – even one accident, when little Tubby Vermeulen from the Transvaal had been brought down so heavily that he had broken his wrist and dislocated his shoulder.

'Come on, Abel, don't just stand there. Get the saddle on Tiger Shark.' Tiger Shark was a young bay stallion with only a year's schooling behind him, an ugly animal with a hammer head and immensely powerful shoulders which gave him a hump-backed appearance. His temperament was equally unattractive. He kicked and bit without provocation or warning, was sometimes almost unmanageable, and he had a vicious aggressive streak that seemed to rejoice in the command to barge in for the ride off; he had never yet flinched from heavy contact. In any other circumstance Shasa would have stayed with Plum Pudding, but Max had saddled Nemesis and Shasa could guess what was coming.

The shaft of his stick had cracked in the final seconds of

the last chukka and he unwound the strap from his wrist and threw it on the ground and called across to his number two as he went to the wagon for a replacement.

'Bunty, you must come up faster and move inside for my cross. Don't keep falling back, man.' Shasa broke off, becoming aware of the hectoring tone of his own voice as he realized that Colonel Blaine Malcomess, the national captain and Shasa's particular demi-god, was watching him. He had come up silently and was now leaning against the rear wheel of the wagon, one ankle crossed over the other, his arms folded over his chest, the wide-brimmed Panama hat canted over one eye and an enigmatic half-smile on his wide mouth. Shasa was sure that it showed disapproval and he tried to smooth over his scowl.

'Hello, sir. We're taking a bit of a drubbing, I'm afraid,' and he forced a rueful and unconvincing smile. No matter what they taught you at Bishops, he didn't like losing, not one little bit.

Far from being censorious of Shasa's bad temper, Blaine was delighted with it. The will to win was the single most important asset, and not only on the polo ground. He had not been sure that Shasa Courtney had it; for a person of his age he covered up very well. Offering a beautiful but urbane face to his elders, deferring attentively to them with the old-fashioned manners drummed into him by his mother and his school, and remaining at all times difficult to fathom.

However, Blaine had been watching him carefully over the last four days. He had seen that Shasa had a strong natural seat on a horse, a marvellous eye and a fluid stroke hinging on a powerful wrist. He was fearless and full of dash, which often meant he was penalized for cutting across the line and for other dangerous play. But Blaine knew that with experience he would learn to disguise his hard play and not make it so apparent to the umpires.

The other requirements for a top international-class

player were great stamina, which would come with age, dedicated application and experience. This last item was so vitally important that a player only reached the high noon of his career at forty years or later. Blaine himself was only just peaking and could look forward to another ten years at the top.

Shasa Courtney had promise, and now Blaine had seen in him the will to win and his bitter anger at the thought of defeat. He smiled as he remembered his own reply when at that age his father had told him: 'Blaine, you must learn to be a better loser.' He had replied from the benefit of all sixteen years of acquired wisdom, 'Yes, sir, but I don't intend to get in enough practice to become really good at it.'

Blaine stifled the smile and spoke softly. 'Shasa, can we have a word, please?'

'Of course, sir.' Shasa hurried to his summons, pulling off his hard cap respectfully.

'You're letting Max rattle you,' Blaine said quietly. 'You've been using your noggin up to now. In the first four chukkas you held them to four goals, but in the last chukka Max knocked in five.'

'Yes, sir.' Shasa scowled again unconsciously.

'Think, lad. What has changed?'

Shasa shook his head and then blinked as it dawned on him. 'He's pulling me across onto his offside.'

'Right,' Blaine nodded. 'He's taking you on his strong side. Nobody has had a go at him from his other side, not once in five days. Change sides with Bunty and come at him on the nearside; come in steeply and barge him hard – just once. Something tells me young Max isn't going to like his own medicine. I think only one dose will be necessary. Nobody has yet seen the true colour of Master Theunissen's liver. My guess is that it has a streak of yellow in it!'

'You mean – foul him, sir?' Shasa stared at him wonderingly. All his life he had been coached in the games of young gentlemen. This was the first time he had received this type of advice.

'Perish the thought!' Blaine winked at him. 'Let's just learn to be good losers, shall we?'

They had established this peculiar accord from the moment Centaine had first introduced them. Of course Blaine's reputation had made it easier for him; he had Shasa's respect and admiration before they had even met and, given Blaine's experience as an officer and politician in the art of bending others to his will, it had been a simple matter for him to make the most of his advantage with one so inexperienced and gullible.

Besides that, Blaine had truly and deeply wanted it to be good between them. Not only for the reason that Shasa was the son of the woman he loved, but because the boy was comely and charismatic, because he was quick-witted and had proved himself fearless and dedicated – and because Blaine did not have, and knew he never would have, a son of his own.

'Stick with him, Shasa, and play him at his own game,' he ended his advice, and Shasa smiled, his face radiant with pleasure and determination.

'Thank you, sir.' He clapped his hard hat on his head and strode away, the shaft of his mallet over his shoulder, the back of his white breeches stained brown with dubbin from the saddle and the sweat drying in salty white crystals between the shoulders of his bright yellow jersey.

'Bunty, we are changing sides,' he called, and when Abel led Tiger Shark up, Shasa punched his shoulder lightly. 'You are right, you old thunder, I did check the girth myself.' He made a show of doing it again, and Abel grinned delightedly when Shasa looked up from the girth buckle and told him, 'Now you can't blame me again.' Without touching the stirrups he swung up onto Tiger Shark's back.

Blaine pushed himself away from the wagon wheel and

sauntered back towards the grandstand, his eyes instinctively sweeping the throng for the bright yellow of Centaine's hat.

She was in a circle of males. Blaine recognized Sir Garry Courtney and General Smuts amongst them, together with three other influential men, a banker, a cabinet minister in the Hertzog government and Max Theunissen's father.

'A pretty average sort of bunch for Madame Courtney.' Blaine winced at the jealous pang he could not harden himself to accept.

Centaine's invitations had been sent out not only to the best players in the country but to all the most influential and important men in every other field: politicians, academics, great landowners and mining magnates, businessmen and newspaper editors, even a few artists and writers.

The château of Weltevreden was unable to house them all and she had taken over every room at the neighbouring Alphen Hotel, once also part of the Cloete family estate, to accommodate the overflow. Together with all her local guests, there were well over two hundred from out of town. She had chartered a special train to bring down the up-country contingent and their ponies, and for five days the entertainment had been continuous.

Junior league polo in the mornings, an *al fresco* banquet at lunch time, senior polo in the afternoon, followed by an elaborate buffet dinner and all-night dancing.

Half a dozen bands played in relays, providing non-stop music through the days and nights. In between there were cabaret turns and fashion shows, a charity sale of art and rare wines, another sale of yearling thoroughbreds, a *concours d'élégance* for motor vehicles and lady drivers, a treasure hunt, a fancy-dress evening, tennis, croquet and bridge tournaments, show-jumping, a motor cyclist on a wall of death, Punch and Judy for the children and a team of professional nannies to keep the little ones occupied.

'And I am the only one who knows what it is all about.' Blaine looked up the stand at her. 'It's crazy and in a way immoral. It's no longer her money to spend. But I love her for her courage in the midst of misfortune.'

Centaine sensed him watching and her head turned quickly to him. For a moment they stared at each other, the distance between them not muting the intensity of their gaze, then she turned back to General Smuts and laughed gaily at what he was saying.

Blaine longed to go to her, just to be near to her, just to smell her perfume and listen to that husky voice with its touch of French accent, but instead he strode determinedly across the front of the stand to where Isabella sat in her wheelchair. This was the first day that Isabella had felt strong enough to attend the tournament and Centaine had arranged for a special ramp to be built to allow her wheelchair to reach the first tier of seats in the stand for a view of the field.

Isabella's silver-haired mother sat on one side of her and she was surrounded by four of her close girl friends and their husbands; but her two daughters came streaking down from the stand as soon as they saw Blaine, holding up their skirts to the knees with one hand and cramming their wide-brimmed beribboned straw hats onto their heads with the other while they gabbled shrilly for his attention and then hopped along on each side of him, clinging to his hands and dragging him up to his seat beside Isabella.

Dutifully Blaine kissed the pale silky cheek that Isabella offered him. The skin was cool, and he caught a whiff of laudanum on her breath. The pupils of her large eyes were dilated from the drug, giving them a touchingly vulnerable look.

'I missed you, darling,' she whispered, and it was the truth.

The moment Blaine had left her, she had looked around

desperately to find Centaine Courtney, her torment only easing a little when she saw Centaine surrounded by admirers higher in the stand.

'I had to chat to the boy,' Blaine excused himself. 'Are you feeling better?'

'Thank you. The laudanum is working now.' She smiled up at him, so tragic and brave that he stooped once more and kissed her forehead. Then as he straightened he glanced guiltily in Centaine's direction, hoping that she had not noticed that spontaneous gesture of tenderness; but she was watching him, and she looked away quickly.

'Papa, the teams are coming out.' Tara tugged him down into his seat. 'Come on, Weltevreden,' she shrieked, and Blaine could concentrate on the match rather than his own dilemma.

Changing sides Shasa led his team past the grandstand, cantering easily down the sideline, standing in the stirrups to adjust the chinstrap of his cap and searching for Blaine in the stand. They caught each other's eye and Shasa grinned as Blaine gave him a laconic thumbs up. Then he dropped back into the saddle and swung Tiger Shark around to face the Natal team as they rode out in their white breeches and caps, black boots and black short-sleeved shirts, looking tough and expert.

Max Theunissen frowned as he realized that Shasa had changed sides, and he circled out and flashed a hand signal to his number two on the far side of the field and then came back around again just as the umpire trotted to the centre and dropped the white bamboo root ball.

The last chukka opened with a confused scrappy mêlée, with hacked shots missing and the ball trampled and rolling under the ponies' hooves. Then it popped clear and Bunty leaned out of the saddle and hit his first good shot of the match, a high forehand drive that lofted well up-field and his pony went after it instinctively, bearing Bunty along on the line whether he liked it or not.

It was Bunty's shot, so he had the right of way and his pony came in perfectly to set him up, but Max Theunissen wheeled Nemesis and the black stallion was at full gallop within two strides. Max's father had not paid £1,000 for nothing, and the big powerful horse came down on Bunty like an avalanche.

Bunty looked over his shoulder and Shasa saw him blanch.

'Your line, Bunty,' Shasa screamed to encourage him. 'Stay on it!' But at the same time he saw Max deliberately press his toe into the back of the stallion's gleaming shoulder, and Nemesis altered his angle. It was a dangerous and menacing attack, and if Bunty had stood up to it, it would have been a blatant foul. But these tactics of terror worked yet again and Bunty sawed his pony's head frantically and broke away, giving up the line. Max swept onto it triumphantly, gathering himself and leaning out of the saddle, lifting his stick high in the foreswing and concentrating all his attention on the white ball that jumped and kicked over the turf directly ahead of him, setting up to take it on the backhand.

He had overlooked Shasa on his nearside, and was unprepared for the blazing burst of speed with which Tiger Shark responded to the drive of Shasa's heels as he came in at a legitimate angle for the ride off.

Neither of them had struck the ball last; it was therefore fair ball, each of them with equal right of way. But as they came together, both horses at full gallop, Tiger Shark just a head behind the big black stallion, Shasa gave him the toe signal behind the shoulder and Tiger Shark responded joyously. He changed angle sharply and barged with all the power of his great misshapen shoulders. The collision was so unexpectedly violent that Shasa was almost unseated himself and was thrown up onto Tiger Shark's neck.

However, Blaine had been right, it was Max Theunissen's

weak side, the one he had so assiduously protected all along, and Tiger Shark had timed the exploitation of his weakness perfectly. Nemesis reeled away and stumbled, his head going down between his front knees, and Max Theunissen was airborne, thrown high over his pony's head, somersaulting in mid-air but with the reins still in his hands, and for a terrible panicky moment Shasa knew he had killed him.

Then with an agility born of fear and natural athletic ability, Max switched around like a cat in the air and landed awkwardly, heavily but on his feet on the turf. For a few moments he was still too terrified and shocked to speak, and Shasa hauled himself back into the saddle and got Tiger Shark in hand as the whistles of the two umpires shrilled from both sides of the field. Max Theunissen started to scream hysterically.

'He fouled me, a deliberate foul. He crossed my line. I could have been killed.' Max was white and shaking, droplets of spittle flying from his quivering lips, and he was jumping up and down on the same spot like a petulant child, wild with frustration and fright.

The umpires were conferring in the middle of the field, and Shasa had an impulse to try and influence them with his own protestations of innocence, but good sense prevailed and he turned Tiger Shark back with all the dignity he could assemble, looking straight ahead, ignoring the roar of the crowd, but sensing that the roar was more an appreciation of justice, a bully caught in his own snare, than the expression of outraged sense of sportsmanship.

The umpires could not agree. They turned and trotted across the field to speak to the referee who came down from the grandstand to meet them.

'Good shot, Shas!' Bunty rode up to him. 'That will give the beggar something to write home about.'

'They might send me off, Bunty,' Shasa replied.

'You never crossed his line,' Bunty defended him hotly. 'I saw it all.'

But the fire in Shasa's blood was cooling and suddenly he thought what his grandfather would say, and even more unpleasant how his mother would react if he were sent off in front of her guests, bringing disgrace to their house. He looked nervously across at the stands, but it was too far to make out the expression on Blaine Malcomess' face. High in the stand he saw the yellow fleck of his mother's hat, and to his fevered eye it seemed to be set at a disapproving angle – but now the umpires were cantering back, one of them coming directly towards Shasa and reining in before him, his expression severe.

'Mr Courtney!'

'Sir!' Shasa straightened in the saddle, ready for the worst.

'This is a formal warning, sir. You are officially warned for dangerous play.'

'I acknowledge your warning, sir.' Shasa tried to match his expression to the forbidding countenance of the umpire, but his heart was singing. He had got away with it.

'Play on, Mr Courtney,' said the umpire, and just before he turned away, Shasa saw the twinkle in his eye.

There were three minutes left in the final chukka as Max rode down to drive the ball deeply into their territory with his penalty shot; but there to pick it up was Shasa's number three and he hit a wobbling, bouncing ball out to the left field.

'Good oh, Stuffs!' Shasa was delighted. Thus far Stuffs Goodman had done nothing to distinguish himself. The relentless Natal attack had dispirited him, and more than once he had been the victim of Max Theunissen's robust play. This was the first time Stuffs had completed a pass and Shasa moved in to receive, then took the ball up field. But Bunty was hanging back again, and without support

415

Shasa's attack was ridden down by a phalanx of Natal riders and the game reverted to an untidy mêlée while the seconds ticked away. The umpire blew up the mêlée and gave the shot to Natal.

'Dashed if we aren't going to hold them to a draw.' Bunty looked at his wristwatch and called across to Shasa as they fell back to receive the next Natal shot.

'Draw isn't ruddy good enough,' Shasa retorted furiously. 'We've got to win.' It was bravado, of course. They hadn't seriously attacked the Natal goal in five chukkas. But Bunty's limited ambitions angered Shasa, and Max Theunissen had definitely faded since his spill, no sign of his old dash and fire, and twice he had fallen back avoiding contact when Shasa brought the ball up field, leaving it to his backs to challenge.

'Only half a minute left!' Despite Shasa's boast, Bunty looked delighted at the term upon their sufferings, but at that moment the ball came to him hard and straight. He missed it and before he could turn the Natal attack swept past him and there was only Stuffs Goodman between them and the goal. As Shasa raced back to try and support him, his heart sank. It was all over. It was too much to hope that Stuffs could hit two clean shots in succession, but despite Shasa's misgivings, Stuffs came in, right into the heart of the Natal attack, white-faced and terrified but game, and he made a wild swing at the ball which never came within two feet of it. But his pony was a crafty old stager, clearly exasperated at the standard of his rider's play, and he trampled down the ball, and kicked it clear, right into Bunty's line. Bunty hit another corker, and chased it up field; but the Natal right back was there, driving in furiously, and the two of them ended up in another untidy waltz, swinging around each other, leaning out and hacking wildly, typical junior league play, neither man strong enough, or with sufficient experience to get another attack under way. The muddle gave both teams time to reorganize themselves and the opposing captains were howling at their men for the ball.

'Let me have it, Bunty!' On the left side of the field Shasa was standing in the stirrups, and Tiger Shark was prancing sideways with nervous anticipation, watching the ball with eyes rolling until the whites showed.

'Here, Digger, here!' howled Max, lying back deep but ready to race up when the ball came clear.

Then Bunty hit his third and last scorcher of the day, right in the sweet spot of the hardwood mallet head, but the ball flew only a few feet before it hit the fore hoof of the Natal back's pony and rebounded under Bunty's stirrups, kicking back into the Weltevreden deep field, right out in the open.

Shasa had anticipated almost instantly and sent Tiger Shark away. He tapped the ball to change its direction and then wheeled Tiger Shark so sharply that the pony went down on his haunches.

'Ha!' Shasa put his heels in and the pony launched himself into full stride with the ball dribbling along just ahead of him.

Shasa leaned out, concentrating all his attention on the little white ball as it popped and flicked erratically, and he got the head of his mallet to it again, putting top spin on the ball so that it came under control and flew low across the turf, aimed at the Natal goal two hundred yards ahead.

Tiger Shark followed it beautifully, easing out to precisely the right distance for Shasa to get a full shot at it. Plum Pudding couldn't have judged it better, and Shasa hit it again with a neat click of wood on wood, and the ball skipped obediently ahead of him. He looked up over the ball and there was the Natal goal dead ahead, only one hundred and fifty yards away, and a kind of savage joy filled him as he realized that instead of merely holding Natal to the draw, they really did have a chance to win.

'Ha!' he called to Tiger Shark, 'Ha!' And the big animal

plunged forward under him. At the same moment Max Theunissen on Nemesis wheeled onto the line ahead and rode directly at him.

'Down the throat,' was the term that described this most hazardous of all interception angles. On two powerful and swift animals they were charging each other down the throat; the roar from the grandstand faded into a horrified hush, and the spectators rose to their feet in unison.

Shasa had only once before witnessed a head-on collision between two big horses at full gallop. That had been at the trials before the Argentinian test match the previous year. He had been in the top row of the stand and he had heard the bones break clearly from there. One of the riders had burst his spleen and died later in hospital; the other had broken both legs. Afterwards they had shot the ponies as they lay in the middle of the field.

'My line!' he yelled at Max Theunissen as they swept towards each other.

'Damn you, Courtney!' Max yelled back defiantly. He had regained his courage, and he glared at Shasa over his pony's head; Shasa saw in his eyes that he was going to force the collision and he shifted slightly in the saddle. Tiger Shark felt it and flinched. They were going to give way – and then without warning Shasa was overwhelmed by the berserker's deadly passion.

Even from the stand Blaine Malcomess sensed it. He recognized that what had seized Shasa was not ordinary courage, rather it was a type of madness – the same madness that had once driven Blaine himself out into no man's land, alone with only a grenade in his hand, straight into the winking red eyes of the German Maxim guns.

He saw Shasa check Tiger Shark's turn and instead force him the opposite way, heading him directly at the black stallion, moving across the line of the ball in a deliberate challenge. It seemed that time slowed for Shasa. His vision was suddenly concentrated to brilliant clarity; he could see the wet pink mucous membrane deep in the flared nostrils of the great stallion in front of him; he could define each minute bubble in the froth that foamed from the corners of his mouth around the snaffle irons, each stiff black bristle in the charcoal velvet of his muzzle, each blood vessel in the lacework that covered the bloodshot corners of the stallion's eyes and each individual lash that surrounded them.

Shasa looked over the black stallion's head into Max's face. It was contorted with fury. He saw the tiny blisters of sweat on Max's chin, and the gap between his square white incisors as his lips were drawn back in a rictus of determination, and he looked into Max's brown eyes and held their gaze.

It was too late, Shasa judged; they had left it too late to avoid the collision, and as he thought it he saw the sudden shock in Max's face, saw his lips crumple and the flesh of his cheeks frost over with terror and watched him jerk back in the saddle and drag Nemesis' head around, pulling him off the line, breaking away right, only just in time.

Shasa swept past him, brushing him aside almost contemptuously, and with the passion still upon him he rose in the stirrups and struck the ball hard and true, driving it between the centre of the posts.

Blaine was still on his feet in the stand as the teams came in, and Shasa was flushed with triumph looking up at him for approbation, and though Blaine gave him only an airy wave and friendly smile, he was almost as exultant as Shasa.

'By God, the lad has the makings,' he told himself. 'He really has got it.' And he sat down again beside Isabella. She saw his expression; she knew him so well. She knew how desperately he had wanted a son – and the reason for his interest in the boy. It made her feel inadequate and useless and angry.

'That child is reckless and irresponsible.' She could not help herself, even though she knew that her censure would have the opposite effect on Blaine. 'He doesn't give a fig for anybody else, but then the Courtneys have always been like that.'

'Some people call it guts,' Blaine murmured.

'An ugly word for an ugly trait.' She knew she was being shrewish; she knew there was a limit to his forbearance, but she could not help this self-destructive urge to try and hurt him. 'He is like his mother—' and she saw the anger snap in Blaine's eyes as he rose to his feet, cutting her off.

'I'll see if I can get you some lunch, my dear.' He strode away, and she wanted to cry after him:

'I'm sorry – it was only because I love you so!'

Isabella ate no red meat, for it seemed to aggravate her condition, so Blaine was contemplating the display of prawns and crayfish, clams and mussels and fish which formed the centrepiece of the buffet, a pyramid taller than his head, such a veritable work of art that it seemed sacrilegious to make the first inroad upon it. He was not alone in his reluctance; the display was surrounded by an admiring cluster of guests exclaiming with delight and admiration so that Blaine was not aware of Centaine's approach until she spoke just behind his shoulder.

'Whatever did you say to my son, Colonel, that turned him into a savage?' And he turned quickly, trying to cover the guilty delight that he felt at her closeness. 'Oh yes, I saw you talking to him before the last chukka,' she went on.

'Man talk, I'm afraid, not for tender ears.'

She laughed softly. 'Whatever it was, it worked. Thank you, Blaine.'

'No need for that – the lad did it himself. That last goal was as plucky an effort as I've seen in a long time. He is going to be good – very good indeed.'

'Do you know what I thought as I watched it?' she asked softly, and he shook his head, leaning closer for her reply.

'I thought *Berlin*,' she told him softly, and he was perplexed for a moment. Then it dawned upon him.

Berlin 1936. The Olympic Games, and he laughed. She must be joking. From junior league to the seniors was the distance to the moon and the stars. Then he saw her expression and he stopped laughing.

'You really are serious!' He stared at her.

'Of course, I won't be able to afford to keep his ponies. But his grandfather loves to watch him play. He will help, and if he had the advice and encouragement of a really top man—' She gave a graceful little shrug, and it was a moment before he could recover from his astonishment sufficiently to reply.

'You never fail to amaze me. Is there nothing you won't reach for?' Then he saw the sudden, sly, lascivious gleam in her eye, and he went on hurriedly, 'I withdraw the question, madam.' For a moment they looked at each other with the veil stripped aside, their eyes and their love naked for anyone to see. Then Centaine broke the contact.

'General Smuts has been asking for you.' She changed direction again in that disconcerting mercurial fashion of hers. 'We are sitting under the oaks behind the stand. Why don't you and your wife join us there?' She turned away from him and the throng of her guests opened before her.

Blaine wheeled Isabella slowly across the smooth carpet of mown Kikuyu grass towards the group under the oaks. The weather had blessed Centaine's tournament; the sky was heron's-egg blue with a silver burst of cloud hanging stationary over the peak of Muizenberg and another thick mattress laid over the massif of Table Mountain that standing cloud known as 'the table cloth'.

It was windy, of course. It was always windy in December, but Weltevreden was tucked into a protected corner of the Constantia valley; passing overhead, the south-easter frou-froued the top leaves of the oaks, barely flickering at the women's skirts, but alleviating what would have been oppressive heat, and sweetening the air to earn its nickname 'the Cape doctor'.

When she saw Blaine coming, Centaine waved the white-jacketed waiter aside and poured champagne with her own hand and brought the glass to Isabella.

'Thank, you, no,' Isabella rebuffed her sweetly, and for a moment Centaine was at a loss, standing before the wheelchair with the scorned crystal glass in her hand.

Then Blaine rescued her. 'If it's going begging, Mrs Courtney.' He took the glass from her, and she smiled quick gratitude, while the others made room for the wheelchair in the circle and the chairman of the Standard Bank, sitting beside Centaine, took up his monologue where it had been interrupted.

'That fellow Hoover and his damned policy of interventionism, he didn't only destroy the economy of the United States but ruined us all in the process. If he had left it alone we'd all be out of this depression by now, but what do we have instead – over five thousand American banks bust this year, unemployment up to twenty-eight millions, trade with Europe at a standstill, the currency of the world in the process of debasement. He has forced one country after another off the gold standard, even Britain has succumbed. We are one of the very few countries that have been able to maintain the gold standard, and believe me it's beginning to hurt. It makes the South African pound expensive, makes our exports expensive, it makes our gold expensive to bring to the surface and God alone knows how long we can hold out.' He glanced across the circle at General Smuts. 'What do you think, *Ou Baas*, how long can we stay on gold?'

And the *Ou Baas* chuckled until his white goatee waggled and his blue eyes sparkled. 'My dear Alfred, you mustn't ask me. I'm a botanist not an economist.' His laughter was infectious, for they all knew that his was one of the most brilliant minds in any field, that this tumultuous twentieth century had so far spewed forth; that he had urged Hertzog to follow Britain's example when she left the gold standard; that he had dined with John Maynard Keynes, the economist of the age, on his last visit to Oxford; and that the two of them corresponded regularly.

'Then you must look at my roses, *Ou Baas*, rather than the gold question,' Centaine ordered. She had judged the mood of her guests and sensed that such heavy discussion was making them uncomfortable. Day to day they had to live with the unpleasant reality of a world tottering on the financial brink and they escaped from it now with relief.

The conversation became light and trivial, but with a superficial sparkle like that of the champagne in the long-stemmed tulip glasses. Centaine led the banter and laughter, but beneath it was that empty feeling of impending disaster, the insistent aching knowledge that all this was ending, that it was unreal as a dream, that this was the last echo of the past as she was carried forward into a future full of menace and uncertainty, a future over which she would no longer have control.

Blaine looked over her shoulder and clapped lightly, and her other guests joined in a splatter of condescending adult applause.

'Hail the conquering hero—' somebody laughed, and Centaine turned in her seat. Shasa was standing behind her, dressed in flannels and blazer, his hair wet from the shower and the marks left by the comb still sharply furrowed through it. He was smiling with just the right degree of modesty.

'Oh *chéri*, I'm so proud of you.' Centaine jumped up and kissed him impulsively and now he blushed with real embarrassment.

'I say, Mater, let's not go all French now,' he remonstrated, and he was so beautiful that she wanted to hug him. But she restrained herself and signalled the waiter to bring Shasa a glass of champagne. He glanced at her quizzically; he was usually restricted to lager, and not more than a pint of that either.

'Special occasion.' She squeezed his arm, and Blaine raised his glass.

'Gentlemen, I give you the famous victory of the Weltevreden juniors.'

'Oh, I say,' Shasa protested. 'We had nine goals start.' But they all drank, and Sir Garry made a place for Shasa beside him.

'Come and sit here, my boy, and tell us how it feels to be champions.'

'Please excuse me, Grandpater, but I have to be with the chaps. We are planning a surprise for later.'

'A surprise?' Centaine sat up. She had lived through some of Shasa's surprise turns. The amateur fireworks show during which the old barn had gone up in a most spectacular but unintended display together with the five acres of plantation behind it was only one of his more memorable efforts. 'What surprise, *chéri?*'

'If I tell you, it won't be a surprise, Mater. But we are going to clear the field just before the prize-giving – I thought I'd let you know.' He gulped the last of the champagne. 'Have to run, Mater. See you later.' She held out a hand to restrain him, but he was already on his way back towards the grandstand where the other members of the victorious Weltevreden Invitation team were eagerly waiting for him. They piled into Shasa's old Ford and went roaring up the long driveway towards the château. She watched them with trepidation until they were out of sight, and when she looked back Blaine and General Smuts had also left the circle and were strolling away amongst the oaks, their heads inclined towards each other talking earnestly. She watched them surreptitiously. They made an interesting and ill-assorted couple, the spry little white-bearded statesman and the tall handsome warrior and lawyer. Their conversation was obviously engrossing, and they were oblivious to all else as they promenaded slowly back and forth, just out of earshot from where Centaine sat.

'When are you returning to Windhoek, Blaine?'

'My wife sails for Southampton in two weeks' time. I will return immediately the mail boat leaves.'

'Can you stay over?' General Smuts asked. 'Say until the New Year? I am expecting developments.'

'May I have an inkling what they are?' Blaine asked.

'I want you back in the House.' Smuts evaded the direct question for the moment. 'I know it will involve sacrifice, Blaine. You are doing an excellent job in Windhoek and building up personal prestige and bargaining power. I am asking you to sacrifice that by resigning the administratorship and contesting the Gardens by-election for the South Africa Party.'

Blaine did not reply. The sacrifice that the *Ou Baas* was asking for was onerous.

The Gardens was a marginal seat. There was a real risk of losing it to the Hertzog party and even with a victory he would gain only a seat on the opposition benches, a heavy price to pay for the loss of the administratorship.

'We are in opposition, *Ou Baas*,' he said simply, and General Smuts struck at the Kikuyu grass with his cane as he pondered his reply.

'Blaine. This is for you only. I must have your word on that.'

'Of course.'

'If you trust me now, you will have a ministry within six months.' Blaine looked incredulous and Smuts stopped in front of him. 'I see I will have to tell you more.' He drew a breath. 'Coalition, Blaine. Hertzog and I are working out a Coalition cabinet. It looks certain and we will announce it in March next year, three months away. I will be taking Justice and it looks as though I will be able to appoint four of my own ministers. You are on my list.'

'I see.' Blaine tried to take it in. The news was stupendous. Smuts was offering him what he had always wanted, a place in the cabinet.

'I don't understand, *Ou Baas*. Why should Hertzog be prepared to negotiate with us now?'

'He knows that he has lost the confidence of the nation and that his own party is becoming unmanageable. His cabinet has become arrogant, if not downright lawless. It is engaging in discretionary rule.'

'Yes, yes, *Ou Baas*. But surely this is our opportunity! Look to this last month alone, look to the by-election at Germiston and the results of the Transvaal provincial elections. We won both decisively. If we can force a general election now, we will win. We don't have to form a coalition with the Nationalists. We could win as the South Africa Party on our own terms.'

The old general was silent for a few moments, his grey beard sunk into his chest and his expression grave. 'You may be right, Blaine. We might win now, but not on our own showing. The vote would go against Hertzog, not for us. A party victory now would be barren and sterile. We could not justify forcing a general election for the national welfare. It would be party political profiteering and I want no part of that.'

Blaine could not reply. Suddenly he felt humbled to be in the confidence of such a man. A man so truly great and good that he would unhesitatingly turn his back on the opportunity to profit from his country's agony.

'These are desperate times, Blaine.' Smuts was speaking softly. 'Storm clouds are gathering all around us. We need a united people. We need a strong coalition cabinet, not a parliament split by party differences. Our economy is tottering on the brink, the gold-mining industry is in jeopardy. At present costs, many of the older mines are already closing down. Others will follow, and when they do it will mean the end of the South Africa that we know and love. In addition to that, the prices of wool and diamonds, our other major exports, have crashed.'

Blaine nodded soberly. All these factors were the basis of nationwide concern.

'I don't have to emphasize the findings of the Wage Commission,' Smuts went on. 'One fifth of our white population has been plunged by drought and primitive farming methods into abject poverty, twenty per cent of our productive lands have been ruined by erosion and abuse, probably permanently.'

'The poor whites,' Blaine murmured, 'a great mass of itinerant beggars and starvelings, unemployed and untrained, without skills, without hope.'

'Then we have our blacks, split by twenty tribal divisions, flocking in from the rural districts in search of the good life, *die lekkerlewe*, and swelling the ranks of the unemployed, finding instead of the good life, crime and illicit liquor and prostitution, building up a pervading discontent, conceiving a fine contempt for our laws and discovering for the first time the sweet attractions of political power.'

'That is a problem we haven't even begun to address or attempt to understand,' Blaine agreed. 'Let us pray our children and our grandchildren do not curse us for our neglect.'

'Let us pray, indeed,' Smuts echoed. 'And while we do so, let us look beyond our own borders for a moment, to the chaos which engulfs the rest of the world.' He stabbed at the earth with his cane to mark each point as he made it. 'In America the system of credit has collapsed and trade with Europe and the rest of the world has come to a standstill. Armies of the poor and dispossessed roam aimlessly across the continent.' He stabbed the point of the cane into the turf. 'In Germany the Weimar Republic is collapsing after ruining the economy. One hundred and fifty billion Weimar marks to one of the old gold marks, wiping out the nation's savings. Now from the ashes has risen a new dictatorship, founded in blood and violence, which has upon it the stench of immense evil.' He struck the earth again, angrily. 'In Russia a ravening monster is murdering millions of his own countrymen. Japan is in the throes of anarchy. The military have run riot cutting down the nation's elected rulers, seizing Manchuria and slaughtering the unfortunate inhabitants by the hundreds of thousands, threatening to walk out of the League of Nations when the rest of the world protests.' Once again the cane hissed as he slashed at the lush Kikuyu grass. 'There has been a run on the Bank of England, Great Britain forced off the Gold Standard, and from the vault of history the ancient curse of anti-Semitism has escaped once more and stalks the civilized world.' Smuts stopped and faced Blaine squarely. 'Everywhere we turn there is disaster and mortal danger. I will not attempt to profit from it and in so doing divide this suffering land. No, Blaine, coalition and cooperation, not conflict.'

'How did it all go wrong so swiftly, *Ou Baas?*' Blaine asked softly. 'It seems just yesterday that we were prosperous and happy.'

'In South Africa a man can be filled with hope at dawn and sick with despair by noon.' Smuts was silent for a moment, and then he roused himself.

'I need you, Blaine. Do you want time to think about it?'

Blaine shook his head. 'No need. You can count on me, *Ou Baas.*'

'I knew I could.'

Blaine looked beyond him to where Centaine sat under the oaks and tried to hide his jubilation and to suppress the sense of shame that underlaid it, shame that unlike this saintly little man before him he was to profit from the agony of his country and the civilized world, shame that only now, out of despair and hardship, he would achieve

428

his cherished ambition of cabinet rank. Added to that he would be returning to the Cape, coming in from the desert lands to this lush and beautiful place, coming in to where Centaine Courtney was.

Then his gaze flicked to the thin pale woman in the wheelchair, her beauty fading under the onslaught of pain and drugs, and his guilt and shame balanced almost perfectly his jubilation.

But Smuts was speaking again.

'I will be staying on here as a guest at Weltevreden for the next four days, Blaine. Sir Garry has bullied me into agreeing to allow him to write my biography and I will be working with him on the first draft. At the same time I will be conducting a series of secret meetings with Barry Hertzog to agree the final details of the coalition. This is an ideal place for us to talk and I would be obliged if you could keep yourself available. I will almost certainly be calling upon you.'

'Of course.' With an effort Blaine set his own emotions aside. 'I will be here as long as you need me. Do you want me to submit my resignation to the administrator's office?'

'Draft the letter,' Smuts agreed. 'I will explain your reasons to Hertzog and you can hand it to him in person.'

Blaine glanced at his watch and the old general said quickly, 'Yes, you will have to prepare for your match. This frivolity in the midst of such dire events is rather like fiddling while Rome burns, but one must keep up appearances. I have even agreed to present the prizes. Centaine Courtney is a persuasive lady. So I hope we will meet later – at the prize-giving when I hand you the cup.'

It was a close thing, but the Cape 'A' team, led by Blaine Malcomess, held off the most determined efforts of the Transvaal 'A' in the final match of the tournament to win by three goals. Immediately afterwards all the teams gathered at the foot of the grandstand where the array of silver cups was set out on the prize table but there was an awkward pause in the proceedings. One team was missing: the junior champions.

'Where is Shasa?' Centaine demanded in a low but furious voice of Cyril Slaine, who was the tournament organizer.

He flapped his hands and looked helpless. 'He promised me he would be here.'

'If this is his surprise—' With an effort Centaine hid her anger behind a gracious smile for the benefit of her interested guests. 'Well, that is it. We begin without them.' She took her place on the front tier of the stand beside the general and held up both hands for attention.

'General Smuts, ladies and gentlemen, honoured guests and dear friends.' She faltered and looked around uncertainly, her voice overlaid by the drone in the air, a sound that rose steadily in volume, becoming a roar, and every face in the crowd was lifted to the sky, searching, some puzzled, others amused or uneasy. Then suddenly over the oaks at the far end of the polo field flashed the wings of a low-flying aircraft. Centaine recognized it as a Puss-Moth, a small single-engined machine. It banked steeply towards the grandstand and came straight at them, no more than head high as it raced across the field. Then, when it seemed it would fly straight into the crowded stand, the nose lifted sharply and it roared over their heads as half the spectators ducked instinctively and a woman screamed.

In the moment that it flashed over her, Centaine saw Shasa's laughing face in the side window of the aircraft's cabin, and the flicker of his hand as he waved, and instantly she was transported back over the years, through time and space.

The face was no longer Shasa's but that of Michael Courtney, his father. In her mind the machine was no longer blue and streamlined but had assumed the gaunt

430

old-fashioned lines, the double deck of wings and wire riggings and the open cockpit and daubed yellow paintwork of a wartime scoutplane.

It banked around in a wide circle, appearing once more over the tops of the oaks, and she stood rigid with shock and her soul was riven by a silent scream of anguish as she watched again the shot-riddled yellow scoutplane trying to clear the great beech trees below the château of Mort Homme, its engine stuttering and missing.

'Michael!' She screamed his name in her head and it was like a blinding flash of agony as once again she watched his mortally wounded machine hit the top branches of the tall copper beech and cartwheel, wing over wing, as it fell out of the air and struck the earth to collapse in a welter of broken struts and canvas. Again she saw the flames bloom like beautiful poisonous flowers and leap high from the shattered machine, and the dark smoke roll across the lawns towards her, and the body of the man in the open cockpit twist and writhe and blacken as the orange flames sucked upwards and the heat danced in glassy mirage and greasy black smoke and filled her ears with drumming thunder.

'Michael!' Her jaws were locked closed, her teeth aching at the pressure, and her lips were rimmed with the ice of horror so that the name could not escape from between them.

Then miraculously the image faded, and she saw instead the small blue machine settle sedately onto the green turf of the polo field, its tail dropping onto the skid, the engine beat dwindling to a polite burbling murmur as it swung around at the far end of the field and then taxied back towards the stand, the wings rocking slightly. It stopped below them and the engine cut out with a final hiccough of blue smoke from the exhausts.

The doors on each side of the cabin were flung open and

out tumbled Shasa Courtney and his three grinning team-mates. It amazed her that they had all crammed into that tiny cockpit.

'Surprise, everybody!' they howled. 'Surprise! Surprise!' And there was laughter and applause and whistles and catcalls from the stand. An aircraft was still a marvellous novelty, able to attract the attention of even such a sophisticated gathering as this. Probably not more than one in five of them had ever flown in one, and this unexpected and noisy arrival had created an excited laughing mood so that the applause and comment was loud and raucous as Shasa led his team up to the prize table to accept the silver cup from General Smuts.

The pilot of the blue aircraft climbed out of the left-hand door, a stocky bald-headed figure, and Centaine glared at him venomously. She had not known that Jock Murphy included flying among his assorted accomplishments, but she determined that he would rue this prank. She had always done all she could to discourage Shasa's interest in aircraft and flying, but it had been difficult. Shasa kept a photograph of his father in flying gear beside his bed and a replica of the SE5a fighter plane hung from the ceiling of his bedroom; over the last few years his questions about flying and his father's military feats had become more insistent and purposeful. She should have been warned by this, of course, but she had been so preoccupied, and it had never occurred to her that he might take to flying without consulting her. Looking back, she realized that she had been deliberately ignoring the possibility, deliberately avoiding thinking about it, and now the shock was all the more unpleasant.

With the silver cup in his hands Shasa ended his short acceptance speech with the specific assurance:

'Finally, ladies and gentlemen, you might have thought that Jock Murphy was flying the Puss-Moth. He was not! He wasn't even touching the controls – were you?' He looked across at the bald-headed instructor, who shook his head in collaboration. 'There you are!' Shasa gloated. 'You see, I have decided that I am going to be a flyer, just like my dad.'

Centaine did not join in the clapping and laughter.

A s suddenly as they had arrived and transformed the life of Weltevreden the hundreds of guests had gone, leaving only the ruined turf of the polo ground, the litter and the mountains of empty champagne bottles and piles of dirty linen in the laundry. Centaine was left also with a feeling of anticlimax. Her last flourish had been made, the last shot in her arsenal fired, and on the Saturday the mail ship docked in Table Bay and brought them an invited but unwelcome visitor.

'Damn fellow reminds me of an undertaker standing in for a tax collector,' Sir Garry huffed and took General Smuts off to the gunroom which he always used as a study when he visited Weltevreden. The two of them were immersed in the initial consultations for the biography and did not appear again until lunchtime.

The visitor came down to breakfast just as Centaine and Shasa arrived back from their early morning gallop, rosy-cheeked and starving. He was examining the hall-marks on the silver cutlery as they entered the dining-room arm in arm through the double doors, laughing at one of Shasa's sallies. However, the mood was instantly shattered, and Centaine bit her lip and sobered when she saw him.

'May I introduce my son, Michael Shasa Courtney. Shasa, this is Mr Davenport from London.'

'How do you do, sir. Welcome to Weltevreden.'

Davenport looked at Shasa with the same appraising stare with which he had been examining the silver.

'It means "well satisfied",' Shasa explained. 'From the Dutch, you know – *Weltevreden*.'

'Mr Davenport is from Sotheby's, Shasa.' Centaine filled the awkward pause. 'He has come to advise me on some of our paintings and furniture.'

'Oh, jolly good,' Shasa enthused. 'Have you seen this, sir?' Shasa pointed out the landscape in soft oils above the sideboard. 'It's my mother's favourite. Painted on the estate where she was born. Mort Homme near Arras.'

Davenport adjusted his steel-framed spectacles and leaned over the sideboard for a closer view so that his considerable stomach drooped into the salver of fried eggs and left a greasy splotch on his waistcoat.

'Signed 1875,' he said sombrely. 'His best period.'

'It's by a chap called Sisley,' Shasa volunteered helpfully, 'Alfred Sisley. He is quite a well-known artist, isn't he, Mater?'

'*Chéri*, I think Mr Davenport knows who Alfred Sisley is.' But Davenport wasn't listening.

'We could get five hundred pounds,' he muttered, and pulled a notebook from his inner pocket to make an entry. A fine dusting of dandruff descended from his lank locks at the movement and sprinkled the shoulders of his dark suit.

'Five hundred?' Centaine demanded unhappily. 'I paid considerably more than that for it.' She poured a cup of coffee, she had never taken to these huge English breakfasts, and carried it to the head of the table.

'That is as maybe, Mrs Courtney. We had a better example of his work on auction only last month, "L'Ecluse de Marly", and it didn't reach the very modest reserve we placed on it. Buyer's market, I'm afraid, very much a buyer's market.'

'Oh don't worry, sir.' Shasa piled eggs onto his plate and crowned them with a wreath of crispy bacon. 'It's not for sale. My mother would never sell it, would you, Mater?'

434

Davenport ignored him and carried his own plate to the vacant seat beside Centaine.

'Now, the Van Gogh in the front salon is another matter,' he told her as he launched into the smoked kippers with more enthusiasm than he had shown for anything since his arrival. With his mouth full he read from his notebook.

'Green and violet wheatfield; furrows lead the eye to golden haloes around the huge orb of the rising sun high in the picture.' He closed the book. 'There is quite a vogue for Van Gogh in America, even in this soft market. Can't tell whether it will last, of course, can't stand him myself, but I will have the picture photographed and send copies to a dozen of our most important clients in the United States. I think we can bank on four to five thousand pounds.'

Shasa had laid down his knife and fork and was staring from Davenport to his mother with a puzzled and troubled expression.

'I think we should talk about this later, Mr Davenport,' Centaine intervened hurriedly. 'I have set aside the rest of the day for you. But let us enjoy our breakfast now.'

The rest of the meal passed in silence, but when Shasa pushed his plate away, half finished, Centaine rose with him. 'Where are you going, *chéri?*'

'The stables. The blacksmith is reshoeing two of my ponies.'

'I'll walk down with you.'

They took the path along the bottom wall of the Huguenot vineyard, where Centaine's best wine grapes were grown, and around the back of the old slave quarters. Both of them were silent, Shasa waiting for her to speak, and Centaine trying to find the words to tell him. Of course, there was no gentle way of saying it and she had delayed too long already. Her procrastination had only made it more difficult for her now.

At the gate of the stable yard she took his arm and turned him into the plantation. 'That man,' she began, and then broke off and started again. 'Sotheby's is the foremost firm of auctioneers in the world. They specialize in works of art.'

'I know,' he smiled condescendingly. 'I'm not a complete ignoramus, Mater.'

She drew him down onto the oak bench that stood at the edge of the spring. Sweet crystal water burbled out of a tiny rocky grotto and splashed down amongst ferns and green moss-covered boulders into the brick-lined pool at their feet. The trout in the pool, as long and as thick as Shasa's forearm, came nosing up to their feet, swirling hopefully for their feed.

'Shasa, *chéri*. He has come here to sell Weltevreden for us.' She said it clearly and loudly, and immediately the enormity of it came down upon her with the brutal force of a falling oak tree, and she sat numb and broken beside him, feeling herself shrinking and shrivelling, giving in at last to despair.

'You mean the paintings?' Shasa asked carefully.

'Not just the paintings, the furniture, the carpets and the silver.' She had to stop to draw breath and control the trembling of her lips. 'The château, the estate, your ponies, everything.'

He was staring at her, unable to comprehend it. He had lived at Weltevreden since he was four years old, as far back as he could remember.

'Shasa, we have lost it all. I have tried since the robbery to hold it together. I was not able to do it. It's gone, Shasa. We are selling Weltevreden to pay off our debts. There will be nothing left after that.' Her voice was cracking again, and she touched her lips to still them before she went on. 'We aren't rich any more, Shasa. It's all gone. We are ruined, completely ruined.' She stared at him, waiting for him to revile her, waiting for him to break as she was about to break, but instead he reached for her and after a moment the stiffness went out of her shoulders and she sagged against him and clung to him for comfort.

'We are poor, Shasa—' and she sensed him struggling to take it all in, trying to find words to express his confused feelings.

'You know, Mater,' he said at last, 'I know some poor people. Some of the boys at school – their parents are pretty hard-up, and they don't seem to mind too much. Most of them are jolly good chaps. It might not be too bad, once we get used to being poor.'

'I'll never get used to it,' she whispered fiercely. 'I will hate it, every moment of it.

'And so will I,' he said as fiercely. 'If only I were old enough – if only I could help you.'

She left Shasa at the blacksmith's shop and returned slowly, stopping often to chat with her coloured folk, the women coming to the stable doors of the cottages with their babies on their hips to greet her, the men straightening up from their labours, grinning with pleasure for they had become her family; to part with them would be more painful even than giving up her carefully accumulated treasures. At the corner of the vineyard she climbed over the stone wall and wandered between the rows of lovingly pruned vines on which the bunches of new grapes already hung weightily, green and hard as musket balls, floury with bloom, and she reached up and took them in her cupped hands as though it was a gesture of farewell and found that she was weeping. She had been able to contain her tears while she had been with Shasa, but now she was alone, her grief and desolation overwhelmed her and she stood amongst her vines and wept.

Despair drained her and eroded her resolve. She had worked so hard, had been alone so long, and now in ultimate failure she was tired, so tired that her bones ached and she knew that she did not have the strength to start all over again. She knew she was beaten and that from now on her life would be a sad and sorry thing, a grinding daily struggle to maintain her pride while she was reduced to the position of a mendicant. For dearly as she loved Garry Courtney, it would be his charity on which she must rely from now on and her whole being quailed at the prospect. For the very first time in her life she could find neither the will nor the courage to go on.

It would be so good to lie down and close her eyes; a strong desire came upon her, the longing for peace and silence.

'I wish it was all over. That there was nothing, no more striving and worrying and hoping.'

The longing for peace became irresistible, filled her soul, obsessed her so that as she left the vineyard and entered the lane she quickened her step. 'It will be like sleeping – sleeping with no dreams.' She saw herself lying on a satin pillow, eyes closed, tranquil and calm.

She was still in breeches and riding-boots, so she could lengthen her stride. As she crossed the lawns she was running, and she flung open the french doors to her study and, panting wildly, ran to her desk and tore open the drawer.

The pistols had been a gift from Sir Garry. They were in a fitted case of royal blue pigskin with her name engraved on a brass plaque on the lid. They were a matched pair, hand-made by Beretta of Italy for a lady, engraved with exquisite gold inlay and the mother-of-pearl butts were set with small diamonds from the H'ani Mine.

She selected one of the weapons and broke it open. The magazine was loaded, and she snapped it closed and cocked the slide. Her hands were steady and her breathing had eased. She felt very calm and detached as she lifted the pistol, placed the muzzle to her temple and took up the slack in the trigger with her forefinger.

She seemed to be standing outside herself, looking on

almost without emotion other than a faint remorse at the waste and a gentle sense of pity for herself.

'Poor Centaine,' she thought. 'What an awful way for it all to end.' And she looked across the room at the gilt-framed mirror. There were tall vases set on each side of the glass filled with fresh long-stemmed yellow roses from the gardens, so that her image was framed within blooms as though she were laid out in her coffin and her face was pale as death.

'I look like a corpse.' She said it aloud, and at the words her longing for oblivion changed instantly to a sickening self-disgust. She lowered the pistol and stared at her image in the mirror, and saw the hot coals of anger begin to burn in her cheeks.

'No, *merde!*' she almost shrieked at herself. 'You don't get out of it that easily.' She opened the pistol and spilled the brass-cased cartridges onto the carpet, threw the weapon onto the blotter and strode from the room.

The coloured maids heard the heels of her riding-boots cracking on the marble treads of the circular staircase and lined up at the door to her suite, smiling happily and bobbing their curtseys.

'Lily, you lazy child, haven't you run my bath yet?' Centaine demanded, and the two maids rolled their eyes at each other. Then Lily scampered for the bathroom in a convincing pantomime of obedience and duty while the pretty little second maid followed Centaine to her dressing-room picking up the clothing that she deliberately dropped on the floor as she went.

'Gladys, you go and make sure Lily runs it deep and hot,' she ordered, and the two of them were standing expectantly beside the huge marble tub as Centaine came through in a yellow silk robe and tested the water with one finger.

'Lily, do you want to make soup out of me?' she demanded, and Lily grinned happily. The water was exactly the right temperature and Centaine's question was acknowledgement of that, a private joke between them. Lily had the bath crystals ready and sprinkled a careful measure on the steaming water.

'Here, give it to me,' Centaine ordered, and emptied half the jar into the bath. 'No more half measures.' Centaine watched the bubbles foam up over the rim of the tub and slide onto the marble floor with a perverse satisfaction, and the two maids dissolved into giggles at this craziness and fled from the room as Centaine threw off the robe and, gasping with the exquisite agony of the heat, settled chin deep in the foaming water. As she lay there, the image of the pearl-handled pistol reformed in her mind but she drove it forcefully away.

'One thing you have never been, Centaine Courtney, is a coward,' she told herself; and when she returned to her dressing-room she selected a dress of gay summer colours and she was smiling as she came down the stairs.

Davenport and Cyril Slaine were waiting for her.

'This is going to take a long time, gentlemen. Let us begin.'

Every single item in the huge mansion had to be numbered and described, the value estimated, the more important pieces photographed and everything entered laboriously in the draft catalogue. All this had to be completed before Davenport went back to England on the mail boat in ten days' time. He would return in three months to conduct the actual sale.

When the time came for Davenport to leave, Centaine surprised them all when she announced her intention of accompanying him around the mountain to the mail ship dock, a duty which would normally have fallen to Cyril.

The sailing of the mail ship was one of the exciting events of the Cape Town social calendar, and the liner swarmed with passengers and the dozens of guests who had come to wish them *bon voyage*.

At the first class entry port Centaine checked the passenger list and found the entry under 'M':

Malcomess, Mrs I. Cabin A 16
Malcomess, Miss T. Cabin A 17
Malcomess, Miss M. Cabin A 17

Blaine's family was sailing as planned. By agreement she had not seen him since the last day of the polo tournament, and surreptitiously she searched for him now through the smoking saloons and lounges of the liner's first class section.

She could not find him and realized that he was probably in Isabella's suite. The idea of their intimate seclusion galled her and she wanted desperately to go up to Cabin A 16 on the boat deck on the pretext of saying farewell to Isabella, but really to prevent Blaine being alone with her for another minute. Instead she sat in the main lounge and watched Mr Davenport demolishing pink gins, while she smiled and nodded at her acquaintances and exchanged banalities with those friends who paraded through the liner's public cabins determined to see and be seen.

She noted with grim satisfaction the warmth and respect of the greetings and attentions showered upon her. It was clear that the wild extravagance of the polo tournament had served its purpose and allayed suspicions of her financial straits. As yet no rumours had been set free to ravage her position and reputation.

That would change soon, she realized, and the thought made her angry in advance. She deliberately snubbed one of the Cape's most determined aspiring hostesses, publicly refusing her obsequious invitation and noting sardonically how the small cruelty increased the woman's respect. But all the time that she was playing these complicated social games, Centaine was gazing over their heads, looking for Blaine.

The liner's siren blared the final warning and the ship's officers, resplendent in white tropical rig, passed amongst them with the polite instruction: 'This vessel is sailing in fifteen minutes. Will all those who are not passengers kindly go ashore immediately.'

Centaine shook hands with Mr Davenport and joined the procession down the steep gangway to the dockside. There she lingered in the jovial press of visitors, staring up the liner's tall side and trying to pick out Isabella or her daughters from the passengers who lined the rail of the boat deck.

Gaily coloured paper streamers fluttered in the south-easter as they were thrown down from the high decks and seized by eager hands on the quayside, joining the vessel to land with a myriad frail umbilical cords – and suddenly Centaine recognized Blaine's eldest daughter. At this distance Tara was looking very grown-up and pretty in a dark dress and with her hair fashionably bobbed. Beside her, her sister had stuck her head through the railings and was furiously waving a pink handkerchief at someone on the dock below.

Centaine shaded her eyes and made out the figure in the wheelchair behind the two girls. Isabella was sitting with her face in shadow, and to Centaine she seemed suddenly to be the final harbinger of tragedy, an inimical force sent to plague her and deny her happiness.

'Oh God, how I wish that she were easy to hate,' she whispered, and her eyes followed the direction in which the two children were waving and she began to edge her way through the crowd.

Then she saw him. He had climbed up onto the carriage of one of the giant loading cranes. He was dressed in a cream-coloured tropical suit with his green and blue regimental tie and a wide-brimmed white Panama hat which he had taken from his head and was waving at his daughters high above him. The south-easter had tumbled his dark hair onto his forehead, and his teeth were very big and white against the dark mahogany of his tanned face.

Centaine withdrew into the crowd, from where she could watch him secretly.

'He is the one thing I will not lose.' The thought gave her comfort. 'I will always have him, after Weltevreden and the H'ani have been taken away.' And then suddenly a hideous doubt assailed her. 'Is that truly so?' She tried to close her mind to it, but the doubt slipped through. 'Does he love me, or does he love what I am? Will he still love me when I am just an ordinary woman, without wealth, without position, with nothing but another man's child?' And the doubt filled her head with darkness and sickened her physically, so that when Blaine lifted his fingers to his lips and blew a kiss up towards the slim, pale, blanket-draped figure in the wheelchair her jealousy struck again with gale force, and she stared at Blaine's face, torturing herself with his expression of affection and concern for his wife, feeling herself totally excluded and superfluous.

Slowly the gap between the liner and the quay opened. The ship's band on the promenade deck struck up. 'God be with you till we meet again'; the bright paper streamers parted one by one and floated down, twisting and turning, falling like her ill-fated dreams and hopes to lie sodden and disintegrating in the murky waters of the harbour. The ship's sirens boomed farewell, and the steam tugs bustled in to take charge and work her out through the narrow entrance of the breakwater. Under her own steam the huge white vessel gathered speed; a bow wave curled at her forefoot and she turned majestically into the north-west to clear Robben Island.

Around Centaine the crowds were drifting away, and within minutes she was alone on the dockside. Above her Blaine still stood on the carriage of the crane, shading his eyes with the Panama hat, staring out across Table Bay for a last glimpse of the tall ship. There was no laughter now, no smile upon that wide mouth that she loved so dearly. He was supporting such a burden of sorrow that perforce she shared it with him, and it blended with her own doubts until the weight of it was unbearable and she wanted to turn and run from it. Then suddenly he lowered the hat and turned and looked down at her.

She felt guilty that she had spied upon him in this unguarded and private moment, and his own expression hardened into something that she could not fathom. Was it resentment or something worse? She never knew for the moment passed. He jumped down from the carriage, landing lightly and gracefully for such a big man, and came slowly to where she waited in the shade of the crane, settling the hat back on his head and shading his eyes with the brim so that she could not be certain what they contained; and she was afraid as she had never been before as he stood before her.

'When can we be alone?' he asked quietly. 'For I cannot wait another minute longer to be with you.'

All her fears, all her doubts, fell away and left her feeling bright and vibrant as a young girl again, almost light-headed with happiness.

'He loves me still,' her heart sang. 'He will always love me.'

General James Barry Munnik Hertzog came out to Weltevreden in a closed car which bore no mark or insignia of his high office. He was an old comrade in arms of Jan Christian Smuts. Both of them had fought with great distinction against the British during the South African War, and they had both taken a part in the peace negotiations at Vereeniging that ended that conflict. After that they had served together on the national convention that led to the Union of South Africa, and they had both been in the first cabinet of Louis Botha's government.

Since then their ways had diverged, Hertzog taking the narrow view with his 'South Africa first' doctrine while Jan Smuts was the international statesman who had masterminded the formation of the British Commonwealth and had taken a leading part in the birth of the League of Nations.

Hertzog was militantly Afrikaner, and had secured for Afrikaans equal rights with English as an official language. His 'Two Streams' policy opposed the absorption of his own *Volk* into a greater South Africa, and in 1931 he had forced Britain to recognize in the Statue of Westminster the equality of the dominions of the empire, including the right of secession from the Commonwealth.

Tall and austere in appearance, he cut a formidable figure as he strode into the library of Weltevreden which Centaine had placed indefinitely at their disposal, and Jan Smuts rose from his seat at the long green-baize-covered table and came to meet him.

'So!' Hertzog snorted as he shook hands. 'We may not have as much time for discussion and manoeuvre as we had hoped.'

General Smuts glanced down the table at Blaine Malcomess and Deneys Reitz, his confidants and two of his nominees for the new cabinet, but none of them spoke while Hertzog and Nicolaas Havenga, the Nationalist minister of finance, settled themselves on the opposite side of the long table. At seventeen years of age Havenga had ridden with Hertzog on commando against the British, acting as his secretary, and since then they had been inseparable. Havenga had held his present cabinet rank since Hertzog's Nationalists had come to power in 1924.

'Are we safe here?' he asked now, glancing suspiciously at the double brass-bound mahogany doors at the far end of the library and then sweeping his gaze around the shelves which rose to the ornately plastered ceiling and were filled with Centaine's collection of books, all bound in Morocco leather and embossed with gold leaf.

'Quite safe,' Smuts assured him. 'We may speak openly without the least fear of being overheard. I give you my personal assurance.'

Havenga looked at his master for further assurance and when the prime minister nodded he spoke with apparent reluctance.

'Tielman Roos has resigned from the Appellate Division,' he announced, and sat back in his seat. It was unnecessary for him to elaborate. Tielman Roos was one of the country's best known and most colourful characters. 'The Lion of the North' was his nickname and he had been one of Hertzog's most loyal supporters. When the Nationalists came to power, he had been minister of justice and deputy premier. It had seemed that he was destined to be Hertzog's successor, the heir apparent, but then failing health and disagreement over the issue of South Africa's adherence to the gold standard had intervened. He had retired from politics and accepted an appointment to the Appellate Division of the Supreme Court.

'Health?' Jan Smuts asked.

'No, the gold standard,' Havenga said gravely. 'He intends coming out against our remaining upon the standard.'

'His influence is enormous,' Blaine exclaimed.

'We cannot let him throw doubt upon our policies,' Hertzog agreed. 'A declaration from Roos now could be disastrous. It must be our first priority to agree upon our joint policy on gold. We must be in a position either to oppose or pre-empt his position. It is vitally important that we offer a united front.' He looked directly at Smuts.

'I agree,' Smuts answered. 'We must not allow our new coalition to be discredited before we have even come into existence.'

'This is a crisis,' Havenga interjected. 'We must handle it as such. May we have your views, *Ou Baas?*'

'You know my views,' Smuts told them. 'You will recall that I urged you to follow Great Britain's example when she went off the gold standard. I don't wish to throw that in your faces now, but I haven't altered my views since then.'

'Please go over your reasons again, *Ou Baas.*'

'At the time I predicted that there would be a flight from the South African gold pound into sterling. Bad money always drives out good money, and I was right. That happened,' Smuts stated simply, and the men opposite looked uncomfortable. 'The resulting loss of capital has crippled our industry and sent tens of thousands of our workers to swell the ranks of the unemployed.'

'There are millions of unemployed in Britain herself,' Havenga pointed out irritably.

'Our refusal to go off gold aggravated unemployment. It has endangered our gold-mining industry. It has sent prices for our diamonds and wool crashing. It has deepened the depression to this tragic level where we now find ourselves.'

'If we go off the gold standard at this late stage, what will be the benefits to the country?'

'First and by far the most important, it will rejuvenate our gold-mining industry. If the South African pound falls to parity with sterling, and that is what should happen immediately, it will mean that the mines will receive seven pounds for an ounce of gold instead of the present four. Almost double. The mines that have closed down will re-open. The others will expand. New mines will open providing work for tens of thousands, whites and blacks, and capital will flow back into this country. It will be the turning point. We will be back on the road to prosperity.'

The arguments for and against were thrown back and forth, Blaine and Reitz supporting the old general, and

447

gradually the two men opposite retreated before their logic until a little after noon Barry Hertzog said suddenly:

'The timing. There will be pandemonium in the stock exchange. There are only three trading days before Christmas. We must delay any announcement until then, do it only when the exchange is closed.' The atmosphere in the library seemed palpable. With Hertzog's statement, Blaine realized that Smuts had finally carried the argument. South Africa would be off gold before the stock exchange re-opened in the new year. He felt a marvellous sense of elation, of achievement. The first act of this new coalition was to set a term to the country's protracted economic agony, a promise of return to prosperity and hope.

'I still have sufficient influence with Tielman to prevail upon him to delay his announcement until after the markets close.' Hertzog was still speaking, but it was only the details that remained to be agreed upon and that evening, as Blaine shook hands with the others in front of the white gables of Weltevreden and went to where his Ford was parked beneath the oaks, he was filled with a sense of destiny.

It was this that had attracted him into the political arena, this knowledge that he could help to change the world. For Blaine this was the ultimate use of power, to wield it like a bright sword against the demons that plagued his people and his land.

'I have become a part of history,' he thought, and the elation stayed with him as he drove out through the magnificent Anreith gates of Weltevreden, the last in the small convoy of vehicles.

Deliberately he let the prime minister's car, followed by the Plymouth that Deneys Reitz was driving, pull even further ahead and then disappear into the bends that snaked up Wynberg Hill. Only then he pulled off onto the verge and sat for a few minutes with the engine idling, watching the rearview mirror to make certain that he was not observed.

Then he put the Ford in gear again and swung a U-turn across the road. He turned off the main road before he reached the Anreith gates, into a lane that skirted the boundary of Weltevreden, and within minutes he was once more on Centaine's land, coming in through one of the back lanes, hidden from the château and the main buildings by a plantation of pines.

He parked the Ford amongst the trees and set off along the path, breaking into a run as he saw the whitewashed walls of the cottage ahead of him gleaming in the golden rays of the setting sun. It was exactly as she had described to him.

He paused in the doorway. Centaine had not heard him. She was kneeling before the open hearth, blowing on the smoky flames that were rising from the pile of pinecones she had set as kindling for the fire. For a while he watched her from the doorway, delighted to be able to observe her while she was still unaware of him. She had removed her shoes and the soles of her bare feet were pink and smooth, her ankles slim, her calves firm and strong from riding and walking, the backs of her knees dimpled. He had never noticed that before and the dimples touched him. He was moved by the deep tenderness that until now he had felt only for his own daughters, and he made a small sound in his throat.

Centaine turned, springing to her feet the instant she saw him. 'I thought you weren't coming.' She rushed to him, holding up her face to him, her eyes shining, and then after a long time she broke off the kiss and still in his arms studied his face.

'You are tired,' she said.

'It has been a long day.'

'Come.' Holding his hand she led him to the chair

beside the hearth. Before he sat, she slipped the jacket off his shoulders and stood on tiptoe to loosen his necktie.

'I've always wanted to do that for you,' she murmured, and hung his jacket in the small yellow-wood cupboard before she went to the centre table and poured whisky into a tumbler, squirted soda onto it from the siphon and brought it to him.

'Is that right?' she asked anxiously, and he sipped and nodded.

'Perfect.' He looked around the cottage, taking in the bunches of cut flowers in the vases, the gleam of new wax on the floors and simple solid furniture.

'Very nice,' he said.

'I worked all day to have it ready for you.' Centaine looked up from the cheroot that she was preparing. 'Anna used to live here, until she married Sir Garry. Nobody else has used it since then. Nobody comes here. It's our place now, Blaine.' She brought the cheroot to him, lit a taper in the fire and held it for him until it was burning evenly. Then she placed one of the leather cushions at his feet and settled upon it, leaning her folded arms on his knee and watching his face in the light of the flames.

'How long can you stay?'

'Well—' he looked thoughtful. 'How long do you want me? An hour? Two? Longer?' and Centaine squirmed with pleasure and clasped his knees tightly.

'The whole night,' she gloated. 'The whole glorious night!'

She had brought down a basket from the kitchen at Weltevreden. They dined on cold roast beef and turkey and drank the wines from her own vineyards. Afterwards she peeled the big yellow Hanepoort grapes and popped them into his mouth one at a time, kissing his lips lightly between each morsel.

'The grapes are sweet,' he smiled, 'but I prefer the kisses.'

'Fortunately, sir, there is no shortage of either.'

Centaine brewed coffee on the open hearth and they drank it sprawled together on the rug in front of the fire, watching the flames, neither of them speaking, but Blaine stroked the fine dark hairs at her temples and at the nape of her neck with his fingertips until slowly the tranquil mood hardened and he ran his fingers down her spine and she trembled and rose to her feet.

'Where are you going?' he demanded.

'Finish your cheroot,' she told him. 'Then come and find out.'

When he followed her into the small bedroom she was sitting in the centre of the low bed.

He had never seen her in a nightdress before. It was of pale lemon satin and the lace at the neck and cuffs was the colour of old ivory that glowed in the candlelight.

'You are beautiful,' he said.

'You make me feel beautiful,' she said gravely, and held out both hands to him.

Tonight their loving, in contrast to the other urgent wildly driven nights, was measured and slow, almost stately. She had not realized that he had learned so much about her body and its special needs. Calmly and skilfully he ministered to them and her trust in him was complete; gently he swept away her last reservations and bore her beyond the sense of self, his body deep in hers and she enfolding him and blending with him so that their very blood seemed to mingle and his pulse beat in time to her heart. It was his breath that filled her lungs, his thoughts that gleamed and glimmered through her brain, and she heard her own words echo in his eardrums:

'I love you, my darling, oh God, how I love you.'

And his voice replied, crying through the cavern of her own throat, his voice upon her lips, 'I love you. I love you.'

And they were one.

He woke before her and the sunbirds were twittering in the bright orange-coloured blooms of the tacoma shrubs outside the cottage window. A beam of sunlight had found a chink in the curtains and it cut through the air above his head like the blade of a golden rapier.

Slowly, very slowly, so as not to disturb her, he turned his head and studied her face. She had thrown aside her pillow and her cheek was pressed to the mattress, her lips almost touching his shoulder, one arm thrown out over his chest.

Her eyes were closed, and there was a delicate pattern of blue veins beneath the soft translucent skin of the lids. Her breathing was so gentle that for a moment he was alarmed, then she frowned softly in her sleep and his alarm gave way to concern as he saw the tiny arrowheads of strain and worry that had been chiselled at the corners of her eyes and mouth during these last months.

'My poor darling.' His lips formed the words without sound, and slowly the splendid mood of the previous night washed away like sand before the incoming tide of harsh reality.

'My poor brave darling.' He had not known grief like this since he stood beside his father's open grave. 'If only there was something I could do to help you, now in this time of your need.' And as he said it the thought occurred to him, and he started so violently that Centaine felt it and rolled away from him in her sleep, frowning again, the corner of her eyelid twitching, and muttered something that he could not understand and then was still.

Blaine lay rigid beside her, every muscle in his body under stress, his fists clenched at his sides, his jaws biting down hard, appalled at himself, angry and frightened that he had even been capable of thinking that thought. His eyes were wide open now. He stared at the bright coin of sunlight on the opposite wall but did not see it, for he was a man on the torturer's rack, the rack of a terrible temptation.

'Honour—' the words blazed in his mind, 'honour and duty.' He groaned silently as on the other side of his brain another word burned as fiercely: 'love'.

The woman who lay beside him had set no price upon her love. She had made no terms, no bargains, but had simply given without asking in return. Rather than demanding she had given him quittance; it was she who had insisted that no other person should be hurt by their happiness. Freely she had heaped upon him all the sweets of her love without asking the smallest price, not the gold band and vows of marriage, not even promises or assurances, and he had offered nothing. Until this moment there had been nothing for him to give her in repayment.

On the other hand he had been singled out by a great and good man who had placed unquestioning trust in him. Honour and duty on one hand – love on the other. This time there was no escape from the lash of his conscience. Who would he betray, the man he revered or the woman he loved? He could not lie still another moment and stealthily he lifted the sheet. Centaine's eyelids fluttered; she made a little mewling sound and then settled deeper into sleep.

The previous evening she had laid out a new razor and toothbrush on the washstand in the bathroom for him, and this little thoughtfulness goaded him further. The agony of indecision scourged him as he shaved and dressed.

He tiptoed back into the bedroom and stood beside the bed.

'I could walk away,' he thought. 'She will never know of my treachery.' And then he wondered at his choice of word. Was it treachery to keep intact his honour, to cleave to his duty? He forced the thought aside and made his decision.

He reached down and touched her eyelids. They fluttered

453

open. She looked up at him, her pupils very black and big and unfocused. Then they contracted and she smiled, a comfortable sleepy contented smile.

'Darling,' she murmured, 'what time is it?'

'Centaine, are you awake?'

She sat up quickly, and exclaimed with dismay. 'Oh Blaine. You are dressed – so soon!'

'Listen to me, Centaine. This is very important. Are you listening?'

She nodded, blinking the last vestiges of sleep from her eyes, and stared at him solemnly.

'Centaine, we are going off gold,' he said, and his voice was harsh, rough with self-contempt and guilt. 'They made the decision yesterday, *Ou Baas* and Barry Hertzog. We'll be off gold by the time the markets re-open in the New Year.'

She stared at him blankly for a full five seconds and then suddenly it struck her and her eyes flared wide open, but then slowly the fire in them faded again.

'Oh God, my darling, what it must have cost you to tell me that,' she said, and her voice shook with compassion, for she understood his sense of honour and knew the depths of his duty. 'You do love me, Blaine. You do truly love me. I believe it now.'

Yet he was glaring at her. She had never seen such an expression on his face before. It was almost as though he hated her for what he had done. She couldn't bear that look, and she scrambled onto her knees in the centre of the rumpled bed and held out her arms in appeal.

'Blaine, I won't use it. I won't use what you have told me—' and he snarled at her, his face contorted with guilt:

'That way you would let me make this sacrifice for nought.'

'Don't hate me for it, Blaine,' she pleaded, and the anger faded from his face.

'Hate you?' he asked sadly. 'No, Centaine, that I could never do.' He turned and strode from the room.

454

She wanted to run after him, to try and comfort him, but she knew that it was beyond even the power of her great love. She sensed that, like a wounded lion, he had to be alone, and she listened to his heavy footfalls receding down the path through the plantation outside her window.

Centaine sat at her desk at Weltevreden. She was alone, and in the centre of her desk stood the ivory and brass telephone.

She was afraid. What she was about to do would place her far beyond the laws of society and the courts. She was at the beginning of a journey into uncharted territory, a lonely dangerous journey which could end for her in disgrace and imprisonment.

The telephone rang and she started, and stared at the instrument fearfully. It rang again and she drew a deep breath and lifted the handset.

'Your call to Rabkin and Swales, Mrs Courtney,' her secretary told her. 'I have Mr Swales on the line.'

'Thank you, Nigel.' She heard the hollow tone of her voice and cleared her throat.

'Mrs Courtney.' She recognized Swales' voice. He was the senior partner in the firm of stockbrokers and she had dealt with him before. 'May I wish you the compliments of the festive season.'

'Thank you, Mr Swales.' Her voice was crisp and businesslike. 'I have a buying order for you, Mr Swales. I'd like it filled before the market closes today.'

'Of course,' Swales assured her. 'We will complete it immediately.'

'Please buy at best five hundred thousand East Rand Proprietary Mines,' she said, and there was an echoing silence in the earphones.

'Five hundred thousand, Mrs Courtney,' Swales repeated

at last. 'ERPM are standing at twenty-two and six. That is almost six hundred thousand pounds.'

'Exactly,' Centaine agreed.

'Mrs Courtney—' Swales stopped.

'Is there some problem, Mr Swales?'

'No, of course not. None at all. You caught me by surprise, that's all. Just the size of the order. I will get onto it right away.'

'I will post you my cheque in full settlement just as soon as I receive your contract note for the purchase.' She paused, and then went on icily, 'Unless, of course, you require me to send you a deposit immediately.' She held her breath. Nowhere could she raise even the deposit that Swales was entitled to ask for.

'Oh dear, Mrs Courtney! I hope you didn't think – I must sincerely apologize for having led you to think that I might question your ability to pay. There is absolutely no hurry. We will post you the contract note in the usual way. Your credit with Rabkin and Swales is always good. I hope to confirm the purchase for you by tomorrow morning at the very latest. As you are no doubt aware, tomorrow is the final trading day before the Christmas recess.'

Her hands were shaking so violently that she had trouble setting the handset of the telephone on its hook.

'What have I done?' she whispered, and she knew the answer. She had committed a criminal act of fraud, the maximum penalty for which was ten years' imprisonment. She had just contracted a debt which she had no reasonable expectation of honouring. She was bankrupt, she knew she was bankrupt, and she had just taken on another half million pounds' obligation. She was taken with a fit of remorse and she reached for the telephone to cancel the order, but it rang before she touched it.

'Mrs Courtney, I have Mr Anderson of Hawkes and Giles on the line.'

'Put him on, please Nigel,' she ordered, and she was

amazed that there was no tremor in her voice as she said, casually, 'Mr Anderson, I have a purchase order for you, please.'

By noon she had telephoned seven separate firms of stockbrokers in Johannesburg and placed orders for the purchase of gold-mining shares to the value of five and half million pounds. Then at last her nerve failed her.

'Nigel, cancel the other two calls, please,' she said calmly, and ran to her private bathroom at the end of the passage with her hands over her mouth.

Just in time she fell to her knees in front of the white porcelain toilet bowl and vomited into it a hard projectile stream, bringing up her terror and shame and guilt, heaving and retching until her stomach was empty and the muscles of her chest ached and her throat burned as though it had been scalded raw with acid.

Christmas Day had always been one of their very special days since Shasa was a child, but she awoke this morning in a sombre mood.

Still in their night clothes and dressing-gowns, she and Shasa exchanged their presents in her suite. He had hand painted a special card for her, and decorated it with pressed wild flowers. His present to her was François Mauriac's new novel *Noeud de Vipères* and he had inscribed on the flyleaf:

> No matter what, we still have
> each other
>
> Shasa.

Her present to him was a leather flying helmet with goggles and he looked at her with amazement. She had made her opposition to flying very plain.

'Yes, *chéri*, if you want to learn to fly, I'll not stop you.'

457

'Can we afford it, Mater? I mean, you know—'

'You let me worry about that.'

'No, Mater.' He shook his head firmly. 'I'm not a child any more. From now on I am going to help you. I don't want anything that will make it more difficult for you – for us.'

She ran to him and embraced him quickly, pressing her cheek to his so that he could not see the shine of tears in her eyes.

'We are desert creatures. We will survive, my darling.'

But her moods swung wildly all the rest of that day as Centaine played the *grande dame*, the châtelaine of Welte- vreden, welcoming the many callers at the estate, serving sherry and biscuits and exchanging gifts with them, laugh- ing and charming, and then on the pretext of seeing to the servants hurrying away to lock herself in the mirrored study with the drawn curtains while she fought off the black moods, the doubts and the terrible crippling forebodings. Shasa seemed to understand, standing in her place when she fell out, suddenly mature and responsible, rallying to her aid as he had never been called upon to do before.

Just before noon one of their callers brought tidings which genuinely allowed Centaine to forget for a short time her own forebodings. The Rev. Canon Birt was the headmaster of Bishops and he took Centaine and Shasa aside for a few moments.

'Mrs Courtney, you know what a name young Shasa has made for himself at Bishops. Unfortunately next year will be his last with us. We shall miss him. However, I am sure it will come as no surprise to you to hear that I have selected him to be head of school in the new term, or that the board of governors have endorsed my choice.'

'Not in front of the Head, Mater,' Shasa whispered, in an agony of embarrassment when Centaine embraced him joyously, but she deliberately kissed both his cheeks in the manner he designated 'French' and pretended to disparage.

'That is not all, Mrs Courtney.' Canon Birt beamed on this display of maternal pride. 'I have been asked by the board of governors to invite you to join them. You will be the first woman – ah, the first lady, ever to sit on the board.'

Centaine was on the point of accepting immediately, but then like the shadow of the executioner's axe the premonition of impending financial catastrophe dulled her vision and she hesitated.

'I know you are a very busy person—' he was about to urge her.

'I am honoured, Headmaster,' she told him. 'But there are personal considerations. May I give you my reply in the new year?'

'Just as long as that is not an outright refusal—'

'No, I give you my assurance. If I can, I will.'

When the last caller had been packed off, Centaine could lead the family, including Sir Garry and Anna and the very closest family friends, down to the polo field for the next act in their traditional Weltevreden Christmas festival.

The entire coloured staff was assembled there, with their children and aged parents and the estate pensioners too old to work, and all the others who Centaine supported. Every one of them was dressed in their Sunday best, a marvellous assortment of styles and cuts and colours, the little girls with ribbons in their hair and the small boys for once with shoes on their feet.

The estate band, fiddles and concertinas and banjoes, welcomed Centaine, and the singing, the very voice of Africa, was melodious and beautiful. She had a gift for each of them, which she handed over with an envelope containing their Christmas bonus. Some of the older women, emboldened by their long service and sense of occasion, embraced her, and so precarious was Centaine's mood that these spontaneous gestures of affection made her weep again, which set the other women off.

It was swiftly becoming an orgy of sentiment and Shasa hastily signalled the band to strike up something lively. They chose 'Alabama', the old Cape Malay song that commemorated the cruise of the confederate raider to Cape waters when she captured the *Sea Bride* in Table Bay on 5 August, 1863.

> There comes the *Alabama*
> *Daar kom die* Alabama –

Then Shasa supervised the drawing of the bung from the first keg of sweet estate wine, and almost immediately the tears dried and the mood became festive and gay.

Once the whole sheep on the spits were sizzling and dripping rich fat onto the coals, the second keg of wine had been broached, the dancing was losing all restraint and the younger couples were sneaking away into the vineyards, Centaine gathered the party from the big house and left them to it.

As they passed the Huguenot vineyard, they heard the giggling and scuffling amongst the vines behind the stone wall and Sir Garry remarked complacently: 'Shouldn't think Weltevreden is going to run short of labour in the foreseeable future. Sounds like a good crop being planted.'

'You are as shameless as they are,' Anna huffed, and then giggled herself just as breathlessly as the young girls in the vineyard as he squeezed her thick waist and whispered something in her ear.

That little intimacy lanced Centaine with a blade of loneliness, and she thought of Blaine and wanted to weep again. But Shasa seemed to sense her pain and took her hand and made her laugh with one of his silly jokes.

The family dinner was part of the tradition. Before they ate Shasa read aloud to them from the New Testament as he had every Christmas Day since his sixth birthday. Then he and Centaine distributed the pile of presents from under the tree, and the salon was filled with the rustle of paper and the ooh's and aah's of delight.

The dinner was roast turkey and a baron of beef followed by a rich black Christmas pudding. Shasa found the lucky gold sovereign in his portion, as he did every year without suspecting that it had been carefully salted there by Centaine during the serving; and when at the end they all tottered away, satiated and heavy-eyed, to their separate bedrooms, Centaine slipped out of the french windows of her study and ran all the way down through the plantation and burst into the cottage.

Blaine was waiting for her and she ran to him. 'We should be together at Christmas and every other day.'

He stopped her from going on by kissing her, and she reviled herself for her silliness. When she pulled back in his arms, she was smiling brightly. 'I couldn't wrap your Christmas present. The shape is all wrong and the ribbon wouldn't stay on. You'll have to take it *au naturel*.'

'Where is it?'

'Follow me, sir, and it shall be delivered unto you.'

'Now that,' he said a little later, 'is by far the nicest present that anybody ever gave me, and so very useful too!'

There were no newspapers on New Year's Day, but Centaine listened to the news every hour on the radio. There was no mention of the gold standard or any other political issue on these bulletins. Blaine was away, occupied all day with meetings and discussions concerning his candidature for the coming parliamentary by-election at the Gardens. Shasa had gone as house guest to one of the neighbouring estates. She was alone with her fears and doubts.

She read until after midnight and then lay in the darkness, sleeping only fitfully and plagued by nightmares, starting awake and then drifting back into uneasy sleep.

Long before dawn she gave up the attempt to find rest and dressed in jodhpurs and riding-boots and her sheepskin coat. She saddled her favourite stallion and rode down in the darkness five miles to the railway station at Claremont to meet the early train from Cape Town.

She was waiting on the platform when the bundles of newspapers were thrown out of the goods van onto the concrete quay, and the small coloured newsboys swarmed over them, chattering and laughing as they divided up the bundles for delivery. Centaine tossed one of them a silver shilling and he hooted with glee when she waved away the change and eagerly unfolded the newspaper.

The headlines took up fully half the front page, and they rocked her on her feet.

SOUTH AFRICA ABANDONS GOLD
STANDARD
HUGE BOOST FOR GOLD MINES

She scanned the columns below, barely able to take in any more, and then, still in a daze, rode back up the valley to Weltevreden. Only when she reached the Anreith gates did the full impact of it all dawn upon her. Weltevreden was still hers, it would always be hers, and she rose in the stirrups and shouted with joy, then urged her horse into a flying gallop, lifting him over the stone wall and racing down between the rows of vines.

She left him in his stall and ran all the way back to the château. She had to talk to someone – if only it could have been Blaine. But Sir Garry was in the dining-room; he was always first down for breakfast.

'Have you heard the news, my dear?' he cried excitedly the moment she entered. 'I heard it on the radio at six o'clock. We are off gold. Hertzog did it! By God, there will be a few fortunes made and lost this day! Anybody who is holding gold shares will double and treble their money. Oh, my dear, is something wrong?'

Centaine had collapsed into her chair at the head of the dining-room table.

'No, no.' She shook her head frantically. 'There is nothing wrong, not any more. Everything is all right – wonderfully, magnificently, stupendously all right.'

At lunchtime Blaine telephoned her at Weltevreden. He had never done so before. His voice sounded hollow and strange on the scratchy line. He did not announce himself but said simply: 'Five o'clock at the cottage.'

'Yes, I'll be there.' She wanted to say more but the line clicked dead.

She went down to the cottage an hour early with fresh flowers, clean crisply ironed linen for the bed and a bottle of Bollinger champagne, and she was waiting for him when he walked into the living-room.

'There are no words that can adequately express my gratitude,' she said.

'That is the way I want it, Centaine,' he told her seriously. 'No words! We will never talk about it again. I shall try to convince myself it never happened. Please promise me never to mention it, never again as long as we live and love each other.'

'I give you my solemn word,' she said, and then all her relief and joy came bubbling up and she kissed him, laughing. 'Won't you open the champagne?' And she raised the brimming glass when he handed it to her and gave him his own words back as a toast:

'For as long as we live and love each other, my darling.'

463

The Johannesburg Stock Exchange re-opened on January the second and in the first hour very little business could be conducted, for the floor was like a battlefield as the brokers literally tore at each other, screaming for attention. But by call-over the market had shaken itself out and settled at its new levels.

Swales of Rabkin and Swales was the first of her brokers to telephone Centaine. Like the market, his tone was buoyant and effervescent.

'My dear Mrs Courtney,' in the circumstances, Centaine was prepared to let that familiarity pass, 'my very dear Mrs Courtney, your timing has been almost miraculous. As you know, we were unfortunately unable to fill your entire purchase order. We were able to obtain only four hundred and forty thousand ERPMs at an average price of twenty-five shillings. The volume of your order pushed the price up two and six. However,' she could almost hear him puffing himself up to make his announcement, 'however, I am delighted to be able to tell you that this morning ERPMs are trading at fifty-five shillings and still rising. I am looking forward to sixty shillings by the end of the week—'

'Sell them,' Centaine said quietly and heard him choke at the end of the line.

'If I may be permitted to offer a word of advice—'

'Sell them,' she repeated. 'Sell all of them.' And she hung up, staring out of the window as she tried to calculate her profits, but the telephone rang again before she reached a total, and one after another her other brokers triumphantly reported on the contracts she had made. Then there was a call from Windhoek.

'Dr Twentyman-Jones, it's so good to hear your voice.' She had recognized him instantly.

'Well, Mrs Courtney, this is a pretty pickle,' Twentyman-Jones told her glumly. 'The H'ani Mine will be back in profit again now, even with the parsimonious quota De Beers is allowing us.'

'We've turned the corner,' Centaine enthused. 'We are out of the woods.'

'Many a slip 'twixt cup and lip.' Gloomily Twentyman-Jones capped cliché with cliché. 'Best not to count our chickens, Mrs Courtney.'

'Dr Twentyman-Jones, I love you.' Centaine laughed delightedly, and there was a shocked silence that echoed across a thousand miles of wire. 'I'll be there just as soon as I can get away from here. There is a lot for us to work on now.'

She hung up and went to look for Shasa. He was down at the stables chatting with his coloured grooms as they sat in the sun dubbining his polo harness and saddlery.

'*Chéri*, I am driving into Cape Town. Will you come with me?'

'What are you going all that way for, Mater?'

'It's a surprise.'

That was the one certain way to gain Shasa's full attention and he tossed the harness he was working on to Abel and sprang to his feet.

Her ebullient mood was infectious and they were laughing together as they walked into Porters Motors showroom on Strand Street. The sales manager came from his cubicle on the run.

'Mrs Courtney, we haven't seen you in far too long. May I wish you a happy and prosperous New Year.'

'It's off to a good start on both counts,' she smiled. 'Speaking of happiness, Mr Tims, how soon can you deliver my new Daimler?'

'It will be yellow, naturally?'

'With black piping, naturally!'

'And the usual fittings – the vanity, the cocktail cabinet?'

'All of them, Mr Tims.'

'I will cable our London office immediately. Shall we say four months, Mrs Courtney?'

'Let us rather say three months, Mr Tims.'

Shasa could barely contain himself until they were on the pavements in front of the showroom.

'Mater, have you gone bonkers? We are paupers!'

'Well, *chéri*, let's be paupers with a little class and style.'

'Where are we going now?'

'The post office.' At the telegraph counter Centaine drafted a cable to Sotheby's in Bond Street:

Sale no longer contemplated. Stop. Please
cancel all preparations.

Then they went to lunch at the Mount Nelson Hotel.

B laine had promised to meet her as early as he was able to escape from the meeting of the proposed new coalition cabinet. He was as good as his word, waiting for her in the pine forest, and when she saw his face her happiness shrivelled.

'What is it, Blaine?'

'Let's walk, Centaine. I've been indoors all day.'

They climbed the Karbonkelberg slopes behind the estate. At the summit they sat on a fallen log to watch the sunset and it was magnificent.

'This was the fairest Cape which we discovered in all our circumnavigation of the earth—' she misquoted from Vasco da Gama's log, but Blaine did not correct her as she had hoped he might.

'Tell me, Blaine.' She took his arm and insisted, and he turned his face to her.

'Isabella,' he said sombrely.

466

'You have heard from her?' Her spirits sank deeper at the name.

'The doctors can do nothing for her. She will be returning on the next mail ship from Southampton.'

In the silence the sun sank into the silver sea, taking the light from the world, and Centaine's soul was as dark.

'How ironic it is,' she whispered. 'Because of you I can have anything in this world except that which I most desire – you, my love.'

The women pounded the fresh millet grain in the wooden mortars into a coarse fluffy white meal and filled one of the leather sacks.

Carrying the sack, Swart Hendrick, followed by Moses his brother, left the kraal after the rise of the new moon and crept silently up the ridge in the night. While Hendrick stood guard, Moses climbed to the old eagle owl nest in the leadwood tree and brought down the cartridge paper packets.

They moved along the ridge until they were beyond all possible chance of observation from the village, and even then they very carefully screened the small fire that they built amongst the ironstone boulders. Hendrick broke open the packets and poured the gleaming stones into a small calabash gourd while Moses prepared the millet meal in another gourd, mixing it with water until it was a soft porridge.

Meticulously Hendrick burned the cartridge paper wrappings in the fire and stirred the ashes to powder with a stick. When it was done he nodded at his younger brother and Moses poured the dough over the coals. As it began to bubble Hendrick buried the diamonds in the unleavened dough.

Moses muttered ruefully as the millet cakes bubbled and

hardened. It was almost an incantation. 'These are death stones. We will have no joy of them. The white men love them too dearly: they are the stones of death and madness.'

Hendrick ignored him and shaped the baking loaves, squinting his eyes against the smoke and smiling secretly to himself. When each round loaf was crisped brown on the underside he flipped it over and let it cook through until it was brick hard; then he lifted it off the fire and set it out to cool. Finally he repacked the crude thick loaves into the leather sack and they returned quietly to the sleeping village.

In the morning they left early and the women went with them the first mile of the journey, ululating mournfully and singing the song of farewell. When they fell behind neither of the men looked back. They trudged on towards the low brown horizon, carrying their bundles balanced on their heads. They did not think about it, but this little scene was acted out every single day in a thousand villages across the southern sub-continent.

Days later the two men, still on foot, reached the recruitment station. It was a single-roomed general-dealer's store, standing alone at a remote crossroad on the edge of the desert. The white trader augmented his precarious business by buying cattle hides from the surrounding nomadic tribes and by recruiting for 'Wenela'.

Wenela was the acronym for the Witwatersrand Native Labour Association, a ubiquitous sprawling enterprise which extended its tentacles into the vastness of the African wilderness. From the peaks of the Dragon Mountains in Basutoland to the swamps of the Zambezi and Chobe, from the thirstlands of the Kalahari to the rain forest of the high plateau of Nyasaland, it gathered up the trickle of black men and channelled them first into a stream and finally into a mighty river that ran endlessly to the fabulous goldfields of the Ridge of White Waters, the Witwatersrand of Transvaal.

The trader looked over these two new recruits in a perfunctory manner as they stood dumbly before him. Their faces were deliberately expressionless, their eyes blank, the only perfect defence of the black African in the presence of the white man.

'Name?' the trader demanded.

'Henry Tabaka.' Hendrick had chosen his new name to cover his relationship to Moses and to throw off any chance connection with Lothar De La Rey and the robbery.

'Name?' The trader looked at Moses.

'Moses Gama.' He pronounced it with a guttural 'G'.

'Have you worked on the mines before? Do you speak English?'

'Yes, *Basie*.' They were obsequious, and the trader grinned.

'Good! Very good! You will be rich men when you come home from *Goldi*. Plenty of wives. Plenty of jig-jig, hey?' He grinned lasciviously as he issued them each with a green Wenela card and a bus ticket. 'The bus will come soon. Wait outside,' he ordered, and promptly lost all interest in them. He had earned his guinea-a-head recruitment fee, good money easily made, and his obligation to the recruits was at an end.

They waited under the scraggy thorn tree at the side of the iron-roofed trading store for forty-eight hours before the railway bus came rattling and banging and blowing blue smoke across the dreary wastes.

It stopped briefly and they slung their meagre luggage up onto the roofrack that was already piled with calabashes and boxes and bundles, with trussed goats and cages of woven bark stuffed with live fowls. Then they climbed into the overloaded coach and squeezed onto one of the hard wooden benches. The bus bellowed and blustered on over the plains and the rows of black passengers, wedged shoulder to shoulder, jolted and swayed in unison as it pitched and rolled over the rutted tracks.

Two days later the bus stopped outside the barbed-wire gates of the Wenela staging post on the outskirts of Windhoek, and most of the passengers, all young men, descended and stood looking about them aimlessly until a huge black overseer with brass plaques of authority on his arm and a long sjambok in his hand chivied them into line and led them through the gates.

The white station manager sat on the stoep of his office building, his boots propped on the half wall of the stoep and a black bottle of German lager at his elbow, fanning himself with his hat. One at a time, the black boss-boy pushed the new recruits in front of him for appraisal. He rejected only one, a skinny little runt of a man who barely had the strength to shuffle up to the verandah.

'That bastard is riddled with TB.' The manager took a gulp of his lager. 'Get rid of him. Send him back where he came from.'

When Hendrick stepped forward he straightened up in his thonged chair and set down the lager glass.

'What is your name, boy?' he asked.

'Tabaka.'

'Ha, you speak English.' The manager's eyes narrowed. He could pick out the troublemakers; that was his job. He could tell by their eyes, the gleam of intelligence and aggression in them. He could tell by the way they walked and carried their shoulders; this big strutting, sullen black was big trouble.

'You in trouble with the police, boy?' he asked again. 'You steal other man's cattle? You kill your brother perhaps – or jig-jig his wife, hey?'

Hendrick stared at him flatly.

'Answer me, boy.'

'No.'

'You call me *Baas* when you speak to me, do you understand?'

'Yes, *Baas*,' Hendrick said carefully, and the manager

opened the police file that lay on the table beside him and thumbed through it slowly, suddenly looking up to catch any sign of guilt or apprehension on Hendrick's face. But he was wearing the African mask again, dumb, and resigned and inscrutable.

'Christ, they stink.' He threw the file back onto the table again. 'Take them away,' he told the black boss-boy, and he picked up his beer bottle and glass and went back into his office.

'You know better than that, my brother,' Moses whispered to him as they were marched away towards the line of thatched huts. 'When you meet a hungry white hyena, you do not put your hand in his mouth,' and Hendrick did not reply.

They were fortunate; the draft was almost full, three hundred black men already gathered in and waiting in the line of huts behind the barbed-wire fence. Some of them had been there ten days and it was time for the next stage of their journey, thus Hendrick and Moses were not forced to endure another interminable wait. That night three railway coaches were shunted onto the spur of line that ran beside the camp and the boss-boys roused them before dawn.

'Gather your belongings. *Shayile!* The hour has struck. The steamer waits to take you to *Goldi*, to the place of gold.'

They formed up in their ranks again and answered to the roll-call. Then they were marched to the waiting coaches.

Here there was another white man in charge. He was tall and sunbrowned, his khaki shirtsleeves rolled up high on his sinewy biceps and wisps of blond hair hanging from under the shapeless black hat that was pulled low down on his forehead. His features were flat and Slavic, his teeth crooked and stained with tobacco smoke and his eyes were light misty blue; he smiled perpetually in a bland idiotic fashion and sucked at a cavity in one of his back teeth. He carried a sjambok on a thong from his wrist, and now and then, for no apparent reason, he flicked the tapered end of the hippohide whip against the bare legs of one of the men filing past him; it was a casual act born of disinterest and disdain rather than calculated cruelty, and though each stroke was feathery light, it stung like a hornet and the victim gasped and skipped and shot up the ladder into the coach with alacrity.

Hendrick drew level with him and the foreman's lips drew back from his bad teeth as he smiled even more widely. The camp manager had pointed the big Ovambo out to him.

'A bad one,' he had warned him. 'Watch him. Don't let him get out of hand.' And now he used his wrist in the stroke that he aimed at the tender skin at the back of Hendrick's knee.

'*Che-cha!*' the overseer ordered. 'Hurry up!' And the lash popped as it wrapped around Hendrick's leg. It did not split the skin, the overseer was an expert, but it left a purple black welt on the dark velvety skin.

Hendrick stopped dead, the other leg lifted to the first rung of the boarding ladder, gripping the rail with his free hand, with the other hand balancing his bundle on his shoulder, and he turned his head slowly until he was staring into the overseer's pale blue eyes.

'Yes!' The overseer encouraged him softly, and for the first time there was a sparkle of interest in his eyes. He altered his stance subtly, coming onto the balls of his feet.

'Yes!' he repeated. He wanted to take this big black bastard, here in front of all the others. They were going to be five days in these coaches, five hot thirsty days during which tempers and nerves would be rubbed raw. He always liked to do it right at the beginning of the journey. It only needed one, and it would save a lot of trouble later if he made an example right here on the siding. That way all of them would know what to expect if they started anything, and in his experience they never did start anything after that.

'Come on, kaffir.' He dropped his voice even lower, making the insult more personal and intense. He enjoyed this part of his work, and he was very good at it. This cocky bastard would not be fit to travel when he had finished with him. He wouldn't be much use to anybody with four or five ribs stoved in, and perhaps a broken jaw.

Hendrick was too quick for him. He went up the ladder into the coach in a single bound, leaving the overseer on the siding, braced and poised for his attack with the sjambok held over-hand, ready to drive the point of the butt into Hendrick's throat as he charged.

Hendrick's move took him completely off balance so that when he aimed a hard cut of the lash at Hendrick's legs as he went up the ladder, he was too late by a full half second and the stroke hissed and died in air.

Following behind his brother, Moses saw the murderous expression on the white overseer's face as he passed. 'It is not yet ended,' he warned Hendrick as they placed their bundles on the overhead racks and settled on the hard wooden bench that ran the length of the coach. 'He will come after you again.'

In the middle of the morning the three coaches were pulled off the spur and coupled to the rear of a long train of goods carriages, and after another few hours of shunting and jolting and false starts, they rumbled slowly up the hills and then ran southwards.

Late in the afternoon the train stopped for half an hour at a small siding and a food barrow was loaded into the leading coach. Under the pale eyes of the white overseer the two black boss-boys wheeled the barrow down the crowded coaches and each of the recruits was handed a small tin dish of white maize cake over which a dollop of bean stew had been spooned.

When they reached Swart Hendrick's seat, the white overseer shouldered the boss-boy aside and took the dish from his hands to serve Hendrick's portion himself.

'We must look after this kaffir,' he said loudly. 'We want him to be strong for his work at *Goldi*.' And he spooned an extra portion of bean stew into the dish and offered it to Hendrick.

'Here, kaffir.' But as Hendrick reached for the dish, he deliberately let it drop onto the floor. The hot stew splashed over Hendrick's feet and the overseer stepped into the mess of maize porridge and ground it under his boot. Then he stood back with one hand on the billy club in his belt and grinned.

'Hey, you clumsy black bugger, you only get one ration. If you want to eat it off the floor, that's up to you.'

He waited expectantly for Hendrick to react, and then grimaced with disappointment when Hendrick dropped his eyes, leaned forward and began to scrape the mashed cake into the dish with his fingers, then scooped a ball of it into his mouth and munched on it stolidly.

'You bloody niggers will eat anything, even your own dung,' he snarled and went on down the coach.

The windows of the coaches were barred, and the doors at both ends were locked and bolted from the outside. The overseer carried the ring of keys on his belt, carefully securing all doors behind him as he passed. From experience he knew that many of the recruits would begin to have misgivings as soon as the journey began, and driven by homesickness and increasing fear of the unknown, by the disturbing unfamiliarity of all about them, would begin to desert, some of them even leaping from the speeding coach. The overseer made his rounds every few hours, meticulously counting heads, even in the middle of the night, and he stood over Hendrick deliberately shining the beam of his lantern into his face, waking him every time he passed down the coach.

The overseer never tired of his efforts to provoke Hendrick. It had become a challenge, a contest between them. He knew it was there; he had seen it in Hendrick's eyes, just a flash of the violence and menace and power, and he was determined to bring it out, flush it into the open where he could crush it and destroy it.

'Patience, my brother,' Moses whispered to Hendrick. 'Hold your anger. Cherish it with care. Let it grow until it is full term, until you can put it to work for you.'

Hendrick was coming to rely more on his brother's advice and counsel with each day that passed. Moses was intelligent and persuasive, his tongue quick to choose the right word, and that special presence which he possessed made other men listen when he spoke.

Hendrick saw these special gifts of his demonstrated clearly in the days that followed. At first he spoke only to the men that sat near him in the hot crowded coach. He told them what it would be like at the place where they were going, and how the white men would treat them, what would be expected of them and what the consequences would be if they disappointed their new employers.

The black faces around him were intent as they listened, and soon those further up the benches were craning to catch his words and calling softly. 'Speak, louder, Gama. Speak, that all of us may hear your words.'

Moses Gama raised his voice, a clear compelling baritone, and they listened with respect. 'There will be many black men at *Goldi*. More than you ever believed possible, Zulus and Xhosas and N'debeles and Swazis and Nyasas, fifty different tribes speaking so many languages that you have never heard before. Tribes as different from you as you are different from the white man. Some of them will be traditional blood enemies of our tribe, waiting and watching like hyenas for a chance to turn upon you and savage you. There will be times when you are deep in the earth, down there where it is always night, that you will be at the mercy of such men. To protect yourselves you must surround yourselves with men you can trust; you must place yourself under the protection of a strong leader; and in return for this protection you must give this chieftain your obedience and loyalty.' And very soon they came to recognize that Moses Gama was this strong leader. Within days he was the undisputed chieftain of all the men in coach three, and while he was talking to them and answering their queries, stilling their fears and misgivings, Moses was in his turn assessing their individual worth, watching and weighing each of them, selecting, evaluating and discarding. He began to rearrange the seating in the coach, ordering those whom he had chosen to move closer to his own seat in the centre, gathering around him the pick of the recruits. And immediately the men he had singled out gained prestige; they formed an élite praetorian guard around their new emperor.

Hendrick watched him doing it, manipulating the men around him, subjecting them to the force of his will and personality, and he was filled with admiration and pride for his younger brother, giving up his own last reservations and willingly according to him his full loyalty and love and obedience.

By association with Moses, Hendrick himself was accorded the respect and veneration of the other men in the coach. He was Moses' captain and henchman and they recognized him as such, and quite slowly it dawned upon Hendrick that in a few short days Moses Gama had forged himself an *impi*, a band of warriors on whom he could rely implicitly, and that he had done it with almost no apparent effort.

Sitting in the crowded coach that was already stinking like an animal cage with the rancid sweat of a hundred hot bodies and with the stench from the latrine cubicle, and mesmerized by the Messianic eyes and words of his own brother, Hendrick thought back to the other great black rulers who had emerged from the mists of African history, to lead first a tiny band, then a tribe and finally a vast horde of warriors across the continent, ravaging and plundering and laying waste.

He thought of Mantatisi and Chaka and Mzilikazi, of Shangaan and Angoni, and with a flash of clairvoyance he saw them at their beginnings, sitting like this at some remote camp-fire in the wilderness, surrounded by a small group of men, weaving the spell over them, capturing their imagination and spirit with a silken noose of words and ideas, inflaming them with dreams.

'I stand at the beginning of an enterprise which I do not yet understand,' he thought. 'All I have done up until this time was only my initiation, all the fighting and killing and striving was but a training. Now I am ready for the endeavour, whatever it may be, and Moses Gama will lead me to it. I do not need to know what it is. It is sufficient only that I follow where it leads.'

And he was listening avidly as Moses spoke names that he had never heard and expounded ideas that were new and strangely exciting.

'Lenin,' said Moses, 'not a man, but a god come down to earth.' And they thrilled to the tale of a land to the north where the tribes had united under this man-god Lenin, had smitten down a king and in doing so had become part of the godhead themselves.

They were enchanted and aroused as he told them of a war such as the earth had never seen before, and their atavistic battlelust scalded their veins and pumped up their hearts, hard and hot as the head of the fighting axe when it comes red and glowing from the ironsmith's forge. The 'revolution' Moses called this war, and as he explained it to them, they saw that they could be part of this glorious battle, they too could be slayers of kings and become part of the godhead.

The door at the head of the coach crashed back on its

slide and the white overseer stepped through and stood with his hands on his hips, grinning mirthlessly at them, and they lowered their heads and stared at the floor, hooding and screening their eyes. But those sitting close to Moses, the chosen ones, the élite, they began to understand then where the battle would be fought and who were the kings that would be slain.

The white overseer sensed the charged atmosphere in the coach. It was thick as the odour of unwashed black bodies and the stink of the latrine in the corner of the coach; it was as electric as the air at noon in the suicide days of November just before the great rains break, and he searched quickly for Hendrick sitting in the centre of the coach.

'One rotten potato,' he thought bitterly, 'and the whole sackful is spoiled.' He touched the billy club in his belt. He had found out the difficult way that the lash of the sjambok was too long to wield effectively in the confines of the coaches. The billy was a stopper, fourteen inches of hard wood, the end drilled and filled with lead shot. He could break bone with it, crush in a skull to kill a man instantly if he needed to, or with a delicate alteration of the weight of the blow merely stun him. He was an artist with the billy club, as he was with the sjambok, but each had its place and time. It was the billy's time now, and he moved slowly down the coach, pretending to ignore Hendrick, examining the faces of each of the other men as he passed, seeing the new rebelliousness in their sullen faces and becoming more angry with the man who had made his task more difficult.

'I should have gone after him at the beginning,' he told himself bitterly. 'I've almost left it too late. Me, who loves the quiet life and the easy way. Well, we'll have to make the best of it now.'

He glanced casually at Hendrick as he passed, and then from the corner of his eye saw the big Ovambo relax slightly as he went on down the aisle between the seats.

'You are expecting it, my boy. You know it has to happen, and I'm not going to disappoint you.'

At the far door of the coach he paused, as if he had an afterthought, and he came back down the aisle slowly, grinning to himself. Now he stopped in front of Hendrick again, and sucked noisily at the cavity in his tooth.

'Look at me, kaffir,' he invited pleasantly and Hendrick lifted his chin and stared at him.

'Which is your *m'pahle?*' he asked. 'Which is your luggage?' and Hendrick was taken off-guard. He was acutely conscious of the treasure of diamonds in the rack above his head and now he glanced up at the leather sack instinctively.

'Good.' The white overseer lifted the sack off the rack and dropped it onto the floor in front of Hendrick.

'Open it,' he ordered, still grinning, one hand on his hip the other on the handle of the billy.

'Come on.' The grin became cold and wolfish as Hendrick sat without moving. 'Open it, kaffir. Let's see what you are hiding.'

It had never failed him yet. Even the most docile of men would react to protect their belongings, no matter how worthless and insignificant.

Slowly Hendrick leaned forward and untied the neck of the leather sack. Then he straightened again and sat passively.

The white overseer stooped, seized the bottom of the sack and straightened up again, never taking his eyes off Hendrick's face. He shook the sack vigorously, spilling the contents onto the floor.

The blanket roll fell out first, and using the toe of his boot the overseer spread it open. There was a sheepskin gilet and other spare clothing in the roll, and a nine-inch knife in a leather sheath.

'Dangerous weapon,' said the overseer. 'You know that no dangerous weapons are allowed in the coaches.' He picked up the knife, pressed the blade into the niche of the window and snapped it off; then he tossed the two separate pieces out between the bars of the window behind Hendrick's head.

Hendrick did not move, although the overseer waited for almost a minute, staring at him provocatively. The only sound was the clackety-clack of the bogey over the cross ties of the steel lines and the faint huffing of the locomotive at the head of the train. None of the other black passengers was watching the small drama develop; they were all staring straight ahead of them, faces closed, eyes unseeing.

'What is this rubbish?' the overseer asked and touched one of the hard flat millet cakes with his toe, and though Hendrick did not move a muscle, the white man saw the first spark in those black smoky eyes.

'Yes,' he thought gleefully. 'That's it. Now he will move.' And he picked up a loaf and sniffed it thoughtfully.

'Kaffir bread,' he murmured. 'Not allowed. Company rules – no food allowed on the train.' And he turned the flat loaf on edge so that it would pass between the bars and he tossed it through the open window. The loaf bounced on the embankment below the racketing steel wheels and then shattered into fragments, and the overseer chuckled and stooped for the next loaf.

It snapped in Hendrick's head. He had held it in check too long and the loss of the diamonds drove him berserk. He went for the white man, launching himself out of the seat, but the overseer was ready for him. He straightened his right arm and drove the point of the billy club into Hendrick's throat. Then, as Hendrick fell back choking and clutching at his throat, he whipped the club into the front of his skull, judging it finely, not a killing blow, and Hendrick's hand dropped from his damaged throat as he toppled forward. However, the overseer would not let him fall, and with his left hand shoved him back against the seat, holding him upright while he worked with the club.

It rang like an axe on wood as it bounced off the bone of Hendrick's skull, and it opened the thin skin of his scalp and the blood sprang up in little ruby-bright fountains. The overseer hit him three times, measured calculated blows, and then he thrust the point of the club into Hendrick's slack gaping mouth, snapping off both his incisor teeth level with the gums.

'Always mark them.' It was one of his maxims. 'Mark them so they don't forget.'

Only then did he release the unconscious man and let him topple, head first, into the centre of the aisle.

Instantly he whipped around and poised on his toes like a puffadder cocking itself into the threatening 'S' of the strike. With the billy club ready in his right hand he stared down the shocked eyes of the black men around him. Quickly they dropped their gaze from his and the only movement was the jerking of their bodies in time to the swaying clatter of the coach beneath them.

Hendrick's blood was puddling under his head, and then running in little dark red snakes across the floor of the aisle. The overseer smiled again, looking down with an almost paternal expression at the recumbent figure. It had been a beautiful performance, quick and complete, exactly as he had planned it, and he had enjoyed it. The man at his feet was his own creation and he was proud of it.

He picked up the other millet loaves out of the blood puddle and one at a time tossed them out between the bars of the window. Finally he squatted over the man at his feet and on the back of his shirt carefully wiped the last traces of blood from his billy. Then he stood up, replaced the club in his belt and walked slowly down the aisle.

It was all right now. The mood had changed, the atmosphere was defused. There would be no more trouble. He had done his job, and done it well.

He went out onto the balcony of the coach, and smiling thinly, locked the sliding door behind him again.

The moment the door closed the men in the carriage came back to life. Moses gave his orders crisply and two of them lifted Hendrick back into his seat; another went to the water tank beside the latrine door, while Moses opened his own pack and brought out a stoppered buckhorn.

While they steadied Hendrick's lolling head, Moses poured a brown powder from the buckhorn into the wounds in his scalp. It was a mixture of ash and herbs, powdered finely, and he rubbed it into the open flesh with his finger. The bleeding stopped, and with a wet cloth he cleaned his brother's broken mouth. Then he cradled his unconscious head in his arms, and waited.

Moses had watched the conflict between his brother and the white man with almost clinical interest, deliberately restraining and directing Hendrick's reaction until the drama had reached this explosive climax. His attachment to his brother was still tenuous. Their father had been a prosperous and lusty man and had brought all of his fifteen wives regularly to the child-bed. Moses had over thirty brothers and sisters. Towards very few of them he felt any special affection beyond vague tribal and family duty. Hendrick was many years his senior and had left the kraal when Moses was still a child. Since then the tales of his exploits had filtered back to him, and Hendrick's reputation had grown on these accounts of wild and desperate deeds. But tales are only tales until they are proven and reputations can be built on words and not deeds.

The testing time was at hand. Moses would consider the results of the test and upon them would depend their future relationship. He needed a hard man as his lieutenant, one of the steely men. Lenin had chosen Joseph Stalin. He would choose a man of steel also, a man like an axe, and with him as a weapon he would hack and shape his own plans out of the hard wood of the future. If Hendrick failed the test Moses would toss him aside with as little compassion as he would an axe whose blade had shattered at the first stroke against the trunk of a tree.

Hendrick opened his eyes and looked at his brother with dilated pupils; he moaned and touched the open wounds on his scalp. He winced at the pain and his pupils shrank and focused, and the rage flamed in their depths as he struggled upright.

'The diamonds?' His voice was low and sibilant as the hiss of one of those deadly little horned adders of the desert.

'Gone,' Moses told him quietly.

'We must go back – find them.' But Moses shook his head.

'They are scattered like the seeds of the grass; there is no way to mark their fall. No, my brother, we are prisoners in this coach. We cannot go back. The diamonds are lost for ever.'

Hendrick sat quietly, with his tongue exploring his shattered mouth, running it over the jagged stumps of his front teeth, considering his brother's cold logic. Moses waited quietly. This time he would give no orders, point no direction, no matter how subtle. Hendrick must come to it of his own accord.

'You are right, my brother,' Hendrick said at last. 'The diamonds are gone. But I am going to kill the man that did this to us.'

Moses showed no emotion. He offered no encouragement. He merely waited.

'I will do it with cunning. I will find a way to kill him, and no man will ever know, except him and us.' Still Moses waited. So far Hendrick was taking the path that he had laid out for him. However, there was still something else he must do. He waited for it, and it came as he had hoped it would.

'Do you agree that I should kill this white dog, my

483

brother?' He had asked for sanction from Moses Gama. He had acknowledged his liege lord, placed himself in his brother's hands, and Moses smiled and touched his brother's arm as though he were placing a mark, a brand of approval, upon him.

'Do it, my brother,' he ordered. If he failed, the white men would hang him on a rope; if he succeeded he would have proved himself an axe, a steely man.

Hendrick brooded darkly in his seat, not speaking for another hour. Occasionally massaging his temples when the throbbing pain of the blows threatened to burst his skull open. Then he rose and moved slowly down the coach examining each of the barred windows, shaking his head and muttering at the pain. He returned to his seat and sat there for a while, and then rose once again and shuffled down the aisle to the latrine cubicle.

He locked himself into the cubicle. There was an open hole in the deck and through it he could see the rushing blur of the stone embankment below the coach. Many of the men using the latrine had missed the hole, and the floor slopped with dark yellow urine and splattered faeces.

Hendrick turned his attention to the single unglazed window. The opening was covered with steel mesh in a wire frame which was screwed into a wooden frame at each corner and at the centre of each side.

He returned to his seat in the carriage and whispered to Moses, 'The white baboon took my knife. I need another.'

Moses asked no questions. It was part of the test. Hendrick must do it alone and, if he failed, accept the full consequences without expecting Moses to share them or attempt to aid him. He spoke quietly to the men around him, and within a few minutes a clasp knife was passed down the bench and slipped into Hendrick's hand.

He returned to the latrine and worked on the retaining screws of the wire frame, careful not to scratch the paintwork around them or leave any sign that they had been tampered with. He removed all eight screws, eased the frame from its seating and set it aside.

He waited until the tracks made a righthand bend, judging by the centrifugal force against his body as the coach turned under him, and then he glanced out of the open window. The train was turning away from him, the leading coaches and goods vans out of sight around the bend ahead, and he leaned out of the window and looked up.

There was a coaming along the edge of the roof of the coach. He reached up and ran his fingers over the ridge and found a handhold. He raised himself, putting his full weight upon it, hanging on his arms, only his feet still inside the latrine window, and the rest of his body suspended outside. He lifted his eyes to the level of the roof and memorized the slope and layout of the top of the coach, then he lowered himself again and ducked back into the latrine. He replaced the mesh over the window but turned the screws only finger tight, then went back to his seat in the coach.

In the early evening the white overseer and his two boss-boys came through the coach with the food barrow. When he reached Hendrick he smiled at him without rancour.

'You are beautiful now, kaffir. The black maids will love to kiss that mouth.' He turned and addressed the silent ranks of black men. 'If any of you want to be beautiful also, just let me know. I will do it for free.'

Just before dark the boss-boys came back to collect the empty dishes.

'Tomorrow night you will be at *Goldi*,' one of them told Hendrick. 'There is a white doctor there who will treat your wounds.' There was a hint of sympathy in his impassive black face. 'It was not wise of you to anger *Tshayela*, the striker. You have learned a hard lesson, friend. Remember it well, all of you.' He locked the door as he left the coach.

Hendrick gazed out of the window at the sunset. In four

485

days of travel the landscape had changed entirely as they had climbed up onto the plateau of the highveld. The grasslands were pale brown, seared by the black frosts of winter, the red earth gouged open with *dongas* of erosion and divided into geometrical camps with barbed-wire. The isolated homesteads seemed forlorn upon the open veld with the steel-framed windmills standing like gaunt sentinels over them, and the lean cattle were long horned and parti-coloured, red and black and white.

Hendrick, who had lived his life in the unpeopled wilderness, found the fences cramping and restrictive. In this place you could never be out of sight of other men or their works, and the villages they passed were as sprawling and populous as Windhoek, the biggest town he had ever conceived of.

'Wait until you see *Goldi*,' Moses told him, as the darkness fell outside and the men around them settled down for the night, wrapping their blankets over their heads for the chill of the highveld blew in through the open windows.

Hendrick waited until the white overseer made his first round of the coaches, and when he shone the beam of his lantern into Hendrick's face made no attempt to feign sleep but blinked up at him blindly. The overseer passed on, locking the door as he left the coach.

Hendrick rose quietly in the seat. Opposite him Moses stirred in the darkness but did not speak, and Hendrick went down the aisle and locked himself in the latrine. Quickly he loosened the screws and worked the frame off its seating. He set it against the bulkhead and leaned out of the window. The cold night air buffeted his head, and he slitted his eyes against the hot smuts that blew back from the coal-burning locomotive and stung his cheeks and forehead as he reached up and found his handholds on the ridge of the coaming.

He drew himself upwards smoothly, and then with a

kick and a heave, flung the top half of his body over the edge of the roof and shot out one arm. He found a grip on the ventilator in the middle of the curved roof and pulled himself the rest of the way on his belly.

He lay for a while panting and with his eyes tightly closed until he got control of the pounding ache in his head. Then he raised himself to his knees and began crawling forward towards the leading edge of the roof.

The night sky was clear; the land was silver with starlight and blue with shadow, and the wind roared about his head. He rose to his feet and balanced against the lurch and sway of the coach. With his feet wide apart and his knees bent he moved forward. A premonition of danger made him look up and he saw the dark shape rush at him out of the darkness and he threw himself flat just as the steel arm of one of the railway water towers flashed over his head. A second later it would have decapitated him, and he shivered with the cold and the shock of near death. After a minute he gathered himself and crawled forward again, not raising his head more than a few inches until he reached the front edge of the roof.

He lay spreadeagled on his belly and cautiously peered over the edge. The balconies of the joining coaches were below him, the gap between the roof about the span of one of his arms. Directly under him the footplates articulated against each other as the train clattered through the curves of the line. Anybody moving from one coach to the next must pass below where Hendrick lay and he grunted with satisfaction and looked behind him.

One of the ventilator pots was just level with his feet as he lay outstretched. He crawled back, drawing the heavy leather belt from the top of his breeches, and buckled it around the ventilator, forming a loop into which he thrust one of his feet as far as the ankle.

Once again he stretched out on the roof, one foot securely anchored by the loop, and he reached down into the space between the coaches. He could just touch the banisters of the guard fence around the balcony. Electric bulbs in wire cages were fixed to the overhang of the balconies so the area below him was well lit.

He drew back and lay flat on the roof, only the top of his head and his eyes showing from below. But he knew that the lights would dazzle anybody who looked upwards into the gap between the roofs and he settled down to wait like a leopard in the tree over the water hole.

An hour passed and then another, but he judged the passage of time only by the slow rotation of the stars across the night sky. He was stiff and freezing cold as the wind thrashed his unprotected body, but he bore it stoically, never allowing himself to doze or lose concentration. Waiting was always a major part of the hunt, of the game of death, and he had played this game a hundred times before.

Suddenly, even over the rush of the train's passage and the rhythm of the cross ties, he heard the click of steel on steel and the rattle of keys in the lock of the door below him, and he gathered himself.

The man would step over the footplates as quickly as he could, not wanting to be in that vulnerable and exposed position for a moment longer than was necessary to make the crossing, and Hendrick would have to be quicker still.

He heard the sliding door slam back against the jamb and the lock turn again, then an instant later the crown of the white overseer's hat appeared below him.

Instantly Hendrick shot his body forward and dropped as far as his waist into the gap between the coaches. Only the leather belt around his ankle anchored him. Lothar had taught him the double lock, and he whipped one arm around the white man's neck, and braced his other hand in the crook of his own elbow, catching the man's head in the vice of his arms, and jerked him off his feet.

488

The white man made a strangled cawing sound and droplets of spittle flew from his lips, sparkling in the electric light as Hendrick drew him upwards as though he were hoisted on the gallows tree.

The white man's hat fell from his head and flitted away into the night like a black bat, and he was kicking and twisting his body violently, clawing at the thick muscled arms that were locked around his neck, his long blond hair fluttering and tumbling in the night wind. Hendrick lifted him until their eyes were inches apart, and he smiled into his face, exposing the mangled black pit of his own mouth, his shattered front teeth still stained with clotted blood, and in the reflection of the balcony lights the white man recognized him. Hendrick saw the recognition flare in his pale dilated eyes.

'Yes, my friend,' he whispered. 'It is me, the kaffir.' He drew the man up another inch and wedged the back of his neck against the edge of the roof. Then very deliberately he put pressure on his spine at the base of his skull. The white man writhed and struggled like a fish on the barbs of the harpoon, but Hendrick held him easily, staring deep into his eyes, and bent his neck backwards, lifting with his forearm under the chin.

Hendrick felt the spine loading and locking at the pressure. It could give no more, and for a second longer he held him at the breaking point. Then with a jerk he pushed the man's chin up another inch and the spine snapped like a dry branch. The white man danced in the air, twitching and shuddering, and Hendrick watched the pale blue eyes glaze over, becoming opaque and lifeless, and over the rush of the wind he heard the soft spluttering release as his sphincter muscle relaxed and his bowels involuntarily voided.

Hendrick swung his dangling corpse like a pendulum and as it cleared the balcony rail he let it drop into the gap between the coaches, directly into the track of the racing wheels. It was sucked away by the spinning steel like a scrap of meat into the blades of a mincing machine.

He lay for a moment recovering his breath. He knew that the overseer's mutilated corpse would be smeared over half a mile of the railway tracks.

He untied his belt from the ventilator and buckled it around his waist, then he crawled back along the roof of the coach until he was directly above the latrine window. He lowered his feet over the sill and with a twist dropped into the cubicle. He replaced the mesh frame over the window and tightened the screws. He went back down the coach to his seat, and Moses Gama was watching him as he wrapped the blanket around his shoulders. He nodded at his brother and pulled the corner of the blanket over his head. Within minutes he was asleep.

He was awakened by the shouts of the boss-boys and the jolting of the coach as it was shunted off the main line. He saw the name of the small village where they had stopped painted on a white board on the platform: 'Vryburg', but it meant nothing to him.

Soon the platform and the coaches were invaded by blue uniformed railway police, and all the recruits were ordered out onto the platform. They lined up, shivering and sleepy under the floodlights, answered to the roll-call. Everyone was present.

Hendrick nudged his brother and with his chin pointed at the wheels and bogey below their coach. The hubs and axles were splattered with blood and tiny slivers and particles of raw red flesh and tissue.

All the following day the coaches stood in the siding while the police individually subjected each of the recruits to a hectoring interrogation in the station master's office. By mid-afternoon it was obvious that they were coming to accept that the overseer's death was accidental and were losing interest in the investigation. The evidence of the locked doors and barred windows was convincing and the testimony of the boss-boys and every one of the recruits was unanimous and unshakable.

In the late afternoon they were loaded back into the coaches and they rumbled on into the night, towards the fabulous Ridge of White Waters.

Hendrick woke to the excited chatter of the men around him, and when he shouldered his way to the crowded window the first thing he saw was a high mountain, so big that it blocked the sky to the north, a strange and wonderful mountain, glowing with a pearly yellow light in the early sun, a mountain with a perfectly flat top and symmetrical sloping sides.

'What kind of mountain is this?' Hendrick marvelled.

'A mountain taken from the belly of the earth,' Moses told him. 'That is a mine dump, my brother, a mountain built by men from the rocks they dig up from below.'

Wherever Hendrick looked there were these flat-topped shining dumps scattered across the undulating grassland or standing along the skyline and near each of them stood tall giraffes of steel, long-necked and skeletal with giant wheels for heads, that spun endlessly against the pale highveld sky.

'Headgears,' Moses told him. 'Below each of those is a hole that reaches down into the guts of the world, into the rock bowels that hold the yellow *Goldi* for which the white men sweat and lie and cheat – and often kill.'

As the train ran on they saw wonder followed by wonder, taller buildings than they had ever believed possible, roads that ran like rivers of steel with growling vehicles, tall chimneys that filled the sky with black thunderclouds, and multitudes upon multitudes, human beings more numerous than the springbok migrations of the Kalahari, black men in silver helmets and knee-high rubber boots, regiments of them, marching towards the tall headgears or, as the shifts changed, wearily swarming back from the shafts splashed from head to foot with yellow mud. There were white men on the streets and platforms, white women in gaily coloured dresses with remote disdainful expressions, human beings in the windows of the buildings which crowded wall to red brick wall right to the verge of the railway tracks. It was too much, too huge and diffuse for them to assimilate at one time and they gaped and exclaimed and pressed to the windows of the coach.

'Where are the women?' Hendrick asked suddenly, and Moses smiled.

'Which women, brother?'

'The black women, the women of our tribe?'

'There are no women here, not the type of women you know. There are only the *Isifebi*, and they do it for gold. Everything here is for gold.'

Once again they were shunted off the main line into a fenced enclosure in which the long white barrack buildings stood in endless rows and the signboard above the gates read:

WITWATERSRAND NATIVE LABOUR
ASSOCIATION
CENTRAL RAND INDUCTION CENTRE

From the coaches they were led to a long shed by a couple of grinning boss-boys and instructed to strip to the buff.

The lines of naked black men shuffled forward under the paternal eyes of the boss-boys, who treated them in a friendly jocular fashion.

'Some of you have brought your livestock with you,' they joked. 'Goats on your scalp, and cattle in your pubic hairs,' and dipping the paint brushes they wielded into buckets of bluebutter ointment, they plastered the heads and crotches of the recruits.

'Rub it in,' they ordered. 'We don't want your lice and crabs and itchy crawlies.' And the recruits entered into the spirit of the occasion and roared with laughter as they smeared each other with the sticky butter.

At the end of the shed they were each handed a small square of blue mottled carbolic soap.

'Your mothers may think you smell like the mimosa in flower, but even the goats shudder when you pass upwind.' The boss-boys laughed and shoved them under the hot showers.

The doctors were waiting for them when they emerged, scrubbed and still naked, and this time the medical examinations were exhaustive. Their chests were sounded and all their bodily apertures probed and scrutinized.

'What happened to your mouth, and your head?' one doctor demanded of Hendrick. 'No, don't tell me. I don't want to know.' He had seen injuries like these before. 'Those bloody animals in charge of the trains. All right, we will send you to the dentist to have those stumps pulled – too late to stitch the head, you'll have a couple of lovely scars! Apart from that, you are a beauty.' He slapped Hendrick's hard shiny black muscles. 'We'll put you down for underground work, and you'll get the underground bonus.'

They were issued grey overalls and hobnailed boots, and then given a gargantuan meal, as much as they could eat.

'It is not like I thought it would be.' Hendrick spooned stew into his mouth. 'Good food, white men who smile, no beatings – not like the train.'

'Brother, only a fool starves and beats his oxen – and these white men are not fools.'

One of the other Ovambo men took Moses' empty dish to the kitchen and returned with it refilled. It was no longer necessary for him to give orders for such menial services. His wants were taken care of by the men around him as if by birthright. Already the death of the white overseer,

Tshayela, the striker, had been embroidered and built into a legend by many repetitions, reinforcing the stature and authority of Moses Gama and his lieutenant; men walked softly around them and inclined their heads respectfully when either Moses or Hendrick spoke directly to them.

At dawn the next morning they were roused from their bunks in the barrack rooms and after a huge breakfast of maize cake and *maas*, the thick clotted sour milk, they were led to the long iron-roofed classroom.

'Men of forty different tribes come from every corner of the land to *Goldi*, men speaking forty different languages, from Zulu to Tswana, from Herero to Basuto, and only one in a thousand of them understands a word of English or of Afrikaans,' Moses explained softly to his brother as the other men respectfully made room for them on one of the classroom benches. 'Now they will teach us the special language of *Goldi*, the tongue by which all men, whether black or white, and of whatever tribe, speak to each other here.'

A venerable old Zulu boss-boy, his pate covered with a cap of shining silver wool, was their instructor in the lingua franca of the gold mines, Fanakalo. The name was taken from its own vocabulary and meant literally 'like this, like that', the phrase that the recruits would have urged upon them frequently over the weeks ahead: 'Do it like this! Work like that! *Sebenza fanakalo!*'

The Zulu instructor on the raised dais was surrounded by all the accoutrements of the miner's trade, set out on display so that he could touch each item with his pointer and the recruits would chant the name of it in unison. Helmets and lanterns, hammers and picks, jumper bars and scrapers, safety rails and rigs – they would know them all intimately before they stood their first shift.

But now the old Zulu touched his own chest and said: '*Mina!*' Then pointed at his class and said: '*Wena!*'

And Moses led them in the chant: 'Me! You!'

'Head!' said the instructor and 'Arm!' and 'Leg!' He touched his own body and his pupils imitated him enthusiastically.

They worked at the language all that morning and then after lunch they were divided into groups of twenty and the group that included Moses and Hendrick was taken to another iron-roofed building similar to the language class-room. It differed only in its furnishings. Long trestle tables ran from wall to wall, and the person that welcomed them was a white man with peculiar bright ginger-coloured hair and moustache and green eyes. He was dressed in a long white coat like those the doctors had worn, and like them he was smiling and friendly, waving them to their places at the tables and speaking in English that only Moses and Hendrick understood, although they were careful not to make their understanding apparent and maintained a pan-tomime of perplexity and ignorance.

'All right you fellows. My name is Dr Marcus Archer and I am a psychologist. What we are going to do now is give you an aptitude test to see just what kind of work you are best suited to.' The white man smiled at them and then nodded to the boss-boy beside him, who translated:

'You do what *Bomvu*, the red one, tells you. That way we can find out just how stupid you are.'

The first test was a blockbuilding exercise which Marcus Archer had developed himself to test basic manual dexter-ity and awareness of mechanical shape. The multicoloured wooden blocks of various shapes had to be fitted into the frame on the table in front of each subject in the manner of an elementary jigsaw puzzle and the time allotted for completion was six minutes. The boss-boy explained the procedure and gave a demonstration and the recruits took their seats at the tables and Marcus Archer called: '*Enza!* Do it!' and started his stop watch.

Moses completed his puzzle in one minute six seconds. According to Dr Archer's meticulous records, to date

116,816 had sat this particular test. Not one of them had completed it in under two and a half minutes. He left the dais and went down to Moses' table to check his assembly of the blocks. It was correct, and he nodded and studied Moses' expressionless features thoughtfully.

Of course, he had noticed Moses the moment he entered the room. He had never seen such a beautiful man in his life, either black or white, and Dr Archer's preference was strongly for black skin. That was one of the main reasons he had come out to Africa five years before, for Dr Marcus Archer was a homosexual.

He had been in his third year at Magdalene College before he admitted this fact to himself, and the man who had introduced him to the bitter-sweet delights had at the same time stimulated his intellect with the wondrous new doctrines of Karl Marx and the subsequent refinements to that doctrine by Vladimir Ilyich Lenin. His lover had secretly enrolled him in the British Communist Party, and after he had left Cambridge introduced him to the comrades of Bloomsbury. However, the young Marcus had never felt entirely at home in intellectual London. He had lacked the spiked tongue, the ready acid wit and the feline cruelty, and after a short and highly unsatisfactory affair with Lytton Strachey, he had been given Lytton's notorious 'treatment' and ostracized from the group.

He had banished himself into the wilderness of Manchester University, to take up the new science of industrial psychology. In Manchester he had begun a long and lyrically happy liaison with a Jamaican trombone player and allowed his connections with the Party to fall into neglect. However, he was to learn that the Party never forgets its chosen ones, and at the age of thirty-one, when he had already made some small reputation for himself in his profession, but when his association with his Jamaican lover had ended acrimoniously and he was dejected and almost suicidal, the Party had reached out one of its tentacles and drawn him gently back into the fold.

They told him that there was an opening in his field with the South African Chamber of Mines working with African mineworkers. His penchant for black skin was by now an addiction. The infant South African Communist Party was in need of bolstering and the job was his if he wanted. It was implied that he had free choice in the matter, but the outcome was never in doubt and within a month he had sailed for Cape Town.

In the following five years he had done important pioneering work with the Chamber of Mines and had received both recognition and deep satisfaction from it. His connections with the Party had been carefully concealed, but the covert work he had done in this area was even more important, and his commitment to the ideals of Marxism had grown stronger as he grew older and saw at first hand the inhumanities of class and racial discrimination, the terrible abyss that separated the poor and dispossessed black proletariat from the enormous wealth and privilege of the white *bourgeoisie*. He had found that in this rich and beautiful land all the gross ills of the human condition flourished as though in a hothouse, exaggerated until they were almost a caricature of evil.

Now Marcus Archer looked at this noble young man with the face of an Egyptian god and a skin of burnt honey, and he was filled with longing.

'You speak English, don't you?' he asked, and Moses nodded.

'Yes, I do,' he said softly, and Marcus Archer had to turn away and go back to his dais. His passion was impossible to disguise, and his fingers were trembling as he took up a stick of chalk and wrote upon the blackboard, giving himself a respite to get his emotions under control.

The tests continued for the rest of the afternoon, the

subjects gradually being sorted and channelled into their various grades and levels on the results. At the end only one remained in the main stream. Moses Gama had completed the progressively more difficult tests with the same aplomb as he had tackled the first, and Dr Archer realized that he had discovered a prodigy.

At five o'clock the session ended and thankfully the subjects trooped from the classroom; the last hour had taxed even the brightest amongst them. Moses alone had remained undaunted and as he filed past the desk Dr Archer said:

'Gama!' He had taken the name from the register. 'There is one more task I would like you to attempt.'

He led Moses down the verandah to his office at the end.

'You can read and write, Gama?'

'Yes, Doctor.'

'It is a theory of mine that a man's handwriting can be studied to find the key to his personality,' Archer explained. 'And I would like you to write for me.'

They sat side by side at the desk, and Dr Archer set writing materials in front of Moses, chatting easily. 'This is a standard text I use.'

On the card he handed Moses was printed the nursery rhyme 'The Cat and the Fiddle'.

Moses dipped the pen and Archer leaned closer to watch. His writing was large and fluent, the characters formed with sharp peaks, forward sloping and definite. All the indications of mental determination and ruthless energy were present.

Still studying the handwriting Archer casually laid his hand on Moses' thigh, intensely aware of the hard rubbery muscle beneath the velvety skin, and the nib spluttered as Moses started. Then his hand steadied and he went on writing. He finished, laid the pen down carefully, and for the first time looked directly into Marcus Archer's green eyes.

'Gama.' Marcus Archer's voice shook and his fingers tightened. 'You are much too intelligent to waste your time shovelling ore.' He paused and moved his hand slowly up Moses' leg.

Moses stared steadily into his eyes. His expression did not change, but he let his thighs fall slowly open, and Marcus Archer's heart was thumping wildly against his ribs.

'I want you to work as my personal assistant, Gama,' he whispered, and Moses considered the magnitude of this offer. He would have access to the files of every worker in the gold-mining industry; he would be protected and privileged, free to pass and enter where other black men were forbidden. The advantages were so numerous that he knew he could not grasp them all in so brief a moment. For the man who made the offer he felt almost nothing, neither revulsion nor desire, but he would have no compunction in paying the price he demanded. If the white man wished to be treated as a woman, then Moses would readily render him this service.

'Yes, Doctor, I would like to work for you,' he said.

On the last night in the barrack room of the induction centre, Moses called all his chosen lieutenants to him. They clustered around his bunk.

'Very soon you will go from here to the *Goldi*. Not all of you will go together for there are many mines along the Rand. Some of you will go down into the earth, others will work on the surface in the mills and the reduction plants. We will be separated for a while, but you will not forget that we are brothers. I, your elder brother, will not forget you. I have important work for you. I will seek you out, wherever you are, and you will be ready for me when I summon you.'

'*Eh he!*' they grunted in agreement and obedience. 'We are your younger brothers. We will listen for your voice.'

'You must know always that you are under my protection, that all trespasses against you will be revenged. You have seen what happens to those who give offence to our brotherhood.'

'We have seen it,' they murmured. 'We have seen it – and it is death.'

'It is death,' Moses confirmed. 'It is death also for any of the brotherhood who betray us. It is death for all traitors.'

'Death to all traitors.' They swayed together, coming once more under the mesmeric spell which Moses Gama wove about them.

'I have chosen a totem for our brotherhood,' Moses went on. 'I have chosen the buffalo for our totem for he is black and powerful and all men fear him. We are the Buffaloes.'

'We are the Buffaloes.' Already they were proud of the distinction. 'We are the black Buffaloes and all men will learn to fear us.'

'These are the signs, the secret signs by which we will recognize our own.'

He made the sign and then individually clasped their right hands in the fashion of the white man, but the grip was different, a double grip and turn of the second finger. 'Thus you will know your brothers when they come to you.'

They greeted each other in the darkened barracks, each of them shaking the hand of all the others in the new way, and it was a form of initiation into the brotherhood.

'You will hear from me soon. Until I call, you must do as the white man requires of you. You must work hard and learn. You must be ready for the call when it comes.' Moses sent them away to their bunks and he and Hendrick sat alone, their heads together, speaking in whispers.

'You have lost the little white stones,' Moses told him. 'By now the birds and the small beasts will have pecked the loaves and devoured the millet bread. The stones will be scattered and lost; the dust will cover them and the grass will grow over them. They are gone, my brother.'

'Yes. They are gone,' Hendrick lamented. 'After so much blood and striving, after all the hardships we endured, they have been scattered like seeds to the wind.'

'They were accursed,' Moses consoled him. 'From the moment I saw them I knew that they would bring only disaster and death. They are white man's toys. What could you have done with the white man's wealth? If you tried to spend it, if you tried to buy white man's things with it, you would instantly have been marked by the white police. They would have come for you immediately and there would have been a rope or a jail cell for you.'

Hendrick was silent, considering the truth of this. What could he have purchased with the stones? Black men could not own their own land. More than a hundred head of cattle and the local chieftain's envy would have been aroused. He already had all the wives – and more – that he wished for, and black men did not drive in motor cars. Black men did not draw attention to themselves in any way, not if they were wise.

'No, my brother,' Moses told him softly. 'They were not for you. Thank the spirits of your ancestors that they were wrested from you and scattered back on the earth where they belong.'

Hendrick growled softly, 'Still it would have been good to have that treasure, to hold it in my hands, even secretly.'

'There are other treasures even more important than diamonds or white man's gold, my brother.'

'What are these treasures?' Hendrick asked.

'Follow me and I will lead you to them.'

'But tell me what they are,' Hendrick insisted.

'You will discover them in good time.' Moses smiled.

501

'But now, my brother, we must talk of first things; the treasures will follow later. Listen to me. *Bomvu*, the red one, my little doctor who likes to be used as a woman, *Bomvu* has allocated you to the *Goldi* called Central Rand Consolidated. It is one of the richest of the *Goldi*, with many deep shafts. You will go underground, and it is best if you make a name for yourself there. I have prevailed on *Bomvu* to send ten of our best men from the Buffaloes to CRC with you. These will be your *impi*, your chosen warriors. You must start with them, but you will build upon them, gathering around you the quick and strong and the fearless.'

'What must I do with these men?'

'Hold them in readiness. You will hear from me soon. Very soon.'

'What of the other Buffaloes?'

'*Bomvu* has sent them, at my suggestion, in groups of ten to each of the other *Goldi* along the Rand. Small groups of our men everywhere. They will grow, and soon we will be a great black herd of buffaloes which even the most savage lion will not dare to challenge.'

S wart Hendrick's initial descent in the earth was the first time in his life that he had been frightened witless, unable to speak or think, so terrified that he could not even scream or struggle against it.

The terror began when he was in the long line of black miners, each of them wearing black rubber gumboots and grey overalls, the unpainted silver helmets on their heads fitted with head lanterns. Hendrick shuffled forward in the press of bodies down the ramp between the poles of the crush, like cattle entering an abattoir, stopping and starting forward again. Suddenly he found himself at the head of the line, standing before the steel mesh gate that guarded the entrance to the shaft.

Beyond the mesh he could see the steel cables hanging into the shaft like pythons with shining scales, and over him towered the steel skeleton of the headgear. When he looked up he could see the huge wheels silhouetted against the sky a hundred feet above his head, spinning and stopping and reversing.

Suddenly the mesh gates crashed open and he was carried on the surge of black bodies into the cage beyond. They packed shoulder to shoulder, seventy men. The doors closed, the floor dropped under his feet and stopped again immediately. He heard the tramp of feet over his head and looked up, realizing that the skip was a double decker and that another seventy men were being packed into the top compartment.

Again he heard the clash of closing mesh gates and he started as the telegraph shrilled, four long rings, the signal to descend, and the skip fell away under him – but this time accelerating so violently that his body seemed to come free and his feet lay only lightly on the steel floor plates. His belly was sucked up against his ribs and his terror was unleashed.

In darkness the skip rocketed downwards, drumming and rattling and racing like an express train in a tunnel, and the terror went on and on, minute after minute, eternity after eternity. He felt himself suffocating, crushed by the thought of the enormous weight of rock above him, his ears popping and crackling at the pressure, a mile and then another mile straight down into the earth.

The skip stopped so abruptly that his knees buckled and he felt the flesh of his face sucked down from the bones of his skull, stretching like rubber. The gates crashed open and he was carried out into the main haulage, a cavern walled with glistening wet rock, filled with men, hundreds of men like rats in a sewer, streaming away into the endless tunnels that honeycombed the bowels of the world.

Everywhere there was water, glistening and shining in the flat glare of the electric light, running back in channels on each side of the haulage, squelching under his feet, hidden water drumming and rustling in the darkness or dripping from the jagged rock of the roof. The very air was heavy with water, humid and hot and claustrophobic so that it had a gelatinous texture, seeming to fill his eardrums and deafen him, trickling sluggishly into his lungs like treacle, and his terror lasted all that long march along the drive until they reached the stopes. Here the men split into their separate gangs and disappeared into the shadows.

The stopes were the vast open chambers from which the gold-bearing ore had already been excavated, the hanging wall above supported now by packed pillars of shoring timber, the footwall under them inclined upwards at an angle following the run of the reef.

The men of his gang trudging ahead of him led Hendrick to his station, and here under a bare electric bulb waited for the white shift boss, a burly Afrikaner flanked by his two boss-boys.

The station was a three-sided chamber in the rock, its number on the entrance. There was a long bench against the back wall of the station and a latrine, its open buckets screened by sheets of burlap.

The gang sat on the bench while the boss-boys called the roll, and then the white shift boss asked in Fanakalo, 'Where is the new hammer boy?' and Hendrick rose to his feet. Cronje, the shift boss, came to stand in front of him. Their eyes were on a level, both big men. The shift boss's nose was crooked, broken long ago in a forgotten brawl, and he examined Hendrick carefully. He saw the broken gap in his teeth and the scars upon his head and his respect was tentative and grudging. They were both hard, tough men, recognizing it in each other. Up there in the sunshine and sweet cool airs they were black man and white man. Down here in the earth they were simply men.

'You know the hammer?' Cronje asked in Fanakalo.

'I know it,' Hendrick replied in Afrikaans. He had practised working the hammer for two weeks in the surface training pits.

Cronje blinked and then grinned to acknowledge the use of his own language. 'I run the best gang of rock breakers on the CRC,' he said, still grinning. 'You will learn to break rock, my friend, or I will break your head and your arse instead. Do you understand?'

'I understand.' Hendrick grinned back at him, and Cronje raised his voice. 'All hammer boys here!'

They stood up from the bench – five of them, all big men like Hendrick. It took tremendous physical strength to handle the jack hammers. They were the élite of the rock-breaking gangs, earning almost double wages and bonus for footage, earning also immense prestige from lesser men.

Cronje wrote their names up on the blackboard under the electric bulb: Henry Tabaka at the bottom of the list and Zama, the big Zulu, at number one. When Zama stripped off his jacket and tossed it to his line boy, his great black muscles bulged and gleamed in the stark electric light.

'Ha!' He looked at Hendrick. 'So we have a little Ovambo jackal come in yipping from the desert.' The men around him laughed obsequiously. Zama was top hammer on the section; everybody laughed when he made a joke.

'I thought that the Zulu baboon scratched his fleas only on the peaks of the Drakensberg so his voice can be heard afar,' Hendrick said quietly, and there was a shocked silence for a moment and then a guffaw of disbelieving laughter.

'All right, you two big talkers,' Cronje intervened, 'let's break some rock.' He led them from the station up the stope to the rockface where the gold reef was a narrow grey horizontal band in the jagged wall, dull and nondescript, without the faintest precious sparkle. The gold was locked away in it.

The roof was low; a man had to double over to reach the face; but the stope was wide, reaching away hundreds of metres into the darkness on either hand, and they could hear the other gangs out there along the rockface, their voices echoing and reverberating, their lanterns throwing weird shadows.

'Tabaka!' Cronje yelled. 'Here!' He had marked the shot holes to be drilled with splashes of white paint, indicating the inclination and depth of each hole.

The blast was a precise and calculated firing of gelignite charges. The outer holes would be charged with 'shapers' to form the hanging wall and foot wall of the stope they would fire first, while the pattern of inner shots fired a second later. These were the 'cutters' that would kick the ore back and clear it from the face.

'*Shaya!*' Cronje yelled at Hendrick. 'Hit it!' and lingered a second to watch as Hendrick stooped to the drill.

It squatted on the rock floor in front of the face, an ungainly tool in the shape of a heavy machine-gun, with long pneumatic hoses attached to it and running back down the slope to the compressed air system in the main haulage.

Swiftly Hendrick fitted the twenty-foot-long steel jumper bit into the lug of the drill and then he and his line boy dragged the tool to the rockface. It took all the strength of both Hendrick and his assistant to lift the tool and position the point of the drill on the white paint mark for the first cut. Hendrick eased himself into position behind the tool, taking the full weight of it on his right shoulder. The line boy stepped back, and Hendrick opened the valve.

The din was stunning, a stuttering implosion of sound that drove in against the eardrums as compressed air at a pressure of 500 pounds a square inch roared into the drill and slammed the long steel bit into the rock.

Hendrick's entire body shuddered and shook to the drive

of the tool against his shoulder but still he leaned his full weight against it. His head jumped on the thick corded column of his neck so rapidly that his vision blurred, but he narrowed his eyes and aimed the point of the drill into the rock at the exact angle that the shift boss had called for. Water squirted down the hollow drill steel, bubbling out of the hole in a yellow mist, splattering into Hendrick's face.

The sweat burst from his black skin, running down his face as though he were standing under a cloudburst, mingling with the slimy mud pouring down his naked back and scattering like rain as his straining muscles fluttered and jumped to the impulse of the pounding steel drill at his shoulder.

Within minutes the entire surface of his body began to itch and burn. It was the hammer boys' affliction; his skin was being scrubbed back and forth a thousand times a minute by the violent shaking motion of the drill, and with each minute the agony became more intense. He tried to close his mind to it but still it felt as though a blowtorch was being played over his body.

The long steel drill sank slowly into the rock until it reached the depth marker painted on it and Hendrick closed the valve. There was no silence, for even though his hearing was dulled, as though his eardrums were filled with cotton wool, yet he could still hear the echoes of the drill thunder resounding against the roof of his skull.

The line boy ran forward, seized the jumper bit and helped him withdraw it from the first shot hole and reposition the tip on the second daubed paint mark. Once again Hendrick opened the valve and the din and the agony began again. However, gradually the itching burn of his body blurred into numbness and he felt disembodied as though cocaine had been injected under his skin.

So he stood to the rock all that shift, six hours without let or relief. When it ended and they trooped back from

507

the face, splattered and coated with yellow mud from head to foot and weary beyond pain or feeling, even Zama the great black Zulu was reeling on his feet and his eyes were dull.

In the station Cronje wrote the total of work completed against their names on the blackboard. Zama had drilled sixteen patterns, Hendrick twelve and the next best man ten.

'*Hau!*' Zama muttered as they rode up to the surface in the crowded skip. 'On his very first shift the jackal is number two hammer.' And Hendrick had just enough strength to reply:

'And on his second shift the jackal will be top hammer.'

It never happened. Not once did he break more rock than the Zulu. But at the end of that first month as Hendrick sat in the company beer hall with the other Ovambos of the Buffalo totem gathered around him, the Zulu came to his table carrying two one-gallon jugs of the creamy effervescent millet beer that the company sold its men. It was thick as porridge, and just as nutritious, though only very mildly alcoholic.

Zama set a one-gallon jug down in front of Hendrick and said: 'We broke some rock together this month, hey, jackal?'

'And we'll break a lot more together next month, hey, baboon?'

And they both roared with laughter and raised the beer jugs in unison and drank them dry.

Zama was the first Zulu to become initiated into the brotherhood of the Buffaloes, not as natural as it sounded for tribal barriers, like mountain ranges, were difficult to cross.

It was three months before Hendrick saw his brother again, but by that time Hendrick had extended his influence throughout the entire compound of black mine workers at the CRC mine property. With Zama as his lieutenant, the Buffaloes now encompassed men from many different tribes, Zulus and Shangaans and Matabeles. The only criterion was that the new initiates should be hard reliable men, preferably with some influence over at least a section of the eight thousand odd black miners, and preferably also appointed by the mine administration to positions of authority on the property: clerks or boss-boys or company police.

Some of the men who were approached resisted the brotherhood's overtures. One of these, a senior Zulu boss-boy with thirty years' service and a misplaced sense of duty to his tribe and the company, fell into one of the ore chutes on the sixtieth level of the main haulage the day after he refused. His body was ground to a muddy paste by the tons of jagged rock that rumbled over it. It seemed that nobody had witnessed the accident.

One of the company police *indunas*, who also resisted the blandishments of the brotherhood, was found stabbed to death in his sentry box at the main gates to the property, while yet another was burned to death in the kitchens. Three Buffaloes witnessed this last unfortunate incident caused by the victim's own clumsiness and inattention and there were no more refusals.

When at last the messenger came from Moses, identifying himself with the secret sign and handclasp, he bore a summons to a meeting, and Hendrick was able to leave the mine property without check.

By government decree the black mine workers were strictly confined within the barbed-wire fences of the compounds. It was the opinion of both the Chamber of Mines and the Johannesburg city fathers that to let tens of thousands of single black males roam the goldfields at will would invite disaster. They had the salutary lesson of the Chinese before them. In 1904, almost fifty thousand Chinese coolies had been brought into South Africa to fill the huge shortage of unskilled labour for the gold mines. However, the Chinese were much too intelligent and restless to be confined to compounds and restricted to unskilled labour and they were highly organized in their secret tong societies. The result was a wave of lawlessness and terror that swept over the goldfields – rapine and robbery, gambling and drugs – so that in 1908, at huge cost, all the Chinese were rounded up and shipped home. The government was determined to avoid a repetition of this terror and the compound system was strictly enforced.

However, Hendrick passed through the gates of the CRC compound as though he were invisible. He crossed the open veld in the starlight until he found the overgrown track and followed it to the old abandoned shafthead. There, parked behind the deserted rusting corrugated iron shed, was a black Ford sedan and as Hendrick approached it cautiously the headlights were switched on, spotlighting Hendrick, and he froze.

Then the lights were switched off and Moses' voice called out of the darkness, 'I see you, my brother.'

They embraced impulsively and then Hendrick laughed. 'Ha! So you drive a motor car now, like a white man.'

'The motor car belongs to *Bomvu*.' Moses led him to it, and Hendrick sank back against the leather seat and sighed comfortably. 'This is better than walking.'

'Now tell me, Hendrick my brother. What has happened at CRC?' And Moses listened without comment until Hendrick finished his long report. Then he nodded.

'You have understood my wants. It is exactly as I wished it. The brotherhood must take in men from all the tribes, not just the Ovambo. We must reach to each tribe, each property, every corner of the goldfields.'

'You have said all this before,' Hendrick growled, 'but

you have never told me why, my brother. I trust you, but the men I have assembled, the *impi* you bid me build, they look to me, and they ask one question. They ask me why? What is the profit in this thing? What is there for us in the brotherhood?'

'And what do you answer them, my brother?'

'I tell them they must be patient.' Hendrick scowled. 'I do not know the answer, but I look wise as if I do. And if they nag me, like children – well, then I beat them like children.' Moses laughed delightedly, but Hendrick shook his head. 'Don't laugh, my brother, I can't go on beating them much longer.'

Moses clapped his shoulder. 'Nor will you have to much longer. But tell me now, Hendrick, what is it you have missed most in the months you have worked at CRC?'

Hendrick answered. 'The feeling of a woman under me.'

'That you shall have before the night is finished. And what else, my brother?'

'The fire of good liquor in my belly, not the weak slop from the company beerhall.'

'My brother,' Moses told him seriously, 'you have answered your own question. These are the things that your men will get from the brotherhood. These are the scraps we will throw our hunting dogs: women and liquor and, of course money, but for those of us at the head of the Buffaloes there will be more, much more.' He started the engine of the Ford.

The gold-bearing reefs of the Witwatersrand form a sprawling arc one hundred kilometres in length. The older properties such as East Daggafontein are in the eastern sector of the arc where the reef originally outcropped; the newer properties are in the west where the reef dips away sharply to great depth; but like Blyvooruitzicht, these deep mines are enormously rich. All the mines are laid out along this fabulous crescent, surrounded by the urban development which the gold wealth has attracted and fostered.

Moses drove the black Ford southwards, away from the mines and the white man's streets and buildings, and the road they followed quickly narrowed and deteriorated, its surface rutted and riven with pot holes and puddles from the last thunderstorm. It lost direction and began to meander, degenerating into a maze of lanes and tracks.

The street lights of the city were left behind them, but out here there was other illumination: the glow of hundreds of wood fires, their orange light muted by their own drifting smoke banks. There was one of these cooking fires in front of each of the shanties of tarpaper and old corrugated iron that crowded so closely that there were only narrow lanes between them, and there was amongst the shacks a feeling of the presence of many unseen people, as though an army were encamped out here in the open veld.

'Where are we?' Hendrick asked.

'We are in a city that no man acknowledges, a city of people who do not exist.'

Hendrick glimpsed their dark shapes as the Ford bumped and pitched over the rough track between the shanties and shacks and the headlights swung aimlessly back and forth illuminating little cameo scenes: a group of black children stoning a pariah dog; a body lying beside the track drunk or dead; a woman squatting to urinate in the angle of one of the corrugated iron walls; two men locked in silent deadly combat; a family at one of the fires eating from tins of bully beef, their eyes huge and shining as they looked up startled into the headlights; and other dark shapes scurrying furtively away into the shadows – hundreds of them and the presence of thousands more sensed.

'This is Drake's Farm,' Moses told him. 'One of the squatter townships that surround the white man's *Goldi*.'

The odour of the amorphous sprawling aggregation of humanity was woodsmoke and sewage, old sweat on hot bodies and charred food on the open wood fires. It was the smell of garbage mouldering in the rain puddles and the nauseating sweetness of bloodsucking vermin in unwashed bedding.

'How many live here?'

'Five thousand, ten thousand. Nobody knows, nobody cares.' Moses stopped the Ford and switched off the headlights and the engine.

The silence afterwards was not truly silence; it was the murmur of multitudes like the sea heard at a distance, the mewling of infants, the barking of a cur dog, the sounds of a woman singing, of men cursing and talking and eating, of couples arguing shrilly or copulating, of people dying and defecating and snoring and gambling and drinking in the night.

Moses stepped out of the Ford and called imperatively into the darkness and half a dozen dark figures came scurrying from amongst the shacks. They were children, Hendrick realized, though their age and sex were obscure.

'Stand guard on my motor car,' Moses ordered, and tossed a small coin that twinkled in the firelight until one of the children snatched it from the air.

'Eh he! Baba!' they squeaked, and Moses led his brother amongst the shacks for a hundred yards and the sound of the women singing was louder, a thrilling evocative sound, and there was the buzz of many other voices and the sour smell of old stale alcohol and meat cooking on an open fire.

They had reached a long low building, a rough shed cobbled together from discarded material. Its walls were crooked and the outline of the roof was buckled and sway backed against the fireglow. Moses knocked upon the door and a lantern was flashed in his face before the door was thrown open

'So my brother,' Moses took Hendrick's arm and drew him into the doorway. 'This is your first shebeen. Here you will have all that I promised you: women and liquor, your fill of both.'

The shed was packed with human beings, jammed so tightly that the far wall was lost in the fog of blue tobacco smoke and a man must shout to be heard a few feet away; the black faces shone with sweat and excitement. The men were miners, drinking and singing and laughing and groping the women. Some were very drunk and a few had fallen to the earth floor and lay in their own vomit. The women were of every tribe, all of their faces painted in the fashion of white women, dressed in flimsy gaudy dresses, singing and dancing and shaking their hips, picking out the men with money and tugging them away through the doors at the back of the shed.

Moses did not have to force his way through this jam of bodies. It opened almost miraculously before him, and many of the women called to him respectfully. Hendrick followed closely behind his brother and he was struck with admiration that Moses had been able to achieve this degree of recognition in the three short months since they had arrived on the Rand.

There was a guard at the door at the far end of the shebeen, an ugly scar-faced ruffian, but he also recognized Moses and clapped his hands in greeting before he pulled aside the canvas screen to allow them to go through into the back room.

This room was less crowded, and there were tables and benches for the customers. The girls in here were still graced with youth, bright-eyed and fresh-faced. An enormous black woman was seated at a separate table in the corner. She had the serene round moon face of the high-bred Zulu but its contours were almost obscured by fat. Her dark amber skin was stretched tightly over this abundance; her belly hung down in a series of fleshy balconies onto her lap, and fat hung in great black dewlaps under her arms and formed bracelets around her wrists. On the table in front of her were neat stacks of coins, silver and copper, and wads of multicoloured bank notes, and the girls were bringing her more to add to the piles each minute.

When she saw Moses her perfect white teeth shone like precious porcelain; she lumbered to her feet, her thighs so elephantine that she waddled with her feet wide apart as she came to him and greeted him as though he were a tribal chief, touching her forehead and clapping with respect.

'This is Mama Nginga,' Moses told Hendrick. 'She is the biggest shebeen keeper and whore mistress on Drake's Farm. Soon she will be the only one on Drake's Farm.'

Only then did Hendrick realize that he knew most of the men at the tables. They were Buffaloes who had travelled on the Wenela train and taken the initiation oath with him, and they greeted him with unfeigned delight and introduced him to the strangers in their midst.

'This is Henry Tabaka. He is the one of the legend. The man who slew *Tshayela*, the white overseer—' and Hendrick noticed the immediate respect in the eyes of these new Buffaloes. They were men from the other mines along the reef, recruited by the original Buffaloes, and Hendrick saw that on the whole they had chosen well.

'My brother has not had a woman or a taste of good liquor in three months,' Moses told them as he seated himself at the head of the central table. 'Mama Nginga, we don't want your *skokiaan*. She makes it herself,' he told Hendrick in a loud aside, 'and she puts in carbide and methylated spirits and dead snakes and aborted babies to give it kick and flavour.'

Mama Nginga screeched with laughter. 'My *skokiaan* is famous from Fordsburg to Bapsfontein. Even some of the white men – the *mabuni* – come for it.'

'It's good enough for them,' Moses agreed, 'but not good enough for my brother.'

Mama Nginga sent one of the girls to them with a bottle

of Cape brandy and Moses seized the young girl around the waist and held her easily. He pulled open the European-style blouse she wore, forcing out her big round breasts so that they shone like washed coal in the lamplight.

'This is where we start, my Buffaloes, a girl and a bottle,' he told them. 'There are fifty thousand lonely men at *Goldi* far from their wives, all of them hungry for sweet young flesh. There are fifty thousand men, thirsty from their work in the earth, and the white men forbid them to slake their thirst with this.' He shook the bottle of golden spirits. 'There are fifty thousand randy thirsty black men at *Goldi*, all with money in their pockets. The Buffaloes will give them what they want.' He pushed the girl into Hendrick's lap and she coiled herself about him with professionally simulated lust and thrust her shining black breasts into his face.

When the dawn broke over the sprawling shanty town of Drake's Farm, Moses and Hendrick picked their way down the reeking convoluted alleys to where they had left the Ford and the children were guarding it still, like jackals around the lion's kill. The brothers had sat all night in the back room of Mama Nginga's shebeen and the preliminary planning was at last done. Each of their lieutenants had been allotted areas and responsibilities.

'But there is still much work to be done, my brother,' Moses told Hendrick as he started the Ford. 'We have to find the liquor and the women. We will have to bring all the little shebeens and brothels like goats into our kraal, and there is only one way to do that.'

'I know how that has to be done,' Hendrick nodded. 'And we have an *impi* to do it.'

'And an *induna*, a general, to command that *impi*.' Moses glanced at Hendrick significantly. 'The time has come for you to leave CRC, my brother. All your time and your strength will be needed now. You will waste no more of your strength in the earth, breaking rock for a white man's pittance. From now on you will be breaking heads for power and great fortune.' He smiled thinly. 'You will never have to pine again for those little white stones of yours. I will give you more, much more.'

Marcus Archer arranged for Hendrick's contract at CRC to be cancelled and for him to be issued travel papers for one of the special trains that carried the returning miners who had worked out their ticket back to the reservations and the distant villages. But Hendrick never caught that train. Instead he disappeared from the white man's records and was absorbed into the shadowy halfworld of the townships.

Mama Nginga set aside one of the shanties at the back of her shebeen for his exclusive use, and one of her girls was always on hand to sweep and wash his laundry, to cook his food and warm his bed.

It was six days after his arrival at Drake's Farm that the Buffalo *impi* opened its campaign. The objective had been discussed and carefully explained by Hendrick and it was simple and clear-cut. They would make Drake's Farm their own citadel.

On the first night twelve of the opposition shebeens were burned to the ground. Their proprietors burned with them, as did those of their customers who were too drunk to crawl out of the flaming hovels. Drake's Farm was far outside the sector served by the white man's fire engines, so no attempt was made to fight the flames. Rather, the inhabitants of Drake's Farm gathered to watch the spectacle as though it was a circus arranged particularly for their entertainment. The children danced and shrilled in the firelight, and screeched with laughter as the bottles of spirits exploded like fireworks.

Nearly all the girls escaped from the flames. Those who had been at work when the fire began ran out naked, clutching their scanty clothing and weeping wildly at the loss of all their worldly possessions and savings. However, there were kindly concerned men to comfort them and lead them away to Mama Nginga's.

Within forty-eight hours the shebeens had been rebuilt on their ashes and the girls were back at work again. Their lot was much improved; they were well fed and clothed and they had their own Buffaloes to protect them from their customers, to make certain they were neither cheated nor abused. Of course, if they in turn shirked or tried to cheat, they were beaten soundly; but they expected that, it made them feel part of the totem and replaced the father and brothers they had left in the reservations.

Hendrick allowed them to keep a fixed proportion of the fee they charged and made sure his men respected their rights to it.

'Generosity breeds loyalty and firmness a loving heart,' he explained to his Buffaloes, and he extended his 'happy house' policy to embrace his customers and everybody else at Drake's Farm. The black miners coming into the township were as carefully protected as his girls were. In very short order the footpads, pickpockets, muggers and other small-time entrepreneurs were routed out. The quality of the liquor improved. From now on all of it was brewed under Mama Nginga's personal supervision.

It was strong as a bull elephant, and bit like a rabid hyena, but it no longer turned men blind or destroyed their brains, and because it was manufactured in bulk, it was reasonably priced. A man could get falling-down drunk for two shillings or have a good clean girl for the same price.

Hendrick's men met every bus and train coming in from the country districts, bringing the young black girls who had run away from their villages and their tribe to reach the glitter of *Goldi*. They led the pretty ones back to Drake's Farm. When this source of supply became inadequate as the demand increased, Hendrick sent his men into the country districts and villages to recruit the girls at the source with sweet words and promises of pretty things.

The city fathers of Johannesburg and the police were fully aware of the unacknowledged halfworld of the townships that had grown up south of the goldfields but, daunted by the prospect of closing them down and finding alternative accommodation for thousands of vagrants and illegals, they turned a blind eye, appeasing their civic consciences by occasional raids, arrests and the wholesale imposition of fines. However, as the incidence of murder and robbery and other serious crime mysteriously abated at Drake's Farm and it became an area of comparative calm and order, so their condescension and forbearance became even more pragmatic. The police raids ceased, and the prosperity of the area increased as its reputation as a safe and convivial place to have fun spread amongst the tens of thousands of black mine workers along the Rand. When they had a pass to leave the compound, they would travel thirty and forty miles, bypassing other centres of entertainment to reach it.

However, there were still many hundreds of thousands of other potential customers who could never reach Drake's Farm, and Moses Gama turned his attention to these.

'They cannot come to us, so we must go to them.' He explained to Hendrick what must be done, and it was Hendrick who negotiated the piecemeal purchase of a fleet of second-hand delivery vans and employed a coloured mechanic to renovate them and keep them in running order.

Each evening convoys of these vehicles loaded with liquor and girls left Drake's Farm, journeying down the length of the goldfields to park at some secluded location close to the big mining properties, in a copse of trees, a valley between the mine dumps, or an abandoned shaft building. The guards at the gate of the mine workers' compound, who were all Buffaloes, made certain that the customers were allowed in and out, and now every member of the Buffalo totem could share in the good fortune of their clan.

'So, my brother, do you still miss your little white stones?' Moses asked after their first two years of operation from Drake's Farm.

'It was as you promised,' Hendrick chuckled. 'We have everything that a man could wish for now.'

'You are too easily satisfied,' Moses chided him.

'There is more?' Hendrick asked with interest.

'We have only just begun,' Moses told him.

'What is next, my brother?'

'Have you heard of a trade union?' Moses asked. 'Do you know what it is?'

Hendrick looked dubious, frowning as he thought about it. 'I know that the white men on the mines have trade unions, and the white men on the railways also. I have heard it spoken of, but I know very little about them. They are white men's business, no concern of the likes of us.'

'You are wrong, my brother,' Moses said quietly. 'The African Mine Workers Union is very much our concern. It is the reason why you and I came to *Goldi*.'

'I thought that we came for the money.'

'Fifty thousand union members each paying one shilling a week union dues – isn't that money?' Moses asked, and smiled as he watched his brother make the calculation. Avarice contorted his smile so that the broken gap in his teeth looked like a black mine pit.

'It is good money indeed!'

Moses had learned from his unsuccessful attempts to establish a mine workers' union at the H'ani Mine. The black miners were simple souls with not the least vestige of political awareness; they were separated by tribal loyalties; they did not consider themselves part of a single nation.

'Tribalism is the one great obstacle in our path,' Moses explained to Hendrick. 'If we were one people we would be like a black ocean, infinite in our power.'

'But we are not one people,' Hendrick pointed out. 'Any more than the white men are one people. A Zulu is as

520

different from an Ovambo as a Scotsman is from a Russian Cossack or an Afrikaner from an Englishman.'

'Ha!' Moses smiled. 'I see you have been reading the books I gave you. When first we came to *Goldi* you had never heard of a Russian Cossack—'

'You have taught me much about men and the world they live in,' Hendrick agreed. 'Now teach me how you will make a Zulu call an Ovambo his brother. Tell me how we are to take the power that is held so firmly in the hands of the white man.'

'These things are possible. The Russian people were as diverse as we black people of Africa. They are Asiatics and Europeans, Tartars and Slavs, but under a great leader they have become a single nation and have overthrown a tyranny even more infamous than the one under which we suffer. The black people need a leader who knows what is good for them and will force them to it, even if ten thousand or a million die in achieving it.'

'A leader such as you, my brother?' Hendrick asked, and Moses smiled his remote enigmatic smile.

'The Mine Workers Union first,' he said. 'Like a child learning to walk, one step at a time. The people must be forced to do what is good for them in the long run even though at first it is painful.'

'I am not sure—' Hendrick shook his great shaven round head on which the ridged scars stood proud like polished gems of black onyx. 'What is it we seek, my brother? Is it wealth or power?'

'We are fortunate,' Moses answered. 'You want wealth and I want power. The way I have chosen, each of us will get what he desires.'

Even with middle-aged contingents of the Buffaloes on each of the mine properties the process of unionization was slow and frustrating. By necessity much of it had to be undertaken secretly, for the government's Industrial Conciliation Act placed severe limitations on black labour association and specifically prohibited collective bargaining by black workers. There was also opposition from the workers themselves, their natural suspicion and antagonism towards the new union shop stewards, all of them Buffaloes, all of them appointed and not elected; and the ordinary workers were reluctant to hand over part of their hard-earned wages to something they neither understood nor trusted.

However, with Dr Marcus Archer to advise and counsel them and with Hendrick's Buffaloes to push the cause forward, slowly the unionization of the workers on each of the various mine properties was accomplished. The miners' reluctance to part with their silver shillings was quelled. There were, of course, casualties, and some men died, but at last there were over twenty thousand dues-paying members of the African Mine Workers Union.

The Chamber of Mines, the association of mining interests, found itself presented with a *fait accompli*. The members were at first alarmed; their natural instinct was to destroy this cancer immediately. However, the Chamber members were first and above all else businessmen, concerned with getting the yellow metal to the surface with as little fuss as possible and with paying regular dividends to their shareholders. They understood what havoc a labour battle could wreak amongst their interests, so they held their first cautious informal talks with the non-existent union and were most gratified to find the self-styled secretary general to be an intelligent articulate and reasonable person.

There was no trace of Bolshevik dialectic in his statements, and far from being radical and belligerent, he was co-operative and respectful in his address.

'He is a man we can work with,' they told each other. 'He seems to have influence. We've needed a spokesman for the workers and he seems a decent enough sort. We could have done a lot worse. We can manage this chap.' And sure enough, their very first meetings had excellent results and they were able to solve a few small vexing long-term problems to the satisfaction of the union and the profit of the mine owners.

After that the informal, unrecognized union had the Chamber's tacit acceptance, and when a problem arose with their labour the Chamber sent for Moses Gama and it was swiftly settled. Each time this happened, Moses' position became more securely entrenched. And, of course, there was never even a hint at strikes or any form of militancy on the union's part.

'Do you understand, my brothers?' Moses explained to the first meeting of his central committee of the African Mine Workers Union held in Mama Nginga's shebeen. 'If they come down upon us with their full strength while we are still weak, we will be destroyed for all time. This man Smuts is a devil, and he is truly the steel in the government's spear. He did not hesitate to send his troops with machine-guns against the white union strikers in 1922. What would he do to black strikers, my brothers? He would water the earth with our blood. No, we must lull them. Patience is the great strength of our people. We have a hundred years, while the white man lives only for the day. In time the black ants of the veld build mountains and devour the carcass of the elephant. Time is our weapon, and time is the white man's enemy. Patience, my brothers, and one day the white man will discover that we are not oxen to be yoked into the traces of his wagon. He will discover rather that we are black-maned lions, fierce eaters of white flesh.'

'How swiftly the years have passed us by since we rode on *Tshayela*'s train from the deserts of the west to the flat shining mountains of *Goldi*.' Hendrick watched the mine dumps on the skyline as Moses drove the old Ford through the sparse traffic of a Sunday morning. He drove sedately, not too slow not too fast, obeying the traffic rules, stopping well in advance of the changing traffic lights, those wonders of the technological age which had only been installed on the main routes within the last few months. Moses always drove like this.

'Never draw attention to yourself unnecessarily, my brother,' he advised Hendrick. 'Never give a white policeman an excuse to stop you. He hates you already for driving a motor car that he cannot afford himself. Never put yourself in his power.'

The road skirted the rolling fairways of the Johannesburg Country Club, oases of green in the brown veld, watered and groomed and mown until they were velvet green carpets on which the white golfers strolled in their four-somes followed by their barefooted caddies. Further back amongst the trees the white walls of the club house gleamed, and Moses slowed the Ford and turned at the bottom of the club property where the road crossed the tiny dry Sand Spruit river and the signpost said 'Rivonia Farm'.

They followed the unsurfaced road, and the dust raised by the Ford's wheels hung behind them in the still dry highveld air and then settled gently to powder the brittle frost-dried grass along the verges a bright theatrical red.

The road served a cluster of smallholdings, each of them five or ten acres in extent, and Dr Marcus Archer's property was the one at the end of the road. He made no attempt to farm the land, he had no chickens, horses or vegetable gardens such as the other small-holders kept. The single building was square and unpretentious, with a tattered thatched roof and wide verandah encompassing all four sides. It was screened from the road by a scraggly plantation of Australian blue gums.

There were four other vehicles parked under the gum trees, and Moses turned the Ford off the track and stopped the engine. 'Yes, my brother. The years have passed swiftly,' he agreed. 'They always do when men are intent on dire purposes, and the world is changing all around us. There are great events afoot. It is nineteen years since the revolution in Russia, and Trotsky has been exiled. Herr Hitler has occupied the Rhineland, and in Europe there is talk of war — a war that will destroy for ever the curse of Capitalism and from which the revolution will emerge victorious.'

Hendrick laughed, the black gap in his teeth making it a grimace. 'These things do not concern us.'

'You are wrong again, my brother. They concern us beyond all else.'

'I do not understand them.'

'Then I will help you.' Moses touched his arm. 'Come, my brother. I am taking you now to the next step in your understanding of the world.' He opened the door of the Ford and Hendrick climbed down on his side and followed him towards the old house.

'It will be wise, my brother, if you keep your eyes and your ears open and your mouth closed,' Moses told him as they reached the steps at the front verandah. 'You will learn much that way.'

As they climbed the steps, Marcus Archer hurried out onto the verandah to greet them, his expression lighting with pleasure as he saw Moses, and he hurried to him and embraced him lovingly then, his arm still around Moses' waist, he turned to Hendrick.

'You will be Henny. We have spoken about you often.'

'I have met you before, Dr Archer, at the induction centre.'

'That was so long ago.' Marcus Archer shook his hand. 'And you must call me Marcus. You are a member of our family.' He glanced at Moses and his adoration was apparent. He reminded Hendrick of a young wife all agog with her new husband's virility.

Hendrick knew that Moses lived here at Rivonia Farm with Marcus and he felt no revulsion for the relationship. He understood how vitally important Marcus Archer's counsel and assistance had been in their successes over the years and approved the price that Moses paid for them. Hendrick himself had used men in the same fashion, never as a loving relationship but as a form of torture of a captured enemy. In his view there was no greater humiliation and degradation that one man could inflict upon another, yet he knew that in his brother's position he would not hesitate to use this strange red-haired little white man as he desired to be used.

'Moses has been very naughty in not bringing you to visit us sooner.' Marcus slapped Moses' arm playfully. 'There are so many interesting and important people here who you should have met ages ago. Come along now, let me introduce you.' He took Hendrick's arm and led him through to the kitchen.

It was a traditional farmhouse kitchen with stone-flagged floor, a black woodburning stove at the far end and bunches of onions, cured hams and polonies hanging from the hooks in the beams of the ceiling.

Eleven men were seated at the long yellow-wood table. Five of them were white, but the rest were black men, and their ages varied from callow youth to grey-haired sage. Marcus led Hendrick slowly down both sides of the table, introducing him to each in turn, beginning with the man at the head of the table.

'This is the Reverend John Dube, but you will have heard him called *Mafukuzela*,' and Hendrick felt an unaccustomed wave of awe.

'*Hau*, Baba!' he greeted the handsome old Zulu with vast respect. He knew that he was the political leader of the Zulu nation, that he was also the editor and founder of the *Ilanga Lase Natal* newspaper, *The Sun of Natal* – but most importantly that he was president of the African National Congress, the only political organization that attempted to speak for all the black nations of the southern African continent.

'I know of you,' Dube told Hendrick quietly. 'You have done valuable work with the new trade union. You are welcome, my son.'

After John Dube, the other men in the room were of small interest to Hendrick, though there was one young black man who could not have been more than twenty years of age but who nevertheless impressed Hendrick with his dignity and powerful presence.

'This is our young lawyer—'

'Not yet! Not yet!' the young man protested.

'Our soon-to-be-lawyer,' Marcus Archer corrected himself. 'He is Nelson Mandela, son of Chief Henry Mandela from the Transkei.' And as they shook hands in the white men's fashion that for Hendrick still felt awkward, he looked into the law student's eyes and thought: 'This is a young lion.'

The white men at the table made small impression on Hendrick. There were lawyers and a journalist, and a man who wrote books and poetry of which Hendrick had never heard, but the others treated his opinions with respect.

The only thing that Hendrick found remarkable about these white men was the courtesy which they accorded him. In a society in which a white man seldom acknowledged the existence of a black except to deliver an order, usually in brusque terms, it was unusual to encounter such concern and condescension. They shook Hendrick's hand without embarrassment, which was in itself strange, and made room for him at the table, poured wine for him from the same bottle and passed food to him on the same plate from which they had served themselves; and when they talked to him it was as an equal and they called him 'comrade' and 'brother'.

It seemed that Marcus Archer was a chef of repute, and he fussed over the woodburning stove producing dishes of food so minced and mixed and decorated and swimming in sauce that Hendrick could not tell either by inspection or taste whether they were fish or fowl or four-footed beast, but the others exclaimed and applauded and feasted voraciously.

Moses had advised Hendrick to keep his mouth filled with food rather than words, and to speak only when directly addressed and then in monosyllables, yet the others kept glancing at him with awe for he was an impressive figure in their midst: his head huge and heavy as a cannonball, the shining cicatrice lumped on his shaven pate and his gaze brooding and menacing.

The talk interested Hendrick very little but he feigned glowering attention as the others excitedly discussed the situation in Spain. The Popular Front Government, a coalition of Trotskyites, Socialists, left-wing Republicans and Communists, were threatened by an army mutiny under General Francisco Franco, and the company at Marcus Archer's luncheon table were filled with joyous outrage at this Fascist treachery. It seemed likely that it would plunge the Spanish nation into civil war and they all knew that only in the furnace of war could resolution be forged.

Two of the white men at the table, the poet and the journalist, declared their intention of leaving for Spain as soon as possible to join the struggle, and the other white men made no effort to disguise their envious admiration.

'You lucky devils. I would have gone like a shot but the Party wants me to remain here.'

There were many references to 'the Party' during the

course of that long Sunday afternoon, and gradually the company turned its concerted attention on Hendrick as though it had been prearranged. Hendrick was relieved that Moses had insisted he read parts of *Das Kapital* and some of Lenin's works, in particular *What is to be Done?* and *On Dual Authority*. It was true that Hendrick had found them difficult to the point of pain and had followed them only imperfectly. However, Moses had gutted these works for him and presented him with the essentials of Marx's and Lenin's thoughts.

Now they were taking it in turns to talk directly at Hendrick, and he realized that he was being subjected to some sort of test. He glanced at Moses, and although his brother's expression did not change, he sensed that he was willing him consciously to a course of action. Was he trying to warn Hendrick to remain silent? He was not certain, but at that moment Marcus Archer said clearly:

'Of course, the formation of a trade union amongst the black mine workers is in itself sufficient to assure the eventual triumph of the revolution—' But his inflection posed a question, and he was watching Hendrick slyly, and Hendrick was not certain from where inspiration came.

'I do not agree,' he growled, and they were all silent, waiting expectantly. 'The history of the struggle bears witness that the workers unassisted will rise only as far as the idea of trade unionism, to combine their resources to fight the employers and the capitalist government. But it needs professional revolutionaries bound by complete loyalty to their ideals and by military-type discipline to carry the struggle to its ultimate victorious conclusion.'

It was almost a verbatim quotation from Lenin's *What is to be Done?* and Hendrick had spoken in English. Even Moses looked amazed by his achievement, while the others exchanged delighted smiles as Hendrick glowered around him and relapsed back into impressive monumental silence.

It was sufficient. He did not have to speak again. By

nightfall, when the others traipsed out into the darkness calling farewells and thanks, climbed into their motor cars with slamming doors and roars of starting engines and drove away down the dusty track, Moses had achieved what he had aimed for in bringing his brother out to Rivonia Farm.

Hendrick had been sworn in as a full member of both the South African Communist Party and of the African National Congress.

Marcus Archer had set the guest bedroom aside for Hendrick. He lay in the narrow truckle bed listening to Moses and Marcus rutting in the main bedroom across the passage, and he was abruptly seized with the conviction that today the seeds of his destiny had been sown: that both the outer limits of his fortune and the time and manner of his own death had been determined in these last few hours. As he fell asleep, he was carried into the darkness on a wave of exultation and of dread.

Moses woke him while it was still dark and Marcus walked out to the Ford with them. The veld was white with frost; it crunched under their feet and had crusted on the windshield of the Ford.

Marcus shook hands with Hendrick. 'Forward, Comrade,' he said. 'The future belongs to us.' They left him standing in the frosty dark, staring after them.

Moses did not drive directly back into the city. Instead he parked the Ford below one of the high flat-topped mine dumps and he and Hendrick climbed the eroded dump side, five hundred feet almost sheer, and reached the top just as the rising sun cleared the horizon and turned the winter veld to pale gold.

'Now do you understand?' Moses asked as they stood shoulder to shoulder on the brink of the precipitous hillside, and suddenly like the sunrise itself Hendrick saw his brother's whole tremendous design.

'You want not a part of it,' he said softly, 'not even the greater part.' He spread his arms in a wide gesture that encompassed all below them from horizon to horizon. 'You want it all. The whole land and everything in it.' And his voice was filled with wonder at the enormity of the vision.

Moses smiled. His brother had at last understood.

They climbed down the mine dump and went in silence to where the Ford was parked. In silence they drove towards Drake's Farm, for there were no words to describe what had happened, as there are no words adequately to describe birth or death. Only as they left the city limits and were forced to stop at one of the level crossings where the railway that served the mine properties crossed the main road, did the mundane world intrude once again.

A ragged black urchin, shivering in the frosty winter high-veld morning, ran to the side window of the Ford and waved a folded newspaper at Moses through the glass. He rolled down the window, flipped the child a copper coin and placed the newspaper on the seat between them.

Hendrick frowned with interest and unfolded the news-sheet, holding it so they could both see the front page. The headlines were full column:

SOUTH AFRICAN TEAM CHOSEN FOR
BERLIN OLYMPIC GAMES
THE NATION WISHES THEM GOOD LUCK

'I know that white boy,' Hendrick exclaimed, grinning gap-toothed as he recognized one of the photographs that accompanied the text.

'So do I,' Moses agreed, but they were looking at different young white faces in the long rows of individual pictures.

Of course, Manfred knew that Uncle Tromp kept the most extraordinary hours. Whenever Manfred's bladder woke him in the small dark hours and he dragged himself out of the toolshed and stumbled down the path to the outhouse against the moroto hedge he would look up and through sleep-blurred eyes see the lamplight burning in the window of Uncle Tromp's study.

Once, more wide awake than usual, Manfred left the path and crept through Aunt Trudi's cabbages to peer in over the sill. Uncle Tromp sat like a shaggy bear at his desk, his beard rumpled from constant tugging and combing with his thick fingers, wire-framed spectacles perched upon his great beak of a nose, muttering furiously to himself as he scribbled on the loose sheets of paper that were tumbled over the desktop like debris after a hurricane. Manfred had assumed he was working on one of his sermons, but had not thought it strange that his labours had continued night after night for almost two years.

Then one morning the coloured postman wheeled his bicycle up the dusty road, burdened by an enormous package wrapped in brown paper and blazoned with stamps and stickers and red sealing-wax. Aunt Trudi placed the mysterious package on the small hall table, and all the children found excuses to creep into the hall and stare at it in awe, until at five o'clock Uncle Tromp drove up in his pony trap and the girls, led by Sarah, ran shrilling to meet him before he could dismount.

'There is a parcel for you, Papa.'

They crowded up behind him while Uncle Tromp made a show of examining the package and reading the label aloud. Then he took the pearl-handled penknife from the pocket of his waistcoat, deliberately tested the edge of the blade with his thumb, cut the strings binding the packet and carefully unwrapped the brown paper.

'Books!' sighed Sarah, and the girls all drooped with palpable disappointment and drifted away. Only Manfred lingered.

There were six thick copies of the same book, all identical, bound in red boards, the titles printed in fake gold leaf but still crisp and shining from the presses. And something in Uncle Tromp's manner and in the intent expression with which he watched Manfred as he waited for his reaction, alerted him to the unusual significance of this pile of books.

Manfred read the title of the top copy and found it long and awkward: *The Afrikaner: His Place in History and Africa.*

It was written in Afrikaans, the infant language still striving for recognition. Manfred found that unusual – all important scholarly works, even when written by Afrikaners, were in Dutch. He was about to remark upon this when his eyes moved down to the name of the author – and he started and gasped.

'Uncle Tromp!'

The old man chuckled with modest gratification.

'You wrote it!' Manfred's face lit with pride. 'You wrote a book.'

'*Ja, Jong* – even an old dog can learn new tricks.' Uncle Tromp swept up the pile in his arms and strode into his study. He placed the books in the centre of his desk and then looked around with astonishment to see that Manfred had followed him into the room.

'I'm sorry, Uncle Tromp.' Manfred realized his trespass.

He had been in this room only once before in his life, and then only by special invitation. 'I didn't ask. May I come in, please, *Oom*?'

'Looks like you are in already.' Uncle Tromp tried to look stern. 'You might as well stay then.'

Manfred sidled up to the desk with his hands behind his back. In this house he had learned immense respect for the written word. He had been taught that books were the most precious of all men's treasures, the receptacles of his God-given genius.

'May I touch one of them?' he asked, and when Uncle Tromp nodded, he gingerly reached out and traced the author's name with his fingertip: 'The Reverend Tromp Bierman'.

Then he picked up the top copy, expecting at any moment the old man to bellow angrily at him. When it did not happen, he opened the book and stared at the small murky print on cheap spongy yellow paper.

'May I read it, please, Uncle Tromp?' he found himself begging, again expecting denial. But Uncle Tromp's expression turned softly bemused.

'You want to read it?' He blinked with mild surprise, and then chuckled. 'Well, I suppose that's why I wrote it – for people to read.'

Suddenly he grinned like a mischievous small boy and snatched the book from Manfred's hand. He sat down at his desk, placed his spectacles on his nose, dipped his pen and scribbled on the flyleaf of the open book, re-read what he had written and then handed it to Manfred with a flourish:

'To Manfred De La Rey,
A young Afrikaner who will help make our people's place in history and Africa secure for all time.
                                        Your affectionate
                                        Uncle Tromp Bierman.'

Clutching the book to his chest, Manfred backed away to the door as though he feared it would be snatched from him again. 'Is it mine – is it truly for me?' he whispered.

And when Uncle Tromp nodded, 'Yes, *Jong*, it's yours,' he turned and fled from the room, forgetting in his haste to voice his thanks.

Manfred read the book in three successive nights, sitting up until long after midnight with a blanket over his shoulders, squinting in the flickering candlelight. It was five hundred pages of close print, larded with quotation from holy scripture, but it was written in strong simple language, not weighed down with adjectives or excessive description and it sang directly to Manfred's heart. He finished it bursting with pride for the courage and fortitude and piety of his people, and burning with anger for the cruel manner in which they had been persecuted and dispossessed by their enemies. He sat with the closed book in his lap, staring into the wavering shadows, living in full detail the wanderings and suffering of his young nation, sharing the agony at the barricades when the black heathen hordes poured down upon them with war plumes tossing and the silver steel of the assegais drumming on rawhide shields like the surf of a gale-driven sea, sharing the wonder of voyaging out over the grassy ocean of the high continent into a beautiful wilderness unspoiled and unpeopled to take it as their own, finally sharing the bitter torment as the free land was wrested from them again by arrogant foreigners in their warlike legions and the final outrage of slavery, political and economic, was thrust upon them in their own land – the land that their fathers had won and in which they had been born.

As though the lad's rage had reached out and summoned him, Uncle Tromp came down the pathway, his footsteps crunching on the gravel, and stooped into the shed. He paused in the doorway, his eyes adjusting to the candlelight, and then he crossed to where Manfred crouched on the bed. The mattress sagged and squeaked as he lowered his bulk upon it.

They sat in silence for a full five minutes before Uncle Tromp asked, 'So, you managed to finish it then?'

Manfred had to shake himself back to the present. 'I think it is the most important book ever written,' he whispered. 'Just as important as the Bible.'

'That is blasphemy, *Jong*.' Uncle Tromp tried to look stern, but his gratification softened the line of his mouth and Manfred did not apologize.

Instead he went on eagerly, 'For the first time ever I know who I am – and why I am here.'

'Then my efforts have not been wasted,' Uncle Tromp murmured and they were silent again until the old man sighed. 'Writing a book is a lonely thing,' he mused. 'Like crying with all your heart into the night when there is nobody out there in the darkness, nobody to hear your cry, nobody to answer you.'

'I heard you, Uncle Tromp.'

'*Ja, Jong*, so you did – but only you.'

However, Uncle Tromp was wrong. There were other listeners out there in the darkness.

The arrival of a stranger in the village was an event; the arrival of three strangers together was without parallel or precedent and raised a storm of gossip and speculation that had the entire population in a fever of curiosity.

The strangers arrived from the south on the weekly mail train. Taciturn and granite-faced, dressed in severe dark broadcloth and carrying their own carpet bags, they crossed the road from the railway siding to the tiny iron-roofed boarding house run by the widow Vorster and were not seen again until Sunday morning when they emerged to stride down the rutted sidewalk, shoulder to shoulder, grim and devout, wearing the white neckties and black suits of deacons of the Dutch Reformed Church and carrying their black leatherbound prayer books under their right arms like sabres, ready to unsheath and wield upon Satan and all his works.

They stalked down the aisle and took the front pew beneath the pulpit as if by right, and the families who had sat on those benches for generations made no demur but quietly found places for themselves at the rear of the nave.

Rumours of the presence of the strangers – they had already been dubbed 'the three wise men' – had permeated to the remotest surrounding districts and even those who had not been inside the church in years, drawn by curiosity, now packed all the pews and even stood against the walls. It was a better turnout even than last Dingaan's Day, the Day of the Covenant with God in thanksgiving for victory over the Zulu hordes and one of the most sacred occasions in the calendar of the Reformed Church.

The singing was impressive. Manfred stood beside Sarah and was so touched by the crystalline beauty of her sweet contralto that he was inspired to underscore it with his untrained but ringing tenor. Even under the deep hood of her traditional Voortrekker bonnet Sarah looked like an angel, golden blonde and lovely, her features shining with religious ecstasy. At fourteen years her womanhood was just breaking into tender uncertain bloom so that Manfred felt a strange breathlessness when he glanced at her over the hymn book they were sharing and she looked up and smiled at him with so much trust and adoration.

The hymn ended and the congregation settled down through a scraping of feet and muted coughing into a tense expectant silence. Uncle Tromp's sermons were renowned throughout South-West Africa, the best entertainment in the territory after the new moving-picture house in Windhoek which very few of them had dared to enter, and

Uncle Tromp was in high fettle this day, provoked by the three sober-faced inscrutable gentlemen in the front row who had not even had the common decency to make a courtesy call at the pastory since arriving. He leaned his great gnarled fists on the rail of the pulpit and hunched over them like a prizefighter taking his guard, then he glanced down on his congregation with outraged contempt and they quailed before him with tremulous delight, knowing exactly what that expression presaged.

'Sinners!' Uncle Tromp let fly with a bellow that rang against the roof timbers and the three dark-suited strangers jumped in their seats as though a cannon had been fired under them. 'The House of God is filled with unrepentant sinners—' and Uncle Tromp was away; he flailed them with dreadful accusations, raking them with that special tone which Manfred thought of privately as 'the voice' and then lulling them with gentle sonorous passages and promises of salvation before again hurling threats of brimstone and damnation at them like fiery spears, until some of the women were weeping openly and there were hoarse spontaneous cries of 'Amen' and 'Praise the Lord' and 'Hallelujah' and in the end they went down trembling on their knees as he prayed for their very souls.

Afterwards they streamed out of the church with a sort of nervous relief, garrulous and gay as though they had just survived some deadly natural phenomenon such as earthquake or gale at sea. The three strangers were the last to leave, and at the door where Uncle Tromp waited to greet them they shook his hand and each of them spoke quietly and seriously to him in their turn.

Uncle Tromp listened to them gravely, then turned to consult briefly with Aunt Trudi before turning back to them.

'I would be honoured if you would enter my home and sit at my board.'

The four men paced in dignified procession up to the pastory, Aunt Trudi and the children following at a respectful distance. She muttered terse instructions to the girls as they walked and the minute they were out of public view they scampered away to open the drapes in the dining-room, which was only used on very special occasions, and to move the dinner setting from the kitchen to the heavy stinkwood dining-table that was Trudi's inheritance from her mother.

The three strangers did not allow their deep erudite discussion to interfere with their appreciation of Aunt Trudi's cooking, and at the bottom of the table the children ate in dutiful but goggle-eyed silence. Afterwards the men drank their coffee and smoked a pipe on the front stoep, the drone of their voices soporific in the midday heat, and then it was time to return to divine worship.

The text that Uncle Tromp had chosen for his second sermon was 'The Lord has made straight a path for you in the wilderness'. He delivered it with all his formidable rhetoric and power, but this time he included passages from his own book, assuring his congregation that the Lord had chosen them particularly as a people and set aside a place for them. It remained only for them to reclaim that place in this land that was their heritage. More than once Manfred saw the three grim-faced strangers sitting in the front pew glance at one another significantly as Uncle Tromp was speaking.

The strangers left on the southbound mail train on Monday morning, and for the days and weeks that followed a brittle sense of expectancy pervaded the pastory. Uncle Tromp, breaking his usual custom, took to waiting at the front gate to greet the postman each morning. Quickly he would peruse the packet of mail, and each day his disappointment became more obvious.

Three weeks passed before he gave up waiting for the

postman. So he was in the toolshed with Manfred, drilling the Fitzsimmons shift into him, honing that savage left hand of Manfred's, when the letter finally arrived.

It was lying on the hall table when Uncle Tromp went up to the house to wash for supper, and Manfred, who had walked up with him, saw him blanch when he observed the seal of the high moderator of the church on the flap of the envelope. He snatched up the envelope and hurried into his study, slamming the door in Manfred's face. The lock turned with a heavy clunk. Aunt Trudi had to wait supper almost twenty minutes before he emerged again, and his grace, full of praise and thanksgiving, was twice its usual length. Sarah rolled her eyes and squinted comically across the table at Manfred, and he cautioned her with a quick frown. At last Uncle Tromp roared 'Amen'. Yet he still did not take up his soupspoon but beamed down the length of the table at Aunt Trudi.

'My dear wife,' he said. 'You have been patient and uncomplaining all these years.'

Aunt Trudi blushed scarlet. 'Not in front of the children, Meneer,' she whispered, but Uncle Tromp's smile grew broader still.

'They have given me Stellenbosch,' he told her, and the silence was complete. They stared at him incredulously. Every one of them understood what he was saying.

'Stellenbosch,' Uncle Tromp repeated, mouthing the word, rolling it over his tongue, gargling it in his throat as though it were the first taste of a rare and noble wine.

Stellenbosch was a small country town thirty miles from Cape Town. The buildings were gabled in the Dutch style, thatched and whitewashed, as dazzling as snow. The streets were broad and lined with the fine oaks that Governor Van Stel had ordered his burghers to plant back in the seventeenth century. Around the town the vineyards of the great châteaux were laid out in a marvellous patchwork and the dark precipices of the mountains rose in a heaven-high backdrop beyond.

A small country town, pretty and picturesque, but it was also the very citadel of Afrikanerdom, enshrined in the university whose faculties were grouped beneath the green oaks and the protecting mountain barricades. It was the centre of Afrikaner intellectualism. Here their language had been forged and was still being crafted. Here their theologians pondered and debated. Tromp Bierman himself had studied beneath Stellenbosch's dreaming oaks. All the great men had trained here: Louis Botha, Hertzog, Jan Christian Smuts. No one who was not Stellenbosch had ever headed the government of the Union of South Africa. Very few who were not Stellenbosch men had even served in the cabinet. It was the Oxford and Cambridge of southern Africa, and they had given the parish to Tromp Bierman. It was an honour unsurpassed, and now the doors would open before him. He would sit at the centre; he would wield power, and the promise of greater power; he would become one of the movers, the innovators. Everything now became possible: the Council of the Synod, the moderatorship itself; none of these were beyond his grasp. There were no limits now, no borders nor boundaries. Everything was possible.

'It was the book,' Aunt Trudi breathed. 'I never thought. I never understood—'

'Yes, it was the book,' Uncle Tromp chuckled. 'And thirty years of hard work. We will have the big manse on Eikeboom Straat and a thousand a year. Each of the children will have a separate room and a place at the university paid for by the church. I will preach to the mighty men of the land and our brightest young minds. I will be on the University Council. And you, my dear wife, will have professors and ministers of government at your table; their wives will be your companions—' he broke off

541

guiltily, 'and now we will all pray. We will ask God for humility; we will ask him to save us from the mortal sins of pride and avarice. Down everybody!' he roared. 'Down on your knees.'

The soup was cold before he allowed them up again.

They left two months later, after Uncle Tromp had handed over his duties to the young dominie fresh from the theology faculty of the university where the old man was now taking them.

It seemed that every man and woman and child from within a hundred miles was at the station to see them off. Manfred had not realized until that moment just how high was the affection and esteem in which the community held Uncle Tromp. The men all wore their church suits and each of them shook his hand, gruffly thanked him and wished him Godspeed. Some of the women wept and all of them brought gifts – they had baskets of jams and preserves, of milk tarts and *koeksisters*, bags of kudu biltong – and enough food to feed an army on the journey southwards.

Four days later the family changed trains at the central Cape Town railway station. There was barely time for them to troop out into Adderley Street and gape up at the legendary flat-topped massif of Table Mountain that towered over the city before they had to rush back and clamber aboard the coach for the much shorter leg of the journey across the Cape flats and through the sprawling vineyards towards the mountains.

The deacons of the church and half the congregation were on the platform at Stellenbosch station to welcome them, and the family discovered very swiftly that the pace of all their lives had changed dramatically.

From almost the first day, Manfred was totally immersed in preparations for the entrance examinations of the university. He studied from early morning until late every night for two months and then sat the examinations over a single painful week and lived through an even more painful week waiting for the results to be posted. He passed first in German language, third in mathematics and eighth overall, the habits of study he had learned over the years in the Bierman household now bearing full fruit, and was accepted into the faculty of law for the semester beginning at the end of January.

Aunt Trudi was strongly opposed to his leaving the manse and entering one of the university residences for men. As she pointed out, he had a fine room to himself now; the girls would miss him to the point of distraction – by implication she was included amongst those who would suffer – and even on Uncle Tromp's now princely stipend, the residence fees would be a burden on the family exchequer.

Uncle Tromp called upon the university registrar and made some financial arrangements which were never discussed in the family and then came down strongly on Manfred's side.

'Living in a house full of women will drive the boy mad in time. He should go where he can benefit from the company of other young men and from the full life of the university.'

So, on 25 January, Manfred eagerly presented himself at the imposing Cape Dutch style residence for gentlemen students, Rust en Vrede. The name translated as 'Rest and Peace', and within the first few minutes of arrival he realized just how ironic was the choice for he was caught up in the barbaric ritual of freshman initiation.

His name was taken from him and he was given instead the sobriquet of *Poep*; which he shared with the nineteen other freshmen of the house. This translated freely as 'flatus'. He was forbidden to use the pronouns 'I' or 'me' but only 'this flatus', and he had to request permission not only

543

of the senior men for every action but also of all inanimate objects he encountered in the residence. Thus he was obliged to utter endless inanities: 'Honourable door, this flatus wishes to pass through,' or 'Honourable toilet, this flatus wishes to sit upon you.'

Within the residence he and his fellow freshmen were not allowed normal means of perambulation but were made to walk backwards, even down stairs, at all times. They were held incommunicado from friends and family and in particular were most strenuously forbidden to talk to anybody of the opposite sex; if they were caught so much as looking in the general direction of a pretty girl a warning notice was hung around their necks and could not be removed even in the bath. 'Beware! Sex maniac at large.'

Their rooms were raided by the seniors every hour, on the hour, from six in the evening until six in the morning. All their bedding was piled in the middle of the floor and soaked with water, their books and possessions were swept from the shelves and turned out of the drawers and piled on the sodden blankets. The senior men performed this duty in shifts until the shivering freshmen took to sleeping on the bare tiles of the passage outside their bedrooms, leaving the chaos within to mould and fester. Whereupon the senior student, a lordly fourth-year honours man named Roelf Stander, held a formal house committee inspection of the rooms.

'You are the most disgusting cloud of flatus ever to disgrace this university,' he told them at the end of the inspection. 'You have one hour in which to make your rooms spotless and put them in perfect order, after which you will be taken on a route march as punishment for your slovenly attitude.'

It was midnight when Roelf Stander finally announced that he was satisfied with the condition of their bedrooms and they were prepared for the route march.

This involved stripping them to their underpants, placing a pillow case over their heads, tying them in Indian file with a rope around their necks and their hands strapped behind their backs and marching them through the streets of the sleeping town and out into the mountains. The chosen route was rough and stony and when one of them fell he brought down the freshmen in front and behind. At four in the morning they were led back into town on bleeding feet and with their throats chafed raw from the coarse hemp rope to find their rooms had been raided once again and that Roelf Stander's next inspection would take place at five o'clock. The first lecture of the university day began at seven. There was no time for breakfast.

All this came under the heading of good clean fun; the university authorities turned a blind eye upon the rites on the grounds that boys will be boys and that the initiation ritual was a 'university tradition', instilling a community spirit into the new arrivals.

However, in this climate of indulgence the bullies and sadists who lurk in any community took full advantage of the sanction accorded them. There were a few merciless beatings, and one freshman was tarred and feathered. Manfred had heard light talk of this punishment, but had not been able to imagine the dreadful agony that it inflicted when the victim's skin was sealed and his scalp and body hair matted and coated with hot tar. The boy was hospitalized and never returned to the university, but the affair was hushed up completely.

Other freshmen dropped out in those first weeks, for the self-appointed guardians of the university tradition made no allowance for delicate physical or mental constitutions. One of the victims, an asthmatic, was judged guilty of insubordination by the seniors and was sentenced to formal drowning.

This sentence was carried out in the bathroom of the residence. The victim was pinioned by four hefty seniors and lowered head first into the toilet bowl of the lavatory.

Two fifth-year medical students were present to monitor the victim's pulse and heartbeat during the punishment, but they had not made allowance for his asthma, and the drowning almost ended as the real thing. Only frantic efforts by the budding doctors and an intravenous injection of stimulant started the boy's heart beating again; he left the university next day, like the other dropouts, never to return.

Manfred, despite his size and physique and good looks, which made him a natural target, was able to bridle his anger and check his tongue. He submitted stoically even to extreme provocation until in the second week of torment a note was pinned on the board in the residence common room:

> All flatus will report to the university
> gymnasium at 4 pm on Saturday to try out
> for the boxing squad.
> Signed: Roelf Stander
> Captain of Boxing

Each of the university residences specialized in some particular sport: one was the rugby football house, another was field and track; but Rust en Vrede's sport was boxing. This, together with the fact that it was Uncle Tromp's old house, was the reason why Manfred had applied for admission in the first place.

It was also the reason why the interest in the freshmen tryout was far beyond anything that Manfred had expected. At least three hundred spectators were assembled, and the seats around the ring were all filled by the time that Manfred and his fellow flatus arrived at the gymnasium. Marshalled by one of the senior men into a crocodile column, they were marched to the changing-rooms and given five minutes to change into tennis shoes, shorts and vests, then lined up against the lockers in order of height.

Roelf Stander strolled down the rank, glancing at the list in his hand and making the matchings. It was obvious that he had been studying them during the preceding weeks and grading their potential. Manfred, the tallest and sturdiest of all the freshmen, was at the end of the line, and Roelf Stander stopped in front of him last.

'There is no other fart as loud and smelly as this one,' he announced, and then was silent for a moment as he studied Manfred. 'What do you weigh, Flatus?'

'This flatus is light heavyweight, sir,' and Roelf's eyes narrowed slightly. He had already singled Manfred out as the best prospect and now the technical jargon heartened him.

'Have you boxed before, Flatus?' he demanded, and then pulled a wry face at the disappointing reply.

'This flatus has never boxed a match, sir, but this flatus has had some practice.'

'Oh, all right, then! I am heavyweight. But as there is no one else to give you a match, I'll go a few rounds with you, if you promise to treat me lightly, Flatus.'

Roelf Stander was captain of the university squad, amateur provincial champion and one of South Africa's better prospects for the team which would go to Berlin for the Olympic Games in 1936. It was a rich joke cracked by a senior student and everybody laughed slavishly. Even Roelf could not hide a grin at his own preposterous plea for mercy.

'All right, we'll begin with the flyweights,' he continued, and led them out into the gymnasium.

The freshmen were seated on a long bench at the back of the hall with an imperfect view of the ring over the heads of the more privileged spectators as Roelf and his assistants, all members of the boxing squad, put the gloves on the first trialists and led them down the aisle to the ring.

While this was going on Manfred became aware of somebody in the front row of seats standing and trying to catch his eye. He glanced around at the senior men who were in charge of them, but their attention was on the ring so for the first time he looked directly at the person in the crowd.

He had forgotten how pretty Sarah was, either that or she had blossomed in the weeks since he had last seen her. Her eyes sparkled and her cheeks were flushed with excitement as she waved a lace handkerchief and mouthed his name happily.

He kept his expression inscrutable, but lowered one eyelid at her in a furtive wink and she blew him a two-handed kiss and dropped back into her seat beside the mountainous bulk of Uncle Tromp.

'They have both come!' The knowledge cheered him enormously; until that moment he had not realized how lonely these last weeks had been. Uncle Tromp turned his head and grinned at him, his teeth very white in the frosted black bush of his beard; then he turned back to face the ring.

The first bout began: two game little flyweights going at each other in a flurry of blows, but one was outclassed and soon there was blood sprinkling the canvas. Roelf Stander stopped it in the second round and patted the loser on the back.

'Well done! No shame in losing.'

The other bouts followed, all of them spirited, the fighters obviously doing their very best, but apart from a promising middleweight, it was all very rough and unskilled. At last Manfred was the only one on the bench.

'All right, Flatus!' The senior laced his gloves and told him: 'Let's see what you can do.'

Manfred slipped the towel off his shoulders and stood up just as Roelf Stander climbed back into the ring from the changing-room end. He now wore the maroon vest and trunks piped with gold that were Varsity colours, and on his feet were expensive boots of glove leather laced high over the ankles. He held up both gloved hands to quieten the whistles and good-natured cheers.

'Ladies and Gentlemen. We do not have a match for our last trialist; no other freshman in his weight division. So if you will be kind enough to bear with me, I'm going to take him through his paces.'

The cheers broke out again, but now there were shouts of 'Go easy on him, Roelf,' and 'Don't kill the poor beggar!' Roelf waved his assurance of mercy at them, concentrating on the section of seats filled with girls from the women's residences, and there were muted squeals and giggles and a tossing of permanently waved coiffures, for Roelf stood six feet, with a square jaw, white teeth and flashing dark eyes. His hair was thick and wavy and gleaming with Brylcreem, his sideburns dense and curling and his moustache dashing as a cavalier's.

As Manfred reached the front row of seats he could not restrain himself from glancing sideways at Sarah and Uncle Tromp. Sarah was hopping her bottom up and down on her seat, and she pressed her clenched fists to cheeks that were rosy with excitement.

'Get him, Manie,' she cried. '*Vat hom!*' and beside her Uncle Tromp nodded at him. 'Fast as a mamba, *Jong!* Brave as a ratel!' he rumbled so that only Manfred could hear; and Manfred lifted his chin and there was a new lightness in his feet as he ducked through the ropes into the ring.

One of the other seniors had taken over the duty of referee: 'In this corner at one hundred and eighty-five pounds the captain of Varsity and amateur heavyweight champion of the Cape of Good Hope – Roelf Stander! And in this corner at one hundred and seventy-three pounds a freshman—' in deference to the delicate company, he did not use the full honorific, ' – Manfred De La Rey.' The timekeeper struck his gong and Roelf came out of his corner dancing lightly, ducking and weaving, smiling thinly over his red leather gloves as they circled each other. Just out of striking distance, around they went, and then back the other way, and the smile left Roelf's lips and they tightened into a straight thin line. His light manner evaporated; he had not expected this.

There was no weak place in the guard of the man who faced him; his cropped golden head was lowered on muscled shoulders, and he moved on his feet like a cloud.

'He's a fighter!' Roelf's anger flared. 'He lied – he knows what he's doing.' He tried once more to command the centre of the ring, but was forced to turn out again as his adversary moved threateningly into his left.

As yet neither of them had thrown a punch, but the cheers of the crowd subsided. They sensed that they were watching something extraordinary; they saw Roelf's casual attitude change, saw deadly intent come into the way he was moving now; and those who knew him well saw the little lines of worry and perturbation at the corners of his mouth and eyes.

Roelf flicked out his left, a testing shot, and the other man did not even deign to duck; he turned it off his glove contemptuously, and Roelf's skin prickled with shock as he sensed the power in that fleeting contact and looked deeply into Manfred's eyes. It was a trick of his, establishing domination by eye contact.

This man's eyes were a strange light colour, like topaz or yellow sapphire, and Roelf remembered the eyes of a calf-killing leopard that his father had caught in a steel spring trap in the hills above the farm homestead. These were the same eyes, and now they altered, they burned with a cold golden light, implacable and inhuman.

It was not fear that clenched Roelf Stander's chest but rather a premonition of terrible danger. This was an animal in the ring with him. He could see the hunger in its eyes, a great killing hunger, and he struck out at it instinctively.

He used his left, his good hand, driving in hard at those pitiless yellow eyes. The blow died in the air and he tried desperately to recover, but his left elbow was raised, his flank was open for perhaps a hundredth part of a second, and something exploded inside of him. He did not see the fist; he did not recognize it as a punch, for he had never been hit like that before. It felt as though it was inside him, bursting through his ribs, tearing out his viscera, imploding his lungs, driving the wind out of his throat in a hissing agony as he was flung backwards.

The ropes caught him in the small of the back and under the shoulderblades and hurled him forward again like a stone from a slingshot. Time seemed to slow down to a trickle; his vision was enhanced, magnified as though there was a drug in his blood, and this time he saw the fist; he had a weird flash of fantasy that it was not flesh and bone but black iron in that glove, and his flesh quailed. But he was powerless to avoid it and this time the shock was even greater – unbelievable, beyond his wildest imaginings. He felt something tear inside him and the bones of his legs melted like hot candlewax.

He wanted to scream at the agony of it, but even in his extremity he choked it off. He wanted to go down, to get down on the canvas before the fist came again, but the ropes held him up and his body seemed to shatter like crystal as the gloved hand crashed into him and the ropes flung him forward.

His hands dropped away from his face and he saw the fist coming yet again. It seemed to balloon before his eyes, filling his vision, but he did not feel it strike.

Roelf was moving into it with all his weight and his skull snapped back in whiplash against the tension of his spinal column and then dropped forward again and he went down on his face like a dead man and lay without a tremor of movement on the white canvas.

It was all over in seconds, the crowd sitting in stunned silence, Manfred still weaving and swaying over the prostrate figure that lay at his feet, his features contorted into a mask of savagery and that strange yellow light glowing in his eyes, not yet human, with the killing sickness still strong upon him.

Then in the crowd a woman screamed and instantly there was consternation and uproar. The men were up on their feet, chairs crashing over backwards, roaring in bewilderment and amazement and jubilation, rushing forward, clambering through the ropes, surrounding Manfred, pounding his back, others on their knees beside the maroon-and-gold-clad figure lying deathly still on the canvas, jabbering instructions at one another as they lifted him gingerly, one of them dabbing ineffectually at the blood; all of them stunned and shaken.

The women were pale-faced with shock, some of them still screaming with delicious horror, their eyes bright with excitement which was tinged with sexuality, craning to watch as Roelf Stander was lifted over the ropes and carried down the aisle, hanging limp as a corpse, his head lolling, blood running back from his slack mouth across his cheek into his gleaming hair – turning to watch Manfred as he was hustled along to the changing-rooms by a group of seniors. The women's faces betrayed fear and horror but some of their eyes smouldered with physical arousal, and one of them reached out to touch Manfred's shoulder as he passed.

Uncle Tromp took Sarah's arm to calm her, for she was capering and shrilling like a dervish, and led her out of the hall into the sunlight. She was still incoherent with excitement.

'He was wonderful – so quick, so beautiful. Oh, Uncle Tromp, I have never seen anything like that in my life. Isn't he wonderful?'

Uncle Tromp grunted but made no comment, listening to her chatter all the way back to the manse. Only when they climbed the front steps onto the wide stoep did he stop and look back, as though to a place or a person that he was leaving with deep regret.

'His life has changed, and ours will change with him,' he murmured soberly. 'I pray Almighty God that none of us ever lives to regret what happened to us this day, for I am the one who brought this about.'

For three more days the ritual of initiation continued, and Manfred was still denied contact with anybody but his fellow freshmen. However, to them he had become a godlike figure, their very hope of salvation, and they crowded to him pathetically through the final humiliations and degradation to take strength and determination from him.

The last night was the worst. Blindfolded and denied sleep, forced to sit unflinching on a narrow beam, a galvanized bucket over their heads against which a senior would crack a club unexpectedly, the night seemed to last for ever. Then in the dawn the buckets and blindfolds were removed and Roelf Stander addressed them.

'Men!' he started, and they blinked with shock at being called that, for they were still in a stupor from lack of sleep and half deafened by the blows on their buckets. 'Men!' Stander repeated. 'We are proud of you – you are the best damned bunch of freshers we've had in this house since I was a fresher myself. You took everything we could throw at you and never squealed or funked it. Welcome to Rust en Vrede; this is your house now, and we are your brothers.' And then the seniors were swarming around them, laughing and slapping their backs and embracing them.

'Come on, men! Down to the pub. We are buying the beer!' Roelf Stander bellowed and, a hundred strong, arms linked, singing the house song, they marched down to the old Drosdy Hotel and pounded on the locked door until the publican in defiance of licensing hours finally gave in and opened up for them.

Light-headed with sleeplessness and with a pint of lager in his belly, Manfred was grinning owlishly and hanging surreptitiously onto the bar counter to keep on his feet when he had a feeling that something was up. He turned quickly.

The crowd around him had opened, leaving a corridor down which Roelf Stander was stalking towards him, grim-faced and threatening. Manfred's pulse raced as he realized that this was to be their first confrontation since that in the ring three days before, and it was not going to be pleasant. He set down his empty tankard, shook his head to clear it and turned to face the other man, and they glowered at each other.

Roelf stopped in front of him, and the others, freshers and seniors, crowded close so as not to miss a single word. The suspense drew out for long seconds, nobody daring to breathe.

'Two things I want to do to you,' Roelf Stander growled, and then, as Manfred braced himself, he smiled, a flashing charming smile, and held out his right hand. 'First, I want to shake your hand, and second, I want to buy you a beer. By God, Manie, you punch like no man I've ever fought before.' There was a howl of laughter and the day dissolved into a haze of beer fumes and good fellowship.

That should have been the end of it, because even though formal initiation had ended and Manfred had been accepted into the Rust en Vrede fraternity, there was still a vast social divide between a fourth-year honours man, senior student and captain of boxing, and a freshman. However, the following evening, an hour before house dinner, there was a knock on Manie's door and Roelf sauntered in dressed in his academic gown and hood, dropped into the single armchair, crossed his ankles on top of Manie's desk and chatted easily about boxing and law studies and South-West Africa geography until the gong sounded, when he stood up.

'I'll wake you at five am tomorrow for roadwork. We've got an important match against the Ikeys in two weeks,' he announced, and then grinned at Manie's expression. 'Yes, Manie, you are on the squad.'

After that Roelf dropped in every evening before dinner, often with a black bottle of beer in the pocket of his gown which they shared out of tooth mugs, and each time their friendship became more relaxed and secure.

This was not lost on the other members of the house, both seniors and freshers, and Manie's status was enhanced. Two weeks later the match against the Ikey team was contested in four weight divisions and Manie donned the university colours for the first time. Ikeys was the nickname for the students at the University of Cape Town, the English-language university of the Cape and traditional rival of Stellenbosch, the Afrikaans-language university whose men were nicknamed Maties. So keen was the rivalry between them that Ikey supporters came out the thirty miles in busloads, dressed in their university colours, full of beer and rowdy enthusiasm, and packed out half the gymnasium, roaring their university songs at the Matie supporters on the other side of the hall.

Manie's opponent was Laurie King, an experienced light-heavy with good hands and a concrete jaw who had never been put down in forty amateur bouts. Almost nobody had ever heard of Manfred De La Rey, and those few who had now discounted his single victory as a lucky punch on an opponent who wasn't taking it seriously anyway.

Laurie King, however, had heard the story and he was taking it very seriously indeed. He kept off for most of the first round until the crowd started to boo with impatience. However, he had now studied Manfred and decided that, although he moved well, he wasn't as dangerous as he had been warned and that he could be taken with a left to the head. He went in to test this theory. The last thing he remembered was a pair of ferocious yellow eyes, burning like a Kalahari sun at midday into his face, and then the harsh canvas grazing the skin from his cheek as he slammed head first into the boards of the ring. He never remembered seeing the punch. Although the gong rang before he was counted out, Laurie King could not come out for the second round; his head was still rolling like a drunkard's. He had to be supported by his seconds back to the dressing-room.

In the front row Uncle Tromp roared like a wounded bull buffalo while beside him Sarah shrieked herself hoarse as tears of joy and excitement wet her lashes and shone upon her cheeks.

The next morning the boxing correspondent of the Afrikaans newspaper *Die Burger*, 'The Citizen', dubbed Manfred 'The Lion of the Kalahari' and mentioned that he was not only the great nephew of General Jacobus Hercules De La Rey, hero of the *Volk*, but also related to the Reverend Tromp Bierman, boxing champion, author, and the new dominie of Stellenbosch.

Roelf Stander and the entire boxing squad were waiting in the quadrangle when Manfred came out of his sociology lecture and they surrounded him.

'You've been holding out on us, Manie,' Roelf accused furiously. 'You never told us that your uncle is *the* Tromp Bierman. Sweet mercy, man, he was national champion for five years. He knocked out both Slater and Black Jephta!'

'Didn't I tell you?' Manie frowned thoughtfully. 'It must have slipped my mind.'

'Manie, you have to introduce us,' the vice-captain pleaded. 'We all want to meet him, please, man, please.'

'Do you think he would coach the team, Manie? Won't you ask him. Hell, if we had Tromp Bierman as coach—' Roelf broke off, awed into silence by the thought.

'I tell you what,' Manie suggested. 'If you can get the whole boxing team to church on Sunday morning, I'm sure that my Aunt Trudi will invite us all to Sunday lunch. I tell you, gentlemen, you don't know what heaven is until you have tasted my Aunt Trudi's *koek-sisters*.'

So scrubbed and shaven and Brylcreemed and buttoned into their Sunday-best suits, the university boxing squad took up a full pew of the church, and their responses and rendition of the hymns shook the roof timbers.

Aunt Trudi looked upon the occasion as a challenge to her culinary skills and she and the girls took all week to prepare the dinner. The guests, all lusty young men in peak physical condition, had existed on university fare for weeks, and they gazed in ravenous disbelief upon the banquet, trying valiantly to divide their attention between Uncle Tromp, who was in top form at the head of the long table recounting his most memorable fights, the tittering blushing daughters of the house who waited upon them and the groaning board piled with roasts and preserves and puddings.

At the end of the meal Roelf Stander, bloated like a python which had swallowed a gazelle, rose to make a speech of thanks on behalf of the team, and halfway through changed it into an impassioned plea to Uncle Tromp to accept the duties of honorary coach.

Uncle Tromp waved away the request with a jovial chortle as though it were totally unthinkable, but the entire team, including Manie, added their entreaties, whereupon he made a series of excuses, each one lamer than the preceding one, all of which were vociferously rebutted by the team in unison, until finally, with a heavy sigh of resignation and forbearance, he capitulated. Then while accepting their fervent gratitude and hearty handshakes, he at last broke down and beamed with unrestrained pleasure.

'I tell you, boys, you don't know what you've let yourselves in for. There are many words I don't understand at all. "I'm tired" and "I've had enough" are just some of them,' he warned.

After the evening service, Manie and Roelf walked back under the dark rustling oaks to Rust en Vrede and Roelf was uncharacteristically silent, not speaking until they had reached the main gates. Then his tone was reflective:

'Tell me, Manie, your cousin – how old is she?'

'Which one?' Manie asked without interest. 'The fat one is Gertrude and the one with pimples is Renata—'

'No! No, Manie, don't be a dog!' Roelf cut him short. 'The pretty one with blue eyes, the one with the silky gold hair. The one I'm going to marry.'

Manfred stopped dead and swung to face him, his head going down on his shoulders, his mouth twisting into a snarl.

'Never say that again!' His voice shook and he seized the front of Roelf's jacket. 'Don't ever talk dirty like that again. I warn you, you talk about Sarah like that again, and I'll kill you.'

Manfred's face was only inches from Roelf's. That terrible yellow glow, the killing rage, was in his eyes.

'Hey, Manie,' Roelf whispered hoarsely. 'What's wrong with you? I didn't say anything dirty. Are you mad? I would never insult Sarah.'

The yellow rage faded slowly from Manfred's eyes and he released his grip on Roelf's lapels. He shook his head as if to clear it, and his voice was bemused when he spoke again. 'She's only a baby. You shouldn't talk like that, man. She's only a little girl.'

'A baby?' Roelf chuckled uncertainly and straightened his jacket. 'Are you blind, Manie. She's not a baby. She is the most lovely—' but Manfred flung away angrily and went storming through the gates into the house.

'So, my friend,' Roelf whispered, 'that's how it is!' He sighed and thrust his hands deeply into his pockets. And then he remembered how Sarah had looked at Manfred during the meal and how he had seen her lay her hand on the back of his neck, furtively and adoringly, as she leaned over him to take his empty plate, and he sighed again, overcome suddenly with a brooding sense of melancholy. 'There are a thousand pretty girls out there,' he told himself with an attempt to throw off the dark mood. 'All of them panting for Roelf Stander—' and he shrugged and grinned lopsidedly and followed Manie into the house.

Manfred won his next twelve matches in an unbroken succession, all of them by knock-out, all of them within three rounds; and all the sports writers had by now adopted the name 'Lion of the Kalahari' in describing his feats.

'All right, *Jong*, win them while you can,' Uncle Tromp admonished him. 'But just remember you aren't going to be young always, and in the long run it's not a man's muscles and fists that keep him on top. It's what's in his skull, *Jong*, and don't you ever forget it!' So Manfred threw himself as enthusiastically into his academic studies as he had into his training routine.

German was by now almost as natural to him as Afrikaans, and he was considerably more fluent in it than in English, which he spoke only reluctantly and with a heavy accent. He found the Roman Dutch Law satisfying in its logic and philosophy and read the Institutes of Justinian like literature; at the same time politics and sociology both fascinated him. He and Roelf debated and discussed them endlessly, cementing their own friendship in the process.

His boxing prowess had made him an instant celebrity on the Stellenbosch campus. Some of his professors treated him with special favour and condescension because of this, while others were at first deliberately antagonistic, acting as though he were a dunce until he proved that he was not.

'Perhaps our well-known pugilist will give us the benefit of his towering intellect and throw some light on the concept of National Bolshevism for us.' The speaker was the professor of Sociology and Politics, a tall austere intellectual with the piercing eyes of a mystic. Though he had been born in Holland his parents had brought him out to Africa at an early age, and Dr Hendrik Frensch Verwoerd was now one of the leading Afrikaans intellectuals and a champion of his people's nationalist aspirations. He lectured first-year political students only once a semester, reserving most of his efforts for his faculty's honour students. Now he was smiling superciliously as Manfred rose slowly to his feet and composed his thoughts.

Dr Verwoerd waited for a few seconds and was about to wave him down again, the fellow was clearly a clod, when Manfred began his reply, speaking with carefully couched grammatical exactitude and in his newly acquired Stellenbosch accent which Roelf was helping him hone – the 'Oxford' accent of Afrikaans.

'As opposed to the revolutionary ideology of conventional Bolshevism created under Lenin's leadership, National Bolshevism was originally a term used in Germany to describe a policy of resistance to the Treaty of Versailles—' and Dr Verwoerd blinked and stopped smiling. The fellow had seen the trap from a mile off, separating the two concepts immediately.

'Can you tell us who was the innovator of the concept?' Dr Verwoerd demanded, a prickle of exasperation in his usual cool tones.

'I believe the idea was first put forward in 1919 by Karl Radek. His forum was an alliance of the pariah powers against the common Western enemies of Britain, France and the United States.'

The professor leaned forward like a falcon bating for its prey. 'In your view, sir, does it, or a similar doctrine, have any currency in the present politics of southern Africa?' They devoted all their attention to each other for the rest of the session, while Manfred's peers, relieved of all necessity to think, listened with varying degrees of mystification or boredom.

The following Saturday night, when Manfred won the university light heavyweight title in the packed gymnasium, Dr Verwoerd was sitting in the second row. It was the first time that he had been seen at any of the university's athletic tournaments, apart, of course, from the rugby football matches which no Afrikaner worthy of the name would have missed.

A few days later the professor sent for Manfred, ostensibly to discuss an essay that he had submitted on the history of liberalism, but their discussion ran for well over an hour and ranged widely. When it ended Dr Verwoerd stopped Manfred at the door. 'Here is a book that you might not have had an opportunity to look at.' He handed it across the desk. 'Keep it as long as you need, and let me know your views when you have finished with it.'

Manfred was in a hurry to get to his next lecture so he did not even read the title, and when he got back to his room he tossed it on his desk. Roelf was waiting to join him on their evening run and he had no chance to look at the book again until he had changed into his pyjamas late that night.

He picked it up from the desk and saw that he had already heard of it, and that it was in the original German. He did not put it down again until dawn was glimmering through the chinks in his curtains and the rock pigeons were cooing on the ledge outside his window. Then he closed the book and re-read the title: *Mein Kampf* by Adolf Hitler.

He passed the rest of the day in a trance of almost

religious revelation and hurried back to his room at lunch-time to read again. The author was speaking directly to him, addressing his German and Aryan bloodlines. He had the weird sensation that it had been written exclusively for him. Why else would Herr Hitler have included such marvellous passages as:

> It is considered as natural and honourable that a young man should learn to fence and proceed to fight duels right and left, but if he boxes, it is supposed to be vulgar! Why? There is no sport that so much as this one promotes the spirit of attack, demanding lightning decisions, and trains the body in steel dexterity . . . but above all the young healthy body must also learn to suffer blows – it is not the function of the *Völkisch* state to breed a colony of peaceful aesthetes and physical degenerates . . . If our entire intellectual upper class had not been brought up so exclusively on upper-class etiquette; if instead they had learned boxing thoroughly, a German revolution of pimps, deserters and suchlike rabble would never have been possible . . .

Manfred shivered with a sense of foreknowledge when he saw his own hardly formulated attitudes to personal moral-ity so clearly explained.

> Parallel to the training of the body, a struggle against the poisoning of the soul must begin. Our whole public life today is a hot-house for sexual ideas and stimulations . . .

Manfred had himself suffered from these torments set like snares for the young and pure. He had been forced to struggle against the evil lustful clamour of his own body when he had been exposed to magazine and cinema posters

– always written in English, that effete degenerate language which he was growing to hate – depicting half-naked females.

'You are right,' he muttered, turning the pages furiously. 'You are laying out the great truths for all of mankind. We must be pure and strong.'

Then his heart bounded as he saw set out in unequivocal language the other truths that he had only before heard lightly hinted at. He was transported back across the years to the hobo camp beside the railway tracks outside Windhoek, and saw again the tattered newspaper cartoon of Hoggenheimer driving the *Volk* into slavery. His outrage was consuming and he trembled with anger when he read:

> With satanic joy in his face, the black-haired Jewish youth lurks in wait for the unsuspecting girl whom he defiles with his blood, stealing her from her people.

In his imagination he saw Sarah's sweet pale body lying spreadeagled under the gross hairy carcass of Hoggenheimer and he was ready to kill.

Then the author lanced a vein of his Afrikaner blood so skilfully that Manfred's soul seemed almost to bleed upon the page.

> It was and is the Jews who bring the negroes into the Rhineland, always with the same secret thought and clear aim of ruining the hated white race by the necessarily resulting bastardization . . .

He shuddered. '*Swartgevaar!* Black danger!' had been the rallying cry of his people over the centuries they had been in Africa, and his atavistic heart beat to that summons once again.

He finished the book shaken and exhausted as he had

never been in the boxing ring. Although it was already late he went to find the man who had loaned it to him, and they talked eagerly and seriously until after midnight.

The next day the professor dropped an approving word to another in a high place: 'I have found one who I believe will be a valuable recruit, one with a good receptive mind who will soon have great influence and standing amongst our young people.'

Manfred's name was laid before the high council of a secret society at its next conclave:

'One of our best young men at the university, the senior student of Rust en Vrede is close to him—'

'Have him recruited,' ordered the chairman of the council.

Five days a week Roelf and Manfred ran a training route through the mountains together, a hard route of steep gradients and rough footing. Five miles out they stopped to drink in the pool below a feathery white waterfall. Roelf watched Manfred kneel on the slippery wet rocks and scoop up a double handful of the clear cold water to pour it into his open mouth.

'He is a good choice,' he agreed silently with the decision of his superiors. The light vest and shorts that Manfred wore showed off his powerful but graceful body, and his lustrous coppery hair and fine features were compelling. But it was the golden topaz eyes that were the key to his personality. Even Roelf felt overshadowed by the younger man's developing confidence and assurance.

'He will be a strong leader, the type we need so desperately.'

Manfred sprang to his feet again, dashing the water from his mouth with his forearm.

'Come on, drag arse,' he laughed. 'Last one back home is a Bolshevik.'

But Roelf stopped him. 'Today I want to talk to you,' he admitted, and Manfred frowned.

'Hell, man, we do nothing but talk anyway. Why here?'

'Because here no one will overhear us. And you are wrong, Manie, some of us are doing more than just talking. We are preparing for action, hard fighting action, the kind of action you love so well.'

Manfred turned back towards him, immediately intrigued, and came to squat in front of him. 'Who? What action?' he demanded, and Roelf inclined his head.

'A secret élite of dedicated Afrikaners, the leaders of our people, men in top places, in government and education and the commercial life of the nation. That's who, Manie. And not only the leaders of today, Manie, the leaders of tomorrow also. Men like you and me, Manie – that's who.'

'A secret society?' Manfred swayed back on his heels.

'No, Manie, much more than that, a secret army ready to fight for our poor downtrodden people. Ready to die to restore our nation to greatness.'

Manfred felt the fine hairs on his arms and at the nape of his neck come erect as the thrill of it coursed through his veins. His response was immediate and unquestioning.

'Soldiers, Manie, the storm-troopers of our nation,' Roelf went on.

'Are you one of them, Roelf?' Manie demanded.

'Yes, Manie, I am one of them, and you also. You have attracted the attention of our supreme council. I have been asked to invite you to join us in our march to destiny, in our struggle to fulfil the manifest destiny of our people.'

'Who are our leaders? What is the name of this secret army?'

'You will know. You will be told everything after you have taken the oath of allegiance,' Roelf promised him, and reached out to seize his arm, pressing powerful fingers into Manie's thick rubber-hard biceps.

'Do you accept the call of duty?' he asked. 'Will you join us, Manfred De La Rey? Will you wear our uniform and fight in our ranks?'

Manfred's Dutch blood, suspicious and broodingly introspective, responded to his promise of clandestine intrigue, while his Germanic side longed for the order and authority of a society of fierce warriors, modern-day Teutonic knights, hard and unrelenting for God and Country. And though he was unaware of it, the streak of flamboyance and love of theatrics he had inherited from his French mother was drawn to the military pomp, uniforms and eagles, that Roelf seemed to offer him.

He reached out and seized Roelf's shoulder and they held each other in the clasp of comrades, staring deeply into each other's eyes.

'With all my heart,' Manfred said softly. 'I will join you with all my heart.'

The full moon stood high above the Stellenbosch mountains, silvering their sheer buttresses and plunging the gullies and ravines into deepest black. In the south the Great Cross stood high, but it was washed out into insignificance by the huge fiery cross that burned closer and fiercer at the head of the open forest glade. It was a natural amphitheatre, screened by the dense conifers that surrounded it, a secret place, hidden from curious or hostile eyes, perfect for the purpose.

Beneath the fiery cross the ranks of storm-troopers were massed and their polished cross belts and buckles glinted in its light and in that of the burning torches each of them held high. There were not more than three hundred troopers present, for they were the elite, and their expressions were proud and solemn as they watched the tiny band of new recruits march out of the forest and down the slope of the glade to where the general waited to greet them.

Manfred De La Rey was the first of them to come to attention before the leaders. He wore the black shirt and riding-breeches, the high polished riding-boots of this secret band of knights, but his head was bare and his uniform unadorned except for the sheathed dagger on his belt.

The high commander stepped forward and stopped only a pace in front of Manfred. He was an imposing figure, a tall man with craggy weathered face and hard jutting jaw. Although thickened around the waist and big-bellied under his black shirt, he was a man in his prime, a black-maned lion in his pride and the aura of command and authority sat easily upon his broad shoulders.

Manfred recognized him immediately, for his was a face often reproduced in the political columns of the national newspaper. He was high in government, the administrator of one of the country's provinces, and his influence was deep and far-reaching.

'Manfred De La Rey,' the commander asked in a powerful voice, 'are you ready to take the blood oath?'

'I am,' Manfred replied clearly, and drew the silver dagger from his belt.

From the ranks behind him Roelf Stander, in full uniform, capped and booted and with the broken cross insignia on his right arm, stepped out and drew the pistol from his holster. He cocked the pistol and pressed the muzzle to Manfred's chest, aiming for the heart, and Manfred did not flinch. Roelf was his sponsor. The pistol was symbolic of the fact that he would also be his executioner should Manfred ever betray the blood oath he was about to swear.

Ceremoniously the commander handed Manfred a sheet of stiff parchment. Its head was illuminated by the crest of the order: a stylized powderhorn like those used by the *Voortrekkers*, the pioneers of his people. Below it was printed the oath, and Manfred took it in one hand and with the other held the bared dagger pointed at his own heart to signify his willingness to lay down his life for the ideals of the brotherhood.

'Before Almighty God, and in the sight of my comrades,' he read aloud, 'I subject myself entirely to the dictates of my people's divinely ordained destiny. I swear to be faithful to the precepts of the *Ossewa Brandwag*, the sentinels of the Afrikaner wagon train, and to obey the orders of my superiors. On my life I swear a deadly oath of secrecy, that I will cherish and hold sacred the affairs and proceedings of the *Ossewa Brandwag*. I demand that if I should betray my comrades, my oath or my *Volk*, vengeance shall follow me to my traitor's grave. I call upon my comrades to hear my entreaty.

> If I advance, follow me.
> If I retreat, shoot me down.
> If I die, avenge me.
> So help me Almighty God!'

And Manfred drew the silver blade across his wrist so that his blood sprang dark ruby in the torchlight, and he sprinkled the parchment with it.

The high commander stepped forward to embrace him, and behind him the black ranks erupted in a jubilant warlike roar of approval. At his side Roelf Stander returned the loaded pistol to its holster, his eyelids stinging with the nettles of proud tears. As the commander stepped back, Roelf rushed forward to take Manfred's right hand in his. 'My brother.' His whisper was choking. 'Now we are truly brothers.'

In mid-November Manfred sat his end-of-year examinations and passed third in a law class of 153.

Three days after the results were posted, the Stellenbosch boxing squad, led by its coach, left to take part in the Inter-Varsity Championships. This year the venue was the University of the Witwatersrand in Johannesburg, and boxers from the other universities of South Africa journeyed from every province and corner of the Union to take part.

The Stellenbosch team travelled up by train, and there was a cheering, singing crowd of students and faculty members to see them off at the railway station on their thousand-mile journey.

Uncle Tromp kissed his women farewell, beginning with Aunt Trudi and working his way down to Sarah, the youngest, at the end of the line, and Manfred followed him. He was wearing his colours blazer and straw basher and he was so tall and beautiful that Sarah could not bear it and she burst into tears as he stooped over her. She flung both arms around his neck and squeezed with all her strength.

'Come along, don't be a silly little duck,' Manfred gruffed in her ear, but his voice was rough with the strange unaccustomed tumult that the contact of her hot silky cheek against his provoked beneath his ribs.

'Oh, Manie, you are going so far away.' She tried to hide her tears in the angle of his neck. 'We have never been parted by such distance.'

'Come on, monkey. People are looking at you,' he chided her gently. 'Give me a kiss and I'll bring you back a present.'

'I don't want a present. I want you,' she sniffed, and then lifted her sweet face and placed her mouth over his. Her mouth seemed to melt in its own heat, and it was moist and sweet as a ripe apple.

The contact lasted only seconds, but Manfred was so intensely aware that she might have been naked in his arms and he was shaken with guilt and self-disgust at his body's swift betrayal and at the evil that seemed to smoke in his blood and burst like a sky rocket in his brain. He pulled away from her roughly, and her expression was bewildered and hurt, her arms still raised as he scrambled up the steps onto the balcony of the coach and joined the noisy banter and horseplay of his team mates.

As the train pulled out of the station she was standing a little apart from the other girls, and when they all turned and trooped away down the platform, Sarah lingered, staring after the train as it gathered speed and ran towards the mountains.

At last a bend in the tracks carried him out of sight of her, and as Manfred drew his head back into the carriage he saw that Roelf Stander was watching him quizzically and now grinned and opened his mouth to speak, but Manfred flared at him furiously and guiltily:

'*Hou jou bek!* Hold your jaw, man!'

T he Inter-Varsity Championships were held over ten days with five heats in each weight division; thus each contestant would fight every second day.

Manfred was seeded number two in his division, which meant that he would probably meet the holder of the champion's belt in the final round. The reigning champion was an engineering student who had just graduated from the Witwatersrand University. He was unbeaten in his career and had announced his intention of turning professional immediately after the Olympics for which he was considered a certain choice.

'The Lion of the Kalahari meets the sternest test of his meteoric career. Can he take the same sort of punishment that he deals out? This is the question everyone is asking, and which Ian Rushmore will answer for us if all goes as expected,' wrote the boxing correspondent of the *Rand Daily Mail*. 'There does not seem to be any contestant in the division who will be able to prevent De La Rey and Rushmore meeting on Saturday night, 20 December 1935. It will be Rushmore's right hand, made of granite and gelignite, against De La Rey's swarming battering two-handed style, and your correspondent would not miss the meeting for all the gold that lies beneath the streets of Johannesburg.'

Manfred won his first two bouts with insulting ease. His opponents, demoralized by his reputation, both dropped in the second round under the barrage of slashing red gloves, and the Wednesday was a rest day for Manfred.

He left the residence on the host university's campus before any of the others were up, missing breakfast to be in time for the early morning train from Johannesburg's Central Station. It was less than an hour's journey across the open grasslands.

He ate a frugal breakfast in the buffet of the Pretoria station and then started out on foot with a leaden reluctance in his gait.

Pretoria Central Prison was an ugly square building and the interior was as forbidding and depressing. Here all executions were carried out, and life imprisonments served.

Manfred went into the visitors' entrance, spoke to the unsmiling senior warder at the enquiries desk and filled in an application form.

He hesitated over the question, 'Relationship to prisoner', then boldly wrote 'Son'.

When he returned the form to the warder, the man read it through slowly and then looked up at him, studying him gravely and impersonally. 'He has not had a visitor, not one in all these years,' he said.

'I could not come before.' Manfred tried to excuse himself. 'There were reasons.'

'They all say that.' Then the warder's expression altered subtly. 'You are the boxer, aren't you?'

'That's right,' Manfred nodded, and then on an impulse he gave the secret recognition signal of the *OB* and the man's eyes flicked with surprise then dropped to the form in front of him.

'Very well, then. Have a seat. I'll call you when he is ready,' he said, and under cover of the counter top he gave Manfred the counter signal of the *Ossewa Brandwag*.

'Kill the *rooinek* bastard on Saturday night,' he whispered, and turned away. Manfred was amazed but elated to have proof of how widely the brotherhood had spread its arms to gather in the *Volk*.

Ten minutes later the warder led Manfred through to a greenpainted cell with high barred windows, furnished only with a plain deal table and three straight-backed chairs. There was an old man sitting on one of the chairs, but he was a stranger and Manfred looked beyond him expectantly.

The stranger stood up slowly. He was bowed with age and hard work, his skin wrinkled and folded and spotted by the sun. His hair was thin and white as raw cotton, wisped over a scalp that was speckled like a plover's egg. His thin scraggy neck stuck out of the coarse calico prison uniform like a turtle's from the opening of its carapace, and his eyes were colourless, faded and red-rimmed and swimming with tears that gathered like dew on his lashes.

'Papa?' Manfred asked with disbelief as he saw the missing arm, and the old man began to weep silently. His shoulders shook and the tears broke over the reddened rims of his eyelids and slimed down his cheeks.

'Papa?' said Manfred, and outrage rose to choke him. 'What have they done to you?'

He rushed forward to embrace his father, trying to hide his face from the warder, trying to protect him, to cover his weakness and tears.

'Papa! Papa!' he repeated helplessly, patting the thin

shoulders under the rough uniform, and he turned his head and looked back at the warder in silent appeal.

'I cannot leave you alone.' The man understood, but shook his head. 'It is the rule, more than my job is worth.'

'Please,' Manfred whispered.

'Do you give me your word, as a brother, that you will not try to help him escape?'

'My word as a brother!' Manfred answered.

'Ten minutes,' said the warder. 'I can give you no more.' He turned away, locking the green steel door as he left.

'Papa.' Manfred led the trembling old man back to the chair and knelt beside him.

Lothar De La Rey wiped his wet cheeks with his open palm and tried to smile, but it wavered and his voice quivered. 'Look at me, blubbering like an old woman. It was just the shock of seeing you again. I'm all right now. I'm fine. Let me look at you, let me just look at you for a moment.'

He drew back and stared into Manfred's face intently. 'What a man you have become – strong and well favoured, just like I was at your age.' He traced Manfred's features with his fingertips. His hand was cold and the skin was rough as sharkskin.

'I have read about you, my son. They allow us to have the newspapers. I have cut out everything about you and I keep them under my mattress. I'm proud, so proud. We all are, everybody in this place, even the narks.'

'Papa! How are they treating you?' Manfred cut him short.

'Fine, Manie, just fine.' Lothar looked down and his lips sagged with despair. 'It's just that – for ever is such a long time. So long, manie, so very long, and sometimes I think about the desert, about the horizons that turn to distant smoke and the high blue sky.' He broke off and tried to smile. 'And I think about you, every day – not a day that I don't pray to God "Look after my son."'

'No, Papa – please,' Manfred pleaded. 'Don't! You will have me weeping too.' He pushed himself off his knees and pulled the other chair close to his father's. 'I've thought about you also, Papa, everyday. I wanted to write to you. I spoke to Uncle Tromp, but he said it was best if—'

Lothar seized his hand to silence him. '*Ja*, Manie, it was best. Tromp Bierman is a wise man; he knows best.' He smiled more convincingly. 'How tall you have grown, and the colour of your hair – just like mine used to be. You will be all right, I know. What have you decided to do with your life? Tell me quickly. We have so little time.'

'I am studying law at Stellenbosch. I passed third in the first year.'

'That is wonderful, my son, and afterwards?'

'I am not sure, Papa, but I think I must fight for our nation. I think I have been called to the fight for justice for our people.'

'Politics?' Lothar asked, and when Manfred nodded, 'A hard road, full of turns and twists. I always preferred the straight road, with a horse under me and a rifle in my hand.' Then he chuckled sardonically. 'And look where that road has led me.'

'I will fight too, Papa. When the time is right, on a battleground of my own choosing.'

'Oh, my son. History is so cruel to our people. Sometimes I think with despair that we are doomed always to be the underdogs.'

'You are wrong!' Manfred's expression hardened and his voice crackled. 'Our day will come, is already dawning. We will not be the underdogs for much longer.' He wanted to tell his father, but then he remembered his blood oath and he was silent.

'Manie.' His father leaned closer, glancing around the cell like a conspirator before he tugged at Manfred's sleeve. 'The diamonds – have you still got your diamonds?' he demanded, and immediately saw the answer in Manfred's face.

'What happened to them?' Lothar's distress was hard to watch. 'They were my legacy to you, all I could leave you. Where are they?'

'Uncle Tromp – he found them years ago. He said they were evil, the coin of the devil, and he made me destroy them.'

'Destroy them?' Lothar gaped at him.

'Break them on an anvil with a sledgehammer. Crush them to powder, all of them.'

Manfred watched his father's old fierce spirit flare up. Lothar leapt to his feet and raged around the cell. 'Tromp Bierman, if I could get my hand on you! You were always a stubborn sanctimonious hypocrite—' He broke off and came back to his son.

'Manie, there are the others. Do you remember – the kopje, the hill in the desert? I left them there for you. You must go back.'

Manfred turned his head away. Over the years he had tried to drive the memory from his mind. It was evil, the memory of great evil, associated with terror and guilt and grief. He had tried to close his mind to that time in his life. It was long ago, and he had almost succeeded, but now at his father's words he tasted again the reek of gangrene in the back of his throat and saw the package of treasure slide down into the cleft in the granite.

'I have forgotten the way back, Papa. I could never find the way back.'

Lothar was pulling at his arm. 'Hendrick!' he babbled. 'Swart Hendrick! He knows – he can lead you.'

'Hendrick.' Manfred blinked. A name, half-forgotten, a fragment from his past; then suddenly and clearly an image of that great bald head, that black cannonball of a head, sprang into his mind. 'Hendrick,' he repeated. 'But he is gone. I don't know where. Gone back into the desert. I could never find him.'

'No! No! Manie, Hendrick is here, somewhere close here on the Witwatersrand. He is a big man now, a chief among his own people.'

'How do you know, Papa?'

'The grapevine! In here we hear everything. They come in from the outside, bringing news and messages. We hear everything. Hendrick sent word to me. He had not forgotten me. We were comrades. We rode ten thousand miles together and fought a hundred battles. He sent word to me, to set a place where I could find him if ever I escaped these damned walls.' Lothar leaned forward and seized his son's head, pulling it close, placing his lips to his ear, whispering urgently and then drawing back. 'You must go and find him there. He will lead you back to the granite hill below the Okavango river – and, oh sweet God, how I wish I could be there to ride into the desert with you again.'

There was the clink of keys in the lock and Lothar shook his son's arm desperately. 'Promise me you will go, Manie.'

'Papa, the stones are evil.'

'Promise me, my own son, promise me that I have not endured these captive years for nothing. Promise me you will go back for the stones.'

'I promise, Papa,' Manfred whispered, as the warder stepped into the cell.

'Time is up. I'm sorry.'

'Can I come and see my father again tomorrow?'

The warder shook his head. 'Only one visit a month.'

'I'll write to you, Papa.' He turned back to embrace Lothar. 'I'll write to you every week from now on.'

But Lothar nodded expressionlessly; his face had closed and his eyes were veiled. '*Ja*,' he nodded. 'You write to me sometime,' he agreed, and shuffled out of the cell.

Manfred stared at the closed green door until the warder

touched his shoulder: 'Come along.' Manfred followed him to the visitors' entrance in a tangle of emotions. Only when he stepped out of the gates into the sunlight and looked up at the towering blue African sky of which his father had spoken so yearningly did one emotion emerge to swamp all the others.

It was rage, blind hopeless rage, and it grew stronger over the days that followed, seeming to climax as he marched down the aisle between the rows of screaming cheering spectators towards the brilliantly lighted ring of rope and canvas, dressed in shimmering silks with the crimson leather on his fists and bloody murder in his heart.

Centaine woke long before Blaine did; she grudged every second they wasted in sleep. It was still dark outside for the cottage was close under the precipice of the high table-topped mountain and screened from dawn's first glow by its bulk, though the birds in the tiny walled garden were already squeaking and chirping sleepily. She had ordered tacoma and honeysuckle to be trained over the stone walls to attract them, and on her orders the feeding-boxes were replenished every day by the gardener.

She had taken months to find the perfect cottage. It had to be discreetly enclosed, with covered parking for her Daimler and Blaine's new Bentley, both vehicles that attracted immediate attention. It had to be within ten minutes' walk of Parliament and Blaine's office in the wing of the imposing Herbert Baker building reserved for cabinet ministers. It had to have a view of the mountain, and must be set in one of the tiny lanes of an unfashionable suburb where none of their friends or business associates or fellow parliamentarians or enemies or members of the press were ever likely to stray. But above all it had to have that special feel.

When at last she walked into it she did not even see the stained and faded wallpaper or the threadbare carpets on the floor. She stood in the central room and smiled softly. 'Happy people have lived here. Yes, this is the one. I'll take it.'

She had registered the title deeds in one of her holding companies, but trusted no architect nor decorator with its renovation. She planned and executed the reconstruction entirely herself.

'It's got to be the most perfect love nest ever built.' She set her usual unattainable standard for herself and consulted with the builder and his carpenters and plumbers and painters every single morning while the work was in hand. They tore down the walls between the four tiny bedrooms and fashioned them into a single boudoir with french windows and shutters opening onto the enclosed garden with its high wall of yellow Table Mountain sandstone and the view of the grey mountain cliff beyond.

She built separate bathrooms for Blaine and herself, his finished in ruby-veined cream Italian marble with gold dolphin taps and fittings, hers like a Bedouin tent draped in rose silk.

The bed was a museum piece, Italian Renaissance workmanship inlaid with ivory and gold leaf. 'We can always play polo on it in the off-season,' Blaine remarked when first he saw it, and she placed her magnificent Turner, all sunlight and golden sea, so that it was in full view from the bed. She hung the Bonnard in the dining-room and lit it with a chandelier which was a shimmering inverted Christmas tree of crystal, and placed the choicest pieces of her collection of Queen Anne and Louis Quatorze silver on the sideboard.

She staffed the cottage with four permanent servants, including a valet for Blaine and a full-time gardener. The chef was a Malay who conjured up the most heavenly pilaffs and *boboties* and *rystafels* that Blaine, who had a spicy palate and was a connoisseur of curries, had ever tasted.

A flowerseller from her pitch outside the Groote Kerk near the parliament buildings had a contract to deliver huge bunches of yellow roses to the cottage each day, and Centaine stocked the small wine cellar with the noblest vintages from Weltevreden's own cavernous cellars and installed, at enormous expense, an electric walk-in cold room in the pantries to keep the hams and cheeses, the potted caviars and smoked Scotch salmon and other such necessities of life in prime condition.

Yet with all her loving attention to detail and lavish planning, they were lucky if they could spend a single night there in a month – although there were other stolen hours, garnered like diamonds, and hoarded by Centaine as though she were the stingiest of misers: a private luncheon when parliament recessed or a midnight interlude after the house had sat late; the occasional afternoon – when his wife, Isabella, believed he was at polo practice or at a cabinet meeting.

Now Centaine rolled her head carefully on the lace pillow and looked at him. The dawn light was silvery through the shutters and his features seemed carved in ivory. She thought that he looked like a sleeping Roman Caesar, with that imperial nose and wide commanding mouth.

'In all but the ears,' she thought, and stifled a giggle. Strange how after three years his presence could make her still feel like a girl. She rose quietly, careful not to rock the mattress and disturb him, picked up her wrap from the couch and slipped through to her bathroom.

Swiftly she brushed her hair into thick dark plumes checking for grey and then, relieved, went on to clean her teeth and wash her eyes with the little blue glass bath of lotion until the whites were clear and sparkling. Then she creamed her face and wiped away the excess. Blaine liked

579

her skin free of cosmetics. As she used her bidet she smiled again at Blaine's mock amazement when he had first seen it.

'Marvellous!' he had cried. 'A horse trough in the bathroom, how jolly useful!'

Sometimes he was so romantic he was almost French. She laughed with anticipation, snatched a fresh silk wrap from the wardrobe and ran through to the kitchen. The servants were all astir, bubbling with excitement because the master was here and they all adored Blaine.

'Did you get them, Hadji?' Centaine demanded, using the title of respect for one who has made the pilgrimage to Mecca, and the Malay chef grinned like a butter-yellow gnome under his tasselled red fez and proudly displayed the pair of thick juicy kippers.

'Come on the mail boat yesterday, madam,' he boasted.

'Hadji, you are a magician,' she applauded. Scotch kippers were Blaine's favourite breakfast. 'You are going to do them his way, aren't you?' Blaine's way was simmered in milk, and Hadji looked pained at the impropriety of the question as he turned back to his stove.

For Centaine it was a marvellous game of make-believe, playing wife, pretending that Blaine truly belonged to her. So with a sharp eye she watched Miriam grind the coffee beans and Khalil finish sponging Blaine's grey pinstripe suit and begin to put a military gleam on his shoes before she left them and crept back into the darkened bedroom.

She felt quite breathless as she hovered beside the bed and studied his features. He still had that effect on her even after all this time.

'I am more faithful than any wife,' she gloated. 'More dutiful, more loving, more—'

His arm shot out so suddenly that she squealed with fright as he plucked her down beside him and flicked the sheet over her.

'You were awake all along,' she wailed. 'Oh, you awful man, I can never trust you.'

They could still, on occasion, drive each other into that mindless frenzy, those writhing sensual marathons that exploded at the end in a great burst of light and colour like the Turner on the wall before them. But more often it had become as it was this morning, a fortress of love, solid and impregnable. They left it with reluctance, coming apart slowly, lingeringly, as the day filled the room with gold and they heard the clink of Hadji's breakfast dishes on the terrace beyond the shutters.

She brought him his robe, full-length brocaded China silk, royal blue lined in crimson with a belt of embroidered seed pearls and velvet lapels. She had chosen it because it was so outlandish, so different from his usual severe style of dress.

'I wouldn't wear it in front of anybody else in the world,' he had told her, holding it gingerly at arm's length, when she presented it to him on his birthday.

'If you do, you'd better not let me catch you at it!' she warned, but after the first shock he had come to enjoy wearing it for her.

Hand in hand they went out onto the terrace and Hadji and Miriam beamed with delight and bowed them to their seats at the table in the morning sunlight.

With a rapid but steely survey, Centaine made sure everything was perfect, from the roses in the Lalique vase to the snowy linen and the Fabergé jug of silver gilt and crystal filled with freshly squeezed grapefruit juice, before she opened the morning paper and began to read to him.

Always in the same order: the headlines and then the parliamentary reports, waiting for him to comment on each, adding her own ideas, and then going on to the financial pages and stock exchange reports, and finally to the sports pages with special emphasis on any mention of polo.

'Oh, I see you spoke yesterday: "a forceful reply from the minister without portfolio", they say.'

And Blaine smiled as he lifted a fillet off his kipper. 'Hardly forceful,' he demurred. '"Pissed off" better describes it.'

'What's this about secret societies?'

'A bit of a flap over these militant organizations, inspired it would seem by the charming Herr Hitler and his gang of political thugs.'

'Anything in it?' Centaine sipped at her coffee. She still couldn't get her stomach to accept these English breakfasts. 'You seem to have dismissed the whole thing rather lightly.' Then she looked up at him with narrowing eyes. 'You were covering up, weren't you?' She knew him so well, and he grinned guiltily at her.

'Don't miss a thing, do you?'

'Can you tell me?'

'Shouldn't really.' He frowned, but she had never betrayed his trust. 'We are very worried indeed,' he admitted. 'In fact the *Ou Baas* considers it the most serious threat since the 1914 rebellion when De Wet called out his commandos to fight for the Kaiser. The whole thing is a political nettle, and a potential minefield.' He paused, and she knew there was more, but she waited quietly for him to make up his mind to tell her. 'All right,' he decided. 'The *Ou Baas* has ordered me to head a commission of enquiry – cabinet level and confidential – into the *Ossewa Brandwag*, which is the most extreme and flourishing of them all. Worse than the *Broederbond* even.'

'Why you, Blaine? It's a nasty one, isn't it?'

'Yes, it's a nasty one, and he picked me as a non-Afrikaner. The impartial judge.'

'Of course, I've heard of the OB. There has been talk for years but nobody seems to know much.'

'Extreme right-wing nationalists, anti-Semitic, anti-black, blaming all the ills of their world on perfidious

Albion, secret blood oaths and midnight rallies, a sort of Neanderthal boy scout movement with *Mein Kampf* as its inspiration.'

'I haven't yet read *Mein Kampf*. Everyone is talking about it. Is there an English or French translation?'

'Not officially published, but I have a Foreign Office translation. It's a rag-bag of nightmares and obscenities, a manual of naked aggression and bigotry. I would lend you my copy but it is appallingly bad literature and the sentiments would sicken you.'

'He may not be a great writer,' Centaine conceded. 'But, Blaine, whatever else he has done, Hitler has put Germany on its feet again after the disaster of the Weimar Republic. Germany is the only country in the world with full employment and a booming economy. My shares in Krupp and Farben have almost doubled in the last nine months.' She stopped as she saw his expression. 'Is something wrong, Blaine?'

He had laid his knife and fork down and was staring at her.

'You have shares in the German armaments industry?' he asked quietly, and she nodded.

'The best investment I have made since gold went off—' She broke off; they had never mentioned that again.

'I have never asked you to do anything for me, have I?' he asked, and she considered that carefully.

'No, you haven't – ever.'

'Well, I'm asking you now. Sell your shares in German armaments.'

She looked puzzled. 'Why, Blaine?'

'Because it is like investing in the propagation of cancer, or like financing Genghis Khan's campaigns.'

She did not reply, but her expression went blank and her eyes went out of focus, crossing into a slightly myopic squint. The first time he had seen that happen he had been alarmed; it had taken him some time to realize that when

583

she squinted like that she was involved in mental arithmetic, and it had fascinated him to see how quickly she made her calculations.

Her eyes flicked back into focus and she smiled agreement. 'On yesterday's prices, I'll show a profit of a hundred and twenty-six thousand pounds. It was time to sell anyway. I'll cable my London broker as soon as the post office opens.'

'Thank you, my love.' Blaine shook his head sorrowfully. 'But I do wish you'd made your profit somewhere else.'

'You may be misjudging the situation, *chéri*,' she suggested tactfully. 'Hitler may not be as bad as you think he is.'

'He doesn't have to be as bad as I think he is, Centaine. He only has to be as bad as he says he is in *Mein Kampf* to qualify for the chamber of horrors.' Blaine took a mouthful of his kipper and closed his eyes with mild ecstasy. She watched him with a pleasure almost equal to his own. He swallowed, opened his eyes, and declared the subject closed with a wave of his fork.

'Enough horrors for such a splendid morning.' He smiled at her. 'Read me the sports pages, woman!'

Centaine rustled the pages portentously and then composed herself to read aloud, but suddenly the colour drained from her face and she swayed in her seat.

Blaine dropped his knife and fork with a clatter and jumped up to steady her. 'What is it, darling?' He was desperately alarmed and almost as pale as she was. She shrugged his hands away and stared at the open newspaper which trembled in her grip.

Blaine moved quickly behind her, and scanned the page over her shoulder. There was an article on the previous weekend's racing at Kenilworth. Centaine's entry, a good stallion named Bonheur, had lost the feature race by a short head, but that could not have occasioned her distress.

Then he saw that she was looking at the foot of the page

and he followed her gaze to a quarter-column photograph of a boxer, in shorts and vest, facing the camera in a formal pose, bare fists raised and a grim expression on his handsome features. Centaine had never evinced the slightest interest in boxing, and Blaine was puzzled. He read the heading of the article which accompanied the photograph:

FEAST OF FISTICUFFS
CLASSY FIELD FOR INTER-VARSITY
CHAMPIONSHIPS

which did nothing to alleviate his puzzlement. He glanced at the footnote beneath the photograph: 'The Lion of the Kalahari, Manfred De La Rey, the Challenger for the Inter-Varsity Light Heavyweight Belt. Hard pounding ahead.'

'Manfred De La Rey.' Blaine said the name softly, trying to remember where last he had heard it. Then his expression cleared and he squeezed Centaine's shoulders.

'Manfred De La Rey! The boy you were looking for in Windhoek. Is this him?'

Centaine did not look round, but she nodded jerkily.

'What is he to you, Centaine?'

She was shaken into an emotional turmoil; otherwise she might have answered differently. But now it was out before she could bite down on the words. 'He's my son. My bastard son.'

Blaine's hands dropped from her shoulders and she heard the sharp hissing intake of his breath.

'I must be mad!' Her reaction was immediate, and she thought, 'I should never have told him. Blaine will never understand. He'll never forgive me.'

She dared not look round at the shock and accusation she knew she would find on his face. She dropped her head and cupped her hands over her eyes.

'I've lost him,' she thought. 'Blaine is too upright, too virtuous to accept it.'

Then his hands touched her again, and they lifted her to her feet and turned her gently to face him.

'I love you,' he said simply, and her tears choked her and she flung herself against his chest and held him with all her strength.

'Oh Blaine, you are so good to me.'

'If you want to tell me about it, I'm here to help you. If you'd rather not talk, then I understand. There is just one thing – whatever it was, whatever you did, makes no difference to me and my feelings for you.'

'I want to tell you.' She fought back her tears of relief and looked up at him. 'I've never wanted to keep secrets from you. I've wanted to tell you for years now, but I am a coward.'

'You are many things, my love, but never a coward.' He seated her again and drew his own chair close so that he could hold her hand while she talked.

'Now tell me,' he commanded.

'It's such a long story, Blaine – and you have a cabinet meeting at nine.'

'Affairs of state can wait,' he said. 'Your happiness is the most important thing in the world.'

So she told him, from the time that Lothar De La Rey had rescued her to the discovery of the H'ani diamond mine and the birth of Manfred in the desert.

She held nothing back: her love for Lothar, the love of a lonely forsaken girl for her rescuer. She explained how it had changed to bitter hatred when she discovered that Lothar had murdered the old Bushman woman who was her foster mother, and how that hatred had focused on Lothar's child that she was carrying in her womb, and how she had refused even to look upon the newborn infant but had made the father take it from the childbed still wet from the act of birth.

'It was wicked,' she whispered. 'But I was confused and afraid, afraid of the rejection of the Courtney family if I brought a bastard amongst them. Oh, Blaine, I have regretted it ten thousand times – and hated myself as much as I hated Lothar De La Rey.'

'Do you want to go to Johannesburg to see him again?' Blaine asked. 'We could fly up to watch the championships.'

The idea startled Centaine. 'We?' she asked. '*We*, Blaine?'

'I couldn't let you go alone. Not to something so disturbing.'

'But can you get away? What about Isabella?'

'Your need is far more important now,' he told her simply. 'Do you want to go?'

'Oh yes, Blaine. Oh yes please.' She dabbed away the last tear with her lace table napkin, and he saw her mood shift. It always fascinated him how she could change moods as other women changed their hats.

Now she was crisp and quick and businesslike. 'I am expecting Shasa back from South-West later today. I'll ring Abe in Windhoek to find out what time they took off. If all is well, we can leave for Johannesburg tomorrow. What time, Blaine?'

'As early as you like,' he told her. 'This afternoon I will clear my desk and make my peace with the *Ou Baas*.'

'The weather should be fine this time of year – perhaps a few thunderstorms on the highveld.' She took his wrist and turned it to see his Rolex watch. '*Chéri*, you can still get to the cabinet meeting if you hurry.'

She went with him to the garage to see him off, still playing the dutiful wife, and kissed him through the open window of the Bentley.

'I'll ring your office as soon as Shasa arrives,' she murmured in his ear. 'I'll leave a message with Doris if you are still in the meeting.' Doris was Blaine's secretary, and one of the very few people in the world that knew about them.

As soon as he was gone, Centaine rushed back into the

bedroom and picked up the phone. The line to Windhoek was noisy with crackles and hisses and Abe Abrahams sounded as though he were in Alaska.

'They left at first light, almost five hours ago,' he told her faintly. 'David is with him, of course.'

'What's the wind, Abe?'

'They should have a tail wind all the way. I'd say twenty or thirty miles an hour.'

'Thank you. I'll wait at the field for them.'

'That might be a little awkward.' Abe sounded hesitant. 'There was a lot of secrecy and deliberate vagueness when they got in from the mine yesterday evening, and I wasn't allowed to see them off from the airfield this morning. I think they might have company – if you will excuse the euphemism.'

As a reflex, Centaine frowned, though she truly could not find it in herself thoroughly to disapprove of Shasa's philanderings. She always excused him with: 'It's his de Thiry blood. He can't help himself,' feeling a covert touch of indulgent pride in her son's effortless successes with the opposite sex. Now she changed the subject.

'Thank you, Abe. I've signed the new Namaqualand leases so you can go ahead and draw up the contract.' They spoke business for five minutes more before Centaine hung up. She made three more calls, all business, then phoned her secretary at Weltevreden and dictated four letters and the cable to her London broker to 'Sell all Krupp and Farben at best.'

She hung up, sent for Hadji and Miriam and gave them instructions for the running of the cottage in her absence. Then she made a quick calculation. The Dragon Rapide, a beautiful blue and silver twin-engined aircraft which Shasa had prevailed on her to buy, could cruise at 150 knots, and with a tail wind of twenty miles an hour they should be at Youngsfield before noon.

'So we will see just how much Master Shasa's taste in women has improved recently.'

She went out to the Daimler and drove slowly around the shoulder of the mountain, below District Six, the colourful Malay quarter, its narrow lanes reverberating to the cries of the muezzin calling the faithful to prayer, the hoot of the fishsellers' horns declaring their wares and the birdlike cries of children, and past the hospital of Groote Schuur and the university which adjoined Cecil Rhodes' magnificent estate, his legacy to the nation.

'It must be the most beautiful situation of any university in the world,' she thought.

The colonnaded stone buildings were set against a backdrop of dark pines and the sheer sky-high cliff of the mountain, while on the meadows abutting them grazed small herds of plains animals, eland and wildebeest and zebra. Sight of the university set her thinking about Shasa again. He had just completed his year, with a respectable second-class.

'I always suspect those who pass first class in everything,' Blaine had remarked when he heard Shasa's results. 'Most of them are too clever for their own good or the good of those around them. I prefer those lesser mortals for whom the achievement of excellence requires considerable effort.'

'You accuse me of spoiling him,' she had smiled. 'But you are always making excuses for Shasa yourself.'

'Being your son, my love, is not the easiest of tasks for a young man,' he had told her, making her bridle furiously.

'You think I am not good to him.'

'You are very good to him. As I have suggested, perhaps too good to him. It's just that you do not leave much for him. You are so successful, so dominant. You have done it all. What can he do to prove himself?'

'Blaine, I am not domineering.'

'I said dominant, Centaine, not domineering. The two

589

are different. I love you because you are dominant. I would despise you if you were domineering.'

'Still I do not always understand this language of yours. I shall look it up in my dictionary.'

'Ask Shasa – English was his only first.' Blaine chuckled and then put his arm around her shoulders. 'You must slacken the rein a little, Centaine, give him space to make his own mistakes and enjoy his own triumphs. If he wants to hunt, even though you do not approve of killing animals that you cannot eat, the Courtneys have all been big-game hunters. Old General Courtney slew elephant in their hundreds and Shasa's father hunted; let the boy try his hand at it. That and polo are the only things you haven't done before him.'

'What about flying?' she challenged.

'I apologize – and flying.'

'Very well, I will let him go and murder beasts. But Blaine, tell me, will he make the polo team for the Olympics?'

'Frankly, my darling – no.'

'But he is good enough! You said so yourself.'

'Yes,' Blaine agreed. 'He is probably good enough. He has all the fire and dash, a marvellous eye and arm, but he lacks experience. If he were chosen he'd be the youngest international ever. However, I don't think he will be. I think Clive Ramsay has to get the ride at number two.'

She stared at him, and he stared back expressionlessly. He knew what she was thinking. As Captain, Blaine was one of the national selectors.

'David will be going to Berlin,' she had followed up.

'David Abrahams is the human version of a gazelle,' Blaine had pointed out reasonably. 'He has the fourth best time in the world for the two hundred metres and the third best for the four hundred. Young Shasa is competing against at least ten of the world's best horsemen for a place.'

'I would give anything in the world for Shasa to go to Berlin.'

'Very likely you would,' Blaine had agreed. She had built a new wing to the engineering faculty at the University of Cape Town, the Courtney Building, when it had finally been decided that Shasa would go there rather than to Oxford; yes, he knew no price was too high for her to pay.

'I assure you, my love, that I will make very certain—' he paused, and she perked up expectantly ' – that I excuse myself from the room when, and if, Shasa's name ever comes up before the selectors.'

'He's so damned virtuous!' she exclaimed aloud now and beat her clenched fist on the steering-wheel of the Daimler with frustration, until a sudden vision of the ivory and gold inlaid bed stopped her and she grinned wickedly. 'Well, perhaps virtuous is not the correct word again.'

The airfield was deserted. She parked the Daimler beside the hangar, where Shasa would not see it from the air. Then she took the travelling rug from the boot and spread it under a tree on the edge of the wide grassy strip.

It was one of those lovely summer days, bright sunlight with only patches of cloud over the mountain, a sharp breeze ruffling the stone pines and taking the edge off the heat.

She settled down on the rug with Aldous Huxley's *Brave New World*, a book that she had been trying to finish for the last week, occasionally glancing up from the page to scan the northern sky.

David Abrahams was almost as enchanted with flying as he was with running. That was what had brought him and Shasa together in the beginning. Though Abe Abrahams had worked for Centaine and been one of her closest personal friends for almost all of David's lifetime, the two boys had really only noticed each other when they went up to university in the same year. Since then they had become inseparable and were founder members of the university flying club, for which Centaine had provided a Tiger Moth trainer.

David was studying law, and it was tacitly understood that when he qualified he would join his father in Windhoek, which meant naturally that he would become one of Centaine's people. She had observed the boy carefully over the years and found no vice in him, so she approved of his friendship with Shasa.

David was taller than his father, with a lean runner's body and an attractively ugly, humorous face, thick curly hair and a large beaky nose which he had inherited from Abe. His best features were his dark Semitic eyes and long sensitive hands, with which he was now manipulating the control column of the Dragon Rapide. He flew with an almost religious dedication, like a priest performing the ritual of some arcane religion. He treated the aircraft as though it were a beautiful living creature, whereas Shasa flew like an engineer – with understanding and great skill, but without David's mystic passion.

David brought that same passion to running and many of the other things in his existence. This was one of the reasons that Shasa loved him so dearly. He spiced Shasa's own life, enhanced the pleasure which Shasa derived from the things they did together. These past weeks might have been dull and anti-climactic without David.

With Centaine's blessing, withheld strenuously for almost a year and then mysteriously given at the last moment, the two of them had taken the Rapide and flown to the H'ani Mine the day after they had written their final examinations.

At the mine Dr Twentyman-Jones had arranged for two four-ton trucks to be waiting for them, fully equipped with camping equipment, camp staff, trackers, skinners and a cook. One of the company prospectors, a man thoroughly versed in the ways of the wild, in bushcraft and hunting big dangerous game, was in charge of the expedition.

Their destination was the Caprivi Strip, that remote ribbon of wilderness, between Angola and Bechuanaland. Entry to this area was severely restricted and hunting was forbidden except in exceptional circumstances. Enviously it was referred to by other sportsmen as the private hunting preserve of the cabinet ministers of the South African government. Blaine Malcomess had arranged entry permits and hunting licences for them.

Under the grizzled old prospector's quiet instruction and firm hand the two young men had come to a closer understanding of, and respect for, the wilderness and the fascinating spectrum of life it contained. In a few weeks he had taught them something of man's place in the fragile balance of nature and instilled in them the principles of ethical hunting.

'The death of each individual animal is sad but inevitable. However, the death of the forest or swamp or plain that supports the entire species is tragedy,' he explained. 'If the kings and noblemen of Europe had not been avid huntsmen, the stag and the boar and the bear would be extinct today. It was the huntsmen who saved the forest from the axe and the plough of the peasants.' And they listened attentively at the camp-fire as he explained. 'Men who hunt for love of the creatures they pursue will protect the breeding females and young from the poachers and save the forests from the goats and cattle. No, my young friends, Robin Hood was a dirty poacher. The sheriff of Nottingham was the real hero.'

So they spent enchanted days in the bush, leaving camp on foot while it was still dark and returning dog-weary after the sun had set. Each of them killed his lion, and experienced the hunter's sadness and elation at the deed, and came out determined to preserve that wild and beautiful country from the predations of unthinking, greedy men. And Shasa, blessed by the chance of birth with the promise of great wealth and influence, came to realize in some small measure how much of that responsibility could one day be his.

The women had been superfluous, as David had warned they would be. However, Shasa had insisted on bringing them, one for himself and one for David.

Shasa's choice was almost thirty years old. 'The best tunes are played on an old fiddle,' he assured David. She was also a divorcée. 'I never break in my own polo ponies.' She had big blue eyes, a ripe red mouth and a pneumatic figure, but was not burdened by an unnecessary amount of brain.

David nicknamed her 'Jumbo', 'Because,' he explained, 'she's so thick that two elephants could walk across her skull side by side.'

Shasa had prevailed upon Jumbo to bring a friend for David, and she had selected a tall dark lady, another divorcée, with trailing locks; her thin arms were loaded with bangles, her long neck with strings of beads. She affected an ivory cigarette-holder and had a smouldering intense gaze but spoke seldom – then usually to ask for another gin.

David dubbed her 'the Camel' for her insatiable thirst. However, the two of them turned out to be ideal, for while they delivered what was expected of them with vigour and expertise when called upon to do so, for the rest they were quite content to remain in camp all day, and in the evening demanded little attention and made no attempt to sabotage the conversation around the camp-fire by joining in.

'That was probably the most enjoyable holiday I will ever spend.' Shasa leaned back in the pilot's seat of the Rapide and stared dreamily ahead, content to let David, in the co-pilot's seat, do the flying. 'But it isn't over yet.' He glanced at his wristwatch. 'Another hour before we reach Cape Town. Keep her on course,' he told David, and unfastened his safety-belt.

'Where are you going?' David demanded.

'I will not embarrass you by replying to that question, but do not be surprised when the Camel comes up to the cockpit to join you.'

'I really am worried about you.' David looked grave. 'You're going to rupture something if you go on like this.'

'Never felt stronger,' Shasa assured him as he wriggled out of the seat.

'Not you, dear boy, it's Jumbo I'm worried about.' David shook his head sadly, and Shasa chuckled, slapped his shoulder and ducked into the rear cabin.

The Camel looked up at him with that dark fanatical gaze and spilled a little gin and tonic down the front of her blouse, while Jumbo giggled and wriggled her fat little rump across the seat to make room for Shasa beside her.

He whispered in her ear and Jumbo looked bewildered, not an unusual expression for her.

'The Mile High Club – what in heaven's name is that?'

Shasa whispered again and she peered out of the side window at the earth below.

'Goodness! I didn't realize we were that high.'

'You get a special brooch when you become a member,' Shasa told her, 'made of gold and diamonds.' And Jumbo's interest flared.

'Oh goody! What kind of brooch?'

'A flying pussy cat, with gold wings and diamond eyes.'

'A pussy cat? Why a pussy—' she broke off as understanding dawned in those china blue eyes. 'Shasa Courtney, you are awful!' She lowered her eyes and blinked demurely, and Shasa winked across the aisle at the Camel.

'I think Davie wants to talk to you.'

The Camel rose obediently, glass in hand, all her bangles and beads jangling as she wobbled from one side of the aisle to the other.

An hour later Shasa brought the Rapide in from the mountain side of the airstrip, and laid her down on the grass as though he were buttering hot toast. He swung her nose around before she had stopped, taxiing back towards the hangars. With a burst of the starboard engine, he brought her up onto the hard stand and cut the motors.

Only then did he notice the yellow Daimler parked in the shadow of the hangar with Centaine standing beside it.

'Oh for the love of Allah, Mater is here. Get those beauties flat on the floor!'

'Too late,' David groaned. 'Jumbo, bless her, is already waving at your mum through the porthole.'

Shasa steeled himself to his mother's wrath as Jumbo came giggling down the boarding ladder, supporting the Camel, whose legs had finally let her down.

Centaine said nothing, but she had a taxi waiting beside the Daimler. How she had known about the girls Shasa would never ask, but she waved the taxi forward and herded the unsteady pair into the back seat with an eye like a stockwhip.

'Get their luggage in the boot,' she ordered Shasa tersely, and the moment it was loaded, she nodded at the taxi-driver. 'Take them wherever they want to go.'

The Camel slumped owl-eyed in her seat, but Jumbo leaned out of the rear window waving and blowing kisses at Shasa until the taxi disappeared through the gates of the airfield, and Shasa bowed his head and waited for his mother's icy sarcasm.

'Did you have a good trip, darling?' Centaine asked sweetly, holding up her face to be kissed, and the two girls were never mentioned again.

'Marvellous!' Shasa's kiss was full of gratitude and relief and genuine pleasure at being with her again, and he began to tell her all about it, but she cut him off.

'Later,' she said. 'Right now I want you to arrange for the Rapide to be refuelled and checked. We are flying up to Johannesburg tomorrow.'

I n Johannesburg they stayed at the Carlton. Centaine owned thirty per cent of the equity in the hotel company, and the royal suite was at her disposal whenever she was in town.

The hotel would soon be in need of major renovation, but it occupied a prime position in the centre of Johannesburg. While she dressed for dinner, Centaine weighed the possibility of having the old building pulled down and redeveloping the site. She would have her architects prepare a report, she decided, as she put business out of her mind and devoted the rest of the evening and all of her attention to Blaine.

Taking a silly chance of alerting the gossips, she and Blaine danced until two in the morning in the nightclub on the top floor of the hotel.

The next day Blaine had a full series of meetings at the Union Buildings in Pretoria, his excuse to Isabella for leaving Cape Town, so Centaine could spend the day with Shasa. In the morning there was a sale of yearlings at the showgrounds, but the prices were ridiculously high and they ended up without having bought a single animal. They lunched at the East African pavilion, where, more than the food, Centaine enjoyed the envious and speculative glances of the women at the surrounding tables.

In the afternoon they went to the zoo. Between feeding the monkeys and rowing on the lake, they discussed Shasa's plans for the future and she was delighted to learn that he had lost none of his determination to take up his duties and responsibilities with Courtney Mining and Finance as soon as he had obtained his Master's degree.

They arrived back at the Carlton with plenty of time to change for the boxing. Blaine, already in his dinner jacket, held a whisky and soda in his hand and he sprawled in one of the armchairs and watched Centaine complete her toilet. She enjoyed that. It was playing at being married again, and she called him to hook in her ear-rings and then paraded for his approval, pirouetting to spread her long skirts.

'I have never been to a boxing match before, Blaine. Aren't we terribly over-dressed?'

'I assure you that black tie is *de rigueur*.'

'Oh God, I'm so nervous. I don't know what I'm going to say to him, even if I get a chance—' she broke off. 'You did manage to get tickets, didn't you?'

He showed them to her and smiled. 'Front row, and I have arranged for a car and driver.'

Shasa drifted into the suite with a white silk scarf draped casually over the shoulders of his dinner jacket, and his black tie minutely and artfully asymmetrical so that it could never be mistaken for one of the modern clip-on monstrosities.

'He looks so magnificent.' Centaine's heart swelled at sight of him. 'How ever am I going to preserve him from the harpies?'

He kissed her before going to the cabinet and pouring her customary glass of champagne.

'Can I freshen your whisky, sir?' he asked Blaine.

'Thanks, but one is my limit, Shasa,' Blaine declined, and Shasa poured himself a dry ginger-ale. That was one thing she didn't have to worry about, Centaine thought, liquor would never be one of Shasa's weaknesses.

'Well, Mater,' Shasa raised his glass, 'here's to your new-found interest in the gentlemanly art of boxing. Are you versed in the general objectives of the game?'

'I think two young men get into a ring and try to kill each other – is that right?'

'That, Centaine, is exactly right,' Blaine laughed. He never used an endearment in front of Shasa, and not for the first time she wondered what Shasa thought of her and Blaine. He must suspect, surely, but she had enough to worry about this evening without opening that dark door. She drank her champagne and then, gorgeous in diamonds and silks, on the arms of the two most important men in her world, she swept out to the waiting limousine.

The streets of the campus of the University of the Witwatersrand around the gymnasium were solid with parked vehicles and others moving nose to tail up the hill, while the sidewalks were packed with a jostling excited crowd of students and fight fans from the general public hurrying towards the hall, so their driver was forced to drop them off two hundred yards short of the entrance, and they joined the throng on foot.

The atmosphere in the hall was noisy and expectant, and as they took their reserved seats Centaine was relieved to see that everyone in the first three rows was wearing evening dress and that there were almost as many ladies as gentlemen in the crowd. She had had nightmares about being the only female in the hall.

She sat through the preliminary bouts, trying to appear interested in the lecture she was receiving from both Blaine and Shasa on the finer points of the contests, but the fighters in the lower weight divisions were so small and scrawny that they reminded her of underfed game cocks, and the flurry of action was fast enough to trick the eye.

Besides, her mind and expectations were racing ahead to her first sight of the man she had come to see.

Another bout ended; the fighters, bruised and slick with sweat, climbed down from the ring, and an expectant hush fell on the hall, and heads began craning around towards the dressing-room.

Blaine checked his programme and murmured, 'This is it!'

Then a bloodthirsty roar went up from the mass of spectators.

'Here he comes.' Blaine touched her arm, but she found she could not turn her head.

'I wish I had never come,' she thought, and shrank down in her seat. 'I don't want him to see me.'

The light heavyweight challenger, Manfred De La Rey, came down to the ring first, attended by his coach and his two seconds, and the block of Stellenbosch students let out a roar and brandished their colour banners, launching into the Varsity war cry. They were immediately answered by the Wits students opposite with cheers and jeers and stamping of feet. The pandemonium was painful to the eardrums as Manfred climbed up into the ring and did a little shuffling dance, holding his gloved hands above his head, the silk gown swinging from his shoulders like a cloak.

His hair had grown longer and unfashionably it was not dressed with Brylcreem, but rippled around his head like a gilded cloud as he moved. His jaw was strong, stopping just short of heaviness, and the bones of forehead and cheek were prominent and cleanly chiselled, but his eyes dominated all his other features – pale and implacable as those of one of the big predatory cats, emphasized by his dark brows.

His shoulders were wide, descending in an inverted pyramid to his hips and the long clean lines of his legs, and

600

his body had been pared of all fat and loose flesh, so that each individual muscle was visible beneath the skin.

Shasa stiffened in his seat as he recognized him. He chewed angrily, grinding his teeth together as he remembered the impact of those fists into his flesh and the suffocating slime of dead fish engulfing him as clearly as if the intervening years had never been.

'I know him, Mater,' he growled between clenched teeth. 'He is the one I fought on the jetty at Walvis Bay.' Centaine laid a hand on his arm to restrain him, but she did not look at him nor speak. Instead, she stole a single glance at Blaine's face, and what she saw distressed her.

Blaine's expression was grim, and she could feel the anger and the hurt in him. He might have been understanding and magnanimous a thousand miles from here, but with the living proof of her wantonness before him, he could only be thinking of the man who had made this bastard on her, and her acquiescence – nay, her joyous participation in the act. He was thinking of her body which should be his alone, used by a stranger, by an enemy against whom he had risked his life in battle.

'Oh God, why did I come?' She tortured herself, and then she felt something melt and change shape inside of her and knew the answer.

'Flesh of my flesh,' she thought. 'Blood of my blood.'

And she remembered the weight of him in her womb, and the spasm of burgeoning life deep within her, and all the instincts of motherhood welled and threatened to choke her, and the angry birth cry rang again in her head, deafening her.

'My son!' she almost cried aloud. 'My own son.'

The magnificent fighting man in the ring turned his head in her direction and saw her for the first time. He dropped his hands to his sides, and he lifted his chin and stared at her with such concentrated venom, with such bitter hatred in those yellow eyes that it was like the blow of a spiked mace in her unprotected face. Then Manfred De La Rey deliberately turned his back on her and strode to his corner.

The three of them, Blaine, Shasa and Centaine, sat rigid and silent in the midst of the roaring, chanting, heaving multitude. Not one of the three looked at the others, and only Centaine moved, twisting the corner of her sequined shawl in her lap and chewing on her lower lip to prevent it quivering.

The champion jumped up into the ring. Ian Rushmore was an inch shorter than Manfred, but broader and deeper in the chest, with long simian arms heavily muscled, and a neck so short and thick that his head seemed to ride directly on his shoulders. Thick, coarse black hair curled out of the top of his vest and he looked powerful and dangerous as a wild boar.

The bell rang and in the blood roar of the crowd the two fighters came together in the middle of the ring. Centaine gasped involuntarily at the thud of gloved fist on flesh and bone. Compared to the flickering blows of the lighter smaller men in the preceding bouts, this was like the meeting of gladiators.

She could not see any advantage between the two men as they wheeled and came together and their fists struck those terrible blows that bounced off solid guards of arms and gloves. Then they weaved and ducked and joined again while the crowd around her bellowed in a mindless frenzy.

As abruptly as it had begun, it ended, and the fighters separated and went back to the little groups of white-clad seconds who hovered over them, tending them lovingly, sponging and kneading their flesh, fanning and massaging and whispering to them.

Manfred took a mouthful from the bottle that his big black bearded coach held to his mouth. He sluiced it around his mouth and then turned and looked at Centaine again, singling her out of the crowd with those pale eyes, and deliberately spat the mouthful of water into the bucket at his feet without breaking his gaze. She knew that it was for her, he was spitting his anger at her. She quailed before his rage and she barely heard Blaine murmur beside her.

'I scored that round as a draw. De La Rey gave nothing away, and Rushmore is wary of him.'

Then the boxers were on their feet again, circling and jabbing and pumping leather-clad fists, grunting like labouring bulls at punches thrown and received, their bodies shining with the running sweat of their exertions and bright red patches glowing on their bodies where blows landed. It went on and on, and Centaine felt a sickness rising in her at the primeval savagery of it, at the sounds and smell and spectacle of violence and pain.

'Rushmore took that one,' Blaine said quietly, as the round ended, and she actually hated him for his calmness. She felt a clammy sweat break out on her face and her nausea threatened to overwhelm her as Blaine went on, 'De La Rey will have to end it in the next two rounds. If he doesn't, Rushmore is going to grind him down. He's getting more confident all the time.'

She wanted to jump to her feet and hurry out of the hall, but her legs would not function. Then the bell rang and the two men were out there again in the glare of floodlights, and she tried to look away but could not – so she stared in sick fascination and saw it happen, saw every vivid detail of it, and knew she would never forget it.

She saw the red leather glove blur as it tore through a tiny gap in the defending circle of arms, and she saw the other man's head snap as though it had reached the limit of the hangman's noose as his body fell through the trap. She saw each individual droplet of sweat burst from his sodden locks, as though a heavy stone had been flung into a deep pool, and the features below twisted grotesquely out of shape by the impact into a carnival mask of agony.

She heard the blow, and the snap of something breaking, teeth or bone or sinew, and she screamed, but her scream was lost and swallowed up in the high surf of sound that burst from a thousand throats around her, and she thrust her fingers into her own mouth as the blows kept coming, so fast that they dissolved before her eyes, so fast that the shocking thuds of impact blended like the sound of an eggbeater in thick cream, and flesh turned to red ruin beneath them. She went on screaming as she watched the terrible killing yellow rage in the eyes of the son she had borne, watched him become a ravening murderous beast, and the man before him wilted and broke, and reeled away on boneless legs, and went down twisting as he fell and rolled onto his back, staring up at the overhead lights with blind eyes, snoring in the thick bright flood that throbbed from his crushed nose into his open mouth. Manfred De La Rey danced over him, still possessed by the killing rage, so that Centaine expected him to throw back his head and howl like a wolf, or throw himself upon the broken thing at his feet and rip the bleeding scalp from its head and brandish it high in obscene triumph.

'Take me away, Blaine,' she sobbed. 'Get me out of this place,' and his arms lifted her to her feet and carried her out into the night.

Behind her the blood roar faded, and she gulped down the cold sweet highveld air as though she had been rescued at the very point of drowning.

'The Lion of the Kalahari writes his own ticket to Berlin,' the headlines crowed, and Centaine shuddered with the memory, and dropped the newspaper over the edge of the bed and reached for the telephone.

'Shasa, how soon can we leave for home?' she demanded,

as soon as his voice, blurred with sleep, sounded in her earpiece, and Blaine came through from the bathroom of the hotel suite with shaving lather on his cheeks.

'You have decided?' he asked as soon as she hung up.

'There is no point in even trying to speak to him,' she replied. 'You saw how he looked at me.'

'Perhaps there will be another time—' he tried to comfort her. But he saw the despair in her eyes and he went to hold her.

D avid Abrahams improved his best time for the 200-metre sprint by almost a second on the first day of the Olympic trials. However, in reaction he did not do as well as expected on the second day when he could only just win his final heat in the 400 by half a metre. Still, his name was high on the list that was read out at the banquet and ball that closed the five days of the track and field trials, and Shasa, who was sitting beside him, was the first to shake his hand and pound him between the shoulder blades. David was going to Berlin.

T wo weeks later the polo trials were held at the Inanda Club in Johannesburg and Shasa was selected for the 'B' team of 'possibles' against Blaine's 'A' team of 'probables' for the last match of the final day.

Sitting high in the grandstand, Centaine watched Shasa play one of the most inspired games of his career, but with despair in her heart knew that it was still not good enough. Shasa never missed an interception, nor mishit a stroke during the first five chukkas, and once even took the ball out from under the nose of Blaine's pony with a display of audacious riding that brought every person in the grand-stand to their feet. Still it was not good enough, she knew.

Clive Ramsay, Shasa's rival for the position of number two in the team that would go to Berlin, had played well all week. He was a man of forty-two years, with a record of solid achievement behind him, and he had seconded Blaine Malcomess in almost thirty international matches. His polo career was just reaching its peak, and Centaine knew that the selectors could not afford to drop him in favour of the younger, more dashing, probably more gifted, but certainly less experienced and therefore less reliable rider.

She could almost see them nodding their heads sagely, puffing their cigars and agreeing. 'Young Courtney will get his chance next time,' and she was hating them for it in advance – Blaine Malcomess included – when suddenly there was a howl from the crowd around her and she jumped to her feet with them.

Shasa, thank God, was out of it, galloping wide down the sideline ready to take the cross as his own number one, another thrusting young player, challenged Clive Ramsay in centre field.

It was probably not deliberate, more likely the conse-quence of a reckless urge to shine, but Shasa's team-mate fouled Clive Ramsay murderously on the interception, knocking his pony onto its knees and sending Clive somersaulting from the saddle onto the iron-hard ground. Later that afternoon X-ray examination confirmed a mul-tiple fracture of Ramsay's femur which the orthopaedic surgeon was subsequently forced to open up and wire.

'No polo for at least a year,' he ordered, when Clive Ramsay came out of the anaesthetic.

So when the selectors went into conclave, Centaine waited anxiously, allowing herself renewed hope. As he had warned Centaine he would, Blaine Malcomess excused himself from the selectors' room when Shasa's name came up. But when he was called back in, the chairman grunted.

'Very well, young Courtney gets the ride in Clive's place.' And despite himself he felt a lift of elation and pride, Shasa Courtney was the closest he would ever get to having a son of his own.

As soon as he could, Blaine telephoned Centaine with the news. 'It won't be announced until Friday, but Shasa has got his ticket.'

Centaine was beside herself. 'Oh Blaine, darling, how will I contain myself until Friday?' she cried. 'Oh, won't it be fun going to Berlin together, the three of us! We can take the Daimler and drive across Europe. Shasa has never visited Mort Homme. We can spend a few days in Paris, and you can take me to dinner at Laserre. There is so much to arrange, but we can talk about it when I see you on Saturday.'

'Saturday?' He had forgotten, she could hear it in his voice.

'Sir Garry's birthday – the picnic on the mountain!' She sighed with exasperation. 'Oh Blaine, it's one of the few times in the year we can be together – legitimately!'

'Is it Sir Garry's birthday again so soon? What happened to the year?' he hedged.

'Oh, Blaine, you did forget,' she accused. 'You can't let me down. It will be a double celebration this year – the birthday, and Shasa's selection for the Games. Promise you will be there, Blaine.'

He hesitated an instant longer. He had already promised to take Isabella and the girls to her mother's home at Franschoek for the weekend.

'I promise, my sweeting, I'll be there.' She would never know what that promise would cost him, for Isabella would make him pay with exquisite refinements of cruelty for the broken pledge.

It was the drug which had wrought this change in Isabella, he kept assuring himself. Beneath it she was still the same sweet and gentle person he had married. It was

607

the unremitting pain and the drug which had ravaged her so, and he tried to maintain his respect and affection for her.

He tried to remember her loveliness, as delicate and ethereal as the bloom on the petals of a new-blown rose, but that loveliness had long since disappeared and the petals of the rose had withered, and the smell of corruption was upon her. The sweet sickly smell of the drug exuded from every pore of her skin and the deep never-healing abscesses in her buttocks and at the base of her spine gave off an odour, faint but penetrating, that he had come to abhor. It made it difficult for him to be near her. The smell and the sight of her offended him but at the same time filled him with helpless pity and corrosive guilt at his infidelity to her.

She had wasted to a skeleton. There was no flesh on the bones of those frail legs, they looked like the legs of one of the wading water birds, perfectly straight and shapeless, distorted only by the lumpy knots of her knees and the useless disproportionately large feet at their extremities.

Her arms were just as thin, and the flesh had receded from the bones of her skull. Her lips had drawn back so that her teeth were prominent and exposed, and looked like those of a skull when she tried to smile or more often grimaced with anger, and her gums were pale, almost white.

Her skin also was pale as ricepaper, and as dry and lifeless, so thin and translucent that the veins of her hands and forehead showed through it in a blue tracery and her eyes were the only living things in her face. They had a malicious glitter in them now, as though she resented him for his healthy lusty body when her own was destroyed and useless.

'How can you, Blaine?' she asked the question with the same accusing high-pitched whine that she had used countless times before. 'You promised me, Blaine. God knows, I see little enough of you as it is. I've been looking forward to this weekend since—' It went on and on, and he tried to shut it out, but he found himself thinking of her body again.

He had not seen her unclothed in almost seven years, then only a month previously he had walked into her dressing-room believing that she was in the gazebo in the garden where she spent most of her day, but she was laid out naked on the white sheet of the massage table with her uniformed day nurse working over her and the shock must have shown clearly on his face as the two women looked up at him, startled.

Every rib stood out of Isabella's narrow chest and her breasts were empty pouches of skin that drooped under her armpits. The dark bush of her pubic hair was incongruous and obscene in the bony basin of her pelvis below which those sticklike legs protruded at a disjointed angle, so shrunken that the gap between her thighs was wider than the span of his hands.

'Get out!' she had screamed at him, and he had torn his eyes from her and hurried from the room. 'Get out! Don't ever come in here again!'

Now her voice had the same ring to it. 'Go to your picnic then, if you must. I know what a burden I am to you. I know you can't bear to spend more than a few minutes in my presence—'

He could not stand it any longer, and he held up a hand to quieten her. 'You are right, my dear. It was selfish of me to even mention it. We won't speak of it again. Of course I will go with you.' He saw the vindictive sparkle of triumph in her eyes, and suddenly for the very first time he hated her, and before he could prevent himself, he thought, 'Why doesn't she die? It would be better for her and everybody about her if she were dead.' Instantly he was appalled at himself and guilt washed over him so that he went to her quickly and stooped over the wheelchair, took that cold bony hand in both of his and squeezed it gently as he kissed her on the lips.

'Forgive me, please,' he whispered – but unbidden the image of her in her coffin appeared to him. She lay there, beautiful and serene as she had once been, her hair once again thick and lustrous auburn spread on the white satin pillow. He shut his eyes tightly to try and drive the image away, but it persisted even when she clung to his hand.

'Oh, it will be such fun to be alone together for a while.' She prevented him pulling away. 'We have so few opportunities to talk any more. You spend so much time in Parliament, and when you aren't about your cabinet duties you are out on the polo field.'

'I see you every day, morning and evening.'

'Oh, I know, but we never talk. We haven't even discussed Berlin yet, and the time is running out.'

'Is there much we should discuss, my dear?' he asked carefully as he disengaged her grip and returned to his own chair on the opposite side of the gazebo.

'Of course there is, Blaine.' She smiled at him, exposing those pale gums behind shrunken lips. It gave her a cunning, almost ferrety, expression which he found disturbing. 'There are so many arrangements to make. When is the team leaving?'

'I may not travel with the team,' he told her carefully. 'I may leave a few weeks earlier and stop off in London and Paris for discussions with the British and French Governments before going on to Berlin.'

'Oh Blaine, we must still make the arrangements for me to go with you,' she said and he had to control his expression for she was watching him carefully.

'Yes,' he said. 'It will need careful planning.'

The idea was insupportable. How he longed to be with Centaine, to be able to get away from all pretence and fear of discovery. 'We shall have to be very certain, my dear, that travelling will not seriously impair your health further.'

'You don't want me with you, do you?' Her voice rose sharply.

'Of course—'

'It's a wonderful chance for you to get away from me, to escape from me.'

'Isabella, please calm yourself. You will do yourself—'

'Don't pretend you care about me – I've been a burden on you for nine years. I'm sure you wish me dead.'

'Isabella—' He was shaken by the accuracy of the accusation.

'Oh, don't play the saint with me, Blaine Malcomess. I may be locked into this chair, but I see things and I hear things.'

'I don't wish to continue like this.' He stood up. 'We'll talk again once you have control—'

'Sit down!' she screeched at him. 'I won't have you running off to your French whore as you always do!' He flinched as though she had struck him in the face, and she went on gloatingly, 'There, I've said it at last. Oh God, you'll never know how close I've been to saying it so many times. You'll never know how good it feels to say it – whore! Doxy!'

'If you continue, I will leave,' he warned.

'Harlot,' she said with relish. 'Slut! Jade!'

He turned on his heel and went down the steps of the gazebo two at a time.

'Blaine,' she screamed after him. 'Come back!'

He continued walking up towards the house, and her tone changed.

'Blaine, I'm sorry. I apologize. Please come back. Please!' and he could not refuse her. Reluctantly he turned back, and found that his hands were shaking with shock and anger. He thrust them into his pockets and stopped at the top of the steps.

'All right,' he said softly. 'It's true about Centaine Courtney. I love her. But it is also true that we have done everything in our power to prevent you being hurt or humiliated. So don't ever talk like that about her again. If she had allowed it, I would have gone to her years ago – and left you. May God forgive me, but I would have walked out on you! Only she kept me here, only she still keeps me here.'

She was chastened and shaken as he was, or so he thought, until she raised her eyes again and he saw that she had feigned repentance merely to lure him back within range of her tongue. 'I know I cannot go to Berlin with you, Blaine. I have already asked Dr Joseph and he has forbidden it. He says the journey would kill me. However, I know what you are planning, you and that woman. I know you have used all your influence to get Shasa Courtney into the team merely to give her an excuse to be there. I know you are planning a wonderful illicit interlude, and I can't stop you going—'

He spread his hands in angry resignation. It was useless to protest and her voice rose again into that harrowing shrillness.

'Well, let me tell you this – it isn't going to be the honeymoon that the two of you think it is. I've told the girls, both Tara and Mathilda Janine, that they are going with you. I've told them already, and they are beside themselves with excitement. It will be up to you. Either you are heartless enough to disappoint your own daughters, or you will be playing baby-sitter and not Romeo in Berlin.' Her voice rose even higher, and the glitter of her eyes was vindictive. 'And I warn you! If you refuse to take them with you, Blaine Malcomess, I will tell them why. I call on God as my witness, I will tell them that their beloved daddy is a cheat and a liar, a libertine and a whoremaster!'

Although everybody, from the most knowledgeable sports writers to the lowliest fight fan, had confidently expected Manfred De La Rey to be on the boxing squad to go to Berlin, when the official announcement of the team was made and he was indeed the light heavyweight selection, but in addition Roelf Stander was the heavyweight choice and the Reverend Tromp Bierman was given the duties of official team coach, the entire town and university body of Stellenbosch erupted in spontaneous expressions of pride and delight.

There was a civic reception and parade through the streets of the town, while at a mass meeting of the *Ossewa Brandwag* the commanding general held them up as an example of Afrikaner manhood and extolled their dedication and fighting skills.

'It is young men such as these who will lead our nation to its rightful place in this land,' he told them, and while the massed uniformed ranks gave the OB salute, the clenched right fist held across the chest, Manfred and Roelf had the badges of officer rank pinned to their tunics.

'For God and the *Volk*,' their high commander exhorted them, and Manfred had never before experienced such pride, such determination to honour the trust that had been placed in him.

Over the weeks that followed, the excitement continued to build up. There were fittings at the official team tailor for the gold and green blazers, white slacks and broad-brimmed Panama hats which made up the uniform in which they would march into the Olympic stadium. There were endless team briefings, covering every subject from German etiquette and polite behaviour to travel arrangements and profiles of the opponents whom they were likely to encounter on the way to the final.

Both Manfred and Roelf were interviewed by journalists from every magazine and newspaper in the country, and a half an hour on the nationally broadcast radio programme 'This is your Land' was devoted entirely to them.

Only one person seemed unaffected by the excitement.

'The weeks you are away will seem longer than my whole life,' Sarah told Manfred.

'Don't be a silly little duck,' he laughed at her. 'It will all be over before you know it, and I'll be back with a gold medal on my chest.'

'Don't call me a silly little duck,' she flashed at him, 'not ever again!'

He stopped laughing. 'You are right,' he said. 'You are worth more than that.'

Sarah had taken on herself the duties of timekeeper and second for Manfred's and Roelf's evening training runs. On flying bare feet she took short cuts up the hillside and through the forest to wait for them at prearranged spots with her stopwatch, borrowed from Uncle Tromp, a wet sponge and a flask of cold freshly squeezed orange juice to refresh them. As soon as they had sponged down, drunk and set off again she would race away, cutting over the crest of the hill or through the valley to wait for them at the next stage.

Two weeks before the sailing date, Roelf was forced to miss one of the evening runs when he was obliged to chair an extraordinary meeting of the students' representative council and Manfred made the run alone.

He took the long steep side of the Hartenbosch mountain at a full run, going with all his strength, flying up the slope with long elastic strides, lifting his gaze to the crest. Sarah was waiting for him there, and the low autumn sun was behind her, crowning her with gold and striking through the thin stuff of her skirts so that her legs were silhouetted and he could see every line and lovely angle of her body almost as though she were unclothed.

He pulled up involuntarily in full stride and stood staring

up at her, his chest heaving and his heart pounding, not only from his exertions.

'She is beautiful.' He was amazed that he had never seen it before, and he walked up the last angle of the slope slowly, staring at her, confused by this sudden realization and by the hollow hunger, the need that he had kept suppressed, whose existence he had never admitted to himself but which now suddenly threatened to consume him.

She came to meet him the last few paces; barefoot she was so much smaller than he was and that seemed only to increase this terrible hunger. She held out the sponge to him, but when he made no move to take it from her, she stepped up close to him and reached up to wipe the sweat from his neck and shoulders.

'I dreamed last night we were back in the camp,' she whispered as she worked, swabbing his upper arms. 'Do you remember the camp beside the railway tracks, Manie?'

He nodded. His throat had closed, and he could not reply.

'I saw my ma lying in the grave. It was a terrible thing. Then it changed, Manie, it wasn't my ma any more, it was you. You were so pale and handsome, but I knew I had lost you – and I was so eaten by my own sorrow that I wanted to die also and be with you for ever.'

He reached out and took her in his arms and she sobbed and fell against him. Her body felt so cool and soft and compliant and her voice shook.

'Oh, Manie. I don't want to lose you. Please come back to me – without you I don't want to go on living.'

'I love you, Sarie.' His voice was hoarse and she jerked in his arms.

'Oh Manie.'

'I never realized it before,' he croaked.

'Oh Manie, I have always realized it. I loved you from

the first minute of the first day, and I will love you until the last,' she cried, and turned her mouth up to his. 'Kiss me, Manie, kiss me or I will die.'

The touch of her mouth ignited something within him, and the fire and the smoke of it obscured reason and reality. Then they were under the pines beside the path, lying on a bed of soft needles, and the sultry autumn air was soft as silk upon his bare back, but not as soft as her body beneath his nor as hot as the liquid depths in which she engulfed him.

He did not understand what had happened until she cried out, in pain and intense joy, but by then it was too late and he found himself answering her cry, no longer able to draw back, carried along on a swirling tidal wave to a place he had never been before – nor had he even dreamed of its existence.

Reality and consciousness returned slowly from far away, and he drew away from her and stared at her in horror, pulling on his own clothing.

'What we have done is wicked beyond forgiveness—'

'No.' She shook her head vehemently and, still naked, reached for him. 'No, Manie, it's not wicked when two people love each other. How can it be wicked? It's a thing from God, beautiful and holy.'

The night before Manfred sailed for Europe with Uncle Tromp and the team, he slept in his old room at the Manse. When the old house was dark and quiet, Sarah crept down the passage. He had left his door unlatched. Nor did he protest as she let her nightdress fall and crept under the sheet beside him.

She stayed until the doves in the oaks outside the stoep began fluttering and softly cooing. Then she kissed him one last time and whispered:

'Now we belong to each other – for ever and always.'

It was only half an hour before sailing and Centaine's stateroom was so crowded that the stewards were forced to pass the champagne glasses over the heads of the guests, and it required a major expedition to get from one side of the cabin to the other. The only one of Centaine's friends who was not present was Blaine Malcomess. They had decided not to advertise the fact that they were sailing on the same mail ship, and had agreed only to meet once they were clear of the harbour.

Both Abe Abrahams, bursting with pride, his arm hooked through David's, and Dr Twentyman-Jones, tall and lugubrious as a marabou stork, were in the party around Centaine. They had come all the way down from Windhoek to see her off. Naturally, Sir Garry and Anna were there, as were the *Ou Baas* General Smuts, and his little fluffy-haired wife with her steel-rimmed spectacles making her look like an advertisement for Mazzawattee tea.

In the far corner Shasa was surrounded by a bevy of young ladies, and was in the middle of a story that was being followed with shrieks of amusement and gasps of incredulous wonder, when suddenly he lost track of what he had been saying and stared out of the porthole beside him. Through it he had a view out onto the boat deck, and what had caught his attention was a glimpse of a girl's head as she passed.

He couldn't see her face, just the side and back of her head, a cascade of auburn curls set on a long slim neck, and a little ear sticking out of the curls at a jaunty angle. It was a fleeting glimpse only, but something about the angle and carriage of that head made him lose immediate interest in the females in front of him.

He went up on his toes, spilling champagne, and stuck his head through the porthole, but the girl had passed by and he only had a back view of her. She had an impossibly narrow waist but a cheeky little rump that switched from side to side and made her skirts swing rhythmically as she walked. Her calves were perfectly turned and her ankles slim and neat. She went round the corner with a last twitch of her bottom, leaving Shasa determined that he must get a look at her face.

'Excuse me, ladies.' His audience gave little cries of disappointment, but he eased himself neatly out of their circle and began working his way towards the door. But before he reached it, the sirens started their booming thunder of warning and the cry went up, 'Last call, ladies and gentlemen – all ashore, those who are going ashore,' and he knew he had run out of time.

'She was probably a dog – a backside like heaven and a face like hell – and she almost certainly isn't sailing, anyway,' he consoled himself. Then Dr Twentyman-Jones was shaking his hand and wishing him luck for the Games, and he tried to forget that bunch of auburn curls and concentrate on his social duties, but it wasn't all that easy.

Out on deck he looked for an auburn head going down the gangway, or in the crowd on the quayside, but Centaine was tugging at his arm as the gap between ship and land opened below them.

'Come, *chéri*, let's go and check the dining-room seating.'

'But you have been invited to the captain's table, Mater,' he protested. 'There was an invitation in the—'

'Yes, but you and David haven't,' she pointed out. 'Come along, David, let's go and find where they have put the two of you, and have it changed if it's not suitable.'

She was up to something, Shasa realized. Normally she would take the seating for granted, secure in the knowledge that her name was all the guarantee of preference that was necessary, but now she was insistent, and she had that look in her eye which he knew so well, and which he called her 'Machiavellian sparkle'.

'Come along then,' he agreed indulgently, and the three of them went down the walnut-panelled staircase to the first class dining-room on the deck below.

At the foot of the stairs a small group of seasoned travellers were being affable to the head waiter; five-pound notes were disappearing like magic into that urbane gentleman's pocket, leaving no bulge, and names were being rubbed out and re-pencilled on the seating plan.

Standing a little apart from the group was a tall familiar figure that Shasa recognized instantly. Something about him, the expectant turn of his head towards the staircase, told Shasa he was waiting for someone, and his dazzling smile as he saw Centaine made it clear who that someone was.

'Good Lord, Mater,' Shasa exclaimed. 'I didn't realize Blaine was sailing today – I thought he would be going later with the others—' he broke off. He had felt his mother's grip on his forearm tighten and the quick catch of her breath as she saw Blaine.

'They have arranged this,' he realized with a flare of amazement. 'That's what her excitement was.' And at last it dawned upon him. 'You never think it of your own mother, but they are lovers. All these years, and I never saw it.' The little things, insignificant at the time but now full of meaning, came crowding back. 'Blaine and the mater, damn me blind! Who would have thought it—' and conflicting emotions assailed him. 'Of all men in the world, I would have chosen him—' In that moment he realized how much Blaine Malcomess had come to stand in the place of the father he had never known, but the thought was followed instantly by a flush of jealous and moral indignation. 'Blaine Malcomess, pillar of society and government, and Mater who is always frowning and shaking her head at me – the naughty little devils, they have been raving away for years without anybody suspecting!'

Blaine was coming towards them. 'Centaine, this is a surprise!'

Mater was laughing and holding out her right hand to

him. 'Gracious me, Blaine Malcomess, I had no idea you were on board.'

Shasa thought wryly: 'What marvellous acting! You have had me and everybody fooled for years. The two of you make Clark Gable and Ingrid Bergman look like a pair of beginners!'

Then suddenly it didn't matter any more. The only thing that was important was that there were two girls following Blaine as he came towards Centaine.

'Centaine, I'm sure you remember my two daughters. This is Tara and this is Mathilda Janine—'

'Tara.' Silently Shasa sang the name in his head. 'Tara – what a lovely name.' It was the girl he had glimpsed on the boat deck, and she was only one hundred times more stunning than he had hoped she might be.

Tara. She was tall, only a few inches below his own six foot, but her legs were like willow wands and her waist was like a reed.

Tara. She had the face of a madonna, a serene oval, and her complexion was a mixture of cream and flower petals, almost too perfect, yet redeemed from insipid vacuity by the smoking chestnut hair, her father's wide strong mouth and her own eyes, resilient as grey steel and bright with intelligence and determination.

She greeted Centaine with the correct amount of deference and then turned to look directly at Shasa.

'Shasa, you too remember Tara,' Blaine told him. 'She came out to Weltevreden four years ago.'

Was this the same noisy little pest? Shasa stared at her – the one in short skirts with scabs on her bony knees who had embarrassed him with her boisterous and childish capers? He could not believe it was, and his voice caught in his throat.

'How good to see you again, Tara, after so long.'

'Remember, Tara Malcomess,' she cautioned herself. 'Be controlled and aloof.' She almost shivered with shame as

620

she remembered how she had gambolled and fawned around him like a puppy begging to be patted. 'What a callow little beast, I was.' But she had been smitten by a crush so powerful at first sight of him that the pain of it still lingered even now.

However, she managed to display the right shade of indifference as she murmured, 'Oh have we met? I must have forgotten, forgive me.' She held out her hand. 'Well, it's pleasant to meet you again – Shasa?'

'Yes, Shasa,' he agreed, and he took the hand as though it were a holy talisman. 'Why haven't we met again since then?' he asked himself, and immediately he saw the answer. 'It was deliberate. Blaine and Mater made damn sure that we never met again in case it complicated their own little arrangement. They did not want Tara reporting back to her mama.' But he was too happy to be angry with them now.

'Have you made your table reservations?' he asked, without relinquishing her hand.

'Daddy is sitting at the captain's table,' Tara pouted lovingly at her father. 'And we are to be left all alone.'

'The four of us could sit together,' Shasa suggested quickly. 'Let's go and talk to the *Maître*.' Blaine and Centaine exchanged relieved glances – it was all going exactly as they had planned, with one twist they had not foreseen.

Mathilda Janine had blushed as she shook hands with David Abrahams. Of the two sisters, she was the ugly duckling for she had inherited not only her father's wide mouth but his large nose and prominent ears as well, and her hair was not auburn but ginger carrot.

'But he's got a big nose too,' she thought defiantly, as she studied David, and then her thoughts went off on a tangent. 'If Tara tells him I'm only sixteen I'll just die!'

The voyage was a tempest of emotions, full of delights and surprises and frustrations and agonies for all of them.

During the fourteen days of the passage to Southampton Blaine and Centaine saw very little of the four youngsters, meeting them for a cocktail beside the ship's pool before lunch and for a duty dance after dinner, David and Shasa each taking a turn at whirling Centaine around the floor while Blaine did the same to his daughters. Then there would be a quick exchange of glances between the four young people and they would make their elaborate excuses before all disappearing down into the tourist class where the real fun was, leaving Blaine and Centaine to their staid pleasures on the upper decks.

Tara in a one-piece bathing costume of lime green was the most magnificent sight Shasa had ever laid eyes upon. Her breasts under the clinging material were the shape of unripe pears and when she came from the pool with water streaming down those long elegant limbs, he could make out the dimple of her navel through the cloth and the hard little marbles of her nipples, and it took all his control to prevent himself groaning out loud.

Mathilda Janine and David discovered a mutual zany and irreverent sense of humour, and kept each other in convulsions of laughter most of the time. Mathilda Janine was up at four-thirty each morning, no matter how late they had got to bed, to give David raucous encouragement as he made his fifty circuits of the boat deck.

'He moves like a panther,' she told herself. 'Long and smooth and graceful.' And she had to think up fifty new witticisms each morning to shout at him as he went bounding past her. They chased each other around the pool and wrestled ecstatically below the surface; once they had managed to fall in locked in each other's arms, but, apart from a furtive pecking kiss at the door of the cabin that Mathilda Janine shared with Tara, neither of them even considered carrying it any further. Although David had benefited from his brief relationship with the Camel, it

622

never occurred to him to indulge in the same acrobatics with someone as special as Matty.

Shasa on the other hand suffered under no such inhibitions. He was vastly more sexually experienced than David, and once he had recovered from the initial awe of Tara's beauty, he launched an insidious but determined assault on the fortress of her virginity. However, his rewards were even less spectacular than David's.

It took him almost a week to work up to the stage of intimacy where Tara would allow him to spread suntan oil on her back and shoulders. In the small hours of the morning when the lights on the dance floor were dimmed for the last dance and the band played the sugary romantic 'Poinciana', she laid her velvet-soft cheek against his, but when he tried to press his lower body against hers, she allowed it for only moments before she arched her back, and when he tried to kiss her at the cabin door she held him off with both hands on his chest and gave him that low tantalizing laugh.

'The silly little witch is totally frigid,' Shasa told his reflection in the shaving mirror. 'She probably has an iceberg in her knickers.' Thought of those regions made him shiver with frustration, and he resolved to break off the chase. He thought of the five or six other females on board, not all of them young, who had looked at him with unmistakable invitation in their eyes. 'I could have any or all of them instead of panting along behind Miss Tin Knickers—' But an hour later he was partnering her in the mixed doubles deck quoit championships, or smoothing suntan oil on that flawless finely muscled back with fingers that trembled with agonized desire, or trying to keep level with her in a discussion of the merits and demerits of the government's plans to disenfranchise the coloured voters of the Cape Province.

He had discovered with some dismay that Tara

Malcomess had a highly developed political conscience, and that even though it was vaguely understood between him and Mater that Shasa would one day go into politics and parliament, his grasp of and interest in the complex problems of the country was not of the same calibre as Tara's. She held views that were almost as disturbing to him as her physical attractions.

'I believe, as Daddy does, that far from taking the vote away from the few black people who have it, we should be giving it to all of them.'

'All of them!' Shasa was appalled. 'You don't really believe that, do you?'

'Of course I do. Not all at once, but on a civilization basis, government by those who have proved fit to govern. Give the vote to all those who have the right standards of education and responsibility. In two generations every man and woman, black or white, could be on the roll.'

Shasa shuddered at the thought, his own aspirations to a seat in the house would not survive that – but this was probably the least radical of her opinions.

'How can we prevent people from owning land in their own country or from selling their labour in the best market, or prohibit them from collective bargaining?'

Trade unions were the tools of Lenin and the devil. That was a fact Shasa had taken in with his mother's milk.

'She's a bolshy – but, God, what a beautiful bolshy!' he thought, and pulled her to her feet to break the unpalatable lecture. 'Come on, let's go for a swim.'

'He's an ignorant fascist,' she thought furiously, but when she saw the way the other women looked at him from behind their sunglasses, she wanted to claw their eyes out of their faces, and at night in her bunk when she thought about the touch of his hands on her bare back, and the feel of him against her on the dance floor, she blushed in the darkness at the fantasies that filled her head.

'If I just let it start – just the barest beginning, I know I won't be able to stop him, I won't even want to stop him—' and she steeled herself against him. 'Controlled and aloof,' she repeated, like a charm against the treacherous wiles of her own body.

B y some extraordinary coincidence it just so happened that Blaine Malcomess had shipped his Bentley in the hold, alongside Centaine's Daimler.

'We could drive to Berlin in convoy,' Centaine exclaimed as though the idea had just occurred to her, and there was clamorous acceptance of the idea from the four younger members of the party, and immediate jockeying and lobbying for seats in the two vehicles. Centaine and Blaine, protesting mildly, allowed themselves to be allocated the Bentley while the others, driven by Shasa, would follow in the Daimler.

From Le Havre they drove the dusty roads of north-western France, through the towns that still had the ring of terror in their names, Amiens and Arras. The green grass had covered the muddy battlefields where Blaine had fought, but the fields of white crosses were bright as daisies in the sunlight.

'May God grant that mankind never has to live through that again,' Blaine murmured, and Centaine reached across and took his hand.

In the little village of Mort Homme they parked in front of the *auberge* in the main street, and when Centaine walked in through the front door to enquire for lodgings, Madame behind the desk recognized her instantly and screeched with excitement.

'Henri, *viens vite! C'est Mademoiselle de Thiry du château*—' and she rushed to embrace Centaine and buss her on both cheeks.

A travelling salesman was ousted, and the best rooms

put at their disposal; a little explanation was needed when Centaine and Blaine asked for separate accommodation, but the meal they were served that night was exquisitely nostalgic for Centaine, with all the specialities – terrines and truffles and *tartes* – with the wine of the region, while Madame stood beside the table and gave Centaine all the gossip, the deaths and births, the marriages and elopements and liaisons of the last nineteen years.

In the early morning Centaine and Shasa left the others sleeping, and drove up to the château. It was rubble and black scorched walls, pierced with empty windows and shell holes, overgrown and desolate, and Centaine stood in the ruins and wept for her father who had burned with the great house rather than abandon it to the advancing Germans.

After the war the estate had been sold off to pay the debts that the old man had accumulated over a lifetime of good living and hard drinking. It was now owned by Hennessy, the great cognac firm; the old man would have enjoyed that little irony, Centaine smiled at the thought.

Together they climbed the hillock beyond the ruined château and from the crest Centaine pointed out the orchard and plantation that marked the old wartime airfield.

'That is where your father's squadron was stationed, on the edge of the orchard. I waited here every morning for the squadron to take off, and I would wave them away to battle.'

'They flew SE5a's didn't they?'

'Only later. At first it was the old Sopwiths.' She was looking up at the sky. 'Your father's machine was painted bright yellow. I called him *le petit jaune*, the little yellow one – I can see him now in his flying helmet. He used to lift the goggles so I could see his eyes as he flew past me. Oh Shasa, how noble and gay and young he was, a young eagle going up into the blue.'

They descended the hillock and drove slowly back between the vineyards. Centaine asked Shasa to stop beside a small stone-walled barn at the corner of North Field. He watched her, puzzled, as she stood for a few minutes in the doorway of the thatched building and then came back to the Daimler with a faint smile on her lips and a soft glow in her eyes.

She saw his enquiring look and told him, 'Your father and I used to meet here.' In a clairvoyant insight Shasa realized that in this rickety old building in a foreign land he had been conceived. The strangeness of this knowledge remained with him as they drove back towards the *auberge*.

At the entrance to the village in front of the little church with its green copper spire, they stopped again and went into the cemetery. Michael Courtney's grave was at the far end, beneath a yew tree. Centaine had ordered the headstone from Africa but had never seen it before. A marble eagle, perched on a tattered battle standard, was on the point of flight, with wings spread. Shasa thought it was a little too flamboyant for a memorial to the dead.

They stood side by side and read the inscription:

SACRED TO THE MEMORY OF
CAPTAIN MICHAEL COURTNEY RFC
KILLED IN ACTION 19 APRIL 1917.
GREATER LOVE HATH NO MAN.

Weeds had grown up around the headstone, and they knelt together and tidied the grave. Then they stood at the foot of it, their heads bowed.

Shasa had expected to be profoundly moved by his father's grave, but instead he felt remote and untouched. The man beneath the headstone had become clay long before he was born. He had felt closer to Michael Courtney six thousand miles from here when he had slept in his bed, worn his old thornproof tweed jacket, handled his Purdey shotgun and his fishing-rods, or used his gold-nibbed pen and his platinum and onyx dress studs.

They went back along the path to the church and found the village priest in the vestry. He was a young man, not much older than Shasa, and Centaine was disappointed for his youth seemed to her a break in her tenuous link to Michael and the past. However, she wrote out two large cheques, one for the repairs to the church's copper spire, and the other to pay for fresh flowers to be placed on Michael's grave each Sunday in perpetuity, and they went back to the Daimler with the priest's fervent benedictions following them.

The following day they all drove on to Paris; Centaine had wired ahead for accommodation at the Ritz in the Place Vendôme.

Blaine and Centaine had a full round of engagements – meetings, luncheons and dinners – with various members of the French government, so the four younger members of the party were left to their own devices and they very soon discovered that Paris was the city of romance and excitement.

They rode to the first *étage* of the Eiffel Tower in one of the creaking elevators and then raced each other up the open steel staircase to the very top and 'oohed' and 'aahed' at the city spread below them. They strolled with arms linked along the footpath on the riverbank and under the fabulous bridges of the Seine. With her baby box Brownie, Tara photographed them on the steps of Montmartre with the Sacré Coeur as a backdrop; they drank coffee and ate croissants in the sidewalk cafés and lunched at the Café de la Paix, dined at La Coupole and saw *La Traviata* at the Opéra.

At midnight when the girls had said goodnight to Centaine and their father and retired demurely and dutifully to their room, Shasa and David smuggled them out over the balcony and they went dancing in the *boites* on the Left Bank or sat listening to jazz in the cellars of Montparnasse, where they discovered a black trombone player who blew a horn that made your spine curl and a little brasserie where you could eat snails and wild strawberries at three in the morning.

In the last dawn, as they crept down the corridor to get the girls back to their room, they heard familiar voices in the elevator cage as it came up to their floor, and only just in time the four of them dived down the staircase and lay in a heap on the first landing, the girls stuffing handkerchiefs into their mouths to stifle their giggles, while just above them Blaine and Centaine, resplendent in full evening dress and oblivious of their presence, left the elevator and arm in arm strolled down the passage towards Centaine's suite.

They left Paris with regret and reached the German border in high spirits. They presented their passports to the French *douaniers* and were waved through to the German side with typical Gallic panache. They left the Bentley and Daimler parked at the barrier and trooped into the German border post where they were struck immediately by the difference in attitude between the two groups of officials.

The two German officers were meticulously turned out, their leather polished to a gloss, their caps set at the exact regulation angle and the black swastikas in a field of crimson and white on their left arms. From the wall behind their desk, a framed portrait of the Führer, stern and moustached, glowered down upon them.

Blaine laid the sheaf of passports on the desk top in front of them with a friendly 'Guten Tag, mein Herr', and stood chatting to Centaine while one of the officials went through the passports one at a time, comparing each of the holders to his or her photograph and then stamping the visa with the black eagle and swastika device, before going on to the next document.

Dave Abrahams' passport was at the bottom of the pile,

and when the officer came to it, he paused and re-read the front cover and then pedantically turned and perused every single page in the document, looking up at David again and scrutinizing his features after each page. After a few minutes of this the group around David fell silent and began exchanging puzzled glances.

'I think something is wrong, Blaine,' Centaine said quietly, and he went back to the desk.

'Problem?' Blaine asked, and the official answered him in stilted but correct English.

'Abrahams, it is a Jewish name, no?'

Blaine flushed with irritation, but before he could reply David stepped up to the desk beside him. 'It's a Jewish name, yes!' he said quietly, and the official nodded thoughtfully, tapping the passport with his forefinger.

'You admit you are Jewish?'

'I am Jewish,' David replied in the same level tone.

'It is not written in your passport that you are Jewish,' the customs officer pointed out.

'Should it be?' David asked. The officer shrugged, then asked, 'You wish to enter Germany – and you are Jewish?'

'I wish to enter Germany to take part in the Olympic Games, to which I have been invited by the German government.'

'Ah! You are an Olympic athlete – a Jewish Olympic athlete?'

'No, I am a South African Olympic athlete. Is my visa in order?'

The official did not reply to the question. 'Wait here, please.' He went through the rear door, carrying David's passport with him.

They heard him speaking to someone in the back office, and they all looked at Tara. She was the only one in the party who understood a little German, she had studied the language for her matriculation examinations and passed it on the Higher Grade.

'What is he saying?' Blaine asked.

'They are talking too fast – a lot about "Jews" and "Olympics",' Tara answered, then the rear door opened and the original official came back with a plump rosy-faced man who was clearly his superior, for his uniform and his manner were grander.

'Who is Abrahams?' he demanded.

'I am.'

'You are a Jew? You admit you are a Jew?'

'Yes, I am a Jew. I have said so many times. Is there something wrong with my visa?'

'You will wait, please.' This time all three officials retired to the rear office, once more taking David's passport with them. They heard the tinkle of a telephone bell, and then the senior officer's voice, loud and obsequious.

'What's going on?' They looked to Tara.

'He's talking to somebody in Berlin,' Tara told them. 'He's explaining about David.'

The one-sided conversation in the next room ended with '*Jawohl, mein Kapitän,*' repeated four times, each time louder, and then a shouted '*Heil Hitler!*' and the tinkle of the telephone.

The three officials filed back into the front office. The rosy-faced superior stamped David's passport and handed it to him with a flourish.

'Welcome to the Third Reich!' he declared, and flung his right hand up, palm open, and extended towards them, and shouted, '*Heil Hitler!*'

Mathilda Janine burst into nervous giggles, 'Isn't he a lark!' Blaine seized her arm and marched her out of the office.

So they drove into Germany, all of them silent and subdued.

They found lodgings in the first roadside inn, and contrary to her usual custom, Centaine accepted them without first inspecting the beds, the plumbing and the kitchens. After dinner nobody wanted to play cards or explore the village and they were in bed before ten o'clock.

However, by breakfast time they had recovered their high spirits, and Mathilda Janine had them laughing with a poem she had composed in honour of the extraordinary feats that her father, Shasa and David were about to perform in the Games ahead of them.

Their good humour increased during the day's easy journey through the beautiful German countryside, the villages and hilltop castles right out of the pages of Hans Andersen fairy tales, the forests of pine trees in dark contrast to the open meadows and the tumbling rivers crossed by arched bridges of stone. Along the way they saw groups of young people in national dress, the boys in lederhosen and feathered loden hats, the girls in *dirndls*, who waved and called greetings as the two big motor cars sped past.

They lunched in an inn full of people and music and laughter, on a haunch of wild boar with roast potatoes and apples and drank a Moselle with the taste of the grape and sunshine in its pale greenish depths.

'Everybody is so happy and prosperous-looking,' Shasa remarked as he glanced around the crowded room.

'The only country in the world with no unemployment and no poor,' Centaine agreed, but Blaine tasted his wine and said nothing.

That afternoon they entered the northern plain on the approach to Berlin, and Shasa, who was leading, swung the Daimler off onto the verge so suddenly that David grabbed for the dashboard and the girls in the back squeaked with alarm.

Shasa jumped out, leaving the engine still running, shouting 'David! David! Just look at them – aren't they the most beautiful things you have ever seen.' The others piled out beside him and stared up at the sky, while Blaine pulled

632

the Bentley in behind the Daimler and he and Centaine climbed out to join them, shading their eyes against the slanting sun.

There was an airfield adjoining the highway. The hangar buildings were painted silver and the windsock waved its long white arm in the small breeze. A stick of three fighter aircraft turned out of the sun, coming around in formation to line up for the strip. They were sleek as sharks, their bellies and lower wings painted sky blue, their upper surfaces speckled with camouflage and the boss of their propellers bright yellow.

'What are they?' Blaine called across to the two young pilots, and they answered as one:

'109s.'

'Messerschmitts.'

The machine-gun snouts bristled from the leading edges of the wings, and the eyes of the cannon peered malevolently from the centre of the spinning propeller bosses.

'What I'd give to fly one of those!'

'An arm—'

'And a leg—'

'And my hope of salvation!'

The three fighters changed formation into line astern and descended towards the airfield.

'They say that they can do 350 mph, straight and level—'

'Oh sweet! Oh sweet! Look at them fly!'

The girls were infected by their excitement, and they clapped and laughed, as the war machines passed low over their heads and touched down on the airstrip only a few hundred yards beyond.

'It would be worth going to war, just to get a shot at flying something like that,' Shasa exulted, and Blaine turned back to the Bentley to hide his sudden anger at the remark.

Centaine slid into the seat beside him and they drove in silence for five minutes before she said: 'He's so young and foolish sometimes – I'm sorry, Blaine, I know how he upset you.'

He sighed. 'We were the same. We called it "a great game" and thought it was going to be the glory of a lifetime that would make us men and heroes. Nobody told us about the ripped guts and the terror and how dead men smell on the fifth day in the sun.'

'It won't happen again,' Centaine said, fiercely. 'Please don't let it happen again!' In her mind's eye she saw once again the burning aircraft, with the body of the man she loved, blackening and twisting and crisping; then the face was no longer Michael's but that of his only son, and Shasa's beautiful face burst open like a sausage held too close to the flames and the sweet young life juices burst from it.

'Please stop the car, Blaine,' she whispered. 'I think I am going to be ill.'

With hard driving they could have reached Berlin that night, but in one of the smaller towns that they were passing through the streets were decorated for some sort of celebration, and Centaine asked and was told that it was the festival of the local patron saint.

'Oh Blaine, let's stay over,' she cried, and they joined in the festival.

That afternoon there was a procession. An effigy of the saint was paraded through the narrow cobbled streets, and a band followed it, with angelic little blond girls in national dress, and small boys in uniform.

'Those are the Hitler Youth,' Blaine explained. 'Something like old Baden-Powell's Boy Scouts, but with a much stronger emphasis on German national aspirations and patriotism.'

After the parade there was torchlit dancing in the town square, and barrows serving foaming tankards of beer or glasses of Sekt, the German equivalent of champagne, and serving-girls with lace aprons and cheeks like ripe apples carrying overflowing platters of rich food, pigs' trotters and veal, smoked mackerel and cheeses.

They found a table at the corner of the square, and the revellers at the neighbouring tables called greetings and merry banter to them; and they drank beer and danced and beat time to the 'oom-pa-pa' band with their beer mugs.

Then quite abruptly the atmosphere changed. The laughter around them became brittle and forced, and there was a wariness in the faces and eyes of revellers at the adjacent tables; the band began to play too loudly and the dancers became feverish in their exertions.

Four men had entered the square. They wore brown uniforms with cross-straps over the chest and the ubiquitous swastika arm-bands. Their brown cloth caps with rounded peaks were pulled low and their leather chin straps were down. Each of them carried a small wooden collection box with a slot in the lid and they spread out and went to each of the tables.

Everybody made a donation, but as they pushed their coins into the slot of the box, they avoided looking at the brown-uniformed collectors. Their laughter was forced and nervous, and they looked into their tankards or at their own hands until the collectors had passed on to the next table, when they exchanged relieved glances.

'Who are these people?' Centaine asked innocently, making no attempt to hide her interest.

'They are the SA,' Blaine replied. 'Storm troopers, the bully boys of the National Socialist Party. Look at that one.' The trooper he had chosen had the bland heavy face of a peasant, dull and brutal. 'Is it not remarkable that there are always people to do this type of work – the need finds the man. Let us pray that his is not the face of the new Germany.'

The storm trooper had noticed their unconcealed interest and he came directly to their table with that menacing deliberate swagger.

'Papers!' he said.

'He wants our papers,' Tara translated, and Blaine handed over his passport.

'Ah! Foreign tourists.' The storm trooper's manner changed. He smiled ingratiatingly and handed back Blaine's passport with a few pleasant words.

'He says, welcome to the paradise of National Socialist Germany,' Tara translated, and Blaine nodded.

'He says, you will see how the German people are now happy and proud – and something else that I didn't catch.'

'Tell him we hope that they will always be happy and proud.' The trooper beamed and clicked the heels of his jackboots as he sprang to attention.

'*Heil Hitler!*' He gave the Nazi salute, and Mathilda Janine dissolved into helpless giggles.

'I can't help it,' she gasped as Blaine gave her a sharp look and a shake of the head. 'It just slays me when they do that.'

The storm troopers left the square, and they could feel the tension ease; the band slackened its frenetic beat and the dancers slowed down. People looked directly at one another and smiled naturally.

That night Centaine pulled the fat goose-down duvet up around her ears and snuggled into the curve of Blaine's arm.

'Have you noticed,' she asked, 'how the people here seemed caught between feverish laughter and nervous tears?'

Blaine was silent for a while and then he grunted, 'There is a smell in the air that troubles me – it seems to me that

636

it is the stench of some deadly plague,' and he shuddered slightly and drew her closer to him.

With the Daimler leading, they streamed down the wide white autobahn into the suburbs of the German capital.

'So much water, so many canals and so many trees.'

'The city's built on a series of canals,' Tara explained. 'Rivers trapped between the old terminal moraines that lie east to west—'

'How is it you always know everything?' Shasa interrupted her, a touch of real exasperation under his teasing tone.

'Unlike some I could name, I am actually literate, you know,' she flashed back, and David winced theatrically.

'Ouch, that hurt, and it wasn't even aimed at me.'

'Very well, little Miss Know-it-all,' Shasa challenged. 'If you are so clever, what does that sign say?' He pointed ahead to a large white signboard beside the autobahn.

The lettering was in black, and Tara read it aloud.

'It says: "Jews! Keep straight on! This road will take you back to Jerusalem, where you belong!"'

As she realized what she had said, she flushed with embarrassment and leaned forward to touch David's shoulder over the back of his seat.

'Oh David, I'm so sorry. I should never have uttered such rot!'

David sat straight, staring ahead through the windscreen, and then after a few seconds he gave a thin little smile.

'Welcome to Berlin,' he whispered. 'The centre of Aryan civilization.'

'Welcome to Berlin! Welcome to Berlin!' The train that had brought them across half of Europe slid into the station, clouds of steam hissing from the vacuum brakes and the cries of greeting almost drowned by the beat of the band playing a rousing martial air.

'Welcome to Berlin!' The waiting crowd surged forward at the moment their coach came to a standstill, and Manfred De La Rey stepped down from the balcony to be surrounded by well-wishers, smiling happy faces and friendly handclasps, laughing girls and wreaths of flowers, shouted questions and popping flash bulbs.

The other athletes, all dressed like him in green blazers with gold piping, white slacks and shoes and Panama hats, were also surrounded and mobbed and it was some minutes before a loud voice rose above the hubbub.

'Attention, please! May I have your attention.' The band beat out a ruffle of drums while a tall man in a dark uniform and steelrimmed spectacles stepped forward.

'First of all let me offer you the warm greetings of the Führer and the German people, and we welcome you to these the eleventh Olympic Games of the modern era. We know that you will represent the spirit and courage of the South African nation, and we wish you all success and many, many medals.' Amidst clapping and laughing, the speaker held up his hands. 'There are motor vehicles waiting to take you to your quarters in the Olympic village, where you will find all preparations have been made to make your stay with us both memorable and enjoyable. Now it is my pleasant duty to introduce the young lady who will be your guide and your interpreter over the next few weeks.' He beckoned to somebody in the crowd, and a young woman stepped out into the space beside him and turned to face the band of athletes. There was a collective sigh and hum of appreciation.

'This is Heidi Kramer.' She was tall and strong, but

unmistakably feminine, with hips and bosom like an hourglass, yet touched with a dancer's grace and a gymnast's poise. Her hair was the colour of the Kalahari dawn, Manfred thought, and her teeth when she smiled were perfect, their edges minutely serrated and translucent as fine bone china, but her eyes were beyond description, bluer and clearer than the high African sky at noon, and he knew without any hesitation that she was the most magnificent woman he had ever seen. At the thought he made a silent guilty apology to Sarah – but compared to this German Valkyrie, Sarah was a sweet little tabby cat beside a female leopard in her prime.

'Now Heidi will arrange for your baggage to be collected and will get you all seated in the limousines. From now on if there is anything you need, ask Heidi! She is your big sister and your stepmother.'

They laughed and whistled and cheered and Heidi, smiling and charming but quick and efficient, took over. Within minutes their baggage had been whisked away by a band of uniformed porters and she led them down the long glass-domed platform to the magnificent entrance portals of the railway station where a line of black Mercedes limousines was waiting for them.

Manfred, Uncle Tromp and Roelf Stander climbed into the back seat of one of them, and the driver was just about to pull away when Heidi waved to him and came running back along the kerb. She wore high heels and they threw tension on her calf muscles, emphasizing their lovely lines and the fine delicacy of her ankles. Neither Sarah nor any of the girls Manfred knew at home wore high heels.

Heidi opened the front passenger door and stuck her head into the Mercedes. 'You gentlemen will object if I ride with you, yes?' she asked with that radiant smile, and they all protested vigorously, even Uncle Tromp joining in.

'No! No! Please come in.'

She slipped into the seat beside the driver, slammed the

door, and immediately wriggled round so that she was facing them, with her arms folded along the back of her seat.

'I am so excited to meet you,' she told them in her accented English. 'I have read so much about Africa, the animals and the Zulus, and one day I will travel there. You must promise to tell me all about your beautiful country, and I will tell you all about my beautiful Germany.'

They agreed enthusiastically, and she looked directly at Uncle Tromp.

'Now, let me guess. You will be the Reverend Tromp Bierman, the team boxing coach?' she asked, and Uncle Tromp beamed.

'How clever of you.'

'I have seen your photograph,' she admitted. 'How could I forget such a magnificent beard?' Uncle Tromp looked highly gratified. 'But you must tell me who the others are.'

'This is Roelf Stander, our heavyweight boxer,' Uncle Tromp introduced them. 'And this is Manfred De La Rey, our light heavyweight.'

Manfred was certain that she reacted to his name, a lift to one corner of her mouth and slight narrowing of the eyes; then she was smiling again. 'We will all be good friends,' she said, and Manfred replied in German.

'My people, the Afrikaners, have always been the loyal friends of the German people.'

'Oh, your German is perfect,' she exclaimed with delight in the same language. 'Where did you learn to speak like a true German?'

'My paternal grandmother and my mother were both pure-blooded Germans.'

'Then you will find much to interest you in our country.' She switched back to English and began to lecture, pointing out the sights of the city as the line of black Mercedes, Olympic pennants fluttering on the bonnets, sped through the streets.

'This is the famous Unter den Linden, the street we Berliners love so dearly.' It was broad and magnificent with linden trees growing down the promenade that divided the double carriageway. 'The street is a mile long. That is the royal palace behind us, and there ahead of us is the Brandenburg Tor.' The tall colonnades of the monument were decked with enormous banners that hung from the quadriga charioteer group of figures on the summit to the ground far below; the crimson and black swastika flanked by the multi-coloured rings of the Olympic symbol billowed and heaved in the light breeze.

'That is the state opera house,' Heidi turned to point through the side window. 'It was built in 1741—' She was entertaining and informative.

'See how the people of Berlin welcome you,' she cried, with that gay brittle enthusiasm which seemed to characterize all the citizens of National Socialist Germany. 'Look! Look!'

Berlin was a city of flags and banners. From every public building, department store, apartment block and private dwelling the flags fluttered and waved, swastikas and the Olympic rings, thousands upon tens of thousands.

When they came at last to the apartment block in the Olympic village that had been set aside for them, an honour guard of the Hitler Youth with burning torches waited to welcome them, and another band drawn up on the sidewalk broke into 'The Voice of South Africa', the national anthem.

Inside the building Heidi issued each of them with a booklet filled with coloured coupons by which every last detail of their personal arrangements were organized, from their room and the bed on which they would sleep, and the buses that would carry them to and from the Olympic complex, to the changing rooms and the numbers of the lockers that they had been allocated at the stadium.

'Here in this house you will have your own chef and

dining-hall. Food will be prepared to your own preference, with due regard to any special diets or tastes. There is a doctor and a dentist available at any hour. Drycleaning and laundry, radios and telephones, a private masseur for the team, a secretary with a typewriter—' It had all been arranged, and they were amazed by the precise, meticulous planning.

'Please find your rooms, your luggage is already there waiting for you. Unpack and relax. Tomorrow morning I will take you on the bus for a tour of the *Reichssportfeld*, the Olympic complex. It is ten miles from here, so we will leave immediately after breakfast at eight-thirty am. In the meantime, if there is anything – anything at all – that you want, you have only to ask me.'

'I know what I'd like to ask her for,' one of the weight-lifters whispered, rolling his eyes, and Manfred clenched his fists with anger at the impertinence, even though Heidi had not heard it.

'Until tomorrow,' she called gaily, and went through to the kitchens to talk to the chef.

'Now that is what I call a woman!' Uncle Tromp growled. 'I give thanks that I am a man of the cloth, old and happily married, and beyond all the temptations of Eve.' There were cries of mock commiserations for Uncle Tromp was by this time everybody's uncle. 'All right!' He was suddenly stern. 'Running shoes, all you lazy young dogs. A quick ten miles before supper, please!'

Heidi was waiting for them when they came down to breakfast, gay and bright and smiling, answering their questions, distributing mail from home, sorting out a dozen small problems quickly and without fuss, and then when they had eaten, taking them off in a group to the bus station.

Most of the athletes from the other countries were in residence, and the village was bustling and full of tense excitement, men and women in sporting attire running through the streets, calling to each other in a multiplicity of tongues, their superb physical condition showing in their bright young faces and in every movement that they made. When they came to the stadium, the size of it awed them all. A huge complex of halls, gymnasiums and covered swimming-pools surrounded the oval track and field theatre. The banks of seating seemed to reach away for ever, and the Olympic altar at the far end with the unlit tripod torch gave a sense of religious solemnity to this temple devoted to the worship of the human body.

It took the morning for them to see it all, and they had a hundred questions between them. Heidi answered them all, but more than once Manfred found her walking beside him, and when they spoke German together it gave them a sense of intimacy, even in the crowd. It was not his imagination alone, for Roelf had noticed the special attention Manfred was receiving.

'How are you enjoying your German lessons?' he asked innocently at lunch, and when Manfred snarled at him he grinned unrepentantly.

Their hosts had arranged sparring partners from the local boxing clubs, and over the days that followed, Uncle Tromp drove them hard towards the pinnacle of their training.

Manfred tore at his opponents, slamming punches into the thick padding that covered their midriffs and heads, so that even with that protection none of them lasted more than a round or two before calling for quarter; and when Manfred went back to his corner and looked around it was usually to find Heidi Kramer watching from somewhere near at hand, a flush on her flawless neck, a strange intent look in those impossibly blue eyes, her lips slightly parted and the tip of her pink tongue held between sharp white teeth.

However, it was only after four days of training that he found himself alone with her. He had finished a hard session in the gymnasium and after showering and changing into grey slacks and a Varsity sweater, he went out through the front entrance of the stadium. He had almost reached the bus station when she called his name and ran to catch up with him.

'I am also going back to the village. I have to talk to the chef – may I ride the bus with you?' She must have been waiting for him and he felt flattered and a little nervous.

She had a free, hip-swinging walk, and her hair swayed around her head like a sheet of golden silk when she looked up at him as they walked down to the bus station.

'I have been watching the boxers from the other countries,' she said, 'especially the light heavyweights, and I have also been watching you.'

'Yes.' He frowned to cover his embarrassment. 'I saw you.'

'You have nobody to fear, except the American.'

'Cyrus Lomax,' he nodded. 'Yes, *Ring Magazine* rates him the best amateur light heavyweight in the world. Uncle Tromp has been watching him also. He agrees that he is very good. Very strong, and being a nigger, he will have a skull like solid ivory.'

'He is the only one you will have to beat for the gold,' she agreed. *The gold* – the sound of it on her lips had a music that quickened his pulse. 'And I will be there cheering for you.'

'Thank you, Heidi.'

They boarded the bus, and when the men in the other seats glanced at Heidi with admiration, he felt proud to have her at his side.

'My uncle is a great follower of boxing. He thinks as I

do, that you have a good chance of beating the American negro. He would like very much to meet you.'

'It is kind of your uncle.'

'He is having a small reception at his home this evening. He asks me to invite you.'

'You know that is not possible,' he shook his head. 'My training schedule—'

'My uncle is an important and very influential man,' she insisted, holding her head on one side and smiling appealingly up at him. 'It will be very early. I promise you will be home before nine o'clock.' She saw him hesitate and went on, 'It will make my uncle – and me – very happy.'

'I have an uncle also, Uncle Tromp—'

'If I get your Uncle Tromp's permission, will you promise to come?'

Heidi was waiting in the Mercedes at the front door of their house in the village at seven o'clock, as she had arranged. The driver held the rear door open for him and Manfred slid onto the leather seat beside her.

She smiled at him. 'You look very handsome, Manfred.'

She had plaited her blond hair into two thick gleaming ropes and piled them on top of her head. Her shoulders and the upper slopes of her stately bosom were bare, and snowy perfection. Her blue taffeta cocktail dress matched the colour of her eyes perfectly.

'You are beautiful,' he said with wonder in his tone. He had never paid a compliment to a woman before, but this was a mere statement of fact. She lowered her eyes, a touchingly modest gesture from someone who must be accustomed to male adulation.

'To the Rupertstrasse,' she ordered the driver.

They drove slowly down the Kurfürstendamm, watching the throngs of merry-makers on the brightly lit sidewalks, then the Mercedes accelerated as they entered the quieter streets of the westerly section of the Grünewald district. This was the millionaires' village on the western outskirts of the sprawling city, and Manfred relaxed and settled back against the leather upholstery and turned to the lovely woman beside him. She was talking seriously, asking him questions about himself and his family, and about his country. Quickly he realized that she had a much better knowledge of South Africa than he could have expected, and he wondered how she had acquired it.

She knew the history of war and conflict and rebellion, the struggle of his people against the barbarous black tribes, and then the subjugation of the Afrikaner by the British, and the terrible threats to their existence as a people.

'The English,' she said, and there was a knife-edge of bitterness in her tone. 'They are everywhere, bringing war and suffering with them – Africa, India, my own Germany. We too have been oppressed and persecuted. If it were not for our beloved Führer, we should still be staggering under the yoke of the Jew and the English.'

'Yes, he is a great man, your Führer,' Manfred agreed and then he quoted: 'What we must fight for is to safeguard the existence and reproduction of our race and our people, the sustenance of our children and the purity of our blood, the freedom and independence of the fatherland, so that our people may mature for the fulfilment of the mission allotted it by the creator of the universe.'

'*Mein Kampf*,' she exclaimed. 'You can quote the words of the Führer!' They had passed a significant milestone in their relationship, Manfred realized.

'With those words he has captured everything that I feel and believe,' he said. 'He is a great man, head of a great nation.'

The house in the Rupertstrasse was set back from the road in large gardens on the bank of one of the beautiful Havel Lakes. There were a dozen chauffeured limousines parked in the driveway, most of them with swastika pennants on their bonnets and uniformed chauffeurs waiting behind the wheels. All the windows of the large house were lit and there was the sound of music and voices and laughter as their own chauffeur let them out of the Mercedes under the portico.

Manfred offered Heidi his arm and they went in through the open front doors, crossed a lobby of black and white chequered marble slabs and panelled walls decorated with a forest of stag antlers, and paused in the doorway of the large reception room beyond. The room was already filled with guests. Most of the men were in dashing uniforms that glittered with the insignia of rank and regiment, while the women were elegant in silks and velvets, with shoulders bare and hair bobbed in the latest style.

The laughter and conversation subsided as they turned to examine the newcomers, and there were interested and calculating appraisals, for Manfred and Heidi made a strikingly handsome couple. Then the conversation picked up again.

'There is Uncle Sigmund,' Heidi exclaimed, and drew Manfred into the room towards the tall uniformed figure who came to meet them.

'Heidi, my dear.' He stooped over Heidi's hand as he kissed it. 'You grow more beautiful each time I see you.'

'Manfred, this is my uncle, Colonel Sigmund Boldt. Uncle Sigmund, may I present Herr Manfred De La Rey, the South African boxer.'

Colonel Boldt shook hands with Manfred. He had pure white hair scraped severely back from the thin face of an academic, with good bone structure and a narrow aristo-cratic nose.

'Heidi tells me that you are of German extraction?' He wore a black uniform with silver death's head insignia on the lapels; and one eyelid drooped, while the eye itself watered uncontrollably and he dabbed at it with the fine linen handkerchief he held in his right hand.

'That is true, Colonel. I have very strong ties to your country,' Manfred replied.

'Ah, you speak excellent German.' The colonel took his arm. 'There are many people here this evening who will want to meet you, but first tell me, what do you think of the black American boxer, Cyrus Lomax? And what will be your tactics when you meet him?'

With discreet social grace, either Heidi or Colonel Boldt were always on hand to steer him from one group of guests to the next, and the wine waiter brought him a glass of mineral water when he refused the champagne that was offered.

However, they left him longer than usual with one guest whom Heidi had introduced as General Zoller, a tall Prussian officer in field grey uniform with an iron cross at the throat who, despite a rather undistinguished and forgettable face with pale sickly features, proved to have a sharp incisive intelligence. He questioned Manfred minutely on the politics and conditions in South Africa, particularly as to the feelings of the average Afrikaner towards their ties to Great Britain and the Empire.

While they spoke, General Zoller chain-smoked a series of thin cigarettes wrapped in yellow paper with a strong herbal odour, and every now and again he wheezed with asthma. Manfred quickly found that he was sympathetic and had an encyclopaedic grasp of African affairs; the time passed very quickly before Heidi came across the room and touched his arm.

'Excuse me, General Zoller, but I have promised the boxing coach that I will have his star back before nine o'clock.'

'I have enjoyed meeting you, young man.' The general shook Manfred's hand. 'Our countries should be good friends.'

Manfred assured him, 'I will do all in my power to bring that about.'

'Good luck for the Games, Herr de La Rey.'

In the Mercedes again Heidi remarked, 'My uncle liked

you very much, and so did many of his friends – General Zoller for one.'

'I enjoyed the evening.'

'Do you like music, Manfred?'

He was a little surprised by the question. 'I enjoy some music, but I am no expert.'

'Wagner?'

'Yes, I like Wagner very much.'

'Uncle Sigmund has given me two tickets to the Berlin Philharmonic Orchestra for next Friday. The young conductor Herbert von Karajan is performing a programme of Wagner. I know you will be fighting your first bout that afternoon, but afterwards we could celebrate.' She hesitated, and then she went on quickly, 'Forgive me, you think me forward, but I assure you—'

'No, no. I would be greatly honoured to accompany you – whether I win or lose.'

'You will win,' she said simply. 'I know you will.'

She dropped him in front of the team house, and waited until he had gone in before she ordered the driver, 'Back to the Rupertstrasse.'

When she got back to the colonel's house most of the other guests were leaving. She waited quietly until he came back from seeing the last of them away and, with an inclination of his silver hair, ordered her to follow him. His treatment of her had altered completely, it was now brusque and superior.

He crossed to the unobtrusive oak door at the far end of the room and went in ahead of her. Heidi entered and closed the door behind her softly, then drew herself to attention and stood waiting. Colonel Boldt left her standing while he poured two balloon glasses of cognac and took one to General Zoller where he sat in the wingbacked chair beside the log fire in the stone fireplace, puffing at one of his herbal cigarettes, with an open file on his knees.

'So, Fräulein,' Colonel Boldt sank into the leather chair

649

and waved Heidi towards the couch, 'sit down. You may relax in your "uncle's" house.'

She smiled politely but sat stiff-backed on the edge of the couch and Colonel Boldt turned back to the general.

'May I ask the general's opinion of the subject?' and General Zoller looked up from the file.

'There seems to be a grey area surrounding the subject's mother. Is it confirmed that his mother was a German, as he claims?'

'I am afraid we do not have confirmation on that. We can establish no proof of his mother's nationality, although I have made exhaustive enquiries amongst our people in South West Africa. The general belief is that she died at childbirth in the African wilderness. However, on his father's side there is definite documented proof that his grandmother was German and that his father fought most valiantly for the Kaiser's army, in Africa.'

'Yes, I see that,' the General said testily, and looked up at Heidi. 'What sentiments has he expressed to you, Fräulein?'

'He is very proud of his German blood, and he looks upon himself as the natural ally of the German people. He is a great admirer of the Führer and can quote at length from *Mein Kampf*.'

The general coughed and wheezed and lit another cigarette with a taper from the fire before turning all his attention back to the red file with the eagle and swastika emblem on the front cover. The others waited quietly for almost ten minutes before he looked up at Heidi.

'What relationship have you established with the subject, Fräulein?'

'On Colonel Boldt's orders, I have made myself agreeable and friendly towards him. I have in small ways conveyed my interest as a woman towards him. I have shown him that I am knowledgeable and interested in the art of boxing, and that I know a great deal about the problems of his fatherland.'

'Fräulein Kramer is one of my best operatives,' Colonel Boldt explained. 'She has been given a thorough grounding in the history of South Africa and the sport of boxing by our department.' The general nodded. 'Proceed, Fräulein,' he ordered, and Heidi went on.

'I have conveyed to him my sympathy for his people's political aspirations and made it clear that I am his friend, with the possibility of more than that.'

'There has been no sexual intimacy between you?'

'No, my General. I judge that the subject would be offended if I were to proceed too rapidly. As we know from his file, he comes from a strict Calvinist religious background. Besides which, I have not received orders from Colonel Boldt to initiate sexual advances.'

'Good,' the general nodded. 'This is a matter of major importance. The Führer himself is aware of our operation. He considers, as I do, that the southern tip of Africa has enormous tactical and strategic importance in our plans for global expansion. It guards the sea routes to India and the East, and in the event that the Suez Canal is denied to our shipping, it is the only route available. In addition, it is a treasure house of raw material vital to our military preparations – chrome, diamonds, the platinum group minerals. With this in mind, and after my meeting with the subject, I am of the firm belief that we must proceed. Therefore, the operation now has full departmental sanction and a "red" rating.'

'Very good, my General.'

'The code name for the operation will be "White Sword" – *Das Weisse Schwart*.'

'*Jawohl*, my General.'

'Fräulein Kramer, you are now assigned exclusively to this operation. You will, at the first opportunity, initiate sexual intimacy with the subject in such a way as not to alarm nor offend him, but rather to strengthen our hold over his allegiance.'

'Very well, my General.'

'In due course it may be necessary for you to enter into a form of marriage with the subject. Is there any reason why you could not do so, if required?'

Heidi did not hesitate. 'None, my General. You can rely on my duty and loyalty entirely. I will do whatever is required of me.'

'Very good, Fräulein.' General Zoller coughed and hunted noisily for breath, and his voice was still rough as he went on, 'Now, Colonel, it will suit our purpose if the subject is a winner of a gold medal at these Games. It will give him a great deal of prestige in his home country, apart from the ideological aspect of a white Aryan triumphing over a person of an inferior black race.'

'I understand, my General.'

'There is not a serious German contender for the light heavyweight title, is there?'

'No, my General, the subject is the only serious white contender. We can make certain that all matches which the subject fights are refereed and judged by members of the Party who are under the control of our department. Naturally, we cannot effect the decision in the case of a knock-out, but—'

'Naturally, Boldt, but you will do all in your power, and Fräulein Kramer will report daily to Colonel Boldt on her progress with the subject.'

B oth the Courtney and Malcomess clans had descended upon the luxurious Bristol Hotel rather than the Olympic village, though David Abrahams had bowed to the dictates of the athletics coach and moved into the apartment house with his team mates, so that Shasa saw little of him during the days of hard training leading up to the opening of the Games.

Mathilda Janine prevailed on Tara to accompany her to most of the field athletic training, in return for equal timeshares of her company at the polo fields, so the two girls spent most of their time dashing from the vast Olympic complex across Berlin to the equestrian centre at high speed, the only rate of progress with which Tara seemed able to conduct her father's green Bentley.

The brief lay-off from training, combined with the imminence of the Games themselves, seemed to have sharpened David's running rather than harmed it. He returned some excellent times during those five days and courageously resisted Mathilda Janine's suggestion that he should sneak out for 'just an hour or two' in the evenings.

'You are in with a chance, Davie,' his coach told him, checking the stopwatch after his last run before the official opening ceremony.

'Just concentrate it all now and you'll have a bit of tin to take home with you.'

Both Shasa and Blaine were delighted with the ponies that their German hosts had provided. Like everything else in the equestrian centre, the grooms, stabling and equipment were all without fault, and under Blaine's iron control, the team settled down to concentrated practice and were soon once more a cohesive phalanx of horsemen.

Between their own long sessions on the practice field, they watched and judged the other teams whom they would have to meet. The Americans, expense not considered, had brought their own mounts across the Atlantic. The Argentinians had gone one better and brought their grooms as well, in flat-brimmed gaucho hats and leather breeches decorated with silver studs.

'Those are the two to beat,' Blaine warned them. 'But the Germans are surprisingly good – and the Brits, as always, will be slogging away at it.'

'We can flatten any of them,' Shasa gave the team the benefit of his vast experience, 'with a little luck.'

Tara was the only one who took the boast seriously, as from the stand she watched him tear down the side field, sitting tall in the saddle, a beautiful young centaur, lean and lithe, white teeth flashing against the dark tan of his face.

'He's so big-headed and cock-sure,' she lamented. 'If only I could just ignore him. If only life wasn't just so *flat* when he's not around.'

B y nine o'clock on the morning of 1 August 1936, the vast Olympic stadium, the largest in the world, was packed with over one hundred thousand human beings.

The turf of the central isle had been groomed into an emerald velvet sheet, and ruled with the stark white lanes and circles that marked out the venue for the field events. The running track around the periphery was of brick-red cinders. High above it rose the 'Tribune of Honour', the reviewing stand for the traditional march-past of the athletes. At the far end of the stadium was the Olympic altar with its tripod torch still cold.

Outside the entrance to the stadium stretched the Maifeld, its open acres of space containing the high bell tower with the legend: '*Ich rufe die Jugend der Welt* – I summon the youth of the world.' And the massed echelons of athletes were drawn up to face down the long boulevard of the Kaiserdamm, renamed for the solemn occasion the

Via Triumphalis. High above the field floated the giant airship, the *Hindenburg*, towing behind it the banner of the Olympics, the five great linked circles.

From afar a faint susurration rose on the cool still morning air. Slowly it grew louder, closer. A long procession of open four-door Mercedes tourers was approaching down the Via Triumphalis, chromework gleaming like mirrors, passing between the closed ranks of fifty thousand brown-uniformed storm troopers who lined both sides of the way, holding back a dense throng of humanity, ten and twenty deep, who roared with adulation as the leading vehicle passed them and threw their right arms high in the Nazi salute.

The cavalcade drew to a halt before the legion of athletes and from the leading Mercedes Adolf Hitler stepped down. He wore the plain brown shirt, breeches and jackboots of a storm trooper. Rather than rending him inconspicuous, this sombre unadorned dress seemed rather to distinguish him in the mass of brilliant uniforms, gold lace, bearskins and stars and ribbons that followed him between the ranks of athletes towards the marathon gate of the stadium.

'So that is the wild man,' Blaine Malcomess thought as Hitler strolled by, not five paces from where he stood. He was precisely as Blaine had seen him portrayed a thousand times, the dark hair combed forward, the small square moustache. But Blaine was unprepared for the intense Messianic gaze that rested upon him for a fleeting part of a second, then passed on. He found that the hair on his forearms had come erect and prickled electrically, for he had just looked into the eyes of an Old Testament prophet – or a madman.

Following close behind Adolf Hitler were all his favourites: Goebbels wore a light summer suit, but Goering was portly and resplendent in the sky-blue full-dress of a *Luftwaffe* marshal and he saluted the athletes casually with his gold baton as he went by. At that moment the great bronze bell high above the Maifeld began to toll, summoning the youth of the world to assembly.

Hitler and his entourage passed out of sight, entering the tunnel beneath the stands, and a few minutes later a great fanfare of trumpets, magnified a hundred times by the banks of loudspeakers, crashed over the field and a massed choir burst into *Deutschland über alles*. The ranks of athletes began to move off, wheeling into their positions for the entry parade.

As they emerged from the gloom of the tunnel into the sunlit arena, Shasa exchanged a glance with David marching beside him. They grinned at each other in shared excitement as the great waves of sound, amplified music from the bands and the choir singing the Olympic hymn and the cheering of one hundred thousand spectators, poured over them. Then they looked ahead, chins up, arms swinging, and stepped out to the grandeur of Richard Strauss's music.

In the rank ahead of Shasa, Manfred De La Rey stepped out as boldly, but his eyes were focused on the brown-clad figure far ahead in the front rank of the Tribune of Honour and surrounded by princes and kings. As they came level, he wanted to fling up his right arm and shout, 'Heil Hitler!' but he had to restrain himself. After lengthy discussion and argument, the counsel of Blaine Malcomess and the other English speakers in the team had prevailed. Instead of the German salute the team members merely snapped their heads around in the 'eyes right' salute as they came level. A low whistle and stamp of disapproval from the largely German spectators followed them. Manfred's eyes burned with tears of shame at the insult he had been forced to offer the great man on the high dais.

His anger stayed with him during the rest of the amazing festivities that followed: the lighting of the Olympic torch and the official speech of opening by the Führer, the sky filled with the white wings of fifty thousand doves released together, the flags of the nations raised simultaneously around the rim of the stadium, the displays of swaying gymnasts and dancers, the searchlights and the fireworks and the music and the fly-past by squadrons of Marshal Goering's *Luftwaffe* that filled and darkened the sky with their thunder.

B laine and Centaine dined alone that evening in her suite at the Bristol and both of them were suffering from an anticlimactic weariness after the day's excitements.

'What a show they put on for the world!' Centaine remarked. 'I don't think any of us expected this.'

'We should have,' Blaine replied, 'after their experience in arranging the Nuremberg rallies, the Nazis are the grand masters of pageantry. Not even the ancient Romans developed the seductive appeal of public spectacle to this refinement.'

'I loved it,' Centaine agreed.

'It was pagan and idolatrous, and blatant propaganda – Herr Hitler selling Nazi Germany and his new race of supermen to the world. But, yes, I have to agree with you, it was unfortunately jolly good fun, with an ominous touch of menace and evil to it that made it even more enjoyable.'

'Blaine, you are a hard-nosed old cynic.'

'My only real virtue,' he conceded, and then changed the subject. 'They have posted the draw for the first-round matches. We are fortunate not to have drawn either the Argentinians or the Yanks.'

They had drawn the Australians, and their hopes of an easy win were dashed almost immediately for the Aussies galloped in like charging cavalry from the first whistle, driving both Blaine and Shasa back in desperate defence, and they kept up that unrelenting attack throughout the first three hard-ridden chukkas, never allowing Blaine's team to gather themselves.

Shasa kept the curb on his own instincts, which were to ride and shine alone, and placed himself completely under the control of his captain, responding instantly to Blaine's calls to 'cut left' or 'cover the fall' or 'break back', drawing from Blaine the only thing which he lacked himself, experience. Now in these desperate minutes the bond of understanding and trust between then, which had taken so long to forge, was tested almost to breaking point, but in the end it held and halfway through the fourth chukka, Blaine grunted as he passed close to his young number two.

'They've shot their bolt, Shasa. Let's see now if they can take what they've been handing out.'

Shasa took Blaine's next high cross shot at full stretch, standing in his stirrups to pull it down out of the air, and then to drive it far up field, drawing off the Aussie backs before sending it back inside in a lazy dropping parabola to fall under the nose of Blaine's racing pony. That was the turning-point, and in the end they rode in on lathered ponies and jumped down from the saddle to pound each other between the shoulder blades, laughing with a triumph touched by a shade of disbelief at their own achievement.

Triumph turned to gloom when they heard that they would meet the Argentinians in the second round.

D avid Abrahams ran a disappointing race in his first heat of the 400-metre dash, coming in fourth and missing the cut. Mathilda Janine refused dinner and went up to bed early that night, but two days later she was bubbling and deliriously excited when David won his heat in the 200 metres and went through to the semi-finals.

M anfred De La Rey's first opponent was the Frenchman, Maurice Artois, unranked in his division.

'Fast as a mamba – brave as a ratel,' Uncle Tromp whispered to Manfred at the gong.

Heidi Kramer was sitting beside Colonel Boldt in the fourth row, and she shivered with unexpected excitement as she watched Manfred leave his corner and come out into the centre. He moved like a cat.

Up to this time it had taken much effort for her to feign an interest in the sport. She had found the sounds and odours and sights associated with it all repellent – the stench of rancid sweat on canvas and leather, the animal grunting and the slogging of padded fists into flesh, the blood and sweat and flying spittle offended her fastidious nature. Now in this company of well-dressed and cultivated spectators, clad herself in fresh silk and lace, perfumed and serene, she found the contrast of violence and savagery before her frightening but at the same time stirring.

Manfred De La Rey, the quiet stern young man, humourless and grave, slightly gauche in unaccustomed clothing and ill at ease in sophisticated company, had been transformed into a magnificent wild beast, and the primeval ferocity he seemed to exude, the blaze of those yellow eyes under the black brows as he slashed the Frenchman's face into a distorted bleeding mask and then drove him down onto his knees in the centre of the sheet of spotless white canvas, excited her perversely so that she found she was clenching her thighs tightly together and her groin was hotly melting and dampening the expensive crêpe-de-chine skirt under her.

That excitement persisted as she sat beside Manfred in the stalls of the state opera house that evening while Wagner's heroic Teutonic music filled the auditorium with thrilling sound. She moved slightly in her seat until her bare upper arm touched Manfred's. She felt him start, begin to pull away, then catch himself. The contact between them was gossamer-light but both of them were intensely aware of it.

Once again Colonel Brandt had placed the Mercedes at her disposal for the evening. The driver was waiting for them when they came down the front steps of the opera house. As they settled into the back seat, she saw Manfred wince slightly.

'What is it?' she asked quickly.

'It is nothing.'

She touched his shoulder with firm strong fingers. 'Here – does it hurt?'

'A stiffness in the muscle – it will be all right tomorrow.'

'Hans, take us to my apartment in the Hansa,' she ordered the driver, and Manfred glanced at her, perturbed.

'Mutti has passed down to me one of her special secrets. It is an embrocation made with wild ferns, and truly magical.'

'It is not necessary—' he protested.

'My apartment is on the way back to the Olympic village. It will not take long and Hans can drop you back home afterwards.'

She had been uncertain as to how she would get him alone without alarming him, but now he accepted her suggestion without further comment. He was silent for the rest of the drive and she could sense the tension in him, though she made no attempt to touch him again.

Manfred was thinking of Sarah, trying to form the image of her face in his mind but it was blurred, a sweet and insipid blur. He wanted to order Hans to drive directly back to the village, but he could not find the will to do so. He knew what they were doing was incorrect – to be alone with a young attractive woman – and he tried to convince himself that it was innocent, but then he remembered the touch of her arm against him and he stiffened.

'It does hurt?' she misinterpreted the movement.

'Just a little,' he whispered, and his voice caught.

It was always most difficult after he had fought. For many hours after a match he was strung up and nervously sensitive, and it was then that his body was likely to play Satan's tricks upon him. He could feel it happening now, and his mortification and guilt forced hot blood up into his face. What would this pure clean German virgin think of him if she guessed at that obscene and wicked tumescence? He opened his mouth to tell her he would not go with her, but she was leaning forward in the seat.

'Thank you, Hans. Drop us here on the corner and you can wait down the block.' She was out of the car and crossing the sidewalk, and he had no option but to follow her.

It was half dark in the entrance lobby of the building.

'I'm sorry, Manfred, I am on the top floor and there is no elevator.'

The climb allowed him to regain control of himself, and she let him into a small one-roomed flat.

'This is my palace,' she smiled apologetically. 'Flats are so difficult to find in Berlin these days.' She gestured to the bed. 'Sit there, Manfred.'

She slipped off the jacket she wore over her white blouse, and stood on tiptoe to hang it in the cupboard. Her breasts swung forward heavily as she lifted her pale smooth arms.

Manfred looked away. There was a shelf of books on one

wall; he saw a set of Goethe's works and remembered how he had been his father's favourite author. Think of anything, he told himself, anything but those big pointed breasts under the thin white cloth.

She had gone through to the little bathroom and he heard running water and the clink of glass. Then she came back with a small green bottle in her hands and stood in front of him smiling.

'You must take off your coat and your shirt,' she said, and he could not reply. He had not thought of that.

'That is not proper, Heidi.'

She laughed softly, a throaty little sound, and through the laughter she murmured, 'Don't be shy, Manfred. Just think of me as a nurse.' Gently she lifted the coat off his shoulders, helping him out of it. Her breasts swung forward again and almost brushed against his face before she stepped back and hung his coat over the back of the single chair and then, a few seconds later, folded his shirt on top of it. She had warmed the bottle in the basin and the lotion was instantly soothing on his skin, her fingers cunning and strong.

'Relax,' she whispered. 'There, I can feel it. It's all hard and knotted. Relax, let the pain just wash away.' Gently she drew his head forward. 'Lean against me, Manfred. Yes, like that.'

She was standing in front of him and she thrust her hips forward so that his forehead was pressed against her lower torso. Her belly was soft and warm and her voice hypnotic, he felt waves of pleasure spreading out from the contact of her kneading fingers.

'You are so hard and strong, Manfred, so white and hard and beautiful—' It was moments before he realized what she had said, but her fingers were stroking and caressing, and all rational thought ebbed out of his mind. He was conscious only of the hands and the murmured endearments and praise, then he was aware of something else, a warm musky odour wafted up from her belly against which his face was pressed. Though he did not recognize it as the smell of a healthy young woman physically aroused and ripe for love, yet his own reaction to it was instinctive and no longer to be denied.

'Heidi,' his voice shook wildly. 'I love you. Forgive me, God, but I love you so.'

'Yes, *mein Schatz*, I know,' she whispered. 'And I love you also.'

She pushed him back gently upon the bed and standing over him began slowly to unbutton the front of the white blouse. As she came over him, her big silky white breasts, tipped with ruby, were the most beautiful things he had ever seen.

'I love you,' he cried so many times during that night, each time in a different voice of wonder and awe and ecstasy, for the things she did with him and for him surpassed all his imaginings.

F or the first day of the finals of the track and field events, Shasa had managed to finagle team tickets for the girls, but the seats were high in the north stand. Mathilda Janine had borrowed Shasa's binoculars and was anxiously scanning the great arena far below them.

'I can't see him,' she wailed.

'He's not out yet,' Shasa reassured her. 'They are running the hundred metres first—' But he was as strung out as she was. In the semi-final heat of the 200-metre dash, David Abrahams had run second to the great American athlete Jesse Owens, 'the Ebony Antelope', and so had secured his place in the final event.

'I'm so nervous I think I am going to have a fit of the

vapours,' Mathilda Janine gasped without lowering the binoculars; on Shasa's other side Tara was as agitated, but for different reasons.

'It's outrageous,' she said, so vehemently that Shasa turned to her surprised.

'What is?'

'Haven't you been listening to a word?'

'I'm sorry, you know David will be coming out at any moment—' He was drowned out by a deafening thunder of applause and the banks of spectators rose to their feet as the finalists in the hundred-metre dash sprang from the blocks and sped down their lanes; as they crossed the finish line, the quality of the sound changed, groans mixed with the ovation for the winner.

'There!' Tara caught Shasa's arm. 'Listen to them.'

Near them in the crowd a voice called, 'Another American negro wins.' And closer still, 'The Americans should be ashamed to let the black animals wear their colours.'

'These bigots are disgusting.' Tara glared around her, trying to identify the speakers in the sea of faces that surrounded them and when she failed turned back to Shasa. 'The Germans are threatening to disallow all medals won by what they call the inferior races, the blacks and the Jews,' she said in a loud voice. 'They are disgusting.'

'Cool down,' Shasa whispered.

'Don't you care?' Tara challenged him. 'David is a Jew.'

'Of course I care,' he said quietly, glancing around in embarrassment. 'But do shut up, Tara, there's a brick.'

'I think—' Tara's voice rose in direct response to Shasa's appeal, but Mathilda Janine screamed even more piercingly.

'There he is – there's David!'

With relief Shasa sprang to his feet. 'There he is – go it, Davie boy. Run like a hairy springbok!'

The finalists for the 200-metre dash had clustered at the far end of the arena and were jogging on the spot, windmilling their arms and going through their warm-up routines.

'Isn't David just indescribable?' Mathilda Janine demanded.

'I think that describes him perfectly,' Shasa agreed, and she punched his arm.

'You know what I mean.'

Then the group of athletes spread out to their blocks and the starter stepped forward. Once more silence descended on the vast arena, and the runners were crouched down, frozen in a rigour of concentration.

The pistol fired, at this distance a pop of sound, and the athletes hurled themselves forward; in a perfect line, long legs flashing, arms pumping high, they sped away on a rising wave of sound, and the line lost its perfection, bulged in the centre; a lean dark panther of a man pulled out ahead and the roar of the crowd became articulate.

'Je-Se O-wens!' repeated in a soaring chant, while the dark man flashed over the finish line pulling a bunch of other runners behind him.

'What happened?' Mathilda Janine screamed.

'Jesse Owens won,' Shasa shouted to make himself heard in the uproar.

'I know that – but David, what happened to David?'

'I don't know. I couldn't see. It was all so close.'

They waited in a fever until the loudspeakers boomed their stentorian command.

'Achtung! Achtung!' and they heard the names in the jumble of German.

'Jesse Owens, Carter Brown—' and then, stunningly, 'David Abrahams.'

Mathilda Janine shrieked. 'Catch me, I'm going to faint. David got the bronze!'

She was still shrieking, and hopping up and down on the spot, tears of wild joy running unheeded down her cheeks and dripping off her chin, while on the green field

665

below a thin gangling figure in shorts and running vest climbed up onto the inferior step of the victors' pyramid and bowed his head as the ribbon with the bronze medal dangling from it was draped around his neck.

The four of them began their celebration that evening in the salon of Centaine's suite at the Bristol. Blaine made a short speech of congratulation while David stood in the middle of the floor looking bashful and self-conscious as they toasted him in champagne. Because it was for David, Shasa drank the whole glass of the magnificent 1929 Bollinger that Centaine provided for the occasion.

He drank another full glass of Sekt at the Café am Kudamm, on the corner of the Kurfürstendamm just down the street from the hotel and then the four of them linked arms and set off down Berlin's notorious fun street. All the signs of decadence that the Nazis had banned – the Coca-Cola bottles on the sidewalk tables, and the strains of jazz from the café bands, the movie posters of Clark Gable and Myrna Loy – were once more in evidence, allowed back under special dispensation for the duration of the Olympics only.

They stopped at another café, and this time Shasa ordered a schnapps.

'Slow down,' David whispered to him, he knew that Shasa seldom drank alcohol, and then never more than a single glass of wine or beer.

'Davie my boy, it's not every day that an old mate of mine wins an Olympic medal.' He was flushed under his tan and his eyes had a feverish glitter.

'Well, I for one refuse to carry you home,' David warned.

They went on down the Ku-damm and Shasa had the girls in fits of giggles at his nonsense humour.

'Ach so, meine lieblings, dis is de famousa Kranzlers coffee house, no? We will enter and drink a leetle champagne, yes?'

'That's Italian, not German,' Tara pointed out. 'And I think you are sloshed.'

'Sloshed is a foul word on fair lips,' Shasa told her, and marched her into the elegant coffee shop.

'Not more champagne, Shasa,' David protested.

'My dear boy, you don't suggest I should drink everlasting life to you in beer, now do you?' Shasa snapped his fingers to summon the waitress and she poured four tulip glasses of the seething yellow wine.

They were all four laughing and chattering so that for some seconds none of them was aware of the sudden tense silence that had descended on the crowded coffee shop.

'Oh dear,' Tara murmured. 'Here come the cavalry.'

Six brown-uniformed storm troopers had entered the room. They had obviously been to some ceremony or function of their regiment, for two of them carried furled banners. It was just as obvious that they had already been drinking; their attitude was bellicose and swaggering, and some of the other customers of the coffee shop hurriedly gathered their hats and coats, paid their bills and left the room.

The six troopers came strutting across to the vacant table next to where the four of them were sitting, and ordered tankards of beer from the waitress. The owner of the coffee shop, anxious to avoid trouble, came to their table, and greeted them obsequiously. They talked for a short while. Then the proprietor took his leave of them by standing at attention and giving the Nazi salute. Immediately the six storm troopers jumped to their feet and returned the salute, cracking the heels of their jackboots together and shouting, '*Heil Hitler!*'

Mathilda Janine, who had drunk at least one full glass of champagne, let out a shriek of laughter and dissolved into helpless giggles, and the full attention of all the troopers was instantly focused upon her.

'Shut up, Matty,' David implored, but that only made it worse. Mathilda Janine rolled her eyes and went scarlet in the face with the effort of trying to contain her giggles, but in the end they exploded out of her with a wild snorting whoop and the storm troopers exchanged glances and then moved across in a bunch and stood shoulder to shoulder surrounding their table.

The leader, a hefty middle-aged sergeant, said something and Tara answered in schoolgirl German.

'Ah,' said the sergeant in heavily accented English, 'you are English.'

'My sister is very young and silly.' Tara glared at Mathilda Janine who let out another muffled snort through her handkerchief.

'They are English,' said the sergeant, an explanation of all madness, and would have turned away, but one of the younger troopers had been staring at David.

Now he asked in passable English, 'You are the runner? You are the winner of the bronze medal. David Abrahams.'

David looked bashful and nodded.

'You are David Abrahams, the Jew runner.' The trooper enlarged on the theme, and David's face went pale and set. The two English-speaking storm troopers explained to the others, the word *Juden* was repeated, and then they all stared at David with hostile faces and fists clenched on their hips as the sergeant asked loudly, 'Are not the English and Americans ashamed to let the Jews and the negroes win their medals for them?'

Before they could answer Shasa had risen to his feet, smiling politely.

'I say, you chaps are barking up the wrong tree. He isn't a Jew at all, he's a Zulu.'

'How is this possible?' The sergeant looked puzzled. 'Zulus are black.'

'Wrong again, old chap. Zulus are born white. They only

go black when they've been left out in the sun. We've always kept this one in the shade.'

'You are joking,' accused the sergeant.

'Of course I am choking!' Shasa imitated his pronunciation. 'Wouldn't you be, looking at what I'm looking at?'

'Shasa, for goodness' sake sit down,' David told him. 'There is going to be trouble.' But Shasa was inebriated with champagne and his own wit and he tapped the sergeant on the chest.

'Actually, my dear fellow, if you are looking for Jews, I am the only Jew here.'

'You are both Jews?' the sergeant demanded, narrowing his eyes threateningly.

'Don't be a clot. I've explained already – he's the Zulu and I'm the Jew.'

'That is a lie,' said the sergeant.

By this time the entire clientele of the coffee shop was listening to this exchange with full attention, and for those who did not understand English their companions were translating.

Shasa was encouraged by all this attention, and reckless with champagne. 'I see I shall have to prove my case to you. Therefore to convince you that I am privy to all the age-old secrets of Judaism, I will reveal one of our best-kept secrets to you. Have you ever wondered what we do with that little piece the rabbi snips off the end of us?'

'Shut up, Shasa,' said David.

'What is he talking about?' Mathilda Janine asked with interest.

'Shasa Courtney, don't be disgusting,' said Tara.

'*Bitte?*' said the storm trooper, looking uneasy, but the other customers of the coffee house were grinning with anticipation. Bawdy humour was common currency on the Ku-damm and they were revelling in the unaccustomed discomfiture of the storm troopers.

'Very well, I shall tell you.' Shasa ignored David and Tara. 'We pack them in salt, like kippers, and send them off to Jerusalem. There in the sacred grove on the Mount of Olives on the day of the Passover, the chief rabbi plants them in rows and makes a magic sign over them and a miracle takes place – a miracle! They begin to grow.' Shasa made a gesture to describe the growing. 'Higher and higher, they grow.' The storm troopers watched his hand rise with mystified expressions. 'Then do you know what happens?' Shasa asked and the sergeant shook his head involuntarily.

'When they have grown into really big thick *schmucks*, we send them to Berlin where they join the Nazi storm troopers.'

They gaped at him, not believing what they had heard and Shasa ended his recital, 'And they teach them to say—' he sprang to attention and raised his right hand '*Heil* – what is that fellow's name again?'

The sergeant let out a bellow and swung a wild right-handed punch. Shasa ducked, but unsteady with champagne he lost his balance and went down with a crash pulling the tablecloth with him, and the glasses shattered. The champagne bottle rolled across the floor, spurting wine, and two storm troopers jumped on top of Shasa and rained punches on his head and upper body.

David leaped up to go to his assistance, and a storm trooper grabbed his arms from behind. David wrenched his right arm free, swung round and belted a beautiful right-hander into the trooper's nose. The man howled and released David to clutch his injured organ, but instantly two other troopers seized David from behind and twisted his arms up behind his back.

'Leave him alone,' screamed Mathilda Janine and with a flying leap landed on the shoulders of one of the troopers. She knocked his cap over his eyes and grabbed a double handful of his hair. 'Leave David, you pig!' She tugged at his hair with all her strength and the trooper spun in a circle trying to dislodge her.

Women were screaming, and furniture was shattering. The proprietor stood in the doorway of his kitchen, wringing his hands, his face working pitifully.

'Shasa Courtney,' Tara yelled furiously. 'You are behaving like a hooligan. Stop this immediately.'

Shasa was half buried under a pile of brown uniforms and swinging fists and made no audible reply. The storm troopers had been taken by surprise, but now they rallied swiftly. Street fighting was their game.

Mathilda was dislodged with a heave of broad brown-shirted shoulders and sent flying into the corner. Three troopers jerked Shasa to his feet, arms twisted up behind his back, and hustled him towards the kitchen door. David received the same treatment, a trooper on each of his arms. The one with the injured nose following close behind, bleeding down his shirt front and cursing bitterly.

The proprietor stood aside hurriedly, and they ran Shasa and David through the kitchens, scattering chefs and serving maids, and out into the alley behind the coffee house, knocking over the garbage cans as Shasa struggled ineffectually.

None of the storm troopers spoke. There was no need to give orders. They were professionals engaged in the sport they loved. Expertly they pinned the two victims to the brick wall of the alley, while a trooper went to work on each of them, switching punches from face to body and back to the face, grunting like pigs at the trough in time to the rhythm of their blows.

Mathilda Janine had followed them out and again she tried to rush to David's defence, but a casual shove sent her reeling back, tripping and falling amongst the garbage cans, and the trooper returned to his task.

Tara was in the kitchen shouting angrily at the café

671

proprietor. 'Call the police, this instant. Do you hear, call the police. They are killing two innocent people out there.'

But the proprietor made a helpless gesture. 'No use, Fräulein. The police will not come.'

Shasa doubled over and they let him fall. Then all three of them started in with the boot. The steel-shod jackboots crashed into his belly and back and flanks.

The storm trooper working on David was sweating and panting with exertion. Now he stepped back, measured the shot carefully, and sent a final upper cut smashing into David's dangling head. It took David full in the mouth and his head jerked backwards, cracking against the brickwork and they let him collapse, face down onto the paving stones.

David lay slack and unmoving, making no effort to avoid the boots that smashed into his inert body, and the storm troopers tired of the sport. It was no fun to kick somebody who was not writhing and doubling up and screaming for mercy. Swiftly they gathered up their caps and banners and in a group trotted away, past the two police constables who were standing at the mouth of the alley trying to look disinterested.

Mathilda Janine dropped on her knees beside David and lifted his battered head into her lap.

'Speak to me, Davie,' she wailed, and Tara came out of the kitchen with a wet dishcloth and stooped over Shasa, trying not to show her anxiety.

It was some minutes before there were signs of life from the victims. Then Shasa sat up and put his head between his knees, shaking it groggily. David pulled himself up on one elbow, and spat out a tooth in a drool of blood-stained spittle.

'Are you all right, Davie my boy?' Shasa asked through crushed lips.

'Shasa, don't ever come to my rescue again,' David croaked. 'Next time you'll get me killed.'

Mathilda Janine helped them to their feet, but now that Shasa had revived, Tara was bleak and disapproving.

'That was the most despicable display I have ever seen, Shasa Courtney. You were obscene and rowdy, and you asked for everything that you got.'

'That's a bit hard, old girl,' Shasa protested, and he and David leaned heavily on each other as they limped down the alley. One of the constables waiting at the corner snarled at them as they passed.

'What did he say?' Shasa asked Tara.

'He says, quite rightly,' she translated frostily, 'that next time you will be arrested for public violence.'

As the two of them made their painful way back down the Ku-damm, bloodied and battered, Mathilda Janine hovering close at hand and Tara marching a dozen paces ahead of them, trying to disassociate herself, they drew the quick horrified glances of passers-by who looked away immediately and then hurried on.

As the four of them rode up in the elevator of the Bristol, Mathilda Janine asked thoughtfully, 'That story of yours, Shasa, you know about growing things on the Mount of Olives. I didn't understand it. Tell me, what is a *schmuck?*'

David and Shasa doubled over with agonized mirth, clutching their injuries. 'Please, Matty, don't say anything more,' David pleaded. 'It hurts so when I laugh.'

Tara turned on her sternly. 'You just wait until I tell Daddy about your part in all this, young lady. He is going to be livid.' She was right, he was, but not as furious as Centaine Courtney.

It turned out that Shasa had broken four ribs and a collar bone and ever afterwards he maintained that his absence from the team accounted directly for the

Argentinian victory over them by ten goals to four in the polo quarter-finals two days later. Apart from two missing teeth, David's injuries were superficial contusions, sprains and lacerations.

'Not too much harm done,' Centaine conceded at last. 'At least there will be no publicity – one of those horrid little newspaper men writing gloating spiteful articles.' She was wrong. Amongst the clientele at the Kranzler coffee house had been the South African correspondent for Reuters, and his article was picked up by the South African *Jewish Times*. It played heavily upon Shasa Courtney's part in defending his Jewish friend, the bronze medalist sprinter, and when they finally got back to Cape Town, Shasa found himself a minor celebrity. Both Shasa and David were asked to speak at a luncheon of the Friends of Zion.

'The law of unforeseen consequence,' Blaine pointed out to Centaine.

'How many Jewish voters do you suppose there are on the rolls?' Centaine squinted slightly as she calculated, and Blaine chuckled.

'You truly are incorrigible, my sweeting.'

The boxing hall in the great complex of the *Reichs-sportfeld* was filled to capacity for the final bout in the light heavyweight division, and there were ranks of brown-uniformed storm troopers lining each side of the aisle from the dressing-rooms, forming an honour guard for the contenders as they came down to the ring.

'We thought it might be necessary to have them,' Colonel Boldt explained to Heidi Kramer as they sat in their ringside seats, and he glanced significantly at the four judges. All of them were Germans, all members of the party, and it had taken some delicate negotiation and trading on Colonel Boldt's part to arrange it so.

Manfred De La Rey was the first contender to enter the ring. He wore green silk shorts and a green vest with the springbok emblem on his chest and his hair was freshly cropped into a golden stubble. He swept a quick glance around the ringside seats as he clasped both gloved fists over his head to acknowledge the tremendous burst of applause that greeted him. The German sporting public had accepted him as one of their heroes; this evening he was the champion of white racial supremacy.

He picked out Heidi Kramer almost immediately, for he knew where to expect her, but he did not smile. She looked back at him as seriously, but he felt the strength flow into his body, absorbed from her presence. Then suddenly his gaze switched away from her, and he scowled, rage mingling with the strength of his love.

That woman was here. He always thought of Centaine Courtney as 'that woman'. She sat only three seats away from his beloved Heidi. Her dense dark plume of hair was unmistakable, and she wore yellow silk and diamonds, elegant and poised; he hated her so strongly that he could taste it in his mouth, like gall and alum.

'Why does she always come to hound me?' he wondered. She had been there in the crowd more than once during the other matches he had fought, and always that tall arrogant man, with large nose and ears, sat beside her.

Centaine was watching him with that disconcerting enigmatic expression in her dark eyes that he had come to recognize so well. He turned his back on her deliberately, trying to convey the full force of his contempt and hatred, and watched Cyrus Lomax climb into the ring across from where he stood.

The American had a well-muscled body the colour of milk chocolate, but his magnificent head was all African, like one of those antique bronze castings of an Ashanti prince, with deep-domed brow and wide-spaced eyes, thick lips sculpted into the shape of an Assyrian war bow, and a broad flat nose. He wore the red, white and blue stars and stripes on his chest and there was an air of menace about him.

'This one is the worst you will ever meet,' Uncle Tromp had warned Manfred. 'If you can beat him, you can beat them all.'

The referee called them to the centre of the ring and announced them and the crowd roared at Manfred's name. He felt strong and indomitable as he went back to his corner. Uncle Tromp smeared Vaseline on his cheeks and eyebrows and slipped the red gumshield into his mouth.

He slapped Manfred's shoulder, an open-handed stinging blow that was like the goad to the bull and he hissed in his ear.

'Fast as a mamba! Brave as a ratel!' Manfred nodded, mouthing the bulky rubber shield, and went out to the chime of the gong, into the hot white glare of lights. The American came to meet him, stalking him like a dark panther.

They fought matched and equal, they fought close and hard, blows with the power to maim and stun slipping by just a shade wide, sensing each other's intention with almost supernatural concentration and shifting the head, pulling back, ducking, using the spring of the ropes, blocking with forearm and glove and elbows, neither ever quite connecting but both of them hostile and quick and dangerous.

The gong tolled the rounds – five, six and seven – Manfred had never been forced to fight this long. Always his victories had come swiftly, ending in that sudden barrage of blows that smashed his opponent into the canvas. However, the hard training that Uncle Tromp had imposed upon him had given him long wind, and toughened his legs and arms. He felt strong and invulnerable still, and he knew it had to come soon. He had only to wait it out. The American was tiring. His punches no longer snapped with quite the same velocity. The mistake must come and Manfred waited for it, containing his passionate hunger to see the American's blood.

It came halfway through the seventh round.

The American threw one of those straight hissing lefts, and not even seeing it, sensing it with animal instinct, Manfred reared back pulling in his chin and the blow brushed his face but stopped short.

Manfred was poised on the balls of his feet, with his weight back but ready to move forward, his right arm was cocked, the fist clenched like a blacksmith's hammer, and the American was a hundredth part of a second slow on the recovery. Seven hard rounds had tired him and he dragged a fraction, and his right side was open. Manfred could not see the opening, it was too minute, too fleeting, but again that instinct triggered him and experience guided his arm; he knew by the set of the American's shoulders, the angle of his arm and the cock of his head where the opening was.

It was too quick for conscious decision, and the punch was already launched before he could think but the decision was made instinctively and it was to end it in one. Not his usual two-handed, swarming battering finish, but the single stroke, decisive and irretrievable, that would end it all.

It began in the great elastic muscles of his calves and thighs, accelerating like a stone in the swing of a slingshot through the twist of his pelvis and spine and shoulders, all of it channelled into his right arm like a wide roaring river trapped in a narrow canyon; it went through the American's guard and burst into the side of his dark head with a force that made Manfred's teeth clash together in his own skull. It was everything he had, all his training and experience, all his strength, all his guts and his heart and every finely tuned muscle was behind that blow, and it landed solid and cleanly.

Manfred felt it go. He felt the bones of his right hand

677

break, snapping and crackling like dry twigs, and the pain was a white electric thing that flared back up his arm and filled his head with flames. But in the pain was triumph and soaring joy for he knew it was over. He knew he had won.

The flames of agony cleared from his vision and he looked to see the American crumpled on the canvas at his feet, but the wild soaring of his heart stopped and turned to a plunging stone of despair. Cyrus Lomax was still on his feet. He was hurt and staggering, his eyes dull and sightless, his legs filled with cotton waste and his skull with molten lead, tottering on the very brink, but he was still on his feet.

'Kill him!' screamed the crowd. 'Kill him!'

Manfred could see how little it needed, just one more with the right hand, for the American was out on his feet – just one more. But there was no more, nothing left. The right hand was gone.

The American was reeling about drunkenly, bouncing off the ropes, knees sagging and then by some immense effort of will recovering again.

'The left hand.' Manfred summoned it all, everything that remained. 'I've got to take him with the left.' And through his own agony he went after him again.

He threw the left hand, going for the head, but the American smothered it with an uncoordinated forward lunge, and he threw both arms around Manfred's shoulders and clinched him, clinging to him like a drowning man. Manfred tried to throw him off and the crowd noise was a berserk thunder, the referee shouting above it 'Break! Break!' but the American held on just long enough.

When the referee got them apart, Cyrus Lomax's eyes were sighted and focused; and he backed away in front of Manfred's desperate efforts to land with the left hand – and the bell rang.

'What is it, Manie?' Uncle Tromp seized him and guided him to his corner. 'You had him beaten. What went wrong?'

'My right,' Manfred mumbled through the pain, and Uncle Tromp touched it, just above the wrist and Manfred almost screamed. The hand was ballooning, the swelling spreading up the arm even as they stared at it.

'I'm throwing in the towel,' Uncle Tromp whispered. 'You can't fight with that hand!'

Manfred snarled at him, 'No!' His eyes were fierce and yellow as he looked across the ring to where they were working on the dazed American, cold compresses and sal volatile, slapping his cheeks, talking to him, talking him round.

The bell rang for the start of the eighth round and Manfred went out and saw with despair the new strength and coordination with which the American was moving. He was still afraid and uncertain, backing off, waiting for Manfred's attack, but getting stronger every minute, obviously puzzled at first by Manfred's failure to use the right hand again, and then realization dawning in his eyes.

'You all gone,' he growled in Manfred's ear in the next clinch. 'No right hand, white boy. I'm going to eat you up now!' His punches started hurting, and Manfred began to back away. His left eye was closing up and he could taste the coppery salt of blood in his mouth.

The American shot out a hard straight left-hander, and instinctively Manfred blocked with his right, catching the blow on his glove; the pain was so intense that blackness shaded his vision and the earth tipped under him, and the next time he was afraid to block with the right and the American's punch got through and slammed into his injured eye. He could feel the swelling hanging on his face like a bloated blood-sucking tick, a fat purple grape that closed the eye completely and the bell rang to end the eighth round.

'Two more rounds,' Uncle Tromp whispered to him, compressing the swollen eye with an ice-pack. 'Can you see it out, Manie?' Manfred nodded and went out to the gong for the ninth and the American came eagerly to meet him – too eagerly, for he dropped his right hand for the big punch and Manfred beat him to it, slamming in a hard left-hander that jolted Lomax back on his heels.

If he had had the use of his right hand Manfred could have taken him yet again, following up in that raging cross storm of blows that no opponent could survive, but the right was maimed and useless, and Lomax ducked away, backing off, recovering and circling in again, working on Manfred's eye, trying to cut it open and with the last punch of the round he succeeded. He slashed the fat purple sac that closed the eye with a glancing left, catching it with the inside of the glove, ripping it open with the cross hatching of the laces, and it burst. A sheet of blood poured down Manfred's face and splashed over his chest.

Before the referee could hold them up to examine the damage, the gong sounded and Manfred staggered back to his corner as Uncle Tromp rushed out to meet him.

'I'm going to stop it,' he whispered fiercely as he examined the terrible wound. 'You can't fight with that – you could lose the eye.'

'If you stop it now,' Manfred told him, 'I will never forgive you.' His voice was low, but the fire in his yellow eyes warned Tromp Bierman that he meant every word. The old man grunted. He cleaned the wound, and applied a styptic pencil. The referee came to examine the eye, turning Manfred's face to the light.

'Can you go on?' he asked quietly.

'For the *Volk* and the Führer,' Manfred answered him softly, and the referee nodded.

'You are a brave man!' he said and signalled for the fight to continue.

That last round was an eternity of agony, the American's

blows sledge-hammered Manfred's body, laying bruises on top of deep seeping bruises, each of them sapping Manfred further, reducing his ability to protect himself from the blows that followed.

Each breath was fresh agony as it stretched the torn muscles and ligaments of his chest and burned the soft tissue of his lungs. The pain in his right hand flowed up his arm and mingled with the pain of each new blow, and darkness lapped the vision of his single remaining eye so that he could not see the punches coming. The agony roared like a rushing wind in his eardrums, but still he stayed on his feet. Lomax pounded him, smashing his face to raw meat, and still he stayed on his feet.

The crowd was outraged, their blood lust turned to pity and then to horror. They were shouting for the referee to stop this atrocity, but still Manfred stayed on his feet, making pathetic fumbling efforts to punch back with his left hand, and the blows kept crashing into his blind face and broken body.

At last, too late – much too late, the gong rang to end it and Manfred De La Rey was still on his feet. He stood in the centre of the ring, swaying from side to side, unable to see, unable to feel, unable to find his way back to his own corner, and Uncle Tromp ran out to him and embraced him tenderly. Uncle Tromp was weeping, tears running shamelessly into his beard as he led Manfred back.

'My poor Manie,' he whispered. 'I should never have let you. I should have stopped it.'

On the opposite side of the ring Cyrus Lomax was surrounded by a crowd of well-wishers. They laughed and slapped his back, and Lomax did a weary little dance of triumph, waiting for the judges to confirm his victory, but shooting troubled glances across the ring at the man he had destroyed. As soon as the announcement was made he would go to him, to express his admiration for such a show of raw courage.

'*Achtung! Achtung!*' The referee had the judges' cards in one hand and the microphone in the other. His voice boomed over the loudspeakers. 'Ladies and gentlemen. The winner of the Olympic Gold Medal on points is – Manfred De La Rey of South Africa.'

There was a tense incredulous silence in the vast hall that lasted for three beats of Manfred's racing heart, and then a storm of protest, a roar of outrage and anger, of booing and foot-stamping. Cyrus Lomax was rushing around the ring like a madman, shaking the ropes, shouting at the judges, dancing with dismay, and hundreds of spectators were trying to climb into the ring to stage an impromptu demonstration against the decision.

Colonel Boldt nodded at somebody near the back of the hall and the squads of brown-shirted storm troopers moved quickly down the aisles and surrounded the ring, driving back the angry mob and clearing a corridor to the dressing-rooms down which Manfred was hustled.

Over the loudspeaker the referee was attempting to justify the decision. 'Judge Krauser scored five rounds to De La Rey, one round drawn and four rounds to Lomax—' but nobody was listening to him, and the uproar almost drowned out the full volume of the loudspeakers.

'The woman must be five or six years older than you are,' Uncle Tromp said carefully, choosing his words. They were walking in the Tegel Gardens and autumn's first chill was in the air.

'She is three years older than I am,' Manfred replied. 'But that makes no difference, Uncle Tromp. All that matters is that I love her and she loves me.' His right hand was still in plaster and he carried it in a sling.

'Manie, you are not yet twenty-one years of age – you cannot marry without the permission of your guardian.'

'You are my guardian,' Manfred pointed out, turning his head to watch him steadily with that disconcerting topaz-yellow gaze and Uncle Tromp dropped his eyes.

'How will you support your wife?' he asked.

'The Reich's Department of Culture has granted me a scholarship to finish my law degree here in Berlin. Heidi has a good job in the Ministry of Information and an apartment, and I will box professionally to earn enough to live on until I can begin my career as a lawyer. Then we will return to South Africa.'

'You have planned it all,' Uncle Tromp sighed, and Manfred nodded; his eyebrow was still knotted with crusty black scab, and he would be scarred for life. He touched the injury now as he asked, 'You will not deny me your permission, will you, Uncle Tromp? We will marry before you leave to go home – and we both want you to be the one to marry us.'

'I am flattered.' Uncle Tromp looked distraught. He knew this lad – how stubborn he was once he had set on a course. To argue further would merely confirm his decision.

'You are a father to me,' Manfred said simply. 'And yet more than a father. Your blessing would be a gift without price.'

'Manie! Manie!' said Uncle Tromp. 'You are the son I never had – I want only what is best for you. What can I say to persuade you to wait a little – not to rush into this thing.'

'There is nothing which will dissuade me.'

'Manie, think of your Aunt Trudi—'

'I know she would want me to be happy,' Manfred cut in.

'Yes, I know she would. But, Manie, think also of little Sarah—'

'What of her?' Manfred's eyes went fierce and cold and he thrust out his jaw, defiant with his own guilt.

683

'Sarah loves you, Manie. She has always loved you – even I have been able to see that.'

'Sarah is my sister, and I love her. I love her with a brother's love. I love Heidi with the love of a man, and she loves me as a woman loves.'

'I think you are wrong, Manie. I have always thought that you and Sarah—'

'Enough, Uncle Tromp. I don't want to hear any more. I will marry Heidi – I hope with your permission and blessing. Will you make those your wedding gifts to us, please, Uncle Tromp?'

And the old man nodded heavily, sadly. 'I give you both my permission and my blessing, my son – and I will marry you with a joyous heart.'

Heidi and Manfred were married on the bank of the Havel Lake in the garden of Colonel Sigmund Boldt's home in the Grünewald. It was a golden afternoon in early September with the leaves turning yellow and red at the first touch of autumn. To be there both Uncle Tromp and Roelf Stander had stayed over when the Olympic teams scattered for home, and Roelf stood up with Manfred as his best man while Uncle Tromp conducted the simple ceremony.

Heidi was an orphan so Sigmund Boldt gave her away, and there were a dozen or so of Heidi's friends – most of them her superiors and colleagues in the Ministry of Propaganda and Information – but there were others, her cousins and more distant relatives in the black dress uniforms of the élite SS divisions, or the blue of the *Luftwaffe* or the field grey of the *Wehrmacht*, and pretty girls, some of them in the traditional peasant-style *dirndls* of which the Nazi Party so strongly approved.

After the short and simple Calvinistic ceremony that Uncle Tromp conducted, there was an *al fresco* wedding banquet provided by Colonel Boldt, under the trees, with a four-piece band wearing Tyrolean hats and lederhosen. They played the popular Party-approved music of the day, alternating with traditional country airs, and the guests danced on the temporary wooden floor which had been laid over the lawn.

Manfred was so absorbed with the lovely new wife in his arms that he did not notice the sudden excitement amongst the other guests, or the way that Colonel Boldt hurried to greet the small party that was coming down from the house, until suddenly the band broke into the stirring marching song of the Nazi Party, the Horst Wessel song.

All the wedding guests were on their feet, standing rigidly to attention, and though he was puzzled, Manfred stopped dancing and stood to attention with Heidi at his side. As the small party of new arrivals stepped onto the temporary wooden dance floor, all the guests raised their arms in the Nazi salute and cried together, '*Heil Hitler!*' Only then did Manfred realize what was happening, the incredible honour that he and Heidi were being accorded.

The man coming towards him wore a white jacket buttoned high at the throat with the simple Iron Cross for valour its only decoration. His face was pale, square and strong; his dark hair was brushed forward over his high forehead, and there was a small clipped moustache under the large well-shaped nose. It was not an extraordinary face, but the eyes were like no others Manfred had ever seen, they seared his soul with their penetrating intensity, they reached to his heart and made him a slave for ever.

His right hand was still encased in plaster as he held the Nazi salute and Adolf Hitler smiled and nodded. 'I have heard that you are a friend of Germany, Herr De La Rey,' he said.

'I am of German blood, a true friend and your most ardent admirer. I can find no words to describe the great but humble honour I feel in your presence.'

'I congratulate you on your courageous victory over the American negro.' Adolf Hitler held out his hand. 'And I congratulate you also on your marriage to one of the lovely daughters of the Reich.' Manfred took the Führer's hand in his own undamaged left hand and he was trembling and filled with awe by the significance of the moment. 'I wish you great joy,' Hitler continued, 'and may your marriage forge iron links between yourself and the German people.'

The Führer's hand was cool and dry, the strong yet elegant hand of an artist, and Manfred's emotions welled up to choke him. 'Always, my Führer, the links between us will last for ever.'

Adolf Hitler nodded once more, shook hands with Heidi, smiled at her joyous tears, and then he was leaving as suddenly as he had arrived, with a word and a smile for a few of the most important guests.

'I never dreamed—' whispered Heidi, clinging to Manfred's arm. 'My happiness is complete.'

'That is greatness,' Manfred said, watching him go. 'That is true greatness. It is hard to think he is mere mortal – and not a god.'

Sarah Bester pedalled down the main street of the little village of Stellenbosch, weaving through the light traffic, smiling and waving at anybody she recognized on the sidewalks. Her school books were strapped on the carrier behind the saddle of her bicycle. The skirt of her gymslip billowed up almost as high as her knees, and she had to keep clutching at her school hat.

That morning her class had been given the results of the previous term's work and she was bursting with the need to tell Aunt Trudi that she had pulled up from fifth to second place. The headmistress had noted on her school report, 'Well done, Sarah, keep up the good work.' It was her last year, in October she would be seventeen and she would write her matriculation the next month.

Manie would be so proud of her. It was his inspiration and encouragement which had done so much to make her one of the top girls in the school. She started to think about him now, daydreaming as she pedalled along under the oaks. He had been away so long, but soon he would be home; then she would tell him and it would all be all right. She wouldn't have to worry and cry alone at night. Manie would be back – strong, kind, loving Manie would make it all right again.

She thought of being married to him, cooking his breakfast, washing his shirts, darning his socks, walking to church at his side, calling him *Meneer* the way Aunt Trudi called Uncle Tromp, lying beside him every night, waking beside him every morning and seeing his beautiful blond head on the pillow beside her, and she knew there was nothing else in all the world she wanted.

'Only Manie,' she whispered. 'Always and only Manie. He is all I have ever had, all I have ever longed for.'

Ahead of her she saw the postman at the gate of the manse and she jumped down off the bicycle and called, 'Have you got anything for us, Mr Grobler?'

The postman grinned at her and took a buff-coloured envelope from his leather purse.

'A telegram,' he told her importantly. 'A telegram from overseas – but it's not for you, little one, it's for your aunt.'

'I'll sign for it!' Sarah scribbled in his receipt book, propped her bicycle on the gate of the manse and flew up the front steps.

'Aunt Trudi!' she screamed. 'A telegram! Where are you?'

She smelt cooking odours, and knew where to look.

'It's a telegram!' Sarah rushed into the kitchen. Aunt Trudi was standing over the long yellow-wood table with the rolling-pin in her hands, flour to her elbows and wisps of silverblond hair tickling her nose so that she blew at them as she straightened. She was glowing moistly from the heat of the kitchen range, and great pots of peach and fig jam bubbled over the flames.

'Goodness me! What a to-do! You must learn to act like a lady, Sarie, you are not a child—'

'A telegram! Look, a real telegram! It's the first we've ever had.'

Even Aunt Trudi was impressed. She reached for it and then paused.

'My hands are covered with flour. Open it, Sarie.'

Sarah tore open the envelope. 'Shall I read it out?' she demanded.

'Yes. Yes, read it – who is it from?'

'It's from Uncle Tromp – he signs it "Your dutiful husband Tromp Bierman".'

'Silly old man! He has paid for four unnecessary words,' Aunt Trudi grumbled. 'Read what he says.'

'He says, "I have to inform you that Manfred was – "' Sarah's voice tailed off into silence and her bright expectant expression crumbled as she stared at the sheet in her hands.

'Go on, child,' Aunt Trudi urged her. 'Read it out.'

Sarah began again, her voice small and whispery. '"I have to inform you that Manfred was today married to a German girl named Heidi Kramer. He plans to study at the University of Berlin and will not be returning home with me. I am sure you wish him happiness as I do. Your dutiful husband Tromp Bierman."'

Sarah lifted her eyes from the form and they stared at each other.

'I cannot believe—' Aunt Trudi breathed. 'Not our Manfred. He wouldn't – he couldn't desert us.' Then she noticed Sarah's face. The child had gone grey as the ashes in the fireplace.

'Oh, my little Sarie.' Aunt Trudi's plump features collapsed with compassion and shared agony and she reached for the girl, but Sarah let the telegram flutter from her fingers to the kitchen floor and whirled and raced from the kitchen.

She snatched up her bicycle from the gate and stepped up into the saddle. She stood up on the pedals so as to drive harder, and her legs pumped to the beat of her heart. Her hat flew off her head and dangled down her back, suspended on the elastic around her neck. Her eyes were wide and dry, her face still grey with shock, as she raced out of the village, turning up past the old Lanzerac estate, heading instinctively for the mountains.

When the track became too steep and rough she dropped the bicycle and went on upwards on foot, through the pine forest until she reached the first crest. There she stumbled off the track and threw herself full length on the damp bed of pine needles, on the exact spot where she had given her love and her body and her soul to Manfred.

Once she had recovered her breath after the hard run up the mountainside, she lay quietly, neither sobbing nor weeping, merely pressing her face into the curve of her own arm. As the afternoon wore on, so the wind veered into the north west and the clouds gathered on the high peaks above where Sarah lay. At dusk it began to rain, and the darkness came on prematurely. The air turned icy, and the wind whimpered in the pines, shaking down droplets onto her prostrate body until her gymslip was soaked through. She never lifted her head, but lay and shivered like a lost puppy and her heart cried out in the darkness.

'Manfred, Manfred, where did you go to? Why did I have to lose you?'

A little before morning broke, one of the search parties from the village, which had scoured the mountainsides all night, stumbled upon her and they carried her down the mountainside.

'It's pneumonia, Mevrou Bierman,' the doctor told Aunt Trudi when she called him to the manse for the second time that next night. 'You are going to have to fight for her life – she doesn't seem to want to fight herself.'

Aunt Trudi would not allow them to take Sarah to the new town hospital. She nursed the girl herself, tending her day and night in the small back bedroom, sponging the sweat and heat from her body while the fever mounted, sitting beside the bed and holding her hot hand through the crisis, not leaving her even when it had broken and Sarah lay pale and wasted with the flesh melted off her face so that her features were bony and gaunt and her lacklustre eyes too large for the bruised cavities into which they had sunk.

On the sixth day, when Sarah was able to sit up and drink a little soup without Aunt Trudi's assistance, the doctor made his final call and behind the closed bedroom door gave Sarah a detailed examination. Afterwards he found Aunt Trudi in the kitchen and spoke to her quietly and seriously. Once he had left the manse Aunt Trudi went back to the bedroom and sat beside the bed, in the same chair on which she had conducted her long vigil.

'Sarah.' She took the girl's thin hand. It was light and frail and cold. 'When did you last have your courses?' she asked.

Sarah stared at her without replying for long seconds, and then for the first time she began to weep. Slow, almost viscous tears welled up from the depths of those haunted bruised eyes and her thin shoulders shook silently.

'Oh, my little girl.' Aunt Trudi reached for her and held her to the bulky pillow of her bosom. 'My poor little girl – who did this to you?'

Sarah wept silently and Aunt Trudi stroked her hair. 'You must tell me—' Suddenly the gentling hand froze on

Sarah's head in midstroke, as understanding crashed in upon her.

'Manie – it was Manie!'

It was not a question, but the confirmation was immediate as a painful sob came exploding up out of Sarah's tortured chest.

'Oh Sarie – oh my poor little Sarie.'

Involuntarily Aunt Trudi turned her head towards a small framed photograph which stood on the table beside the sick girl's bed. It was a studio photograph of Manfred De La Rey in boxer's shorts and vest, crouched in the classic pugilist's pose with the silver championship belt around his waist. The inscription read, 'To little Sarie. From your big brother, Manie.'

'What a terrible thing!' Aunt Trudi breathed. 'What will we do now?'

The following afternoon while Aunt Trudi was in the kitchen, larding a leg of venison which was a gift from one of the parishioners, Sarah came in on bare feet.

'You should not be out of bed, Sarie,' Aunt Trudi told her sternly, then was silent as Sarah did not even glance in her direction.

The thin white cotton nightdress hung loosely on her wasted frame, and she had to steady herself on the back of a kitchen chair for she was weak from her sick bed.

Then she gathered herself and crossed like a sleepwalker to the kitchen range. With the tongs she lifted the round black cast-iron cover off the fire box, and orange points of flame flickered through the opening. Only then did Aunt Trudi realize that Sarah had the photograph of Manfred in her hand. She had removed it from the frame and she held it up in front of her eyes and studied it for a few seconds. Then dropped it into the opening of the firebox.

Rapidly the square of cardboard curled and blackened. The image upon it faded to ghostly grey and then was obscured by flames. With the points of the fire-tongs Sarah stabbed at the scrap of soft ash that remained, crushing and pounding it to powder. Even then she went on striking the irons into the flames with unnecessary force, until there was nothing left. Then she replaced the cast-iron cover over the firebox and dropped the tongs. She swayed on her feet and might have toppled forward onto the hot stove, but Aunt Trudi caught her and steered her to a kitchen chair.

Sarah sat staring across the kitchen at the stove for many minutes before she spoke.

'I hate him,' she said softly, and Aunt Trudi bowed her head over the haunch of venison to hide her eyes.

'We have to talk, Sarie,' she said softly. 'We have to decide what to do.'

'I know what to do,' Sarah said and the tone chilled Aunt Trudi. It was not the voice of a bright sweet child, but that of a woman hardened and embittered and coldly angry with what life had offered her.

Eleven days later Roelf Stander returned to Stellenbosch, and six weeks later he and Sarah were married in the Dutch Reformed Church. Sarah's son was born on the 16th March 1937. It was a difficult birth, for the infant was big-boned and she was small-hipped and her body still not fully recovered from the pneumonia.

Roelf was allowed into the delivery room immediately after the birth. He stood over the cot staring down at the mottled swollen face of the newborn infant.

'Do you hate him, Roelf?' she asked from the bed. Sarah's hair was sodden with sweat and she was drawn and exhausted. Roelf was silent for a few moments while he considered the question. Then he shook his head.

'He is a part of you,' he said. 'I could never hate anything that is you.'

She held out her hand to him, and he came to stand beside the bed and took it.

'You are a kind person. I will be a good wife to you, Roelf. I promise you that.'

'I know exactly what you are going to say, Daddy.' Mathilda Janine sat opposite Blaine in his panelled ministerial office in the Parliament building.

'You do, do you?' Blaine asked. 'Then let's hear from you exactly what I'm going to say.'

'Firstly,' Mathilda Janine held up her index finger, 'you are going to say that David Abrahams is a fine young man, a brilliant law student and a sportsman of international reputation who won one of the only two medals which this country was awarded at the Berlin Olympics. You are then about to say that he is gentle, considerate and kind, that he has a marvellous sense of humour and dances beautifully, that he is handsome in a funny sort of way and would make any girl a wonderful husband. Then you will say "but" and look grave.'

'I was going to say all that, was I?' Blaine shook his head with wonder. 'All right. Now I say "but" and look grave. Please continue for me, Matty.'

'But, you say gravely, he is Jewish. You will notice the inflexion, and now you look not only grave but significantly grave.'

'This puts a certain amount of strain on my facial muscles – significantly grave. Very well, continue.'

'My darling Daddy would not be so callow as to add, "Don't get me wrong, Matty, some of my best friends are Jews." You would never be as gauche as that, would you?'

'Never.' Blaine tried not to grin, even though he was still seriously worried by the proposition. He could never resist the impishness of his plain carrot-headed but beloved youngest daughter. 'I would never say that.'

'"But," you would say, "mixed marriages are very difficult, Matty. Marriage is a hard business without complicating it by different religions and customs and ways of life."'

'How wise of me,' Blaine nodded. 'And how would you reply?'

'I would tell you that for the past year I have been taking instruction with Rabbi Jacobs and by the end of next month I will be a Jewess.'

Blaine winced. 'You have never kept anything from me before, Matty.'

'I told Mummy.'

'I see.'

She smiled cheerily, still trying to make a game of it. 'Then you would say, "But, Matty, you are still a baby."'

'And you would reply, "I will be eighteen next birthday."'

'And you would look gruff and say, "What are David's prospects?"'

'And you would tell me, "David starts work with Courtney Mining and Finance at the end of the year with a salary of two thousand a year."'

'How did you know that?' Matty was stunned. 'David only told me—' She broke off as she realized what his source had been and she fidgeted in her seat. Her father's relationship with Centaine Courtney troubled her more than she could ever tell him.

'Do you love him, Matty?'

'Yes, Daddy. With all my heart.'

'And you have already obtained your mother's permission – that I can be sure of.' Over the years both Mathilda Janine and Tara had become adept at playing Isabella and Blaine off against each other.

Mathilda Janine nodded guiltily, and Blaine selected a cheroot from the humidor on his desk. While he prepared it, he frowned thoughtfully.

'It's not a thing to go into lightly, Matty.'

694

'I am not going into it lightly. I've known David two years.'

'I always thought you might make a career—'

'I am, Daddy. My career is going to be making David happy and giving him lots and lots of babies.'

He lit the cheroot and grumbled. 'Well then, you'd better send your David to see me. I want to warn him what will happen to him if he doesn't look after my little girl.'

Mathilda Janine shot round the desk, dumped herself into his lap and flung both arms around his neck. 'You are the most wonderful father any girl ever had!'

'When I give in to you!' he qualified the compliment, and she hugged him until her arms and his neck ached.

S hasa and David flew up to Windhoek in the Rapide to fetch Abe Abrahams and his wife down for the wedding. The rest of David's family and most of his friends, including Dr Twentyman-Jones, came down by train. Together with the friends and family of Mathilda Janine Malcomess this made up a multitude that filled the great synagogue in the Gardens suburb to capacity.

David would dearly have liked Shasa to act as his best man. However, it had taken some delicate persuasion to get the strictly orthodox Rabbi Jacobs to perform the ceremony for a bride who had clearly converted to the Faith for the express purpose of marriage rather than out of purely religious commitment. David could not therefore try to smuggle a gentile best man into the *Schul*, and Shasa had to be content with the position of pole-holder at one corner of the *huppah* canopy. However, Shasa made a hilariously funny speech at the reception which Blaine gave at the house in Newlands Avenue, with David as the butt of his wit.

The wedding reception provided Shasa with an opportunity

to effect one of his periodic reconciliations with Tara Malcomess. Their relationship over the two years since the Berlin Olympics had been storm and sunny weather alternating so rapidly that even the two protagonists themselves were not always certain as to how matters stood between them at any given time.

They managed to occupy opposing grounds on almost every issue; though politics was their favourite subject of dissension, the plight of the poor and oppressed in a land where there were plenty of both of these classes was another perennial winner.

Tara could usually find plenty to say about the insensitivity of the privileged rich white ruling classes, and the iniquity of a system which enabled a young man, whose only proven distinctions were a beautiful face and a rich and indulgent mother, to number amongst his playthings fifteen polo ponies, an SS Jaguar in British racing green with the special three and a half litre engine, and a De Havilland Tiger Moth biplane, while thousands of black children had their little bellies bloated with malnutrition and their legs bowed and deformed by rickets.

These subjects did not exhaust their genius at finding contentious issues. Tara had strong views on so-called 'sportsmen' who went out into the veld armed with high-powered rifles to blast the innocent and beautiful animals and birds; nor did she approve of the obvious relish with which some witless young men regarded the slow but inexorable approach of war clouds for the promise of excitement that they seemed to offer. She was scornful of anyone who was satisfied with a second-class degree when it was apparent that with just a little application they could have finished an expensive education, denied to tens of thousands of others, with a *cum laude* degree in engineering.

On the other hand, Shasa thought it sacrilege that a girl who had the face and body of a goddess should try to disguise these facts in an attempt to be taken for a daughter of the proletariat. Nor did he approve of this same young woman spending most of her waking hours either in study, or in the slums and shanty towns that had sprung up on the Cape Flats, dishing out to snot-nosed piccaninnies free soup the ingredients of which she had helped obtain by standing on street corners with a beggar's box.

He especially did not like the medical students and newly qualified young doctors, bolsheviks one and all, with whom she spent so much time in her capacity as an unpaid and untrained nurse in the volunteer clinics, tending unwashed and highly infectious brown and black patients suffering from tuberculosis, syphilis, infant dysentery, scabies, the secondary effects of chronic alcoholism and all the other unlovely consequences of poverty and ignorance.

'St Francis of Assisi was lucky he didn't have you to compete with – you'd have made him look like Attila the Hun.'

He found her friends boring in their serious single-mindedness, and ostentatious in their left-wing beards and shoddy dress.

'They just lack any style or class, Tara. I mean, how can you bear to walk in the street with one of them?'

'Their style is the style of the future, and their class is the class of all humanity.'

'Now you are even talking like one of them, for cat's sake!'

However, these differences were mild and without real substance when compared to their truly monumental disagreement on the subjects of Tara Malcomess' chastity and virginity.

'For God's sake, Tara, Queen Victoria has been dead for thirty-seven years. This is the twentieth century.'

'Thank you for the history lesson, Shasa Courtney, but if you try to get your hand into my bloomers again I am going to break your arm in three separate and distinct places.'

697

'What you have got in there isn't so bloody special. There are plenty of other young ladies—'

'"Ladies" is a euphemism, but let that pass. I suggest that in the future you confine your attentions to them and leave me alone.'

'That is the only sensible suggestion you have made all evening,' Shasa told her in an icy fury of frustration and started the Jaguar sports car with a thunder of exhausts and superchargers that echoed through the pine forests and startled all the other couples parked in the darkness about the pseudo-Greek temple that was the memorial to Cecil John Rhodes.

They drove down the winding mountain road at a savage pace, and Shasa skidded the big sports car to a halt in the gravel in front of the double mahogany doors of the Malcomess home.

'Don't bother to hold the door for me,' Tara said coldly, and slammed it so hard that he flinched.

That had been two months before, and there hadn't been a day since then that Shasa hadn't thought of her. When he was sweating in the heat of the great pit of the H'ani Mine or poring over a contract with Abe Abrahams in the Windhoek office or watching the muddy brown waters of the Orange river being transformed into sheets of silver by the spinning overhead sprinklers of the irrigation equipment, Tara's image would pop uninvited into his mind.

He tried to erase it by flying the Tiger Moth so low that the landing wheels raised puffs of dust from the surface of the Kalahari, or by absorbing himself in precise and intricate aerobatic evolutions, the spin and barrel roll and stall turn, but as soon as he landed Tara's memory was waiting for him.

He hunted the red-maned Kalahari lions in the desert wilderness beyond the mystic hills of the H'ani, or immersed himself in the multifarious affairs of the Courtney companies, studying under his mother, watching her methods and absorbing her thinking, until she trusted him sufficiently to put him in control of some of the smaller subsidiaries.

He played the game of polo with almost angry dedication, pushing himself and the horses under him to the outer limits, and brought the same singleminded determination to the pursuit and seduction of a daunting procession of women – young and not so young, plain and pretty, married and single, more and less experienced – but when he saw Tara Malcomess again he had the strange hollow feeling that he had only been half alive during those months of separation.

For her sister's wedding, Tara had put aside the pretentiously drab uniform of the left-wing intellectual, and as a bridesmaid she was dressed in grey silk with a blue sheen to it which, beautiful as it was, could not quite match the steely grey of her eyes. She had changed her hairstyle, cutting it short; the thick smoky curls formed a neat cap around her head, leaving the back of her long neck bare, and this seemed to emphasize her height and the length and perfection of her limbs.

They looked at each other for a moment across the length of the crowded marquee, and it seemed to Shasa that lightning had flashed across the tent; for an instant he knew that she had missed him as much and thought about him as often. Then she nodded politely and turned her full attention back to the man beside her.

Shasa had met him once before. His name was Hubert Langley and he was one of Tara's bleeding-heart brigade. He wore a shabby tweed jacket with leather elbow patches when most of the other male guests were in morning dress. He was an inch shorter than Tara, with steel-rimmed spectacles and prematurely thinning blond hair. His beard was the colour and texture of the plumage of a day-old chicken, and he lectured in sociology at the university.

Tara had once confided in Shasa. 'Huey is actually a card-carrying member of the Communist Party, isn't that remarkable?' Her voice was awed. 'He is totally committed and he has an absolutely brilliant mind.'

'One might call him a shining jewel in a greasy and grubby setting,' Shasa remarked, thereby precipitating another of their periodic estrangements.

Now he watched as Huey laid one of his freckled paws on Tara's unblemished forearm, and when he touched Tara's cheek with his wispy moustaches and whispered one of the gems from that absolutely brilliant mind into her pink shell-like ear, Shasa realized that slow strangulation was too good for him.

He sauntered across the tent to intervene and Tara greeted him coolly, perfectly hiding the fact that her pulse was thumping loudly in her ears. She hadn't realized how intensely she had missed him until she watched him making his speech, urbane and self-assured, amusing and so infuriatingly good-looking.

'However, we are not climbing on the same old merry-go-round again,' she warned herself, and put up all her defences as he took the chair on the other side of her and smiled at her and teased her lightly while looking at her with open admiration, which was so hard to resist. They had shared so much together, friends and places and fun and fights, and he knew exactly how to tickle her sense of humour. She realized that once she started to laugh it was all over, and she held out against it, but he worked on her defences with skill and perfect timing, adroitly breaking them down as swiftly as she set them up, until at last she surrendered with a tinkle of laughter which she could no longer contain, and he followed up swiftly, cutting her out from Huey's side.

From the balcony Mathilda Janine singled out her elder sister and tossed her bouquet directly at her. Tara made no effort to catch it but Shasa snatched it out of the air and handed it to Tara with a bow, while the other wedding guests applauded and looked knowing.

As soon as David and Matty had departed, dragging a bunch of old shoes and tin cans behind David's old bull-nosed Morris, Shasa worked Tara out of the marquee and spirited her away in the Jaguar. He didn't make the mistake of taking her back up the mountain to the Rhodes memorial, scene of their last historic battle. Instead he drove out to Hout Bay and parked on the top of the precipitous cliffs. While the sun set in a silent bomb-burst of orange and red into the sombre green Atlantic, they fell upon each other in a frenzy of reconciliation.

Tara's body was divided into two zones by an invisible but distinct line around her waist. On occasions of extreme goodwill such as this, the area above the line was, after a suitable show of resistance, made available to him. However, the area south of the line was inviolate, a restriction that left them both strung up with nervous tension when in the dawn they finally and reluctantly parted with one last lingering kiss at Tara's front door.

This latest reconciliation lasted four months which was a new record for them, and after preparing an emotional balance-sheet on which the many advantages of bachelor-hood were overbalanced by one single weighty consideration – 'I cannot live without her', Shasa formally proposed marriage to Tara Malcomess and was devastated by her reply.

'Don't be silly, Shasa, apart from a sort of vulgar animal attraction, you and I have absolutely nothing in common.'

'That is the most utter bilge, Tara,' he protested. 'We come from the same backgrounds, we speak the same language, laugh at the same jokes—'

'But Shasa you don't care.'

'You know that I plan to enter Parliament.'

'That is a career decision, not a thing of the heart, that isn't caring for the poor and the needy and the helpless.'

701

'I care for the poor—'

'You care for Shasa Courtney, that's who you really care for.' Her voice rasped like a stiletto drawn from its sheath. 'For you the poor is anybody who can afford to run only five polo ponies.'

'Your papa had fifteen nags in training at the last count,' he pointed out tartly.

'You leave my father out of this,' she flashed at him. 'Daddy has done more for the black and brown people of this country—'

He held up both hands to stop her. 'Come on, Tara! You know I am Blaine Malcomess's most ardent admirer. I was not trying to insult him, I was simply trying to get you to marry me.'

'It's no good, Shasa. It's one of my unshakable convictions that the vast wealth of this land must be redistributed, removed from the hands of the Courtneys and the Oppenheimers and given—'

'That's Hubert Langley speaking, not Tara Malcomess. Your little Commie pal should think of generating new wealth rather than divvying up the old. When you take everything we have, the Courtneys and the Oppenheimers, and share it out equally, there would be enough for a square meal for everybody, twenty-four hours later we would all be starving again, the Courtneys and the Oppenheimers included.'

'There you are!' She was triumphant. 'You are quite happy to see everybody starve but yourself.'

He gasped at the injustice, and rallied to launch a full-scale counterattack, but just in time he saw the steely grey battle light in her eyes and checked himself.

'If you and I were married,' he made his voice humble, 'you could influence me, persuade me to your way of thinking—'

She had been poised for one of their marvellously

exhilarating shouting matches, and now she looked slightly crest-fallen.

'You crafty little capitalist!' she said. 'That's not fighting fair.'

'I don't want to fight with you, my dear girl. In fact, what I want to do with you is diametrically the opposite of fighting.'

Despite herself, she giggled. 'That's another thing I have against you, you carry your mind around in your underpants.'

'You still haven't answered my question: will you marry me?'

'I have an essay to hand in by nine o'clock tomorrow morning, and I am on duty at the clinic from six o'clock this evening. Please take me home now, Shasa.'

'Yes or no?' he demanded.

'Perhaps,' she said, 'but only after I detect a vast improvement in your social conscience, and certainly not before I have obtained my master's degree.'

'That's another two years.'

'Eighteen months,' she corrected him. 'And even then it's not a promise, it's only a big fat "perhaps".'

'I don't know if I can wait that long.'

'Then bye-bye, Shasa Courtney.'

They never extended their record beyond four months, for three days later Shasa received a phone call. He was at a meeting with his mother and the new winemaker that Centaine had recently brought out to Weltevreden from France. They were discussing the designs for the labels on the latest vintage of Cabernet Sauvignon when Centaine's secretary came through to her office.

'There is a phone call for you, Master Shasa.'

'I can't come now. Take a message and I'll call back.' Shasa did not even look up from the display of labels on Centaine's desk.

'It's Miss Tara, and she says it's urgent.'

Shasa glanced sheepishly at Centaine. It was one of her strict maxims that business came first, and did not mix with any of his social or sporting activities, but this time she gave him a nod.

'I won't be a minute.' He hurried out and was back within seconds.

'What on earth is it?' Centaine stood up quickly when she saw his face.

'Tara,' he said. 'It's Tara.'

'Is she all right?'

'She's in jail.'

In December of the year 1838 on a tributary of the Buffalo river, the Zulu King Dingaan had sent his impis of warriors armed with rawhide shield and assegai against the circle of wagons of the Voortrekkers, the ancestors of the Afrikaner people.

The wheels of the wagons were bound together with trekchains and the spaces between them blocked with thorn branches. The Voortrekkers stood to the barricade with their long muzzle loaders, all of them veterans of a dozen such battles, brave men and the finest marksmen in the world.

They shot down the Zulu hordes, choking the river from bank to bank with dead men and turning its waters crimson, so that for ever after it was known as Blood river.

On that day the might of the Zulu empire was shattered, and the Voortrekker leaders, standing bare-headed on the battlefield, made a covenant with God to celebrate the anniversary of the victory with religious service and thanksgiving for all time.

This day had become the most holy date in the Calvinistic Afrikaner calendar after the day of Christ's birth. It celebrated all their aspirations as a people, it commemorated their sufferings and honoured their heroes and their forefathers.

Thus the hundredth anniversary of the battle had peculiar significance for the Afrikaners and during the protracted celebrations the leader of the Nationalist Party declared, 'We must make South Africa safe for the white man. It is shameful that white men are forced to live and work beside lesser breeds; coloured blood is bad blood and we must be protected from it. We need a second great victory if white civilization is to be saved.'

Over the months that followed, Dr Malan and his Nationalist Party introduced a series of racially orientated bills to the House. These ranged from making mixed marriages a crime, to the physical segregation of the whites from men of colour, whether Asiatic or African, and disenfranchising all coloured persons who already had the vote while ensuring that those who did not have it, remained without it. Up until the middle of 1939 Hertzog and Smuts had managed to head off or defeat these proposals.

The South African census distinguished between the various racial groups, 'the Cape-coloured and other mixed breeds'. These were not, as one might believe, the progeny of white settlers and the indigenous tribes, but were rather the remnants of the Khoisan tribes, the Hottentots and Bushmen and Damaras, together with descendants of Asiatic slaves who had been brought out to the Cape of Good Hope in the ships of the Dutch East India Company.

Taken together they were an attractive people, useful and productive members of a complex society. They tended to be small-boned and light-skinned with almond eyes in faintly oriental features. They were cheerful, clever and quick-witted, fond of pageant and carnival and music, dextrous and willing workers, good Christians or devout Muslims. They had been civilized in Western European fashion for centuries and had lived in close and amiable association with the whites since the days of slavery.

The Cape was their stronghold and they were better off than most other coloured groups. They had the vote, albeit on a separate roll from the whites, and many of them, as skilled craftsmen and small traders, had achieved a standard of living and affluence surpassing that of many of their white neighbours. However, the majority of them were domestic servants or urban labourers surviving just above or below subsistence level. These people now became the subject of Dr Daniel Malan's attempts to enforce segregation in the Cape as well as every other corner of the land.

Hertzog and Smuts were fully aware that many of their own followers sympathized with the Nationalists, and that to oppose them rigidly might easily bring down the delicate coalition of their United Party. Reluctantly they put together a counter-proposal, for residential segregation, which would disrupt the delicate social balance as little as possible and which, while making law a situation which already existed, would appease their own party and cut the ground from under the Nationalist opposition's feet.

'We aim to peg the present position,' General Jan Smuts explained, and a week after this explanation a large orderly crowd of coloured people, joined by many liberal whites, gathered in the Greenmarket Square in the centre of Cape Town peaceably to protest against the proposed legislation.

Other organizations, the South African Communist Party and the African National Congress, the Trotsky National Liberation League and the African Peoples Organization, scented blood in the air and their members swelled the ranks of the gathering, while in the front row centre, right under the hastily erected speakers' stand, auburn hair shining and grey-blue eyes flashing with righteous ardour, stood Tara Malcomess. At her side, but slightly below her level, was Hubert Langley, backed by a group of

Huey's sociology students from the university. They stared up at the speaker, enthralled and enchanted.

'This fellow is very good,' Hubert whispered. 'I wonder why we have never heard of him before.'

'He is from the Transvaal,' one of his students had overheard and leaned across to explain. 'One of the top men in the African National Congress on the Witwatersrand.'

Hubert nodded. 'Do you know his name?'

'Gama – Moses Gama. Moses, the name suits him – the one to lead his people out of captivity.'

Tara thought that she had seldom seen a finer-looking man, black or white. He was tall and lean, with the face of a young pharaoh – intelligent, noble and fierce.

'We live in time of sorrow and great danger,' Moses Gama's voice had a range and timbre that made Tara shiver involuntarily. 'A time that was foreseen in the Book of Proverbs.' He paused and then spread his hands in an eloquent gesture as he quoted. 'There is a generation, whose teeth are as swords, and their jaw teeth as knives to devour the poor from the earth, and the needy from among men.'

'That's magnificent!' Tara shivered again.

'My friends, we are the poor and the needy. When each of us stands alone we are weak – alone we are the prey for those with teeth like swords. But together we can be strong. If we stand together, we can resist them.'

Tara joined in the applause, clapping until the palms of her hands were numb, and the speaker stood calmly waiting for silence. Then he went on, 'The world is like a great pot of oil slowly heating. When it boils over there will be turmoil and steam and it will feed the fire beneath it. The flames will fly up to the sky and afterwards nothing will be the same again. The world we know will be altered for ever, and only one thing is certain, as certain as the rise of tomorrow's sun. The future belongs to the people, and Africa belongs to the Africans.'

Tara found she was weeping hysterically as she clapped and screamed her adulation. After Moses Gama, the other speakers were dull and halting and she was angry with their ineptitude, but when she looked for him in the crowd Moses Gama had disappeared.

'A man like him dare not stay too long in one place,' Hubert explained. 'They have to move like the will-o'-the-wisp to keep ahead of the police. A general never fights in the front line. They are too valuable to the revolution to be used as cannon-fodder. Lenin only returned to Russia after the fighting was over. But we will hear of Moses Gama again – mark my words.'

Around them the crowd was being marshalled to form up into a procession behind a band, a fifteen-piece marching band – any gathering was an excuse for the Cape-coloured people to make music, and in ranks four and five abreast the demonstration began to snake out of the square. The band played 'Alabama', setting a festive mood, and the crowd was laughing and singing; it seemed a parade rather than a demonstration.

'We will be peaceful and orderly,' the organizers reinforced their previous orders, passing them down the column. 'No trouble – we want no trouble with the police. We are going to march to the Parliament building and hand a petition to the prime minister.'

There were two or three thousand in the procession, more than they had hoped for. Tara marched in the fifth rank just behind Dr Goollam Gool and his daughter Cissie and the other coloured leaders.

With the band leading them, they turned into Adderley Street, the main city thoroughfare. As they marched up towards the Parliament building, the ranks of the procession were swelled by the idlers and the curious, so that as their leaders attempted to turn into Parliament Lane, they were followed by a column of five thousand, a quarter of a mile long, almost half of whom were there for the fun and the excitement, rather than from any political motives.

At the entrance to Parliament Lane a small detachment of police was waiting for them. The road had been barricaded, and there were more police armed with batons and sjamboks, those long black whips of hippohide, being held in reserve further up the road in front of the fence of cast-iron palings which protected the Parliament building.

The procession came to a ragged halt at the police barrier and Dr Gool signalled the band to silence, then went forward to parley with the white police inspector commanding the detail while the photographers and reporters from local newspapers crowded around them to record the negotiations.

'I wish to present a petition to the prime minister on behalf of the coloured people of the Cape Province,' Dr Gool began.

'Dr Gool, you are conducting an unlawful assembly and I must ask you to get your people to disperse,' the police inspector countered. None of his men had been issued with firearms and the atmosphere was almost friendly. One of the trumpet-players blew a loud raspberry and the inspector smiled at the insult and wagged his finger like a schoolmaster at the culprit; the crowd laughed. This was the kind of paternal treatment which everybody understood.

Dr Gool and the inspector haggled and argued in a good-natured fashion, undeterred by pleasantries from the wags in the crowd, until finally a parliamentary messenger was sent for. Dr Gool handed him the petition and then returned to address the procession.

By this time many of the idlers had lost interest and drifted away; only the original nucleus of the procession remained.

'My friends, our petition has been conveyed to the prime minister,' Dr Gool told them. 'We have achieved our object and we can now rely on General Hertzog, as a good man and a friend of the people, to do the just thing. I have promised the police that we will all go home quietly now, and that there will be no trouble.'

'We have been insulted,' Hubert Langley called out loudly. 'They will not even deign to speak to us.'

'Make them listen to us,' another voice called and there was loud agreement and equally loud dissent. The procession began to lose its orderly form and to heave and sway.

'Please! My friends—' Dr Gool's voice was almost drowned in the uproar, and the police inspector called an order and the reserves moved down the street and formed up behind the barricade, batons at the ready, facing the head of the procession.

For some minutes the mood was ugly and confused, and then the coloured leaders prevailed and the procession began to break up and disperse – except for a hard core of three or four hundred. All of these were young, many of them students, both black and white, and Tara was one of the few females amongst them.

The police moved forward and firmly herded them away from the barricade, but spontaneously they re-formed into a smaller but more cohesive band and began marching back towards District Six, the almost exclusively coloured area of the city which abutted onto the central commercial area, but whose diffuse and indistinct boundaries would be one of the subjects of the proposed legislation physically to segregate the racial groups.

The younger, more aggressive marchers linked arms and began to chant and sing, and the police detachments shadowed them, firmly frustrating their efforts to turn back into the central area of the city, shepherding them towards their own areas.

'Africa for the Africans,' they chanted as they marched.

'We are all the same colour under the skin.'

'Bread and freedom.'

Then Hubert Langley's students became more lyrical and picked up the ancient refrain of the oppressed that he had taught them:

> When Adam delved and Eve span
> Who was then the gentleman?

The band began to play the more modern protest:

'Mine eyes have seen the glory of the coming of the Lord.' And after that they launched into: '*Nkosi sikelela Africa* – God Save Africa.'

As they entered the narrow lanes and higgledy-piggledy alleys of District Six, the street gangs emerged to watch with interest, and then to join the fun. In the crowded streets were those with personal scores to settle, and there were also the blatantly criminal and opportunistic gang members.

A half brick came sailing in a high arc out of the packed ranks and crashed through the plate-glass window front of one of the white general dealers, a man notorious for overcharging and restricting credit. The crowd was galvanized, a woman screamed, men began to howl like wolves in a pack.

Somebody reached through the jagged hole in the shop window and grabbed an armful of men's suits. Further down the street another window went with a shattering of glass shards, and the police grouped more tightly and moved forward.

Tara was trying desperately to help restore order, pleading with the laughing looters as they stampeded into the shops, but she was shoved aside and almost knocked down and trampled underfoot.

'Go home, whitey,' one of the gang members shouted in her face. 'We don't want you here.' Then he ducked into the doorway of the shop and picked up a new Singer sewing-machine in his arms.

'Stop it!' Tara met him as he came back through the door of the shop. 'Put it back. You are spoiling everything. Don't you see that's what they want you to do?' She beat her clenched fists on the man's chest, and he recoiled before her fury. However, the lane was jammed with humanity, looters, gang members, ordinary citizens and political protesters, confused and angry and afraid. From the end of the lane the police charged in a phalanx; batons rising and falling, sjamboks swinging, they began to sweep the mob down the street.

Tara ran out of the looted store just at the moment when a large constable in dark blue uniform was laying on his baton with a will, his target a skinny little Malay tailor who had scampered out of his shop to try to retrieve a bolt of looted cloth.

The constable hit the tailor with a full swing of the baton, crushing his red pillbox fez, and when the little man dropped on the paving stones, stooped over him to aim another blow at his head. Tara launched herself at the policeman. It was a reflex action, like a lioness protecting one of her cubs. The policeman was bent forward, his back to her, and Tara took him off balance. He went down sprawling, but Tara had a death grip on his baton and the wrist-strap parted.

Suddenly she found herself armed and triumphant with the blue-jacketed enemy of the proletariat, minions of the bourgeoisie, before her.

She had come in behind the rank of advancing police as they passed the shop, and their backs were turned to her. The thuds of the swinging batons and the terrified squeals of the victims infuriated her. There were the poor and the needy and the oppressed and here were the oppressors – and here also with raised baton was Tara Malcomess.

Normally it would have taken Shasa little over half an hour to drive the Jaguar from the Anreith gates of Weltevreden to the charge office in Victoria Street. This afternoon it took him almost an hour and a good deal of fast talking.

The police had cordoned off the area from Observatory Main Road right to the old fort on the extreme south end of the Grand Parade. An ominous shroud of black smoke hung over District Six and drifted out over Table Bay and the police at the roadblocks were tense and on edge.

'You can't go in there, sir,' a sergeant flagged down the Jaguar. 'Nobody allowed in there. Those black bastards are throwing bricks and burning everything in sight.'

'Sergeant, I have just had a message. My fiancée is in there and she needs me. She's in terrible trouble – you have to let me go to her.'

'Orders, sir, I'm sorry.' There were half a dozen constables at the barricade, four of them coloured municipal police.

'Sergeant, what would you do if it were *your* wife or mother who needed you?'

The sergeant glanced around him sheepishly. 'I tell you what I'll do, sir. My men are going to open the roadblock for one minute and we are going to turn our backs. I never saw you and I don't know nothing about you.'

The streets were deserted but littered with debris, loose stones and bricks and broken glass that crunched under the tyres of the Jaguar. Shasa drove fast, appalled at the destruction he saw around him, slitting his eyes against the drifts of smoke that obscured his vision every few hundred yards. Once or twice he saw figures lurking in the alleys, or watching from the upper windows of the undamaged buildings, but nobody attempted to stop him or attack him. Nevertheless, it was with intense relief that he reached the police station in Victoria Road, and the protection of the hastily marshalled police riot squads.

'Tara Malcomess.' The sergeant at the front desk of the charge office recognized the name immediately. 'Yes, you could say that we know about her! After all, it took four of my men to carry her in here.'

'What are the charges, Sergeant?'

'Let me see—' He consulted the charge sheet. 'So far we have only got attending an unlawful assembly, wilful destruction of property, inciting to violence, using abusive and threatening language, obstructing the police in the execution of their duty, assaulting a policeman and/or policemen, common assault, assault with an offensive weapon and/or assault with intent.'

'I will put up her bail.'

'That, sir, will cost a pretty penny, I should say.'

'Her father is Colonel Malcomess, the cabinet minister.'

'Well, why didn't you say so before? Please wait here, sir.'

Tara had a blackened eye and her blouse was torn; her auburn hair stood up in tangled disarray as she peered out at Shasa between the bars of her cell.

'What about Huey?' she demanded.

'Huey can cook in Hades for all I care.'

'Then I'm going to cook with him,' Tara declared truculently. 'I'm not leaving here without him.'

Shasa recognized the obstinate set of her madonnalike features, and sighed. So it cost him one hundred pounds – fifty for Tara and fifty for Huey.

'I'll be damned if I will give him a lift though,' Shasa declared. 'Fifty quid is enough for any little bolshevik. He can walk back to his kennel from here.'

Tara climbed into the front seat of the Jaguar and folded her arms defiantly. Neither of them spoke as Shasa gunned the motor and pulled away with unnecessary violence, burning blue smoke off the back tyres.

Instead of heading back towards the affluent white

southern suburbs, he sent the Jaguar roaring up the lower slopes of Devil's Peak and parked at one of the viewpoints overlooking the smoking and damaged buildings of District Six.

'What are you doing?' she demanded, as he switched off the engine.

'Don't you want to have a look at your handiwork?' he asked coldly. 'Surely you are proud of what you have achieved.'

She shifted uneasily in her seat. 'That wasn't us,' she muttered. 'That was the *skollie* boys and the gangsters.'

'My dear Tara, that is how revolution is supposed to work. The criminal elements are encouraged to destroy the existing system, to break down the rule of law and order, and then the leaders step in and restore order again by shooting the revolutionaries. Haven't you studied the teachings of your idol Lenin?'

'It was the fault of the police—'

'Yes, it's always the fault of the police – that's also part of Lenin's plan.'

'It isn't like that—'

'Shut up,' he snapped at her. 'Just for once shut up and listen to me. Up to now I've put up with your Joan of Arc act. It was silly and naive but I tolerated it because I loved you. But when you start burning down people's homes and throwing bricks and bombs, then I don't think it's so funny any more.'

'Don't you dare condescend to me,' she flared.

'Look, Tara, look down there at the smoke and flames. Those are the people you pretend to care for, those are the people who you say you want to help. Those are their homes and livelihoods that you have put the torch to.'

'I didn't think—'

'No, you certainly didn't think. But I am going to tell you something now and you'd better remember it. If you try to destroy this land I love and make its people suffer, then you become my enemy and I will fight you to the death.'

She was silent for a long time, her head turned away from him and then at last she said softly, 'Will you take me home, please?'

He took the long way home over Kloof Nek and along the Atlantic coast, circling around the far side of Table Mountain to avoid the riot-torn areas and they never spoke again until he parked at last in front of the Malcomess home in Newlands.

'Perhaps you are right,' Tara said. 'Perhaps we really are enemies.' She climbed out of the Jaguar and stood looking down at him as he sat behind the wheel in the open cockpit.

'Goodbye Shasa,' she said softly, sadly, and went into the house.

'Goodbye, Tara,' he whispered. 'Goodbye, my beloved enemy.'

All the Courtneys were gathered in the front room of Weltevreden.

Sir Garrick and Anna sat on the long sofa which was covered with striped Regency patterned damask. They had come down from Natal for Sir Garry's birthday, and the week before they had all climbed Table Mountain for the traditional birthday picnic. It had been a merry occasion and the *Ou Baas*, General Jan Christian Smuts, had been with them, as he nearly always was.

Sir Garry and Lady Anna had planned to return home a few days previously, but then the ghastly news of the German invasion of Poland had broken and they had stayed on at Weltevreden. It was only right that the family should be together in these desperate days.

The two of them held hands like young lovers as they sat close together. Since his last birthday, Sir Garry had grown a small silver goatee beard, perhaps in unconscious imitation of his old friend General Smuts. It increased his scholarly mien and added a little touch of distinction to his pale aesthetic features. He leaned slightly forward on the sofa, inclined towards his wife but with his attention on the radio cabinet over which Shasa Courtney was fussing, twiddling the tuning knobs and frowning at the crackle and whine of static.

'The BBC is on the forty-one-metre band,' Centaine told him sharply and glanced at her diamond-studded wristwatch. 'Do be quick, *chéri*, or we will miss the transmission.'

'Ah!' Shasa smiled as the static cleared and the chimes of Big Ben rang out clearly. As they died away the announcer spoke.

'Twelve hundred hours Greenwich Mean Time and in place of the news we are broadcasting a statement by Mr Neville Chamberlain the prime minister—'

'Turn it up, *chéri*,' Centaine ordered anxiously, and the fateful words, measured and grave, boomed into the elegant room.

They listened to it all in complete silence. Sir Garry's beard quivered, and he took the steel-rimmed spectacles off his nose and absentmindedly chewed on one of the side frames. Beside him Anna wriggled forward onto the edge of the sofa, her thick thighs spread under their own weight; her face slowly turned a deeper shade of brick and her grip on her husband's hand tightened as she stared at the radio in its mahogany cabinet.

Centaine sat in the tall wingbacked chair beside the huge stone fireplace. She looked like a young girl in a white summer dress with a wide yellow ribbon around her slim waist. She was thirty-nine years old, but there was not yet a single thread of silver in the dense dark curls of her hair and her skin was clear, the faint crow's feet at the corners of her eyes smoothed almost entirely by expensive oils and creams. She leaned an elbow on the arm of the chair, and while with one finger she touched her cheek, she never took her eyes off her son.

Shasa paced the long room, moving from the radio cabinet in its niche between the long flowered curtains, across the highly polished parquet floor with its scattering of oriental carpets until he reached the grand concert piano that stood against the main wall of bookcases at the far end of the room, then turning and coming back with quick restless paces, his hands clasped behind his back, his head bowed in concentration.

She thought how he looked so much like his father. Though Michael had been older and not quite so handsome, yet they had the same quality of grace. She remembered how she had believed Michael to be immortal, a young god, and she felt the terror enter her soul again – that same helpless crippling terror – as she heard the words of war echo through this beautiful home that she had built as a fortress against the world.

'We are never safe – there is no refuge,' she thought. 'It is coming again, and I cannot save those I love. Shasa and Blaine – they will both go and I cannot keep them from it. Last time it was Michael and Papa, this time it's Shasa and Blaine – and, oh God, I hate it. I hate war and I hate the evil men who make it. Please God spare us this time. You took Michael and Papa, please spare Shasa and Blaine. They are all I have – please don't take them from me.'

The deep slow voice spoke into the room, and Shasa froze in the centre of the floor, turning his head to stare over his shoulder at the radio as the voice said:

'And so, it is with the deepest regret that I have to inform you that a state of war now exists between Great Britain and Germany.'

718

The transmission ended and was replaced by the slow sad strains of chamber music.

'Turn it off, *chéri*,' Centaine said softly, and there was complete silence in the room.

Nobody moved for many seconds. Then abruptly Centaine rose to her feet. She was smiling gaily as she linked her arm through Shasa's.

'Lunch is ready everybody,' she cried lightly. 'In such lovely weather we will eat on the terrace. Shasa will open a bottle of champagne, and I have managed to get the first oysters of the season.'

She kept up a bright and cheery monologue until they were all seated at the table and the wine glasses were filled and then suddenly her act collapsed, and she turned to Sir Garry with a tortured expression.

'We won't have to go in, will we, Papa? General Hertzog promised he would keep us out. He says it's an English war. We won't have to send our men again – not this time, will we, Papa?'

Sir Garry reached across and took her hand. 'You and I know what the price was last time—' his voice choked off and he could not mention Michael's name. After a moment he gathered himself. 'I wish I could give you comfort, my dear. I wish I could say what you want to hear.'

'It's not fair,' said Centaine miserably. 'It just isn't fair.'

'No, I agree it isn't fair. However, there is a monstrous tyranny abroad, a great evil which will swallow us and our world if we do not resist it.'

Centaine sprang up from the table and ran into the house. Shasa rose quickly to follow her, but Sir Garry restrained him with a hand on his arm, and ten minutes later Centaine came out again. She had washed her face and refreshed her make-up and she was smiling, but there was a feverish glitter in her eyes as she took her place at the head of the table.

'We are all going to be gay,' she laughed. 'That's an order. No brooding, no morbid thoughts or words – we are all going to be happy—' she broke off and the laughter wobbled. She had been about to say, 'for it may be the last time we will all be happy together ever again.'

O n 4 September 1939, the day after Great Britain and France had declared war on Nazi Germany, General Barry Hertzog rose to address the Parliament of the Union of South Africa.

'It is my sad and painful duty to inform the house that the cabinet of the Government is divided on the question of this country's position in the state of war that exists at present between Britain and France on the one hand and Germany on the other hand.' He paused and replaced his spectacles to scrutinize the faces of the men who sat beside him on the government front benches, and then went on gravely.

'It is my firm belief that the ultimatum given to Germany by the British Government concerning the occupation of Poland by the German *Wehrmacht* is not binding upon this country, nor does the German occupation of Poland constitute a threat to the security of the Union of South Africa—' A great roar of approval went up from the opposition benches and Dr Daniel Malan, froglike and bespectacled, smiled benignly, while on the government benches Smuts and his supporters registered their protest as loudly.

'It is rather a local matter between Germany and Poland,' Hertzog went on, 'and it gives this country no cause to join in the declaration of war. Accordingly I propose that South Africa remain neutral; that it cede the naval base at Simonstown to Britain, but in all other respects continue its present relationship with all the belligerents as if no war were being waged.'

The ageing prime minister was a fluent and persuasive speaker and as he continued enlarging his case for neutrality, Blaine Malcomess on the front bench of the government side was covertly watching the reaction of the Smuts supporters around him.

He knew which of them were as firmly committed as himself and the *Ou Baas* to stand by Britain, and which of them were wavering and uncertain. As Hertzog continued speaking, he sensed the swing of emotions towards the old general's side, and with a sense of disbelief and rising shame he foresaw the ignominious decision that the House was about to take. His anger rose to keep pace with his shame.

General Hertzog was still speaking, and Blaine was now only listening with half an ear as he scribbled a note to pass across to the *Ou Baas*, when abruptly his full attention flashed back to what the prime minister was saying.

'Finally, coming to the ethics of the German invasion of Poland, a case could very well be made out for the justification of this action if it were taken into consideration that the security of the German state—'

Blaine felt his spirits soar, and he sensed rather than saw the sudden shock and revulsion of feeling amongst those who had begun to waver towards the side of neutrality.

'He has gone too far,' Blaine wrote on a fresh sheet of his notepad. 'He is defending Hitler's aggression. We have won.'

He tore the sheet from the pad and handed it to General Smuts, who read it and nodded slightly, and rose to his feet to put the other side of the argument.

'Britain is our friend, our oldest and our best friend. We must stand by her to the end,' he said in his high-pitched voice, rolling his r's in his distinctive Malmesbury bray.

'Far from being a local dispute, the Polish invasion has consequences that reach far beyond Danzig and the corridor, into the hearts and souls of free men in every corner of the globe.'

When, at last, the motion, for war or neutrality, was put to the vote, Dr Malan's Nationalists voted as a block for neutrality, and one third of Hertzog's own party, together with three of his cabinet ministers, followed his lead.

However, Smuts and his own men – Reitz and Malcomess and Stuttaford and the others – carried the day and by the slim margin of eighty votes to sixty-seven, South Africa declared war on Nazi Germany.

In a last desperate bid to thwart the declaration, General Hertzog called for dissolution of Parliament and a general election, but the governor-general, Sir Patrick Duncan, refused the request and instead accepted the old general's resignation and invited General Jan Christian Smuts to form a new government and take the nation to war.

'The *Ou Baas* won't let me go,' Blaine said bitterly, and Centaine ran to him across the bedroom of their cottage and stood on tiptoe to embrace him.

'Oh thank God, Blaine my darling. I prayed and prayed and He answered me. I couldn't bear to lose you both. Not you and Shasa – I could never have survived it.'

'I'm not proud that I will stay at home while others go.'

'You have fought once, bravely, unselfishly,' she told him. 'You are a thousand times more valuable here than lying dead on a battlefield in a foreign land.'

'The *Ou Baas* has convinced me of that,' he sighed. With an arm around her waist he led her through to the sitting-room, and she knew that tonight for once they would not make love. His distress was too great. She knew that tonight he wanted only to talk, and it was her duty to listen to him while he poured out his doubts and fears and regrets.

They came out in a jumble, without logical sequence,

722

and she sat close to him so he could touch her merely by stretching out a hand as she listened quietly.

'Our position is so precarious – how can we wage a war when we command a majority of only thirteen votes in the House, while against us we have a solid opposition who hate the *Ou Baas* and what they call his English war? They will fight us every step of the way, while the people also are deeply divided against us. We have within our own borders an enemy as vicious as the Nazis, the *Ossewa Brandwag* and the Black Shirts and the Grey Shirts, the *Deutsche Bund* in South West Africa, enemies within and without.'

She poured him another whisky and soda and brought him the Stuart crystal tumbler. It was his second drink that evening and she had never before seen him take more than one.

'Pirow has betrayed us. He is one of them now, but for all those years he has been in a position of trust.' Oswald Pirow had been the Minister of Defence under the Hertzog government. 'We gave him a defence budget of fifty-six million and a brief to build up an effective modern army, but instead he treacherously gave us a paper army. We believed his reports and his assurances, but now that he has gone we find ourselves without modern weapons, a handful of obsolete tanks and venerable aircraft and an army of fewer than fifteen hundred in the permanent force. Pirow refused to arm the nation for a war which he and Hertzog were determined we would never fight.'

The night wore on but both of them were too strung up to think of sleeping, and when he refused a third whisky she went through to the kitchen to make a pot of coffee and he followed her. He stood behind her with his arms around her waist while they waited for the water to come to the boil.

'General Smuts has given me the Interior Ministry in the new cabinet. One of the reasons he chose me was that

I have already chaired the commission of enquiry into the *Ossewa Brandwag* and the other subversive organizations. It will be one of my major concerns to suppress their efforts to disrupt our preparations for war. The *Ou Baas* himself has taken the Ministry of Defence, and he has already promised Britain an army of fifty thousand volunteers ready to fight anywhere in Africa.'

They took the coffee tray through to the sitting-room and as Centaine poured, the telephone rang, shrill and shocking in the silent cottage. She started and spilled steaming coffee over the tray.

'What time is it, Blaine?'

'Ten minutes to one.'

'I won't answer it – let it ring,' Centaine shook her head, staring at the insistent instrument, but he stood up.

'Only Doris knows I'm here,' he said. 'I had to let her know in case—' He didn't have to explain further. Doris was his secretary, the only one in their confidence, and of course she had to know where to find him. Centaine picked up the telephone.

'Mrs Courtney speaking.' She listened for a moment. 'Yes, Doris, he is here.' She handed the telephone to Blaine and turned away. He listened for a few moments, then said quietly, 'Thank you, Doris, I'll be there in twenty minutes.' He hung up and looked up at Centaine.

'I'm sorry, Centaine.'

'I'll fetch your coat.'

She held it for him and he slipped his arms into the sleeves and turned to face her, buttoning it as he said, 'It's Isabella.' He saw her surprise and went on, 'The doctor is with her. They need me. Doris wouldn't say more, but it sounds serious.'

After Blaine had gone, she took the coffee pot and cups through to the kitchen, and rinsed them in the sink. Seldom had she felt so lonely. The cottage was silent and cold and she knew she could not sleep. She went back into the lounge and put a gramophone record on the turntable. It was an aria from Verdi's *Aida*, always one of her favourites, and as she sat and listened to it the memories it aroused came stealing back out of the past – Michael and Mort Homme and the other long-ago war – and her melancholy swamped her.

She slept at last, sitting in the armchair with her legs curled up under her, and the telephone woke her with a start. She reached for it before she was properly awake.

'Blaine!' She recognized his voice instantly. 'What time is it?'

'It's four o'clock – a few minutes after.'

'Is something wrong, Blaine?' She came fully awake.

'Isabella,' he said. 'She is asking for you.'

'For me?' Centaine was confused.

'She wants you to come here.'

'I can't, Blaine. That's not possible, you know that.'

'She's dying, Centaine. The doctor says she won't last out the day.'

'Oh God, Blaine, I'm so sorry.' And with wonder at herself, she realized she truly was. 'Poor Isabella—'

'Will you come?'

'Do you want me to, Blaine?'

'It is her last request. If we refuse it, our guilt will be so much harder to bear.'

'I'll come,' she said and hung up.

She took only a few minutes to bathe her face and change and put on light make-up. She drove through the almost deserted streets, and Blaine's big gabled home was the only one in Newlands Avenue with lights burning.

He met her at the mahogany double front doors and he did not embrace her, but said simply, 'Thank you, Centaine.' Only then she saw his daughter standing in the hall behind him.

'Hello, Tara,' she greeted her. The girl had been weeping. Her big grey eyes were puffy and swollen and rimmed with red, and her face was so pale that her dark auburn hair seemed to burn like a bush fire. 'I'm so sorry to hear about your mother.'

'No, you aren't.' Tara stared at her with a flat hostile expression which suddenly wavered and cracked. She sobbed and ran down the passageway. A door slammed in the back of the house.

'She's very upset,' Blaine said. 'I apologize for her.'

'I understand,' Centaine answered. 'I deserve at least part of that.'

He shook his head to deny it, but said simply, 'Please come with me.'

They climbed the circular staircase side by side and Centaine asked softly, 'What is it, Blaine?'

'A degeneration of the spine and nervous system, a process that has been going on slowly over the years. Now there is pneumonia, and she can no longer resist.'

'Pain?' Centaine asked.

'Yes,' he replied. 'She has always had pain, more than the average person could bear.'

They went down the wide carpeted passageway and Blaine tapped on the door at the end and then opened it.

'Come in, please.'

The room was large and furnished in cool restful greens and blues. The curtains were closed and a night lamp burned on the bedside table. The man standing beside the bed was clearly a doctor. Blaine led Centaine to the four-poster bed and though she had tried to prepare herself, still she started when she saw the figure that lay upon the banked pillows.

She remembered Isabella Malcomess' serene and gentle beauty. Now a death's head stared at her from sunken eye-sockets, and the fixed grin of yellowish teeth, the rictus of shrunken lips, was somehow obscene. The effect was heightened by the contrast of thick auburn hair which formed a cloud about the ravaged head.

726

'It was kind of you to come.' Centaine had to lean closer to the bed to hear the thin voice.

'I came as soon as I heard you wanted me.'

The doctor intervened quietly. 'You may stay only a few minutes – Mrs Malcomess must rest.' But Isabella fluttered her hand impatiently, and Centaine saw that it was a bird's claw of fragile bones covered with skin the colour of tallow and a ropy network of blue veins.

'I wish to speak in private,' she whispered. 'Please leave us, Doctor.'

Blaine leaned over her to adjust the pillows under her head.

'Please don't tire yourself, dear,' he said, and his gentleness towards the dying woman gave Centaine a jealous pang she could not suppress.

Blaine and the doctor left quietly, and closed the door with a click of the latch. They were alone together for the first time. Centaine was overcome by a sense of unreality. For so many years this woman had bulked large in her life, her very existence had meant that Centaine had to suffer all the vile emotions from guilt to jealousy, from anger to hatred. But now that she stood beside her deathbed, they had all evaporated. All she felt was a vast sense of pity.

'Come nearer, Centaine,' Isabella whispered, beckoning her with another feeble flutter of her wasted hand. 'Talking is such an effort.'

Impulsively Centaine went down on her knees beside the bed so that their eyes were only inches apart. She felt a terrible need to repent for all the unhappiness she had caused and to ask for Isabella's forgiveness, but Isabella spoke first.

'I told Blaine that I wanted to make my peace with you, Centaine. I told him I understood that the two of you had not been able to help falling in love, and that I realized you had tried to spare me as much as possible. I told him I knew that you were never vindictive, that although you could have taken him away, you never inflicted that final humiliation upon me, that although I was no longer a woman, you allowed me to retain the last shreds of my dignity.'

Centaine felt the pity flood her soul and fill her eyes. She wanted to take this frail dying creature in her arms and hold her, but something in Isabella's eyes prevented her, it was a fierce proud light and Centaine simply bowed her head and remained silent.

'I told Blaine that you had filled his life with the happiness I could not give him, but despite that and because of your generosity, I was still able to keep part of him for myself.'

'Oh, Isabella, I don't know how to tell you—' Centaine's voice choked and Isabella gestured her to silence.

She seemed to be gathering herself for some enormous effort. A faint flush of colour came back into her cheeks and the fierce light in her eyes flared up. Her breath quickened and when she spoke again her voice was stronger, harsher.

'I told him all these things to persuade him to bring you here. If he had guessed what I truly intended, he would not have allowed you to come.' She raised her head from the pillow and her voice became a serpent's hiss.

'Now I can tell you how deeply I have hated you every waking hour of every long year, how my hatred kept me alive this long so that I could prevent you from having him as your husband, and now that I am dying that hatred is magnified a hundred times—' She broke off and panted for breath, as Centaine recoiled before her glare. She realized that Isabella was a woman driven to madness by the agony she had endured, by the long corrosion of hatred and jealousy.

'If a dying woman's curse has any force,' Isabella spoke again, 'then I curse you, Centaine Courtney, with my last breath. May you experience the same torture you have inflicted upon me, may you know pain as I have known it. The day you stand before the altar with my husband I will reach out to you from beyond the grave—'

'No!' Centaine stumbled to her feet, and backed towards the door. 'Stop it! Please, stop it!'

Isabella laughed, a shrill and taunting sound. 'I curse you, and let my curse blight your adulterous passion. I curse every minute the two of you spend together when I have gone. I curse whatever seed he places in your womb, I curse each kiss and touch – I curse you and I curse your brat. I curse all your issue. An eye for an eye, Centaine Courtney. Heed my words – an eye for an eye!'

Centaine ran across the room and flung herself against the door. Throwing it open, she ran down the passage. Blaine was coming up the staircase at a run. He tried to hold her, but she tore herself from his grasp and rushed out through the front doors to where the Daimler was parked.

She had been driving for many hours, driving fast with the accelerator pressed to the floorboards, keeping the great seven-litre engine at a long sustained bellow, sending a tall pale column of dust into the sky behind her, before she consciously realized she was going back into the desert, back to the dreaming mystical hills that the little Bushmen called 'The Place of all Life'.

It was two months before Centaine came back out of the Kalahari Desert. For all that time she had thwarted Blaine's efforts to contact her, refusing to reply to the letters he wrote or the telephone calls he made to both Abe Abrahams and Dr Twentyman-Jones.

She read the death notices for Isabella Malcomess in the obituary columns of the newspapers which reached the H'ani Mine only weeks after publication, but they served to increase her feeling of isolation and the brooding premonition of disaster and tragedy which Isabella's death curse had left with her.

She returned to Weltevreden in the end only at Shasa's insistence. When she arrived her hair was floury with dust from the long journey and she was darkly tanned by the Kalahari sun, but tired and dispirited still.

Shasa must have received her telegram and been expecting her. He must have heard the Daimler's motor as she came up the avenue to the château, but he was not on the front steps to meet her, and she realized why when she went into her study. He turned from the window from where he had watched her arrival and now he crossed the room to meet her. He was in uniform.

She stopped in the doorway, and an icy stillness froze her. She watched him come towards her – and in her memory she was carried back down the years and across space to another meeting with a tall and impossibly handsome young man in the same khaki tunic, with the polished belt and Sam Browne cross-strap, the peaked cap set at a jaunty angle, and the airman's wings on his chest.

'Thank God, you've come, Mater,' Shasa greeted her. 'I had to see you before I left.'

'When?' she breathed the question, terrified to hear the answer. 'When do you go?'

'Tomorrow.'

'Where? Where are they sending you?'

'First we go to Roberts Heights,' that was the airforce training base in the Transvaal, 'for conversion to fighters, and after that wherever they send us. Wish me luck, Mater.'

She saw that he wore orange flashes on the epaulettes of his tunic, the insignia of those who had volunteered to fight beyond the country's borders.

'Yes, my darling, I wish you luck,' she said, and knew that her heart would break to see him go.

The roar of the Rolls-Royce Merlin engine filled his head even through the earphones of the radio telephone that Shasa wore over his leather flying helmet. The cockpit canopy of the Hawker Hurricane fighter aircraft was open, so the slipstream buffeted his head, but it gave him an uninterrupted view of the blue African sky around him. The three fighters flew in a loose arrowhead formation. The dun-coloured desert camouflage could not disguise their beautiful deadly lines.

Shasa led the flight. His promotion had been rapid. Command came naturally to him, he had learned that lesson well from Centaine Courtney. It had taken only eighteen months for him to reach the rank of squadron leader.

He flew in a short-sleeved khaki tunic, khaki shorts and with velskoen on his bare feet, for the summer heat of Abyssinia was brutal. Around his waist was belted a Webley service revolver, an archaic weapon for the pilot of a modern pursuit aircraft, but all of them had taken to wearing side-arms since the intelligence section had circulated those obscene photographs. One of the motorized recce units had overrun a village in the mountains and found the remains of two South African pilots who had been forced down and captured by the Abyssinian irregulars – the *shufta*, wild hill bandits. The pilots had been given to the women of the village. They had first been emasculated, then flayed with hot irons and disembowelled so skilfully that they were still living as their viscera was drawn from them. Finally, their jaws had been wedged open with thorn branches and the women had urinated into their open mouths until they drowned. So all the pilots carried sidearms now, to defend themselves first, and then to make certain they were never captured alive.

Today the air was clear and bright under a cloudless azure sky, and visibility was unlimited. Below and ahead stretched the rugged Abyssinian highlands, precipitous

Ambas, the huge table-topped mountains, the dark deep gorges between, desert and rock, dry and sun-bleached to the dun colour of an old lion's scarred hide.

The three fighters bored upwards, striving for height. They had scrambled from the dusty forward airstrip at Yirga Alem only minutes before, in response to a faint but desperate appeal over the field radio from the advancing infantry, and Shasa wheeled the flight onto the northern heading and picked out the thin pale thread of the road winding through the mountains far below them.

Immediately he resumed the fighter pilot's scan, his head pivoting and turning, eyes darting and flicking, never allowed to fix and focus short, up and around and down in a regular never ceasing motion and he saw them first.

They were tiny specks, a cloud of black midges against the aching blue.

'Popeye flight, this is leader. Tally ho!' he said into the microphone of his radio telephone. 'Eleven o'clock high! Ten plus – and they look like Capronis. Buster! Buster!' 'Buster' was the order to go to full throttle.

'I have them,' Dave Abrahams answered immediately. It was extraordinary that they had been able to keep together, from the training days at Roberts Heights through all the vagaries of the East African campaign, until now they were fighting with Dan Pienaar's South African Corps, driving the Duke of Aosta's Italians back through the mountains towards Addis Ababa.

Shasa glanced across at him. David had brought his Hurricane up on Shasa's starboard wingtip. He also had his canopy open, and they flashed a grin across at each other. David's large beaky nose had been burned raw and pink by the sun, and the straps of his helmet hung unbuckled under his chin. It was a good feeling to have him on his wing. Then both of them closed their canopies in preparation for the attack and looked ahead. Shasa brought the flight around into a gentle turn, climbing up into the sun, the classic fighter tactics.

The distant midges resolved swiftly into the familiar silhouettes of three-engined Caproni bombers. Shasa counted twelve, four sticks of three. They were going for the crossroads at Kerene again, where the South African advance was bottled into the pass between the soaring walls of the high Ambas, and at that moment Shasa saw the bombs drop away from below the leading bombers.

Still under full throttle, the Rolls-Royce engines screamed in protest as they climbed out, turning into the sun that blinded the Italian gunners. Shasa winged over and went down into the attack.

He could see the bomb-bursts now, tiny fountains of pale dust, spurting up around the crossroads, falling amongst the antlike column of vehicles in the gut of the hills. Those poor bastards down there were taking a pounding, and as they tore down the sky the second flight of Capronis released their bombloads. The fat grey eggs, finned at one end, went down with a deceptively slow wobbling motion, and Shasa twisted his head around in one last sweep of the heavens, squinting into the sun, checking that the Italian fighters were not waiting up there, lying in ambush; but the sky was unsullied blue, and he switched his full attention back to his gunsight.

He picked out the leading Caproni in the third flight, hoping his attack would spoil the bomb-layer's aim, and he touched left rudder and rotated the Hurricane's nose downwards a hair's breadth until the silver and blue Caproni swam gently in the rose of his gunsight.

Six hundred yards and he held his fire. He could see the insignia of the fasces on the fuselage, the bundled rods and axe of imperial Rome. The heads of the two pilots in the cockpit were inclined earthwards, watching for the fall of the bombs. The twin machine-guns in the revolving power turret were trained aft.

Five hundred yards. He could see the head and shoulders of the turret gunner. The back of his helmet was towards Shasa. He had not yet spotted the three deadly machines screaming down onto his starboard quarter.

Four hundred yards – so close that Shasa could see the scorching of fumes around the exhaust ports of the Caproni's engines, and the gunner still was unaware.

Three hundred yards. The bomb bay of the Caproni began to open under her swollen belly, pregnant with death. Now Shasa could make out the rows of rivet heads along the silver fuselage and on the wide blue wings. He settled his grip on the joystick between his knees and slipped the safety-lock on the firing button, readying the eight Browning machine-guns in his wings.

Two hundred yards. He played the rudder bars with his toes and the gunsight drifted over the Caproni's fuselage. He stared through it, frowning slightly with concentration, his lower lip caught between his front teeth. Suddenly a line of bright fiery phosphorescent beads strung across the nose of his Hurricane. The gunner of the second Caproni had spotted him at last, and fired a warning burst across his nose.

One hundred yards. The gunner and both pilots in the leading Caproni, alerted by the burst of fire, had looked round and seen him. The turret gunner was traversing frantically trying to bring his guns to bear. Through the gunsight Shasa could see his white face, contorted with terror.

Eighty yards. Still frowning, Shasa pressed down with his thumb on the firing-button. The Hurricane shuddered and slowed to the recoil of eight Brownings, and Shasa was thrown gently forward against his shoulder-straps by the deceleration. Bright streams of tracer, sparkling like electricity, hosed into the Caproni, and Shasa watched the strike of shot, directing it with quick subtle touches of his controls.

The Italian gunner never fired his turret guns. The Perspex canopy disintegrated around him and concentrated fire tore him to shreds. Half his head and one of his arms were pulled off like those of a careless child's rag doll, and went spinning and bouncing away in the propeller wash. Instantly Shasa switched his aim, picking up the silver coin of the spinning propeller and the vulnerable wing root of the Caproni in his sights. The crisp silhouette of the wing dissolved like wax in a candleflame. Glycerine and fuel vapour poured from the motor in liquid sheets, and the whole wing pivoted slowly backwards on its root, and then tore away and spun off, a dead leaf in the slipstream. The bomber flipped over on its back and went down in a flat inverted spiral, unbalanced by the missing wing, weaving irregular zigzag patterns of smoke and vapour and flame down the sky, and Shasa turned all his attention to the next formation of bombers.

He brought the Hurricane round still under full throttle, and he pulled his turn so tightly that the blood drained away from his brain and his vision turned grey and shadowy. He tensed his belly muscles and clenched his jaw to resist the drainage of blood, and levelled out on a head-on course with the next Caproni in line.

The two aircraft raced together with terrifying speed. The nose of the Caproni swelled miraculously to fill all Shasa's vision, and he fired into it at pointblank range and then pulled up his nose and they flashed past each other so close that he felt the bump and jar of the bomber's slipstream. He came round again, hard and furiously, breaking up the Italian formations, scattering them across the sky, turning and diving and firing until with that abruptness that is so much part of aerial combat, they were all gone.

He was alone in an enormously blue and empty sky and he was sweating with adrenalin reaction. His grip on the control column was so tight that it hurt his knuckles. He throttled back and checked his fuel gauge. Those desperate minutes at full throttle had burned over half a tankful.

'Popeye flight, this is leader. Come in all units.' He spoke into his microphone and the response was immediate.

'Leader, this is three!' That was the third Hurricane, with young Le Roux at the controls. 'I'm down to quarter of a tank.'

'All right, three, return independently to base,' Shasa ordered. And then he called again. 'Popeye two, this is leader. Do you read me?'

Shasa was searching the sky around him, trying to pick up David's aircraft, feeling the first prickle of anxiety.

'Come in, Popeye two,' he repeated, and looked down, searching for smoke rising from a wrecked aircraft in the broken brown land below. Then his pulse jumped as David's voice came in clearly through his headphones.

'Leader, this is two, I have damage.'

'David, where the hell are you?'

'Approximately ten miles east of Kerene crossroads, at eight thousand feet.'

Shasa glanced into the easterly quarter and almost instantly picked out a thin grey line being swiftly drawn above the blue horizon towards the south. It looked like a feather.

'David, I see smoke in your area. Are you on fire?'

'Affirmative. I have an engine fire.'

'I'm coming, David, hold on!'

Shasa flung the Hurricane's wing up in a steep turn and rammed the throttle open to its stop.

David was a little below him, and he went screaming down the sky.

'David, how bad is it?'

'Roast turkey,' David said laconically, and ahead of him Shasa made out the burning Hurricane.

David had his stricken machine in a steep side slip, so that the flames were not streaming back over the cockpit canopy but were being blown out to one side. He was going down fast, trying to build up speed to the critical point when the fire would be starved of oxygen and would extinguish itself spontaneously.

Shasa bore down on him and then eased back his own speed and kept slightly above and two hundred yards off. He could see the bullet holes in the other machine's engine cowling and wing. One of the Italian gunners had got in a good burst at David. The paintwork was blackening and blistering back down the Hurricane's fuselage, almost as far as the cockpit, and David was struggling with the Perspex canopy, trying to open it.

'A jammed canopy and David will cook,' Shasa thought, but at that moment the canopy came free and slid back easily and David looked across at him. The air around his head was distorted by the shimmering heat of invisible flames and a brown patch appeared on the sleeve of David's tunic as the khaki cotton scorched.

'No good! I'm hitting the silk, Shasa.' He saw David's lips move and his voice echoed in Shasa's earphones, but before he could reply, David pulled the helmet from his head and released his shoulder-straps. He lifted one hand in a farewell salute, and then turned the burning Hurricane onto its back and fell out of the open cockpit.

He went down with arms and legs spread in an untidy sprawling starfish, beginning to turn like a cartwheel until suddenly a cascade of silk burst from his parachute pack, bloomed into a glistening snowy flower over him and he was jerked backwards, his fall broken, and he drifted away towards the parched, dung-coloured earth five thousand feet below, the light breeze carrying his parachute away towards the south.

Shasa throttled his Hurricane back until he was losing height at the same rate as the descending parachute, and he circled David slowly, keeping two or three hundred yards separation from his dangling body, craning his head over the side of his open cockpit, trying to estimate where David would land, and then glancing anxiously at the fuel gauge on his instrument panel. The needle hovered just above the red line.

David's burning Hurricane smashed into the dusty plain below the soaring Ambas and exploded in a quick dragon's breath of smoke, and Shasa surveyed the ground.

Directly below were ridges of iron grey which peaked into cones of darker rock. Between the ridges were stony hollows, rough as a crocodile's skin, and then, just beyond the last ridge, a softer smoother valley; as they descended he made out the regular furrows of primitive cultivation on the gentle slopes of the valley. David would come down on or very close to the final ridge.

Shasa's eyes narrowed. Human habitation! There was a tiny group of thatched huts at the end of the valley, and for a moment his spirits rose. Then he remembered the photographs – those mutilated and desecrated lumps of human flesh, and his jaw clenched as he looked across at David, swaying and swinging on the parachute shrouds.

He banked the Hurricane away, turning and dropping down towards the valley, and he levelled out at fifty feet above the ground, and flew back between the rock ridges up the shallow valley. He roared over the rude fields of cultivation, scraggly stalks of sorghum standing in ragged lines, stunted and browned by drought, and then ahead of him he saw human figures.

A group of men were running down the valley from the village, twenty or more figures in long dirty grey robes that flapped around their bare black legs as they ran. Their hair was teased up into fuzzy dark bushes, and all of them were armed, some with modern carbines probably looted from the battlefield, others with the long muzzle-loading jezails.

As the Hurricane roared low over their heads, three or four of them stopped running and threw their rifles to their shoulders, pointing them up at Shasa. He saw the flash of black powder smoke as they fired, but he did not feel the bullets hit his aircraft.

Shasa needed no further evidence of their hostile intentions. The armed men were streaming along the bottom of the ridge, waving their rifles, racing to intercept the tiny figure on the floating parachute.

Shasa dropped down again, lined up the running group and at five hundred yards, opened up with the eight Brownings. Sheets of tracer and dust flew up around the group of robed figures in a raging storm, and he saw four or five of them picked up and flung down again by the hail of machine-gun fire.

Then he was forced to climb out to miss the hills at the head of the valley, and as he came around once more he saw that the *shufta* had regrouped and were once again running to intercept David who was at less than a thousand feet now. It was clear that he would fall on the slope of the ridge.

Shasa dropped in for a second attack, but this time the *shufta* scattered before the approaching Hurricane and from the cover of the rocks they turned a furious fusillade on Shasa as he roared over their heads. His own machine-gun fire threw up clouds of dust and rock fragments, but did little execution.

He climbed up and levelled out, swivelling his head to watch David land. The parachute drifted over the ridge, missing it by only a few feet, then it hit the down-draught of the back slope and dropped sharply.

He saw David land heavily and tumble head over heels, bumping across the rocky slope until the parachute jerked him to his feet again. He struggled with the tangled shrouds and the billowing folds of silk, sawing and tipping it, spilling air from it until the parachute collapsed in a silvery heap and David threw off the harness.

He stood and stared down the slope towards the band of running howling *shufta* and Shasa saw him unbuckle the flap of his holster and draw his service pistol, then shade his eyes and look up at the circling Hurricane.

Shasa dropped down almost to his level, and as he passed he pointed urgently down the slope. David stared up at him without comprehension. He looked very small and abandoned on the desert hillside, and Shasa was close enough to see the resignation on his face as he waved farewell to Shasa and turned to face the savage band coming up to take him.

Shasa fired another burst at the *shufta* as he roared towards them, and again they scattered for cover. They were still half a mile from David; he had delayed them for precious seconds. He put the Hurricane into a maximum-rate turn, his wingtip brushing the thorn scrub of the ridge as he came around, and the instant he levelled out he let down his undercarriage. With landing-wheels hanging he roared back over the spot where David stood and repeated his urgent signal, pointing down into the valley.

He saw understanding lighten David's face. He turned and ran down the slope with long bounding strides, so that he seemed to float above the dark rocks, skimming them lightly.

Shasa turned at the bottom end of the valley and lined up on the roughly ploughed strip of land at the foot of the slope. He saw that David was already halfway down and that the *shufta* were trying to head him off – but then he needed all his wits for the touch down.

At the last moment he pulled on full flap and held the Hurricane off, letting her float in, bleeding off speed – back, back, back with the stick. Two feet off the ploughed earth she stalled and dropped in with a crash, bounced and hit again, and bounced, caught a wheel in the rough and her tail went up. She almost nosed in, then checked and ran out, kicking and jolting, throwing Shasa cruelly against his shoulder-straps.

He was down. He had given himself even odds on getting her down without breaking her, but here he was down and David had almost reached the bottom of the ridge.

David wasn't going to make it, he realized almost immediately. Four of the strongest runners amongst the *shufta* had pulled ahead, and they were going to cut David off before he reached the ploughed land. The other *shufta* had stopped and were shooting at long range. Shasa saw bullets kick up little dust feathers along the slope, some of them fell frighteningly close to David's racing form.

Shasa turned the Hurricane, standing on one rudder to force her wheels over the rough furrows. When her nose was pointed directly at the four leading *shufta*, he gave the Hurricane a burst of full throttle and her tail lifted. For a moment she was level and her Brownings could bear. He fired a full burst, and a tornado of shot swept across the field, scything down the dry sorghum stalks and catching the group of running men, blowing two of them into sodden bundles of red rags, spinning a third in a giddy little *danse macabre* veiled by a curtain of flying dust. The remaining bandit threw himself flat to the earth, and the Hurricane's tail dropped back onto the tail wheel. The machine-guns could no longer bear.

David was only a few hundred yards away now, coming on fast, his long legs flying and Shasa swung the Hurricane to point back down the valley. The down slope would add speed to their take-off run.

Shasa leaned out of the cockpit.

'Come on, Davie,' he yelled. 'Gold medal this time, boyo!'

Something hit the cowling just in front of the canopy with a metallic twang and then went screaming off in ricochet, leaving a silver smear through the paintwork. Shasa looked back. The *shufta* were into the edge of the field, running forward, then stopping to kneel and fire. Another bullet cracked past his head, forcing him to flinch and duck.

'Come on, Davie.' He could hear David's panting breath above the idling beat of the Rolls-Royce engine, and a bullet slapped into the wing, punching a neat round hole through the fabric.

'Come on, Davie.' Sweat had stained David's tunic and greased his flushed face. He reached the Hurricane and jumped up onto the wing. The aircraft dipped under his weight.

'On my lap,' Shasa yelled. 'Get in!' David scrambled in on top of him, grunting for breath.

'I can't see ahead,' Shasa shouted. 'You take the stick and the throttle – I'll work the rudders.'

He felt David's hands on the joystick and the throttle lever, and relinquished both of them. The engine beat quickened and the Hurricane began to roll forward.

'A touch of left rudder,' David called, his voice broken and rough with fatigue, and Shasa pushed on an inch of left rudder.

In a gale of sound and dust the Rolls-Royce engine built up to full power, and they were bumping and bouncing over the field, steering an erratic course as Shasa worked the rudders blindly, over-correcting to David's instructions.

Shasa could not see ahead. David was crushing him down in the seat and totally obscuring his forward vision. He twisted his head and looked over the edge of the cockpit, watching the ground begin to blur past him as their speed built up, responding quickly to David's calls for left or right rudder. The dry sorghum stalks whipped against the leading edges of the wings; the sound they made was almost as ugly as the snap and flute of bullets passing close. All the remaining *shufta* were still firing at them, but the range was opening rapidly.

The Hurricane hit a hump in the field and it kicked

them into the air. The jolting and thudding ceased abruptly and they were airborne, climbing away.

'We made it!' Shasa shouted, amazed at their achievement, and as the words left his lips something hit him in the face.

The bullet was a piece of hammered-iron pot-leg, as long and thick as a man's thumb. It had been fired from a 1779 Tower musket by a handful of black powder. It struck the metal frame of the canopy beside Shasa's head, and the pot leg mushroomed and tumbled as it ricocheted. Spinning, it smashed into the side of Shasa's face, its velocity sharply reduced by the impact on the frame. Striking side-on, it did not penetrate to the brain.

Shasa did not even lose consciousness. It felt as though he had been hit in the outer corner of his left eye with a full swing of a hammer. His head was knocked across so that it struck the opposite side of the canopy.

He felt the supra-orbital margin of the frontal bone of his skull shatter, and hot blood drenched his eye and tatters of his own skin and flesh hung down over his face like a curtain.

'David!' he screamed. 'I'm hit! I can't see!'

David twisted around and looked back at Shasa's face and he cried out in horror. Blood was spurting and dribbling and splashing, blown by the slipstream into pink veils that spattered into David's face.

'I can't see,' Shasa kept repeating. His face was raw meat running red. 'I can't see, oh God Davie, I can't see.'

David pulled the silk scarf from around his own neck and pushed it into one of Shasa's groping hands.

'Try and stop the bleeding,' he shouted above the roar of the engine, and Shasa bundled the scarf and pressed it into the hideously ragged wound, while David gave all his attention to getting them home, keeping low, skimming the wild brown hills.

It took them fifteen minutes back to the airstrip at Yirga

Alem and they came in at treetop level. David slammed the Hurricane onto the dusty strip and taxied tail up to the waiting field ambulance that he had called for from the air.

They lifted Shasa out of the blood-spattered cockpit. Then David and a medical orderly half-carried, half-led him, stumbling like a blind man to the ambulance. Within fifteen minutes Shasa was anaesthetized and laid out on the operating table in the hospital tent and an airforce doctor was working over him.

When he came round from the anaesthetic, all was dark.

He lifted his hand and touched his face. It was swathed in bandages, and panic rose in him.

'David!' he tried to scream, but it came out in a drunken slur from the chloroform.

'All right, Shasa, I'm here.' The voice was close by and he groped for him.

'Davie! Davie!'

'It's all right, Shasa, it's all going to be just fine.'

Shasa found his hand and clung to it. 'I can't see. I'm blind.'

'The bandages, that's all,' David assured him. 'The doctor is delighted with you.'

'You're not lying to me, David?' Shasa pleaded. 'Tell me I'm not blind.'

'You are not blind,' David whispered, but mercifully Shasa could not see his face as he said it. Shasa's desperate grip relaxed slowly, and after a minute the painkillers took effect and he drifted back into unconsciousness.

David sat beside his cot all that night; even in darkness the tent was hot as an oven. He wiped the glistening sweat from Shasa's neck and chest, and held his hand when he whimpered in his sleep and muttered, 'Mater? Are you there, Mater?'

After midnight the doctor ordered David to leave him and get some rest, but David refused.

'I have to be here when he wakes – I have to be the one to tell him. I owe him that much at least.'

Outside the tent the jackals yipped at the dawn, and when the first glow struck through the canvas, Shasa woke again, and asked immediately, 'David?'

'I'm here, Shasa.'

'It hurts like hell, Davie, but you told me it's going to be all right. I remember that, you did tell me, didn't you?'

'Yes, that's what I said.'

'We'll be flying together soon, won't we, Davie boy? The old team, Courtney and Abrahams back in business?'

He waited for the reply, but when it did not come Shasa's tone changed. 'I'm not blind, am I? We will be flying again?'

'You are not blind,' David said softly. 'But you won't be flying again. You're going home, Shasa.'

'Tell me!' Shasa ordered. 'Don't try and spare me, that will only make it worse.'

'All right, I'll tell you straight. The bullet burst your left eyeball. The doctor had to remove it.'

Shasa lifted his hand and touched the left side of his face disbelievingly.

'You will still have full vision in the right eye, but you won't be flying Hurricanes again. I'm sorry, Shasa.'

'Yes,' Shasa whispered. 'So am I.'

David came to visit him again that evening. 'The CO has put you up for the DFC. You'll get it, for sure.'

'That's charming of him,' Shasa said. 'Bloody charming.' And they were silent for a while, then David spoke again.

'You saved my life, Shasa.'

'Oh shut up, Davie, don't be a bore.'

'They are flying you down to the coast tomorrow morning in the transport Dakota. You'll be in Cape Town for Christmas. Give Matty and the baby a kiss for me, you lucky sod.'

'I'd change places any day,' Shasa told him. 'But we'll give you one hell of a party when you come home.'

'Is there anything I can do for you – anything you need?' David asked as he stood up.

'As a matter of fact, there is. Do you think you could get your hands on a bottle of whisky for me, Davie?'

The commander of the submarine straightened up from the eye-piece of the telescope and nodded to Manfred De La Rey.

'Look, please!' he said, and Manfred took his place at the telescope, pressing his forehead against the rubber pad and staring into the lens.

They were lying two miles offshore and on the surface it was late evening. The sun was setting behind the land.

'Do you recognize the landmarks?' the U-boat commander asked in German and Manfred did not answer immediately, for he found it difficult to speak. His emotions were too strong.

Five years, five long years since he had set eyes on this beloved coast, and his joy was abundant. He knew that he could never be truly happy anywhere but in his Africa.

However, the intervening years had not been unhappy. There had always been Heidi, and in this last year his son, Lothar, named after his own father. The two of them had formed the pivot of his existence. And there had also been his work – two tasks running side by side, each of them demanding and utterly fulfilling.

His law studies had culminated in a Master's degree in Roman Dutch Law and International Law at the University of Berlin.

There had also been his military preparations. Sometimes these had kept him from his new family for months at a time, but now he was a highly trained and dedicated operative of the German *Abwehr*. He had acquired unusual and diverse skills. He had become a radio operator, and an expert in explosives and small arms; he had made ten parachute jumps, five of these in darkness, and he could pilot a light aircraft; he was versed in cipher and coding, he was a deadly marksman with rifle or sidearms, an exponent of unarmed combat, a trained assassin, both body and mind honed to a razor's edge of preparedness. He had learned the art of persuasive public speaking and rhetoric, and had studied the political and military structures of South Africa until he knew all the vulnerable areas and how to exploit them. He was now ready in every way that he and his masters could foresee for the task that lay ahead of him. Not one man in a million, he knew, would ever have an opportunity such as he was being given – the opportunity to mould history and to turn the detestable order of the world upon its head. Greatness had been thrust upon him, and he knew himself equal to that challenge.

'Yes,' he replied in German to the U-boat commander, 'I recognize the landmarks.'

He had spent one happy, carefree summer holiday on this sparsely populated stretch of the south-eastern coast of Africa. Here Roelf Stander's family owned five thousand hectares, and five miles of this foreshore.

Manfred and Roelf had fished from that rocky headland, pulling the big silver kabeljou from the creaming green surf that broke over the black boulders. They had climbed that low range of hills to hunt the speckled bushbuck amongst the flowering ericas and magnificent blooms of the wild protea shrubs. In that quiet cove with its rind of smooth yellow sand they had swum naked, and afterwards lain on the beach to discuss the future and fantasize about their own particular roles in it. There below the hills, gleaming in the last rays of the sun, stood the whitewashed walls of the small holiday cottage in which they had lived.

'Yes,' he repeated. 'This is the rendezvous.'

'We will wait for the agreed time,' the U-boat commander said, and gave the order to lower the periscope.

Still two miles offshore, the submarine lay twenty metres below the surface, suspended in the dark waters with its engines stopped, while above it the sun sank below the horizon and night fell over the African mainland. Manfred went down the narrow passageway to the tiny cubicle he shared with two of the U-boat's junior officers and began his final preparations for landing.

In the weeks since they had left Bremerhaven, he had come to hate this sinister craft. He hated the cramped quarters and the close intimate proximity of other men, he hated the motion and the ceaseless vibration of the engines. He had never become accustomed to the knowledge that he was locked in an iron box deep under the cold oceanic waters, and he hated the stink of diesel and oil and the reek of the other men trapped down here with him. He longed with all his soul for the clean night air in his lungs and the hot African sun on his face.

Quickly he stripped off the white rollneck jersey and the navy blue peajacket and dressed instead in the worn and shapeless clothing of a country Afrikaner, a *bywoner* or poor white squatter. He was still darkly tanned from his training in the mountains and he had allowed his hair to grow out over his collar and his beard to become thick and curly, adding many years to his age. He looked at himself now in the small mirror on the bulkhead above his bunk.

'They will never recognize me,' he said aloud. 'Not even my own family.'

He had dyed his hair and beard black, the same colour as his eyebrows, and his nose was thickened and twisted. It had never set properly after the American Cyrus Lomax had broken it in the Olympic final, and one eyebrow was lumpy and scarred. He looked entirely different from the young, clean-cut, blond athlete who had sailed from Africa five years before. He pulled the stained felt hat low over his eyes and nodded at his image with satisfaction, then turned from the mirror and went down on his knees to reach the equipment that had been stowed beneath his bunk.

It was packed in rubber waterproofed containers and sealed with tape. He checked off each numbered package on his list, and a German seaman carried them away and stacked them at the foot of the ladder in the submarine's conning tower.

Manfred checked his watch. There was just time for a quick meal and then he would be ready. The bosun called him from the galley, and with a mouth still full of bread and sausage, Manfred hurried to the U-boat's control room.

'There are lights ashore.' The captain stood up from the periscope and gestured Manfred to take his place.

It was fully dark on the surface and through the lens Manfred picked out immediately the three beacon fires, one on each horn of the headlands and one on the sheltered beach.

'That is the correct recognition signal, Captain.' He straightened up and nodded. 'We should surface now and make the reply.'

To the thunder and crackle of compressed air purging the diving tanks, the U-boat rose up like Leviathan through the dark depths and burst out through the surface.

While the submarine still wallowed in her own froth, the captain and Manfred climbed the ladder and went out onto the bridge. The night air was cool and sweet, and Manfred drew deep breaths of it as he peered through his binoculars at the black loom of the shore.

The captain gave a quiet order to the signals yeoman, and he worked the handle of the Addis lamp, clattering out quick beams of yellow light across the dark silver-flecked ocean, spelling out the Morse letters 'W S', the abbreviation of 'White Sword'. After a short pause one of the beacon fires on the headland was snuffed out, and a few minutes later the second fire was extinguished, leaving only the one on the beach still burning.

'That is the correct response,' Manfred grunted. 'Please have my equipment brought on deck, Captain.'

They waited almost half an hour until out of the darkness close at hand a voice hailed them.

'White Sword?'

'Come alongside,' Manfred called back in Afrikaans, and a small open fishing-boat crept towards them on its long oars.

Quickly Manfred shook hands with the U-boat captain and gave him the Nazi salute, '*Heil Hitler!*'

Then he scrambled down onto the lower deck. The moment the wooden hull of the fishing-boat touched, Manfred leapt lightly across and balanced easily on the central thwart.

The rower in the forward seat rose to greet him.

'Manie, is that you?'

'Roelf!' Manfred embraced him briefly. 'It's so good to see you! Let's get my equipment aboard.'

The rubber canisters were swung across by the U-boat's deck crew and stowed in the bottom of the fishing-boat, and at once they pushed off. Manfred took the oar beside Roelf and they gave way swiftly, then rested on their oars to watch the black submarine shark below the surface and disappear in a rash of white water.

Once again they began pulling towards the shore, and Manfred asked softly, 'Who are the others?' He indicated the three other oarsmen with his chin.

'All our people – local farmers from the district. I've known them since I was a child. They are completely trustworthy.'

They did not speak again until they had run the boat in through the low surf to the beach, dragged it up the sand and hidden it amongst the salt bush.

'I will fetch the truck,' Roelf muttered, and a few minutes later the yellow headlights came down the rough track to the beach. Roelf parked the battered green four-tonner beside the fishing-boat.

The three farmers helped them transfer Manfred's equipment to the back of the truck and cover the canisters with bales of dried lucerne and a tattered old tarpaulin. Then they climbed up on top of the load while Manfred took the passenger seat in the cab.

'Tell me all the news of my family, first,' Manfred burst out. 'We have plenty of time for business later.'

'Uncle Tromp is just the same. What a sermon that man can preach! Sarie and I go every Sunday—'

'How is Sarah?' Manfred demanded. 'And the baby?'

'You are out of date,' Roelf laughed. 'Three babies now. Two boys and a little girl of three months. You'll meet them all soon.'

One at a time they dropped the other men off along the winding dirt road with a word of thanks and a quick handshake, until at last they were alone. A few miles further on they reached the main coastal road near the village of Riversdale, and turned westwards towards Cape Town two hundred miles away, and ran on through the night, stopping only to refuel the truck at the little town of Swellendam and to spell each other at the wheel of the truck.

Four hours later they crossed the mountains and went down the steep narrow pass to the wide littoral. They stopped again a few miles outside Stellenbosch, at one of the co-operative winery companies. Although it was three o'clock in the morning, the manager was waiting for them and he helped them unload the rubber canisters and carry them down into the cellar.

'This is Sakkie Van Vuuren,' Roelf introduced the manager. 'He is a good friend, and he has prepared a safe place for your equipment.'

He led them to the rear of the cellar, to the last row of wooden casks. These were massive oak containers each holding a thousand gallons of immature red wine, but the manager thumped the palm of his hand against one of them and when it gave out a hollow sound, he smiled.

'I did the work myself,' he said and opened the front of the cask. It was hinged like a door and the cask beyond was empty. 'Nobody will ever find the goods here.'

They packed the rubber canisters into the cask and closed the hinged lid. It was indistinguishable from any other of the massive wine-filled casks in the row.

'We will be ready to move when the time is ripe,' the winemaker told Manfred. 'When will it be?'

'Soon, my friend,' Manfred promised him. 'Very soon,' and he and Roelf drove on into the village of Stellenbosch.

'It's good to be home.'

'You will only stay here tonight, Manie,' Roelf told him. 'Even with your new black beard and broken nose, you are too well-known. You will be recognized.'

He parked the truck in the yard of a secondhand car dealer down near the railway tracks and left the key under the floor mat. Then the two of them walked the last mile, through the deserted streets to Roelf's home, a cottage in a row of small thatched cottages. Roelf let them in through the back door into the kitchen, and a familiar figure rose up from his seat at the kitchen table to greet them.

'Uncle Tromp!' Manfred cried. The old man held open his arms, and Manfred ran into his embrace.

'What a terrible ruffian you are with that beard,' Uncle Tromp laughed. 'And I see the American did a permanent job on your nose.'

Manfred looked over Uncle Tromp's shoulder and there was a woman standing in the doorway of the kitchen. That was what misled him – a woman, not a girl. Her face was marked by a kind of sad wisdom, and her expression was pinched and without joy.

'Sarah?' Manfred left Uncle Tromp and went towards here. 'How are you, my little sister?'

'I was never your little sister, Manfred,' she said. 'But I am very well, thank you.' She made no effort to embrace him and Manfred was clearly disturbed by the coolness of her welcome.

'Are you happy, Sarah?'

'I have a fine man and three beautiful babies,' she said, and looked at Roelf.

'You will be hungry now,' she told him. 'Sit down. You can talk while I make your breakfast.'

The three men seated themselves at the kitchen table and every once in a while Manfred glanced surreptitiously at Sarah as she worked over the stove, and his expression was troubled, ridden by old memories and guilt. Then he gathered himself and concentrated once more on what the others were saying.

'The news is all good – the British smashed and broken at Dunkirk, France has fallen and the Netherlands. The German U-boats are winning the battle of the Atlantic and even the Italians are victorious in North Africa—'

'I did not know you were one of us, Uncle Tromp,' Manfred cut in on the discussion.

'Yes, my son. I am a patriot as you are. The *Ossewa Brandwag* is forty thousand strong now. Forty thousand picked men in positions of power and authority, while Jannie Smuts has sent one hundred and sixty thousand of the English-lovers with their little orange tabs on their shoulders out of the country. He has put himself at our mercy.'

'Our leaders know of your arrival, Manie,' Roelf told him. 'They know that you bring a message from the Führer himself, and they are eager to meet you.'

'Will you arrange a meeting,' Manfred asked, 'as soon as possible? There is much work to do. Glorious work to do.'

Sarah Stander stood quietly at the kitchen stove,

breaking eggs into the frying pan, turning the chops under the grill. She did not look round or draw attention to herself, but she thought:

'You have come to bring sadness and suffering into my life again, Manfred De La Rey. With your every word and look and gesture you open the wounds I thought had healed. You have come to destroy what little life has left me. Roelf will follow you blindly into folly. You come to threaten my husband and my babies—' And her hatred of him was made stronger and more venomous as it fed on the corpse of the love that he had murdered.

Manfred travelled alone. There was no control of personal movement, there were no roadblocks, police searches or demands for identification papers. South Africa was so far from the main war centres that there were not even significant shortages of consumer goods, apart from petrol rationing and a ban on the milling of white flour, therefore no need for ration books or other documentation existed.

Carrying a small valise, Manfred merely purchased a second-class railway ticket for Bloemfontein, the capital town of the Orange Free State province, and he shared a compartment with five other travellers on the five hundred mile journey.

Ironically, the meeting to subvert the elected government of the nation took place in the provincial government building at the foot of Artillery Hill. When Manfred entered the imposing administrator's office, he was reminded how wide was the influence of their secret organization.

The commander of the OB came to meet him at the door. He had changed little since he had administered the blood-oath to Manfred in that midnight torchlit ceremony.

Still paunchy and craggy-featured, he was now dressed in a sombre double-breasted civilian suit. He greeted Manfred warmly, clasping his hand and patting his shoulder, smiling broadly.

'I have been expecting you, brother, but first let me congratulate you on your achievements since last we met, and the magnificent work you have accomplished so far.'

He led Manfred into the room and introduced him to the five other men seated at the long table.

'All of us have taken the blood oath. You may speak freely,' he told Manfred who knew now that he was addressing the highest council of the brotherhood.

He sat at the bottom of the table facing the commander and gathered his thoughts for a moment before beginning. 'Gentlemen, I bring you personal greetings from the Führer of the German people, Adolf Hitler. He has asked me to assure you of the close friendship that has always existed between the Afrikaner and the German nation, and to tell you that he is ready to support us in every possible way in our struggle to win back what is rightfully ours, to regain for the Afrikaner the land that belongs to him by right of birth and conquest.' Manfred spoke forcefully and logically. He had prepared this address with the help of the experts of the German propaganda department and had rehearsed it until his delivery was perfect; he could judge his success by the rapt expressions of the men listening to him.

'The Führer is fully aware that this country has been stripped of almost all men of military age who have sympathy with the Smuts government and the British. Almost one hundred and sixty thousand men have been sent north to serve beyond our borders. This makes the task easier.'

'Smuts has called in all weapons in private hands,' one of the men interrupted him. 'He has taken the sporting rifles and shotguns, even the memorial cannons from the town squares. There will be no rising without weapons.'

'You have seen to the centre of the problem,' Manfred agreed. 'To succeed we need money and weapons. We will get those.'

'The Germans will send them to us?'

'No.' Manfred shook his head. 'This has been considered and rejected. The distance is too great, the difficulty of landing great quantities of arms on an inhospitable coast is not acceptable and the ports are well guarded. However, immediately we have control of the ports, supplies of heavy arms will be rushed to us by U-boats of the German navy, and in return we will throw open our harbours to the German U-boats. We will deny the Cape route to the British.'

'Then where will we get the arms we need for the rising?'

'From Jannie Smuts,' Manfred told them, and they stirred uncomfortably and glanced at one another doubtfully.

'With your approval, naturally, I will recruit and train a small élite striking force of our *stormjagters*. We will raid the government arms and ammunition dumps and seize what we need – the same with money. We will take it from the banks.'

The enormity of the concept, the boldness and sweep of it, amazed them. They stared in silence and Manfred went on.

'We will act swiftly and ruthlessly, seize the arms and distribute them. Then at a given signal we will rise, forty thousand patriots, to seize all the reins of power, the police and the army, the communications system, the railways, the harbours. In all of these we have our people already in place. All of it will be done at the pre-arranged signal.'

'What will that signal be?' asked the commander of the OB.

'It will be something that will turn the entire country on its head – something staggering, but it is too early to speak of it. It is necessary only to say that the signal has been chosen and the man who will give the signal.' Manfred looked at him steadily, seriously. 'I will have that honour. I have trained for the task, and I will do it alone and unaided. After that it will only remain for you to take up the reins, to swing our support to the side of the victorious German army, and to lead our people to the greatness that has been denied them by our enemies.'

He was silent then as he studied their expressions, and he saw the patriotic fervour on their faces and the new light in their eyes.

'Gentlemen, do I have your approval to proceed?' he asked, and the commander looked at each of them in turn, and received a curt nod of the head.

He turned back to Manfred. 'You have our approval and our blessing. I will see that you have the support and assistance of every single member of the brotherhood.'

'Thank you, gentlemen,' Manfred said quietly. 'And now if I may give you the words of Adolf Hitler himself from the great book *Mein Kampf*, "Almighty God, bless our arms when the time is ripe. Be just as Thou has always been. Judge now whether we be deserving of freedom. Lord, bless our battle."'

'Amen!' they cried, leaping to their feet and giving the O B salute of clenched fist across the chest. 'Amen!'

The green Jaguar was parked in the open, beside the road where it skirted the top of the cliff. The vehicle looked abandoned, as though it had stood here for days and weeks.

Blaine Malcomess parked his Bentley behind it and walked to the cliff's edge. He had never been here before, but Centaine had described the cove to him and how to find the pathway. He leaned out now and looked down the cliff. It was very steep but not sheer; he could make out the path zigzagging down three hundred feet to Smitswinkel Bay, and at the bottom he saw the roofs of three or four rude huts strung out along the curve of the bay, just as Centaine had described.

He shrugged out of his jacket and threw it onto the front seat of the Bentley. The climb down the pathway would be warm work. He locked the door of the car and set off down the cliff path. He had come, not only because Centaine had pleaded with him to do so, but because of his own affection and pride and sense of responsibility towards Shasa Courtney.

At various times in the past he had anticipated that Shasa would be either his stepson or his son-in-law. As he climbed down the pathway he felt again the deep regret – no, more than regret, the deep sorrow – that neither expectation had been fulfilled thus far.

He and Centaine had not married, and Isabella had been dead for almost three years now. He remembered how Centaine had fled from him on the night Isabella died, and how for many months afterwards she had avoided him, frustrating all his efforts to find her. Something terrible had happened that night at Isabella's deathbed. Even after they had been reconciled, Centaine would never talk about it, never even hint at what had taken place between her and the dying woman. He hated himself for having put Centaine in Isabella's power. He should never have trusted her, for the damage she had done had never healed. It had taken almost a year of patience and gentleness from Blaine before Centaine had recovered from it sufficiently to take up again the role of lover and protectress which she had so revelled in before.

However, she would not even discuss with him the subject of marriage, and became agitated and overwrought when he tried to insist. It was almost as if Isabella were still alive, as if she could from her long-cold grave assert some malevolent power over them. There was nothing in life he wanted more than to have Centaine Courtney as his lawful wife, his wife in the eyes of God and all the world, but he was coming to doubt it would ever be so.

'Please Blaine, don't ask me now. I cannot – I just cannot talk about it. No, I can't tell you why. We have been so happy just the way we are for so many years. I can't take the chance of ruining that happiness.'

'I am asking you to be my wife. I'm asking you to confirm and cement our love, not to ruin it.'

'Please, Blaine. Leave it now. Not now.'

'When, Centaine, tell me when?'

'I don't know. I honestly don't know, my darling. I only know I love you so.'

Then there were Shasa and Tara. They were like two lost souls groping for each other in darkness. He knew how desperately they needed each other, he had recognized it from the very beginning, and how close they had come to linking hands. But always they failed to make that last vital contact, and drifted, pining, apart. There seemed to be no reason for it, other than pride and pigheadedness, and without each other they were diminishing, neither of them able to fulfil their great promise, to take full advantage of all the rare blessings that had been bestowed upon them at birth.

Two beautiful, talented young people, full of strength and energy, frittering it all away in a search for something that never existed, wasting it on impossible dreams or burning it up in despair and despondency.

'I cannot let it happen,' he told himself with determination. 'Even if they hate me for it, I have to prevent it.'

He reached the foot of the path and paused to look around. He did not need to rest, for although the descent had been arduous and although he was almost fifty years old, he was harder and fitter than most men fifteen years younger.

Smitswinkel Bay was enclosed by a crescent of tall cliffs;

only its far end was open to the wider expanse of False Bay. Protected on all sides, the water was lake-calm and so clear he could follow the stems of the kelp plants down thirty feet to where they were anchored on the bottom. It was a delightful hidden place and he took a few moments longer to appreciate its tranquil beauty.

There were four shacks built mostly of driftwood, each of them widely separated from the others, perched upon the rocks above the narrow beach. Three were deserted, their windows boarded up. The last one in the line was the one he wanted, and he set off along the beach towards it.

As he drew closer he saw the windows were open, but the curtains, faded and rotted by salt air, were drawn. There were crayfish nets hanging over the railing of the stoep and a pair of oars and a cane fishing-rod propped against one wall. A dinghy was drawn up on the beach above the highwater mark.

Blaine climbed the short flight of stone steps and crossed the stoep to the front door. It was open and he stepped into the single room.

The small Devon stove on the far wall was cold, and a frying pan stood on it, greasy with congealed leftovers. Dirty plates and mugs cluttered the central table, and a column of black ants was climbing one leg to reach them. The wooden floor of the shack was unswept, gritty with beach sand. There were two bunks set against the side wall, opposite the window. The bare boards of the upper bunk were without a mattress, but in the lower bunk was a jumble of grey blankets and a hard coir mattress with a stained and torn cover. On top of it all lay Shasa Courtney.

It was a few minutes before noon and he was still asleep. An almost empty bottle of whisky and a tumbler stood on the sandy floor within reach of Shasa's dangling arm. He wore only a pair of old rugby shorts and his body was burned to the colour of oiled mahogany, a dark beach-comber's tan; the hair on his arms was sunbleached to gold, but on his chest it remained dark and curly. It was obvious that he had not shaved in many days and his hair was long and unkempt on the dirty pillow. Yet the deep tan covered all the more obvious signs of debauchery.

He slept quietly, no sign on his face of the turmoil which must have driven him from Weltevreden to this squalid shack. He was still in all respects but one a magnificent-looking young man – that was why the left eye was even more shocking. The top ridge of the eye-socket was depressed on the outside corner where the bone had shattered; the scar through his dark eyebrow was shiny white and ridged. The empty eye-socket was sunken, and the eye-lids drooped apart, exposing wet red tissue in the gap between his thick dark lashes.

It was impossible to look on the hideous injury without feeling pity, and it took Blaine a few seconds to steel himself to what he had to do.

'Shasa!' He made his voice harsh. Shasa groaned softly and the lid of his empty eye twitched.

'Wake up, man.' Blaine went to the bunk and shook his shoulder. 'Wake up. We've got some talking to do.'

'Go away,' Shasa mumbled, not yet awake. 'Go away and leave me alone.'

'Wake up, damn you!'

Shasa's good eye flickered open and he peered up at Blaine blearily. His eye focused and his expression altered.

'What the hell are you doing here?' He rolled his head away, hiding the bad eye as he groped amongst the tangled bedclothes until he found a scrap of black cloth on a black elastic band. With his face still averted, he fitted the patch over the damaged eye and looped the band over his head before he turned back to look at Blaine again. The eye patch gave him a piratical panache, and in some perverse way highlighted his good looks.

'Got to pump ship,' he blurted and tottered out onto the stoep.

While he was away Blaine dusted one of the stools and set it against the wall. He sat down on it, leaned back, and lit one of his long black cheroots.

Shasa came back into the shack, pulling up the front of his rugby shorts, and sat down on the edge of the bunk, holding his head with both hands. 'My mouth tastes like a polecat pissed in it,' he muttered, and he reached down for the bottle between his feet and poured what remained of the whisky into the glass, licked the last drop from the neck and trundled the empty bottle across the floor in the general direction of the overflowing garbage bucket beside the stove.

He picked up the glass. 'Offer you one?' he asked, and Blaine shook his head. Shasa looked at him over the rim.

'That look on your face can mean only one of two things,' Shasa told him. 'Either you have just smelled a fart or you don't approve of me.'

'I take it the coarse language is a recent accomplishment, like your new drinking habits. I congratulate you on both. They suit your new image.'

'Bugger you, Blaine Malcomess!' Shasa retorted defiantly, and raised the glass to his lips. He swished the whisky through his teeth, rinsing his mouth with it. Then he swallowed and shuddered as the raw spirit went down his throat and he exhaled the fumes noisily.

'Mater sent you,' he said flatly.

'She told me where I could find you, but she didn't send me.'

'Same thing,' Shasa said, and held the glass to his lips, letting the last drop run onto his tongue. 'She wants me back, digging diamonds out of the dirt, picking grapes, growing cotton, pushing paper – damn it, she just doesn't understand.'

'She understands much more than you give her credit for.'

'Out there men are fighting. David and my other mates.

They are in the sky – and I am down here in the dirt, a cripple, grovelling in the dirt.'

'You chose the dirt.' Blaine looked around the filthy shack scornfully. 'And you are doing the whining and grovelling.'

'You'd better get the hell out of here, sir,' Shasa told him. 'Before I lose my temper.'

'A pleasure, I assure you.' Blaine stood up. 'I misjudged you. I came to offer you a job, an important war job, but I can see that you are not man enough for it.' He crossed to the door of the cottage and paused. 'I was going to issue an invitation as well, an invitation to a party on Friday night. Tara is going to announce her engagement to marry Hubert Langley. I thought it might amuse you – but forget it.'

He went out with his long determined stride and after a few seconds Shasa followed him out onto the stoep and watched him climb the cliff path. Blaine never looked back once, and when he disappeared over the top, Shasa felt suddenly abandoned and bereft.

He had not until that moment realized how large Blaine Malcomess bulked in his life. How much he had relied on Blaine's good counsel and experience, both on and off the polo field.

'I wanted to be like him so much,' he said aloud. 'And now I never will be.' He touched the black patch over his eye.

'Why me?' He gave the eternal cry of the loser. 'Why me?' And he sank down onto the top step and stared out over the calm green waters to the entrance of the bay.

Slowly the full impact of Blaine's words sank home. He thought about the job he had offered, an important war job – then he thought about Tara and Hubert Langley. Tara – he saw her grey eyes and smoking red hair, and self-pity washed over him in a cold dark wave.

Listlessly he stood up and went into the shack. He opened the cupboard above the sink. There was a single bottle of Haig left. 'What happened to the others?' he asked himself. 'Mice?'

He cracked the cap on the bottle, and looked for a glass. They were all dirty, piled in the sink. He lifted the bottle to his lips, and the fumes made his eye smart. He lowered the bottle before he drank and stared at it. His stomach heaved and he was filled with a sudden revulsion, both physical and emotional.

He tipped the bottle over the sink, and watched the golden liquid chug and spurt into the drainhole. When it was gone, once it was too late, his need for it returned strongly and he was seized by dismay. His throat felt parched and sore and the hand that held the empty bottle began to shake. The desire for oblivion ached in every joint of his bones, and his eye burned so that he had to blink it clear.

He hurled the bottle against the wall of the shack and ran out into the sunshine, down the steps to the beach. He stripped off the eye-patch and his rugby shorts and dived into the cold green water and struck out in a hard overarm crawl. By the time he reached the entrance to the cove, every muscle ached and his breathing scorched his lungs. He turned and without slackening the tempo of his stroke headed back to the beach. As soon as his feet touched bottom he turned again, and swam out to the headland, back and forth he ploughed, hour after hour, until he was so exhausted that he could not lift an arm clear of the surface and he was forced to struggle back the last hundred yards in a painful side-stroke.

He crawled up the beach, fell face down on the wet sand and lay like a dead man. It was the middle of the afternoon before he had recovered the energy to push himself upright and limp up to the shack.

He stood in the doorway and looked around at the mess he had created. Then he took the broom from behind the door and went to work. It was late afternoon before he had finished. The only thing he could do nothing about was the dirty bed linen. He bundled the soiled blankets with his dirty clothes for the dhobi wallah at Weltevreden to launder. Then he drew a kettle of fresh water from the rainwater tank beside the back door and heated it over the stove.

He shaved carefully, dressed in the cleanest shirt and slacks he could find and adjusted the patch over his eye. He locked the shack and hid the key; then, carrying the bundle of dirty laundry he climbed the pathway to the top. His Jaguar was dusty and streaked with sea salt. The battery was flat and he had to run it down the hill and start it on the fly.

Centaine was in her study, seated at her desk, poring over a pile of documents. She sprang to her feet when he came in and would have rushed to him, but with an obvious effort she restrained herself.

'Hello, *chéri*, you look so well. I was worried about you – it's been so long. Five weeks.'

The patch over his eye still horrified her. Every time she saw it she remembered Isabella Malcomess' last words to her:

'An eye for an eye, Centaine Courtney. Heed my words – an eye for an eye.'

As soon as she had herself under control again she went calmly to meet him and lifted her face for his kiss.

'I'm glad you are home again, *chéri*.'

'Blaine Malcomess has offered me a job, a war job. I'm thinking of taking it.'

'I am sure it is important,' Centaine nodded. 'I am happy for you. I can hold the fort here until you are ready to return.'

'I am sure you can, Mater,' he grinned wryly. 'After all you have been doing pretty well for the last twenty-two years – holding the fort.'

765

The long line of goods trucks drawn by a double coupling of steam locomotives climbed the last slope of the pass. On the steep gradient, the locomotives were sending bright silver columns of steam spurting from their valves, and the Hex river mountains echoed to the roar of their straining boilers.

With a final effort they crested the head of the pass and burst out onto the high plateau of the open karoo; gathering speed dramatically they thundered away across the flatlands and the line of closed trucks snaked after them.

Forty miles beyond the head of the pass the train slowed and then trundled to a halt in the shunting yards of the intermediate railway junction of Touws river.

The relief crews were waiting in the stationmaster's office and they greeted the incoming crews with a little light banter and then climbed aboard to take their places on the footplates. The leading locomotive was uncoupled and shunted onto a side spur. It was no longer needed, the rest of the run, a thousand miles northwards to the goldfields of the Witwatersrand, was across comparatively flat land. The second locomotive would return down the mountain pass to link up with the next goods train and assist it up the steep gradients.

The incoming crews, carrying their lunch pails and overcoats, set off down the lane towards the row of railway cottages, relieved to be home in time for a hot bath and dinner. Only one of the drivers lingered on the platform and watched the goods train pull out of the siding, gathering speed swiftly as it headed northwards.

He counted the trucks as they passed him, verifying his previous count. Numbers twelve and thirteen were closed trucks, painted silver to distinguish them and to deflect the heat of the sun's rays. On the side of each was blazoned a crimson cross, and in letters six feet tall that ran the full length of each truck, the warning: 'EXPLOSIVES.' They had each been loaded at the Somerset West factory of African Explosives and Chemical Industries with twenty tons of gelignite consigned to the gold mines of the Anglo American Group.

As the guard's van passed him the driver sauntered into the stationmaster's office. The stationmaster was still at the far end of the platform, his pillbox cap on his head and his furled flags of red and green under his arm. The driver lifted the telephone off its bracket on the wall and spun the handle.

'Central,' he said into the voicepiece, speaking in Afrikaans, 'give me Matjiesfontein eleven sixteen.'

He waited while the operator made the connection. 'You are through. Go ahead.' But the driver waited for the click of the operator going off the line before he said,

'Van Niekerk here.'

'This is White Sword.' The reply, though he had been expecting it, made the hair on the back of his neck prickle.

'She is running twenty-three minutes late. She left here two minutes ago. The trucks are numbers twelve and thirteen.'

'Well done.'

Manfred De La Rey replaced the telephone and checked his wrist-watch before he smiled at the two women who watched him apprehensively across the farmhouse kitchen.

'Thank you, *Mevrou*,' he addressed the older of the two. 'We are grateful for your help. No trouble will come to you out of this, I give you my word.'

'Trouble is an old acquaintance, *Meneer*,' the proud old woman replied. 'In ninety-nine the *rooinekke* burned my farm and killed my husband.'

Manfred had parked the motorcycle behind the barn. He started it and rode back down the track a mile or so until he joined the main road. He turned north, and a few miles further on he was riding parallel to the railway line.

At the base of a rocky hill the lines and the road diverged. The railway tracks climbed the shoulder of the hill and then disappeared behind it.

Manfred stopped the motorcycle and checked that the road was clear, ahead and behind, then he turned off onto another farmtrack, and followed the railway tracks around the back of the hill. Again he stopped, propped the bike on its foot rest, and checked the locale.

They were far enough from the widow's farmhouse not to attach suspicion to the old woman. The hill hid this section of the tracks from the main road, but the road was close enough to offer a swift escape route in either direction. The gradient would slow the approaching locomotive to almost walking pace. He had watched while other goods trains passed the spot.

He turned the cycle off the road, following the tracks of other wheels that had flattened the grass. In the first fold of the land, hidden in a cluster of thorn trees, the trucks were parked. Four of them – a three-tonner, two four-tonners and a big brown Bedford ten-tonner. Getting fuel rationing coupons to fill their tanks had been difficult.

It was a mere hundred paces to the railway line from where the trucks stood and his men were waiting beside them, resting, lying in the grass, but they scrambled up as the motorcycle bumped and puttered over the fold of ground and they crowded around him eagerly. Roelf Stander was at their head.

'She'll be here at nine-thirty,' Manfred told him. 'The trucks are twelve and thirteen. Work that out.'

One of his band was a railway man, and he made the calculations of distance between the locomotive and the explosive trucks. Roelf and Manfred left the others hidden and went out onto the line to mark out the distances. Manfred wanted to stop the goods train so that the two laden trucks were directly opposite the waiting vehicles in the clump of thorn trees.

They paced it out from this point and Manfred set the charges under the fish plates in a joint of the tracks. Then he and Roelf went back and laid the red warning flares, using the railwayman's calculations of speed and distance as a guide.

It was dark by the time they had finished, so they could proceed to the next step. They moved the men out into their positions. They were all young, picked for their size and physical strength. They were dressed in rough clothing of dark colours and armed with a motley collection of weapons that had survived the call-in by the Smuts government – shotguns and old Lee Enfields and Mannlichers from other long-ago wars. Only Roelf and Manfred were armed with modern German Lugers, part of the contents of the rubber canisters from the U-boat.

Manfred took charge of the smaller group while Roelf waited with the work party that would unload the trucks, and they settled down in darkness to wait.

Manfred heard it first, the distant susurration in the night, still far off, and he roused them with three sharp blasts on his whistle. Then he armed the battery box and connected the wires to the brass screw terminals. The huge Cyclops eye of the approaching locomotive glared across the plain below the hill. The waiting men adjusted their face masks and lay hidden in the grassy ditch beside the railway line.

The beat of the locomotive engine slowed and became deeper as it ran onto the slope. It climbed laboriously, running past the first group of waiting men, and then it hit the first of the warning flares. The flare ignited with a sharp crack and lit the veld for fifty yards around with red flickering light.

Manfred heard the metallic squeal of brakes, and he relaxed slightly. The driver was acting reflexively, it would not be necessary to blow out the tracks. The second flare ignited, shooting out long tongues of red flame from under

769

the driving wheels, but by now the locomotive was pulling up sharply, brakes grinding metal on metal and steam flying from the emergency vacuum tubes in screaming white jets.

While it was still moving, Manfred leapt onto the footplates, and thrust the Luger into the astonished faces of the driver and his fireman.

'Shut her down! Switch off the headlight!' he yelled through his mask. 'Then get down from the cab!'

With the brakes locked, the railwaymen scrambled down and lifted their hands high. They were immediately searched and trussed up. Manfred ran back down the train, and by the time he reached the explosives trucks, Roelf's men had already forced the doors and the wooden cases of gelignite were being handed along a human chain to be loaded into the first lorry.

'What about the guard at the rear of the train?' Manfred asked.

'We have got him tied up,' Roelf answered, 'and Manfred ran back to the head of the train. Swiftly he defused and lifted the explosive charges he had laid, delighted that it had not been necessary to fire them. By the time he got back, the first lorry was fully loaded with cases of explosives.

'Take her away!' Roelf yelled, and one of his men climbed into the cab, started the engine and with lights extinguished, drove it away.

The second vehicle reversed up to the explosives trucks and they began to load it.

Manfred checked his watch. 'Twelve minutes,' he muttered. They were ahead of schedule.

The driver, the guard and the fireman were tied securely and locked in the guard's van while the loading of explosives went on smoothly and swiftly.

'All finished,' Roelf shouted. 'We can't load any more.'

'Forty-eight minutes,' Manfred told him. 'Well done. All right, move out everybody!'

'What about you?'

'Go!' Manfred ordered. 'I'll look after myself.'

He watched the Bedford truck pull away and waited until it reached the farm road and switched on its headlights. The sound of its engine dwindled. He was alone. If Roelf or the others had known what he intended to do now, they might have baulked and tried to prevent it.

Manfred climbed into the open door of the explosives truck. It was half filled with the white wooden cases. They had only been able to carry away a part of the load, while the second truck had not been touched. There were still at least twenty-five tons of explosive remaining on board.

He set the timing device with a delay of fifteen minutes and placed it in the gap between the stacked cases and the steel side of the truck, pushing it far back where it could not be readily seen. Then he jumped down to the ground and ran forward to the locomotive. None of the three men locked in the caboose of the guard's van were members of the *Ossewa Brandwag*. Left alive they would be certain to give damaging evidence to the police. He felt little pity for them. They were casualties of war.

He climbed into the cab of the locomotive and disengaged the wheel brakes; then he opened the throttle gradually. The wheels spun, then found purchase and the train jolted forward with the couplings clanking. It began to pull away jerkily up the slope.

Manfred eased the throttle open to the halfway notch and locked it there. Then he jumped down to the ground, and watched the trucks rumble past where he stood. They were gaining speed gradually. When the caboose passed, he walked back down the tracks to the clump of thorn trees, and sat astride the seat of the motorcycle.

He waited impatiently, glancing at his watch every few minutes.

The explosion, when at last it came, was a brief orange flare, like sheet lightning over the northern horizon, followed after a long pause by the puff of the shockwave against his face and a sound like distant surf breaking on a rocky shore.

Manfred kick-started the motorcycle and drove southwards into the night.

It was a good beginning, he thought, but there was so much still to do.

B laine looked up as Shasa entered his office and hesitated in the doorway. He was neatly dressed in airforce uniform, medal ribbons on his chest, DFC and Africa Star, and the badges of rank on his shoulders.

'Morning, Shasa,' Blaine nodded bleakly. 'Ten o'clock. May I offer you a whisky?'

Shasa winced. 'I came to apologize for my behaviour the other day, sir. It was inexcusable.'

'Sit down.' Blaine pointed at the buttoned leather armchair against the bookcase. 'We all act like blithering idiots at some time in our lives. The trick is to know when you are doing it. Apology accepted.'

Shasa sat down and crossed his legs, then uncrossed them. 'You mentioned a job, sir?'

Blaine nodded and stood up. He moved to the window and stood staring down into the gardens. An old woman was feeding the pigeons from a paper bag. He watched her as he made his final decision. Was he letting his concern for Centaine Courtney and her son cloud his sense of duty? What he had in mind was critical to the welfare of the state. Was Shasa too young and inexperienced for the task? he wondered. But he had gone over this many times already, and he turned back to his desk.

He picked up a plain unmarked black folder. 'This is highly classified,' he said as he weighed the folder in his right hand. 'A most secret and sensitive report and appreciation.' He handed it to Shasa. 'It is not to leave this office. Read it here. I have a meeting with Field Marshal Smuts.' He pulled back his sleeve and glanced at his watch. 'I will be back in an hour. We'll talk again then.'

He was longer than an hour, and when he returned Shasa was still reading. He looked up at Blaine from the armchair with the open folder in his hands, and his expression was troubled and grave.

'What do you make of it?' Blaine asked.

'Of course, I have heard of the OB,' Shasa replied. 'But I had no idea it was anything like this. It's a secret army, sir, right in our midst. If it were ever to be fully mobilized against us—' he shook his head, trying to find the words. 'A revolution, a civil war, while most of our own fighting men are up north.'

'They have begun to move,' Blaine said softly. 'Until now they have been procrastinating, in typical Afrikaner style, squabbling amongst themselves, but something has happened recently to give them new purpose—' he broke off, thought for a moment, then went on. 'It goes without saying, Shasa, that nothing we discuss must be repeated to anybody, not even closest family.'

'Of course, sir.' Shasa looked aggrieved.

'You read about the explosion of a dynamite train on the Touws river line two weeks ago?'

'Yes, sir, a frightful accident. The driver and his crew went up with it.'

'We have new evidence. We don't believe it was an accident. The crew were all in the guard's van, and there are indications that at least one of them was bound hand and foot. We believe that a large quantity of explosives was hijacked from the train, and afterwards the remainder was detonated to cover the theft.'

Shasa whistled softly.

'I believe this was merely a beginning. I believe that a

new phase has begun and that it is going to escalate swiftly from now onwards. As I said, something has happened to trigger it – we have to find out what it is and crush it.'

'How can I help, sir?'

'This thing is big – nationwide. I have to keep close contact with the police chiefs of each of the various provinces together with military intelligence. The entire operation must be closely co-ordinated. I need a personal assistant, a liaison officer. I'm offering you the job.'

'I'm honoured, sir, but I can't see why you have chosen me. There must be dozens of other better qualified—'

'We know each other well, Shasa,' Blaine interrupted him. 'We have worked together over many years. We make a good team. I trust you. I know you have both brains and guts. I don't need a policeman. I need someone who understands my thinking and who I know will follow my orders implicitly.' Suddenly Blaine grinned. 'Besides which, you need a job. Am I right?'

'You are right, sir. Thank you.'

'You are on convalescent leave at the moment, but I will have you seconded from the airforce to the Department of the Interior immediately. You will keep your rank and pay as squadron leader, but you will report directly to me from now on.'

'I understand, sir.'

'Shasa, have you flown since you lost your eye?' He came right out and spoke about the eye without evasion. Nobody, not even Mater, had done that. Shasa's regard for him was reinforced.

'No, sir,' he said.

'Pity. You may be required to move around the country pretty damned quickly.' He watched Shasa's face, saw his jaw clench determinedly.

'It's only a matter of judging distance accurately,' Shasa muttered. 'Just practice.' Blaine felt a glow of gratification.

'Try hitting a polo ball again,' he suggested off-handedly.

'Good practice in developing judgement – but let's discuss more serious business now. The police officer in overall charge of the investigation is Chief Inspector Louis Nel, here at the Cape Town Central Station. I'll introduce you. He's a first-rate chap, you'll like him.'

They talked and planned for another hour before Blaine dismissed him. 'That's enough for you to get on with. Report back to me here at eight-thirty tomorrow morning.' But when Shasa reached the door he stopped him.

'By the way, Shasa, Friday night. The invitation is still open. Eight o'clock. Black tie or mess kit. Try and make it, won't you?'

S arah Stander lay alone in the brass-framed bed in the darkness. The older children were sleeping in the next room. The baby in the cot beside her bed snuffled contentedly in her sleep.

The town hall clock struck four o'clock. She had listened to it chime every hour since midnight. She thought she would go through to the other room to make sure the children were covered – little Petrus always kicked off his blankets – but at that moment she heard the kitchen door open stealthily and she went rigid and held her breath to listen.

She heard Roelf come through and begin undressing in the bathroom, the double thump-thump as he dropped his boots, then a little later the bedroom door creaked and the bed tipped under his weight. She pretended to be sleeping. It was the first time he had ever stayed out this late. He had changed so much since Manfred had returned.

She lay unsleeping in the darkness and thought, 'He is the bringer of trouble. He will destroy us all. I hate you, Manfred De La Rey.'

Beside her she knew Roelf was not sleeping either. He

was restless and strung up. The hours passed slowly, and she forced herself to lie still. Then the baby whimpered and she took her into the bed and gave her one of her breasts. Sarah's milk had always been strong and good, and the baby drank and burped and dropped back to sleep. She returned her to the cot, and the moment she slipped back under the sheet Roelf reached for her. Neither of them spoke, and she steeled herself to accept him. She hated this. It was never like it had been on those well-remembered occasions with Manfred. However, tonight Roelf was different. He mounted her quickly, almost brutally, and ended swiftly with a hoarse wild cry and he fell off her into a deep sleep. She lay and listened to him snore.

At breakfast she asked him quietly, 'Where were you last night?'

Instantly he was angry. 'Hold your mouth, woman,' he shouted at her, using the word *bek*, the mouth of an animal not a human being. 'You are not my keeper.'

'You are involved in some dangerous foolishness.' She ignored the warning. 'You have three little ones, Roelf. You cannot afford stupidity—'

'Enough, woman!' he yelled at her. 'This is man's business. You keep out of it.'

Without another word he left for the university, where he was a lecturer in the law faculty. She knew that in ten years he could have the chair, if only he didn't get into trouble before that.

After she had cleaned the house and made the beds, she put the children into the big double pram and pushed them down the sidewalk towards the centre of the village. She stopped once to talk with one of the other university wives, and again to buy sugar suckers for the two big children. Then, as she was paying for the candy, she noticed the headlines of the newspapers piled on the counter.

'I'll take a *Burger* as well.' She crossed the road and sat on a park bench while she read the story of the explosion of a goods train somewhere in the karoo. Then she folded the paper neatly and sat thinking.

Roelf had left after lunch the previous day. The explosion had occurred at a little before ten-thirty p.m. She worked out times and distances, and slowly a cold crippling dismay made her belly cramp. She put the children back in the pram and crossed to the post office. She parked the pram beside the glass telephone booth where she could keep an eye on it.

'Central, please give me the main police station in Cape Town.'

'Hold the line.'

Suddenly the enormity of what she was about to do broke in upon her. How could she turn Manfred De La Rey over to the police without betraying her own husband to them at the same time – and yet she knew it was her duty to stop Roelf doing these terrible things that must lead to disaster. It was her duty to her husband and to her babies.

'This is the Cape Town central police station. May I help you?'

'Yes,' Sarah stuttered, and then 'No, I'm sorry. It doesn't matter. It isn't important.' She hung up, ran out of the booth and wheeled the pram determinedly back towards the cottage. She sat at the kitchen table and wept softly, bewildered and alone and uncertain. Then after a while she wiped her eyes on her apron and made herself a cup of coffee

S hasa parked the Jaguar across the road from Blaine Malcomess' home, but he did not get out at once. He sat and considered what he was about to attempt.

'Probably make an idiot of myself again,' he thought, and tilted the rearview mirror so that he could see himself in it. He ran a comb through his hair and adjusted the eye-patch carefully. Then he climbed out.

Vehicles were parked bumper to bumper down both sides of Newlands Avenue. It was a big party, two or three hundred guests, but then Blaine Malcomess was a big man and his daughter's engagement an important event.

Shasa crossed the road. The front doors were wide open, but still it was difficult to get into the house. Even the lobby was crowded, and the party was in full swing. A coloured band was belting out 'The Lambeth Walk' and Shasa could see into the lounge where the dancers were prancing around merrily. He pushed his way through to the bar. Even Blaine Malcomess couldn't offer whisky, it just wasn't obtainable any longer. Nowadays it was considered patriotic to drink Cape brandy, but Shasa ordered a ginger ale.

'My drinking days have come and gone,' he thought wryly and, glass in hand, eased his way through the packed rooms, shaking hands with old friends, kissing the cheeks of the women, many of whom he had at one time or another kissed with more purpose.

'So good to see you back, Shasa.' They tried not to notice the black eye-patch, and after a few seconds he moved on, searching for her.

She was in the dining-room with the coloured chef and two maids, supervising the final touches to the elaborate buffet dinner.

She looked up and saw him and froze. She was wearing a filmy light evening dress the colour of ash of roses, and her hair was down to her shoulders. He had forgotten how her eyes could shine like mother-of-pearl, grey mother-of-pearl.

She made a gesture dismissing the servants, and he went slowly to meet her.

'Hello, Tara, I'm back,' he said.

'Yes, I heard. You've been back five weeks. I thought you might—' she stopped and studied his face. 'I heard you were decorated,' she touched the ribbon on his chest. 'And that you were wounded.'

She studied his face frankly, not avoiding looking at his left eye. Then she smiled. 'It makes you look very dashing.'

'It doesn't make me feel dashing.'

'I can sense that,' she nodded. 'You have changed.'

'Do you think so?'

'Yes, you aren't so—' she shook her head, irritated that she could not find the precise word. 'Not so brash, so cocksure.'

'I want to talk to you,' he said. 'Seriously.'

'All right,' she nodded. 'What is it?'

'Not here,' he said. 'Not with all these people.'

'Tomorrow?'

'Tomorrow will be too late. Come with me now.'

'Shasa, are you mad? This is my party – my engagement party.'

'I'll bring the Jag around to the tradesmen's entrance,' he said. 'You'll need a wrap, it's cold out.'

He parked the Jag close in against the wall. This was where they used to conduct those long lingering farewells. He switched off the headlights. He knew she would not come, but nevertheless, he waited.

His surprise was genuine, his relief intense when she pulled open the door and slid into the passenger's seat. She had changed into slacks and a rollneck sweater. She wasn't going back to the party.

'Drive!' she said. 'Get away from here.'

They were silent for a while, and he glanced at her every time a street lamp lit the interior. She was looking straight ahead, smiling faintly, and at last she spoke.

'You never needed anything or anyone before. That was the one thing I couldn't stand about you.'

He did not reply.

'I think you need me now. I sensed it the very moment I saw you again. You truly need me at last.'

He was silent, words seemed superfluous. Instead he reached across and took her hand.

'I'm ready for you now, Shasa,' she said. 'Take me somewhere we can be alone, entirely alone.'

There was enough moon to light the pathway. She clung to him for support and they laughed breathlessly with excitement and stopped halfway down the cliff to kiss.

He let them into the shack and lit the paraffin lamp. With relief Shasa saw that the servants from Weltevreden had followed his orders. There was fresh linen on the bunk, and the floor had been polished.

Tara stood in the centre of the floor, her hands clasped protectively in front of her, her eyes huge and luminous in the lamplight, and she began to tremble when he took her in his arms.

'Shasa, please be gentle,' she whispered. 'I'm so scared.'

He was patient and very gentle, but she had no yardstick by which to recognize how immensely skilled and certain he was. She only knew that he seemed to sense each nuance of change in her feelings, anticipating each response of her body so that she felt no shame at her nakedness, and all her other fears and doubts dissolved swiftly under his tender hands and soft loving lips. At last she found herself running ahead of him, learning swiftly to guide and encourage him with subtle little movements and small gasps and cries of approval.

So that at the end she gazed up at him with wonder, and whispered, huskily, 'I never thought – I never dreamed it would be like that. Oh, Shasa, I'm so glad you came back to me.'

The Fordsburg branch of the Standard Bank serviced all the gold mines of the Central Rand complex. All the wages of the tens of thousands of weekly paid black mine workers were drawn from this branch and the senior accountant was a member of the OB.

His name was Willem De Kok, a small pasty-faced runt of a man with myopic misty eyes behind thick lenses, but his looks were deceptive. Within a few minutes of their meeting Manfred De La Rey found he had a quick mind, a complete dedication to the cause and almost too much courage for his small body.

'The money comes in on Thursday afternoon, between five and six o'clock. They use an armoured car and there is a police escort on motorcycles. That isn't the time to do it. There would almost certainly be shooting.'

'I understand,' Manfred nodded. 'Before you go on, please tell us how much money is usually transferred.'

'Between fifty thousand and seventy thousand pounds – except on the last Thursday of each month, when we make provision for the monthly paid workers on the mine properties. Then it will be closer to a hundred thousand. In addition there is always our ordinary cash float of approximately twenty-five thousand.'

They were gathered in the home of one of the mine officials of the Crown Deep gold mines. The same man had recruited the local *stormjagters* for the operation. He was a big red-faced man named Lourens, with the look of a heavy drinker. Manfred was not entirely happy with him; although so far he had found no real cause for his mistrust, he felt the man would be unreliable under stress.

'Thank you, Meneer De Kok, please go on.'

'The bank manager, Mr Cartwright, opens the back door of the building and the money is brought in. Of course, at this time in the afternoon the bank is closed to normal business. Mr Cartwright and I, together with our two senior tellers, count the money and issue a receipt. It is then deposited in the vault and locked up for the night. I have one key and half of the combination. Mr Cartwright keeps the other key and has the other half of the combination.'

'That would be the time,' Manfred anticipated. 'After the police escort has left, but before the vault is locked.'

'That is a possibility,' De Kok nodded. 'However, at that time it will still be light. Many people on the streets. Mr Cartwright is a difficult man – many things could go wrong. May I tell you how I would arrange it, if I were in command?'

'Thank you, Meneer De Kok. I'm glad of your assistance.'

It was ten minutes before midnight when Mr Peter Cartwright left the Freemason hall at the end of the meeting. He was the master of the lodge and he was still wearing his apron over his dinner jacket. He always parked his Morris in the lane behind the hall, but tonight as he sat in the driver's seat and fumbled with the ignition key, something hard was pressed into the back of his neck and a cold voice said quietly, 'This is a pistol, Mr Cartwright. If you do not do exactly as you are told, you will be shot in the back of the head. Drive to the bank, please.'

Terrified for his life and following the instructions of the two masked men in the back seat of the Morris, Peter Cartwright drove to the bank building and parked the Morris near the back door. There had been a spate of bank robberies over the last few months, at least four on the Witwatersrand and during one of them a bank guard had been shot dead. Cartwright was in no doubt as to the danger of his position or the ruthlessness of his captors.

As soon as he climbed out of the Morris, they closed on each side of him, pinning his arms and hustling him to the back door of the bank. One of them tapped upon it with the butt of his pistol and to Cartwright's astonishment it opened immediately. Only when he was inside did he realize how the robbers had gained access. His senior accountant Willem De Kok was already there, in pyjamas and dressing-gown, his hair tousled and his face slack and ashen with terror. He had obviously been dragged from his bed.

'I'm sorry, Mr Cartwright,' he blubbered. 'They forced me.'

'Pull yourself together, man,' Cartwright snapped at him, his own fear making him brusque – then his expression changed as he saw the two women: De Kok's fat little wife and his own beloved Mary in hair curlers and pink full-length dressing-gown with artificial pink roses down the front.

'Peter,' she wailed. 'Oh Peter, don't let them do anything.'

'Stop that, Mary. Don't let them see you like that.'

Cartwright looked around at his captors. There were six of them, including the two who had waylaid him, but his training in character judgement enabled him to pick out the leader almost immediately, a tall, powerfully built man with a dense black beard curling out from under his cloth face-mask, and above the mask a pair of strangely pale eyes, like those of one of the big predatory cats. His fear turned to real terror when he looked into those yellow eyes, for he sensed that there was no compassion in them.

'Open the vault,' the man said. His English was heavily accented.

'I don't have the key,' Cartwright said, and the man

with yellow eyes seized Mary Cartwright by the wrist and forced her to her knees.

'You wouldn't dare,' Cartwright blustered, and the man placed the muzzle of his pistol to Mary's temple.

'My wife is going to have a baby,' Cartwright said.

'Then you will want to spare her any further unpleasantness.'

'Open it for them, Peter. Let them have it. It's not our money,' Mary screamed. 'It's the bank's. Give it to them.' And she began to urinate in little spurts that soaked through the skirts of her dressing-gown.

Cartwright went to the green Chatwood steel door of the vault and drew his watch chain from his fob pocket with the key dangling on the end of it. Anger and humiliation seethed in him as he tumbled the combination and turned the key. He stood back while De Kok came forward to do the same. Then, while all their attention was on the vault door as it swung open, he glanced across at his desk. He kept the pistol in the top right-hand drawer. It was a .455 service Webley and there was always a round under the hammer. By now his outrage at the treatment of his wife outweighed his terror.

'Get the money!' the leader with the pale eyes ordered and three of the robbers, carrying canvas kit bags, hurried into the vault.

'My wife,' Cartwright said, 'I must see to her.' Nobody interfered as he lifted her to her feet and helped her to the desk. Tenderly he settled her into the chair, keeping up a flow of reassurance that covered the soft scrape as he opened the drawer.

He lifted the pistol and slipped it into the pocket of his masonic apron.

Then he backed away, leaving his wife at the desk. He had both hands raised to shoulder level in an attitude of surrender as he rejoined De Kok against the far wall. Both women were out of the line of his fire, but he waited until the three robbers re-emerged from the vault, each of them lugging a kitbag stuffed with wads of banknotes. Again all attention was on those bulging canvas bags, and Cartwright reached into the pocket of his white leather apron, brought out the pistol and his first shot crashed across the room in a long spurt of blue gunsmoke. He kept firing as the Luger bullets smashed into his body, and he was flung back against the wall. He fired until the hammer of the Webley snapped down on a spent cartridge, but his last bullet had gone into the concrete floor between his feet, and he was dead as he slumped down the bullet-pocked wall and huddled at the foot of it, with his blood puddling under him.

SHOOT-OUT AT RAND BANK
TWO DEAD
ROBBERY LINKED TO OB

The letters OB caught Sarah Stander's eye on the placard outside the news-stand. She went in and bought candy for the children, as she always did, and then, as an apparent afterthought, she took a copy of the newspaper.

She crossed to the park and while the two toddlers romped on the lawn and she absently rocked the pram with her foot to keep the baby quiet, she read the front-page article avidly.

Mr Peter Cartwright, the manager of a bank in Fordsburg, was last night shot dead while attempting to prevent a robbery at the bank's premises. One of the robbers was also shot dead, while a second man was seriously wounded and taken into custody by the police.

First estimates are that the four remaining robbers fled with cash in excess of £100,000.

A police spokesman said this morning that preliminary

interrogation of the wounded robber had established definite involvement by members of the *Ossewa Brandwag* in the outrage.

The Minister of the Interior, Colonel Blaine Malcomess, announced from his office in the House of Parliament in Cape Town that he had ordered an enquiry into the subversive activities of the OB and that any member of the public with information to offer should contact the nearest police station or telephone the following numbers: Johannesburg 78114, Cape Town 42444. The minister gave the assurance that all information would be treated in the strictest confidence.

She sat for almost an hour, trying to reach a decision, torn between loyalty to her family and her patriotic duty to her own people. She was confused, terribly confused. Was it right to blow up trains and rob banks and kill innocent people in the name of freedom and justice? Would she be a traitoress if she tried to save her husband and her babies? And what about those other innocents who were certain to die if Manfred De La Rey were allowed to continue? She could readily imagine the strife and chaos that would result if the entire country were to be plunged into civil war. She looked at the newspaper again and memorized the telephone number.

She stood up, called the children and wheeled the pram across the road. As she reached the far sidewalk and started towards the post office, she noticed old Mr Oberholster, the postmaster, watching her from the window of his office. She knew that he was one of them, she had seen him in OB uniform when he came to the cottage to pick Roelf up for one of their meetings.

Immediately she felt panicky with guilt. All telephone calls went through the post office exchange. Oberholster might easily listen in on her conversation, or the operator might recognize her voice. She turned away and pushed the pram down towards the butcher as though that had originally been her intention. She bought two pounds of pork chops, Roelf's favourite dinner, and hurried back to the cottage, eager to be off the street, to be alone so she could think.

As she let herself into the kitchen she heard men's voices in the front room that Roelf used as a study. He was back early from the university today, and then her pulse quickened as she heard Manfred's voice. She felt guilty and disloyal that he could still have that effect upon her. Manfred had not been to the cottage for almost three weeks, and she realized that she had missed him and thought about him almost every day with feelings that oscillated from bitter hatred and resentment to tremulous physical arousal.

She began to prepare dinner for Roelf and the children, but the men's voices carried quite clearly from the front room. Occasionally Sarah paused to listen, and once she heard Manie say, 'While I was in Jo'burg—' So he had been in Johannesburg. The bank robbery had taken place the night before last – time enough since then for him to come down by road or on the mail train. She thought about the two men who had been killed. She had read in the paper that the bank manager had a pregnant wife and two small children. She wondered how the woman felt now, with her husband gone, and three little ones to care for.

Then she was distracted by the men's voices again, and she paused to listen. What she heard filled her with foreboding.

'Where will this thing end?' she brooded. 'Oh I wish they would stop. I wish Manie would go away and leave us alone—' But the thought of that filled her with a sense of hopelessness.

Shasa flew down alone from the Witwatersrand in the Rapide and landed at Youngsfield after dark. He drove directly from the airfield to Blaine's home in Newlands Avenue.

Tara opened the door to him, her face lighting when she realized it was him. 'Oh, darling, I missed you!' They kissed rapturously until Blaine's voice made them start apart.

'Look here, Shasa, I don't like to interrupt anything important, but when you can spare a moment I'd like to hear your report.'

Tara was blushing furiously. 'Daddy, you were spying on us!'

'Public display, my dear. No spying necessary. Come along, Shasa.' He led the way to his study and waved Shasa to a chair.

'Drink?'

'I'd like a ginger ale, sir.'

'How are the mighty fallen!' Blaine poured a little of his hoarded whisky for himself and handed Shasa the ginger ale. 'Now what is it that you couldn't talk about on the telephone?'

'We just might have had a bit of luck at last, sir.' On Blaine's orders Shasa had flown up to Johannesburg as soon as the Fordsburg bank robbery had been linked to the *Ossewa Brandwag*. He had been at Marshall Square, the headquarters of the CID, while the captured bank robber was being interrogated. 'As you know, the fellow is an official on the Crown Mines. Thys Lourens is his name, and sure enough he was on our list of known OB members. Not one of the big fish, however, but quite a formidable-looking chap, although I'd expect him to be a bit of a boozer. I told the police inspector that you wanted answers—'

'No rough stuff.' Blaine frowned.

'No, sir. It wasn't necessary. Lourens wasn't as tough as he looked. We only had to point out that the penalty for armed robbery and accessory to murder was the gallows, but that we were prepared to do a deal and he started to gush. I gave you most of what he told us when I telephoned you this morning.'

'Yes. Go on.'

'Then he gave us the names of the other men involved in the robbery, that is, three of them. We were able to make the arrests before I left Johannesburg. However, the leader of the gang was a man he had only met three days before the robbery. He did not know his name, or where we could find him.'

'Did he give you a description?'

'Yes. Big man, black hair and beard, crooked nose, scar over one eye – a pretty detailed description, but he gave us something else which may be vital.'

'What is that?'

'A code name. The leader is known only as *Die Wit Swaard*, the White Sword, and they were ordered to co-operate with him from the very top level of the *stormjagters*.'

'White Sword,' Blaine mused. 'Sounds like something out of *Boy's Own Paper*.'

'Unfortunately not so childish,' Shasa went on. 'I impressed upon the inspector in charge that the code name and the description must be withheld until he had orders from you personally.'

'Good.' Blaine sipped his drink, pleased that his trust in Shasa Courtney had been so soon vindicated. 'White Sword – I wonder if this is the trigger we have been looking for, the catalyst that has at last brought the OB to the point of action.'

'It could very well be, sir. All the arrested members of the gang are obviously very much in awe of the man. He was clearly the force behind the entire thing, and he has disappeared completely. There is no trace of the missing money – incidentally, we have established that it is over one hundred and twenty-seven thousand pounds.'

'A tidy sum,' Blaine murmured, 'and we must presume that it has gone into the war chest of the OB, probably along with the gelignite from the railway hijacking.'

'As far as this code name goes, sir, I would like to suggest that we continue to keep it from the press and everybody not directly concerned with the investigation.'

'I agree. However, let me hear your reasons – see if they are the same as mine.'

'Firstly, we don't want to alert the quarry. We don't want him to know that we are on his track.'

Blaine nodded. 'Quite so.'

'The other reason is that it will confirm the reliability of any informant who uses the code name.'

'I don't follow you,' Blaine frowned.

'Your appeal to the public for assistance has resulted in a flood of telephone calls, but unfortunately most of them are bogus. If we let the code name become general knowledge, they'll all be using it.'

'I see. Use of the code name will establish the callers' credentials.'

'That's it, sir.'

'All right then, we'll keep it under the hat for the time being. Is there anything else?'

'Not at present.'

'Then let me tell you what has happened here while you were away. I have met the prime minister and we have decided to declare the OB a political organization. All civil servants, including the police and the army, will be obliged to resign their membership immediately.'

'That won't alter their sympathies,' Shasa pointed out.

'Of course not,' Blaine agreed. 'We will still have something like forty or fifty per cent of the country against us and for Nazi Germany.'

'It can't go on like this, sir. You and the *Ou Baas* will have to force a showdown.'

'Yes, we know that. As soon as our investigations are complete, as soon as we have a pretty comprehensive list of the ringleaders, we will swoop.'

'Arrest them?' Shasa was startled.

'Yes. They will be interned for the duration of the war as enemies of the state.'

Shasa whistled softly. 'Pretty drastic, sir. That could lead to real trouble.'

'That is why we have to scoop them all up in the net at one time – we cannot afford to miss any of them.' Blaine stood up. 'I can see you are exhausted, Shasa, and I am sure there are a few things that Mademoiselle Tara has to say to you. I'll expect you at my office at eight-thirty sharp tomorrow morning.' They moved to the study door and Blaine added as an afterthought, 'By the way, your grandfather, Sir Garry, arrived at Weltevreden this morning.'

'He has come down for his birthday,' Shasa smiled. 'I look forward to seeing him. I hope you and Field Marshal Smuts will be coming to the birthday picnic as usual.'

'Wouldn't miss it for the world!' Blaine opened the study door, and across the lobby Tara was hovering innocently, pretending to be selecting a book from the shelves in the library.

Blaine grinned, 'Tara, you let Shasa get some sleep tonight, do you hear me? I refuse to work with a zombie tomorrow.'

The meeting in Blaine's office the following morning lasted longer than either of them expected, and later moved down the passageway to the prime minister's office where Field Marshal Smuts personally questioned Shasa. His questions were so searching that Shasa felt drained by the effort of keeping pace with the *Ou Baas'* mercurial mind. He escaped with relief, Smuts's admonition following him.

'We want this fellow "White Sword" whoever he is, and we want him before he can do any more damage. Get that message across to everybody involved.'

'Yes, sir.'

'And I want those lists on my desk before the weekend. We must have these fellows locked up and out of harm's way.'

It was mid-morning before Shasa arrived at CID headquarters and parked the Jaguar in the reserved bay that had been set aside for him.

The special operations room had been set up in one of the extensive basement areas. There was a constable on duty at the door and Shasa signed the register. Entry was restricted to persons on the list. Many of the police force were known *OB* members, or sympathizers. Inspector Louis Nel had chosen his team with extreme care.

He was a balding, taciturn man whose age and job classification had prevented him from volunteering for overseas military service, a fact that he bitterly resented. However, Shasa had soon discovered that he was an easy man to like and respect, though a difficult one to please. They had quickly established a working rapport.

Nel was in his shirt-sleeves, a cigarette dangling from his lips as he talked into the telephone, but he covered the mouthpiece and summoned Shasa with an imperious wave.

'Where the hell have you been? I was going to send out a search party,' he reprimanded him. 'Sit down. I want to talk to you.'

Shasa perched on the corner of his desk while the inspector continued his telephone call, and he stared through the window into the busy operations room. Inspector Nel had been allocated eight detectives and a bevy of female stenographers. The room was full of cigarette smoke and the clatter of typewriters as they worked. One of the other telephones on the inspector's desk rang, and he glanced up at Shasa. 'Take that – damned switchboard keeps putting everything through to me.'

Shasa picked up the receiver. 'Good morning, this is CID headquarters. May I help you?' he said, and when there was silence, he repeated it in Afrikaans.

'Hello, I want to talk to somebody—' the caller was a woman, a young woman and very agitated, she was speaking Afrikaans, and her voice was breathless and uncertain. 'In the paper they said you wanted to know about the *Ossewa Brandwag*. I want to talk to somebody.'

'My name is Courtney,' Shasa said in Afrikaans. 'Squadron-Leader Courtney. I am grateful that you want to assist the police. You can tell me everything.' He tried to make his voice warm and reassuring. He could sense that the woman was afraid, perhaps on the point of changing her mind and ringing off. 'Take your time. I'm here to listen to you.'

'Are you the police?'

'Yes, madam. Would you like to give me your name?'

'No! I won't tell you—'

He realized his mistake. 'That's perfectly all right. You don't have to give your name,' he told her quickly, and there was a long silence. He could hear her breathing.

'Take your time,' he repeated gently. 'You just tell me what you want to.'

'They are stealing the guns.' The woman's voice sank to a whisper.

'Can you tell me what guns?' Shasa asked carefully.

'From the gun factory in Pretoria, the railway workshop.'

Shasa sat up straighter and held the telephone receiver with both hands. Almost all the military arms and munitions manufacture was being undertaken in the railway workshops in Pretoria. It was the only establishment with the heavy equipment, highspeed lathes and steam presses, capable of turning out barrels and blocks for rifles and machine-guns. The cartridge cases for the munitions were being stamped out at the Pretoria Mint, but they were despatched to the railway workshops for final processing.

'What you are saying is important,' he told her carefully. 'Can you tell me how they are stealing the guns?'

'They are putting scrap iron in the cases, and stealing the guns,' the woman whispered.

'Can you tell me who is doing this, please? Do you know who is responsible?'

'I don't know the people in the workshop, but the one who is in charge. I know who he is.'

'We must know his name,' Shasa told her persuasively, but she was silent. He could sense that she was struggling with herself, and that if he pushed her now he would lose her.

'Do you want to tell me who he is?' he asked. 'Just take your time.'

'His name—' the woman hesitated, was silent a moment longer, and then she blurted out, 'they call him *Wit Swaard* – White Sword.'

Shasa felt his skin crawl as though it were infested with vermin, and his heart seemed to check, miss a beat, then race away wildly.

'What did you say?'

'White Sword – his name is White Sword,' the woman repeated and there was a crackle and click as the connection was broken.

'Hello! Hello!' Shasa shouted into the receiver. 'Are you there? Don't hang up!' But the hiss of static on the empty line mocked him.

Shasa stood beside Blaine Malcomess' desk while he made the call to the commissioner of police at Marshall Square in Johannesburg.

'As soon as you have the search warrant you are to close the workshops. No one allowed to enter or leave. I have already spoken to the military commander of the Transvaal. He and his quartermaster-general will give you full co-operation. I want you to begin the search right away, open all the weapons cases in the stores and check every item against the factory production sheets. I will be flying up, leaving immediately. Please have a police car meet me at Roberts Heights airfield at—' he glanced at Shasa for a time, ' – five o'clock this evening. In the meantime, I want you to impress utter secrecy on all your men involved in the search. One other thing, Commissioner, please select only men who you are satisfied are not members of any subversive organizations, particularly the *Ossewa Brandwag*.'

Shasa drove them out to Youngsfield in the Jaguar and as they parked behind the hangar Blaine unfolded his long legs and climbed out of the sportscar.

'Well, at least the most gruelling part of the journey is over with,' he remarked.

There was a police inspector waiting for them on the hard stand below the Roberts Heights control tower as Shasa taxied the Rapide in and cut the engines. He came forward to meet them as Blaine and Shasa came down the landing steps.

'How is the investigation going?' Blaine demanded immediately after they had shaken hands. 'What have you found so far?'

'Nothing, Minister.' The inspector shook his head. 'We have checked over six hundred cases of rifles. It's a time-consuming job. But so far everything seems to be in order.'

'How many cases in the stores?'

'Nine hundred and eighty.'

'So you have checked over half.' Blaine shook his head. 'Let's go and have a look anyway.'

He settled his hat on his head and buttoned his overcoat to the neck for there was a cold wind sweeping across the airstrip, bringing memories of the snows of the Drakensberg mountains, and the highveld grass was bleached silvery by the frosts of late winter. He and Shasa climbed into the back seat of the black police Packard and neither of them spoke on the short journey into the centre of Pretoria.

At the gates to the railway workshops there was a double guard of police and military personnel. They checked the occupants of the Packard carefully, not visibly impressed by Blaine's status.

The chief inspector in charge of the investigation was in the office of the workshop manager and his report had little to add to what they already knew. They had so far been unable to find any irregularity in the production or packaging of weapons.

'Give me the tour,' Blaine ordered grimly, and the entire party – Blaine, Shasa, the chief inspector and the workshop manager – went out on to the main production floor.

'Workshop' was hardly a correct description of the large factory that they entered. Originally built to service and repair the rolling stock of the state-owned railway, it had been expanded and modernized until it was capable of building its own locomotives from scratch. Now the long production line along which they picked their way was turning out armoured cars for the desert war in North Africa.

The working of the factory had not been halted by the police investigation and the cavernous sheds roofed with corrugated iron echoed to the thunder of the steam presses and the cacophony of the lathes and turret head drills.

'How many men do you employ?' Blaine had to shout to make himself heard in the uproar.

'Almost three thousand altogether – we are working three shifts now. Wartime production.'

The manager took them through to the furthest building.

'This is where we turn out the small arms,' he shouted. 'Or rather the metal parts. Barrel and blocks. The woodwork is manufactured by outside contractors.'

'Show us the finished articles and the packing,' Blaine ordered. 'That's where the trouble is, if there is trouble.'

After assembly and checking, the completed rifles, British Long Service No 4 Mark 1 in .303 calibre, were greased and wrapped in yellow grease-proof paper, then packed in the long WD green wooden cases, ten rifles to a case. Finally the cases were loaded onto steel pallets and trundled through to the despatch stores.

When they entered the despatch stores, there were a dozen uniformed police constables working with at least fifty factory employees in blue overalls. Each case was being taken down from the tall stacks and opened by one of the constables, then the wrapped rifles were taken out and counted, repacked and the case lids relocked. The checked cases were being stacked at the far end of the storehouse, and Shasa saw immediately that only about fifty cases remained to be opened and inspected.

The chief storekeeper hurried across from his desk and challenged Blaine indignantly. 'I don't know who you are – but if you are the bloody fool who ordered this, you need your arse kicked. We have lost a day's production. There is a goods train at the siding and a convoy waiting in Durban harbour to take these weapons to our boys up north.'

Shasa left the group and went across to watch the working constables. 'No luck?' he asked one of them.

'We're wasting our time,' the man grunted without looking up, and Shasa silently reviled himself. A day's war production lost because of him, it was a dire responsibility and his sense of despondency increased as he stood and watched the remaining cases opened, checked and resealed.

The constables assembled at the door of the stores and the overalled factory employees went out through the tall sliding doors to resume their posts on the production line. The police inspector came back to where they stood in a small disconsolate group.

'Nothing, Minister. I'm sorry.'

'We had to do it,' Blaine said, glancing at Shasa. 'Nobody is to blame.'

'Too bloody true somebody is to blame,' the chief storeman broke in truculently. 'Now that you've had your fun, can I get on with loading the rest of the shipment?'

Shasa stared at him. There was something about the man's behaviour that set off a little warning tingle down his spine – the blustering defensive manner, the shiftiness of his gaze.

'Of course,' he thought. 'If there was a switch, this is where it would take place, and this fellow would be in it to his neck.' His mind was starting to slough off the inertia of disappointment and anticlimax.

'All right,' Blaine agreed. 'It was a wild-goose chase. You can get on with your work.'

'Hold on, sir,' Shasa intervened quietly, and he turned back to the storeman. 'How many railway trucks have you loaded already?'

There it was again – the shift of the man's eyes, the slight hesitation. He was going to lie. Then he glanced involuntarily at the sheaf of papers in the clipboard that lay on his desk beside the doors that led out onto the loading bays.

Shasa crossed quickly to the desk and picked up the sheaf of loading manifests. 'Three trucks have already been loaded,' he read from the manifest. 'Which are they?'

'They have been shunted away,' the storeman muttered sulkily.

'Then let's have them shunted back here right away,' Blaine intervened briskly.

Blaine and Shasa stood together under the arc lamps on the concrete loading quay while the first of the closed railway goods trucks was unlocked and the sliding door opened. The interior of the truck was loaded to the roof with green rifle cases.

'If they are here, they will be at the bottom of the load,' Shasa suggested. 'Whoever is responsible would get rid of the evidence as soon as possible. He'd make damned sure they were the first cases loaded.'

'Get down to the bottom cases,' Blaine ordered sharply, and the top cases were carried out and stacked on the quay.

'Right!' Blaine pointed to the back of the truck. 'Get that case out and open it.'

The lid came up and the constable let it fall to the concrete floor with a clatter.

'Sir!' he exclaimed. 'Look at this.'

Blaine stepped up beside him and stared down into the open box, and then he looked up again quickly.

The chief storekeeper was hurrying across the floor of the shed towards the doors at the far end.

'Arrest that man!' Blaine shouted urgently, and two constables ran forward and seized him. He was struggling angrily as they dragged him out onto the loading quay.

Blaine turned to Shasa, his expression grim and his eyes flinty. 'Well, my boy, I hope you are satisfied. You've given us a mountain of work and a lot of sleepless nights ahead,' he said.

Fifteen grave men sat around the long polished stinkwood table in the panelled cabinet office and listened silently as Blaine Malcomess made his report.

'There is no way of establishing with any certainty exactly how many weapons are missing. Two other large shipments have been sent out since the first of the month and as yet neither of these has reached its destination in Cairo. They are still in transit, but we must expect that weapons are missing from both shipments. I estimate some two thousand rifles together with a million and a half rounds of ammunition.'

The men around the table stirred uneasily, but nobody spoke.

'This is alarming, of course. However, the truly disturbing aspect of the business is the theft of some thirty to fifty Vickers machine-guns from the same source.'

'This is incredible,' Deneys Reitz muttered. 'That is enough to launch a nationwide rebellion. It could be 1914 all over again. We must make sure no word of this gets out. It will cause panic.'

'We should also consider,' Blaine went on, 'the tons of explosives hijacked in the karoo. Those would almost certainly be used to disrupt communications and prevent deployment of our limited military strength. If there was to be a rebellion—'

'Please tell us, Blaine,' the prime minister held up a finger. 'Firstly, do we have any indication of when we can expect them to come out into the open and attempt their *coup d'état?*'

'No, Prime Minister. The best I can do is an estimate based on our probable discovery of the weapons theft. They must have realized that the theft would be discovered as soon as the first consignment reached Cairo, and almost certainly they plan to move before that time.'

'When would the shipment have reached Cairo?'

'Two weeks from now approximately.'

'So we must expect that they will make the attempt within days, rather than weeks?'

'I'm afraid so, Prime Minister.'

'My next question, Blaine. How complete is your investigation? Do you have a full list of the ringleaders of the OB and the *stormjagters?*'

'Not a full list, we have only about six hundred names so far. I think it includes almost all their key men – but, of course, we can't have any way of being sure of that.'

'Thank you, Blaine.' The prime minister tugged thoughtfully at his small silver goatee beard. His expression was almost serene, his blue eyes calm and unworried. They all waited for him to speak again.

'How sensitive are the names on the list?' he asked.

'There is the administrator of the Orange Free State.'

'Yes, we know about him.'

'Twelve members of Parliament, including one former cabinet minister.'

'Parliamentary privilege,' Field-Marshal Smuts murmured. 'We can't touch them.'

'Then there are church leaders, at least four high-ranking army officers, top civil servants, one assistant police commissioner.' Blaine read the list through, and by the time he had finished, the prime minister had already made up his mind.

'We can't afford to wait,' he said. 'With the exception of the members of parliament, I want detention and internment orders prepared for all the others on the list of suspects. I'll sign them as soon as they are drafted. In the meantime I want you to plan the simultaneous arrests of all of them, and make provision for their incarceration.'

'There are the concentration camps built for Italian prisoners of war at Baviaanspoort and Pietermaritzburg,' Blaine pointed out.

'Good,' Field-Marshal Smuts agreed. 'I want these men all safely behind barbed-wire as soon as possible. And I want the missing weapons and explosives found, and found quickly.'

'We cannot afford to wait,' Manfred De La Rey said carefully. 'Every hour is dangerous, every day brings us closer to the brink, a week could spell disaster.'

'We are not ready. We need time,' one of the other men in the first-class railway compartment cut in. There were eight men, including Manfred, in the compartment. They had boarded the southbound express separately at different stops over the last two hundred miles. The conductor of the train was a sympathizer, and there were *stormjagters* in the corridors outside the compartment, acting as sentries. Nobody could reach them or eavesdrop on their conversation.

'You promised us another ten days in which to complete the final preparations.'

'We haven't got ten days, man. Haven't you listened to what I am telling you?'

'It can't be done,' the man repeated stubbornly.

'It can be done,' Manfred· raised his voice. 'It has to be done!'

The administrator intervened sternly. 'Enough of that, gentlemen. Let's keep the fighting for our enemies.'

With an obvious effort Manfred moderated his tone. 'I apologize for my outburst. However, I repeat that we have no time to spare. The removal of the weapons from the railway workshops has been discovered, ten of our men there have been arrested. One of our men at Marshall Square has told us that they have received detention orders for over two hundred of our senior members and that these are to be served on Sunday – that is four days from now.'

'We are aware of all that,' the administrator intervened

again. 'What we must do now is decide whether we can afford to put the entire plan forward – or if it should be abandoned. I will listen to each of your opinions and then we will vote. We shall stand by the majority decision. Let us hear first from Brigadier Koopman.'

They all looked to the army general. He was in civilian clothing but his military bearing was unmistakable. He spread a large-scale map on the fold-down table, and used it to illustrate his report in a professionally dispassionate voice. First he set out the order of battle of the army, and the dispositions of the troops, aircraft and armoured cars that remained in the country and then went on, 'So you see that the two main troop concentrations are at the infantry training barracks at Roberts Heights and at Durban awaiting shipment for overseas duty. With almost one hundred and sixty thousand outside the country, these do not amount to more than five thousand men. There are no modern aircraft, other than the fifty Harvard trainers. This makes it feasible to immobilize the troops at their present positions at least for the first few crucial days that it will take to seize control. This can be achieved by destroying all major road and railway bridges, particularly those over the Vaal river, the Orange river and the Umzindusi river.'

He went on talking for another ten minutes, and then summed up, 'We have our men placed in positions of command, right up to the general staff, and they will be able to cushion us from any forthright action by the army. After that they will arrest and hold the Smuts men on the general staff and bring the army in on our side to support the new republican government.'

One after another the other men present made their reports. Manfred was last to speak.

'Gentlemen,' he began. 'Within the last twelve hours I have been in direct radio contact with the German *Abwehr* through their representative in Portuguese Angola. He has relayed to us the assurances of the German High Command

and of the Führer himself. The German submarine supply vessel *Altmark* is at present within three hundred nautical miles of Cape Town carrying over five hundred tons of armaments. She awaits only the signal to steam to our aid.' He spoke quietly but persuasively, and he sensed the mood swing in his favour.

When he finished there was a short but profound silence and then the administrator said, 'We have all the facts before us now. We must make the decision. It is this. Before the government can arrest and imprison us and the other legitimate leaders of the *Volk*, we put into effect the plan. We rise and depose the present government and take the power into our own hands to put our nation back on the course to freedom and justice. I will ask each of you in turn – do you say "Yes" or do you say "No"?'

'*Ja*,' said the first man.

'*Ek stem ja*. I say yes.'

'*Ek stem ook ja*, I also say yes.'

At the end the administrator summed up for them. 'We are all agreed – there is not one of us against the enterprise.' He paused and looked at Manfred De La Rey. 'You have told us of a signal to launch the rising. Something that will turn the country on its head. Can you tell us now what that signal will be?'

'The signal will be the assassination of the traitor Jan Christian Smuts,' Manfred said.

They stared at him in silence. It was clear that even though they had anticipated something momentous, none of them had expected this.

'The details of this political execution have been carefully planned,' Manfred went on to assure them. 'Three different contingency plans were drawn up in Berlin, each for a different date, depending on the dictates of circumstances. The first plan, the earliest date, suits our present purpose exactly. Smuts will be executed this coming Saturday. Three days from now – the day before the detention orders are served on our leaders.'

The silence drew out a minute longer, then the administrator asked, 'Where? How will it be done?'

'You do not need to know that. I will do what is necessary, alone and unaided. It will be up to you to act quickly and forcibly as soon as the news of Smuts' death is released. You must step into the void he leaves and seize the reins of power.'

'Let it be so,' said the administrator quietly. 'We will be ready for the moment when it comes, and may God bless our battle.'

Of the eight men in the compartment, only Manfred remained aboard when the express pulled out of Bloemfontein station and began its long run southwards towards Cape Town.

'I have a permit to keep a firearm on the estate,' Sakkie Van Vuuren, the winery manager, told Manfred. 'We use it to shoot the baboons that come down from the mountains to raid the vineyards and orchards.'

He led the way down the steps into the cool gloom of the cellars.

'Anybody who hears a few shots coming from the mountains will take no notice of them – but if you are challenged, tell them you are employed by the estate and refer them to me.' He opened the false front of the wine cask and stood back while Manfred knelt and opened one of the waterproof canisters.

First he lifted out the radio transmitter and connected the new batteries which Van Vuuren had procured for him. The radio was fitted into a canvas rucksack and was readily portable.

He opened the second canister and brought out the rifle case. In it was a sniper's model 98 Mauser, with that superb action which permitted such high breech pressure levels that the velocity of the 173 grain bullet could be pushed up over 2500 feet per second. There were fifty rounds of the 7–57 mm ammunition which had been specially hand-loaded by one of the expert technicians at *Deutsche Waffen und Munitionsfabrik*, and the telescopic sight was by Zeiss. Manfred fitted the telescopic sight to the rifle and filled the magazine. The rest of the ammunition he repacked and then stowed the canisters away in the false-fronted cask.

Van Vuuren drove him up into one of the valleys of the Hottentots Holland mountains in his battered old Ford halftonner, and when the track at last petered out, left him there and drove back down the rocky winding trail.

Manfred watched him out of sight and then hefted his pack and rifle and began to climb upwards. He had plenty of time, there was no need to hurry, but the hard physical exertion gave him pleasure and he went up with long elastic strides, revelling in the flood of sweat on his face and body.

He crossed the first range of the foothills, went down into the wooded valley and then climbed again to one of the main peaks beyond. Near the crest he stopped and set up the radio, stringing his aerials from the tops of two cripplewood trees and orientating them carefully towards the north.

Then he settled down with his back to a boulder and ate the sandwiches that little Sarah had made for him. The contact time with the *Abwehr* agent in Luanda, the capital of Portuguese Angola, was 1500 hours Greenwich Mean Time, and he had almost an hour to wait.

After he had eaten he took the Mauser in his lap and handled it lovingly, refamiliarizing himself with the weapon's feel and balance, working the bolt action, bringing the butt to his shoulder and sighting through the lens of the telescope at objects down the slope.

In Germany he had practised endlessly with this same rifle, and he knew that at any range up to three hundred metres he could choose in which eye he would shoot a man. However, it was essential that he check the rifle to make absolutely certain that the sights were still true. He needed a target as close to that of a human form as possible, but he could find nothing suitable from where he sat. He laid the rifle carefully aside, checked his wristwatch and transferred his attention to the radio.

He set up the Morse key and turned to the page of his notebook on which he had already reduced the message to code. He flexed his fingers and began to send, tapping the brass key with a fluid rapid movement, aware that the operator at Luanda far in the north would recognize his style and would accept that rather than his code name as proof of his identity.

'Eagle Base, this is White Sword.' On the fourth call he was answered. The signal in his headphones was strong and clear.

'Go ahead, White Sword.'

'Confirm plan one in force. Repeat plan one. Acknowledge.'

There was no need for a long message that could increase the chances of being traced or intercepted. Everything had been arranged with Teutonic attention to detail before he left Berlin.

'Understand plan one. Good luck. Over and out from Eagle Base.'

'Over and out White Sword.'

He rolled the aerial wires, repacked the transmitter, and was about to swing it on his shoulder when an explosive barking cough echoed along the cliffs and Manfred sank down flat behind the rock and reached for the Mauser. The wind favoured him and he settled down to wait.

He lay for almost half an hour without moving, still and intent, scanning the valley floor below, before he saw the first movement amongst the jumbled lichen-covered rocks and stunted protea bushes.

The baboons were moving in their usual foraging order, with half a dozen young males in the van, the females and young in the centre, and three huge grey patriarchal males in the rearguard. The infants were slung upside down below their mothers' bellies, clinging with tiny paws to the thick coarse belly fur and peering out with pink hairless faces. The larger youngsters rode like jockeys perched on the backs of their dams. The three fighting bulls at the rear of the troop followed them, swaggering arrogantly, knuckling the ground as they moved forward on four legs, their heads held high, almost doglike, their muzzles long and pointed, their eyes close-set and bright.

Manfred chose the largest of the three apes and watched him through the lens of the sight. He let him come on up the slope until he was only three hundred metres from where he lay.

The bull baboon suddenly loped forward and with an agile bound reached the top of a grey boulder the size of a small cottage. He sat there, perched on his hindquarters, resting his elbows on his knees, almost human in his pose, and he opened his jaws in a cavernous yawn. His fangs were pointed and yellow and as long as a man's forefinger.

Carefully Manfred took up the slack in the rear trigger until he felt the hair trigger engage with an almost inaudible click, then he settled the cross hairs of the telescopic sight on the baboon's forehead, and held his aim for the hundredth part of a second. He touched the front trigger, while he still concentrated fixedly on the baboon's sloping furry forehead and the rifle slammed back into his shoulder. The shot crashed out across the valley. The echoes rang back from the cliffs in a descending roll of thunder.

The bull baboon somersaulted backwards from his seat on the boulder, and the rest of the troop fled back down the slope in screaming panic.

Manfred stood up, hoisted the pack onto his shoulders and picked his way down the slope. He found the ape's carcass huddled at the base of the rock. It still twitched and quivered in reflex but the top of the animal's skull was missing. It had been cut away as though by an axe stroke at the level of the eyes and bright blood welled up through the base of the brain pan and dribbled over the rocks.

Manfred rolled the carcass over with his foot and nodded with satisfaction. The special hollow-tipped bullet would decapitate a man just as neatly, and the rifle had held true to within a finger's breadth at three hundred metres.

'Now I am ready as I will ever be,' Manfred murmured and went down the mountain.

Shasa had not been home to Weltevreden, nor had he seen Tara since he and Blaine had flown home from Pretoria in the Rapide after the discovery of the stolen weapons.

He had not left CID headquarters during that time. He ate at the police canteen and snatched a few hours' sleep in the dormitory that had been set up on the floor above the operations room. The rest of the time he had been engrossed entirely in the preparations for the planned police swoop.

There were almost a hundred and fifty suspects to be dealt with in Cape Province alone, and for each the warrant had to be drawn, the expected whereabouts of subjects charted, and police officers delegated to make each separate arrest.

Sunday had been selected deliberately for almost all of the subjects were devout Calvinists, members of the Dutch

Reformed Church, and would attend divine service that morning. Their whereabouts could be anticipated with a high degree of certainty and they would in all probability be unsuspecting, in a religious frame of mind, and not in the mood to offer any resistance to the arresting officers.

It was midday Friday before Shasa remembered that his grandfather's birthday picnic was the following day and he rang Centaine at Weltevreden from the police operations room.

'Oh *chéri*, that is terrible news, Sir Garry will be so disappointed. He has asked for you every day since he arrived – and we are all so looking forward to seeing you.'

'I'm sorry, Mater.'

'Can't you get away to join us – even for an hour?'

'That's just not possible. Believe me, Mater, I am as disappointed as anyone.'

'You don't have to come up the mountain, Shasa. Just drink a glass of champagne with us at Weltevreden before we leave. You can go back immediately and do whatever it is you are doing that is so important. For my sake, *chéri*, won't you try?'

She sensed that he was wavering. 'Blaine and Field-Marshal Smuts will be here. They have both promised. If you come at eight o'clock, just to wish your grandfather a happy birthday, I promise you can leave again before eight-thirty.'

'Oh, all right, Mater,' he capitulated, and grinned into the telephone. 'Don't you find it boring always to get your own way?'

'It is something I have learned to bear, *chéri*,' she laughed back at him. 'Until tomorrow.'

'Until tomorrow,' he agreed.

'I love you, *chéri*.'

'I love you too, Mater.'

He hung up, feeling guilty at having given in to her, and was about to ring Tara to tell her that he wouldn't be able to escort her to the picnic when one of the sergeants across the room called him.

'Squadron Leader Courtney, this call is for you.'

'Who is it?'

'She didn't say, it's a woman,' and Shasa smiled as he crossed the room. Tara had anticipated him and called him first.

'Hello, is that you Tara?' he said into the mouthpiece, and there was silence except for the soft sound of somebody breathing nervously. His nerves snapped tight, and he lowered his voice, trying to make it friendly and encouraging as he switched into Afrikaans.

'This is Squadron Leader Courtney speaking. Is that the lady I spoke to before?'

'*Ja*. It is me.' He recognized her voice, young, breathless and afraid.

'I am very grateful to you. What you have done has saved many lives – the lives of innocent people.'

'I saw nothing about the guns in the newspapers,' the woman whispered.

'You can be proud of what you have done,' he told her, and then on inspiration added, 'Many people would have died, perhaps even women and little children.'

The words 'little children' seemed to decide her and she blurted out, 'There is still great danger. They are planning something terrible, White Sword is going to do something. Soon, very soon. I heard him say that it will be the signal, and it will turn the nation on its head—'

'Can you tell me what it is?' Shasa asked, trying not to frighten her, keeping his voice low and reassuring. 'What is this thing he plans?'

'I don't know. I only know it will be very soon.'

'Can you find out what it is?'

'I don't know – I can try.'

'For the sake of everybody, the women and little children, will you try to find out what it is?'

'Yes, I will try.'

'I will be here at this telephone—' then suddenly he remembered his promise to Centaine ' – or at this other number—' and he gave her the number at Weltevreden. 'Try here first, and the other number if I am not here.'

'I understand.'

'Can you tell me who White Sword is?' He took a calculated risk. 'Do you know his real name?' Immediately the connection crackled and was broken. She had hung up. He lowered the telephone and stared at it. He sensed that he had frightened her off for good with that last question, and dismay overwhelmed him.

'Something that will turn the nation on its head.' Her words haunted him, and he was filled with an ominous sense of impending disaster.

Manfred drove sedately along the De Waal Drive past the university buildings. It was past midnight, and the streets were almost deserted except for a few Friday-night revellers wending their unsteady way homeward. The car he was driving was a nondescript little Morris and the rifle was in the boot under a tattered piece of tarpaulin. He was dressed in a railwayman's blue overalls over which he wore a thick fisherman's jersey and a heavy greatcoat.

He was moving into position now to avoid the danger of being seen on the mountain during daylight carrying a rifle. On a weekend the slopes of Table Mountain were favoured by hikers and rock climbers, birdwatchers and picnickers, boy scouts and lovers.

He passed the forestry station and turned into Rhodes Avenue, then followed the road up past the Kirstenbosch Botanical Gardens with the bulk of the mountain blotting out half the starry night sky. The road wound around the bottom slopes through the dark forests. Before he reached the Constantia Nek pass he slowed down, and checked in his rearview mirror to make certain there was no vehicle following him. Then he switched off his headlights and turned off sharply onto the forestry track.

He drove at a walking pace, keeping in low gear until he reached the forestry gate. Then he stopped and, leaving the engine idling, went to the gate and tried his key in the lock. Roelf had given him the key and assured him that the forester was a friend. It turned easily, and Manfred drove the Morris through and closed the gate behind him. He hooked the staple of the padlock through the chain, but did not lock it.

He was on the bottom stretch of the bridle path now and drove on up the narrow track as it ascended the slope in a series of tight hairpins. He passed the contour path that girdled the mountain three hundred metres above sea level. A mile further on, just below the summit he reversed the Morris off the bridle path so that it was out of sight of a casual hiker. From the boot he took the Mauser and wrapped it carefully in a light tarpaulin. Then he locked the doors of the Morris and went back down towards the contour path carrying the rifle across his shoulder. He used his flashlight as little as possible and then only for quick glimpses of the pathway, shielding the beam with his body.

Within twenty minutes he intercepted the pathway that climbed directly up Skeleton Gorge and he flashed his light onto the square concrete signpost and read the legend printed on it.

SMUTS TRACK

The concrete block resembled a tombstone rather than a signpost, and he smiled grimly at the appropriateness of the name upon it. The old field-marshal had made this ascent the most famous of all routes to the summit.

Manfred climbed quickly, without resting, 1200 feet up Skeleton Gorge until he came up past Breakfast Rock over the crest, onto the tableland. Here he paused for a moment to look back. Far below him the Constantia valley huddled in the night, lit by only a star dusting of lights. He turned his back upon it and began his final preparations. He had scouted the site two days previously, and he had chosen the stance from which he would fire and paced out the exact range from there to the point on the pathway where a man would become visible as he came out onto the summit.

Now he moved into his stance. It was a hollow between two boulders, lightly screened by mountain scrub. He spread the tarpaulin over the low wiry bracken and then lay full length upon it, flattening the plants into a comfortable mattress under him.

He wriggled into firing position, cradled the butt of the Mauser into his cheek and aimed at the head of the pathway 250 metres away. Through the Zeiss lens he could make out the individual branches of the bush that grew beside the path starkly silhouetted against the soft glow of light from the valley beyond.

He laid the weapon on the tarpaulin in front of him, ready for instant use. Then he pulled the collar of the greatcoat up around his ears and huddled down. It was going to be a long cold wait, and to pass the time he reviewed all the planning that had led him to this place, and the odds that tomorrow morning, at a little before or a little after ten-thirty, his quarry would come up the path that bore his name and step into the cross hairs of the Zeiss scope.

The dossier on Jan Christian Smuts meticulously assembled by the *Abwehr* in Berlin, which he had studied so avidly, had shown that for the last ten years, on every anniversary of this date, the field-marshal had kept this arrangement with an old friend, and now the fate of a nation depended on him doing so once again.

Shasa drove through the Anreith gates and up the long driveway to the château. There were a dozen motor cars parked in front of Weltevreden, Blaine's Bentley amongst them. He parked the Jag beside it and checked his wristwatch. It was ten minutes past eight o'clock. He was late and Mater was going to be huffed, she was an absolute stickler for punctuality.

She surprised him again by springing up from the long table in the dining-room and running to embrace him. The entire party of twenty was assembled for one of Weltevreden's celebrated breakfasts. The buffet sideboard groaned under the weight of silver and food. The servants in their long white *kanzas* and red pillbox fezes burst into beaming grins when they saw Shasa and a welcoming buzz of pleasure went up from the guests seated at the stinkwood table.

They were all there, everybody Shasa loved – Grandpater Garry at the head of the table, sprightly as a pixie; Anna beside him, her red face creasing into an infinity of smiles like a friendly bulldog; Blaine; Tara, as lovely as this spring morning; Matty, all freckles and carroty red hair; the *Ou Baas*; and of course Mater. Only David was missing.

Shasa went to each of them in turn, laughing and exchanging banter, embracing and shaking hands and kissing. There were whoops and whistles when he pecked Tara's blushing cheek. He handed Grandpater Garry his present and stood beside him as he unwrapped the specially bound first editions of *Burchell's Travels* and exclaimed with delight. He shook hands with the *Ou Baas* respectfully and glowed with pleasure at his quiet commendation, 'Good work you are doing, *Kêrel*.' Finally he exchanged a quick word with Blaine before loading his plate at the sideboard and taking the chair between Tara and Mater.

He refused the champagne – 'I've got work to do today' – and played with Tara's foot under the table while he joined in the hilarity that resounded around the long table.

Too soon they were all rising and the women went to

815

get their coats while the men went out to the cars and made certain that the rugs and picnic baskets were loaded.

'I'm sorry you can't come with us, Shasa.' Grandpater Garry took him aside. 'I hoped we could have a chat, but I've heard from Blaine how important your work is.'

'I'll try and get back here tomorrow night. The pressure should be off by then.'

'I won't go back to Natal until we've been able to spend a little time together. You are the one to carry on the Courtney name, my one and only grandson.'

Shasa felt a rush of deep affection for this wise and gentle old man; in some strange way the fact that they had both suffered mutilation, Sir Garry's leg and Shasa's eye, seemed to have forged an even stronger bond between them.

'It's years since I have been up to visit you and Anna at Theuniskraal,' Shasa burst out impulsively. 'May I come to spend a couple of weeks with you?'

'Nothing would give us greater pleasure,' Sir Garry hugged him, and at that moment Field-Marshal Smuts came across.

'Still talking, old Garry, do you ever stop? Come along now, we have a mountain to climb, and the last one to the top gets sent to an old-age home.'

The old friends smiled at each other. They could have been brothers, both slight of build but wiry and dapper, both with little silver goatee beards and disreputable old hats upon their heads.

'Forward!' Sir Garry brandished his cane, linked his arm through the field-marshal's and led him to the back seat of Centaine's yellow Daimler.

The Daimler led the procession, followed by Blaine's Bentley and Tara blew Shasa a kiss as it passed. He stood on the front steps of Weltevreden and it was very quiet after they had all gone.

He turned back into the house and went upstairs to his own room, selected a batch of clean shirts, socks and underpants from his drawers and stuffed them into a grip.

On the way downstairs he turned aside, went into Centaine's study and picked up the telephone. One of the duty sergeants in the operations room at CID headquarters answered.

'Hello, Sergeant. Have there been any messages for me?'

'Hold on, sir, I'll have a look.' He was back in a few seconds. 'Only one, sir, ten minutes ago. A woman – wouldn't leave her name.'

'Thank you, Sergeant,' Shasa hung up quickly. He found that his hand was trembling and his breath had shortened. A *woman – wouldn't leave her name.* It had to be her. Why hadn't she called him here? She had the number.

He stood over the phone, willing it to ring. Nothing happened. After five minutes he began to pace the floor – moving restlessly between the wide french windows and the huge ormolu Louis Quatorze desk, watching the silent telephone. He was undecided, should he go back to CID headquarters in case she called there again, but what if she came through here? Should he ring the sergeant – but that would block the line.

'Come on!' he pleaded. 'Come on!' He glanced at his wristwatch – thirty-five minutes he had wasted in indecision.

'I'll have to pack it up. Can't stand here all day.'

He went to the desk. He reached for the instrument, but before he could touch it, it rang. He hadn't been ready for it, the sound raked his nerves shrilly, and he snatched it up.

'Squadron Leader Courtney,' he spoke in Afrikaans. 'Is that you, *Mevrou?*'

'I forgot the number – I had to go back to the house to fetch it,' she said. Her voice was rough with exertion, she had been running. 'I couldn't call before – there were people, my husband—' she broke off. She had said too much.

'That is all right. Don't worry, everything is all right.'

'No,' she said. 'It's terrible what they are going to do. It's just terrible.'

'Do you want to tell me?'

'They are going to kill the field-marshal—'

'The field-marshal?'

'The *Ou Baas* – Field-Marshal Smuts.'

He could not speak for a moment, and then he rallied. 'Do you know when they plan to do it?'

'Today. They will shoot him today.'

'That's not possible—' he did not want to believe it. 'The *Ou Baas* has gone up Table Mountain today. He's on a picnic with—'

'Yes! Yes!' The woman was sobbing. 'On the mountain. White Sword is waiting for him on the mountain.'

'Oh my God!' Shasa whispered. He felt as though he were paralysed. His legs were filled with concrete and a great weight crushed his lungs so that for a moment he could not breathe.

'You are a brave woman,' he said. 'Thank you for what you have done.'

He dropped the telephone onto its cradle and snatched open the drawer of Centaine's desk. The gold-engraved Beretta pistols were in their presentation case. He lifted one of them out of its nest of green baize and checked the load. There were six in the magazine and an extra magazine in a separate slot in the case. He thrust the pistol into his belt and the magazine into his pocket and turned for the door.

The pistol was useless at anything farther than point-blank range, but the hunting rifles were locked in the cabinet in the gunroom, the ammunition was kept separately, his key was in the Jag – it would take precious minutes to fetch it, open the cabinet, unchain his 9.3 Mannlicher, find the ammunition – he could not afford the time. The picnic party had a start of nearly forty minutes on him. They might be halfway up the mountain by now. All the people he loved were there – and an assassin was waiting for them.

He sprinted down the steps and sprang into the open cockpit of the Jag. She started with a roar; he spun her in a tight circle, gravel spraying from under the back tyres, and went down the long drive with the needle climbing quickly to the eighty mph notch. He went out through the Anreith gates, and into the narrow curves and dips as the road skirted the base of the mountain. More than once he nearly ran out of road as the Jag snarled and screeched through the turns, but it was fully fifteen minutes before he snaked her in through the gates of Kirstenbosch Botanical Gardens and at last pulled into the parking area behind the curator's office. The other vehicles were there, parked in a straggling line, the Daimler and the Bentley and Deneys Reitz's Packard, but the parking area was deserted.

He took one quick look up at the mountain that towered 2000 feet above him. He could make out the path as it climbed out of the forest and zigzagged up the gut of Skeleton Gorge, passing the pimple of Breakfast Rock on the skyline and then crossing the rim onto the tableland.

There was a line of moving specks on the pathway, just emerging from the forest. The *Ou Baas* and Grandpater were setting their usual furious pace, proving to each other how fit they were, and as he shaded his eyes he recognized Mater's yellow dress, and Tara's turquoise skirt, just tiny flecks of colour against the grey and green wall of the mountain. They were trailing far behind the leaders.

He began to run. He took the first easy slope at a trot, pacing himself. He reached the 300-metre contour path and paused beside the concrete signpost to draw a few long breaths. He surveyed the track ahead.

It went up very steeply from here, jigging through the forest, following the bank of the stream, a series of uneven rocky steps. He went at it fast, but his town shoes had thin leather soles and gave him little purchase. He was panting wildly and his shirt was soaked through with sweat as he came out of the forest. Still almost 1000 feet to the top, but he saw immediately that he had gained on the picnic party.

They were strung out down the pathway. The two figures leading were Grandpater and the *Ou Baas* – at this distance it was impossible to distinguish between them, but that was Blaine a few paces behind them. He would be hanging back so as not to force the older men to a pace beyond their strength. The rest of the party were in groups and singles, taking up half the slope, with the women far in the rear.

He drew a deep breath and shouted. The women paused and looked back down the slope.

'Stop!' he yelled with all his lung power. 'Stop!'

One of the women waved – it was probably Matty – then they began to climb again. They had not recognized him, nor had they understood the command to stop. They had taken him for another friendly hiker. He was wasting time, the leaders were just under the crest of the summit.

Shasa began to climb with all his strength, leaping over the uneven footing, forcing himself to ignore the burning of his lungs and the numbing exhaustion of his legs, driving himself upwards by sheer force of will.

Tara looked back when he was only ten feet below her.

'Shasa!' she cried, delighted but surprised. 'What are you doing – ?'

He brushed past her. 'Can't stop,' he grunted, and went on up, passing Anna and then Mater.

'What is it, Shasa?'

'Later!' There was no wind for words, his whole existence was in his agonized legs, and the sweat poured into his eye, blurring his vision.

He saw the leaders make the last short traverse before going over the top, and he stopped and tried to shout again. It came out as an agonized wheeze, and as he watched Grandpater and the *Ou Baas* disappeared over the crest of the slope with Blaine only twenty paces behind them.

The shot was dulled by distance, but even so Shasa recognized the sharp distinctive crack of a Mauser.

From somewhere he found new strength and he flew at the slope, leaping from rock to rock. The single shot seemed to echo and re-echo through his head, and he heard somebody shouting, or perhaps it was only the wild sobbing of his breath and the thunder of his blood in his own eardrums.

Manfred De La Rey lay all that night in his hide. At sunrise he stood up and swung his arms, squatted and twisted to loosen his muscles and banish the chill that had soaked through the overcoat into his bones. He moved a few paces back and emptied his bladder.

Then he stripped off the overcoat and the jersey – both had been bought from a second-hand clothes dealer on the Parade. They were unmarked and could never be traced to him. He bundled them and stuffed them under a rock. Then he settled back in his hide, stretched out on the tarpaulin. A few blades of grass were obscuring his line of fire and he broke them off and aimed at the head of the path.

His aim was clear and uninterrupted. He worked a cartridge from the magazine into the breech of the Mauser, checking it visually as it slid home, and he locked the bolt down.

Once more he took his aim, and this time he curled his finger round the rear trigger and carefully set the hair trigger with that crisp satisfying little click. Then he pushed the safety-catch over with his thumb and laid the rifle on the tarpaulin in front of him.

He froze into immobility. Patient as a leopard in a tree above a water-hole, only his yellow eyes alive, he let the hours drift by, never for an instant relaxing his vigil.

When it happened, it happened with the abruptness that might have taken another watcher by surprise. There was no warning, no sound of footsteps or voices. The range was too long for that. Suddenly a human figure appeared on the head of the path, silhouetted against the blue of the sky.

Manfred was ready for it. He lifted the rifle to his shoulder with a single fluid movement and his eye went naturally to the aperture of the lens. He did not have to pan the telescopic sight, the image of the man appeared instantly in his field of vision, enlarged and crisply focused.

It was an old man, with thin and narrow shoulders, wearing an open-neck white shirt and a Panama hat that was yellow with age. His silver goatee beard sparkled in the bright spring sunshine. The unwavering cross hairs of the telescope were already perfectly aligned on the exact centre of his narrow chest, a hand's breadth below the vee of his open shirt. No fancy head shot, Manfred had decided, take him through the heart.

He touched the hair trigger and the Mauser clapped in his eardrums, and the butt drove back into his shoulder.

He saw the bullet strike. It flapped the loose white shirt against the skinny old chest and Manfred's vision was so heightened that he even saw the bullet exit. It flew out of the old man's back on a long pink tail of blood and living tissue like a flamingo's feather, and as the frail body was plucked out of sight into the grass, the cloud of blood persisted, hanging in the clear morning air for the thousandth part of a second before it settled.

Manfred rolled to his feet and started to run. He had

plotted every yard of his escape route back to the Morris, and a savage elation gave strength to his legs and speed to his feet.

Behind him somebody shouted, a plaintive bewildered sound, but Manfred did not check or look back.

S hasa came over the crest at a full run. The two men were kneeling beside the body that lay in the grass at the side of the track. They looked up at Shasa, both their faces stricken.

Shasa took one look at the body as it lay face down. The bullet must have been a dum-dum to inflict such a massive exit wound. It had carved a hole through the chest cavity into which he could have thrust both his fists.

There was no hope. He was dead. He hardened himself. There would be time for grief later. Now was the time for vengeance.

'Did you see who did it?' he gasped.

'Yes.' Blaine jumped to his feet. 'I got a glimpse of him. He cut back around Oudekraal Kop,' he said, 'dressed in blue.'

Shasa knew this side of the mountain intimately, every path and cliff, every gorge and gully between Constantia Nek and the Saddle.

The killer had turned around the foot of the kop – he had a start of less than two minutes.

'The bridle path,' Shasa gasped. 'He is heading for the bridle path. I'll try and cut him off at the top of Nursery Ravine.' He started to run again, back towards Breakfast Rock.

'Shasa, be careful!' Blaine yelled after him. 'He has the rifle with him – I saw it.'

The bridle path was the only way a vehicle could reach the tableland, Shasa reasoned as he ran, and this had been so carefully planned that the killer must have an escape vehicle. It had to be parked somewhere on the bridle path.

The footpath made a wide loop around Oudekraal Kop, then came back to the edge and ran along the cliff top past the head of Nursery Ravine until it intersected the bridle path half a mile farther on. There was another rough, little-used path that cut this side of the Kop, along the cliff top. The beginning was difficult to find and a mistake would lead into a dead end against the precipice – but if he found it he could cut a quarter of a mile off the route.

He found the path and turned off onto it. At two places the track was overgrown and he had to struggle through interlaced branches, at another spot at the edge the track had washed away. He had to back up and take a run at it, jumping over the gap with five hundred feet of open drop below him. He landed on his knees, clawed himself to his feet and kept running.

He burst out unexpectedly into the main footpath and collided at full tilt with the blue-overalled killer coming in the opposite direction.

He had a fleeting impression of the man's size and the breadth of his shoulders, and then they were down together, locked chest to chest, grappling savagely, rolling down the slope of the path. The impact had knocked the rifle out of the killer's hand, but Shasa felt the springy hardness and the bulk of his muscle, and the first evidence of the man's strength shocked him. He knew instantly that he was outmatched. Against his fiercest resistance the man rolled him onto his back and came up on top of him, straddling him.

Their faces were inches apart. The man had a thick dark curling beard that was sodden with sweat, his nose was twisted and his brows were dense and black, but it was the eyes that struck terror into Shasa. They were yellow and somehow dreadfully familiar. However, they galvanized Shasa, transforming his terror into superhuman strength.

He wrenched one arm free and rolled the killer over far enough to yank the Beretta pistol from his own belt. He had not loaded a cartridge into the chamber, but he struck upwards with the short barrel, smashing it into the man's temple, and he heard the steel crack on the bone of the skull.

The man's grip slackened and he fell back. Shasa wriggled to his knees, fumbling to load the Beretta. With a metallic snicker the slide pushed a cartridge into the chamber, and he lifted the barrel. He had not realized how close they had rolled to the clifftop. He was kneeling on the very brink, and as he tried to steady his aim on that bearded head, the killer jack-knifed his body and drove both feet into Shasa's chest.

Shasa was hurled backwards. The pistol fired but the shot went straight into the air, and he found himself falling free as he went over the edge of the cliff. He had a glimpse down the precipice; there was open drop for hundreds of feet, but he fell less than ten of those before he wedged behind a pine sapling that had found a foothold in a cleft of the rock.

He hung against the cliff face, his legs dangling free, winded and dazed, and he looked up. The killer's head appeared over the edge of the cliff, those strange yellow eyes glared at him for an instant and then disappeared. Shasa heard his boots scrabble on the pathway, and then the unmistakable sound of a rifle bolt being loaded and cocked.

'He is going to finish me off,' he thought, and only then realized that he still had the Beretta in his right hand.

Desperately he hooked his left elbow over the pine sapling and pointed the Beretta up at the rim of the cliff above his head.

Once more the killer's head and shoulders appeared against the sky, and he was swinging the long barrel of the Mauser downwards; but the weapon was awkward to point at this angle and Shasa fired an instant before it could bear. He heard the light bullet of the pistol strike against flesh, and the killer grunted and disappeared from view. A moment afterwards he heard someone else shout from a distance, and recognized Blaine's voice.

Then the killer's running footsteps moved swiftly away as he set off along the path once more, and a minute later Blaine looked down at Shasa from the clifftop.

'Hold on!' Blaine's face was flushed with exertion and his voice unsteady. He pulled the thick leather belt from his trouser top and buckled it into a loop.

Lying flat on his belly at the top of the cliff, he lowered the looped belt and Shasa hooked his arm through it. Even though Blaine was a powerful man with abnormal arm and chest development from polo practice, they struggled for minutes before he could drag Shasa over the top of the cliff.

They lay together for a few moments; and then Shasa pulled himself unsteadily to his feet and staggered off along the pathway in pursuit of the fugitive. Within a dozen paces Blaine pulled ahead of him, running strongly and his example spurred Shasa. He kept up, and Blaine gasped over his shoulder.

'Blood!' He pointed to the wet red speckles on a flat stone in the pathway. 'You hit him!'

They came out onto the wide bridle path, and started down, running shoulder to shoulder now, helped by the gradient of the descent, but they had not reached the first hairpin bend when they heard an engine start in the forest below.

'He's got a car!' Blaine panted as the engine whined into a crescendo, then the sound of it receded swiftly. They pulled up and listened to it dwindle into silence. Shasa's legs could hold him up no longer. He sank into a heap in the middle of the road.

There was a telephone at the Cecilia Forestry Station

and Shasa got through to Inspector Nel at CID head-quarters and gave him a description of the killer.

'You'll have to move fast. The man has obviously got his escape planned.'

The mountain club kept a lightweight stretcher at the forestry station, for this mountain took many human lives each year. The forester gave them six of his black labourers to carry it, and accompanied them back up the bridle path and along the mountain rim to the head of Skeleton Gorge.

The women were there. Centaine and Anna were in tears, clinging to each other for comfort. They had spread one of the rugs over the dead man.

Shasa knelt beside the body and lifted the corner of the rug. In death Sir Garry Courtney's features had fallen in, so that his nose was arched and beaky, his closed eyelids were in deep cavities, but there was about him a gentle dignity so that he resembled the death mask of a fragile Caesar.

Shasa kissed his forehead and the skin was cool and velvety smooth against his lips.

When he stood up, Field-Marshal Smuts laid a hand of comfort on his shoulder. 'I'm sorry, my boy,' the old field-marshal said. 'That bullet was meant for me.'

Manfred De La Rey pulled off the road, steering with one hand. He did not leave the driver's seat of the Morris, and he kept the engine running while he unbuttoned the front of his overalls.

The bullet had entered just below and in front of his armpit, punching into the thick pad of the pectoral muscle and it had angled upwards. He could find no exit wound, the bullet was still lodged in his body, and when he groped gently around the back of his own shoulder, he found a swelling that was so tender that he almost screamed involuntarily as he touched it.

The bullet was lying just under the skin, but it did not appear to have penetrated the chest cavity. He wadded his handkerchief over the wound in his armpit and buttoned the overalls. He checked his watch. It was a few minutes before eleven o'clock, just twenty-three minutes since he had fired the shot that would set his people free.

A sense of passionate soaring triumph overrode the pain of his wound. He pulled back onto the road and drove sedately around the base of the mountain, down the main road through Woodstock. At the gates of the railway yards he showed his pass to the gatekeeper and went through to park the Morris outside the restrooms for off-duty firemen and engine drivers.

He left the Mauser under the seat of the Morris. Both the weapon and the vehicle would be taken care of. He crossed quickly to the back door of the restroom and they were waiting for him inside.

Roelf leapt to his feet anxiously as he saw the blood on the blue overalls.

'Are you all right? What happened?'

'Smuts is dead,' Manfred said, and his savage joy was transmitted to them. They did not cheer or speak, but stood quietly, savouring the moment on which history would hinge.

Roelf broke the silence after a few seconds. 'You are hurt.'

While one of the *stormjagters* went out and drove the Morris away, Roelf helped Manfred strip off his soiled overalls. There was very little blood now, but the flesh around the wound was swollen and bruised. The bullet-hole itself was a black puncture that wept watery pink lymph. Roelf dressed and bound it up with bandages from a railway first-aid kit.

Because Manfred had very little use of his left arm, Roelf lathered the black beard and shaved it off with a straight

828

razor for him. With the beard gone Manfred was years younger, handsome and clean-cut once again, but pale from loss of blood and the weakness of his wound. They helped him into a clean pair of overalls and Roelf set the fireman's cap on his head.

'We will meet again soon,' Roelf told him. 'And I am proud to be your friend. From now on glory will follow you all the days of your life.'

The engine driver came forward. 'We must go,' he said. Roelf and Manfred shook hands and then Manfred turned away and followed the driver out of the restroom and down the platform to the waiting locomotive.

The police stopped the northbound goods train at Worcester Station. They opened and searched all the trucks and a constable climbed into the cab of the locomotive and searched that also.

'What is the trouble?' the engine driver demanded.

'There has been a murder. Some bigwig was shot on Table Mountain this morning. We've got a description of the killer. There are police roadblocks on all the roads and we are searching every motor vehicle and ship and train—'

'Who was killed?' Manfred asked, and the constable shrugged.

'I don't know, my friend, but judging by the fuss it's somebody important.' He climbed down from the cab, and a few mintues later the signals changed to green and they rolled out of the station heading north.

By the time they reached Bloemfontein, Manfred's shoulder had swollen into a hard purple hump and the pain was insupportable. He sat hunched in a corner of the cab, moaning softly, teetering on the brink of consciousness, the rustle of dark wings filling his head.

Roelf had telephoned ahead, and there were friends to meet him and smuggle him out of the Bloemfontein railway yards.

'Where are we going?'

'A doctor,' they told him, and reality broke up into a patchwork of darkness and pain.

He was aware of the choking reek of chloroform, and when he woke he was in a bed in a sunny but monastically furnished room. The shoulder was bound up in crisp white bandages, and despite the lingering nausea of the anaesthetic, he felt whole again.

There was a man sitting in the chair beside the window, and as soon as he realized Manfred was awake, he came to him.

'How do you feel?'

'Not too bad. Has it happened – the rising? Have our people seized power?'

The man looked at him strangely. 'You do not know?' he asked.

'I only know that we have succeeded—' Manfred began, but the man fetched a newspaper and laid it on the bed. He stood beside Manfred as he read the headlines:

ASSASSINATION ON TABLE MOUNTAIN
OB BLAMED FOR KILLING OF PROMINENT
    HISTORIAN
SMUTS ORDERS ARREST AND
    INTERNMENT OF 600

Manfred stared uncomprehendingly at the news-sheet, and the man told him, 'You killed the wrong man. Smuts has the excuse he wanted. All our leaders have been seized, and they are searching for you. There is a manhunt across the land. You cannot stay here. We expect the police to be here at any minute.'

Manfred was passed on and he left the city riding in the back of a truck under a load of stinking dry hides. The *Ossewa Brandwag* had been decimated by the arrests, and those members remaining at liberty were shaken and afraid, all of them running for cover. None of them wanted to take the risk of harbouring the fugitive. He was passed on again and again.

The plan had seen no further ahead than the assassination and successful revolt, after which Manfred would have emerged as a *Volk* hero and taken his rightful place in the councils of the republican government. Now it was run and hide, sick and weak, a price of five thousand pounds on his head. Nobody wanted him; he was a dangerous risk and they passed him on as quickly as they could find someone else to take him.

In the published lists of those arrested and interned in the government crackdown, he found many names he knew, and with dismay he read Roelf's name, and that of the Reverend Tromp Bierman amongst them. He wondered how Sarah, Aunt Trudi and the girls would fare now, but he found it difficult to think or concentrate, for despair had unmanned him, and he knew the terror of a hunted and wounded animal.

It took eight days to make the journey to Johannesburg. He had not deliberately set out for the Witwatersrand, but circumstances and the whim of his helpers led him that way. By rail and truck and, later, when the wound began to heal and his strength returned, at night and on foot across the open veld, he at last reached the city.

He had an address, his last contact with the brotherhood and he took the tramcar from the main railway station along the Braamfontein ridge and watched the street numbers as they passed.

The number he needed was 36. It was one in a row of semi-detached cottages, and he started to rise to leave the tramcar at the next stop. Then he saw the blue police uniform in the doorway of number 36 and he sank down in his seat again and rode the tramcar to its terminus.

He left it there and went into a Greek café across the road. He ordered a cup of coffee, paying for it with his last few coins, and sipped it slowly, hunched over the cup, trying to think.

He had avoided a dozen police roadblocks and searches in these last eight days, but he sensed that he had exhausted his luck. There was no hiding-place open to him any longer. The road led from here on to the gallows.

He stared out of the greasy plate-glass window of the café and the street sign across the road caught his eye. Something stirred in his memory, but it eluded his first efforts to grasp it. Then suddenly he felt the lift of his spirits and another weak glimmer of hope.

He left the café and followed the road whose name he had recognized. The area deteriorated quickly into a slum of shanties and hovels and he saw no more white faces on the rutted unmade street. The black faces at the windows or in the reeking alleyways watched him impassively across that unfathomable void which separates the races in Africa.

He found what he was looking for. It was a small general dealer's store crowded with black shoppers, noisy and laughing, the women with their babies strapped upon their backs, bargaining across the counter for sugar and soap, paraffin and salt, but the hubbub descended into silence when a white man entered the shop, and they gave way for him respectfully, not looking directly at him.

The proprietor was an elderly Zulu with a fluffy beard of white wool, dressed in a baggy Western-style suit. He left the black woman he was serving and came to Manfred, inclining his head deferentially to listen to Manfred's request.

'Come with me, *Nkosi*.' He led Manfred through to the storeroom at the back of the shop.

'You will have to wait,' he said, 'perhaps a long time,' and he left him there.

Manfred slumped down on a pile of sugar sacks. He was hungry and exhausted and the shoulder was starting to throb again. He fell asleep and was roused by a hand on his shoulder and a deep voice in his ear.

'How did you know where to look for me?'

Manfred struggled to his feet. 'My father told me where to find you,' he answered. 'Hello, Swart Hendrick.'

'It has been many years, little Manie.' The big Ovambo grinned at him through the black gap of missing teeth; his head, laced with scars, was black and shiny as a cannonball. 'Many years, but I never doubted we would meet again. Never once in all those years. The gods of the wilderness have bound us together, little Manie. I knew you would come.'

The two men sat alone in the back room of Swart Hendrick's house. It was one of the few brick-built dwellings in the shanty town of Drake's Farm. However, the bricks were unbaked and the building was not so ostentatious as to stand out from the hovels that crowded close around it. Swart Hendrick had long ago learned not to draw the attention of the white police to his wealth.

In the front room the women were cooking and working, while the children bawled or shouted with laughter round their feet. As befitted his station in life, Swart Hendrick had six town wives who lived together in an amiable symbiotic relationship. The possessive jealousy of monogamistic Western women was totally alien to them. Senior wives took a major part in the selection of the junior wives and gained considerable prestige from their multiplicity, nor did they resent the maintenance sent to the country wives and their offspring or their spouse's periodic visits to the country kraal to add to the number of those offspring. They considered themselves all part of one family. When the children from the country were old enough to be sent into the city for the furtherance of their education and fortune, they found themselves with many fostermothers and could expect the same love and discipline as they had received in the kraal.

The smaller children had the run of the house and one of them crawled mother-naked into Swart Hendrick's lap as he sat on his carved stool, the sign of rank of a tribal chieftain. Although he was deep in discussion with Manfred, he fondled the little one casually, as he would a favourite puppy, and when the beer pot was empty, he clapped his hands and one of the junior wives, the pretty moon-faced Zulu or the nubile Basuto with breasts as round and hard as ostrich eggs, would bring in a new pot and kneel before Hendrick to present it to him.

'So, little Manie, we have spoken of everything, and said all that is to be said, and we come back to the same problem.' Swart Hendrick lifted the beer pot and swallowed a mouthful of the thick white bubbling gruel. He smacked his lips, then wiped the half moon of beer from his upper lip with the back of his forearm and handed the pot across to Manfred. 'That problem is this. At every railway station and on every road the white police are searching for you. They have even offered a price for you – and what a price, little Manie. They will give five thousand pounds for you. How many cattle and women could a man buy with that amount of money?' He broke off to consider the question and shook his head in wonder at the answer. 'You ask me to help you to leave Johannesburg and to cross the great river in the north. What would the white police do if they caught me? Would they hang me on the same tree as they hang you – or would they only send me to break rocks in the prison of *Ou Baas* Smuts and King Georgy?' Swart Hendrick sighed theatrically. 'It is a heavy question, little Manie. Can you give me an answer?'

'You have been as a father to me, Hennie,' Manfred said

quietly. 'Does a father leave his son for the hyena and the vultures?'

'If I am your father, little Manie, why then is your face white and mine black?' Hendrick smiled. 'There are no debts between us, they were all paid long ago.'

'My father and you were brothers.'

'How many summers have burned since those days,' Hendrick mourned the passage of time with a sorrowful shake of his head. 'And how the world and all those in it have changed.'

'There is one thing that never changes – not even over the years, Hennie.'

'What is that, oh child with a white face who claims my paternity?'

'A diamond, my black father. A diamond never changes.'

Hendrick nodded. 'Let us speak then of a diamond.'

'Not one diamond,' Manfred said. 'Many diamonds, a bagful of diamonds that lie in a faraway place that only you and I know of.'

'T'he risks are great,' Hendrick told his brother. 'And doubt lurks in my mind like a man-eating lion lying in thick bush. Perhaps the diamonds are where the white boy says they are, but the lion of doubt still waits for me. The father was a devious man, hard and without mercy – I sense that the son has grown to be like the father. He speaks of friendship between us, but I no longer feel the warmth in him.'

Moses Gama stared into the fire; his eyes were dark and inscrutable. 'He tried to kill Smuts,' he mused aloud. 'He is of the hard Boers like those of old, the ones that slaughtered our people at Blood river and shattered the power of the great chiefs. They have been defeated this time, as they were in 1914, but they have not been destroyed. They will rise to fight again, these hard Boers, when this white men's war across the sea ends, they will call out their impis and carry the battle to Smuts and his party once again. It is the way of the white man – and I have studied his history – that when peace comes, they often reject those who fought hardest during the battle. I sense that in the next conflict the whites will reject Smuts and that the hard Boers will triumph – and this white boy is one of them.'

'You are right, my brother,' Hendrick nodded. 'I had not looked that far into the future. He is the enemy of our people. If he and his kind come to power then we will learn a bitter lesson in slavery. I must deliver him to the vengeance of those who seek after him.'

Moses Gama raised his noble head and looked across the fire at his elder brother.

'It is the weakness of the multitudes that they cannot see the horizon – their gaze is fixed only as far ahead as their bellies or their genitals,' Moses said. 'You have admitted to that weakness – why, my brother, do you not seek to rise above it? Why do you not raise your eyes and look to the future?'

'I do not understand.'

'The greatest danger to our people is their own patience and passivity. We are a great herd of cattle under the hand of a cunning herdsman. He keeps us quiescent with a paternal despotism, and most of us, knowing no better, are lulled into an acceptance which we mistake for content-ment. Yet the herdsman milks us and at his pleasure eats of our flesh. He is our enemy, for the slavery in which he holds us is so insidious that it's impossible to goad the herd to rebel against it.'

'If he is our enemy, what of these others that you call the hard Boers?' Hendrick was perplexed. 'Are they not a fiercer enemy?'

'Upon them will depend the ultimate freedom of our

people. They are men without subtlety and artifice. Not for them the smile and kind word that disguises the brutal act. They are angry men filled with fear and hatred. They hate the Indians and the Jews, they hate the English, but most of all they hate and fear the black tribes, for we are many and they are few. They hate and fear us because they have what is rightly ours, and they will not be able to conceal their hatred. When they come to power, they will teach our people the true meaning of slavery. By their oppressions, they will transform the tribes from a herd of complacent cattle into a great stampede of enraged wild buffalo before whose strength nothing can stand. We must pray for this white boy of yours and all he stands for. The future of our people depends upon him.'

Hendrick sat for a long time staring into the fire, and then slowly raised his great bald head and looked at his brother with awe.

'I sometimes think, son of my father, that you are the wisest man of all our tribe,' he whispered.

Swart Hendrick sent for a *sangoma*, a tribal medicine man. He made a poultice for Manfred's shoulder that when applied, hot and evil-smelling, proved highly efficacious and within ten days Manfred was fit to travel again.

The same *sangoma* provided a herbal dye for Manfred's skin which darkened it to the exact hue of one of the northern tribes. The eyes, Manfred's yellow eyes, were not a serious handicap. Amongst the black mine workers who had worked out their Wenela contract and were returning home, there were certain symbols which confirmed their status as sophisticated men of the world, tin trunks to hold the treasures they had acquired, the pink post office savings books filled with the little numbers of their accumulated wealth, the silver metal mine helmets which they were allowed to retain and which would be worn with pride everywhere from the peaks of Basutoland to the equatorial forests, and lastly a pair of sunglasses.

Manfred's travel papers were issued by one of Hendrick's Buffaloes, a clerk in the pay office of ERPM, and they were totally authentic. He wore his dark sunglasses when he boarded the Wenela train and his skin was dyed the same hue as the black workers who surrounded him closely. All these men were Hendrick's Buffaloes, and they kept him protected in their midst.

He found it strange but reassuring that the few white officials that he encountered on the long slow journey back to South West Africa, seldom looked at him directly. Because he was black, their gaze seemed to slide by his face without touching it.

Manfred and Hendrick left the train at Okahandja and with a group of other workers climbed onto the bus for the final hot dusty miles to Hendrick's kraal. Two days later they set out again, this time on foot, heading north and east into the burning wilderness.

There had been good rains during the previous season and they found water in many of the pans in the southern Kavango and it was two weeks before they saw the kopjes humped like a caravan of camels out of the blue heat haze along the desert horizon.

Manfred realized as they tramped towards the hills how alien he was in this desert. Hendrick and his father had belonged here, but since childhood Manfred had lived in towns and cities. He would never have been able to find his way back without Hendrick's guidance; indeed he would not have survived more than a few days in this harsh and unforgiving land without the big Ovambo.

The kopje that Hendrick led Manfred towards seemed identical to all the others. It was only when they scaled the steep granite side and stood upon the summit, that the memories came crowding back. Perhaps they had been deliberately suppressed, but now they emerged again in stark detail. Manfred could almost see his father's features ravaged by fever and smell again the stench of gangrene from his rotting flesh. He remembered with fresh agony the harsh words of rejection with which his father had driven him to safety, but he closed his mind to the ache of them.

Unerringly he went to the crack that split the granite dome and knelt over it, but his heart sank when he peered down and could distinguish nothing in the deep shadows that contrasted with the sunlight and its reflection from the rock around him.

'So they have gone, these famous diamonds,' Hendrick chuckled cynically when he saw Manfred's dismay. 'Perhaps the jackals have eaten them.'

Manfred ignored him and from his pack brought out a roll of fishing-line. He tied the lead sinker and the stout treble fish hook to the end and lowered it into the crack. Patiently he worked, jigging the hook along the depth of the crack while Hendrick squatted in the small strip of shade under the summit boulders and watched him without offering encouragement.

The hook snagged something deep in the crack, and cautiously Manfred applied pressure on the line. It held and he took a twist around his wrist and pulled upwards with gradually increasing strength. Something gave, and then the hook pulled free. He drew the line in hand over hand. One point of the treble hook had opened under the strain, but there was a shred of rotted canvas still attached to the barb.

He bent the tine of the hook back into shape and lowered it once again into the crack. He plumbed the depths, working each inch from side to side and up and down. Another half hour of work and he felt the hook snag again.

This time the weight stayed on it, and he eased the line

in, an inch at a time. He heard something scraping on the rough granite, then slowly a shapeless lumpy bundle came into view deep down. He lifted it slowly, holding his breath as it came up the last few feet. Then as he swung it clear, the canvas of the old rucksack burst open and a cascade of glittering white stones spilled onto the granite top around him.

They divided the diamonds into two equal piles as they had agreed, and drew lots for the first choice. Hendrick won and made his selection. Manfred poured his share into the empty tobacco pouch he had brought for the purpose.

'You told the truth, little Manie,' Hendrick admitted. 'I was wrong to doubt you.'

The following evening they reached the river and slept side by side beside the fire. In the morning they rolled their blankets and faced each other.

'Goodbye, Hennie. Perhaps the road will bring us together again.'

'I have told you, little Manie, that the gods of the wilderness have linked us together. We will meet again, that I am certain of.'

'I look forward to that day.'

'The gods alone will decide whether we meet again as father and son, as brothers – or as deadly enemies,' Hendrick said and slung his pack over his shoulder. Without looking back he walked away into the southern desert.

Manfred watched him out of sight, then he turned and followed the bank of the river into the north-west. That evening he came upon a village of the river people. Two of the young men in their dugout canoe ferried him across to the Portuguese side. Three weeks later Manfred reached Luanda, capital of the Portuguese colony, and rang the bell on the wrought-iron gates of the German consulate.

He waited in Luanda three weeks for orders from the German *Abwehr* in Berlin, and slowly it dawned upon him that the delay was deliberate. He had failed in the task they had set him, and in Nazi Germany failure was unforgivable.

He sold one of the smallest diamonds from his hoard at a fraction of its real value and waited out his punishment. Each morning he called at the German consulate and the military attaché turned him away with barely concealed contempt.

'No orders yet, Herr De La Rey. You must be patient.'

Manfred spent most of his days in one of the water-front cafés and his nights in his cheap lodgings, endlessly going over each detail of his failure, or thinking about Uncle Tromp and Roelf in the concentration camp, or about Heidi and the child in Berlin.

His orders came at last. He was issued a German diplomatic passport and he sailed on a Portuguese freighter as far as the Canary Islands. From there he flew on a civilian Junkers aircraft with Spanish markings to Lisbon.

In Lisbon he encountered the same deliberate contempt. He was dismissed casually to find his own lodgings and await those orders which seemed never to come. He wrote personal letters to Colonel Sigmund Boldt and to Heidi. Although the consulate attaché assured him that these had gone out in the diplomatic bag to Berlin, he received no reply.

He sold another small diamond and rented pleasant spacious lodgings in an old building on the bank of the Tagus river, passing the long idle days in reading, study and writing. He began work on two literary projects simultaneously, a political history of southern Africa and an autobiography, both for his own edification and with no intention of ever publishing. He learned Portuguese, taking lessons from a retired schoolmaster who lived in the same building. He kept up a rigorous physical training schedule, as though he were still boxing professionally, and he came to know all the secondhand book stores of the city where he purchased every law book he could find and read them in German, English and Portuguese. But still the time hung heavily on his hands and he chafed at his inability to take part in the conflict that raged around the globe.

The conflict swung against the Axis powers. The United States of America had entered the war and Flying Fortresses were bombing the cities of Germany. Manfred read of the terrible conflagration that had destroyed Cologne and he wrote again to Heidi for perhaps the hundredth time since he had arrived in Portugal.

Three weeks later, on one of his regular calls at the German consulate, the military attaché handed him an envelope and with a surge of joy he recognized Heidi's handwriting upon it. It told him that she had received none of his previous letters and had come to believe that he was dead. She expressed her wonder and thankfulness at his survival and sent him a snapshot of herself and little Lothar. In the photograph he saw that she had put on a little weight, but in a stately manner she was even more handsome than when last he had seen her – and in a little over three years his son had grown into a sturdy youngster with a head of blond curls and features that showed promise of strength as well as beauty. The photograph was black and white and did not show the colour of his eyes. Manfred's longing for them both threatened to consume him. He wrote Heidi a long passionate letter explaining his circumstances and urging her to make all possible efforts to procure a travel pass and to join him with the child in Lisbon. Without being specific, he was able to let her know that he was financially able to take care of them, and that he had plans for a future that included them both.

Heidi De La Rey lay awake and listened to the bombers. They had come on three successive nights. The centre of the city was devastated, the opera house and the railway station totally destroyed, and from the information which she had access to in the Department of Propaganda, she knew of the Allied successes in France and Russia, she knew the truth of the hundred thousand German troops captured by the Russians at Minsk.

Beside her Colonel Sigmund Boldt slept restlessly, rolling over and grunting so she was even more disturbed by him than by the distant American bombers. He had reason to worry, she thought. All of them were worried since the abortive attempt to assassinate the Führer. She had seen the films of the execution of the traitors, every minute detail of their agony as they hung on the meat hooks, and General Zoller had been one of them.

Sigmund Boldt had not been one of the conspirators, she was certain of that, but he was close enough to the plot to be caught up in the tidal wave that flowed from it. Heidi had been his mistress for almost a year now, but she had begun to notice the first signs of his waning interest in her, and she knew that his days of influence and power were numbered. Soon she would be alone again, without special food rations for herself and little Lothar.

She listened to the bombers. The raid was over, and the sound of their motors dwindled away to a mosquito hum, but they would be back. In the silence after their departure, she thought about Manfred and the letters he had written to which she had never replied. He was in Lisbon, and in Portugal there were no bombers.

She spoke to Sigmund the next day at breakfast. 'It is only little Lothar I am thinking of,' she explained, and she thought she saw a glimmer of relief in his expression. Perhaps he had already been calculating how he could be rid of her without a fuss. That afternoon she wrote to

Manfred, care of the German consulate in Lisbon, and she enclosed a photograph of herself and Lothar.

Colonel Sigmund Boldt moved quickly. He still had influence and power in the department sufficient for him to procure her travel pass and documents within a week, and he drove her out to Tempelhof airport in the black Mercedes and kissed her goodbye at the foot of the boarding ladder of the Junkers transport aircraft.

Three days later Sigmund Boldt was arrested in his home at Grünewald and a week later he died under interrogation in his cell at the Gestapo headquarters, still protesting his innocence.

L ittle Lothar De La Rey caught his first glimpse of Africa peering between the rails of the Portuguese freighter as it steamed into Table Bay. He stood between his father and mother, holding their hands and chuckling with delight at the steam tugs that came bustling out to welcome their ship.

The war had ended two years ago, but Manfred had taken extraordinary precautions before bringing his family to Africa. First he had written to Uncle Tromp who had been released from internment at the end of the war, and from him learned all the family and political news. Aunt Trudi was well and both the girls were married now. Roelf had been released at the same time as Uncle Tromp and had returned to his job at the university. He and Sarah were happy and well and expecting another addition to their family before the year's end.

Politically the news was promising. Although the *Ossewa Brandwag* and the other para-military organizations had been discredited and disbanded, their members had been absorbed into the National Party under Dr Daniel Malan, and the Party was rejuvenated and strengthened by their numbers. Afrikaner unity had never been more solid, and the dedication of the massive Voortrekker monument on a kopje above Pretoria had rallied the *Volk* so that even many of those who had joined Smuts' army and fought in North Africa and Italy were flocking to the cause.

A backlash was developing against Smuts and his United Party. The feeling was that he placed the interests of the British Commonwealth, which he had done so much to bring into being, before the interests of South Africa.

Furthermore, Smuts had made a political misjudgement by inviting the British Royal Family to visit the country, and their presence had served to polarize public feelings between the English-speaking jingoists and the Afrikaners. Even many of those who had been Smuts men were offended by the visit.

Doctor Hendrik Frensch Verwoerd who had left his teaching post at Stellenbosch University to become editor of *Die Vaderland* allowed only one reference to the royal visit in his newspaper. He warned his readers that there might be some disruption of traffic in Johannesburg owing to the presence of foreign visitors in the city.

On the occasion of the loyal address at the opening of the South African Parliament, Dr Daniel Malan and all his Nationalist members had absented themselves from the House in protest.

Uncle Tromp ended his letter, 'So we have come through the storm strengthened and purified as a *Volk*, and more determined than ever in our endeavours. There are great days ahead, Manie. Come home. We need men like you.'

Still Manfred did not move immediately. First he wrote to Uncle Tromp again. In veiled terms he asked what the position was with regard to a white sword he had left behind, and after a delay he received assurance that nobody knew anything about his sword. Discreet enquiries through friends in the police force had elicited the information that although the dossier on the missing sword was still open, it was no longer under active investigation and nobody knew its whereabouts or to whom it belonged. It must be assumed that it would never be found.

Leaving Heidi and the boy in Lisbon, Manfred travelled by train to Zürich where he sold the remainder of the diamonds. In the post-war euphoria prices were high, and he was able to deposit almost £200,000 in a numbered account with Crédit Suisse.

When they reached Cape Town the family went ashore without attracting attention, although as an Olympic gold medallist Manfred could have found himself the centre of a great deal of publicity if he had wished. Quietly he felt his way, visiting old friends, former OB members and political allies, making certain that there were no nasty surprises in store for him before he gave his first interview to the *Burger* newspaper. To them he explained how he had passed the war in neutral Portugal because he had declined to fight for either side, but now he had returned to the land of his birth to make whatever contribution he could to political progress towards what was every Afrikaner's dream, a Republic of South Africa, free from the dictates of any foreign power.

He had said all the right things, and he was an Olympic gold medallist in a land where athletic prowess was venerated. He was handsome and clever and devout, with an attractive wife and son. He still had friends in high places and the number of those friends was increasing each day.

He purchased a partnership in a prosperous Stellenbosch law firm. The senior partner was an attorney named Van Schoor, very active in politics and a luminary of the Nationalist Party. He sponsored Manfred's entry into the Party.

Manfred devoted himself to the affairs of Van Schoor and De La Rey and just as single-mindedly to those of the Cape Nationalist Party. He showed great skills as an organizer and as a fund-raiser, and by the end of 1947 he was a member of the *Broederbond*.

The *Broederbond*, or brotherhood, was another secret society of Afrikaners. It had not replaced the defunct *Ossewa Brandwag*, but had existed concurrently, and often in competition with it. Unlike the *OB* it was not flamboyant and overtly militant, there were no uniforms or torchlit rallies.

It worked quietly in small groups in the homes and offices of powerful and influential men for membership was only bestowed upon the brightest and the best. It considered its members to be an elite of super-Afrikaners, whose end object was the formation of an Afrikaner Republic. Like the disbanded *OB*, the secrecy surrounding it was iron-clad. Unlike the *OB*, a member must be much more than merely a pure-blooded Afrikaner. He must be a leader of men, or at the very least a potential leader, and an invitation to join the brotherhood held within it the promise of high political preference and favour in the future Republic.

Manfred's first rewards of membership came almost immediately, for when the campaign for the general election of 1948 opened, Manfred De La Rey was nominated as the official Nationalist candidate for the marginal seat of Hottentots Holland.

Two years previously, in a by-election, the seat had been won for Smuts' United Party by a young war-hero from a rich English-speaking Cape family. As the incumbent, Shasa Courtney had been nominated by the United Party as their candidate to contest the general election.

Manfred De La Rey had been offered a safer seat but he had deliberately chosen Hottentots Holland. He wanted the opportunity to meet Shasa Courtney again. He recalled vividly their first meeting on the fish jetty at Walvis Bay. Since then their destinies seemed to have been inextricably bound together in a knot of Gordian complexity, and Manfred sensed that he had to face this adversary one more time and unravel that knot.

To prepare himself for the campaign as well as to satisfy his brooding enmity towards them, Manfred began an investigation of the Courtney family, in particular Shasa and his mother Mrs Centaine de Thiry Courtney. Almost immediately he found areas of mystery in the woman's past, and these grew deeper as his investigations continued. Finally he was sufficiently encouraged to employ a Parisian firm of private investigators to examine in detail Centaine's family background and her origins.

On his regular monthly visit to his father in Pretoria Central Prison, he brought up the Courtney name and begged the frail old man to tell him everything he knew about them.

When the campaign opened, Manfred knew that his investigations had given him an important advantage, and he threw himself into the rough and tumble of a South African election with gusto and determination.

Centaine de Thiry Courtney stood on the top of Table Mountain, a little apart from the rest of the party. Since Sir Garry's murder the mountain always saddened her, even when she looked at it from the windows of her study at Weltevreden. This was the first time that she had been on the summit since that tragic day, and she was here only because she could not refuse Blaine's invitation to act as his official partner. 'And, of course, I am still enough of a snob to relish the idea of being introduced to the king and the queen of England!' She was truthful with herself.

The *Ou Baas* was chatting to King George, pointing out the landmarks with his cane. He was wearing his old

Panama hat and baggy slacks, and Centaine felt a pang at his resemblance to Sir Garry. She turned away.

Blaine was with the small group around the royal princesses. He was telling a story and Margaret Rose laughed delightedly. 'How pretty she is,' Centaine thought. 'What a complexion, a royal English rose.' The princess turned and said something to one of the other young men. Centaine had been introduced to him earlier; he was an airforce officer as Shasa was, a handsome fellow with a fine sensitive face, she thought, and then her female instincts were alerted as she caught the secret glance the couple exchanged. It was unmistakable, and Centaine felt that little lift of her spirits she always enjoyed when she saw two young people in love.

It was followed almost immediately by a return of her sombre mood. Thinking of love and young lovers, she studied Blaine. He was unaware of her gaze, relaxed and charming, but there was silver in his hair, shining silver wings above those sticky-out ears she loved so well, and there were deep creases in his tanned face, around the eyes and at the corners of his mouth and his big aquiline nose. Still his body was hard and flat-bellied from riding and walking, but he was like the old lion, and with a further slide of her spirits she faced the fact that he was no longer in his prime. Instead he stood at the threshold of old age.

'Oh, God,' she thought, 'even I will be forty-eight years old in a few months,' and she lifted her hand to touch her head. There was silver there also, but so artfully tinted that it seemed merely a bleaching of the African sun. There were other unpalatable truths that her mirror revealed to her in the privacy of her boudoir, before she hid them with the creams and powders and rouges.

'How much more time is there, my darling?' she asked sadly but silently. 'Yesterday we were young and immortal, but today I see at last that there is a term to all things.'

At that moment Blaine looked across at her, and she

saw his quick concern as he noticed her expression. He murmured an apology to the others and came to her side.

'Why so serious on such a lovely day?' he smiled.

'I was thinking how shameless you are, Blaine Malcomess,' she answered, and his smile slipped.

'What is it, Centaine?'

'How can you blatantly parade your mistress before the crowned heads of Empire,' she demanded. 'I have no doubt it is a capital crime, you could have your head struck off on Tower Green!'

He stared at her for a moment, and then the grin came back, boyish and jubilant. 'My dear lady, there must be some way I can escape that fate. What if I were to change your status – from scarlet mistress to demure wife?'

She giggled. She very seldom did that, but when she did, he found it irresistible. 'What an extraordinary time and place to receive a proposal of marriage, and an even more extraordinary time and place to accept one.'

'What do you think their majesties would say if I were to kiss you here and now?' He leaned towards her and she leapt back startled.

'Crazy man, you just wait until I get you home,' she threatened. He took her arm and they went to join the company.

'Weltevreden is one of the loveliest homes in the Cape,' Blaine agreed. 'But it doesn't belong to me – and I want to carry my bride over the threshold of my own home.'

'We cannot live in Newlands House.' Centaine did not have to say more, and for a moment Isabella's ghost passed between them like a dark shadow.

'What about the cottage?' He laughed to banish Isabella's memory. 'It's got a magnificent bed, what else do we need?'

'We'll keep that,' she agreed. 'And every now and then we will slip away to revisit it.'

'Dirty weekends, good-oh!'

'You are vulgar, do you know that?'

'So where shall we live?'

'We will find a place. Our own special place.'

It was five hundred acres of mountain, beach and rocky coastline with a profusion of protea plants and grand views across Hout Bay and out to the cold green Atlantic.

The house was a huge rambling Victorian mansion, built at the turn of the century by one of the old mining magnates from the Witwatersrand, and in desperate need of the attention that Centaine proceeded to lavish upon it. However, she kept the name Rhodes Hill. For her one of its chief attractions was that a mere twenty minutes in the Daimler took her over the Constantia Nek pass and down to the vineyards of Weltevreden.

Shasa had taken over the chairmanship of Courtney Mining and Finance at the war's end, although Centaine kept a seat on the board and never missed a meeting. Now Shasa and Tara moved into the great château of Weltevreden that she had vacated, but Centaine visited there every weekend and sometimes more often. It gave her a pang when Tara rearranged the furniture that she had left and relandscaped the front lawns and gardens, but with an effort she managed to hold her tongue.

Often these days she thought of the old Bushman couple who had rescued her from the sea and the desert, and then she would sing softly the praise song that O'wa had composed for the infant Shasa:

> His arrows will fly to the stars
> and when men speak his name

it will be heard as far –
And he will find good water,
    wherever he travels, he will find good water.

Although after all these years the clicks and tones of the
San language tripped strangely on her tongue, she knew
that the blessing of O'wa had borne fruit. That, and her
own rigorous training had led Shasa to the good waters of
life.

Gradually Shasa with the help of David Abrahams in
Windhoek had instilled into the sprawling Courtney
Mining and Finance Company a new spirit of youthful
vigour and adventure. Although the old hands, Abe Abrahams and Twentyman-Jones, grumbled and shook their
heads and although Centaine was occasionally forced to
side with them and veto Shasa's wilder more risky projects,
the company regained direction and increased in stature.
Each time that Centaine examined the books or took her
seat below her son at the boardroom table, there was less
to complain about and more cause for self-congratulation.
Even Dr Twentyman-Jones, that paragon of pessimists, had
been heard to mutter, 'The boy has got a head on his
shoulders.' And then appalled at his own lapse, he had
added morosely, 'Mind you, it will take a full day's work
from all of us to keep it there.'

When Shasa had been nominated as the United Party
candidate for the parliamentary by-election of Hottentots
Holland and had snatched a close-fought victory from his
Nationalist opponent, Centaine saw all her ambitions for
him becoming reality. He would almost certainly be offered
something more important after the next general election,
perhaps the job as deputy minister of mines and industry.
After that, a full seat in the cabinet, and beyond that? She
let the idea of it send little thrills up her spine, but did not
allow herself to dwell on it in case the thought brought ill-
fortune on the actuality. Still it was possible. Her son was

well favoured, even the eye-patch added to his individuality, he spoke amusingly and articulately, and he had the trick of making people listen and like him. He was rich and ambitious and clever – and he had herself and Tara behind him. It was possible and more than possible.

By some remarkable dialectic contortion Tara Malcomess Courtney had retained her social conscience intact while taking up the management of the Weltevreden household as though to the manner born.

It was typical that she retained her maiden name, and that she could rush from the elegant surroundings of Weltevreden to the slum clinics and feeding centres for the poor out on the Cape flats without missing a step, taking with her larger charitable donations than Shasa really liked to part with.

She threw herself into the duties of motherhood with equal abandon. Her first three efforts were all male, healthy and rumbustious. In order of seniority they were Sean, Garrick and Michael. With her fourth visit to the childbed she produced, with little effort and time wasted in labour, her masterpiece. This one Tara named after her own mother, Isabella, and from the moment he first picked her up and she puked a little sour clotted milk on his shoulder, Shasa was totally besotted with her.

Up to this time it was Tara's spirit and intriguing individuality that had kept Shasa from growing bored and responding to the subtle and less than subtle invitations that were showered on him by circling female predators.

Centaine, fully aware that Shasa's veins were charged with hot de Thiry blood, agonized that Tara seemed oblivious of the danger and dismissed her veiled warnings with an offhand, 'Oh, Mater, Shasa isn't like that.' Centaine knew that was exactly the way he was. 'Mon Dieu, he started at fourteen.' But she relaxed after the other woman finally entered his life in the shape of Isabella de Thiry Malcomess Courtney. It would have been so easy for a fatal slip to spoil it all, to dash the sweet cup from her lips just as she was able to savour it to the full, but now at last Centaine was secure.

She sat under the oaks beside the polo practice grounds of Weltevreden, a guest on the estate she had built up and cherished, but an honoured guest and well content. The coloured nannies had charge of the babies, Michael just a year and a bit and Isabella still at the breast.

Sean was out in the middle of the field. He sat on the pommel of Shasa's saddle, shrieking with excitement and delight, as his father ran the pony at a full gallop down between the far goal posts, brought him up short in a swirl of dust, pivoted and came back in a crescendo of hoof beats. Meanwhile Sean, secure in the circle of Shasa's left arm, urged him 'Faster! Faster, Papa! Go faster!'

On Centaine's knee Garrick bounced impatiently, 'Me!' he yelled. 'Now me!'

Shasa brought the pony in still at full gallop, then reined him down to a dead stop. He lifted Sean off the pommel against his best effort to stick like a bush tick. Garrick slipped off Centaine's lap and toddled to his father.

'Me, Daddy, my turn!'

Shasa leaned out of the saddle, swung the child up in front of him and they were off again at a gallop. It was a game of which they never tired; they had already exhausted two ponies since lunchtime.

There was the sound of a motor vehicle coming down from the château, and Centaine sprang to her feet involuntarily as she recognized the distinctive beat of the Bentley's engine. Then she composed herself and went to meet Blaine with a little more dignity than her eagerness dictated, but as he stepped out of the vehicle she saw his expression and she quickened her step.

'What is it, Blaine?' she demanded as he kissed her cheek. 'Is something wrong?'

'No, of course not,' he assured her. 'The Nationalists

have announced their candidates for the Cape constituencies, that's all.'

'Who have they put up against you?' She was all attention now. 'Old Van Schoor again?'

'No, my dear, new blood. Someone you have probably never heard of, Dawid Van Niekerk.'

'Who have they nominated for Hottentots Holland?' When he hesitated, she was immediately insistent. 'Who is it, Blaine?'

He took her arm and began to walk her slowly back to join the family at the tea-table under the oaks.

'Life is a strange thing,' he said.

'Blaine Malcomess, I asked you for an answer, not a few gems of homespun philosophy. Who is it?'

'I'm sorry my dear,' he murmured regretfully. 'They have nominated Manfred De La Rey as their official party candidate.'

Centaine stopped dead, and she felt the blood drain from her face. Blaine tightened his grip on her arm to steady her as she swayed on her feet. Since the beginning of the war Centaine had heard or seen nothing of her second, unacknowledged, son.

Shasa began his campaign with an open meeting in the Boy Scouts hall of Somerset West.

He and Tara drove out the thirty miles from Cape Town to this beautiful little village which nestled at the foot of Sir Lowry's Pass beneath the rugged barrier of the Hottentots Holland mountains. Tara insisted that they take her old Packard. She never felt comfortable in Shasa's new Rolls.

'How can you bear to drive around on four wheels that cost enough to clothe, educate and feed a hundred black children from the cradle to the grave?'

For once Shasa saw the practical wisdom of not flaunting his wealth in front of his constituents. Tara was really tremendous value for money, Shasa reflected. An aspiring politician could not ask for a better running mate – a mother of four lovely children, outspoken, holding strong opinions and possessing a natural shrewdness that anticipated the prejudices and fickle enthusiasm of the herd. She was also strikingly beautiful with all that smouldering auburn hair and a smile that could light up a dreary meeting, and despite four childbirths in almost as many years, her figure was still marvellous, small waist, good hips – only her bosom had burgeoned.

'I'd back her in a showdown with Jane Russell – tit for tat she'd win by a length going away.' Shasa chuckled aloud, and she looked across at him.

'That's your dirty laugh,' she accused. 'Don't tell me what you are thinking. Let me hear your speech instead.'

He rehearsed it for her, with appropriate gestures and she made an occasional suggestion on content and delivery. 'I would pause longer there,' and, 'look fierce and determined,' or, 'I wouldn't make too much of that bit about the Empire. Not really in fashion any more.'

Tara still drove furiously and the journey was soon over. There were larger-than-life posters of Shasa pasted at the entrance and the hall was gratifyingly full. All the seats were taken and there were even a dozen or so younger men standing at the back – they looked like students, Shasa doubted they were old enough to vote.

The local United Party organizer, a Party rosette on his lapel, introduced Shasa as a man who needed no introduction and extolled the fine work he had done for the constituency during his previous short term of office.

Then Shasa rose, tall and debonair in a dark blue suit that was not too new or fashionably cut, but with a crisp white shirt – only spivs wore coloured shirts – and an airforce tie to remind them of his war record. The eye-patch further emphasized what he had sacrificed for his country and his smile was charming and sincere.

'My friends—' he began, and got no further. He was drowned out by a pandemonium of stamping and chanting and jeering. Shasa tried to make a joke of it, pretending to conduct the orchestrated abuse, but his smile became steadily less sincere as the uproar showed no signs of abating, instead becoming louder and more vindictive as the minutes passed. Finally he began to deliver his address, bellowing it out to be heard above the din.

There were about three hundred of them, taking up the entire back half of the hall, and they made clear their allegiance to the Nationalist Party and its candidate, waving Party banners that depicted the powder horn insignia and holding up posters of Manfred De La Rey's gravely handsome portrait.

After the first few minutes a number of the elderly and middle-aged voters in the front of the hall, sensing the violence that was coming, helped their wives from their seats and scuttled out of the side entrance to a renewed outburst of jeers.

Suddenly Tara Courtney leapt to her feet beside Shasa. Flushed with anger, her grey eyes hard and glittering as bayonets, she yelled at them, 'What kind of men are you? Is this fair? You call yourselves Christians? Where is your Christian charity? Give the man a chance!'

Her voice carried, and her furious beauty checked them. Their inherent sense of chivalry began to take effect, one or two of them sat down and grinned sheepishly, the noise began to abate, but a big dark-haired man leapt up from the audience and rallied them.

'Kom kêrels, come on, boys, let's see the Soutie back to England where he belongs.'

Shasa knew the man, he was one of the local Party organizers. He had been on the Olympic team back in 1936 and had spent most of the war in an internment camp. He

857

was a senior lecturer in Law at Stellenbosch University and Shasa challenged him in Afrikaans:

'Does Meneer Roelf Stander believe in the rule of law and the right of free speech?'

Before he could finish, the first missile was thrown. It came sailing in a high parabola from the back of the hall and burst on the table in front of Tara, a brown paper bag filled with dog turds, and immediately there was a bombardment of soft fruit and toilet rolls, dead chickens and rotten fish.

From the front of the hall the United Party supporters stood up and shouted for order, but Roelf Stander waved his men forward and joyously they surged up to give battle. Seats were overturned, and women screamed, men were shouting and swearing and wrestling and falling over one another.

'Keep close behind me,' Shasa told Tara. 'Hold onto my coat!' He fought his way towards the door, punching any man who stood in his way.

One of them went down before Shasa's right hook, and protested plaintively from the floor, 'Hey, man, I'm on your side,' but Shasa dragged Tara out of the side door and they ran to the Packard.

Neither of them spoke until Tara had them back on the main road, headlights pointing towards the dark bulk of Table Mountain. Then she asked, 'How many of them did you get?'

'Three of theirs – one of ours,' and they burst into nervously relieved laughter.

'It looks as though this is going to be a lot of fun.'

The election of 1948 was fought with increasing acrimony as across the land a realization began to dawn that the nation had reached some fateful crossroads.

The Smuts men were flabbergasted by the depth of feeling the Nationalists had managed to engender amongst the Afrikaner people, and they were totally unprepared for the almost military mobilization of all the forces at the command of the Nationalist Party.

There were few black voters and of all white South Africans the Afrikaners formed a small majority. Smuts had relied for his support upon the English-speaking electorate together with the moderate Afrikaner faction. As polling day drew closer, this moderate support was slowly seduced by the wave of Nationalistic hysteria, and the gloom in the United Party deepened.

Three days before polling day, Centaine was in her new garden, supervising the marking out and planting of a hundred additional yellow rose bushes when her secretary came hurrying down from the house.

'Mr Duggan is here, ma'am.'

Andrew Duggan was the editor of the *Cape Argus*, the English-language newspaper with the largest readership in the Cape. He was a good friend of Centaine's, a regular house guest, but still it was most inconsiderate of him to call unannounced. Centaine's hair was a bushy fright, despite her headscarf, and she was flushed and sweaty and without make-up.

'Tell him I'm not at home,' she ordered.

'Mr Duggan sends his apologies, but it's a matter of extreme urgency. He used the term "life and death", ma'am.'

'Oh, very well. Go tell him I will be with him in five minutes.'

She changed from slacks and sweater into a morning dress and made a few perfunctory dabs with a powder puff, then she swept into the front room where Andrew Duggan stood by the french doors looking out over the Atlantic.

Her welcome to him was less than effusive, and she did not offer her cheek for him to kiss, a small token of her displeasure. Andrew was apologetic.

'I know how you feel, Centaine, this is damned cheeky of me barging in here, but I simply had to speak to you and I couldn't use the telephone. Tell me I am forgiven, please.'

She softened and smiled. 'You are forgiven and I'll give you a cup of tea to prove it.'

She poured the orange pekoe tea, brought the paper-thin Royal Doulton cup to him and sat beside him on the sofa.

'Life and death?' she asked.

'More correctly – life and birth.'

'You intrigue me. Please go on, Andy.'

'Centaine, I have received the most extraordinary allegations, supported by documents which appear on the surface to be genuine. If they are, then I shall be obliged to print the story. The allegation concerns you and your family, but especially you and Shasa. They are most damaging allegations—' he trailed off and looked at her for permission to continue.

'Go on, please,' Centaine said with a calm she did not feel.

'Not to put too fine a point on it, Centaine, we have been told that your marriage to Blaine was your first and only marriage—' Centaine felt the leaden weight of dismay crush down upon her ' – which, of course, means that Shasa is illegitimate.'

She held up her hand to stop him. 'Answer me one question. Your informant is the Nationalist Party candidate in the Hottentots Holland constituency or one of his agents. Is my guess correct?'

He bowed his head slightly in assent but said, 'We do not reveal our sources. It's not the policy of our newspaper.'

They were silent for a long while and Andrew Duggan studied her face. What an extraordinary woman she was, indomitable even in the face of catastrophe. It saddened him to think that he must be the one who would destroy her dream. He had guessed at her ambitions and empathized with them. Shasa Courtney had much of value to give the nation.

'You have the documents, of course?' Centaine asked, and he shook his head.

'My informant is holding them against my firm undertaking to print the story before polling day.'

'Which you will give him?'

'If I cannot have something from you to refute the allegations, then I must print. It is material and in the public interest.'

'Give me until tomorrow morning,' she asked, and he hesitated. 'As a personal favour, please Andy.'

'Very well,' he agreed. 'I owe you that at least.' He stood up. 'I'm sorry, Centaine, I have taken too much of your time already.'

Immediately Andrew Duggan had left, Centaine went upstairs and bathed and changed. Within half an hour she was in the Daimler and heading for the town of Stellenbosch.

It was long after five when she parked in front of the law offices of Van Schoor and De La Rey, but the front door opened to her touch and she found one of the partners working late.

'Meneer De La Rey left a little early today. He took a brief home to work undisturbed.'

'My business is most urgent. Can you give me his home address?'

It was a pleasant but modest gabled house on an acre of ground on the banks of the river, adjoining the spreading Lanzerac estate. Somebody had taken a great deal of care with the garden and it was filled with flowers even this late in the year, with the first snows of winter on the mountains.

A woman opened the door to Centaine, a big blond woman with a heavily handsome head and a high full bosom. Her smile was reserved and she opened the door only halfway.

'I would like to speak to Meneer De La Rey,' Centaine told her in Afrikaans. 'Will you tell him Mrs Malcomess is here.'

'My husband is working. I do not like to disturb him – but come in, I will see if he will speak to you.'

She left Centaine in the front room with its flocked wallpaper of dark red, velvet curtains and heavy Teutonic furniture. Centaine was too keyed up to sit down. She stood in the centre of the floor and looked at the paintings on the fireplace wall without really seeing them, until she became aware of being observed herself.

She turned quickly and a child stood in the doorway, studying her with unblinking frankness. He was a lovely boy, probably seven or eight years old, with a head of blond curls but with incongruously dark eyes under dark brows.

The eyes were her own, she recognized them immediately. This was her grandchild – she knew it instinctively, and the shock of it made her tremble. They stared at each other.

Then she gathered herself and approached him slowly. She held out her hand and smiled.

'Hello,' she said. 'What is your name?'

'I am Lothar De La Rey,' he answered importantly. 'And I am nearly eight years old.'

'Lothar!' she thought, and the name brought all the memories and heartaches back to swamp her emotions. Still she managed to hold the smile.

'What a big fine boy—' she began, and she had almost touched his cheek when the woman appeared in the door behind him.

'What are you doing here, Lothie?' she scolded. 'You have not finished your dinner. Back to the table this instant, do you hear?'

The child bolted from the room and the woman smiled at Centaine.

'I'm sorry. He is at the inquisitive age,' she apologized. 'My husband will see you, *Mevrou*. Please come with me.'

Still shaken from her brief encounter with her grandchild, Centaine was unprepared for the additional shock of meeting her son face to face. He stood behind a desk that was strewn with documents and he glared at her with that disconcerting yellow gaze.

'I cannot tell you that you are welcome in this house, Mrs Malcomess.' He spoke in English. 'You are a blood enemy of my family, and of mine.'

'That is not true.' Centaine found her voice was breathless, and she tried desperately to regain control.

Manfred made a dismissive gesture. 'You robbed and cheated my father, you crippled him, and through you he has spent half his life in prison. If you could see him now, an old man broken and discarded, you would not come here seeking favours from me.'

'Are you certain I came for a favour?' she asked, and he laughed bitterly.

'For what other reason? You have hounded me – from the day I first saw you in the courtroom at my father's trial. I have seen you watching me, following me, stalking me, like a hungry lioness. I know you seek to destroy me as you destroyed my father.'

'No!' She shook her head vehemently, but he went on remorselessly.

'Now you dare to come and beg my favour. I know what you want.' He pulled open the drawer of his desk and lifted out a file. He opened it and let the papers it contained spill upon the desktop. Amongst them she recognized French birth certificates and old newspaper clippings.

'Shall I read all these to you or will you read them yourself? What other proof do I need to show the world that you are a whore and your son a bastard?' he asked, and she flinched at the words.

'You have been very thorough,' she said softly.

'Yes,' he agreed. 'Very thorough. I have all the evidence—'

'No,' she contradicted him. 'Not all the evidence. You know about one bastard son of mine — but there is another bastard. I will tell you about my second bastard.'

For the first time he was uncertain, staring at her, at a loss for words. Then he shook his head.

'You are shameless,' he marvelled. 'You flaunt your sins before the world.'

'Not before the world,' she said. 'Only before the person they concern most. Only before you, Manfred De La Rey.'

'I do not understand.'

'Then I shall explain why I followed you — as you put it — hounded and stalked you like a lioness. It was not the way a lioness stalks her prey, it was the way a lioness follows her cub. You see, Manfred, you are my other son. I gave birth to you in the desert and Lothar took you away before I had seen your face. You are my son and Shasa is your halfbrother. If he is a bastard, so are you. If you destroy him with that fact, you destroy yourself.'

'I do not believe you!' He recoiled from her. 'Lies! All lies! My mother was a German woman of noble birth. I have her photograph. There! Look there on the wall!'

Centaine glanced at it. 'That was Lothar's wife,' she agreed. 'She died almost two years before you were born.'

'No. It's not true. It cannot be true.'

'Ask your father, Manfred,' she said softly. 'Go to Windhoek. The date of that woman's death will be registered there.'

He saw it was true, and he slumped down into his chair and buried his face in his hands.

'If you are my mother – how can I hate you so bitterly?'

She went and stood over him. 'Not as bitterly as I have hated myself for renouncing and abandoning you.'

She bent and kissed his head. 'If only—' she whispered. 'But now it is too late – far too late. As you have said, we are enemies separated by a void as wide as the ocean. Neither of us can ever cross it, but I do not hate you, Manfred, my son. I have never hated you.'

She left him slumped at his desk and walked slowly from the room.

A t noon the following day Andrew Duggan telephoned her.

'My informant has retracted his allegations, Centaine. He tells me that the papers – all the papers connected to the case – have been burned. I think somebody got at him, Centaine, but I cannot for the life of me think who.'

O n 25 May 1948, the day before polling for the general election, Manfred addressed a huge crowd in the Dutch Reformed Church hall in Stellenbosch. All of them were staunch Nationalist supporters. No opposition was allowed to enter the hall, Roelf Stander and his action squad saw to that.

Yet when Manfred rose to speak, he also was prevented from doing so. The standing ovation that the crowd gave him kept him silent for fully five minutes. However, when it was over, they sat and listened in attentive silence as he gave them a vision of the future.

'Under Smuts this land of ours will become peopled by a coffee-coloured race of half-bred mongrels, the only white ones left will be the Jews – those same Jews who at this very moment in Palestine are murdering innocent British soldiers at every turn. As you well know, Smuts has hastened to recognize the new state of Israel. That is only to be expected. His paymasters are the Jewish owners of the gold mines—'

Now the crowd cried: '*Skande* – Scandal!' and he paused impressively before he went on.

'What we offer you instead is a plan, nay more than a plan – a vision, a bold and noble vision which will ensure the survival of the pure untainted bloodlines of our *Volk*. A vision that will at the same time protect all the other people of this land, the Cape coloureds, the Indians, the black tribes. This grand concept has been drawn up by clever men working with dedication and without self-interest – men like Dr Theophilus Dönges and Dr Nicolaas Diederichs and Dr Hendrik Frensch Verwoerd – brilliant men every one of them.'

The crowd roared their agreement, and he sipped a glass of water and shuffled his notes until they quieted.

'It is an idealistic, carefully worked out and completely infallible concept that will allow all the different races to live in peace and dignity and prosperity and yet allow each of them to retain its separate identity and culture. For this reason we have named the policy 'Separateness'. That is our vision that will carry our land to greatness, a vision at which the world will wonder, an example to all men of good will everywhere. That is what we call *Apartheid*. That, my beloved people, is the glorious mantle which we have prepared to place upon our country. *Apartheid*, my dear friends, that is what we offer you, the shining vision of *Apartheid*.'

He could not speak for many minutes, but when there was silence, he went on in a brisker more businesslike tone.

'Of course, it will first be necessary to disenfranchise

those black and coloured people who are already registered on the voters' roll—'

When he ended an hour later they carried him on their shoulders from the hall.

T ara stood close beside Shasa as they waited for the electoral officers to finish counting the votes and announce the result in the Hottentots Holland constituency.

The hall was filled with an excited crowd. There was laughter and singing and horseplay. The Nationalist candidate was at the far side of the hall with his tall blond wife beside him, surrounded by a restless overwrought knot of his supporters all sporting Nationalist rosettes.

One of the United Party organizers beckoned frantically at Shasa over the heads of the crowd, but he was chatting gaily to a bevy of female enthusiasts, and Tara slipped away to answer the summons. She came back only seconds later and when Shasa saw her face he broke off his conversation and went to meet her, forcing his way through the throng.

'What is it, darling? You look as though you have seen a ghost.'

'It's the *Ou Baas*,' she whispered. 'A telephone call from the Transvaal. Smuts has lost Standerton. The Nationalists have won it.'

'Oh God, no.' Shasa was appalled. 'The *Ou Baas* has held that seat for twenty-five years. They cannot discard him now.'

'The British discarded Winston Churchill,' Tara said. 'They don't want heroes any more.'

'It's a sign,' Shasa muttered. 'If Smuts goes, we all go with him.'

Ten minutes later the news was telephoned through.

Colonel Blaine Malcomess had lost the Gardens by almost a thousand votes.

'A thousand votes—' Shasa tried to accept it, 'but that's a swing of almost ten per cent. What happens now?'

The electoral officer climbed onto the stage at the end of the hall. He had the results in his hand, and the crowd fell silent but edged forward eagerly.

'Ladies and gentlemen, the results of the election for the constituency of Hottentots Holland,' he intoned. 'Manfred De La Rey, Nationalist Party: 3,126 votes. Shasa Courtney, United Party: 2,012 votes. Claude Sampson, Independent: 196 votes.'

Tara took Shasa's hand and they went out to where the Packard was parked. They sat side by side on the front seat, but Tara did not start the engine immediately. They were both shaken and confused.

'I just cannot believe it,' Tara whispered.

'I feel as though I am on a runaway train,' Shasa said. 'Heading into a long dark tunnel, no means of escape, no way of stopping it.' He sighed softly. 'Poor old South Africa,' he murmured. 'God alone knows what the future holds for you.'

Moses Gama was surrounded by men. The small room with walls of galvanized corrugated iron was packed with them. They were his praetorian guard, and Swart Hendrick was chief amongst them.

The room was lit only by a smoky paraffin lamp, and the yellow flame highlighted Moses Gama's features.

'He is a lion among men,' Hendrick thought, reminded again of one of the old kings – of Chaka or Mzilikazi, those great black elephants. Thus must they have called the war chiefs to council, thus they must have ordered the battle.

'Even now the hard Boers vaunt their victory across the

land,' Moses Gama said. 'But I tell you, my children, and I tell you true that below the leaping flames of their pride and avarice lie the ashes of their own destruction. It will not be easy and it may be long. There will be hard work, bitter hard work and even bloody work – but tomorrow belongs to us.'

The new Deputy Minister of Justice left his office and went down the long corridor in the Union Buildings, that massive fortresslike complex designed and built by Sir Herbert Baker on a low kopje overlooking the city of Pretoria. It was the administrative headquarters of the South African Government.

Outside it was dark, but there were lights burning in most of the offices. All of them were working late. Taking over the reins of power was an onerous business, but Manfred De La Rey revelled in every tedious detail of the task he had been given. He was sensible of the honour for which he had been selected. He was young, some said too young, for the post of a deputy minister, but he would prove them wrong.

He knocked on the minister's door and opened it to the command, 'Kom binne – enter!'

Charles Robberts 'Blackie' Swart was tall almost to the point of deformity with huge hands that now lay on the desk top in front of him.

'Manfred.' He smiled like a crack appearing in a granite slab. 'Here is the little present I promised you.' He picked up an envelope embossed with the crest of the Union of South Africa and handed it across the desk.

'I will never be able to express my gratitude, Minister.' Manfred took the envelope. 'I hope only to demonstrate it to you by my loyalty and hard work in the years ahead.'

Back in his own office Manfred opened the envelope

and unfolded the document it contained. Slowly savouring each word of it, he read through the free pardon granted to one Lothar De La Rey, convicted of various crimes and sentenced to life imprisonment.

Manfred folded the document and slipped it back into its envelope. Tomorrow he would deliver the pardon to the prison governor in person, and he would be there to take his father's hand and lead him out into the sunshine again.

He stood up and went to his safe, tumbled the combination and swung open the heavy steel door. There were three files lying on the top shelf, and he took them down and laid them on his desk. One file was from military intelligence, the second from CID headquarters, the third from his own Department of Justice. It had taken time and careful planning to have all three on his desk and all record of their existence removed from the archive registers. They were the only existing files on 'White Sword'.

He took his time and read each one through carefully. It was long after midnight when he finished, but now he knew that nowhere in those files had any person made the connection between 'White Sword' and Manfred De La Rey, Olympic gold medallist and now Deputy Minister of Justice.

He picked up the three files and carried them through to the outer office where he switched on the shredding machine. As he fed each separate page into the shredder and watched the thin strips of paper come curling out the far side like spaghetti, he considered what he had learned from them.

'So there was a traitoress,' he murmured. 'I was betrayed. A woman, a young woman, speaking in Afrikaans. She knew everything, from the guns in Pretoria to the ambush on the mountain. There is only one young woman who knew all that.' There would be retribution in time, but Manfred was in no hurry – there were many scores to settle, many debts to pay.

When the last page of the reports was reduced to minute slivers, Manfred locked his office and went down to where the new black Ford sedan that went with his rank was parked.

He drove back to his sumptuous official residence in the elegant suburb of Waterkloof. As he went upstairs to the bedroom he was careful not to wake Heidi. She was pregnant again, and her sleep was precious.

He lay in the darkness unable to sleep himself. There was too much to think about, too much planning to do, and he smiled and thought, 'So at last the sword of power is in our hands – and we will see, with a vengeance, who are the underdogs now.'

THE DIAMOND HUNTERS

For DEE

His flight had been delayed for three hours at Nairobi, and despite four large whiskies he slept only fitfully until the intercontinental Boeing touched down at Heathrow. Johnny Lance felt as though someone had thrown a handful of grit in each eye, and his mood was ugly as he came through the indignity of Customs and Immigration into the main hall of the international terminus.

The Van Der Byl Diamond Company's London agent was there to meet him.

'Pleasant trip, Johnny?'

'Like the one to Hell,' Johnny grunted.

'Good practice for you.' The agent grinned. The two of them had seen some riotous times together.

Reluctantly Johnny grinned back at him.

'You got me a room and a car?'

'Dorchester – and Jag.' The agent handed over the car keys. 'And I've got two first-class seats reserved on tomorrow's nine o'clock flight back to Cape Town. Tickets at the hotel reception desk.'

'Good boy.' Johnny dropped the keys into the pocket of his cashmere overcoat and they started for the exit. 'Now where is Tracey van der Byl?'

The agent shrugged. 'Since I wrote to you she has dropped out of sight. I don't know where you can start looking.'

'Great, just great!' said Johnny bitterly as they came out into the car park. 'I'll start with Benedict.'

'Does the Old Man know about Tracey?'

Johnny shook his head. 'He's a sick man. I didn't tell him.'

1

'Here's your car.' The agent stopped by the pearl-grey Jaguar. 'Any chance of a drink together?'

'Not this trip, sorry.' Johnny slipped in behind the wheel. 'Next time.'

'I'll hold you to that,' said the agent and walked away.

It was almost dark by the time Johnny crossed the Hammersmith flyover in the moist smoky grey of the evening, and he lost himself twice in the maze of Belgravia before he found the narrow mews behind Belgrave Square and parked the Jaguar.

The exterior of the flat had been lavishly redecorated since his last visit, and Johnny's mouth twisted. He might not be so hot at earning the stuff – but our boy Benedict certainly was a dab hand at spending it.

There were lights burning and Johnny hit the door knocker half a dozen lusty cracks. It echoed hollowly about the mews, and in the silence that followed Johnny heard the whisper of voices from behind the curtains, and a shadow passed quickly across the window.

Johnny waited three minutes in the cold, then he stepped back into the middle of the mews.

'Benedict van der Byl,' he bellowed. 'I'll give you a count of ten to get this door open. Then I'll kick the bloody thing down.'

He drew breath, and bellowed again.

'This is Johnny Lance – and you know I mean it.'

The door opened almost immediately. Johnny pushed his way through it, not glancing at the man who held it, and started for the lounge.

'Dammit, Lance. You can't go in there.' Benedict van der Byl started after him.

'Why not?' Johnny glanced back at him. 'It is a Company flat – and I'm the General Manager.'

Before Benedict could reply, Johnny was through the door.

One of the girls picked up her clothing from the floor

2

and ran naked into the bedroom passage. The other pulled a full-length caftan over her head and glared at Johnny sulkily. Her hair was in wild disorder, fluffed out into a grotesque halo of stiff curls.

'Nice party,' said Johnny. He glanced at the movie projector on the side table, and then at the screen across the room. 'Films and all.'

'Are you the Fuzz?' demanded the girl.

'You've got an infernal cheek, Lance.' Benedict van der Byl was beside him, tying the belt of his silk dressing-gown.

'Is he Fuzz?' the girl demanded again.

'No,' Benedict assured her. 'He works for my father.' With the statement he seemed to gather self-assurance, drawing himself up to his full height and smoothing his long dark hair with one hand. His voice regained its polish and lazy inflection. 'Actually, he is Daddy's messenger boy.'

Johnny turned to him, but he addressed the girl without looking at her.

'Beat it, girlie. Follow your friend.'

She hesitated.

'Beat it!' Johnny's voice crackled like a bush fire, and she went.

The two men stood facing each other. They were the same age, in their early thirties – both tall, both dark-haired – but different in every other way.

Johnny was big in the shoulder and lean across the hips and belly, his skin polished and browned by the desert sun. The line of his heavy jawbone stood out clearly, and his eyes seemed still to seek far horizons. His voice clipped and twanged with the accents of the other land.

'Where is Tracey?' he asked.

Benedict lifted one eyebrow in a pantomine of arrogant surprise. His skin was pale olive, unstained by sunlight for it was months since he had last visited Africa. His lips were very red, as though they had been painted, the classical lines of his features were blurred by flesh. There were soft little pouches under his eyes, and a plumpness beneath the silk dressing-gown that suggested he ate and drank often and exercised infrequently.

'My dear chap, what on earth makes you think I know where my sister is? I haven't seen her for weeks.'

Johnny turned away and crossed to one of the paintings on the far wall. The room was hung with good original South African artists – Alexis Preller, Irma Stern and Tretchikof – an unusual mixture of techniques and styles, but someone had convinced the Old Man they were sound investments.

Johnny turned back to face Benedict van der Byl. He studied him as he had the paintings, comparing him with the clean young athlete he had been a few years before. A clear mental image in his mind pictured Benedict moving with leopard grace across the green field of play under the packed grandstands, turning smoothly beneath the high floating arc of the ball to gather it neatly, head high, and break back infield to open the line for the return kick.

'You're getting fat, Laddy Buck,' he said softly, and Benedict's anger stained his cheeks dull red.

'Get out of here,' he snapped.

'In a minute – tell me about Tracey first.'

'I've told you – I don't know where she is. Whoring it up around Chelsea, I expect.'

Johnny felt his own anger surge fiercely, but his voice remained level.

'Where is she getting the money, Benedict?'

'I don't know – the Old Man—'

Johnny cut him short. 'The Old Man is keeping her on an allowance of ten pounds a week. From what I hear she's throwing more than that around.'

'Christ, Johnny,' Benedict's tone became conciliatory, 'I don't know. It's not my business. Perhaps Kenny Hartford is—'

4

Again Johnny interrupted impatiently. 'Kenny Hartford is giving her nothing. That was part of the divorce agreement when they split up. Now I want to know who is subsidizing her trip to oblivion. How about it, big brother?'

'Me?' Benedict was indignant. 'You know there is no love wasted between us.'

'Must I spell it out?' Johnny asked. 'All right, then. The Old Man is dying – without losing his horror of all weakness and sin. If Tracey turns into a drug-soaked little tramp – then there's a good chance that our boy Benedict will come back into full favour. It would be a good gamble on your part to lay out a few thousand now, to send Tracey to Hell. Cut her off completely from her father – and all those nice fat millions.'

'Who said anything about drugs?' Benedict blustered.

'I did.' Johnny stepped up to him. 'You and I have a little unfinished business. It would give me intense pleasure to take you to pieces and see what makes you work.'

He held Benedict's eyes for long seconds, then Benedict looked down and fiddled with the cord of his dressing-gown.

'Where is she, Benedict?'

'I don't know, damn you!'

Johnny moved softly across to the movie projector and picked up a reel of film from the table beside it. He peeled off a few feet of celluloid from the reel and held it up to the light.

'Pretty!' he said, but the line of his mouth tightened with disgust.

'Put that down,' snapped Benedict.

'You know what the Old Man thinks about this sort of thing, don't you, Benedict?'

Suddenly Benedict went pale.

'He wouldn't believe you.'

'Yes, he would.' Johnny tossed the reel on the table and turned back to Benedict. 'He believes me because I've never lied to him.'

Benedict hesitated, wiped his lips nervously with the back of his hand.

'I haven't seen her for two weeks. She was renting a place in Chelsea. Stark Street. No. 23. She came to see me.'

'What for?'

'I lent her a couple of pounds,' Benedict muttered sulkily.

'A couple of pounds?' Johnny asked.

'All right, a couple of hundred. After all, she is my sister.'

'Damn decent of you,' Johnny lauded him. 'Write down the address.'

Benedict crossed to the leather-topped writing desk and scribbled on a card. He came back and handed the card to Johnny.

'You like to think you're big and dangerous, Lance.' His voice was pitched low but it shook with fury. 'Well, I'm dangerous too – in a different sort of way. The Old Man can't live for ever, Lance. When he's gone I'm coming after you.'

'You frighten the hell out of me.' Johnny grinned at him, and went down to the car.

The traffic was solid in Sloane Square as Johnny eased the Jaguar slowly down towards Chelsea. There was plenty of time to think; to remember how close they had been – the three of them. He and Tracey and Benedict.

Running together as wild young things with the endless beaches and mountains and sun-washed plains of Namaqualand as their playground. That was before the Old Man made the big strike on the Slang River, before there was money for shoes. When Tracey wore dresses made from flour sacks sewn together, and they rode to school each day, all three of them bare-back on a single pony like a row of bedraggled little brown sparrows on a fence.

He remembered how the long sun-drenched weeks while the Old Man was away were spent in laughter and secret games. How they climbed the *kopje* behind the mud-walled shack each evening and looked towards the north across

6

the limitless land, flesh-coloured and purple in the sunset, searching for the wisp of dust in the distance that would mean the Old Man was coming home.

Then the almost painful excitement when the dusty, rackety Ford truck with its mudguards tied on with wire was suddenly there in the yard, and the Old Man was climbing down from the cab, a sweat-stained hat on the back of his head and the dust thick in the stubble of his beard, swinging Tracey squealing above his head. Then turning to Benedict, and lastly to Johnny. Always in that order – Tracey, Benedict, Johnny.

Johnny had never wondered why sometimes he was not first. It was always that way. Tracey, Benedict, Johnny. The same way as he had never wondered why his name was Lance and not van der Byl. Then it had come to an end suddenly, the whole brightly sunlit dream of childhood was gone and lost.

'Johnny, I'm not your real father. Your father and mother died when you were very young.' And Johnny had stared at the Old Man in disbelief.

'Do you understand, Johnny?'

'Yes, Pa.'

Tracey's hand groped for his beneath the table top like a little warm animal. He jerked his own hand away from it.

'I think you'd better not call me that any more, Johnny.' He could remember the exact tone of the Old Man's voice, neutral, matter of fact, as it splintered the fragile crystal of his childhood to fragments. The loneliness had begun.

Johnny accelerated the Jaguar forward and swung into the King's Road. He was surprised that the memory hurt so intensely – time should have mellowed and softened it.

His life from then on had become a ceaseless contest to win the Old Man's approval – he dare not hope for his love.

Soon there were other changes, for a week later the old Ford had come roaring unexpectedly out of the desert in the night, and the barking of the dogs and the Old Man's shouted laughter had brought them, sleepy-eyed, tumbling from their bunks.

The Old Man had lit the Petromax lamp and sat them on the kitchen chairs about the scrubbed deal table. Then with the air of a conjuror he had lain something that looked like a big lump of broken glass on the table.

The three sleepy children had stared at it solemnly, not understanding. The harsh glare of the Petromax was captured within the crystal, captured, repeated, magnified and thrown back at them in fire and blue lightning.

'Twelve carats – ' gloated the Old Man, 'blue-white and perfect, and there is a cartload more where that came from.'

After that there were new clothes and motor cars, the move to Cape Town, the new school and the big house on Wynberg Hill – but always the contest. The contest that did not earn the Old Man's approval as it was designed to do, but earned instead Benedict van der Byl's jealousy and hatred. Without his drive and purpose, Benedict could not hope to match Johnny's achievements in the classroom and on the sports field. He fell far behind the pace that Johnny set – and hated him for it.

The Old Man did not notice for he was seldom with them now. They lived alone in the big house with the thin silent woman who was their housekeeper, and the Old Man came infrequently and for short periods. Always he seemed tired and distracted. Sometimes he brought presents for them from London and Amsterdam and Kimberley, but the presents meant very little to them. They would have liked it better had it stayed the way it was in the desert.

In the void left by the Old Man the hostility and rivalry between Johnny and Benedict flourished to such proportions that Tracey was forced to choose between them. She chose Johnny.

In their loneliness they clung to each other.

The grave little girl and the big gangling boy built

together a castle against the loneliness. It was a bright secure place where the sadness could not reach them – and Benedict was excluded from it.

Johnny swung the Jaguar out of the line of traffic into Old Church Street, down towards the river in Chelsea. He drove automatically and the memories came crowding back.

He tried to recapture and hold the castle of warmth and love that he and Tracey had built so long ago, but instantly his mind leapt to the night on which it had collapsed.

One night in the old house on Wynberg Hill Johnny had come awake to the sound of distant weeping. He had gone barefooted in his pyjamas, following that heart-rending whisper of grief. He was afraid, fourteen years old and afraid in the dark house.

Tracey was weeping into her pillow and he had stooped over her.

'Tracey. What is it? Why are you crying?'

She had jumped up, kneeling on the bed, and flung both arms about his neck.

'Oh, Johnny. I had a dream, a terrible dream. Hold me, please. Don't go away, don't leave me.' Her whisper was still thick and muffled with tears. He had gone into her bed and held her until at last she slept.

Every night after that he had gone to her room. It was innocent and completely childlike, the twelve-year-old girl and the boy who was her brother, in fact if not in name. They held each other in the bed, and whispered and laughed secretly until sleep carried them both away.

Then suddenly the castle was blasted by the bright electric glare of the overhead light. The Old Man was standing in the door of the bedroom, and Benedict was behind him in his pyjamas dancing with excitement and chanting triumphantly.

'I told you, Pa! I told you so!'

The Old Man was shaking with rage, the bush of grey

hair standing erect like the mane of a wounded lion. He had dragged Johnny from the bed, and struck away Tracey's clinging hands.

'You little whore,' he bellowed, holding the terrified boy easily with one hand and leaning forward to strike his daughter in the face with his open hand. Leaving her sobbing, face down on the bed, he dragged Johnny down the passages to the study on the ground floor. He threw him into the room with a violence that sent him staggering against the desk.

The Old Man had gone to the rack and taken out a light Malacca cane. He came to Johnny and, taking a handful of his hair, threw him face down over the desk.

The Old Man had beaten him before, but never like this. Mad with rage the Old Man's blows had been unaimed, some fell across Johnny's back.

Yet in the agony it was deadly important to the boy that he should not cry out. He bit through his lip so the taste of blood was salt and copper in his mouth. He must not hear me cry! And he choked back the moans feeling his pyjama trousers hanging heavy and sodden with blood.

His silence served only as a goad to the Old Man's fury. Flinging the cane aside, he pulled the boy upright and attacked him with his hands. Slamming Johnny's head from side to side with full, open-handed blows that burst in Johnny's skull with blinding flashes of light.

Still Johnny kept on his feet, clinging to the edge of the desk. His lips broken and swollen and his face bloated and darkening with bruises, until at last the Old Man was driven far beyond the borders of sanity. He bunched his fist and drove it into Johnny's face – and with a wonderful sense of relief Johnny felt the pain go out in a warm flood of darkness.

Johnny heard voices first. A strange voice:

' – As though he's been savaged by a wild beast. I'll have to inform the police.'

Then a voice he recognized. It took him a little time to place it. He tried to open his eyes but they seemed locked tight, his face felt enormous, swollen and hot. He forced the fat lids of his eyes back and recognized Michael Shapiro, the Old Man's secretary. He was talking quietly to the other man.

There was the smell of antiseptic and the doctor's bag lay open on the table beside the bed.

'Listen, Doctor. I know it looks bad – but hadn't you better talk to the boy before you stir up the police?'

They both looked towards the bed.

'He's conscious.' The doctor came to him quickly. 'What happened to you, Johnny? Tell us what happened. Whoever did this to you will be punished – I promise you.'

The words were wrong. Nobody must ever punish the Old Man.

Johnny tried to speak but his lips were stiff and swollen. He tried again.

'I fell,' he said. 'I fell. Nobody! Nobody! I fell down.'

When the doctor had gone Mike Shapiro came and stood over him. His Jewish eyes were dark with pity, and something else – anger perhaps, or admiration. 'I'm taking you to my house, Johnny. You will be all right now.'

He stayed two weeks under the care of Michael Shapiro's wife, Helen. The scabs came away, the bruises faded to a dirty yellow, but his nose stayed crooked with a lump at the bridge. He studied his new nose in the mirror, and liked it. It made him look like a boxer, he thought, or a pirate, but it was many months before the tenderness passed and he could finger it freely.

'Listen, Johnny, you are going to a new school. A fine boarding-school in Grahamstown.' Michael Shapiro tried to sound enthusiastic. Grahamstown was five hundred miles away. 'In the holidays you'll be going to work in Namaqualand – learning all about diamonds and how to mine them. You'll enjoy that, won't you?'

Johnny had thought about it for a minute, watching Michael's face and reading in it his shame.

'I won't be going home again then?' By home he meant the house on Wynberg Hill. Michael shook his head.

'When will I see—' Johnny hesitated as he tried to find the right words, ' – when will I see them again?'

'I don't know, Johnny,' Michael answered him honestly.

As Michael had promised it was a fine school.

On his first Sunday after the church service, he had followed the other boys back to their classroom for the session of compulsory letter-writing. The others had immediately begun dashing off hasty scribbles to their parents. Johnny sat miserably until the master in charge stopped at his desk.

'Aren't you going to write home, Lance?' he asked kindly. 'I'm sure they'll all want to hear how you are.'

Johnny picked up his pen obediently, and puzzled over the blank writing-pad.

He wrote at last:

Dear Sir,
    I hope you will be pleased to hear that I am now at school. The food is good, but the beds are very hard.
    We go to church every day and play rugby football.
                              Yours faithfully,
                                        Johnny.

From then until he left school and went up to University three years later, he wrote every week to the Old Man. Every letter began with the same salutation and went on, 'I hope you will be pleased to hear—' There was never a reply to any of these letters.

Once each term he received a typewritten letter from

Michael Shapiro setting out the arrangements that had been made for the school holidays. Usually these involved a train journey hundreds of miles across the Karroo to some remote village in the vast dry wasteland, where a light aircraft belonging to Van Der Byl Diamonds was waiting to fly him still deeper into the desert to one of the Company's concession areas. Again, as Michael Shapiro had promised, he learned about diamonds and how to mine them.

When the time to move on to University arrived, it was completely natural that he chose to take a degree in Geology.

During all that time he was an outcast from the van der Byl family. He had seen none of them – not the Old Man, nor Tracey, nor even Benedict.

Then, in one long eventful afternoon, he saw all three of them. It was his final year at University. His degree was a certainty. He had headed the lists at every examination from his first year onwards. He had been elected the senior student of Stellenbosch University, but now there was a further honour almost within his grasp.

In ten days' time the National Selectors would announce the rugby team to meet the New Zealand All Black touring team – and Johnny's place at flank forward was as certain as his degree in Geology.

The sporting press had nicknamed Johnny 'Jag Hond' after that ferocious predator of the African wilds, the Cape hunting dog; an animal of incredible stamina and determination that savages its prey on the run. The nickname had stuck fast, and Johnny was a favourite of the crowds.

In the line-up of the team from Cape Town University was another crowd-pleaser whose place in the National Side to meet the All Blacks seemed equally assured. From his position at full back Benedict van der Byl dominated the field of play with a grace and artistry that were almost god-like. He had grown tall and wide-shouldered, with long powerful legs and dark brooding good looks.

13

Johnny led the visiting team out on to the smooth green velvet field, and while he jogged and flexed his back and shoulders he looked up at the packed stands seeking assurance that the high priests of rugby football were all there. He saw Doctor Danie Craven sitting with the other selectors in their privileged position below the Press enclosure. While in front of the Doctor, leaning back to exchange a few words with him, sat the Prime Minister.

This meeting between the two universities was one of the high spots of the rugby season, and the *aficionados* travelled thousands of miles to watch it.

The Prime Minister smiled and nodded, then leaned forward to touch the shoulder of the big white-headed figure that sat in the row below him.

Johnny felt an electric tingle run up his spine as the white head lifted and looked directly at him. It was the first time he had seen the Old Man in the seven years since that terrible night.

Johnny lifted an arm in salute, and the Old Man stared at him for long seconds before he turned away to speak with the Prime Minister.

Now the drum majorettes came out in ranks on to the field. White-booted, dressed in Cape Town University colours with short swinging skirts and tall hats, they high-stepped and paraded, lovely young girls flushed with excitement and exertion.

The roar of the crowd drummed with the blood in Johnny's ears, for Tracey van der Byl was leading the first rank. He knew her instantly, despite the passage of years in which she had grown to young womanhood. Her legs and arms were sun-bronzed and her dark hair hung glossily to her shoulders. She cavorted and kicked and stamped shouting the traditional cheers, jiggling her firm young bottom with innocent abandon while the crowds screamed and writhed, beginning already to work themselves into an hysterical frenzy. Johnny watched Tracey. He stood com-

14

pletely still in the thunderous uproar. She was the most beautiful woman he had ever seen.

Then the show was over, the drum majorettes retreating back through the stadium entrance, and the home team trotted on to the field.

The presence of the Old Man and Tracey added intensity to the glare of hatred that Johnny turned on the tall white-clad figure that fell back to take control of the Cape Town back field.

Benedict van der Byl reached his position and turned. From inside his calf-length sock he took a comb and ran it through his dark hair. The crowd bellowed and whistled, loving this little theatrical gesture. Benedict returned the comb to his sock and posed with one hand on his hip, his chin lifted arrogantly as he surveyed the opposition.

Suddenly he intercepted Johnny's glare, and the pose altered as he dropped his eyes and shuffled his feet a little.

The whistle fluted, and play began. It was everything the crowds had hoped for, a match that would long be remembered and gloated over. Massive Panzer offensives by the forwards, long probing raids by the backs with the oval ball flickering from hand to hand, until a bone-jarring tackle smashed the carrier to the turf. Hard and fast and clean play swung from side to side, a hundred times the crowd came up on its feet as one, eyes and mouths wide in screaming unbearable tension, to sink back with a groan as the ball was held by a desperate defence within inches of the try line.

No score and three minutes of play left, Cape Town attacking from a set scrummage, driving through a gap in the defence and then putting the ball in the air with a long raking pass, taken cleanly by the Cape Town wing without a break in his stride. His feet twinkled across the green turf, and again the crowd came up with a gasp.

Johnny hit him low, just above the knee, with his shoulder. The two of them rolled together out of the field of play lifting a puff of white lime from the line and the crowd groaned and sank back.

While they waited to receive the throw, Johnny whispered hoarse orders. His gold and maroon jersey was soaked with sweat, and blood from a grazed hip stained his white shorts.

'Get it back fast. Don't run with it. Give it to Dawie. Kick high and deep, Dawie.'

Johnny leapt high to the flight of the thrown ball, with a bunched fist he punched it back accurately into Dawie's hands, at the same moment twisting his body to block the attackers.

Dawie fell back two paces and kicked. The power of the kick swung his right foot above his head, and the impetus flung him forward to put his forwards 'on side'.

The ball climbed slowly, flying like a dart with no wobble or roll in the air, reaching the zenith of its trajectory high over mid-field, then floating back to earth.

Twenty thousand heads followed its flight, a hush had fallen over the field – and in the unnatural silence Benedict van der Byl was drifting back deep into his own territory, anticipating the drop of the ball with deceptively unhurried strides, yet timing it with the precision of the gifted athlete.

The ball slotted neatly into his arms, and he began moving lazily infield to open his angle for the return kick. Still a tense throbbing mesmeric hush hung over the field, Benedict van der Byl was at the focus of attention.

'Jag Hond!' A single voice in the crowd alerted them, and twenty thousand heads swung downfield.

'Jag Hond!' A roar now. Johnny was well clear of the pack, arms pumping and legs churning as he bore down on Benedict. It was a futile effort, he could not hope to intercept a player of Benedict's calibre from such long range, yet Johnny was burning the last of his physical reserves in that charge. His face was a sweat-shining mask

16

of determination, and clods of torn grass flew from under his savagely driving boots.

Then something happened which was unaccountable, almost past belief. Benedict van der Byl glanced round and saw Johnny. He broke his stride, two clumsy shuffling paces, and tried to pivot away deeper into his own ground. All the assurance had gone from his body, all the skill and grace. He tripped and stumbled, almost fell and the ball popped out of his hands, bouncing awkwardly.

Benedict scrambled after it, groping blindly, looking back over his shoulder. Now on his face was an expression of naked terror. Johnny was very close. Grunting at each stride like a gut-shot lion, massive shoulders already bunching for the strike, his lips drawn back into a murderous parody of a grin.

Benedict van der Byl dropped to his knees and covered his head with both arms, cringing down on to the green turf.

Johnny swept past him without a check, stooping easily in his run to gather the bouncing ball.

When Benedict uncovered his head and, still kneeling, looked up, Johnny stood ten yards away between the goal posts watching him. Then, deliberately, Johnny placed the ball between his feet to complete the formality of the touchdown.

Now, as if by agreement, both Johnny and Benedict looked towards the main grandstand. They saw the Old Man rise from his seat and make his way slowly through the ecstatic crowds towards the exit.

The day after the match, Johnny went back into the desert.

He was down in the bottom of a fifteen-foot prospect trench that had been dug across the grain of the country rock. It was oppressively hot in the confines of the trench and Johnny was stripped to a skimpy pair of khaki shorts, his sun-browned muscles oily with sweat, but he worked steadily at his sampling. He was establishing the contours and profile of an ancient marine terrace that the ages had buried beneath the sand. It was here on the bedrock that he expected to find the thin layer of diamond-bearing gravel.

He heard the Jeep pull up at ground level above him, and the crunch of footsteps. Johnny straightened up and held his aching back muscles.

The Old Man stood at the edge of the trench and looked down at him. He held a folded newspaper in his hand. This was the first time Johnny had seen him at close range in all the years, and he was shocked at the change. The mass of bushy hair was so white, and his features were folded and creased like those of a mastiff, leaving the big hooked nose standing like a hillock from his face. But there was no wasting or deterioration in his body, and his eyes were still that chilling enigmatic blue.

He dropped the newspaper into the trench and Johnny caught it, still staring up at the Old Man.

'Read it!' said the Old Man. The paper was folded to the sports page, and the headline was thick and bold.

JAG HOND IN. VAN DER BYL OUT.

The shock was as delicious as the plunge into a mountain stream. He was in – he would carry the gold and green, and wear the leaping Springbok on his blazer pocket.

He looked up, proud and happy, standing bare-headed in the sun waiting for the Old Man to speak.

'Make up your mind,' said the Old Man softly. 'Do you want to play ball – or work for Van Der Byl Diamonds? You

18

can't do both.' And he walked back to the Jeep and drove away.

Johnny cabled his withdrawal from the team to the Doctor personally. The storm of outraged protest and abuse in the national press, and the hundreds of viperous letters Johnny received accusing him of cowardice and treachery and worse made him thankful for the sanctuary of the desert.

Neither Johnny nor Benedict had ever played the game again. Thinking about it, even at this remove of time, Johnny felt the sting of disappointment. He had wanted that green and gold badge of honour so very deeply. Brusquely he pulled the Jaguar off the road and scanned the street map of London and found Stark Street tucked away off the King's Road. He drove on remembering how it had been after the Old Man had taken it from him. The agony of mind had been scarcely endurable.

His companions in the desert were Ovambo tribesmen from the north, and a few of those taciturn white men that the desert produces, as hardy and uncompromising as her vegetation or her mountain ranges.

The deserts of the Namib and the Kalahari are amongst the loneliest places on earth, and the desert nights are long. Not even the day's unremitting physical labour could tire Johnny sufficiently to drug his dreams of a lovely girl in a short white skirt and high boots – or an old white-headed man with a face like a granite cliff.

Out of those long days and longer nights came solid achievements to stand like milestones marking the road of his career. He brought in a new diamond field, small but rich, in country which no one else had believed would yield diamonds. He pegged a uranium lode which Van Der Byl

Diamonds sold for two and a half millions, and there were other fruits from his efforts as valuable if not as spectacular.

At twenty-five, Johnny Lance's name was whispered in the closed and forbidding halls of the diamond industry as one of the bright young comers.

There were approaches – a junior partnership in a firm of consulting geologists, field manager for one of the struggling little companies working marginal ground in the Murderers' Karroo. Johnny turned them down. They were good offers, but he stayed on with the Old Man.

Then the big Company noticed him. A century ago the first payable pipe of 'blue ground' in Southern Africa was discovered on a hard scrabble farm owned by a Boer named De Beer. Old De Beer sold his farm for £6,000, never dreaming that a treasure worth £300,000,000 lay beneath the bleak dry earth. The strike was named De Beers New Rush, and a horde of miners, small businessmen, drifters, chancers, rogues and scoundrels moved in to purchase and work minute claims, each the size of a large room.

From this pretty company of fortune's soldiers two men rose high above the others, until between them they owned most of the claims in De Beers New Rush. When these two, Cecil John Rhodes and Barney Barnato, at last combined their resources, a formidable financial enterprise was born. From such humble beginnings the Company has grown to awesome respectability and dignity. Its wealth is fabled, its influence immeasurable, its income is astronomical. It controls the diamond supply to the world. It controls also mineral concessions over areas of Central and Southern Africa which total hundreds of thousands of square miles, and its reserves of unmined precious and base minerals cannot be calculated. Small diamond companies are allowed to co-exist with the giant until they reach a certain size – then suddenly they become part of it, gobbled up as a tiger shark might swallow any of its pilot fish who become too large and daring. The big Company can afford to buy the best prospects, equipment – and men. It reached out one of its myriad tentacles to draw in Johnny Lance. The price they set on him was twice his present salary, and three times his future prospects.

Johnny turned it down flat. Perhaps the Old Man did not notice, perhaps it was mere coincidence that a week later Johnny was promoted Field Manager of Beach Operation. The nickname that went with the job was 'King Canute'.

Van Der Byl Diamonds had thirty-seven miles of beach concession. The tiny ribbon of shoreline, one hundred and twenty feet above high-water mark, and one hundred and twenty feet below low-water mark. Inland the concession belonged to the big Company. It had purchased the land, a dozen vast ranches, simply to obtain the mineral rights. The sea concessions, territorial up to waters twelve miles off shore, belonged to them also. Granted to them by Government charter twenty years before. But Van Der Byl Diamonds had the Admiralty strip – and it was 'King Canute's' job to work it.

The sea-mist came smoking in like ground pearl dust off the cold waters of the Benguela current. From out of the mist bank the high unhurried swells marched in towards the bright yellow sands and the tall wave-cut cliffs of Namaqualand.

The swells peaked up sharply as they felt the land. Their crests trembled and turned luminous green, began to dissolve in plumes of wind-blown spray, arched over and slid down upon themselves in the roar and rumble of white water.

Johnny stood on the driver's seat of the open Land-Rover. He wore a sheepskin jacket against the chill of the dawn mist, but his head was bare and his dark hair fluttered nervously against his forehead in the wind.

His heavy jaw was thrust forward, and his hands in the pockets of the sheepskin jacket were balled into fists. He scowled aggressively as he measured the height and push of the surf. With his crooked nose he looked like a boxer waiting for the gong.

Suddenly with an awkward angry movement he jerked his left hand from his pocket and looked down at the dial of his wrist watch. Two hours and three minutes to low tide. He pushed his fist back into his pocket, and swivelled quickly to look at his bulldozers.

There were eleven of them, big bright yellow D.8 Caterpillars, lined up along the high-water mark. The operators sat goggled and tense in their high stern seats. They were all watching him anxiously.

Beyond them, standing well back, were the earthloaders. They were ungainly, pregnant-looking machines with swollen bellies, and heavily lugged tyres that stood taller than a man. When the time came they would rush in at thirty miles an hour, drop a steel blade beneath their bellies and scrape up a fifteen-ton load of sand or gravel, race back inland and drop their load, turn and rush back for another gargantuan bite out of the earth.

Johnny was steeling himself, judging the exact moment in which to hurl a quarter of a million pounds' worth of machinery into the Atlantic Ocean, in the hope of recovering a handful of bright pebbles.

The moment came, and Johnny spent half a minute of precious time in scrutinizing his preparations before committing himself to action.

Then 'GO!' he shouted into his loudhailer and wind-milled his right arm in the unmistakable command to advance.

'Go!' he shouted again, but his voice was lost. Even the sound of the wild surf was lost in the bull bellow of the diesels. Lowering their massive steel blades, a chorus line of steel monsters, they crawled forward.

Now the golden sand curled before the scooped blades, like butter from the knife. It built up before the monstrous

22

machines, becoming a pile and then a high wall. Thrusting, pulling back, butting, worrying, the bulldozers swept the wall of sand forward. The arms of the operators pumping the handles of the controls like mad barmen drawing a thousand pints of beer, the diesels roaring and muttering and roaring again.

The wall of sand met the first low push of sea water up the beach and smothered it. In seeming astonishment and uncertainty the sea pulled back, swirling and creaming before the advancing dyke of sand.

The bulldozers were performing a complicated but smoothly practised ballet now. Weaving and crossing, blades lifting and falling, backing and advancing, all under the supervision of the master choreographer, Johnny Lance.

The Land-Rover darted back and forward along the edge of the huge pit that was forming, with Johnny roaring orders and instructions through the electric loudhailer.

Gradually a sickle-shaped dyke of sand was thrown out into the sea, while behind it the bulldozer blades cut down, six, ten, fifteen feet through the loose yellow sand.

Then suddenly they hit the oyster line, that thin layer of fossilized oyster shell that so often covers the diamond gravels of South West Africa.

Johnny saw the change in the character of his pit, saw the shell curling from the blades of the bulldozers.

With half a dozen orders and hand signals he had his 'dozers flatten a ramp at each end of his pit, to give the earthloaders access. Then he ordered them away to hold the dyke against the sea.

He glanced at his watch. 'One hour thirteen minutes,' he muttered. 'We're running tight!'

Quickly he checked his pit. Two hundred yards long, fifteen feet deep, the overburden of sand stripped away, the oyster line showing clean and white in the sun, the bulldozers clear of the pit bottom – fighting back the sea.

'Right,' he grunted. 'Let's see what we've got.'

He turned to face the two earthmovers waiting expectantly above the high-water mark.

'Go in and get it!' he shouted, and gave the windmill arm signal.

Nose to tail the earthloaders roared forward, swinging wide at the head of the pit, then swooping down the ramp and dashing along the bottom. They scooped up a load of shell and gravel without checking their speed and went bellowing up the far ramp, swinging again to race up and deposit their load below the cliff, but above the high-water mark.

Round they went, and round again, chasing their tails, while the bulldozers held back the sea which was now becoming angry – sending its cohorts to skirmish along the dyke, seeking a weak place to attack.

Johnny glanced at his watch again.

'Three minutes to low water,' he spoke aloud, and grinned. 'We're going to make it – I think!'

He lit a cigarette, relaxing a little now. He dropped into the driving seat and swung the Land-Rover up the beach, parking it beyond the mountain of gravel that the earthloaders were building.

He climbed out and took up a handful of the gravel.

'Lovely!' he whispered. 'Oh sweet! Sweet!'

It was right. All the signs were good. In the single handful he identified a small garnet, and a larger lump of agate.

He scooped another handful.

'Jasper,' he gloated. 'And banded ironstone!'

All these stones were the team-mates of the diamond, you found them together.

The shape was right also, the stones polished round and shiny as marbles, not flattened like coins which would mean they had washed in only one direction. Round stones meant a wave action zone – a diamond trap!

'We've hit a jewel box – I'll take Lysol on that!'

24

From thirty-seven miles of beach Johnny had picked a two-hundred-yard stretch, and hit it right on the nose. A choice not by luck, but by careful study of the configuration of the coastline, aerial photographs of the wave patterns and bottom contours of the sea, an analysis of the beach sands, and finally by that indefinable 'feel' for ground that a good diamond man has.

Johnny Lance was mightily delighted with himself as he climbed back into the Land-Rover. The earthloaders had scraped the gravel down to bedrock. Their job was finished, and they pulled out of the pit and stood with panting exhausts beside the enormous pile of gravel they had recovered.

'Bottom boys!' roared Johnny, and the patient army of Ovambo tribesmen who had been squatting above the beach came swarming down into the pit. Their job was to sweep and clean the pit bottom, for a high proportion of the diamonds would have worked their way down through the gravel into the crevices and irregularities of the bedrock.

The sea changed its mood, furious at the brutal rape of its beaches it came hissing and tearing at the sand dyke. The tide was making now, and the bulldozers had to redouble their efforts to keep it out.

In the pit the Ovambos worked in a frenzy of activity, sparing only an occasional apprehensive glance for the wall of sand that held the Atlantic at bay.

Now Johnny was tensing up again. If he pulled them out early he would be leaving diamonds down there, if he left them in too late he might drown machinery – and men.

He cut it fine, just a fraction too fine. He pulled the bottom boys out with the sea beginning to break over the dyke, and to seep through under it.

Then he began to pull out his bulldozers, ten of them out – one still coming infinitely slowly, waddling across the wide bottom of the empty pit.

The sea broke through, it broke simultaneously in two places and came boiling into the pit in a waist-high wave.

The bulldozer operator saw it, hesitated one second, then his spirit failed him and he jumped down from his machine; abandoning it to the sea he sprinted ahead of the wave, making for the steep nearest side of the pit.

'Bastard!' swore Johnny as he watched the operator scramble to safety. 'He could have made it.' But his anger was against himself also. His decision to withdraw had been too long delayed, that was £20,000 worth of machinery he had sacrificed to the sea.

He slammed the Land-Rover into gear, and put her to the pit. She went off the edge like a ski jump, falling fifteen feet before she hit the bottom, but her fall was cushioned by the slope of sand and she sprang forward bravely to meet the rush of sea water.

It broke over the bonnet, slewing the vehicle viciously, but Johnny fought her head round and kept her going towards the stranded bulldozer.

The engine of the Land-Rover had been sealed and water-proofed against just such an emergency, and now she ploughed forward throwing a sheet of water to each side. But her forward rush faltered as the green water poured over her.

Now suddenly the entire sand dyke collapsed under the white surf and the Atlantic took control. The tall wave of green water that raced across the pit hit the Land-Rover, upending her, throwing Johnny into the jubilant frothing water, while the Land-Rover rolled over on her back, pointing all four wheels to the sky in surrender.

Johnny went under but came up immediately. Half swimming, half wading, battered by the boisterous sea he struggled on towards the yellow island of steel.

The sea struck him down, and he went under again. Found his feet for a moment, then had them cut from under him once more.

Then suddenly he had reached the bulldozer and was dragging himself up over the tracks to the driver's seat. He was coughing and vomiting sea water, as he reached the controls.

The bulldozer sat immovable, held down by her own twenty-six tons of dead weight on to the hard bedrock of the pit. Although the sea burst over her, and swirled through her tracks, it could not move her.

Through eyes blurred and swimming with salt water and his own tears, Johnny briefly checked the gauges on the instrument panels. She had oil pressure and engine revs, and high above his head the exhaust pipe chugged blue smoke.

Johnny coughed again. Vomit and sea water shot up his throat in a scalding jet, but he pushed the throttle wide and threw in both clutch levers.

Ponderously the great machine ground forward, almost contemptuously shouldering the sea aside, her tracks solidly gripping the bedrock.

Johnny looked about him quickly. The sand ramps at each end of the pit were washed away. The sides were sheer now, and behind him the sea was rushing unimpeded into the pit.

A wave broke over his head, and Johnny shook the water from his hair like a spaniel and looked around with mounting desperation for an avenue of escape.

With a shock of surprise he saw the Old Man. He had thought him to be four hundred miles away in Cape Town, but here he was on the edge of the pit. The white hair shone like a beacon.

Instinctively Johnny swung the bulldozer in his direction, crawling through the turbulent waters towards him.

The Old Man was directing two of the other bulldozers, reversing them as close as he dared to the lip of the bank of sand, while from the service truck parked below the cliff a line of Ovambos came staggering down the beach with the heavy tractor tow chain over their shoulders. They shuffled bow-legged under the tremendous weight of the chain, sinking ankle deep into the sand with each step.

The Old Man roared at them, urging them on, but the words were lost in the thunder of diesel engines and the ranting of the wind and the sea. Now he turned back to Johnny.

'Get her in close,' the Old Man yelled through cupped hands. 'I'll bring the end of the chain down to you!'

Johnny waved an acknowledgement, then grabbed at the controls as the force of the next wave pushed even the giant tractor off its line, and Johnny felt the diesel falter for the first time – the water had found its way in through the seals at last.

Then he was under the high bank of yellow sand that towered twenty feet above him and he scrambled forward over the engine bonnet to meet the Old Man.

The Old Man was poised on the lip of the pit with the end of the chain draped in a loop over both shoulders. He was stooped beneath its weight, and when he stepped forward the sand crumpled away beneath him and he came sliding and slipping down the steep incline, buried waist deep, the great chain snaking after him.

Judging the rush of the sea Johnny jumped down to help him. Together, battered by the sea, they dragged the chain to the bulldozer.

'Fix it on to the blade arm,' grunted the Old Man, and they got a double turn of chain around the thick steel arm.

'Shackle!' Johnny snapped at him, and while the Old Man untied the length of rope which secured the steel shackle around his waist, Johnny looked up at the cliff of sand that hung over them.

'Christ!' he said softly, the sea was attacking it – and now it was soft and trembling above them, ready to collapse and smother them.

The Old Man passed him the huge shackle, and Johnny

began with numbed hands to secure the end of the chain. He must pass the thick case-hardened pin through two links and then screw it closed. It was a Herculean task under these conditions, with the surf bursting over his head, the drag of the sea on the chain, and the cliff of sand threatening to fall on them at any moment. From twenty feet above them Johnny's foreman was watching anxiously, ready to pass the word to the two waiting bulldozers to throw their combined weights on the chain.

The thread of the pin caught, half a dozen turns would secure it, he would have finished the job by the time the word was passed to the 'dozer operators.

'Okay,' he nodded and gasped at the Old Man. 'Pull!'

The Old Man lifted his head and bellowed up the bank, 'Pull!'

The foreman acknowledged with a wave.

'Okay.' And his head disappeared behind the bank as he ran back to the bulldozers, and at that moment the surf swung the chain. A movement of a few inches, but enough to catch Johnny's left index finger between two of the links.

The Old Man saw his face, saw him struggling to free himself.

'What is it?'

Then the water sucked back for a moment, and he saw what had happened. He waded forward to help – but from above them came the throaty roar of the diesels and the chain began running away, snaking and twisting up the bank like a python.

The Old Man reached Johnny and caught him about the shoulders to steady him. They braced themselves in horror, staring at the captive hand.

The chain jerked taut, severing the finger cleanly in a bright burst of scarlet, and Johnny reeled back into the Old Man's arms. The great yellow bulk of the bulldozer was dragged relentlessly down on top of them, threatening to crush them both, but using the next break and push of the sea the Old Man dragged Johnny clear – and they were carried sideways along the bank, tumbled helplessly by the strength of the water out of the bulldozer's path.

Johnny clutched his injured hand to his chest, but it hosed a bright stream of blood that discoloured the water about them. His head went under and salt water shot down his throat into his lungs. He felt himself drowning, the strength oozing out of him.

He surfaced again, and through bleary eyes saw the glistening wet bulldozer half-way up the sand bank. He felt the Old Man's arms about his chest and he went under again relaxing as the darkness closed over his eyes and brain.

When the darkness cleared from his eyes, he was lying on the dry sand of the beach and the first thing he saw was the Old Man's face above him, furrowed and pouched, his silver white hair plastered across his forehead.

'Did we get her out?' Johnny asked thickly.

'Ja,' the Old Man answered. 'We got her out.' And he stood up, walked to the Jeep, and drove away, leaving the foreman to tend to Johnny.

Johnny grinned at the memory, and lifting his left hand off the driving-wheel of the Jaguar he licked the shiny stump of his index finger.

'It was worth a finger,' he murmured aloud, and still searching for road signs he drove on slowly.

He smiled again comfortably, shaking his head with amusement as he remembered his hurt and disappointment when the Old Man had walked away and left him lying on the beach. He had not expected the Old Man to fall on his shoulders sobbing his gratitude and begging forgiveness for all the years of misery and loneliness – but he had expected something more than that.

After a two-hundred-mile round Jeep-journey through the desert night to the nearest hospital where they had trimmed and bound the stump, Johnny was back at the workings the next day in time to watch the first run of gravel from the beach.

In his absence, the gravel had been screened to sieve off all the over-size rock and stone, then it had been puddled through a tank of silicon mud to float off all the material with a specific gravity less than 2.5, then finally what was left had been run through a ball mill – a long steel cylinder containing steel balls the size of baseballs. The cylinder revolved continually and the steel balls crushed to powder all substance softer than 4 on Mohs hardness scale.

Now there was a residue, a thousandth part of the gravel they had won from the sea. In this remainder would be the diamonds – if diamonds there were.

When Johnny arrived back at the shed of galvanized iron and wood on the cliff above the beach that housed his separation plant, he was still half groggy from the anaesthetic and lack of sleep.

His hand throbbed with the persistence of a lighthouse, his eyes were reddened and a thick black stubble covered his jaws.

He went to stand beside the grease table that filled half the shed. He was swaying a little on his feet, as he looked around at the preparations. The massive bin at the head of the table was filled with the concentrated diamond gravels, the plates greased down, and his crew was standing ready.

'Let's go!' Johnny nodded at his foreman, who immediately threw in the lever that set the table shaking like an old man with palsy.

The table was a series of steel plates, each slightly inclined and thickly coated with dirty yellow grease. From the bin at the head of the shuddering table a mixture of gravel and water began to dribble, its consistency and rate of flow carefully regulated by the foreman. It spread over the greased table like spilled treacle, dropping from one plate to the next, and finally into the waste bin at the end of the table.

A diamond is unwettable, immerse it in water, scrub it, – but it comes out dry. A coat of grease on a steel plate is also unwettable, so wet gravel and sea shell will slide over it and keep moving across the agitating, sloping table.

But a diamond when it hits grease sticks like a half-sucked toffee to a woollen blanket.

In the excitement and anxiety of the moment Johnny felt his weariness recede, even the pain in his stump was muted by it. His eyes and whole attention were fastened on that glistening yellow sheet of grease.

The little stuff under a carat in weight, or the industrial black diamond and boart would not be visible on the table; the agitation was too rapid – blurring with speed, and the flow of loose material would disguise them.

So complete was his absorption that it was some seconds before he was aware of a presence beside him. He glanced up quickly.

The Old Man was there, standing with the wide stance and tension-charged attitude that was his own special way.

Johnny was acutely conscious of the Old Man's bulk beside him – and he felt the first flicker of alarm. What if this was a barren run? He needed diamonds now – as he had never needed anything in his life. He scanned the blurring plates of yellow grease, seeking the purchase price that could buy back the Old Man's esteem. The speckled gravel flowed imperturbably across the plates, and Johnny felt a flutter of panic.

Then from across the table the foreman let out a whoop, and pointed.

'Thar she blows!'

Johnny's eyes darted to the head of the table. There beneath the outlet from the bin, half buried in the thick grease by its own weight, anchored solidly while the worthless gravel washed past it, was a diamond.

A big fat five-carat thing, that glowed sulky and yellow, like a wild animal resenting its captivity.

Johnny sighed softly and darted a sideways glance at the Old Man. The Old Man was watching the table without expression, and though he must have been conscious of Johnny's scrutiny, he did not look up. Johnny's eyes were dragged irresistibly back to the table.

By some freakish chance, the next diamond fell from the bin directly on to the one already anchored in the grease.

When diamond strikes diamond it bounces like a golf ball off a tarmac road.

The second diamond, a white beauty the size of a peach pip, clicked loudly as it struck the other then spun head high in the air.

Both Johnny and the foreman laughed involuntarily with delight at the beauty of that twinkling drop of solid sunlight.

Johnny reached across the table with his good hand, and snatched it out of the air. He rubbed it between his fingers – revelling in the soapy feel of it, then turned and offered it to the Old Man.

The Old Man looked at the diamond, nodded in acknowledgement. Then he pulled back the cuff of his coat and checked his wrist watch.

'It's late. I must get back to Cape Town.'

'Won't you stay for the rest of the run, sir?' Johnny realized his tone was too eager. 'We could have a drink together afterwards.' He remembered after he had spoken, that the Old Man abhorred alcohol.

'No.' The Old Man shook his head. 'I have to get back by this evening.' Now he looked steadily into Johnny's eyes. 'You see, Tracey is getting married tomorrow afternoon and I must be there.'

Then he smiled, watching Johnny's face, but nobody could ever guess the meaning of a smile on the Old Man's lips – for it never showed in his eyes.

'Didn't you know?' he asked, still smiling. 'I thought you had received an invitation.' And he went out of the shed to where his Jeep stood in the bright sunshine waiting to take him out to the aircraft landing-strip among the sand dunes.

The pain in his injured hand, and the Old Man's words denied Johnny the sleep he so desperately needed, but it was two o'clock in the morning before he threw back his blankets and lit the lamp beside his camp bed.

'He said I had been invited – and, by God, I'll be there.'

He drove through the night, and the next morning. The first two hundred miles were on desert tracks of sand and stone, then he reached the metalled highway in the dawn and turned south across the great plains and over the mountains. It was noon before he saw the squat blue silhouette of Table Mountain on the skyline dwarfing the city that huddled beneath it.

He checked in at the Vineyard Hotel, and hurried to his room to bath and shave and change into a suit.

The grounds of the old house were crowded with expensive automobiles, and the overflow was parked along both sides of the street outside, but he found a space for the dusty Land-Rover. He walked up through the white gates and across the green lawns.

There was a band playing in the house, and a hubbub of voices and laughter drifted out through the windows of the ballroom.

He went in through the side door. The passages were thronged with guests, and he made his way amongst them seeking a familiar face in the groups of loud-voiced gesticulating men and giggling women. At last he found one.

'Michael.' And Michael Shapiro looked round, recognizing him and letting the conflicting emotions of pleasure, surprise and alarm show clearly on his face.

'Johnny. It's good to see you.'

'Is the ceremony over?'

'Yes, and the speeches also – thank God.' He took Johnny's arm and led him aside. 'Let me get you a glass of

34

champagne.' Michael hailed a waiter and put a crystal glass into Johnny's hand.

'Here's to the bride,' Johnny murmured and drank.

'Does the Old Man know you are here?' Michael came out with the question that was burning his mouth, and when Johnny shook his head, Michael's expression became thoughtful.

'What's he like, Michael, Tracey's husband?'

'Kenny Hartford?' Michael considered the question. 'He's all right, I suppose. Nice-looking boy, plenty of money.'

'What's he do for a crust of bread?'

'His daddy left him the whole loaf – but to fill in the time he does fashion photography.' And Johnny pulled down the corners of his mouth.

Michael frowned. 'He's all right, Johnny. The Old Man picked him carefully.'

'The Old Man?' Johnny's jaw thrust out.

'Of course, you know him – he wouldn't leave an important decision like that to anybody else.'

Johnny finished his champagne in silence, and Michael watched his face anxiously.

'Where is she? Have they left yet?'

'No.' Michael shook his head. 'They're still in the ballroom.'

'I think I'll go and wish luck to the bride.'

'Johnny.' Michael caught hold of his elbow. 'Don't do anything stupid – will you?'

Johnny stood at the head of the marble staircase that led down into the ballroom. The floor was crowded with dancing couples and the music was loud and merry. The bridal party sat at a raised table across the floor.

Benedict van der Byl saw Johnny first. His face flushed and he leaned quickly to whisper to the Old Man, then began to rise from his seat. The Old Man placed a restraining hand on Benedict's shoulder, and smiled across the room at Johnny.

Johnny went down the stairs and made his way through the dancers. Tracey had not seen him. She was talking to the silky-faced young man who sat beside her. He had wavy blond hair.

'Hello, Tracey.' She looked up at Johnny and caught her breath. She was more beautiful than he remembered.

'Hello, Johnny.' Her voice was almost a whisper.

'May I dance with you?' She was pale now, and her eyes went to the Old Man, not to her new husband. The gleaming white bush of hair nodded slightly, and Tracey stood up.

They made one circuit of the dance floor before the band stopped playing. Johnny had planned a hundred different things to say to her, but he was dumb until the music ended and the opportunity was passing. Hurriedly now in the few seconds that were left Johnny told her: 'I hope you will be happy, Tracey. But if you ever need help – ever – I will come, I promise you that.'

'Thank you.' Her voice was husky, and for a moment she looked like the little girl who had cried in the night. Then he took her back to her husband.

The promise had been made five years ago, and now he had come to London to honour it.

Number 23 Stark Street was a neat double-storeyed cottage with a narrow front. He parked outside it. It was dark now and lights burned on both floors. He sat in the parked Jaguar, suddenly reluctant to go further. Somehow he knew that Tracey was here, and he knew it would not be pretty. For a moment he recaptured the image of her as a lovely young woman in a wedding dress of white satin, then he climbed out of the Jaguar and went up the steps to the front door. He reached for the bell before he noticed with surprise that the door was ajar. He pushed it open and walked into a small sitting-room furnished with feminine taste.

The room had been hastily ransacked, one of the curtains was spread on the floor and on it were piled books and ornaments. Pictures had been taken down from the walls and stacked ready for removal.

Johnny picked up one of the books, and opened the cover. On the fly leaf was a handwritten name. 'Tracey van der Byl.' He dropped it back on the pile as he heard footsteps on the stairs from the floor above.

A man came down the stairs. He was dressed in soiled green velvet trousers, sheepskin boots, and shabby frock coat of military cut frogged with tarnished gold braid. He was carrying an armful of women's dresses.

He saw Johnny and stopped nervously, his pink lips opened in vacant surprise but his eyes were beady and bright under the thatch of lank blond hair.

'Hello,' Johnny smiled pleasantly. 'Are you moving out?' And he drifted quietly closer to the man on the stairs and stood looking up at him.

Suddenly from the floor above a low wail echoed down the stairs. It was an eerie sound, without passion or pain, as though steam were escaping from a jet, only just recognizable as human. Johnny went rigid at the sound, and the man on the stairs glanced nervously over his shoulder.

'What have you done to her?' Johnny asked softly, without menace.

'No. Nothing! She's on a trip. A bad trip.' The man's denial was frantic. 'It's her first time on acid.'

'So you're cleaning the place out, are you?' Johnny asked mildly.

'She owes me plenty. She can't pay. She promised – and she can't pay.'

'Oh,' said Johnny. 'That's different. I thought you were hitting the place.' He reached into his overcoat and brought out his wallet, riffling the wad of banknotes. 'I'm a friend of hers. How much does she owe you?'

'Fifty nicker.' The man's eyes sparkled when he saw the wallet. 'I gave her credit.'

Johnny counted off ten fivers, and held them out. The

man dropped the bundle of clothing over the banisters and came eagerly down the last few stairs.

'Did you sell her the stuff – the acid?' Johnny asked, and the man stopped a pace from him, his expression stiffening with suspicion.

'Oh, for God's sake.' Johnny grinned. 'We are not children – I know the score.' He offered the banknotes. 'Did you get the stuff for her?'

The man grinned back at him weakly, and nodded as he reached for the money. Johnny's free hand snapped closed on the thin wrist and he swung him off his feet, forcing his wrist up between his shoulder-blades.

Johnny stuffed the money into his pocket, and marched him up the stairs.

'Let's go and have a look, shall we?'

There was a mattress on the iron bedstead covered with a grey army blanket. Tracey sat cross-legged on the blanket. She wore only a thin cotton slip and her hair hung lank and lustreless to her waist. Her arms crossed over her chest were thin and white as sticks of chalk. Her face also was pale, the skin translucent in the light of the electric bulb. She was rocking gently back and forth and wailing softly, her breath steaming in the icy cold room.

It was her eyes that shocked Johnny the most. They seemed to have expanded to an enormous size, and beneath each was a dark bruised-looking smear. The pupils of the eyes were distended and glittery with the same adamant sheen as uncut diamonds.

The big glittery green eyes fastened on Johnny and the man in the doorway, and the wail rose abruptly to a shriek. The shriek died away, and she bowed forward and buried her face in her hands, covering her eyes.

'Tracey,' said Johnny softly. 'Oh God, Tracey!'

'She'll be all right,' the man whimpered and twisted in his grip. 'It's the first time – she'll be all right.'

'Come.' Johnny dragged him out of the room, and pushed

38

the door closed with his foot. He held him against the wall, and his face was set and pale, his eyes merciless – but he spoke quietly, patiently as though he was explaining to a child.

'I'm going to hurt you now. I'm going to hurt you very badly. Just as badly as I can without killing you. Not because I enjoy it, but because that girl is a very special person to me. In the future when you think about giving poison to another girl – I want you to remember what I did to you tonight.'

Johnny held him with his left hand against the wall and he used his right hand, punching up under the ribs at an angle to tear the stomach muscles. With three or four blows he was too high, and he felt ribs crack and snap under his fist.

When he stepped back the man sagged slowly face forward, and Johnny caught him cleanly in the mouth snapping his teeth off at the gums, splitting his lips open like the petals of a rose. The man had made a lot of noise. Johnny looked into Tracey's room to make sure she had not been disturbed, but she was still bowed forward, rocking rhythmically on her haunches.

He found the bathroom and dampened his handkerchief to wipe the blood off his hands and the front of his overcoat. He came out into the passage again and stooped over the unconscious body to check the pulse. It was strong and regular, and he felt a lift of relief as he dragged the man's face out of the puddle of his own vomit and blood to prevent him drowning.

He went through to Tracey and, despite her frantic struggles, wrapped her in the greasy army blanket and carried her down to the Jaguar.

She quietened down and lay like a sleeping child in the back seat while he tucked the blanket round her, then he went back into the house and phoned 999, giving the address and hanging up immediately.

He left Tracey in the car outside the Dorchester, while he went in to speak to the reception clerk. Within minutes Tracey was in a wheelchair on her way up to the two-bedroom suite on the second floor. The doctor was there fifteen minutes later.

After the doctor had gone Johnny bathed, and carrying a tumbler of Chivas Regal in one hand he went into Tracey's room and stood by her bed. Whatever the doctor had given her had put her out cleanly. She lay gaunt and pale – yet with a strangely fragile beauty that seemed enhanced by the bruised discoloration of her eye sockets.

He stooped to brush the hair from her cheek, and her breath was light and warm on his hand. He felt such an infinity of tenderness for her then as he had never known for any other person, he was amazed by the strength of it.

He stooped over her and gently brushed her lips with his own. Her lips were dry and flaky white, and their touch was harsh as sandpaper.

Johnny straightened up and went to the armchair across the room. He sank into it wearily, and sipped the whisky, feeling its warmth spread from his belly and untie the knots in his muscles. He watched the pale ruined face on the pillows.

'We are in a hell of a mess, you and I,' he spoke aloud, and felt anger again. For long minutes it was undirected, but slowly it gelled and found an object to focus on.

For the first time in his life he was angry with the Old Man.

'He has brought you to this,' he said to the girl on the bed. 'And me—'

The reaction was swift, his loyalty was a thing grown part of his existence. Always he had trained himself to believe that the Old Man's machinations were just and wise – even if at times the justice and wisdom were hidden from him. Mortal man does not doubt the omnipotence of his gods.

Sickened by his own treachery, he began to examine the Old Man's motives and actions under the bright light of reason.

Why had the Old Man sent Michael Shapiro to fetch him out of the desert?

'He wants you in Cape Town, Johnny. Benedict didn't measure up. The Old Man has given him the London Office, it's a form of exile. He's picked you to take over the Company,' Michael explained. 'Tracey is out of the way. She and her husband are in London also. I guess the Old Man thinks it's safe to have you back in Cape Town now.'

Michael watched Johnny's undisguised joy and went on slowly.

'I'm speaking out of turn, perhaps. Mr van der Byl is a strange man. He's not like other people. I know how you feel about him, I've watched it all, you know – but listen, Johnny, you can go anywhere on your own now. There are a lot of other companies that want you—' But he had seen the expression on Johnny's face, and stopped ' – okay, Johnny. Forget I ever said it. I only spoke because I like you.'

Thinking on it now, there had been substance in Michael's warning. Certainly he was General Manager of Van Der Byl Diamonds, but he was no nearer to the Old Man than he had ever been. He lived under the mountain but the mountain was remote and he had not been able to scale the lowest slopes.

He had found the city as lonely as the desert, and he was ripe for the first attractive woman who set her snares for him.

Ruby Grange was tall and slim with hair the colour they call 'Second Cape' in a diamond, like sunlight through a crystal glass of champagne.

He wondered now at his own naïvety. That he should be so easily misled, and should have rushed so headlong into her web. After the wedding she had revealed herself, exposing the deeply calculating greed, the driving hunger for flattery and material possessions which was her mainspring, and her complete absorption with herself – Johnny had not been able to believe it. For months he fought off the growing certainty until it could be denied no longer, and he looked with chilled dismay on the shallow selfish little creature he had married.

He had withdrawn from her and flung all his energies into the Company.

This, then, was his life and he saw that it was an empty thing, hollowed out by the Old Man's hand.

For the first time his mind skirted the idea that it was a carefully calculated and sadistic revenge for the innocent action of a half-grown boy.

As though it were an escape from thoughts too dreadful to be borne, he fell asleep in the chair and the glass fell from his hand.

Jacobus Isaac van der Byl sat in a leather chair before the X-ray viewer. Fear had blasted the granite of his features, leaving them cracked and sagging, recognizable but subtly alerted below the gleaming white mane.

Fear was in his eyes also, moving below the surface like slimy water creatures in the pale blue pools. With the fear chilling and numbing his limbs he watched the cloudy and swirling images on the screen.

The specialist was talking softly, impersonally, as though he were lecturing one of his classes.

' – enveloping the thymus here, and extending beyond the trachea.'

The point of his gold pencil followed the ghostly outline on the screen. The Old Man swallowed with an effort. It seemed to be swelling in his throat as he listened, and his voice was hoarse and blurred to his own ears.

'You will operate?' he asked, and the specialist paused in his explanation. He glanced at the surgeon across the desk. The exchange was as guilty as that of conspirators.

The Old Man swivelled his chair and faced the surgeon.

'Well?' he demanded harshly.

'No.' The surgeon shook his head apologetically. 'It's too late. If only you had—'

'How long?' The Old Man overrode his explanation.

'Six months, not more.'

'You are certain?'

'Yes.'

The Old Man's chin sank on to his chest and he closed his eyes. There was complete silence in the room, they watched him with professional pity and interest as he reached his own personal acceptance of death.

At last the Old Man opened his eyes and stood up slowly. He tried to smile but his lips would not hold the shape.

'Thank you, gentlemen,' he croaked in this new rough voice. 'Will you excuse me, please. There are many things to arrange now.'

He went down to where the Rolls waited at the entrance. He walked slowly, shuffling his feet and the chauffeur came to him quickly, but the Old Man shrugged away his helping hands and climbed into the back seat of the car.

Michael Shapiro was waiting for him in the study of the big house. He saw the change in him immediately and jumped up from his chair. The Old Man stood in the doorway, his body seemed to have shrunk.

'Six months,' he said. 'They give me six months.' He said it as though he had expected to buy off death, and they had tricked him. He closed his eyes again, and when he opened them there was a glint of cunning in them, even his face had a pinched foxy look to it.

'Where is he? Is he back yet?'

'Yes, the Boeing got in at nine this morning. He's at the

43

office now.' Michael was shocked, it was the first time he had seen the Old Man without the mask.

'And the girl?' He had not called her 'daughter' since the divorce.

'Johnny has her in a private nursing home.'

'Worthless slut,' said the Old Man softly, and Michael stilled the protest before it reached his lips. 'Get your pad. I want you to take something down.' The Old Man chuckled hoarsely. 'We'll see!' he said, making it sound like a threat. 'We'll see!'

Johnny's doctor was waiting at Cape Town airport.

'Take her, Robin. Dry her out, and fatten her up. She's up to her gills with drugs and she probably hasn't eaten for a month.'

Tracey showed her first spark of spirit.

'Where do you think—'

'Into a nursing home.' Johnny anticipated her questions. 'For as long as is necessary.'

'I'm not—'

'Oh, yes, you bloody well are.' He took her arm, and Robin grabbed the other. They walked her, still protesting weakly to the car park.

'Thanks, Robin Old Soldier, give her the full workout.'

'I'll send her back to you like new,' Robin promised and drove away. Johnny took a few moments to look at the massive square silhouette of the mountain – his own private home-coming ceremony. Then he fetched the Mercedes from the airport garage, and hesitated between home or the office, decided he was not up to an interrogation from Ruby and chose the office. He kept a clean shirt and shaving tackle in his private bathroom there.

They descended on him like a tribe of man-eating Amazons as he came in through the glass doors into the lusciously furnished and carpeted reception area of Van Der Byl Diamonds head office.

The two pretty little receptionists began yipping joyously in chorus.

'Oh, Mr Lance, I have a whole sheaf of messages—'

'Oh, Mr Lance, your wife—'

Trying not to run he made it to within ten feet of his own door, when the Old Man's secretary popped out of ambush from behind her frosted-glass panel.

'Mr Lance, where on earth have you been? Mr van der Byl has been asking—'

Which alerted Lettie Pienaar, his own secretary.

'Mr Lance, thank goodness you're back.'

Johnny stopped and held up his hands in an attitude of surrender.

'One at a time, ladies. There is enough to go round – don't panic.'

Which broke the reception team into a quivering jelly of giggles, and sent the Old Man's watchdog back behind her panel sniffing disgustedly.

'Which is the most important, Lettie?' he asked as he went to his desk and flipped through his mail, shrugged out of his coat and began stripping tie and shirt as he headed for his bathroom.

They shouted at each other through the open door of the bathroom, as Johnny shaved quickly and showered, Lettie bringing him up to date on every aspect of Company and domestic business.

'Mrs Lance has phoned regularly. She called me a liar when I told her you were at Cartridge Bay.' Lettie was silent a moment, then as Johnny came out of the bathroom she asked, 'By the way, where have you been?'

'Don't you start that.' Johnny stood over the desk, and began flipping through the accumulated papers. 'Get my wife on the phone, please – no, hold it. Tell her I'll be home at seven.'

Lettie saw she had lost his attention, and she stood and went out. Johnny settled down behind his desk.

Van Der Byl Diamonds was a sick company. Despite Johnny's protests the Old Man had been drawing off its reserves and feeding them into his other ventures – the property-developing company, the clothing factory, Van Der Byl fisheries, the big irrigation scheme on the Orange River – and now the cupboard was almost bare.

The beach concessions were reaching the end of a short but glorious life. They were starting to work break-even ground. The Old Man had sold the Huib Hoch concession to the big Company for a quick profit – but the profit had been just as quickly transferred out of Johnny's control.

There was only one really fat goose left in his pen, and it wasn't laying eggs yet.

Eighteen months earlier Johnny had purchased two offshore diamond grounds from a company which had died in attempting to work them. It had been strangled by its own inefficiency.

Taking diamonds from the sea is about eight times more expensive than working them from a dry opencast. One must dredge the gravel from the wild and unpredictable waters of the Skeleton Coast, load it into dumb barges, tow the barges to a safe base, off-load it and then begin the recovery process – or rather, that was the method the defunct company had attempted.

Johnny had dreamed up, and then ordered a vessel which was completely self-contained. It could lie out at sea, suck up the gravel and process it, spilling the waste gravel back into the sea as rapidly as it was sucked aboard. It was fitted with a sophisticated recovery plant that was completely computerized and contained within the ocean-going hull. It needed only a small crew, and it could work in all weather conditions short of a full tornado.

The *Kingfisher* was lying at Portsmouth dockyards rapidly

nearing completion. Her trials were scheduled for early August.

Financing the building of this vessel had been a nightmare for Johnny. The Old Man had been unhelpful, when he wasn't being downright obstructive. He never discussed the venture without that little smile twitching at his lips. He had restricted Van Der Byl Diamonds' monetary involvement in the project so severely that Johnny had been forced to raise two millions outside the company.

He had found the money, and the Old Man had smiled again.

Kingfisher should have been lying on the grounds three months ago, sucking up diamonds. The whole financial structure of the scheme was based on her completion on schedule, but *Kingfisher* was running six months behind and now the foundations were shivering.

Sitting at his desk Johnny was working out how to shore up the whole edifice and keep it from collapsing before he could get *Kingfisher* working. The creditors were rumbling and creaking, and Johnny had only his own enthusiasm and reputation left to keep them quiet.

Now he must ask them to defer their interest payments for another three months. He picked up the telephone.

'Get me Mr Larsen at Credit Finance,' he said, steeling himself as he did so, jutting out his jaw and thrusting one bunched fist into his jacket pocket.

At five o'clock he stood up from his desk and went to the cabinet. He poured three fingers of whisky and went back to lower himself wearily into his swivel chair. He felt no elation at having won another reprieve, he was too tired.

The unlisted telephone on his desk rang and he picked it up.

'Lance,' he said.

'How was London?' he recognized the voice instantly, feeling no surprise that the Old Man knew about his journey. The Old Man knew everything. Before he could answer the hoarse croak came again, 'Come up to the house – now!' And the receiver clicked dead.

Johnny looked at the whisky in his hand regretfully and set it down untouched. The Old Man would smell it and smile.

Cloud was blowing over the mountain, and the setting sun turned it to the colour of tangerine and peaches. The Old Man stood at the window and watched the cloud cascade down into the valley, dispersing as it fell.

He turned from the window as Johnny entered the study and instantly Johnny was aware that something momentous had taken place in his absence.

He glanced quickly at Michael Shapiro for a cue, but Michael's grey-streaked head was bowed over the papers he held on his lap.

'Good evening.' Johnny addressed the Old Man.

'Sit there.' The Old Man indicated the Spanish leather chair opposite his desk.

'Read it,' the Old Man ordered Michael, and Michael cleared his throat and patted the papers into a neat square before he began.

The Old Man sat with his eyes on Johnny's face. It was a candid, intimate scrutiny, but Johnny felt no discomfort under it. It was almost as though the Old Man's eyes were caressing him.

Mike Shapiro read intelligently, bringing out the meaning of the involved and convoluted legal phrases. The document was the Old Man's Last Will and Testament, and it took twenty minutes for Mike to complete the reading of it. When he had finished there was silence in the room, and the Old Man broke it at last.

'Do you understand?' he asked. There was a gentleness about him that there had never been before. He seemed to have shrunk, the flesh withering on his bones and leaving them dry and light – like the sun-dried bones of a long dead seabird.

'Yes, I understand.' Johnny nodded.

'Explain it to us simply, not in your lawyer's gobbledy-gook, just to be certain,' the Old Man insisted, and Mike began to speak.

'Mr van der Byl's private estate, with the exception of his shares in Van Der Byl Diamond Co. Ltd, after taxes and expenses, is placed in Trust for his two children, Tracey—'

The Old Man interrupted impatiently, swatting Mike's words out of the air as though they were flies.

'Not that. The Company. Tell him about the shares in the Company.'

'Mr van der Byl's shares in the Company are to be divided equally between you and the two van der Byl children, Tracey—'

Again the Old Man interrupted.

'He knows their names, dammit.'

It was the first time ever that either of them had heard him swear. Mike grinned ruefully at Johnny, as though asking for his sympathy, but Johnny was intent on the Old Man, studying his face, feeling the deep satisfying thrill swelling within his chest.

A third share in Van Der Byl Diamonds was no great fortune – nobody knew that better than Johnny.

However, by placing Johnny's name on the list with Tracey and Benedict – he had made him his own. This was what he had worked for all these years. The declaration was public, an acknowledgement to the world.

Johnny Lance had a father at last. He wanted to reach out and touch the Old Man. His chest felt swollen, tight with emotion. Behind his eyelids was a slow soft burning. Johnny blinked.

'This is—' His voice was ragged, and he coughed. 'I just don't know how to tell you—'

The Old Man interrupted him impatiently, silencing him with an imperious gesture, and he croaked at Mike.

'Now read him the codicil to the Will. No, don't read it. Explain it to him.'

Michael's expression changed; he looked down at his papers as he spoke, as though reluctant to meet Johnny's eyes. He cleared his throat unnecessarily and shifted in his seat.

'"By the codicil to the Will, dated the same date, and duly signed by Mr van der Byl the bequest of shares in Van Der Byl Diamond Co. Ltd to JOHN RIGBY LANCE, is made conditional on the issue by the said JOHN RIGBY LANCE of a personal guarantee for the debts of the company, including the present loan account and amounts outstanding to tributary companies for royalties and options."'

'Christ,' said Johnny, stiffening in his chair and turning to stare incredulously at the Old Man. The tightness in his chest was gone. 'What are you trying to do to me?'

The Old Man dismissed Mike Shapiro quietly, without even looking at him. 'I'll call you when I want you.' And when he had gone he repeated Johnny's question.

'What am I trying to do to you?' he asked. 'I am trying to make you responsible for debts totalling about two and a half million Rand.'

'No creditor would come to me for half a million, I would be hard pressed to raise ten thousand on my personal account.' Johnny shook his head irritably, the whole thing was nonsensical.

'There is one creditor who could come to you, and subject you to the full process of law. Not to receive payment in cash – but in personal satisfaction. He would smash you – and delight in doing so.'

Johnny's eyes narrowed disbelievingly. 'Benedict?'

The Old Man nodded. 'For once Benedict will hold the top cards. He won't be able to dislodge you from the management of the company, because Tracey will support you as she always has done – but he will be able to watch every move you make from his seat on the Board of Directors. He will be able to hound you, bring you and the Company down without suffering financial loss himself. And when you fall – you know better than to expect mercy from him. You will be devoured by the ogre you have created.'

'Created?' Johnny's voice was shocked. 'What do you mean?'

'You turned him into what he is now. You broke his heart, made him weak and useless—'

'You are crazy.' Johnny came to his feet. 'I have never done anything to Benedict. It was he who—'

But the Old Man's husky croak brushed aside Johnny's protests. 'He tried to run with you – but could not. He gave up, became small and vicious. Oh, I know about the way he is – how you made him.'

'Please, listen to me. I did not—'

But the Old Man went on remorselessly. 'Tracey also, you have ruined her life. You enslaved her, in your sin—'

'That night!' Johnny shouted at him. 'You never let me explain. We never—'

Now the Old Man's voice was a whiplash.

'Silence!' And Johnny could not defy him, the habit was too deeply engrained. The Old Man was trembling, his eyes glittering with passion. 'Both my children! You have plagued me and my family. My son is a weak-willed drifter, trying to hide his hurt in a hunt for pleasure. I have given him the instruments to destroy you, and when he does so perhaps he will become a man.'

The Old Man's voice was strained now, rusty and pain-racked. He swallowed with an effort, his throat convulsing – but there was no softening of the glitter in his eyes.

'My daughter also, torturned by her lust. A lust which you awakened – she also seeks an escape from her guilty passion. Your destruction will be her release.'

'You're wrong,' Johnny cried out, half in protest, half in entreaty. 'Please, let me explain—'

'This is how it will work. I have made you vulnerable, linking you to a crippled and foundering enterprise. This time we will be rid of you.' He stopped to pant quickly, like a running dog. His breathing was strangled, harsh-sounding. 'Benedict will cut you down, and Tracey will have to watch you go. She cannot help you, her inheritance is carefully tied up, she has no control of the capital. Your only hope is the *Kingfisher*. The *Kingfisher* will turn into a vampire and suck your life blood! You asked why I was systematically transferring the assets of Van Der Byl Diamonds to my other companies? Well, now you know the answer.'

Johnny's lips moved. He was very pale. His voice came out small and whispery.

'I could refuse to sign the guarantee.'

The Old Man smiled bleakly, a drawing back of the lips that was without warmth or humour.

'You will sign it.' His voice was wheezy. 'Your pride and conceit will not let you do otherwise. You see, I know you. I've studied you all these years. But if you refuse to sign the guarantee, I will still have smashed you. Your shares will go to Benedict. You will be out. Out! Gone! We will be finished with you at last.' Then his voice dropped, 'But you will sign. I know it.'

Involuntarily Johnny lifted his hands towards the Old Man, a gesture of supplication. 'In all this time. When I stayed with you, when I—' His voice went husky and dried up. 'Did you never feel anything for me – anything at all?'

The Old Man sat up in his chair. He seemed to regain his bulk and he began to smile. He spoke quietly now, he did not have to shout.

'Get out of my nest, Cuckoo. Get out and fly!' he said.

Slowly Johnny's expression changed, the line of his jaw hardened, thrusting out aggressively. His shoulders went back. He pushed his hands into his pockets, balling his fists into bony hammers.

He nodded once in understanding.

'I see.' He nodded again, and then he started to grin. It was an unconvincing grin, that twisted his mouth out of shape and left his eyes dark and haunted.

'All right, you mean old bastard, I'll show you.'

He turned and walked from the room without looking back.

The Old Man's expression lit in deep satisfaction. He chuckled, then his breath caught. He began to cough, and the pain ripped his throat with a violence that left him clinging weakly to the edge of his desk.

He felt the crab of death move within his flesh, sinking its claws more deeply into his throat and lungs – and he was afraid.

He called out in his pain and fear, but there was nobody in the old house to hear him.

Kingfisher was launched in August and ran her trials in the North Sea. Benedict was aboard, by the Old Man's express command. With a vessel of such complexity, and of such revolutionary design, it would have been a miracle had she functioned perfectly. August that year was not the month for miracles. At the end of the trials Johnny had compiled a list of twenty-three modifications that were necessary.

'How long?' he asked the representative of the shipyard.

'A month.' The reply was hesitant.

'You mean two,' said Benedict and laughed out loud. Johnny looked at him thoughtfully, he guessed that the Old Man had spoken to him.

'I'll tell you something, Johnny.' Benedict was still laughing. 'I'm glad this cow isn't my dream of paradise.'

Johnny froze. Those words were the Old Man's, repeated parrot fashion. It was all the confirmation that he needed.

Johnny flew back to Cape Town to find his creditors on the verge of mutiny. They wanted to sell out, and take the loss.

Johnny spent two whole precious days on Larsen's wine farm at Stellenbosch calming his fears. When Fifi Larsen, twenty years younger than her husband, squeezed Johnny's thigh under the lunch table he knew it would be all right – for another two months.

During the next hectic, strength-sapping week of argument and negotiation, Johnny made time to see Tracey.

She had been out of the nursing-home for a month now, staying with friends on a small farm near Somerset West.

When Johnny climbed out of the Mercedes, and Tracey came down from the stoop to greet him, he had his first real lift of pleasure in a long time.

'God,' he said. 'You look great.'

She was dressed in a cotton summer dress with open sandals on her feet. Her friends were away for the day, so they walked through the orchards. He studied her openly, noticing how her cheeks and arms had filled out and the colour had come back into them. Her hair was bright and springing with lights in the sun, but there were still the dark smears under her eyes, and she smiled only once when he picked a sprig of peach blossoms for her. She seemed to be afraid of him, and unsure of herself.

At last he faced her and placed his hands on her shoulders. 'All right. What's eating you?'

It came out in a quick staccato rush of words.

'I want to thank you for coming to find me. I want to explain why I was – like that. In that state. I don't want you to believe – well, bad things about me.'

'Tracey, you don't have to explain to me.'

'I want to. I must.' And she told him, not looking at his face, twisting and tearing the blossoms in her hands.

'You see, I didn't understand, I thought all men were like that. Not wanting, I mean not doing it—' She broke off, and started again. 'He was kind, you understand. And there were lots of parties and friends around all the time, every night. Then he wanted to go to London – for his career. There was not enough scope here. Even then I didn't know. Well, I knew he had lots of men friends and that some of them were different – but . . . Then I went to his studio and found them, and they laughed, Kenny and the boy twined together like snakes. "But you must have known," he said. Something just snapped in my head, I felt spoiled, dirty and horrible and I wanted to die. There was nobody to go to and I didn't want anybody – I just wanted to die.' She stopped and stood waiting for him to speak.

'Do you still want to die?' he asked gently, and she looked up startled and shook her shining hair.

'I don't want you to die either.' And suddenly they were both laughing. After that it was good between them and they talked with all the strangeness gone until it was almost dark.

'I must go,' Johnny said.

'Your wife?' she asked, the laughter fading.

'Yes. My wife.'

It was dark when Johnny went in through the front door of the new split-level ranch type in Bishopscourt which was his house but not his home; the telephone was ringing. He picked up the receiver.

'Johnny?'

'Hello Michael.' He recognized the voice.

'Johnny, get up here to the old house right away.'

Michael Shapiro's voice was strained.

'Is it the Old Man?' Johnny asked anxiously.

'No talk – just come, quickly!'

The curtains were drawn, and a log fire roared on the stone hearth. But the Old Man was cold. The coldness was deep inside him where the flames could not warm it. His hands shook as he picked sheets of paper from the open document box, glanced at them and then dropped them into the fire. They exploded into orange flame, then curled and blackened to ash. At last the box was empty but for a thick wad of multi-coloured envelopes bound together with a ribbon. He loosened the knot, picked out the first envelope, and slipped from it a single sheet of writing-paper.

'Dear Sir,
I hope you will be pleased to hear that I am now at school. The food is good but the beds are very hard—'

He dropped both envelope and letter on the fire and selected another. One at a time he read and then burned them.

'—that I have been selected to play for the first fifteen—'

Sometimes he smiled, once he chuckled.

'—I was top in all subjects except history and religious teaching. I hope to do better next—'

When there was one envelope left he held it a long time in his blue-veined bony hands. Then with an impatient flick of his wrist he threw it on to the fire and reached up to the mantelpiece to pull himself to his feet. As he stood he looked into the gilt-framed mirror above the fireplace.

He stared at his reflection, mildly surprised by the change that the last few weeks had wrought in his appearance. His eyes had lost the sparkle of life, fading to a pale dirty brownish blue – the colour of putrefaction. They bulged from the sockets, in the glassy startled stare which is peculiar to the later stages of terminal cancer.

The watery feeling of limb, and the coldness were not the result of the pain-killing drugs, he knew. Nor was the shuffling feet-dragging gait with which he crossed the thick Bokhara carpet to the stinkwood desk.

He looked down at the oblong leather case with its brass-bound corners, and he coughed, a single flesh-tearing bark. He caught at the desk to steady himself, waiting for the pain to pass before he sprang the catch on the case and laid the lid back.

His hands were quite steady as he took the barrel and butt section of the Purdy Royal twelve-bore shotgun from the case and fitted them together.

He died the way he had lived – alone.

'God, how I hate black.' Ruby Lance stood in the centre of the bedroom floor, staring at the clothing laid out on the double bed. 'It makes me look so washed out.'

She swung her head from side to side, setting the champagne-coloured cascade of her hair swinging. She turned and moved lazily across the room to the tall mirrors. She smiled at herself, a languid slanting of the eyes, and then she spoke over the shoulder of her own image.

'You say that Benedict van der Byl has arrived from England?'

'Yes,' Johnny nodded. He sat slumped in the chair beside his dressing-room door, pressing his fingers into his eyes.

Ruby came up on her toes, pulling in her stomach and pushing forward her small hard breasts.

'Who else will be there?' she asked, cupping her hands under her breasts and squeezing out the nipples between thumb and forefinger, inspecting them critically. Johnny took his hand from his eyes.

'Did you hear me?' Ruby's voice took on a sharp admonishing note. 'I'm not talking to myself, you know.'

She turned away from the mirror to face him. Standing long and slim and golden as a leopard, even her eyes had the yellow intentness of a leopard's stare. She gave the impression that at any moment she would draw her lips back in a snarl.

'It's a funeral,' he said quietly. 'Not a cocktail party.'

'Well, you can't expect me to die of sorrow. I couldn't stand him.' She crossed to the bed and picked up the pair of peach-coloured panties and rubbed the glossy material against her cheek. Then she stepped into them with two long-legged strides.

'At least I can wear something pretty under the weeds.' She snapped the elastic against her sun-gilt belly, and the almost colourless blonde curls were flattened beneath the sheer silk.

Johnny stood up slowly, and went into his dressing-room. Scornfully she called after him. 'Oh for God's sake, Johnny Lance, stop dragging that long face around as though it's the end of the world. Nobody owes that old devil a thing – he collected all his debts long before they fell due.'

They were a few minutes early, and they stood together beneath the pine-trees outside the entrance to the chapel.

When the pearl-grey Rolls drew up at the gate and brother and sister stepped down and came up the paved path, Ruby could not contain her interest.

'Is that Benedict van der Byl?'

Johnny nodded.

'He's very good-looking.'

But Johnny was looking at Tracey. The change in her appearance since he had last seen her was startling. She walked like a desert girl again, straight and proud. She came directly to Johnny and stopped in front of him. She removed her dark glasses, and he could see she had been weeping, for her eyes were slightly puffy. She wore no make-up, and with the dark scarf framing her face she looked like a nun. The marks that sorrow had left gave her face maturity.

'I did not think this day would ever come,' she said softly.

'No,' Johnny agreed. 'It was as though he would live for ever.'

Tracey moved a step closer to him, she reached out as if to touch Johnny's arm but her fingers stopped within inches of his sleeve. Johnny understood the gesture, it was a sharing of sorrow, an understanding of mutual loss, and an unstated offer of comfort.

'I don't think we have met.' Ruby used her sugar and arsenic tone. 'It is Miss van der Byl, isn't it?'

Tracey turned her head and her expression went flat and neutral. She replaced the dark glasses, masking her eyes.

'Mrs Hartford,' she said. 'How do you do.'

Mike Shapiro stood beside Johnny in the pew. He spoke without moving his lips, just loud enough for Johnny to catch the words.

'Benedict knows the conditions of the Will. You can expect his first move immediately.'

'Thanks, Mike.'

Johnny kept his eyes on the massive black coffin. The candlelight glinted and sparkled on the elaborate silver handles.

As yet he could find no interest for the conflict that lay

ahead. That would come. Now he was too deeply involved in the passing of an era, his life had reached another point of major departure. He knew it would change, had already changed.

He looked across the aisle suddenly, his gaze drawn intuitively.

Benedict van der Byl was watching him, and at that moment the priest asked for the pallbearers.

They went to stand beside the coffin, Benedict and Johnny on opposite sides of the polished black casket among the massed display of arum lilies. They watched each other warily. It seemed to Johnny that the whole scene was significant. The two of them standing over the Old Man's corpse, facing each other, with Tracey looking on anxiously.

Johnny glanced back into the body of the church, looking for Tracey. Instead he found Ruby. She was watching them both, and Johnny knew suddenly that the board had changed more than he realized. A new piece had been added to the game.

He felt Mike Shapiro nudge him, and he stooped forward and grasped the silver handle. Between them they carried the Old Man out into the sunshine.

The handle had cut into his palm with the weight of the coffin. He went on massaging it, even after the coffin had gone down into the pit. The crude mounds of fresh earth were covered with blankets of bright green artificial grass. The mourners began to drift away, but Johnny went on standing there bare-headed. Until Ruby came to touch his arm.

'Come on.' Her voice pitched low, but stinging. 'You're making a fool of yourself.'

Benedict and Tracey were waiting under the pine-trees by the churchyard gate, shaking hands and talking quietly to the departing mourners.

'You are Ruby, of course.' Benedict took her hand, smiling a little, urbane and charming. 'The flattering reports I've had of you hardly do you justice.' And Ruby glowed, seeming like a butterfly to spread her wings to the sun.

'Johnny.' Benedict turned to him, and Johnny was taken off balance by the friendly warmth of his smile and the grip of his hand. 'Michael Shapiro tells me that you have accepted my father's legacy and the conditions attached to it – you have signed the guarantee. It's wonderful news. I don't know what we would have done without you in Van Der Byl Diamonds. You are the only one that can pull the Company though this difficult period. I want you to know I am behind you all the way, Johnny. I intend becoming much more involved with the Company now, giving you all the help you need.'

'I knew I could depend on you, Benedict.' Johnny accepted the challenge as smoothly as it was thrown down. 'I think everything is going to turn out all right.'

'We have a meeting on Monday, then I must return to London on Thursday – but I hope you can have dinner with me before then – you and your lovely wife, of course.'

'Thank you.' Ruby seeing the refusal on Johnny's lips, interrupted quickly. 'We'd enjoy that.'

'Y ou were going to refuse, weren't you?' She sat with her legs curled up sideways under her, watching him from the passenger seat of the Mercedes with the slanting eyes of a Persian cat.

'You're damn right.' Johnny nodded grimly.

'Why?'

'Benedict van der Byl is poison.'

'You say so.'

'Yes, I say so.'

'Could be you're jealous of him.' Ruby lit one of her gold-tipped cigarettes, putting the smoke through her lips.

'Good God!' Johnny gave one harsh snort of laughter, then they were silent awhile, both staring ahead.

'I think he's pretty dreamy.'

'You can have him.' Johnny's tone was disinterested, but her retort was shrill.

'I could too – if I wanted to. Anyway you and that Tracey creature mooning—'

'Cut it out, Ruby.'

'Oh my, I've said the wrong thing. The precious Mrs Hartford—'

'Cut it out, I said.' Johnny's tone was sharp.

'Little Miss Fancy Pants – God! She almost had them down for you in the bloody graveyard—'

'Shut up, damn you.'

'Don't you swear at me.' And she lashed out at him flat-handed, leaning forward across the seat to strike him in the mouth. His lower lip smeared against his teeth, and the taste of blood seeped into his mouth. He took the handkerchief from his breast pocket and held it to his mouth, steering the Mercedes with one hand.

Ruby sat curled in her corner of the seat, puffing quickly at the cigarette. Neither of them spoke again until he drew up in front of the double garage. Then Ruby slipped out of the Mercedes and ran across the lawns to the front door. She slammed it behind her, with a force that rattled the full-length glass panel.

Johnny parked the Mercedes, closed the garage door and followed her slowly into the house. She had kicked off her shoes on the wall-to-wall carpet in the lounge, and run through on to the patio beside the swimming pool. She stood barefooted staring down into the clear water, hugging herself about the shoulders.

'Ruby.' He came up behind her, forcing the anger out of

his voice with an effort, trying to keep it conciliatory. 'Listen to me—'

She spun around to face him, eyes blazing like a cornered leopard.

'Don't try and gentle talk me, you bastard. What do you think I am – your damned servant. When did I last get to do anything I wanted?'

With Ruby he had long ago realized that placation was the short cut to peace, so he was roused by the implication.

'I've never stopped you from—'

'Good! That's just fine! Then you won't stop me going away.'

'What do you mean?' He was caught between shock and a sneaking sense of hope. 'Are you talking about divorce—'

'Divorce? Are you out of your little mind! I know all about the big bagful of goodies the Old Man left you in his will. Well, little Ruby is getting her pinkies into that bag – starting right now.'

'What do you want exactly?' His voice was cold and flat.

'A new wardrobe, and a quick whip around all those nice places you go to all the time – London, Paris and the rest. That will do for a start.'

He thought a moment, assessing how far he could stretch his overdraft; since his marriage his bank statement had seldom been typed in black. It was worth it, he decided. He could afford no distraction over the next few months. He could move faster and think quicker without having Ruby Lance sitting between his shoulder-blades – much better she should go.

'All right,' he nodded. 'If that's what you want.'

Her eyes narrowed slightly and her mouth pinched in as she studied his face.

'That was too easy,' she said. 'You want to get rid of me? Don't get any ideas, Johnny boy, you put one finger – or anything else – out of line and I'll chop it off.'

'There is a Mrs Hartford to see you, sir.' Lettie Pienaar's voice whispered through on the intercom, then just audibly she added, 'Lucky you!'

Johnny grinned. 'You're fired for insolence – but send her in before you go.'

He stood up as Tracey came in, and went around his desk to meet her. She wore a no-nonsense grey suit, with her hair scraped back from her face. She should have looked like a school marm – but she didn't.

'You've got your times mixed up, Tracey. The Directors' meeting is at two this afternoon.'

'That's a sweet greeting.' She sat down in an egg-shaped swivel chair, crossing long legs which Johnny dragged his eyes off with an effort. 'I've come looking for a job.'

'A job?' He stared at her blankly.

'Yes, a job. You know – work? Employment?'

'What on earth for?'

'Well, now that you've dragged me back from the bright lights with all the finesse of a caveman – you don't expect me to sit around until I drop dead of boredom. Besides, your tame doctor feels that good healthy employment is essential to the completion of my – ah – cure.'

'I see.' He sank back into his own chair. 'Well – what can you do?'

'Mr Lance.' Tracey widened her eyes suggestively, but made her voice prim. ' – Really!'

'All right,' Johnny chuckled. 'What are your qualifications?'

'You may or may not know that I have a law degree from the University of Cape Town.'

'I didn't.'

'Also, it occurred to me that during the next few months you might need someone around whom you can trust.' She was serious now, and Johnny's smile faded also. 'Like the old days.' She added quietly. They were silent for a few seconds.

'It just so happens that we are looking for a personal assistant in our legal department,' Johnny murmured, and then softly, 'Thanks, Tracey.'

The Board Room of Van Der Byl Diamonds was furnished in soft forest colours, browns and greens. A long luxurious room that reflected the opulence of the days when the Company had been glutted with capital. But now the air was charged with a tension that crackled in the air like static electricity.

The subject of debate was the diamond recovery vessel, *Kingfisher*. The Company's last hope. Her only substantial asset, and Johnny's personal cross.

'This vessel should have been in operation nine months ago. All the estimates were based on that assumption – yet, she is still lying awaiting completion on the slips at Portsmouth.' Benedict was speaking with unconcealed relish. 'In consequence, the interest charges that are accruing put us in a position—'

'The shipyard was out on strike for a total of four months during construction – in addition they were working to rule for—' Johnny's jaw was thrust out, he was ready to fight.

'Ah! I don't think we are particularly interested in the unpredictability of the British workman – the contract should have gone to the Japanese company. Their tender was lower—'

'It would have,' grated Johnny, 'if your father had not insisted—'

'Please, let us not attempt to lay the blame at the door of a dead man.' Benedict's tone was sanctimonious. 'Let us rather try and rectify a grievous situation. When will *Kingfisher* be ready for sea?'

'On the thirteenth of September.'

'It had better be.' Benedict dropped his eyes to his notes.

'Now, this man whom you have engaged to captain the vessel – Sergio Caporetti – let us hear a little about him, please.'

'Fifteen years' experience on offshore oil-drilling vessels in the Red Sea. Three years as Captain of Atlantis Diamonds' offshore dredger operating off the West Coast. He's one of the best, no doubt about it.'

'All right.' Almost reluctantly Benedict accepted this, and consulted his notes. 'Now, we have two sea-concession areas. No. 1 area off Cartridge Bay; No. 2 some twenty miles north of that. Judging by your prospecting results you will elect to work No. 1 area first.'

Johnny nodded, waiting for the next attack to develop. Benedict sat back in his chair.

'Atlantis Diamonds Ltd went broke working our No. 1 area – what makes you think you can succeed where they failed?'

'We've been over this before,' Johnny snapped.

'I wasn't there, remember? Humour me, please. Go over it again.'

Quickly Johnny explained that Atlantis Diamonds' costs had been inflated by their method of operation. Their dredgers were not self-propelled but had to be towed by tugs. The gravel they recovered had been stored, taken into Cartridge Bay in bulk, transhipped ashore to be processed at a land-based plant. *Kingfisher* was a self-propelled and self-contained vessel. She would suck up the gravel, process it through the most sophisticated system of cyclone and X-ray equipment and dump the waste overboard.

'Our costs will be one quarter those of Atlantis Diamonds,' he finished.

'And our loan account is a mere two millions,' Benedict murmured dryly. Then he looked towards Mike Shapiro at the bottom of the table. 'Mr Secretary, please note the following motion – "That this Company proceed to sell the vessel *Kingfisher* presently building at Portsmouth. That it then sells all diamond concessions at the most advantageous terms negotiable, and goes into voluntary liquidation forthwith." Have you got that?'

It was a direct frontal attack. Clearly if the motion succeeded the Company was worthless. They could not recover the price of the *Kingfisher* on a forced sale. There would be a shortfall – and Johnny had signed the guarantee. It was a straight test that Benedict was making. A setting of the lines of battle. Tracey held the balance between Johnny and Benedict. He was forcing her to declare herself.

Benedict watched her while the motion was put to the vote. He leaned forward in the padded leather chair, a slightly amused smile on the full red lips. Beautifully groomed and tailored, with the grace that wealth and position give to a man and which cannot be counterfeited. But the clean athletic lines of his body were fractionally blurred by indulgence, and there was a little too much flesh along the line of his jaw that gave him the petulant look of a spoilt child.

Tracey voted with Johnny Lance, not hesitating a second before lifting her hand. Returning Benedict's smile levelly, and watching her brother's smile alter subtly – become wolfish, for Benedict did not like to lose.

'Very well, my darling sister. Now we know how we stand at least.' He turned easily to Johnny. 'I presume you wish me to continue with my duties in London.'

For years now Benedict had handled the London sales of the Company's stones. It was an unexacting task, which the Old Man had judged within his capabilities.

'Thank you, Benedict,' Johnny nodded. 'Now, I have a proposal to put to the meeting – "That the Directors of this Company, as a gesture of solidarity, agree to waive their rights to Directors' fees until such time as the Company's financial position is on a more sound footing."'

It was a puny counter-attack, but the best he could mount at the moment.

Take-off was in the first light from Youngsfield, and Johnny swung the twin-engined Beechcraft on to a northerly heading, leaving the blue massif of Table Mountain on the left hand.

Tracey wore an anorak over her rose-coloured shirt, and the bottoms of her denim pants were tucked into soft leather boots, her dark hair caught at the nape of her neck with a leather thong.

She sat very still, looking ahead through the aircraft's windshield at the dawn-touched contours of the land ahead. At the bleak lilac and purple mountains and the great lion-coloured plains spreading down to meet the mists that hung over the cold Atlantic.

In her stillness Johnny sensed her excitement and found it infectious.

The sun exploded over the horizon, washing golden and bright over the plains, and tipping the mountains with flame.

'Namaqualand.' Johnny pointed ahead.

She laughed with excitement, like a child at Christmas, turning in the seat to face him.

'Do you remember—' She began, then stopped in confusion.

'Yes,' said Johnny. 'I remember.'

They landed before noon on a rough airstrip bulldozed out of the wilderness. There was a Land-Rover waiting to take them down to the beach to inspect the progress of the workings.

There was little remaining along the thirty-seven-mile Admiralty strip worth working. It was a clean-up and shut-down operation.

When the reigning 'King Canute' handed over the parcel of diamonds that made up the month's recovery, he was apologetic.

'You took out all the plums, Johnny. It's not like the old days.'

Johnny prodded the pathetic pile of small, low-grade stones with his forefinger.

'No, it's not,' he agreed. 'But every little bit helps.'

They climbed back into the Beechcraft and flew on northwards.

Now they passed over areas where the desert had been scratched and torn over wide areas.

The tractors had left centipede tracks in the soft earth.

'Ours?' asked Tracey.

'I wish they were. We'd have no worries then. No, all this belongs to the big Company.'

Johnny checked his watch, automatically comparing the progress of the flight to his estimates. Then he lifted the microphone from the R/T set.

'Alexandra Bay Control. This is Zulu Sugar Peter Tango Baker.'

He knew that they had him on the radar plot, and were watching him – not because they were worried about his safety, but because he was now over the Proclaimed Diamond Area of South West Africa – that vast jealously guarded tract of nothingness.

The radio crackled back at him instantly, demanding his permit number, his flight plan, querying his intentions and his destination.

Having convinced Control of his innocence, and received their permission to continue his flight, he switched off his R/T set, and grimaced at Tracey.

He felt ruffled by this small brush with Olympus. He knew that most of it was professional jealousy. He smarted under the knowledge that he was working ground that the big Company would despise as not sufficiently lucrative to bother about.

Sometimes Johnny dreamed about discovering a fault in a land title, or an error in a survey that had been casually performed seventy years previously before the value of this parched denuded earth had been realized. He imagined himself being able to claim the mineral rights to a few square miles plumb in the middle of the big Company's richest field. He shivered voluptuously at the thought, and Tracey looked at him enquiringly.

He shook his head, then his line of thought took him on to a further destination.

He banked the aircraft, crossing the coastline with its creamy lines of surf running in on the freezing white sands of the beach.

'What?' She was expectant, receptive to the new tone in his voice.

'Thunderbolt and Suicide,' he said, and she made a small grimace of incomprehension.

'There.' He pointed ahead, and through the light smoke of the sea mist she saw them show bare – white and shiny, like a pair of albino whales.

'Islands?' she asked. 'What's so special about them?'

'Their shape,' he answered. 'See how they lie like the mouth of a funnel, with a small opening between them.'

She nodded. The two islands were almost identical twins, two narrow wedges of smooth granite, each about three miles long, lying in a chevron pattern to each other – but not quite meeting at the peak. The mighty Atlantic swells bore up from the south and ran into the mouth of the funnel. Finding themselves trapped in this granite corral, the swells reared up wildly and hurled themselves on the cliffs in massive bomb-bursts of spray before streaming out in white foam through the narrow opening between the two islands.

'I can see how Thunderbolt gets its name.' Tracey eyed the wild booming surf with awe. 'But how about Suicide?'

'The old guano collectors must have called it that, after they tried landing on it.'

'Guano,' Tracey nodded. 'That accounts for the colour.'

Johnny put the Beechcraft into a shallow dive, hurtling in low over the green water. Ahead of them the seabirds rose in alarm, streaming in a long black smear into the sky, the cormorants and gannets whose excreta through the ages had painted the rocks that glaring white.

As they flashed through the gap below the level of the cliffs, Tracey exclaimed, 'There's some sort of tower there – look! In the back of the island.'

'Yes,' Johnny agreed. 'It's an old wooden gantry they used for loading the guano into the longboats.'

He pulled the Beechcraft up in a climbing turn, gaining height to look down on the two islands.

'Do you see where the surf comes through the gap? Now look beneath the surface, can you see the reefs under the water?'

They lay like long dark shadows through the green water, at right angles to the drift of white foam.

'Well, you are looking at the most beautifully designed natural diamond trap in the world.'

'Explain,' Tracey invited.

'Down there,' he pointed south, 'are the big rivers. Some of them dried up a million years ago, but not before they had spat the diamonds they carried into the sea. The tide and the wind has been working them up towards the north for all these ages. Throwing some of them back on the beach but carrying others up this way.'

He levelled the Beechcraft out and resumed their interrupted flight northwards.

'Then suddenly they run up against Thunderbolt and Suicide. They are concentrated and squeezed through the gap, then they are confronted by a series of sharp reefs across their path. They cannot cross them – they just settle down in the gullies and wait for someone to come and suck them out.'

He sighed like a man crossed in love.

'My God, Tracey. The smell of those diamonds reeks in my nostrils. I can almost see the shine of them through a hundred and sixty feet of water.'

He shook himself as though waking from a dream.

'I've been in the game all my life, Tracey. I've got the "feel", the same as a water-diviner has. I tell you with absolute certainty there are millions of carats of diamonds lying in the crotch of Thunderbolt and Suicide.'

'What's the snag?' Tracey asked.

'The concession was granted twenty years ago to the big Company.'

'By whom?'

'The Government of South West Africa.'

'Why aren't they mining it?'

'They will – sometime in the next twenty years. They aren't in any hurry.'

They lapsed into silence, staring ahead, though once Johnny clucked his tongue irritably and shook his head – still thinking about Thunderbolt and Suicide.

To distract him Tracey asked, 'Where do they come from in the first place – the diamonds?'

'Volcanic pipes,' Johnny answered. 'There are more than a hundred known pipes in Southern Africa. Not all yield stones, but then some do. New Rush – Finsch – Dutoitspan – Bulfontein – Premier – Mwadui. Great oval-shaped treasure chests, filled with the legendary "Blue Ground" – the mother lode of the diamond.'

'There are no pipes here – surely?' Tracey turned towards him in his seat.

'No,' Johnny agreed. 'We are after the alluvial stones. Some of those ancient pipes exploded with the force of a hydrogen bomb, spraying diamonds over hundreds of square miles. Others were sub-marine pipes that discharged their treasure into the restless sea. Others of the more passive volcanic pipes were simply eroded away by wind and water and the diamonds were exposed.'

'Then they were washed down to the sea?' she guessed.

Johnny nodded. 'That's right. Over millions of years they

were moved infinitely slowly by landslides, floods, rivers and rainwater. Where all the other pebbles and stones were abraded and worn away to nothingness – the diamonds, four hundred times harder than any other natural substance on earth, were unmarked. So at last they reached the sea and mingled with the others from the sub-marine pipes, to be laid down by wave action on the beaches, or finally to come up against a place like Thunderbolt and Suicide.'

Tracey opened her mouth to ask another question, but Johnny interrupted.

'Here we are. There is Cartridge Bay.' And he pushed the nose of the aircraft down slightly. It was more a lagoon than a bay. Separated from the sea by a narrow sandspit, it spread away into the treeless waste, an enormous extent of quiet shallow water in tranquil contrast to the unchecked surf that burst on the sandspit. There was a deep water entrance through the sandspit, and a channel meandered across the lagoon to where a cluster of lonely whitewashed buildings sprang up on the edge of the desert.

Johnny banked steeply towards the buildings, and below them flocks of black and white pelicans and pink flamingoes rose in panic from the shallows.

Johnny landed and taxied across to the waiting Land-Rover with the white lightning insignia of Van Der Byl Diamonds painted on its side.

Lugging the cool box that contained their lunch, Johnny led Tracey to the vehicle and introduced her to his foreman. Then they climbed in and went bumping down to the buildings on the lagoon. Johnny received from his foreman a report on progress of the work. The buildings had been abandoned by the defunct Atlantis Diamond Company. Johnny was renovating them to serve as a base for the *Kingfisher*; a rest and recreation centre for the crew, a radio centre, a refuelling depot and a workshop to handle running maintenance and repairs. In addition he was putting a jetty out into the lagoon for the converted seventy-foot pilchard trawler that would be *Kingfisher*'s service boat – acting as tender and ferry.

They ran an extensive inspection of the base. Johnny was pleased with the interest Tracey showed, and he enjoyed answering her questions for his own enthusiasm was high. It was nearly two o'clock before they had finished.

'How are the watchtowers coming?' Johnny asked.

'All up, ready and waiting.'

And suddenly Johnny had a two-edged inspiration.

'Might as well go and have a look.' He made it casual.

'Okay, I'll fetch the Land-Rover,' the foreman agreed.

'I know the way.' Johnny put him off. 'You go and get your lunch.'

'It's no trouble—' the foreman began, caught Johnny's frown, cut himself short, then glanced at Tracey. 'Yeah! Sure! Fine! Okay – here are the keys.' He handed Johnny the Land-Rover keys, and disappeared into his own quarters.

Johnny checked the grub box, and they climbed into the open Land-Rover.

'Where are we going?' Tracey asked.

'Inspect the watchtowers along the sandspit.'

'Watchtowers?'

'We've put up a line of fifty-foot wooden towers along the beach. From them we will take continual bearings on *Kingfisher* when she is working offshore. By radio we will be able at any time to give her the exact position over the bottom to within a few feet, as a check to the computer.'

'My, you are clever.' Tracey fluttered her eyelashes at him in mock admiration.

'Silly wench,' said Johnny, and let out the clutch. He swung down past the radio shack on to the hard wet sand at the edge of the lagoon; accelerating he hit second then third and they went away around the curve of the lagoon, headed towards the great yellow wind-carved dunes that lined the coast.

Tracey stood up on her seat, clutching the edge of the windscreen, and the wind snatched at her hair. She pulled the retaining thong from it, and shook it out into a shiny black flag that snapped and snaked behind her.

'Look! Look!' she cried as the flocks of startled flamingoes lurched into flight, streaming white and pink and black over the glossy silver water.

Johnny laughed with her, and swung the Land-Rover towards the dunes.

'Hold on!' he shouted, and she clung to the windscreen, shrieking in delicious terror as they flew up the steep side of a dune, spinning a cloud of sand from the rear wheels and then dropped over the crest in a stomach-churning swoop. They crossed the sandspit and hit the beach, racing along it, playing tag with the waves that shot up the sand.

Five miles up the beach Johnny parked above the high-water mark and they ate cold chicken and drank a bottle of chilled white wine sitting side by side in the sand, leaning against the seat cushions from the Land-Rover. Then they went down to the edge of the sea to wash the chicken grease from their fingers.

'Yipes! It's cold.' Tracey scooped a double handful of sea water. Then she looked at Johnny and her expression became devilish.

He backed away, but not quickly enough. The icy water hit him in the chest, and he gasped.

'War!' It was their childhood cry.

Tracey whirled and went off long-legged along the beach, with Johnny pounding after her. She sensed him gaining on her, and shouted.

'It was a mistake! I didn't mean it! I'm sorry!'

At the last moment as he reached out to grip her shoulder, she jinked and ran knee-deep into the sea. Turning at bay to face him, she kicked a spray of water at him, shouting defiance and laughter.

'All right, come on then!'

Braving the flying spray, he reached her and picked her up kicking and struggling and waded out waist deep.

'No, no – please. Johnny. I give in – I'll do anything.'

At that moment a freak wave, bigger and stronger than the others, knocked Johnny's legs out from under him. They went under, and were rolled up the beach, to stagger out, completely soaked, clinging together, helpless with laughter.

They stood beside the Land-Rover trying to wring the water out of their clothing.

'Oh, you beast!' sobbed Tracey through her laughter. Her hair was a sodden mass, and drops of sea water clung in her eyelashes like dew.

Johnny took her in his arms and kissed her, and they stopped laughing.

She went loose against his chest, her eyes tightly closed and her lips, salty with sea water, opened against his.

The radio telephone in the Land-Rover beside them began to bleat fretfully, flashing its little red warning light.

They drew apart slowly, reluctantly, and stared at each other with dazed, bemused eyes.

Johnny reached the Land-Rover, unhooked the microphone and lifted it to his lips.

'Yes?' his voice cracked. He cleared his throat and repeated. 'Yes?'

The foreman's voice was distorted and scratchy through the speaker.

'Mr Lance, I'm sorry to have—' he was clearly about to finish ' – interrupted you.' But he stopped abruptly, and began again. 'It's just that I think you should know we've had a gale warning. Northerly gale building up quickly. If you want to get back to Cape Town you had better get airborne before it hits us – otherwise you could be shut in for days.'

'Thanks. We'll be back right away.' He hung up, and

Tracey smiled shakily. Her voice was also husky and unnatural-sounding.

'And a damn good thing too!'

Tracey's hair was still damp, and the borrowed polo-neck jersey swamped her. The grey trousers were also borrowed, rolled up to show her bare feet.

She sat very quietly and thoughtfully in the passenger seat of the Beechcraft. Far below them a small fishing vessel lay with a white cloud of seabirds hovering over it, and she watched it with exaggerated attention. There was a heavy feeling of restraint between them now, they could no longer meet each other's eyes.

'Pilchard trawler.' Johnny noticed her gaze.

'Yes,' said Tracey, and they were silent again.

'Nothing happened.' Johnny spoke again gruffly.

'No,' she agreed. 'Nothing happened.' Then shyly she reached out and took his hand. Lightly she rubbed the stump of his missing finger.

'Still friends?' she asked.

'Still friends.' He grinned at her with relief, and they flew on towards Cape Town.

Hugo Kramer watched the aircraft through his binoculars, balancing easily against the roll and pitch of the bridge.

'Police patrol?' asked the man at the helm beside him.

'No,' Hugo replied without lowering the glasses. 'Red and white twin Beechcraft. Registration ZS – PTB. Private aircraft, probably one of the diamond companies.'

He lowered the glasses, and crossed to the wing of the bridge. 'Anyway, we are well outside territorial waters.'

The drone of the aircraft engine faded away, and Hugo transferred his attention to the frantic activity on the deck below him.

The trawler, *Wild Goose*, lay heeled over under the weight of fish that filled her purse seine-net; at least a hundred tons of seething silver pilchards bulging the net out alongside the trawler into a round bag fifty feet across. While above it a shrieking canopy of seabirds swirled and wheeled and dived, frantic with greed.

Three of the crew on a scoop-net which hung from the overhead derrick were dipping the fish out of the net, swinging a ton of fish at each scoop over the side, and dropping them like a silver cloudburst into the trawler's hold. The donkey engine on the winch clattered harshly in time to their movements.

Hugo watched with satisfaction. He had a good crew, and although the fishing was only a cover for the *Wild Goose* – yet Hugo took pride in his teutonic thoroughness which dictated that the cover should be as solid as possible. In any case, all profits from fishing were for his personal account. It was part of the agreement with the Ring.

He packed the binoculars carefully into their leather case, and hung them behind the chartroom door. Then he clambered swiftly down the steel ladder to deck level, moving with catlike grace despite the heavy rubber hip boots he wore.

'I'll take her here for a while,' he told the man at the winch controls. He spoke in Afrikaans, but his accent was shaded with the German of South West Africa.

Wide-shouldered under the blue fisherman's jersey, he worked with smooth economic movements. His hands on the winch control were rough and reddened by wind and sun, for his skin was too fair to weather. The skin of his face was also red, and half-boiled, peeling so there were pinky raw places on his cheeks and black scabs on his lips.

The hair that hung out under his cap was white as

bleached sisal, and his eyelashes were thick and colourless, giving him a mild near-sighted look. His eyes were the palest of cornflower blue, yet without being weak and watery as those of most albinos; they were slitted now, as he judged the roll and dip of the boat – engaging the clutch to meet the movement, or pulling on the drum brake.

'Skipper!' A shout from the bridge above him.

'Ja.' Hugo did not allow his attention to waver as he replied, 'What is it?'

'Gale warning! There is a northerly buster building up.'

And Hugo grinned, pulled on the brake and shut the throttle.

'All right, clean up. Cut the purse rope, let the fish go free.'

He turned and swarmed up the ladder to the bridge, and went to his chart table.

'It will take us three hours to get in position,' he muttered aloud, leaning over the chart, then he barged out on to the wing of the bridge again to chase up his crew.

They had cut the purse rope on the net, allowing the net to fall open like a woman's skirt, and the fish were pouring out, a dark spreading stain through the gap. Two men had the pressure hose on, washing loose fish from the deck into the sea, others were slamming the hatch-covers closed.

Within forty minutes *Wild Goose* was running south under full throttle to take up her waiting station.

The diamond coast of South West Africa lies in the bolt of the Trades. The prevailing wind is the south-easter, but periodically the wind system is completely reversed and a gale comes out of the north, off the land.

It is a Scirocco-type wind like the 'Khamsin' of the Libyan desert, or the 'Simoom' of Tripoli.

It was the same searing dry wind out of the desert, filling the sky with brooding dust and sand clouds, smothering everything beneath a hellish pall like the smoke from a great battlefield.

The dust clouds were part of the design, the Ring had taken account of them when they planned the system – for the north wind lifted into the sky such a quantity of mica dust that the radar screens of the diamond security police were cluttered and confused, throwing up phantom echoes and making it impossible to pick up the presence of a small airborne object.

Turn Back Point was three miles inland, and sixty miles north of the Orange River. The name was given by the first travellers, and expressed their views on continuing a journey northwards. Those old travellers had not known that they stood in the centre of an elevated marine terrace, an ancient beach now lifted above the level of the sea, and that it was the richest prospect of an area so diamond-rich that it was to be ring-fenced, patrolled by Jeep and dog and aircraft, guarded by gun and radar, a laager so secure that a man leaving it would have to submit to X-ray, and take nothing out with him but the clothes he wore.

At Turn Back Point was one of the four big separation plants where all the gravel from the big Company's workings from miles around was processed. The settlement was comparatively large, with plant, workshops and stores, and accommodation for five hundred men and their families. Yet not all the Company's efforts to make it attractive and liveable could alter the fact that Turn Back Point was a hell-hole in a savage and forbidding desert.

Now with the north wind blowing, what had been unpleasant before was almost unbearable. The buildings were tightly sealed, even the joints around the windows and doors were plugged with cloth or paper – and yet the red dust seeped in to powder the furniture, the desks, the bed linen, even the interior of the refrigerators, with a thin gritty film. It settled in the hair, was sugary between the teeth, clogged the nostrils – and with it came that searing heat that seemed to dry the moisture from the eyeballs.

Outside the dust was a red glittering fog which reduced visibility to a dozen yards. Men who were forced out into that choking dry soup wore dust goggles to protect their eyes, and the mica dust covered their clothing with a shiny coating that glittered even in that dun light.

Beyond the settlement a man moved now through the fog, carrying a small cylindrical object. He leaned forward into the wind, moving slowly away into the desert. He reached a shallow depression and went down into it. Setting his burden on the sand, he rested a moment. Then he knelt over the cylinder. He appeared monstrous under his leather jacket and cap, his face covered by goggles and a scarf.

The fibre-glass cylinder was painted with yellow fluorescent paint. At one end was a transparent plastic bubble which housed an electric globe, at the other end was a folded envelope of rubberized nylon material attached to the cylinder by a stainless steel coupling, and linked to the coupling was a small steel bottle of hydrogen gas. The whole assembly was eighteen inches long, and three inches in diameter. It weighed a few ounces more than fifteen pounds.

Within the cylinder were two separate compartments. The larger contained a highly sophisticated piece of transistorized electronic equipment which would transmit a homing signal, light or extinguish its lamp on long-distance radio signal command, and also at command it would control the inflow of hydrogen gas into the nylon balloon through the connecting coupling.

The smaller compartment held simply a sealed plastic container into which were packed twenty-seven diamonds. The smallest of these stones weighed fourteen carats, the largest a formidable fifty-six carats. Each of these stones had been selected by experts for colour, brilliance, and perfection. These were all first-water diamonds, and once they were cut they would fetch in the open market between seven hundred thousand and a million pounds – depending on the skill of the cutting.

There were four members of the Ring at Turn Back Point. Two of them were long service and trusted diamond sorters employed behind the guarded walls of the processing plant. They worked together, to check each other, for the Company operated a system of employee double check – which was completely useless when there was collusion. These men selected the finest stones and got them out of the plant.

The third member of the Ring was a diesel mechanic in the Company workshops. It was his job to receive and assemble the equipment which arrived concealed in a marked drum of tractor grease. He also packed the stones into the cylinder and passed it on to the man who was now kneeling out in the desert, preparing to launch the cylinder into the swirling dust fog.

His final check completed, the man stood up and went to the lip of the depression and peered out into the dust storm. At last he seemed satisfied, and hurried back to the yellow cylinder. With an incisive twist of the bevelled release ring he opened the valve on the bottle of hydrogen gas. There was a snakelike hiss, and the nylon balloon began to inflate. The folds of material crackled as they filled. The balloon lifted, eager to be gone, but the man restrained it with difficulty until the balloon was smooth and tight. He let go, and the balloon with its dangling cylinder leapt into the sky, and almost instantly was gone into the dust clouds.

The man stood with his face lifted to the dark furnace-red sky. His goggles glinted blindly, but his attitude was one of triumph, and when he turned away he walked lightly with the step of a man freshly released from danger.

'One more package,' he promised himself. 'Just one more,

and I'll pull out. Buy that farm on the Olifants River, do a bit of fishing, take a shooting trip every year—'

He was still dreaming when he reached the parked Land-Rover and climbed into the driver's seat. He started the engine, switched on the headlights, and drove slowly down the track towards the settlement.

The sign on the rear of the departing Land-Rover was in white paint so that it showed clearly through the haze of red dust.

'SECURITY PATROL,' it read.

*W*ild Goose lay on station, with her diesels throbbing softly, ticking over to hold her head into the wind. Even twenty miles out at sea the wind was searing hot and the occasional splatter of spray on Hugo's face was refreshing.

He stood in the corner of the bridge where he could watch the sea and the helmsman, but he was anxious. *Wild Goose* had been lying on station for fifteen hours now, during ten of which the norther had howled dismally through her rigging.

He was always anxious at the beginning of a pick-up. There was so much that could have gone wrong, anything from a police sweep to a tiny electrical fault in the equipment.

'What time is it, Hansie?' he shouted and the helmsman glanced up at the chronometer above his head.

'Three minutes after six, skipper.'

'Dark in half an hour,' Hugo grunted disgustedly, slitted those pale-lashed eyes into the wind once more, then shrugged and ambled back into the bridge house.

He stopped at the console beside his chart table. Even to an experienced eye the machine was an ordinary 'Fish-Finder', an adaptation of the old wartime anti-submarine device, the ASDIC, to the more prosaic business of plotting

83

the depth and position of the pilchard shoals beneath the surface.

However, this model had undergone a costly and specialized conversion. The Ring had flown an expert out from Japan to do the work.

Now that the set hummed softly, its control panel lit soft green by the internal light, but the sound was neutral, and the circular glass screen was blank.

'You want some coffee, Hansie?' Hugo asked the old coloured man at the wheel. His crew were handpicked, loyal and trusted. They had to be – one loud mouth could blow a multi-million pound business.

'Ja dankie, skipper.' The old man creased his weather-battered face in appreciation, and Hugo shouted down the companionway to the galley.

'Cooky, how's it for a pot of coffee?'

But the reply was lost, for at that moment the console came to life dramatically. A row of lights blinked on above the control panel, the muted hum changed to a rapid beep-beep signal, and the screen glowed ghostly green.

'She's up!' Hugo shouted his relief, and ran to the set. His first mate rushed through from his cabin behind the bridge, tucking his shirt into unbuttoned trousers, his face puckered with sleep.

'About bloody time,' he blurted, groggily.

'Take over from Hansie,' Hugo told him, and he settled into the padded seat in front of the ASDIC set.

'Right, bring her round two points to port and open her up.'

The *Wild Goose* swung her head into the sea, and her motion changed from easy swoop and glide to a crabbing butting lunge, and the spray burst over the glass of the bridge.

Sitting before the console Hugo was tracking the flight of the balloon and keeping *Wild Goose* on an interception course.

Driven by the forty-knot norther the balloon crossed the coastline, climbing swiftly to three thousand feet. Hugo manipulated the knob on the console which sent the balloon a command to release gas and maintain altitude. Her response was recorded immediately on the screen.

'Good,' Hugo whispered. 'Good girl.' Then louder. 'Bring her round a bit, Oscar – the balloon is drifting to the south.'

For twenty minutes more they butted through the swells.

'Okay,' Hugo broke the silence. 'I'm going to ditch her.' He twisted the knob clockwise slowly, expelling all the gas from the nylon balloon.

'*Ja*. That's it. She's down.' He looked out of the window above the set. The dust-laden clouds had brought the night on prematurely. It was dark outside, with a low black ceiling through which no star showed.

Hugo turned his attention back to the set.

'That's it, Oscar. You're right on course. Hold her there.'

Then he glanced across at old Hansie and another younger crewman. They were sitting patiently on the bench against the far bulkhead. Both of them were clad in full oilskins, shiny yellow plastic from head to ankle, with gumboots below that.

'Okay, Hansie,' Hugo nodded. 'You can get up in the bows. We are only a mile or so away now.'

They climbed down on to the wave-swept deck, and Hugo watched them scuttling forward between each green burst of water and crouching in the bows. Both of them ducking each time another swell poured over the top of them, their yellow plastic suits showing clearly in the murky deck lights.

'I'm going to switch her on now,' Hugo warned the helm. 'We should have her on visual.'

'Right.' Oscar peered ahead, and Hugo flicked a switch on the panel, commanding the balloon to turn on her guide light.

Almost immediately there was a shout from Oscar.

'There she is. Dead ahead!'

Hugo jumped up and ran forward. It took a few seconds for his eyes to adjust, then he made out the tiny red firefly of light ahead of them in the vast blackness of sea and sky. It showed for a second then was gone in the trough of the next wave.

'I'll take her.' Hugo replaced Oscar at the wheel. 'You get on the spotlight.'

The beam of the spotlight was a solid white shaft through the darkness. The fluorescent yellow paint of the cylinder glowed in the circle of the spot.

Hugo lay *Wild Goose* upwind of the cylinder, and then allowed her to drift down gently on it. Hansie and his assistant were ready with the twenty-foot boat-hook.

Delicately Hugo manoeuvred down over the bobbing yellow cylinder, and grunted with satisfaction as the boat-hook slipped through the recovery ring and the cylinder was hauled in over the bows.

He watched while the two dripping oilskin-clad figures clambered back up the ladder into the wheelhouse, and laid the cylinder on the chart table.

'Good! Good!' Hugo slapped their backs heartily. 'Now, go and get dry – both of you!' They climbed down the companionway, and Hugo handed the wheel over to Oscar.

'Home!' he instructed him. 'As quick as you like.' And he carried the cylinder through into his cabin.

Sitting at the fold-down table in his cabin, Hugo unscrewed the lower section of the cylinder and took out the plastic container. He opened it and spilled the contents out on the table top.

He whistled softly, and picked up the biggest stone. Although he was no expert he knew instinctively that it was a brilliant of exceptional quality. Even the roughness of its exterior could not mask the fire in its depths.

To him it was worthless, there was nowhere he could market a stone like that. There was no temptation to take it out of the Ring – all it would mean for him was fifteen years at hard labour.

The Ring was based on this mutual reliance, no one part of it could function without all the others – yet each part was self-contained and watertight. Only one man knew all its parts, and nobody knew who that one man was.

From the drawer beside him Hugo took out his tools and set them on the table. He lit the spirit stove and set the pot of paraffin wax in the gimbal above it to heat.

Then he poured the diamonds into a shiny metal can. It was the type of ordinary commercial can used for packing and preserving foodstuffs.

Balancing against the ship's motion, he lifted the pot from the stove, and poured the steaming liquid wax over the diamonds, filling the can to rim level.

The wax cooled and solidified quickly, turning opaque and white. The stones were now incorporated in a cake of wax that would prevent them rattling, and would give the sealed can authentic weight.

Hugo lit a cigarette and crossed the cabin to look out into the wheelhouse. The helmsman winked at him and Hugo smiled.

He went back to the table, the can was cool enough to handle. He placed the circular lid over it, and moved to the portable Jenny bolted to a chest of drawers. Carefully he clinched the lid into place, his eyes squinting at the smoke from the cigarette that dangled from his lips.

Satisfied at last he set the sealed can on the table, while he went to where his jacket hung on the door. From the inside pocket he pulled out a manilla envelope, then from the envelope he drew a printed, colour-screened label. He came back to the bench and meticulously pasted the label around the can. On the label was a highly glamorized artist's conception of a leaping pilchard, making it look like a Scottish salmon.

'Pilchards in Tomato Sauce.' Hugo read the label aloud,

as he leaned back to admire his work. 'A product of South West Africa.' He smiled with satisfaction and began packing his equipment away.

'How much?' The foreman of the fish pump called across the narrowing gap between *Wild Goose* and the jetty.

'About fifty tons,' Hugo shouted back. 'Then the norther chased us home.'

'*Ja*. None of the boats stayed out.' The foreman watched his gang secure the mooring ropes, and swing the hose of the vacuum pump over *Wild Goose*'s hold to begin pumping out her pilchards.

'Take over, Oscar.' Hugo picked up his jacket and cap. 'I'll be back tomorrow.' He jumped down on to the jetty and strode down towards the canning factory with its awesome stink of pilchard oil. His jacket was slung over his shoulder, one finger hooked through the tag.

He went down an alley between the boiler rooms and the fish-drying plant, across a wide yard where the bags of fish meal were piled to the height of a double-storey building. He turned in through the double doors of the cavernous warehouse filled to roof height with cardboard cartons, each stencilled with the words:

1 gross cans.   Pilchards in tomato sauce.
Consign to: Vee Dee Bee Agencies Ltd.
                32, Bermondsey Street,
                London, S.E.1.

He went into the cubicle that served the warehouse storeman as an office.

'Hello, Hugo. Good trip?' The storeman was Hugo's brother-in-law.

'Fifty ton.' Hugo hung his coat casually on the hook behind the door. 'I've got to take a leak,' he said, and went to the latrine across the floor of the warehouse.

He came back, and drank a cup of tea with his brother-in-law. Then he stood and said, 'Jeannie will be waiting.'

'Give her my love.'

'She don't need yours. She's going to get plenty of mine!' Hugo winked, and took his coat from the hook. It was lighter now, the can was gone from the pocket.

He went through the main gates of the harbour, exchanging a casual greeting with the customs officer, and went to the battered early model convertible in the car park.

He kissed the girl at the driving-wheel, threw his coat on the back seat and climbed in over the door.

'You drive,' he told her, grinning. 'I want both hands free.'

She squeaked and pulled his hand out of her skirts.

'Can't you wait till we get home?'

'I've been at sea for five days and I'm hungry as hell.'

'You're a caution, you are.' She laughed at him and started the car.

This was Sergio Caporetti, the man Johnny had chosen to captain *Kingfisher*. He was a round man, the same shape as a snowman. He filled the doorway of Johnny's office, and his great belly bulging into the room ahead of him. His face was round also, like a baby's – but the beautiful dark Italian eyes fringed with thick lashes like a girl's.

'Come in, Sergio,' Johnny greeted him. 'Nice to see you.'

The Italian crossed the room deceptively quickly, and Johnny's hand was completely engulfed by the enormous hairy paw.

'So, at last we are ready,' Sergio grunted. 'Three months

I sit on bum – do nothing. Look at me – ' He slapped his belly with a sound like a pistol shot. ' – fat! No good.'

'Well, not quite ready.' Johnny qualified the statement. He was flying Sergio and his crew over to England well ahead of time. He wanted the big Italian to have plenty of opportunity to study and get to know the revolutionary new equipment with which *Kingfisher* was fitted. Then when the vessel was ready for sea, Sergio would sail her out to Africa.

'Sit down, Sergio. Let's go over the crew list—'

When Sergio left an hour later, Johnny went as far as the lift with him.

'If you have any problems phone me, Sergio.'

'Si.' Sergio shook hands. 'Don't worry – Caporetti is in charge. All is well.'

On his way back Johnny stopped at the reception desk.

'Is Mrs Hartford in today?' he asked one of the little receptionists, and both of them replied in chorus like Tweedledum and Tweedledee.

'No, Mr Lance.'

'Has she phoned to say where she is?'

'No, Mr Lance.'

Tracey had disappeared. Five days now there had been no sign of her, her new office was deserted and unused. Johnny was worried and angry. He was worried that she had gone on another binge, and he was angry because he missed her.

He was scowling ferociously as he went back into his office.

'Goodness me.' Lettie Pienaar stood beside his desk with a batch of mail in her hand. 'We do look happy. Here's something to cheer you.'

She handed him a postcard with a colour picture of the Eiffel Tower. It was the first word from Ruby since she had left. Johnny read it quickly.

'Paris – ' he said, ' – is fun, it seems.' He tossed the card on to the desk and plunged back into the day's work.

He worked late, stopped at a steakhouse to eat, then drove back to the silent house in Bishopscourt.

The crunch of tyres on the gravel drive and headlights flashing across the bedroom wall woke him. He sat up in bed as the front-doorbell began a series of urgent peals and he switched on the bedside light. Two o'clock – Christ!

He pulled a dressing-gown over his nudity and tottered down the passage, switching on lights as he went. The doorbell kept ringing.

He turned the front door key. The door flew open and Tracey came in like a strong wind, clutching a briefcase to her chest.

'Where the hell have you been?' Johnny was suddenly fully awake, angry and relieved.

'Johnny! Johnny!' She was dancing with excitement, incoherent, her cheeks flaming and eyes shining. 'I've got them – at least, it, both of them.'

'Where have you been?' Johnny was not to be so easily sidetracked, and with an obvious effort Tracey brought her excitement under control, but she was still smiling and gave the impression of humming like an electric motor.

'Come.' She took his hand and dragged him into the lounge. 'Get yourself a large whisky and sit down,' she ordered, imperious as a queen.

'I don't want a whisky, and I don't—'

'You'll need one,' she interrupted, and went to the open liquor cabinet, poured a massive whisky into a crystal glass, squirted soda into it, and brought it back to Johnny.

'Tracey, what the hell is going on?'

'Please, Johnny. It's so wonderful, don't spoil it for me. Just sit there, please!'

Johnny sank reluctantly into the chair, and Tracey

slipped the catch on her briefcase and drew out a sheaf of documents. She stood in the centre of the floor, and took up the pose of a Victorian actress.

'This – ' she explained, ' – is a translation from the original German of a proclamation by Governor in Council dated 3rd May 1899 and issued at Windhoek. I will leave out the preamble and go straight to the meat.'

She cleared her throat and began reading:

'In consideration of the sum of 10,000 marks which is hereby paid and received, the rights to mine, win, recover, collect or carry away all metals, whether base or precious, stones whether base, semi-precious or precious, minerals, guano, vegetation and other substances organic or inorganic for a period of Nine Hundred and Ninety-Nine years is granted to Messrs Farben, Hendryck and Mosenthal S.A., Guano Merchants of 14 Bergenstrasse, Windhoek, in respect of a circular area ten kilometres in radius whose centre shall be a point situated at the highest elevation of the island lying on latitude 23° 15′ South and longitude 15° 12′ East.'

Tracey paused and looked at Johnny. He was frozen, stony-faced, staring at her with all his attention. She went on quickly, gabbling it out.

'All the old German mineral concessions and rights were ratified by the Union Parliament when the Union of South Africa took over the mandate after the Great War.'

He nodded, unable to speak. Tracey's smile kept breaking out.

'That concession still has all the force of law behind it. The grant of any subsequent rights is invalid, and although the original grant was mainly for the recovery of guano – yet it covers precious stones also.'

Again Johnny nodded, and Tracey put the document at the bottom of the sheaf of papers in her hand.

'The concession Company, Farben, Hendryck and

Mosenthal S.A., is still in existence. The Company's only remaining asset, apart from any long-forgotten concessions, is an old building at 14 Bergenstrasse, Windhoek.'

Tracey seemed to change the subject suddenly.

'You asked me where I have been, Johnny. Well I've been to Windhoek, and over most of the worst roads in South West Africa.

'The Farben, Hendryck and Mosenthal Company is owned by the brothers Hendryck, a couple of Karakul fur farmers. They are a pair of horrible old men, and when I saw them slitting the throats of those poor little Persian lambs just to prevent the fur uncurling, well—' Tracey paused, and gulped. 'Well, I didn't explain to them about the concession. I just offered to buy the Company, and they asked twenty thousand and I said "sign", and they signed and I left them chuckling with glee. They thought they'd been terribly clever. There! It's all yours!'

Tracey handed the Agreement to Johnny and while he read it she went on.

'I made the Agreement in the name of Van Der Byl Diamonds, I signed it as a Director – I hope you don't mind.'

'Christ!' Johnny took a long deep swallow of whisky, then set the glass down and stood up.

'Mind?' he repeated. 'You bring me the concession to Thunderbolt and Suicide – and ask me if I mind.'

He reached for her and eagerly she went to him.

'Tracey, you're wonderful.' They hugged each other ecstatically, and Johnny swung her off her feet. Without either of them planning it they were suddenly lying, still in each other's arms, on the couch. Then they were kissing, and the laughter dwindled into small murmurs and incoherent sounds.

Tracey pulled away from him at last, and slipped off the couch. She stood in the centre of the floor. Her breathing was ragged. Her hair was a dark tangle.

'Whoa! That's enough.'

'Tracey.' He started up from the couch, wild for her, but she held him at the full stretch of her arms, her hands flat on his chest, backing away in front of him.

'No, Johnny, no!' She shook her head urgently. 'Listen to me.'

He stopped. The wild look faded from his eyes.

'Look, Johnny, God knows I'm no saint, but – well, I don't want us to – well, not on a couch in some other woman's house. That's not how I want it to be.'

B enedict eased the big honey-coloured Bentley out of the traffic stream that clogged Bermondsey Street and turned into the gates of the warehouse. He parked beside the loading bay and climbed out.

As he pulled off his gloves, he glanced along the bank. Mountains of goods were stacked ready for distribution. Cases of Cape wine and spirits, canned fruit in brown cartons, canned fish, forty-gallon drums of fish oil, bundles of raw hides stiff as boards, and cases of indefinable goods – all of it the produce of Southern Africa.

Vee Dee Bee Agencies had grown out of all recognition in the ten years since Benedict had launched it.

Benedict climbed the steps to the bank three at a time, and strode down between the towering stacks of goods that reached up into the murk of the high ceiling. He walked with the assurance of a man on his own ground, the skirts of his overcoat swirling about his knees, broad-shouldered and tall. The storemen and porters greeted him deferentially as he passed, and when he entered the main office there was a stirring and whispering among the ranks of typists as though a wind had blown through a forest.

The Managing Director hurried out of his office to greet Benedict and usher him in.

'How are you, Mr van der Byl? There's tea coming now.' And he stood behind Benedict to take his coat.

The meeting lasted half an hour, Benedict reading through the weekly sales and cost reports, querying an item here, remarking on a figure with pleasure or displeasure as it deserved. Many people watching him work would have been startled. This was not the indolent playboy they thought they knew, this was a hard-eyed businessman coldly and unemotionally milking the maximum profit from his enterprise.

There would have been others who wondered where Benedict had found the capital to finance a business of this magnitude, especially if they had known that he owned the premises, and that Vee Dee Bee Agencies was by no means his only stake in the world of business. He had not received money from his father – the Old Man had not believed Benedict capable of successfully negotiating the purchase of a pound of butter.

The meeting ended, and Benedict stood up and shrugged on his overcoat, while his Managing Director went to the grey steel safe in the corner, tumbled the combination and swung the heavy door open.

'The shipment arrived yesterday,' he explained as he reached into the safe and brought out the can. 'On the SS *Loch Elsinore* from Walvis Bay.'

He handed the can to Benedict, who examined it briefly, smiling a little at the painting of the leaping fish and the lettering 'Pilchards in Tomato Sauce'.

'Thank you.' He slipped the can into his briefcase, and the Managing Director walked with him back to the Bentley.

B enedict left the Bentley in a garage in Broadwick Street, and walked through the jostle of Soho until he reached the grimy brick building behind the square. He pressed the bell opposite the card that read Aaron Cohen, Manufacturing Jeweller, and when the door opened he climbed the stairs to the top and fourth floor. Again he rang, and after a while an eye peeped at him through the peephole – but the door opened almost immediately.

'Hello, Mr van der Byl. Come in! Come in!' The young doorman welcomed him in and locked the door behind him. 'Papa is expecting you!' he went on as they both looked up at the eye of the closed-circuit TV camera above the wrought-iron grille that barred the passage.

Whoever was viewing the screen was satisfied, for there was an electrical buzz and the grille swung open. The doorman led Benedict down the passage.

'You know the way. Papa is in his office.'

Benedict was in a shabby little reception room, with a threadbare carpet and a pair of chairs that looked like Ministry of Works rejects. He turned to the right-hand door and went through it into a long room that clearly occupied most of the top floor of the building.

Along one side of the room ran a narrow bench, to which were bolted twenty small lathes. Each machine ran off a belt from a central drive below the bench. The man tending the machines wore a white dust jacket, and he grinned at Benedict. 'Hello, Mr van der Byl, Papa is expecting you.' But Benedict delayed a moment to watch the operation of the saws. In the jaws of each lathe was set a diamond, and spinning against the diamond was a circular blade of phosphor bronze. As Benedict watched, the man turned back to the task of spreading a fine paste of olive oil and diamond dust on to the cutting edge of each blade – for it was not the bronze that cut. Only a diamond will cut a diamond.

'Some nice stones, Larry,' Benedict remarked, and Larry Cohen nodded.

'All of them between four and five carats.'

Benedict leaned close and examined one of the diamonds. The line of the cut was marked with Indian ink on the stone. Benedict knew what heart-searching and discussion, what examination and drawing upon the rich storehouses of experience had preceded the positioning of that ink line. It might take two days to saw through each diamond, so Benedict left the bench and moved on.

In a row down the other side of the room sat the other Cohen brothers. Eight of them. Old Aaron was a great breeder of boys. They ranged in age from nearly forty to nineteen years and there were a couple who were still in school and hadn't yet come into the business.

'How do you like this one, Mr van der Byl?' Michael Cohen looked up as Benedict approached. Michael was shaping a fine diamond, cutting it into a round using a lesser stone as a blade. A small tray beneath the lathe caught the dust from the two stones. This dust would be used later for sawing and polishing.

'A beauty,' said Benedict. These men were of the brotherhood, working with diamonds all their lives and loving them as other men loved women or horses and fine paintings.

He moved on down the room, greeting each of the brothers, stopping to watch for a minute the loving care with which the elder boys, master craftsmen each of them, were cutting the precisely angled facets that make up the perfect round brilliant. The fifty-eight facets – table, stars, pavillons and the others which endow a cut stone with its mystic 'life' and 'fire'.

Leaving them crouched over their wheels, so similar to those of a potter, he went through the door at the end of the room.

'Benedict, my friend.' Aaron Cohen came from his desk

to embrace him. He was a tall thin man in his late sixties with a thick silver-grey mane of hair, round-shouldered from years of crouching over a diamond wheel. 'I did not know you were in London, they told me you were in Cape Town. Yesterday was Ruby's birthday. If we had known—'

Benedict took the envelope from his pocket and shook twenty-seven diamonds on to the blotter of the desk.

'What do you think of those, Papa?'

'*Shu! Shu!*' Papa patted his own cheeks with delight, and he reached instinctively for the biggest stone.

'I should live to see such a stone!' He screwed a jeweller's *loupe* into his eye, turning to catch the natural light from the high windows, and scrutinized the diamond through the eyepiece.

'Ah, yes. There is a feather*, but small. V.V.S.I.† But we will cut through it. Yes, we will take two gems from this stone. Two perfect diamonds of ten or twelve carats each, and perhaps five smaller ones.' More than half a diamond's bulk is lost in the cutting.

'Yes! Yes! From this stone we will sell a hundred thousand pounds' worth of polished diamonds!'

Aaron crossed to the door. 'Boys! Come see! I will show you a prince among diamonds.' And his sons crowded into the office. Michael took it first and gave his opinion. 'A good stone, yes. But not of the same water as the stone we had in the last batch. You remember that octahedron crystal—'

'What you talking!' his father interrupted. 'You wouldn't know a diamond from a piece of gorgonzola cheese already!'

'He is right, Papa.' Larry joined in the discussion. 'The other stone was better.'

'So the Big Lover argues with his father! Little shiksas with skirts up around their tochis you know all about.

* Semi-transparent veinlike flaw.
† Very very slight imperfection.

98

Dancing the Watsui and the Cha-Cha. Yes! But diamonds you know from nothing.' This declaration precipitated a full-scale, family argument in which each of the brothers joined with gusto.

'Shuddup! Shuddup! Back to work all of you! Out! Out!' Aaron broke up the meeting, driving his sons from the office and slamming the door behind them.

'*Shu!*' He looked to heaven. 'What a business! Now we can weigh the stones.'

When they had weighed and tallied the stones, and Aaron had locked them into the safe, Benedict told him:

'I am thinking of breaking up the Ring.'

Aaron froze and looked across the desk at Benedict. Between them there was always the pretence that their relationship was legitimate. They never spoke about the Ring, or where the unregistered stones came from, or how the finished gems were sent to Switzerland.

'Why?' Aaron asked carefully.

'I am a rich man now. With my father's money, and what I have made from the Ring and invested. A very rich man. I no longer need to take the risks.'

'Such problems I wish I had. But perhaps you are wise – I would not think to argue with you.'

'There will be one or two more packages. Then it will be finished.'

Aaron nodded. 'I understand,' he said. 'Like all good things it must end.'

I t was a little after noon when Benedict parked the Bentley outside the mews flat off Belgrave Square. He went to shower immediately he was home. In all the years he had lived here he had never grown accustomed to London's grime-laden atmosphere, and he bathed or showered at least three times a day.

He sang in the shower, and then enveloped in a huge bath towel he left a string of damp footprints through to the lounge where he mixed a Martini, and screwed up his eyes at the first stinging taste of the drink.

The phone rang.

'Van der Byl,' he said into the mouthpiece, and then his expression changed as he listened. Quickly he put down the glass and used both hands to hold the telephone receiver.

'What on earth are you doing here?' His tone of astonishment was not faked.

'What a wonderful surprise. When can I see you? How about right now – for lunch? That's great! No, nothing I can't put off – this is a pretty special occasion, you know. Where are you staying? The Lancaster. Fine. Look, give me forty-five minutes, and I'll meet you in the Looking-Glass Room on the top floor. Yes, ten past one. God, what a delightful – I've said that already. See you in three-quarters of an hour.'

He replaced the receiver, swallowed the remains of his Martini and headed for his bedroom suite. This would make a good day into a truly remarkable one, he thought, as he quickly selected a silk shirt. He looked at his reflection in the mirror and grinned.

'The ball has really started bouncing your way, Benedict,' he whispered.

She was not at the bar, nor in the Looking-Glass Room. Benedict crossed to the tall picture windows for a glimpse of one of London's finest views across Hyde Park and the Serpentine. It was a smoky blue day, and the pale sun added bronze to the autumn shades of gold and red in the park.

He turned from the windows, and she was crossing the room towards him. His stomach swooped with delight for she also was pale gold with the coppery sheen of sun on her long legs and bare arms. The grace of her carriage was as he remembered it, the precise lifting and laying down of narrow feet on the thick pile of the carpet.

He stood quite still, letting her come to him. Heads turned all across the room, for she was a splendid golden creature. Benedict knew suddenly and clearly that he wanted this woman for himself.

'Hello, Benedict,' she said, and he stepped forward to take her hand in both of his.

'Ruby Lance!' He squeezed her long fingers gently. 'It's so good to see you again.'

The use of her surname was the clue to the strength of his reaction. She belonged to the one man in the world that Benedict most envied and hated. For this reason she was infinitely desirable.

'Let us celebrate with a little drink. I think the occasion deserves at the very least a champagne cocktail.'

She sat with those long slim legs neatly crossed, leaning back in her chair, holding the stemmed glass with tapering fingers. Her hair hung straight to her shoulders, like some rare silken tapestry in white gold, and her eyes watched him with a catlike candour, a calm feline intentness that seemed to look into his soul.

'I should not have bothered you,' she said. 'But I know so few people here.'

'How long can you stay?' He brushed aside the disclaimer. 'I must cancel my other arrangements.'

'A week.' She made it sound like an offer that was subject to negotiation.

'Oh, no!' His voice was mock distressed. 'You can do better than that – we won't be able to do half what I had planned in so short a time. You can stay longer, surely?'

'Perhaps,' she agreed, and lifted the glass an inch. 'It's good to see you.'

'And you.' Benedict agreed with emphasis. They sipped the sparkling wine watching each other's eyes.

Where others must wait weeks and months Benedict went in immediately as though it were his right. A smile and a murmured word, and theatre tickets were his or the doors of fashionable restaurants opened magically.

That first night he took her to the National Theatre, then for dinner at Le Coeur de France where a very famous movie actor stopped at their table.

'Hello, Benedict. We are all going on to the yacht later for a bit of a party. Join us, won't you?' And those legendary eyes turned to Ruby. 'And bring your beautiful friend with you.'

They ate breakfast under the awning on the after-deck of the yacht, eggs and bacon and Veuve Clicquot champagne, and watched the hubbub of dawn traffic on the wondrously smelly old Thames. Ruby was the only girl in the party without a fur to cheat the chill of the river dawn. Benedict made a mental note of the fact.

On the way home she sat with those long legs curled under her in the seat of the Bentley, still sleek and golden despite the night's exertions, but with the lightest touch of blue beneath her eyes.

'I can't remember having enjoyed an evening so much, Benedict.' She patted a tiny pink-lipped yawn. 'You're a wonderful companion.'

'Tonight again?' he asked.

'Yes, please,' she murmured.

She sensed an urgency in him, when she came down into the lobby of the Lancaster that evening. He came quickly to meet her as she stepped out of the lift, and the quiet assurance with which he kissed her cheek and took her arm surprised her.

They were silent as he snaked the Bentley through the

evening traffic. Ruby realized that at the tips of her long tapered fingers, within touching distance, was a fortune such as she had never before allowed herself to dream about. She was deadly afraid. A wrong move, even a wrong word might drive that fortune beyond her grasp for ever. She would never have a chance like this again, and she was afraid to move, almost paralysed with fear. The decision she knew she would have to make very soon would be fateful. Must she encounter his advance with withdrawal, or must she meet it as frankly as it was made.

She was so deeply involved with her thoughts that when the Bentley came to a standstill she looked up with surprise. They were parked in a mews outside an expensive-looking flat.

Benedict came round and opened her door, and led her without protest into the flat.

She looked about her curiously, recognizing some of the art works on display in the entrance hall. Benedict took her through into the long lounge and settled her solicitously into the tapestry-covered chair which dominated the room like a throne, and suddenly her fear was gone. She felt queenlike in her control. She knew with certainty that this would all be hers.

Benedict stood in the centre of the room, almost a petitioner in his attitude, and he began to speak. She listened quietly, her expression showing no hint of the triumphant surge of her spirits, and when he stopped to wait for her reply she did not hesitate.

'Yes,' she said.

'I will be with you when you tell him,' Benedict promised.

'It won't be necessary,' Ruby assured him. 'I can handle Johnny Lance.'

'No.' Swiftly Benedict crossed to her chair and took her hands, drawing her to her feet. 'I must be there with you. Promise me that.'

Then it became suddenly evident to Ruby that the strength of her position was unassailable. Benedict needed her not for any physical reasons – but merely because she belonged to Johnny Lance.

Looking steadily into Benedict's eyes she determined to test her intuition.

'He does not have to know about you,' she said. 'I could arrange a divorce with him.'

'He *must* know about me. That's what I want, don't you see?'

'Yes, I see.' She was secure.

'It is agreed?' He could barely conceal his anxiety.

'Yes,' she nodded. 'It's agreed.' And they smiled at each other – each completely satisfied.

'Come.' He led her almost reverently into his bedroom, and Ruby stopped in the doorway with a little cry of delight.

The double bed was a mountain of glowing fur in a score of shades ranging from soft pinkish cream, through beige and oyster, pale smoky blue to midnight and jet glossy black.

'Choose one!' he ordered her. 'To seal our bargain.'

She moved like a sleepwalker towards the bed, but as she reached the centre of the Khedive carpet Benedict called out softly.

'Wait.'

She stopped obediently and he came up behind her. She felt his hands on the back of her neck, and she lowered her chin, shaking her hair forward so that he could unhook the clasp and draw down the fastening of her dress.

She stepped out of the dress as it dropped around her ankles, then waited passively as he carefully removed her brassiere.

'Now,' he said. 'Try them on.'

In her stockings and high-heeled shoes she went to the bed, subtly emphasizing the lilt of her movements, and took up the first fur.

Benedict was sprawled in the wing-back chair across the room as she glanced back at him. His face was gloating and flushed, so that his features seemed swollen and coarsened as he stared at her. She understood now that this was a form of ritual in which they were engaged. Like a victorious Roman general, Benedict was conducting his own personal triumph, reviewing the spoils and the plunder. It had no basis in sexual or physical desire, but was rather a service of worship to Benedict himself. She was the priestess of this rite.

Yet, knowing this, Ruby felt no resentment. Rather, she found herself excited by the cold perversity of the pageant. As she paraded and postured, turned and swirled and flared the skirts of a wild mink, she was very conscious of his eyes upon her body. She knew it was perfect, and his scrutiny stirred her physically for the first time in her life. She felt her blood quicken and pound, felt her heart flutter within its cage of ribs like a captive bird, and her loins tighten like a clenching first. For her also the ritual was narcissistic – satisfying her own deep emotional need.

As she discarded each of the coats she dropped it in the centre of the floor, until there was a knee-high pile of precious fur.

At last she faced him, hugging the soft creamy cloud tightly about her body. Then she opened her arms, and the coat also, standing on tip-toe to tighten and highlight the hard muscle in her legs and flanks.

'This one,' she whispered, and he came out of the chair, picked her up in his arms and laid her, still wrapped in mink, on the great pile of furs.

Ruby woke in the double bed to a feeling of excitement and enormous well-being such as she had not experienced since she was a schoolgirl on the first morning of a holiday.

The morning was far advanced, pale sunshine in a square shaft poured through the open window like a stage effect.

Benedict in a yellow silk dressing-gown stood beside the bed watching her with an unfathomable expression which changed immediately he realized that she was awake.

'My man has collected your luggage from the Lancaster. Your toilet things are in the bathroom, your clothing in the dressing-room.'

He sat down carefully on the edge of the bed, and leaned forward to kiss her forehead and then each cheek.

'We will breakfast when you are ready.' He sat back and watched her eyes; clearly he was waiting for her to say something important. Immediately she was on guard, wary of making a mistake, seeking a clue in his expression.

'Last night,' he asked. 'Was it as good for you, as it was for me?'

Understanding washed over her in a warm wave. He wanted assurance, a comparison between himself and Johnny Lance.

'I have never in my life – ' She placed the emphasis carefully. ' – experienced anything like it.'

He nodded, relieved, pleased – and stood up.

'After breakfast we will go to town.'

This morning, Edmund, Benedict's man, chauffeured the Bentley. When they alighted at the north end of Bond Street and walked arm in arm along the pavement, Edmund tailed them at a dignified crawl, steadfastly ignoring the abuse of other drivers.

The morning was cool enough for Ruby to wear her new cream mink, and the looks of admiration and envy she drew from the other strollers delighted Benedict. He wanted to impress her, he wanted to flaunt his wealth.

'The wife of a diamond man must have diamonds.' He spoke on impulse as they came up to an expensive-looking jewellers. Ruby squeezed his arm and turned to look into the window.

'Good Lord,' Benedict laughed. 'Not here!' And Ruby looked at him with surprise.

Mockingly Benedict began reading the signs in the window.

'"Paradise Jewellers. A large selection of blue-white gems. Certificate of flawlessness with every diamond. Perfect flawless stones at bargain prices as advertised on T.V. and in the national Press. Small deposit secures your ring now. A diamond is forever – show her you really care."'

'But they are such a well-known firm. They have branches all over the world – even in South Africa!' Ruby protested, and bridled a little as Benedict smiled patronizingly.

'Let me explain about diamonds. They are bought for two reasons by two different types of people. Firstly by rich men as investments that will not erode and can only increase in value. These men buy notable stones on the advice of experts, the best of the gem diamond production goes to them. So when Richard Burton buys Liz a £300,000 diamond he is not being extravagant – on the contrary he is being ultra-conservative and thrifty with his money.'

'That's the kind of meanness I like,' Ruby laughed, and Benedict smiled at her honesty.

'You may find me as thrifty,' he promised.

'Go on,' she said, 'tell me more about diamonds.'

'Well, there is another type who buys diamonds. Usually just one in his life, luckily for him – and he very seldom tries to resell it again or he would get a nasty shock. This type is Joe Everybody – who wants to get married. He usually goes to somebody like Paradise Jewellers.' Benedict poked a derisive finger at the sign in the window. 'Because he has seen it on telly and he can get a ring on the instalment plan. In many cases the deposit covers the dealer for the cost of the stone – the rest goes on advertising, finance charges and, of course, profit.'

'How do you know Paradise Jewellers are that type?' Ruby's attention was wide-eyed and girlish.

'You recognize them firstly by the big advertising splurge, then by their language.' Again he studied the notices in the window. '"A large selection of blue-white gems" – of every thousand stones of jewellery quality produced only one is fine enough in colour to be termed blue-white. It is unlikely they have a large selection. "Gem" is a special term reserved for a diamond which is in every way superb. "Flawless stones at bargain prices" – the lack of flaws in a diamond is only one of many factors governing its value. As for bargain prices – there ain't no such animal. Prices are maintained at the lowest level by fierce competition among expert and canny dealers, and there are no "sales" or special prices for anyone.'

'But where should a person buy a diamond?' Ruby was impressed and dismayed despite herself.

'Not here.' Benedict chuckled. 'Come, I will show you.' And before she could protest he had taken her arm and swept her into the shop, to be greeted with enthusiasm by the manager who must have noticed Ruby's mink and the attendant Bentley, which was causing a small traffic jam outside the shop.

'Good morning, madam and sir. May I be of service to you?'

'Yes,' Benedict turned to Ruby, as they settled down in the manager's office with a tray of diamond rings in front of them. 'You cannot examine a diamond properly in its setting.'

He selected the biggest diamond, took from his pocket a

gold-plated penknife fitted with a special tool and prised open the claws of the setting to a chorus of horrified squeals from the staff.

'I will make good any damage,' he snapped, and they subsided as Benedict took the loose stone and laid it on the velvet-covered tray.

'Firstly, size. This stone is about one carat.' He looked for confirmation to the manager who nodded. 'Let us say the value of this stone is £500. Ten similar stones will be worth £5,000, right? However, a ten-carat stone may be worth as much as £75,000. So the price per carat rises sharply as the total weight of the stone increases. If I were investing I would not touch a stone under three carats.'

The staff were listening now with as much attention as Ruby.

'Next, colour,' said Benedict, and glanced at the manager. 'A sheet of clean white paper, please.'

The manager scratched in his drawer and laid a sheet of paper in front of Benedict who placed the stone upon it, bottom upwards.

'We compare the colour it "draws" from white paper in good natural light.' He looked up at the manager. 'Switch off the fluorescent lights, and open those curtains, please.'

The manager obeyed with alacrity.

'This is a matter of experience. The colour is judged by a standard. We forget about the fancy rare colours like blue and red and green, and take our top standard as blue-white. A stone so white as to appear slightly blue, after which the distinctions drop to "fine white", and "white". Then stones which "draw" a yellowish tinge which we call "Cape" – in different shades, then finally stones which "draw" a brown colour – which will reduce the value of a stone by up to eighty per cent.'

Benedict fished in his fob pocket and pulled out a guinea case which he opened.

'Every expert carries a special diamond which he uses as

109

a gauge for colour by which to judge all other stones. This is mine.'

The staff exchanged apprehensive looks as Benedict placed a small diamond beside the other. He studied them a moment then replaced his gauge in the case.

'Second Silver Cape, I'd say,' he grunted, and the staff looked suitably abashed. 'Now we consider the stone's perfection.' He looked at the manager. 'Please lend me your *loupe*.'

'*Loupe?*' The manager was mystified.

'Yes, your jeweller's glass.'

'I—' the manager was deeply embarrassed.

'You sell diamonds – yet you do not own a *loupe*.' Benedict shook his head in disapproval. 'No matter, I have my own.'

Benedict took the glass from his inner pocket and placed it in his eye.

'Imperfections can be almost negligible – a "natural" at the girdle, or a bubble or pinpoint of carbon in the stone, on the other hand they can be gross "cracks", "clouds", "ice", or "feathers" which will ruin the value of the stone. But this one is flawless – so when the certificate of flawlessness is issued there will be no misrepresentation.' Benedict closed the glass and tucked it back into his pocket. 'However, in order to produce a flawless stone, the cut has been squeezed.'

He held up the stone between thumb and forefinger.

'The cut or "make" of a stone is the fourth and final decider of its value. The "make" should conform closely to the "ideal". This stone has been cut to exclude a flaw, and in consequence it is badly proportioned – heavy and out of round. I would prefer to see a graceful stone which includes a slight imperfection rather than a grotesque little cripple like this.'

He put the diamond down on the desk.

'The asking price by Paradise Jewellers for this stone is

£500 – which would be fair and correct for a gem. However, the colour is poor and although it is flawless it is of ungainly make. Its true value would be about – ah, let's see – £185 approximately.'

There was another chorus of protest from the assembled staff, led by the manager.

'I assure you, sir, that all our stones have been most carefully appraised.'

'How long have you been with Paradise Jewellers?' Benedict demanded brusquely. 'Four months, isn't it?'

The manager gaped at him.

'Before that you were a salesman in the showroom of a large firm of embalmers and undertakers.'

'I, well – I mean.' The manager fluttered his hands weakly. 'How did you know that?'

'I like to know about all my employees.'

'Employees?' The manager looked stunned.

'That's correct. My name is Benedict van der Byl. I own Paradise Jewellers.'

Ruby clapped her hands and cooed her applause.

'What a bundle of surprises you are!' she exclaimed.

Benedict smiled in acknowledgement and inclined his head.

'Now,' he said, as he rose and helped Ruby to her feet. 'We will go and buy some real diamonds.'

Aaron Cohen sold them two fine white twin marquise-cut brilliants, and Ruby chose the mounting for a pair of white-gold earrings from a leather-bound catalogue.

Benedict gave Aaron his cheque for twenty thousand pounds, then turned to Ruby.

'Now,' he said. 'We'll have lunch at the Celeste Grill-room. The food is bloody awful – but the decor is stupendous. We had best phone and reserve a table – it isn't really necessary but they get terribly hurt if you don't.'

As they settled back in the lush upholstery of the Bentley, Benedict instructed the chauffeur.

'Go past Trafalgar Square, Edmund. I want to pick up the newspapers from South Africa House.'

Edmund double-parked outside the Ambassador's entrance, and the doorman recognized the car and hurried inside to fetch the bundle of newspapers.

As they pulled away around the square towards Haymarket, Benedict selected a copy of the *Cape Argus*.

'Let's see what's happened at home.' He glanced at the front page, and stiffened perceptibly.

'What is it?' Ruby leaned towards him anxiously, but he ignored her. His eyes were darting across the page like the shuttle of a loom. She saw the colour fade from his face, leaving it white and intent. He finished reading, and pushed the paper towards her. She spread the page.

'VAN DER BYL DIAMONDS WIN VALUABLE CONCESSION.
APPEAL COURT SUPPORTS KAISER'S MINERAL GRANT.
LANCE GETS THUNDERBOLT AND SUICIDE.
  Bloemfontein, Thursday.

'In an urgent application by the Central Diamond Mines Ltd, to prevent Van Der Byl Diamonds Ltd prospecting and mining a concession area off the South West African Coast, Mr Justice Tromp today dismissed the application with costs stating in his judgment: "The original concession granted by German Imperial Decree in 1899, and subsequently ratified by Act of the Union Parliament in Act 24 of the 1920 must hold good in law, and will take precedent over any subsequent grant or concession purporting to have been made by the Minister of Mines to any other party."

'The area in dispute covers 100 square kilometres surrounding two small islands lying some fifteen miles south of Cartridge Bay and five miles offshore. The islands are known as Thunderbolt Island and Suicide Island, and at the turn of the century were the site of considerable exploitation by

112

a German guano company. Mr John Rigby Lance, the General Manager of Van Der Byl Diamond Co. Ltd, acquired the rights to the concession when he took over the inoperative guano company.

'In Cape Town today Mr Lance stated: "It's the opportunity I have waited for all my life. All indications are that Thunderbolt and Suicide will prove to be one of the richest marine diamond fields in the world."

'Van Der Byl Diamond Co. had a diamond-dredging vessel nearing completion in the United Kingdom, and Mr Lance stated that he hoped to begin recovery operations off Thunderbolt and Suicide Islands before the end of the year.'

R uby lowered the paper and looked at Benedict. What she saw was an intense physical shock. Benedict had crumpled down in the seat. Gone was all the assurance and *savoir faire*. His face was deathly pale, but now his lips trembled and with disgust she saw that his eyes were swimming with tears. He hunched forward over his hands, shaking his head gently and hopelessly.

'The bastard,' he whispered, and his voice was soggy and muffled. 'He does it every time. I thought that I had him at last but – Oh God, I hate him.'

He looked at her, his face soft with self-pity. 'He does it every time. Often I've thought I had him, but he just—'

She was mystified by his reaction.

'Aren't you pleased? Van Der Byl Diamonds will make millions—'

'No! No!' he cut in savagely, and then the years of hatred and frustration and humiliation began pouring out. Ruby listened quietly, slowly beginning to understand it all, marvelling at the accumulation of pain and hatred that he exposed for her. He remembered conversations from twenty

113

years ago. Small childhood episodes, innocent remarks that had festered and rankled for a decade.

'You don't want him to succeed, is that it?' she asked.

'I want to crush him, break him, humiliate him.'

For ten seconds Ruby was silent.

'Well, what are we going to do about it?' she asked flatly.

'Nothing, I suppose.' Benedict's tone irritated her. 'He always comes out on top, you just can't—'

'Nonsense,' Ruby snapped. She was angry now. 'Let's go over it carefully, and see how we can stop him. He is only human, and you have shown me enough to prove you are a brilliant and successful businessman.'

Benedict's expression changed, becoming trusting and animated. He turned to her almost eagerly: he blinked his eyes. 'Do you really believe that?'

The bunk was too narrow, Sergio Caporetti decided, much too narrow. He would have one of the carpenters alter it today.

He lay on his back, wedged in firmly, with the blanket-covered mound of his belly blocking his view southwards. He lay and assessed his physical condition. It was surprisingly good. There was but a small blurred pain behind his eyes and the taste of stale cigars and rank wine in the back of his throat was bearable. The leaden feeling in his lower limbs alarmed him until he realized that he was still wearing his heavy fisherman's boots. He remembered one of the girls complaining about that.

He hoisted himself on one elbow, and looked at the girls. One on each side of him, jamming him solidly into the bunk with magnificent hillocks of pink flesh. Big strong girls both of them, he had chosen them with care, neither of them an ounce under twelve stone. Sergio sighed happily – it had been a wonderful weekend. The girls were snoring, in such harmony that it might have been a rehearsed stage act. He listened to them with mild admiration for a few minutes, then crawled over the outside girl and stood in the centre of the cabin, clad only in his heavy boots. He yawned extravagantly, scratching the thick black wiry curls that covered his chest and belly, and cocked an eye at the bulkhead clock. Four o'clock on a Monday morning, but it had been a truly memorable weekend.

The table was hidden under a forest of empty wine bottles, and dirty plates. There was a congealed mass of cold spaghetti bolognaise in a dish and he picked it up. As he clumped out of the cabin on to *Kingfisher*'s bridge he was scooping up spaghetti with his fingers and cramming it into his mouth.

He stood at the rail of the bridge, a naked hairy figure in tall black boots clutching a dish of spaghetti to his chest, and looked around the dockyard.

Kingfisher was in stocks undergoing the modifications that Johnny Lance had ordered. She was standing high above the level she would attain when she was launched. Although she was a vessel of a mere 3,000-ton displacement, she appeared black and monstrous in the floodlights that illuminated the ship-builders' yard. It was obvious from her unusual silhouette that she was designed for a special purpose. Her superstructure was situated well aft like that of an oil tanker, while her foredeck was crowded by the huge gantry which would control the dredge, and by the massive storage tanks for the compressed air.

At this hour of the morning the shipyard was deserted, and wisps and tendrils of sea mist drifted about *Kingfisher*'s bulk.

Standing fifty feet above the dry dock, still wolfing cold spaghetti, Sergio urinated over the rail – deriving a simple honest pleasure from the long arching stream and the tinkle of liquid striking the concrete far below.

He clumped back into his cabin, and looked down fondly

on his two sleeping Valkyries while he finished the last of the spaghetti. Then he wiped his fingers carefully on his chest hair and called to them gently.

'Come, my kittens, my little doves, the time for play she has passed – the time for work she commences.'

With Latin gallantry he bundled them into a taxi at the dockyard gates, pressing on to each of them a lusty kiss, a banknote, a bottle of Chianti, protestations of deep affection, and the promise of another party next Friday night.

He picked his way back through the dockyard jungle of machinery and buildings, lighting a long black cigar and inhaling smoke pleasurably until he came in sight of *Kingfisher* and halted with surprise and annoyance. There was a big honey-coloured Bentley parked near the gangway that led up to *Kingfisher*'s deck. He resented visits from the Company bosses, especially this one, and especially at this ridiculous hour on a Monday morning.

T he hose spiralled down into greenness, and they followed it down holding hands. Tracey was still a little nervous. This was not like the Mediterranean, a warm blue friendly embrace of waters to welcome the diver – it was the wild Atlantic, coldly menacing, green and untamed. It frightened her, and Johnny's hand gave her comfort.

Their Draeger demand valves repeated their breathing in a singing metallic wheeze, and icy leaks and rivulets kept finding their way into the cuffs and neck of Tracey's rubber suit.

Sixty feet below the surface Johnny paused, and peered into the glass window of her mask. He grinned at her, his mouth distorted by the bulky mouthpiece, and she gave him a thumbs-up sign. They both looked upwards. The surface was silvered like an imperfect mirror, and the black cigar shape of the boat was lapped in strange light. The hose and anchor chain pierced the silver ceiling and hung down into the shady green depths.

Johnny pointed downwards, and she nodded. They put their heads down, pointed their flippers to the surface, and still hand in hand they paddled steadily towards the sea bed.

Tracey was aware of a crackling hissing sound now, and from out of the greeny blackness below them scudded clouds of silver bubbles twisting and writhing towards the surface. She strained her eyes downwards, following the line of the hose, and slowly out of the murk materialized the black rubber-clad forms of the two men working at the end of the hose; they appeared weird and mystical like black priests performing a satanical mass.

She and Johnny reached the sea bed and hung just above it, a little way off from the two men on the hose. Johnny indicated the depth gauge that he wore like a wrist watch. It showed a depth of 120 feet. Then he turned and by a hand signal showed her the direction of the reefs.

They were in a valley between these long peaked underwater ridges of black rocks, the same reefs that Tracey had seen from the air. There was a distinct pull of water as the current drifted at right angles to the direction of the reefs.

Johnny squeezed her hand, and then pulled her down. They lay on their bellies on the floor of the sea, and Johnny scooped a handful of the white sand, washed it quickly so that the smaller particles were carried away in a cloud on the current, then he showed her the coarse gravel which remained. Again he grinned, and she returned his smile.

Still leading her by the hand, he swam slowly towards the two men working on the hose, and stopped to watch them.

Attached to the end of the hose was a rigid steel pipe two inches in diameter, and twenty feet long – although now only half of its length was visible above the sand bottom. The two divers were forcing it down through sand and gravel to reach bedrock. The hose itself was attached to a compressor on the deck of the boat which was generating a vacuum in the hose and sucking up the sand and gravel as the steel pipe was forced downwards.

They were prospecting the Thunderbolt and Suicide field. Taking these two-inch samples at 500-foot intervals to ascertain the depth of water, the thickness of the over-burden, and the content of the gravel beds. They were also mapping and plotting the reefs, so that by the time *Kingfisher* arrived they would have a fairly clear picture of the top-ography and aspect of the field. They would know where to begin dredging, and roughly what to expect when they did.

So far the results had endorsed Johnny's most optimistic expectations. There was a good thick catchment of gravel in all the gullies between the reefs. As he had expected, the heavier gravels had been laid down in the gullies closest to the gap between Thunderbolt and Suicide, and the smaller and lighter gravels had been carried further. In some of the gullies the gravel beds were fifteen feet deep, and the types of stone present were all highly promising. He had isolated garnet, jasper, ironstone, beryl chips and titanium dust.

However, the conclusive and definite proof had also come up through that two-inch hose out of the depths. They had already pulled the first diamonds from the Thunderbolt and Suicide fields. When you considered the odds against finding a stone in a two-inch sample at 500-foot centres and that payable gravel contained one part diamond in fifty million, it was exciting and encouraging that they had already recovered four diamonds. Small stones, to be sure, not one of them more than half a carat, but diamonds for all that, and some of them of excellent quality.

One of the men on the hose turned and gave Johnny a flat-handed cut-out sign. The pipe was on bedrock. Johnny nodded and jerked a thumb upwards, and drawing Tracey with him, started for the surface.

They climbed the ladder over the survey boat's counter, moving clumsily under the weight of the air bottles strapped to their backs, but there were willing hands to help them aboard and strip off the heavy equipment, and unzip the clinging rubber suits.

Tracey accepted a towel gratefully from one of the crew, and while she tilted her head to dry her sodden mane of hair, she looked across half a mile of green sea to the two white whale-backed islands with their attendant clouds of seabirds. The wave bursts on the cliffs sounded like distant artillery, or far thunder.

'God, this is a wild and exciting place.' Her voice bubbled with excitement as she scrubbed at her hair. 'It makes one come alive.'

Johnny understood her feelings, it was the forbidding restless sea and the harsh land that promised danger and adventure. He was about to reply, but the two hose men came aboard at that moment, the taller of them spitting out his mouthpiece and letting it fall to his chest.

'We'll move up to the next point, if it's okay by you, Mr Lance?' The man pulled off his mask and hood, exposing white-blond hair and a sun-broiled face.

'Fine, Hugo,' Johnny agreed, and watched approvingly as Hugo Kramer gave the orders to get the anchor and the hose up before taking *Wild Goose* seawards to her next prospecting point. Johnny had been reluctant to charter *Wild Goose* as the prospecting vessel and as the service boat for *Kingfisher*. He did not know Hugo Kramer, and Benedict van der Byl's insistence on the man had made him suspicious.

However, it was natural that they should use a skipper from the van der Byl fleet and Johnny was now prepared to admit he had been wrong. Kramer was an intelligent and willing worker, resourceful and trustworthy, a fine seaman who handled *Wild Goose* with all the skill it would need to bring her alongside *Kingfisher* in a heavy sea. His unfortunate physical appearance Johnny hardly noticed any more, although the original shock of that pink face, white hair and those blind-looking eyes had been considerable.

Tracey was not so charitable. The man made her uneasy. There was a wild-animal ferocity about him, a barely controlled violence. The way he looked at her sometimes made her skin prickle. He did it now; turning back from issuing his orders he ran his eyes over her body. In the black silk costume her good round breasts showed at their best, and Hugo Kramer looked at them with those white-fringed bland eyes. Instinctively she covered them with the towel, and it seemed as though his lips twitched with amusement as he turned to Johnny.

'They tell me this dredger of yours is something special, Mr Lance?'

'She is, Hugo. Not like the other half-baked barges and bastardized conversions that have been tried by other companies. She's the first diamond recovery vessel designed expressly for the job.'

'What's different about her?'

'Nearly everything. Her hose is operated off a gantry on the foredeck, it goes out through a well pierced through her hull.'

'What kind of hose?'

'Eighteen-inch armoured woven steel with rubber liner. We can get it down to a hundred fathoms, and it has a compensating section in it to stop it plunging with the wave action of the hull.'

'Eighteen inches is pretty big. How will you build up vacuum?'

'That's the point, Hugo. We don't suck – we blow! We evacuate water from the hose by purging it with compressed

120

air, the inrush of water into the opening of the hose sucks in the gravel.'

'Hey, that's neat. So the deeper you work the more effective it will be!'

'Right.'

'What about the actual recovery? Are you going to have the usual screening, ball mill, and grease table arrangement?'

'That's what killed the other companies – trying to separate by the old methods. No. We've got a cyclone to start with.'

'Cyclone?'

'You know a cream separator?'

'Yeah.'

'Same principle. Just spin the gravel in a circular tank and float off everything with a specific gravity of less than 2.5. Take what is left, dry it, spread it on a conveyor belt and run it under an X-ray machine which pinpoints every single diamond. As you know, diamonds fluoresce under X-rays and they show up crisply. The X-ray machine reports the diamond to the central computer. . . ' Johnny's voice and whole attitude was charged with enthusiasm which was impossible for his listeners to resist. Tracey was carried along with him, watching his eyes and his mouth as he talked, smiling when he smiled, her lips following his faithfully.

'This is the cyclone room,' Benedict van der Byl explained as, with a hand on her elbow, he helped Ruby Lance down off the last rung of the ladder. 'I explained to you how it worked.'

'Yes.' Ruby nodded, and looked around the room with interest. The roughly riveted and grey painted plating of *Kingfisher*'s hull formed a square metal box, in the centre of which stood the cyclone. It was also painted battleship grey, a ten-foot-high cone-shaped circular tower.

'The gravel is blown in through here.' Benedict indicated the eighteen-inch pipe which entered the cyclone room through the forward bulkhead, then connected to the bottom of the cyclone. 'Up it goes.' Benedict flung his hand upwards. 'And round it goes.' He made a stirring motion. 'The heavy stuff is thrown off and led away through that.' A smaller pipe emerged from the shoulder of the cyclone and disappeared through the farther bulkhead. 'While the lighter stuff shoots out through the top and is sprayed overboard again.'

'I understand. Now, where is the weak spot?' Ruby asked.

'Come.' Benedict led her across the room, picking their way among the litter left by the workmen who still swarmed through *Kingfisher*. They reached a steel door in the bulkhead.

'Watch your head.' They ducked into a long passageway with doors at both ends. On their right hand was an enclosed tunnel that ran the length of the room.

'This is the conveyor room,' Benedict explained. 'The concentrated gravels fall through a hot air draught from an electric furnace to dry them. They are gathered on a conveyor belt, concealed in that tunnel, and carried through into the X-ray room.'

'This is where you will fit it?' Ruby asked.

'Yes. In the conveyor tunnel. It will mean moving that inspection hatch back twelve feet to give us the space.'

Ruby nodded. 'The man who will do the work – can you trust him?'

'Yes. He has worked for me before.' Benedict did not add that the same man had designed the electronic equipment for the balloons used by the Ring, and had flown out from Japan to convert the ASDIC equipment on *Wild Goose*.

'All right.' Ruby seemed satisfied. More and more she was becoming the driving force in the alliance, bolstering

Benedict's resolution when he showed timidity or when he tried to evade the actions which must, in time, lead to a confrontation with Johnny Lance.

'Let's see the X-ray room.'

It was a tiny cupboard-like compartment. The floor, roof and all four walls were clad with thick sheet lead. Suspended from the roof was the X-ray machine, and under it a circular table the surface of which was covered with a honeycomb-patterned stainless steel sheet.

'The concentrated gravel spills on to the table, and the table revolves under the X-ray machine which fluoresces each diamond and the computer picks it up and reports its size and exact position on the table. The computer then commands one of those – ' Benedict pointed to a forest of hard plastic tubes, each attached to a metal arm, ' – to swing out over the table exactly above the diamond and suck it up. The computer selects the correct diameter of tube for the size of the diamond – and, after the tube has obeyed the computer, the table passes under a second X-ray machine which confirms that the diamond has been collected. If, by chance, the tube fails to suck up the stone, then the computer automatically sends the table on another circuit. If, however, the diamond is safely gathered then the waste material is scraped from the table and it swings round to pick up more gravel from the cyclone room – and repeat the whole process. The system is 100 per cent effective. Every single diamond is recovered by it. Even stones as small as sugar grains.'

'Where is the computer?' Ruby asked.

'There.' Benedict pointed through the small leaded glass window which overlooked the X-ray table. Beyond it was another small compartment. Ruby flattened her nose against the glass, and peered in. The computer occupied most of the room, a huge glossy enamelled cabinet not unlike a refrigerator despite the switches and dials. Benedict peered in beside her.

'The computer runs the entire operation. It controls the flow of compressed air into the dredger pipe, it regulates the cyclone, runs the X-ray machine and the table, it weighs and counts the diamonds recovered before depositing them in a safe, and it even navigates the *Kingfisher* and reports to the bridge her exact position over the sea bed, it checks the lubrication and temperature of the engines and power plant and on request will make a complete and immediate report of the whole or any part of the operation.'

Ruby was still peering into the computer room.

'What happens to the diamonds once they have been picked off the revolving table?' she asked.

'They are sucked through an electronic scale which weighs each stone, then they are carried through into the computer room and deposited in that safe.' Benedict pointed out the steel door set in the bulkhead. 'The safe has a time and combination lock. So the system works without a diamond being touched by human hand.'

'Let's go and talk to the Italian peasant,' suggested Ruby, and as she turned from the window Benedict slipped his arm about her shoulders and hugged her possessively.

'Not now,' snapped Ruby irritably, shrugging off his arm, and she led the way out of the X-ray compartment, passing the locked door of the computer control room opposite the door to the conveyor room. She was impressed with the ingenuity of the system – but the fact that it had been constructed by Johnny Lance made her angry.

Her loyalties had changed completely, going to the highest bidder.

124

Sergio Caporetti felt a small twinge of pity when he looked at Ruby Lance. So thin, and with a backside like a boy. She would be little comfort to a man on a cold night. Sergio worked the cheroot from one corner of his mouth to other, anointing the stub with saliva in the process. Also she was cold-blooded, he decided. Sergio had a very sensitive intuition when it came to judging the temperature of a woman's passion. Cold like a snake, he decided, his pity giving way to revulsion. He repressed a small shudder as he watched her settle on to the day couch in his cabin, and cross her long golden legs precisely. Just like a snake, she would eat a man as though he were a little hopping frog. Sergio had admiration for Johnny Lance, but – he decided – not even he would be safe with a woman like this.

'You like my ship?' he asked, an attempt at friendliness. 'She is *very* fine ship.'

Sergio actually used a more forceful adjective than *very*, one that suggested *Kingfisher* was capable of procreation, and Ruby's lips curled with disgust. She ignored the question and lit a cigarette, swinging one leg impatiently, and turned her head to stare through the porthole.

Sergio was hurt by the rebuff, but he had no time to brood on it for Benedict van der Byl came to stand in the centre of the cabin with his hands clasped lightly behind his back.

'Mr Caporetti—' he asked quietly. 'How much do you like money?'

Sergio grinned, and pushed the grubby maritime cap to the back of his head. 'I like it pretty good, I like it better than mother – and I love my mother like my life,' he said.

'Would you like to become a rich man?' Benedict asked, and Sergio sighed wistfully.

'*Si!*' he nodded. 'But it is the impossible thing. There is too much *vino*, too much lovely girls, and the cards they are cruel like – ' Sergio paused to find a suitable simile and

125

glanced at Ruby, ' – like a thin woman. No. Money she does not stay long, she comes and she goes.'

'What would you do for £25,000?' Benedict asked.

'For twenty-five thousand – ' Sergio's eyes were dark liquid and lovely as those of a dying gazelle or a woman in love, ' – there is nothing I will not do.'

*K*ingfisher sailed for Africa on the 4th of October. As the representative of the owners, Benedict van der Byl drove down from London to bid her *bon voyage*, and he spent an hour behind locked doors with Sergio Caporetti before the departure of the vessel.

Kingfisher made good time southwards on her first leg of the voyage, but the unscheduled delay of ten days at the island of Las Palmas infuriated Johnny. His urgently cabled enquiries from Cape Town elicited the reply that there were teething troubles in *Kingfisher's* engine room which were being attended to in the Las Palmas dockyards. The voyage would be resumed as soon as the repairs had been effected.

The Japanese gentleman who welcomed *Kingfisher* to Las Palmas was named Kaminikoto. This was too much for Sergio's tongue, so he called him 'Kammy'.

Sergio's crew was sent ashore with the excuse that the work on *Kingfisher* was dangerous. They were installed in the best tourist hotel and liberally supplied with intoxicating liquor. Sergio did not see them for the next ten days that he and Kammy were busy on the modifications to *Kingfisher's* computer, and recovery equipment.

During those ten days Sergio and Kammy discovered that despite physical appearances they were brothers.

Kammy had mysterious packing-cases brought on board and they worked like furies from dawn until after dark each day. Then they relaxed.

Kammy was half Sergio's size with a face like a mischievous monkey. At all times he wore a Homburg hat. On the one occasion that Sergio saw him in his bath without his headgear he discovered that Kammy was as bald as St Peter's dome.

Kammy's abundant tastes in women were identical to Sergio's. This made the hiring of partners an easy matter, for what suited the one suited the other. Sergio took south with him fond memories of the little Japanese clad only in his Homburg hat, uttering bird-like cries of encouragement and excitement, while perched like a jockey on top of a percheron mare.

When at last Sergio shepherded his debauched crew back aboard *Kingfisher* the only obvious sign of their labours was that the inspection hatch on the conveyor tunnel had been moved back twelve feet.

'It is my best work,' Kammy told Sergio. Already he was sad at the prospect of parting. They were brothers. 'I signed my name. You will remember me when you see it.'

'You good guy, Kammy. The best!' Sergio embraced him, lifting him off his feet and kissing him heartily on each cheek while Kammy clutched desperately at his Homburg.

They left him standing on the wharf, a forlorn and solitary figure, while *Kingfisher* butted out into the Atlantic and swung away southwards.

Ruefully Johnny Lance glanced over at the mountain of empty champagne bottles beyond the barbecue pits. The bill for this little party would be in the thousands, but it was not an extravagance. The guest list included all Van Der Byl Diamond Company's major creditors and their wives. Johnny Lance was showing them all what they were getting for their money. To appear prosperous was almost as reassuring to a creditor as being prosperous. He was going to stuff them full of food and champagne, show them over the *Kingfisher* and fly them back home, hoping sincerely that they would be sufficiently impressed to stop badgering him for a while – and let him get on with the business of taking the Company out into the clear.

Tracey caught his eye. Her humorous roll of the eyes was a plea for sympathy, for she was surrounded by a pack of middle-aged bankers and financiers whom champagne had made susceptible to her charms. Johnny winked at her in reply, then glanced around guiltily to find Ruby, and was relieved that she was in deep conversation with Benedict van der Byl in a far corner of the marquee.

He made his way out of the crowd to the edge of the dune, and lit a cigarette while he looked back across Cartridge Bay.

The chartered Dakotas that had flown the guests and caterers up from Cape Town were standing on the airstrip beyond the buildings.

The marquee was situated on the crest of a sand dune overlooking the narrow entrance to the bay. The dune had been bulldozed to accommodate the tent, the laden tables, and the barbecue pits around which white-clad servants were busy, and the spitted carcasses of three sheep and a young ox were already browning crisply and emitting a cloud of fragrant steam.

Tracey watched Johnny standing out on the edge of the dune. He looked tired, she thought. The strain of the last few months had worn him down. Looking back on it now she realized that every few days had thrust a crisis upon him. The terrible worry of the court case that had won them Thunderbolt and Suicide had barely ended before Johnny had faced the delays in the construction of *Kingfisher*, the bullying of creditors, the sniping of Benedict and a hundred other worries and frustrations.

He was like a prize-fighter coming out to the bell of the last round, she thought tenderly, as she studied the profile of his face now staring out to sea. His stance was still aggressive, the big jaw pushed out and the hand with the missing finger that held the cigarette balled into a fist, but there were blue shadows under his eyes and lines of tension at the corners of his mouth.

Suddenly, there was an alertness in Johnny's attitude, he shaded his eyes with a hand before turning back towards the marquee.

'All right, everyone!' he called, stilling the babble of their voices. 'Here she comes.'

Immediately the uproar was redoubled and the whole party trooped out into the sunlight, their excitement and the shrillness of their voices enhanced by the Pommery they had been walloping back since mid-morning.

'Look! There she is!'

'Where? Where?'

'I can't see her.'

'Just to the left of that cloud on the horizon.'

'Oh yes! Look! Look!'

Tracey took a second glass of champagne from one of the waiters, and carried it across to Johnny.

'Thanks.' He smiled at her with the ease that now existed between them.

'It's taken her long enough to get here.' Tracey picked out the faraway speck on the green ocean that was *Kingfisher*. 'When will she begin working?'

'Tomorrow.'

'How long will it be before we know – well, if it has come off?'

'A week.' Johnny turned to her. 'A week to be certain, but we'll know in a day or two how it's shaping up.'

They were silent then, staring out at the gradually approaching speck. The crowd lost interest quickly and drifted back to the liquor, and the fragrant steaming platters of golden-brown meat that were coming from the barbecue pits.

Tracey broke the long friendly silence at last. She spoke hesitantly, as though reluctant to bring up a painful subject.

'How long has Ruby been back now – ten days?'

'About that,' Johnny agreed, glancing at her quickly. 'I haven't seen much of her,' he admitted. 'But she seems to be a lot more relaxed – and at least she's kept off my back.'

'She and Benedict seem to have become very pally.' Tracey glanced across to where the other couple were now included in a boisterous circle of revellers.

'She bumped into him in London,' Johnny agreed, sounding offhand. 'She tells me they had lunch a couple of times.'

She waited for him to continue, to express some suspicion or reservation, but he seemed to have no further interest in the subject; instead he began running over the day's further arrangements with her.

'I'm relying on you to take charge of the wives when we go aboard. Keep an eye on Mrs Larsen particularly – she's up to her gills in bubbly.'

For the next two hours that it took *Kingfisher* to make her approach and enter the channel of Cartridge Bay, Johnny hardly took his eyes from her unusual silhouette. She was not a pretty vessel but the white lightning insignia of Van Der Byl Diamonds on her funnel gave her a special beauty in his eyes. As she passed below them and entered the bay, Larsen proposed a toast to her successful career, then they all descended the dune and climbed into the waiting Land-Rovers and drove round the bay to meet her. By the time they arrived *Kingfisher* had made fast alongside the jetty, and Captain Sergio Caporetti was waiting to welcome them aboard.

He stood at the head of the gangway, and sensible to the importance of the moment he was decked in his finest and best; a double-breasted suit with a cream and lilac pinstripe set off the tomato-red silk tie, but his two-tone black and white crocodile skin shoes drew attention to his large feet and his gait was that of an emperor penguin. A liberal application of a hair pomade with a penetrating smell of violets had flattened his black hair into a shiny slick, bisected by the ruler-straight line of white scalp which was his parting. However, the aroma of the pomade was at odds with the particularly stinky cheroot of a brand which Sergio reserved for weddings, funerals and other special occasions.

His beautiful gazelle eyes became passionate and dark as they lit on Fifi Larsen. Mrs Larsen's tight-fitting slacks moved as though they were full of live rabbits and her pink sweater was straining its seams. Her eyes were sparkling with champagne and she giggled without apparent reason, flushing under Sergio's scrutiny.

The tour of *Kingfisher* began, Sergio Caporetti taking up an escort position directly behind Mrs Larsen. They had hardly descended the first ladder when Mrs Larsen let out a small squeak and shot about eighteen inches into the air, before coming back to earth with all her plentiful womanhood aquiver.

'My dear Fifi, whatever is wrong?' Her husband was all solicitude, while behind her Sergio Caporetti wore an expression of cherubic innocence. Johnny felt dizzy with alarm, for he had seen Sergio's great hairy paw settling comfortably on to those majestic buttocks. Mrs Fifi Larsen had been thoroughly goosed.

In relieved disbelief Johnny heard her reply, which was preceded by another giggle.

'I seem to have twisted my ankle. Perhaps there is somewhere I could sit down.'

Johnny looked around frantically for Tracey to get Mrs Larsen out of Sergio's clutching range, but before he could signal her, Fifi was limping away on Sergio Caporetti's arm, bravely declining all offers of help.

'Please don't let me spoil your fun. I'll just sit in the Captain's cabin for a few minutes.'

Quickly Johnny moved up beside the silver-haired Larsen

and resolved to stay close beside him. Even if he could not prevent Fifi visiting Sergio's quarters, he was going to make good and sure that the husband didn't join the party.

'This is the explosives locker.' Johnny took Larsen's arm and led him away. 'We keep a store of plastic explosives for underwater blasting—'

Larsen's concern at his wife's injury dissolved and he became immersed in the tour of *Kingfisher*. Johnny followed the line of production for him from the moment the gravel was sucked in through the dredge.

As they left the cyclone room Johnny preceded him, holding the steel door open for Larsen.

'From the cyclone the concentrates pass through here into—' He stopped with surprise as they entered the narrow compartment beyond the cyclone.

'What's wrong, Lance?' Larsen demanded.

'No. It's nothing,' Johnny assured him. After the surprise of finding that the inspection plate in the conveyor tunnel had been moved he realized that it was as well from a security angle. Probably the marine architects had ordered the modification. 'The concentrates are carried through into the next compartment to the X-ray room. This way, please.'

As Johnny led the way to the next door he resolved to check with the architects. Larsen asked a question and he replied and the conveyor tunnel was forgotten. They went through into the X-ray room.

'He noticed it.' Benedict puffed quickly and nervously at the cigarette cupped in his hand. 'He doesn't miss a thing. The bastard.'

'He noticed it, yes. But he accepted it.' Ruby was definite. 'I know him. I was watching him. He was disturbed for a second then he rationalized it. I could almost see his mind work. He accepted it.'

They stood together on the exposed angle of *Kingfisher*'s bridge. Suddenly Ruby laughed.

'Don't look so worried,' she warned him merrily. 'We are being watched by your sister again. She's down on the foredeck. Come.'

Still smiling she led him around the angle of the bridge house, and out of sight she was immediately deadly serious again.

'That sister of yours is getting suspicious. We must keep away from each other until you tell Johnny.'

Benedict nodded.

'When are you going to tell him?' she demanded.

'Soon.'

'How soon?' Ruby would not be able to rest until it was out in the open, until Benedict had committed himself, yet she must not push him too hard.

'As soon as *Kingfisher* runs the Company under. I will pick the moment that he is beaten financially, then I will tell him. I want it to be the *coup de grâce*.'

'When will it be, Benedict darling? I am so anxious to be with you – without all this subterfuge.'

Benedict opened his mouth to reply and froze like that, his expression changing slowly into that of a man who doubts the evidence of his own eyes. He was staring over Ruby's shoulder.

Ruby turned quickly. The curtain across the Captain's porthole behind her was open a chink. She looked in upon a spectacle of such whole-hearted rubicund magnitude that it should have occurred only to Olympus between Jupiter and Juno.

In the cabin Fifi Larsen was receiving treatment for her sprained ankle.

'Well, you've got your toy now. Let's hope for all our sakes you can do something with it,' Benedict smiled pleasantly as he came across to where Johnny stood with Larsen under the great gallows-shaped gantry on the foredeck of *Kingfisher* that would raise and lower the dredging head.

'Toy, Mr van der Byl?' Larsen's white eyebrows bristled. 'Surely you have no doubts? I mean, now that you've got this Thunderbolt and Suicide concession?'

'Oh, I wouldn't say doubts, Mr Larsen. Reservations perhaps, but not really doubts. Mr Lance has been the champion of this venture. His enthusiasm has carried it – in the face of all opposition. Even that of my late father.' Benedict turned to Larsen smoothly.

'Your father opposed the scheme? I didn't know that!' Larsen was perturbed.

'Not opposed it, Mr Larsen.' Benedict smiled reassuringly. 'Not really opposed it. But you will notice that he was prepared to risk your money – not his own. That will give you some idea of how he felt.'

There was a chilled silence, before Larsen turned to Johnny.

'Well, Lance, thank you for an interesting day. Very interesting. I'll be watching your progress with attention – close attention.' And he turned away and strode to where a subdued and demure Fifi was waiting with a group of the other wives.

'Thanks.' Johnny gave Benedict a bleak grin.

'Don't mention it.' Benedict smiled that charming boyish smile.

'At the end of this week I'll take that little speech of yours, roll it into a ball and ram it down your throat,' Johnny promised him softly, and Benedict's expression changed. His eyes slitted and his grin showed his teeth and tightened the soft line of his jaw.

'You're pretty slick with your mouth, Lance.'

They glared at each other, the antagonism so apparent, as elemental as a pair of rutting stags, that they were suddenly the centre of all attention. The guests stared curiously, aware of the drama but not understanding it.

Ruby started forward quickly to intervene, taking Johnny's elbow, her voice sugary.

'Oh, Benedict, do you mind if I talk to Johnny a moment? I have to know if he's returning to Cape Town with me this evening.'

She led him away, and the tension dissolved. The disappointed guests began drifting to the gangplank and filing down on to the jetty.

In the confusion of embarkation aboard the two Dakotas, Johnny managed to exchange a last word with Tracey.

'You'll stay here until you know?' she asked. He nodded.

'Good luck, Johnny. I'll pray for you,' she whispered, then followed Ruby Lance up into the fuselage of the Dakota.

Johnny watched the two big aircraft taxi down to the end of the strip, turn in succession and roar away into the purple and red sky of evening.

After they had gone it was very still, and the silence of the desert was complete. Johnny sat in the open Land-Rover and smoked a cigarette while the night came down around him.

He was uneasy, aware of a deep-down tickle of apprehension and foreboding which he could not pin down.

The last glow of sunset faded from the western sky, and the desert stars were bright and hard and close to the earth, silvering the dome of space with the splendour that the city-dweller would never guess at.

Still Johnny hunched in the seat of the open Land-Rover trying to explore the source of his uneasiness, but with so little success that at last he must attribute it to the strain and fatigue of the last few months, his involvement with Tracey, his steadily worsening relationship with Ruby – and the latest clash with Benedict.

He flicked the stub of his cigarette away, watching morosely the explosion of red sparks as it struck the earth, then he started the Land-Rover and drove slowly down towards the jetty.

Kingfisher's lights were smeared in paths of yellow and silver across the still waters of the bay. Every porthole was lit brightly, giving her the festive air of a cruise ship.

Johnny left the Land-Rover at the head of the jetty, and walked out to her. The muted throb of her engines cheered him a little, the knowledge that the vessel was preparing for the morrow.

On deck he paused beside the gigantic compressed air tanks, each the size of a steam locomotive, and checked the pressure gauges. The needles were moving perceptibly around the dials, and his mood lightened a little.

He went up the ladder to the bridge, and into the chartroom where Sergio and Hugo were drinking coffee.

'Not my fault, Mr Lance,' Sergio began defensively. 'I am a gentleman – I cannot refuse a lady.'

'You'll dig your own grave with that spade of yours one day,' Johnny warned him grimly, as he went to the chart table and hung over it.

'Now let's get cracking.' Johnny's sense of dread lifted completely as he looked down at the large-scale Admiralty chart. The twin humps of Thunderbolt and Suicide were clearly marked. 'Hugo, have you got the prospecting schedules?'

'There, on the table.' Hugo and Sergio came to stand on each side of Johnny while he opened the bound file of typewritten sheets.

'The soundings we made differ from the Admiralty chart. We'll put in our figures, before we plot the dredging pattern.'

The three of them settled over the chart with dividers

and parallels to begin marking in the path that *Kingfisher* would follow through the maze of reefs and gullies.

It was long after midnight before Johnny made his way wearily to the guest cabin below the bridge. He kicked off his shoes, lay on the bunk to rest a moment before undressing and fell into a deathlike sleep of exhaustion.

He was awakened by one of the crew with a mug of coffee and he pulled on a windbreaker before hurrying on to the bridge.

Kingfisher was just passing out through the channel of Cartridge Bay into the open sea, and Sergio grinned at him from where he stood beside the helm.

Dawn was only a lemon-coloured promise over the desert behind them, and the sea was black as washed anthracite, kicked into a chop by the small morning wind. They stood on the darkened bridge and sipped steaming coffee, cupping their hands around the enamel mugs.

Then they turned and ran south, parallel to the desert which was now touched with hot orange and violet. The seabirds were up, a flight of malgas turned to glowing darts of fire by the early sun as they winged swiftly across the bows.

With a dramatic suddenness the sun came up over the horizon, and highlighted the chalk-white cliffs of Thunderbolt and Suicide far ahead so that they shone like beacons on the cold green sea. The curtains of spray that burst on the islands flashed and faded as they shot into the sky and fell again.

Wild Goose was waiting for them lying under the lee of the islands, but she came out to meet them, staggering and plunging theatrically over the short uneasy sea that hooked around the islands or boiled through the gap between them.

The radio telephone began crackling and squawking as the sighting reports from Johnny's watchtowers on the shore started coming in, cross-referencing to give *Kingfisher* her position over the ground. There were short exchanges between Sergio and Hugo on *Wild Goose* as they came together, and the little trawler worked in close, ready to give assistance with the laying of the cables if she were needed.

But standing in the angle of the bridge, Sergio Caporetti had the situation under his control. The grubby marine cap pushed to the back of his head and a long black cheroot stuck in the side of his mouth, he stood balanced on the balls of his feet, his eyes darting from judging the set of the sea surf to the repeater of the computer which was feeding him his soundings and position – yet attentive to the R/T reports from shore and from *Wild Goose*.

Johnny was contented with his choice of man as he watched Sergio at work. *Kingfisher* crept slowly up into the lee of Suicide Island, half a mile from the pearly white cliffs, then she hung there a moment before Sergio punched one of the buttons on her control panel.

From forward there was the harsh metallic roar of an anchor cable running out, and as *Kingfisher* backed away leaving a yellow-painted buoy the size of a barrage balloon bobbing under the cliffs of Suicide so one of the massive deck winches began automatically paying out its six-inch steel cable.

Kingfisher backed and crept forward, drifted down on the current or butted up against it while she went through the laborious but delicate operation of laying her four anchors at each point of the compass. Chained above each anchor floated the huge yellow buoys, and from each buoy the steel cables led to the winches on *Kingfisher*'s deck. On instructions from the computer the winches on each quarter would pay out or reel in the cable to hold *Kingfisher* steady over the ground while she worked.

It was mid-afternoon before *Kingfisher* was ready, pinned down like an insect to a board, and the computer reported that she was directly over the gully that Johnny had selected as the starting point. She had twenty-five fathoms of water under her – and then the thick bank of gravel.

'All is ready.' Sergio turned to Johnny, who had stood by quietly all this time – not interfering in the task of positioning. 'You will begin the programme now?'

'Yes.' Johnny stirred himself.

'I would like to watch,' Sergio suggested, and Johnny nodded.

'All right, come.' Sergio handed over the bridge to the helmsman and they went down to the armoured door of the computer room.

Johnny opened the lock. There were only two keys to this compartment. Johnny had one and Benedict van der Byl had the other. He had insisted on having the duplicate, and Johnny had reluctantly agreed not knowing that the key would be used in Las Palmas.

The heavy steel door swung back, and Johnny stepped over the coaming and seated himself before the console of the computer. Covered in cellophane and suspended on a clip above the keyboard of the computer were the cards containing the various programme codes.

Johnny selected the sheet headed: PRIMARY OPERATION: DREDGING AND RECOVERY, and began feeding the code into the computer, punching it on the keyboard.

'Beta, stroke, oh, oh, seven, alpha.'

And within the enamelled console, a change of sound heralded the beginning of the new programme, the hum of her reels and the click of the selectors, while on her control panel the lights blinked and flashed.

Now the computer's screen began to answer the instruction, spelling out her response like a typewriter.

'New programme.'
'Primary Operation. Dredging and Recovery.'
'Phase One.'

'Initiate safety procedure:—
a) Report air pressure . . . 1
b) Report air pressure . . . 2'

Johnny leaned back in the padded stool and watched the exhaustive check that the computer now made of *Kingfisher*'s equipment, typing out the results on the screen.

'What she do now?' Sergio asked curiously, as though he had never spent ten days in this compartment assisting his Japanese friend. Johnny explained the procedure briefly.

'How come you know this so good?' Sergio enquired.

'I spent a month at the Computer Company's head office in America last year while they designed this machine.'

'You the only one in the Company who can work it?'

'Mr Benedict van der Byl has done the course as well as I.' Johnny told him, then he leaned forward again. 'Now she is set.'

The screen on the computer reported itself satisfied.

'Phase One Completed.
Initiate Phase Two.
Lowering and siting of dredge head.'

Johnny stood up. 'Okay, let's get upstairs.'

He locked the door of the computer room and followed Sergio up to the bridge.

Johnny went to stand beside the repeater screen on the bridge, which was relaying the computer's signals exactly as they were printed on the main screen in the compartment below. He could see out through the windows of the wheelhouse, and he watched the automatic response of the heavy equipment on the foredeck.

The gantry swung forward, and the steel arms picked the dredge head from its chocks, and lifted it with the armoured suction hose dangling behind it. Then the gantry swung back, and with a jerky mechanical movement lowered the head through the square opening in the deck. This well pierced the hull, and through it the hose began to snake – a monstrous black python sliding into its hole. The huge reels that held the hose revolved smoothly, as the dredge was lowered to the sea bed.

'Head on bottom.'

The computer screen reported, and the hose reels stopped abruptly.

'Phase Two Completed.
Initiate Phase Three.
Cyclone Revolutions 300.
Vent dredge pump.'

There was a rising high-pitched whine now, like the approach of a jet aircraft. The sound reached a peak, and steadied – and immediately another sound overlaid it. The dull roar of high-pressure air through water, a sound of such power and excitement that Johnny felt the hair on his forearms prickle erect. He stood still as a statue, his expression rapt and his lips set in a small secret smile. That sound was the culmination of two years of planning and endeavour, the sweet reward of the driving dedication that had made a dream into reality.

Suddenly he wished that Tracey was with him to share this moment, and then he knew instinctively that she had deliberately left him alone to savour his moment of triumph.

He grinned then, as he watched the thick black hose engorge and pulse with internal life, like a great artery – pumping, pumping, pumping.

In his imagination Johnny could see the rich porridgy mixture of sea water and mud and gravel that shot up the hose into the spinning cyclone, he could imagine the steel head on the sea bed below the hull surging rhythmically to stir the sand and pound loose any gravel that pressure had welded into a conglomerate.

From the waste pipe over *Kingfisher*'s stern poured a solid steam of dirty yellow water mixed with the sand and gravel that had been rejected and spun out of the cyclone. It stained the green sea with a cloudy fecal discharge, like the effluent from a sewage outlet.

For three days and two nights *Kingfisher*'s pumps roared, and she inched forward along the marine gully like a fussy housewife vacuuming every speck of dust from her floor. As the third evening spread its dark cloak over her, Johnny Lance sat on the padded seat in front of the computer console. He sat forward on the stool with his elbows on his knees and his face in his hands for a full hour. He sat like that in the attitude of despair.

When he lifted his head, his face was haggard and the lines of defeat were clearly cut into his features with the cold chisel of failure.

From the meagre recovery of small diamonds that *Kingfisher* had made in the last three days it was clear beyond reasonable doubt that despite all the indications the Thunderbolt and Suicide field would not support the running costs of the vessel, let alone cover the overheads, or the interest charges and capital repayments on the loan account.

Van Der Byl Diamond Company was finished – and Johnny Lance was financially ruined beyond any possibility of ever finding redemption.

It remained only for the jackals to assemble and squabble over the carcass.

S ergio Caporetti leaned over the railing of the bridge, blowing long streamers of blue cheroot smoke from mouth and nostrils to help foul a morning which was already thick and grey with sea-fret. The islands of Thunderbolt and Suicide were blanketed by the mist, but the surf broke against their hidden cliffs like distant artillery and the seabirds' voices were plaintive and small lost souls in the void.

Wild Goose came bustling up out of the mist, swinging in under *Kingfisher*'s side to hover there under power with two of her crew fending off.

Hugo Kramer stuck his white blond head out of the wheelhouse window, and shouted up at the deck.

'Okay, boss. Come on!'

Sergio watched the tall figure on *Kingfisher*'s deck rouse and look around like a man waking from sleep. Johnny Lance lifted his head and looked up at the bridge, and Sergio noticed that he was unshaven, a new beard darkened his jaw and emphasized its prominence. He looked as though he had not slept, and he hunched into the windbreaker with the collar turned up against the mist. He did not smile, but lifted one hand in farewell salute to Sergio – who noticed incongruously that the index finger was missing from the hand. Somehow, that pathetic little detail struck Sergio. He was sorry, truly sorry. But there is always a loser in every game, and twenty-five thousand pounds is a lot of money.

'Good luck, Johnny.'

'Thanks, Sergio.' Johnny went to the rail lugging his briefcase and swung over it; he dropped swiftly down the steel rungs set in *Kingfisher*'s hull and jumped the narrow gap of surging water to *Wild Goose*'s deck.

The trawler's engine bellowed, and she pulled away, rounding on to a course for Cartridge Bay. Johnny Lance stood on her open deck looking back at *Kingfisher*.

'He's a good guy.' Sergio shook his head with regret.

'He's a boss,' the helmsman grunted. 'No boss is any good.'

'Hey, you! I am also a boss,' Sergio challenged him.

'Like I said.' The helmsman suppressed a grin.

'I kiss your mother,' Sergio insulted him with dignity, then changed the subject. 'I go below now, take over.'

Sergio opened the door to the control room with the duplicate key. He closed the door behind him, seated himself at the console and took from his pocket a sheet of paper headed: KAMINIKOTO SECONDARY RECOVERY PROGRAMME.

Ten minutes later he came out of the control room and locked the door.

'Kammy, I love you,' he chuckled as he closed off the watertight doors that isolated this deck from the one above. He wound the locking bars into position to ensure that he was not interrupted by one of his own crew.

From the tool cupboard on the bulkhead he selected a pair of set spanners and went through into the conveyor room. It took him twenty minutes to unscrew the heavy, deeply threaded bolts that secured the hatch. It had been designed to resist easy entry – a deterrent to casual investigation, but at last Sergio could lift the steel plate off its seating.

He eyed the small square opening with distaste, and reflexively sucked in his pendulous belly. The hatch had not been designed to afford passage to a man of his dimensions.

He took off his cap and jacket and hung them on the cock of one of the pipes, then he ground out his cheroot under his heel and brushed back the hair from his forehead with both hands, checked that his flashlight was in his pocket, and committed himself to the hatch.

He wriggled and kicked, and grunted and built up a heavy sweat for five minutes before he had squeezed through into the conveyor belt tunnel. He squatted on his haunches, panting heavily and flashed his torch along the tunnel. Above his head the conveyor belt carrying the gravel ran smoothly, but the residual heat from the driers made it unbearably hot. He began to crawl rapidly to the end of the tunnel.

From the inside it was impossible to tell, without measuring, that the conveyor belt tunnel was shorter by twelve feet than the external length.

The end of the tunnel was false, and beyond it was a secret cubicle only just large enough to house Kaminikoto's equipment through which all the gravel passed on its journey to the X-ray room.

The Japanese genius for miniaturization was demonstrated by the equipment in this secret cubicle. It was an almost exact copy of the sorting equipment in the main X-ray compartment – except that it had been scaled down to one tenth of the size without affecting its efficiency; in addition, this miniature plant could discriminate in the diamonds it selected. It would not allow a stone over four carats to pass through, and it screened out fixed percentages of the smaller stones – allowing only a proportion of the smaller and less valuable diamonds to proceed through into the main X-ray room.

It was an amazing piece of electronic engineering, but Sergio was unimpressed as he lay on his side in the cramped hot tunnel and began laboriously to unscrew another smaller plate in the false bulkhead.

At last it was open, and he reached through the opening; after a few seconds of fiddling and groping and heavy breathing he brought out a stainless steel cup with a capacity of about two pints. There were clamps on the cup to hold it in position below the chute under Kaminikoto's machine.

The metal cup was heavy, and Sergio placed it carefully on the deck beside him before propping himself on an elbow and shining the flashlight into the cup and took something out of it, stared at it a moment then dropped it back.

'By the blood of all the martyrs!' he gasped with shock, and then immediately contrite for his blasphemy he crossed himself awkwardly with the hand holding the flashlight. Then again he shone the torch into the cup, and shook his head in disbelief. Quickly he pulled a canvas drawstring bag from his pocket, and lying on his side he carefully poured the contents of the cup into the bag, drew the string tight and stuffed it back into his pocket where it made a big hard bulge on his hip like a paper sack of rock-candy. He clamped the stainless steel cup back into position, screwed the coverplate over the opening, and backed away down the tunnel on hands and knees.

He very badly needed a cheroot.

Four hours later Hugo Kramer shinned up the ladder on to *Kingfisher*'s deck while his helmsman took the trawler down to leeward to wait for him.

Sergio shouted down from the bridge.

'Johnny he has gone?'

'*Ja!*' Hugo shouted back. 'He should almost be in Cape Town by now. That Beechcraft is a fast plane.'

'Good.'

'How did it go with you?' Hugo countered.

'Come up – I'll show you.'

Sergio led him into his cabin behind the bridge and locked the door carefully. Then he went to each of the portholes and drew the curtains across them, before crossing to his desk and switching on the reading lamp.

'Sit down.' Sergio indicated the chair opposite the desk. 'You want a drink, or something?'

'Come on,' Hugo grated impatiently. 'Stop mucking around, let's have a look.'

'Ah!' Sergio looked at him sadly. 'You Germans, you are always too much hurry. You cannot rest, enjoy life—'

'Cut the crap!' Hugo's pale eyes were on his face, and Sergio was suddenly aware that this man was dangerous, like a tiger-shark. Coldly dangerous, without malice or passion. Sergio was surprised he had not noticed it before. I must be careful with this one, he thought, and he unlocked the drawer of his desk and took out the canvas bag.

He loosened the drawstring and poured the diamonds on to the blotter. The smallest was the size of a match head – perhaps point one of a carat, and the poorest quality was black and granular-looking, ugly little industrial stones, for Kammy had been careful not to take out only the best and so distort the *Kingfisher*'s recovery as to arouse suspicion. There were hundreds of these tiny crystals and chips which would fetch a few pounds in the industrial market; but there were other stones in the full range of quality and shapes and sizes – as big as green peas, or as marbles, and a few bigger than that. Some of them were perfect octahedron crystals, others water-worn, chipped or amorphous in shape.

They formed a dully glittering pile in the centre of the blotter, in all perhaps five hundred diamonds, yet all of these were dwarfed by one single stone that lay in the centre of the pile, rising out of it the way Mount Everest rises from her foothills.

There are freak diamonds so large or unusual that they become legend. Diamonds who have their own names and whose histories are recorded and invested with romance. The great 'paragons' – stones of the first water whose cut and finished weight exceed one hundred metric carats.

Africa has produced many of them: the *Jonker Diamond*, a 726-carat rough cut to a brilliant of 125 carats that hangs about the throat of the Queen of Nepal; The *Jubilee Diamond*, a superb 245-carat cushion of unearthly fire fashioned out of 650-carat rough – then the biggest of them all, a monstrous rough stone of 3,106 carats, the *Cullinan* which yielded not one, but two paragons. The

Great Star of Africa at 530 carats and *The Cullinan II* at 317 carats. Both these stones grace the Crown Jewels of England.

Now on Sergio Caporetti's desk lay a rough stone which would add yet another paragon to the list.

'Have you weighed it?' asked Hugo, and Sergio nodded.

'How much?'

'Three hundred and twenty carats,' Sergio said softly.

'Jesus!' whispered Hugo, and Sergio crossed himself quickly to dissociate from the use of names.

Reverently Hugo Kramer leaned forward and picked up the big diamond. It filled the palm of his hand, the cleavage plane that formed its base was smooth and clean as an axe-stroke. There were bigger diamonds in history, but this diamond had a special feature which would set it in a niche of its own and endow it with peculiar value.

Its colour was the serene blue of a high summer sky.

This stone could pay half the total bill for *Kingfisher's* construction – if it were ever used for that purpose.

Hugo replaced the blue diamond on the desk and lit a cigarette without taking his eyes from it.

'This field – it is bigger – richer, far richer than we had guessed.'

Sergio nodded.

'In three days we have taken diamonds that I hoped to see once in five years,' Hugo went on as he began picking out the larger diamonds from the pile and laying them in a line across the desktop in approximate order of size, while Sergio opened his desk drawer and took out a box of his special occasion cheroots.

'We must tell the boss,' Hugo decided. He began arranging the diamonds in a neat circle about the big blue, thinking deeply. 'He must know how rich it is before he talks to Lance. He must make arrangements. He will know what to do – he's a clever one.'

'What about these?' Sergio indicated the treasure on the desk. 'Are you going to take them off?'

Hugo hesitated. 'No,' he decided. 'We could never get rid of this big Blue through the usual channel, it is too big, too distinctive. We will keep it aboard. When the boss takes over the Company again – then we will just declare it all nice and legal. No trouble.' He stood up. 'Look after them. I must hurry if I am to get a message to Cape Town in time.'

T he Company bears my father's name, Mr Larsen. It's as simple as that.' Benedict's voice was husky with emotion, and he looked down at his hands. 'I have a duty to my father's memory.'

'My boy, well—' Larsen came to lay his hand on Benedict's arm. 'Well, I just don't know what to say. Honour is a rare and precious thing these days.' With his free hand he was groping almost frantically for the bell on the desk behind him. He must get this signed up solid before the youngster changed his mind.

'I tried to warn you, Mr Larsen. My father and I never had any faith in this marine recovery scheme. Lance pushed it through—'

'Yes, quite so,' Larsen agreed, and turned to his assistant who came into the office at the trot in response to the bell. 'Ah, Simon. The Van Der Byl Diamond loan. Will you have an agreement made out immediately – Mr van der Byl will take over the capital amounts, and the outstanding interest as well.' By rolling his eyes Larsen tried to convey to his assistant the deadly urgency of the situation. The young man understood and fifteen minutes later laid the Agreement on Larsen's desk. Larsen unscrewed the cap of his pen and handed it to Benedict.

Larsen and three of his young men ushered Benedict out through the glass doors of the bank and across the pavement to where the Rolls stood in the reserved parking bay in Adderley Street.

Benedict settled into the back seat, acknowledged the bank official's farewells, and tapped on the chauffeur's window. As they pulled away, Ruby Lance slipped her hand through his arm and squeezed it.

'Did you get it?' she asked.

Benedict grinned happily. 'I frightened five years' growth out of old Larsen. He almost broke his neck in the hurry to give it to me.'

'Now you've got it all.' Ruby snuggled a little closer to him on the soft leather upholstery. Benedict nodded, and checked his watch.

'The meeting is set for fifteen minutes' time. I'll go up the front way, but I want you to go up in the private lift from the basement garage, and wait in my office. We will be in the Board Room. I will ring you at the right moment.'

The Rolls picked its way slowly down around the Heerengracht and double-parked outside the building. The chauffeur came to open the door, but before he alighted Benedict smiled into Ruby's face.

'This will be one of the high moments of my life,' he said softly. 'This time I've got the bastard cold.'

'I'll be waiting for you,' Ruby said, and he climbed out of the Rolls. He waited until it had turned into the entrance ramp of the basement garage, then he crossed the pavement into the main lobby of the skyscraper. He strode to the elevator with long eager strides, and his mouth kept pulling into a small excited smile.

The Board Room was set high, and the picture windows looked up at the great squat mountain, whose sheer cliffs dropped directly to the wooded slopes up which the first buildings of the city straggled.

Johnny Lance stood at the head of the table. He had lost weight in the last few days, so that his shoulders appeared bony and gaunt under the white silk shirt. He had discarded his jacket, and pulled the knot of his tie down an inch. The bones of his cheeks and jaw made harsh angles that were accentuated and not softened by the deep shades of fatigue that darkened his eyes. His hands were thrust deep into his pockets, and he spoke without reference to the sheaf of paper that lay on the table before him.

'Our working costs are as close as dammit to a hundred pounds an hour; right Mike?' And Michael Shapiro nodded. 'Well, we worked the Suicide main gully for sixty-six hours, and we recovered a princely 200 carats of the lousiest pile of junk I've ever seen. If we get a thousand quid for the lot we'll be doing well. This for an expenditure of six and a half thousand.'

Johnny paused, and looked around the table. Michael Shapiro was doodling on his note pad with fierce concentration, Tracey van der Byl was pale, her eyes never left Johnny's face and her expression ached with pity and helpless compassion; Benedict van der Byl was looking out of the window at the mountain, he was slumped comfortably in his chair, smiling a little and listening politely.

'The Suicide main gully is one of the five most likely parts of the entire concession. It's no good, so the rest of the field may be useless. We have the two other concessions, the original fields, to try. However, it will take three or four days to get *Kingfisher* moved up the coast.' Johnny paused, and Benedict swivelled his chair, still with the small smile on his lips.

'The interest payments fall due on the 30th – three days'

time. Where are you going to find one hundred and fifty thousand Rand?'

'Yes,' Johnny nodded. 'I think I can persuade Larsen to extend for a few weeks; he will bloody well have to if he wants to protect his—'

'Hold on,' Benedict murmured. 'Larsen has got nothing to do with it.'

Johnny was silent, watching him warily. 'Explain,' he invited.

'I've taken over the loan from Larsen,' Benedict told him. 'I'm not interested in extending.'

'Larsen wouldn't have negotiated without warning me.' Johnny was stricken, his disclaimer was wrung from him in pain.

'Shapiro?' Benedict turned to Michael Shapiro for confirmation.

'Sorry, Johnny. It's true. I've seen the documents.'

'Thanks, Michael.' Johnny's voice was bitter with accusations. 'Thanks for letting me know.'

'He showed me a few minutes before the meeting, Johnny. I swear I didn't know.' Michael's expression was distressed.

'Right.' Benedict straightened up in his chair, his voice was brisk. 'Let's get down to first principles. You've ruined my father's Company, Lance – but, thank God, I may be able to retrieve the situation. Call it sentiment or what you like, but I want your shares and yours.' He turned to Tracey and nodded at her.

'No,' said Tracey sharply.

'Right.' Benedict smiled at her. 'Then I'm going to hammer Johnny Lance for his full obligations. That way I get the Company anyway, but I'll make damn sure he remains an unrehabilitated bankrupt for the rest of his life.'

Tracey lifted her hand to her throat, and turned her eyes to Johnny. Waiting for him to set a lead. There was a long stark silence, then Johnny Lance dropped his eyes.

'I've still got three days.' His voice was gruff and tired.

'Three days you have.' Benedict grinned coldly. 'And you're welcome to them.'

Johnny picked up his papers and put them under one arm; he took his jacket off the back of the chair and swung it over his shoulder.

'Wait,' ordered Benedict.

'What for?' Johnny's grin was twisted. 'You've had your fun.'

Benedict lifted the receiver of the telephone on the table and dialled swiftly.

'Come through, please, darling.' He spoke into the mouthpiece and smiled at Johnny as he hung up. Then as the door opened he went to meet Ruby Lance, and kissed her on the mouth. The two of them stood, arm in arm, and looked at Johnny.

'The Company is not the only thing I've taken from you,' Benedict said softly.

'I want a divorce.' Ruby looked steadily into Johnny's face. 'Benedict and I are going to get married.'

They were all watching Johnny, and they saw him flinch. He looked from one face to the other, then his mouth tightened and his forehead furrowed.

Tracey saw his anger mounting, and her eyes flicked to Benedict's face. He was leaning forward expectantly, his lips quivering with expectation, his eyes alight with triumph. Tracey wanted to scream out a warning to Johnny, stop him falling into the trap that Benedict had set so carefully.

Johnny took a pace forward, coming up on to the balls of his feet. He was about to make his defeat total and ineradicable. Then Benedict spoiled it for himself, he goaded once more.

'Game, set and match, Johnny Lance,' he crowed.

The effort of will that Johnny made to recover his reason was not shown on his face, he made the step forward seem natural and he continued towards the door.

'The house is in your name, of course, Ruby, so would you please send my things down to the Tulbagh Hotel,' he asked quietly.

He stopped in front of the couple and spoke to Ruby.

'You'll want to protect your reputation, of course, so I'll not sue for adultery. We'll call it desertion.'

'You're eating your guts out,' jeered Benedict. 'Lance can't keep his woman. Van der Byl took her away from him. Go on, sue for adultery – let the world hear it.'

'As you wish,' Johnny agreed.

And he walked out of the Board Room to the elevators.

Johnny flopped on to the bed fully dressed, and rubbed his closed eyes with his fingertips. He felt confused and off-balance, the edge of his mind which usually slashed quickly and incisively through a problem was dulled. This problem was so multiplied and tangled that he felt like a man in a thicket of African ebony trying to cut his way out with a blunt machete.

Without opening his eyes he groped for the telephone, and the girl on the hotel switchboard downstairs answered. He gave her a number in Kimberley.

'Person to person, Mr Ralph Ellison.'

'Fifteen minutes' delay, Mr Lance,' the girl told him.

'Okay,' Johnny replied. 'Ask room service to send me up a Chivas Regal and soda.' He suddenly needed liquor, something to dull the pain. 'Make that a double, honey – no, make it two doubles.'

He had drained both glasses by the time his Kimberley call came through.

'Ralph?' Johnny spoke into the receiver.

'Johnny, how nice of you to call.' There was an echo like distant laughter beneath those cool ambassadorial tones in Ralph Ellison's voice and Johnny knew instantly that the word was out. Damn it, he was slow – of course Benedict would have blocked him.

'Are you still interested in a deal on the Thunderbolt and Suicide Concession?' Johnny loosed a despairing long-range shot.

'Of course, you know we are always interested,' Ralph replied.

'The price is two million.' Johnny lost interest and lay back on the bed, closing his eyes again. He knew Ralph was having his revenge – you didn't take this boy to court and win without sowing yourself a minefield to retreat over.

'Two million,' Ralph murmured. 'Now that's a little high – for a field that's yielding 200 carats of small industrial diamonds per 10,000 loads, that's definitely on the high side. Of course we wouldn't want that battleship of yours either – we are not starting our own navy.' Ralph chuckled juicily. 'We could talk around fifty to a hundred grand – no more than that, Johnny.'

'Okay, Ralph.' Johnny spoke wearily. 'Thanks all the same. We'll have a drink together sometime.'

'Any time, Johnny,' Ralph agreed. 'Any time at all. You call me.'

Johnny dropped the receiver back on its hook and looked at the ceiling. He had heard that a gunshot wound was numb at first – he felt numb now. All that energy had seeped out of him, he had lost direction.

The telephone shrilled and he picked it up. The girl on the switchboard asked politely:

'Are you finished, Mr Lance?'

'Yes,' said Johnny. 'You might say that.'

'Is there anything else you require?' The girl sounded puzzled.

'Yes, honey, send up the hemlock.'

'I beg your pardon?'

'Two more big fat whiskies, please.'

He drank them in the bath, and while he dried himself

155

the doorbell tinkled. He wound the bath towel round his waist and went through to open the door.

Tracey stepped into the bedroom and closed the door behind her. They stood looking at each other for a long moment. Her eyes were big and dark, reflecting his agony faithfully.

'Johnny—' Her voice was husky, and she reached out and laid the palm of her hand on his cheek. His shoulders sagged, and he moved close to her, his forehead sinking on to her shoulder. He sighed, a ragged broken exhalation of breath.

'Come,' she said, and led him to the bed. Leaving him there she went to the windows and closed the curtains.

It was warm and safe in the half dark of the curtained room, and they held each other as they had done long years before. Clinging together, so their breathing mingled, and it was not necessary to speak.

When they became lovers it seemed that they had waited all their lives for that moment.

Afterwards he lay in her arms and he felt strength flowing back into him, drawing it from her. When he sat up in the bed the bemused, almost dazed expression had gone. His jaw was out and his eyes were bright.

'We've still got three days,' he said.

'Yes.' She sat up beside him. 'Go, Johnny. Go quickly, don't waste another moment.'

'I'll pull *Kingfisher* out of the main gully. I'll find those diamonds. They are there. I *know* they are there. I'll take her right down into the jaws of Thunderbolt and Suicide, I'll find those bloody diamonds – damned if I won't.' He swung his legs off the bed, reached for his clothes, glancing at his wrist watch as he did so. 'Four o'clock. I can get to Cartridge Bay a few minutes after dark. Will you call the communications office, ask them to radio Cartridge Bay and have a flare path set for me, and *Wild Goose* standing by to run me out?'

'I'll phone them from here. Then I'll take a bath – you go on. Don't waste time.' Tracey nodded eagerly, and Johnny let his eyes drop down over her body. He reached out and touched one big white breast almost diffidently.

'You are beautiful – I hate to go.'

'It will all be here, waiting for you, when you get back.'

'It wasn't the way I'd planned it. It wasn't good the way I'd dreamed about it.' Benedict paced angrily over the floor of the Old Man's study, swinging towards the windows and pausing to stare out at the mountain across the valley.

'You hurt him. You crushed him.' Ruby moved restlessly in her chair across the room from him, curling her long golden legs defensively under her, sitting like a cat in the big chair. She was worried, and it showed in the tiny crows' feet at the corners of her eyes and the way she held her lips pursed. She should have anticipated this reaction from him, she should have known that this moment of triumph could never match his anticipation of it – and that revenge must always be followed by sour distaste and a feeling of disappointment. She realized that her safest course was to leave him alone now, she should never have returned with him to the old house on Wynberg Hill. She stood up.

'Darling.' She crossed to him. 'I'm going home now. I want to pack his clothes and get rid of them. I want to wipe out every memory of him. From now on it's you and I – together.'

She stretched up to kiss him, but Benedict turned his face away.

'Oh! So you're going, are you?' His expression was petulant, his lips pouting spitefully.

'We're both tired, darling. Let us both rest a while – and I'll come back later this evening.'

157

'So now you're giving the orders, are you?' He laughed nastily.

'Darling—'

'And cut out all the darlings. We pulled a deal and it didn't work out. You were meant to be a club to break his skull – and do you know something? He didn't give a damn. I was watching him, he was pleased – yes! He was bloody well delighted to get rid of you.'

'Benedict—' She stepped back.

'Listen.' He stepped close to her, and pushed his face towards hers. 'If you're so bloody anxious to go, why don't you bloody well go – and keep going. If he doesn't want you – then I sure as hell don't want you either.'

'Benedict,' she whispered. The colour faded from her face, leaving it washed white as beach sand. She stared at him in horror, as her dreams began to fall into ruins around her. 'You don't mean that.'

'I don't? Is that so?' He threw back his head and laughed again. 'Listen, you got some nice diamonds and a mink coat. You got a big house in Bishopscourt – now, that's pretty good pay for a whore.'

'Benedict—' She gasped at the insult, but he wasn't listening.

'I proved I could have you, didn't I? I proved I could take you away from him – and that's what it was all about. Now, why don't you go on home like a good girl.'

'The machine. I know about that thing in *Kingfisher*.' It was a mistake. Until then she still had a chance. His face changed shape and the blood flooded into it. His voice when he spoke was unsteady, thick with rage for his lips seemed to have swollen.

'Try it,' he whispered back at her. 'Go on, try it. They'll give you fifteen years in a woman's prison, my beauty. And think about this also—' He showed her his hand, holding it like a blade before her eyes. 'I'll kill you. I swear before

God, I'll kill you with my bare hands. You know I'll do it – you know enough about me now.'

She backed away from him, and he followed her still holding his hand at her throat.

'You've been paid. Now get out.'

A few seconds longer she stood before him, and he was not too far gone in rage to see the fear in her eyes mingle with something else that made her eyes slit and drew her lips back to show the little white teeth.

'All right,' she said. 'I'll go.' And she walked from the room, stepping daintily, the long yellow hair swinging against her shoulders.

R uby drove slowly for her vision was blurred with her tears. Twice other drivers hooted at her but she kept both hands clenched on the wheel and stared ahead, following the De Waal Drive around the lower slopes of the mountain. Before she reached the University she swung off the road and drove up through the pine forests until she reached the car park behind the Cecil Rhodes Memorial. She left the car and walked down on to the wide paved terrace below the Greek columns and stone steps where the mounted statue eternally searched the horizon with one hand lifted to shade his eyes.

She went to the parapet and looked across to the far blue mountains of the Helderberg. She hugged herself about the shoulders for the wind through her silk summer dress was as cold as her misery.

Now the tears broke over her lids and slid down her cheeks to fall unheeded on to the silken front of her dress. They were tears of self-pity, but also the tears of an anger as searing cold as dry ice.

'The swine,' she whispered through lips that trembled.

Near her two young students sitting on the parapet, kicking their legs over the drop beneath them and hugging each other in the abandon of first love, turned to glance at her.

The boy whispered to the girl, and she giggled in unthinking cruelty – but looked away as Ruby directed a long venomous glare at her. Then in embarrassment the couple scrambled off the parapet and moved away, leaving her alone.

Never for one moment did she consider standing aside. Benedict's threats meant nothing – her only concern was to take the action which would injure him most severely. The consequences to herself were not part of her calculations. She wanted only to select the swiftest and most terrible vehicle of retribution. As the dark clouds that fogged her reason slowly cleared, the means came to her readily.

Johnny was staying at the Tulbagh Hotel.

She turned and ran back to her car, the long yellow banner of her hair floating behind her like the pennant at the tip of a cavalry lance. She drove fast until she hit the downtown rush-hour crowds. The tears dried on her face as she crawled, fuming with impatience, along the slow river of traffic.

It was after five when she parked in a loading zone outside the entrance to the Tulbagh and ran into the lobby.

'What room is Mr Lance in?' she demanded of the girl at the desk.

'Mr Lance checked out an hour ago.' Curiously the girl examined Ruby's ruined make-up.

'Did he say where he was going?' Ruby snapped at her, feeling the sickening slide of disappointment within her.

'No, Madam.' The girl shook her head. 'But he was in a hurry.'

'Damn! Damn!' Ruby swore bitterly. She turned from the desk undecided where next to look. Perhaps Johnny had gone back to the office.

Across the lobby the elevator doors slid open and Tracey

Hartford stepped out. Even in her impatience Ruby recognized in the glow that seemed to emanate from her that Tracey was a girl freshly risen from the bed of the man she loved. There was not a vestige of doubt in Ruby's mind as to the identity of that man.

The shock of it paralysed her for a moment. Then she felt the urge to cross the floor and claw that smug smile from Tracey's face. She fought it down, and instead she stepped into her path as Tracey started for the glass outer doors.

'Where is Johnny?' she demanded, and Tracey came up short. Her little gasp of guilt confirmed Ruby's suspicion.

'Where is he, damn you!' Ruby's voice was pitched low but brittle with emotion.

'He's not here.' Tracey recovered herself, quickly masking her expression.

'Where has he gone? I must see him.'

'He's flown up to Cartridge Bay.'

'When did he leave? It's important – terribly important.'

'An hour ago. He'll be airborne already.'

'Can you get a message to him?' In her impatience Ruby caught Tracey's wrist, holding her in a grip that marked the skin.

'I can radio him—' Tracey pulled her hand free.

'No,' Ruby cut in quickly. She could not have her message shouted across the ether for all to hear. 'Can you follow him – charter plane?'

Tracey shook her head. 'They won't fly to an unscheduled airfield after dark.'

'Then you must follow him – by car. You must drive up there.'

'Why?' Tracey stared at her, puzzled by this strange insistence, noticing the dried tears and the wild look in Ruby's eyes. 'It's an eight-hour drive.'

'I'll tell you. Can we use Johnny's room?'

Tracey hesitated, remembering the unmade bed. Then

the hotel manager came into the lobby and Tracey turned to him with relief.

The Beechcraft bucked suddenly and dropped a wing, instinctively Johnny corrected the lunge with stick and rudder then glanced quickly at his instrument panel for an explanation. There was none to be found there, so he looked over the wing and for the first time noticed the dust on the great plains below him; it was moving low against the earth in long streamers like mist, and the setting sun turned it to mauve and old gold. With a prickle of alarm he scanned the horizon ahead, and saw it coming down from the north like a great moving range of blue mountains. Even as he watched it, it rolled across the low sun, turning it into a sullen red orb. The light in the cockpit changed to a weird glow as though the door to a furnace had been thrown open.

Again the Beechcraft crabbed awkwardly as another gust of high wind hit her, and at the same moment the radio crackled and came alive.

'Zulu Sugar Peter Tango Baker this is Alexandra Bay Control, come in please.'

The voice of the controller was almost unintelligible with storm static. Johnny reached for the transmit switch of the radio, then stopped his hand. He thought quickly. He could guess they were trying to reach him to cancel his flight approval. That was a big northern boiling down out of the desert. They would abort his flight, and divert him out of the path of the storm.

He checked his wrist watch. Twenty minutes' flying time to Cartridge Bay. No – he was flying full into the eye of the wind, say twenty-five or thirty minutes. Quickly he searched the coast on his port side and saw the long white lines of surf stretched ahead into the thickening purple gloom. The coast was still clear, it might stay that way for another thirty minutes.

'Zulu Sugar Peter Tango Baker this is Alexandra Bay. I say again – come in. Come in. Zulu Sugar Peter Tango Baker.' The agitation in the controller's voice came through over the static.

There was a fair chance of getting in to Cartridge Bay, racing the storm and winning. He could edge out to the westward and come in from the sea, pick up *Kingfisher*'s riding lights as a beacon and sneak in under the leading edge of the dust clouds. If he missed he could turn and run with the wind for home. The radio was hissing and crackling angrily now, the controller's voice sometimes lost in the interference, sometimes coming through strongly.

' – Cancelled. I say again: your flight approval is cancelled. Do you read me, Zulu Sugar Peter Tango Baker. Come in, please. – Beaufort force seven. – visibility in the storm area – I say again, there is nil visibility in—'

The norther would roar for days now and with it would blow away his last chance of working the gap at Thunderbolt and Suicide.

Johnny switched off the radio, cut off contact with Control and immediately it was strangely quiet in the cockpit. He settled himself down into the bucket seat, and eased open the throttles, watching the needles creep up around the dials of the rev counters.

Now he was down to an altitude of three hundred feet and the Beechcraft was leaping about like a hooked marlin. He was flying her on instruments for outside the cockpit it was completely dark. He could not see his own wingtips, but above him the stars still showed. He was riding the vanguard of the storm, and the dust clouds were ahead, racing to meet him and blanket the flare path at Cartridge Bay.

Every few seconds he darted a quick glance ahead, hoping to pick up the lights, then his eyes flew back to the instrument panel.

'Now,' he thought grimly. 'It should be now. I should be over the grounds. Thirty seconds more and I'll know I've missed her.'

He looked up again, and there was *Kingfisher* dead ahead. All her lights were ablaze, a burning beacon of hope in the darkness. She appeared to be riding easily, for the wind had not yet had time to thrash the sea into a frenzy.

He flashed over her, seeming to graze her superstructure in passing, and now he was searching anxiously for the glow of the flare path on the land beyond.

It came up as a path of lesser darkness in the absolute blackness of the night. He steadied on course towards it, watching it change to a long double line of oil-burning flares that smoked and fluttered in the wind.

He flew her in fast, high above the stall and the shock of touchdown threatened to tear the undercarriage off her.

Then he was jolting and trundling down the earthen runway with the flares flashing past his wingtips.

'Lance, old man,' he murmured thankfully, 'that was a very shaky do!'

The wind hum against the body of the car, and the snarl of rubber on tarmac as the Mercedes snaked through the bends of the twisting mountain road were sounds to match the racing of Tracey's blood and the hammer of her heart.

She drove with an inspired abandon, watching the bends leap out at her out of the darkness, sensing the massive crags and cliffs that hung over the road and blotted out half the night sky.

The silver sheet of Clanwilliam Lake reflected the stars,

and then was left behind. Down from the mountains she went and over the Olifants River to make a brief fuel stop at Vanrynsdorp and scan the road map anxiously in the light of the gasoline pumps. She read with a sinking feeling the mileage figures printed along the little red ribbon of the road, and knew that for her each mile would be multiplied by her own urgency.

Then once more behind the wheel she faced the vast emptiness of Namaqualand – and sent the Mercedes flying across it.

' – There is some type of machine, I don't know how it works, but it filters out the diamonds. Benedict had it installed at Las Palmas—'

The headlights were puny little white shafts, and the road a long blue smear that went on endlessly. Tracey lit a cigarette with one hand, hearing Ruby's voice again in her ears.

' – There is one diamond amongst them. He called it "The Big Blue". Benedict says it's worth a million—' Tracey was not sure she believed it. It was the enormity of the treachery and deceit that she could not accept.

' – The Italian, the Captain, be careful of him. He works for Benedict. The other one also – Hugo – they are all in it. Warn Johnny.'

Benedict! Weak, spoiled Benedict, the playboy, the spendthrift. Could he have planned and carried this through?

A gust of wind hit the car from the side, taking her unawares, pushing the Mercedes off the tar on to the gravel. Tracey fought to hold the skid. Dust and gravel roared out in a cloud from under the wheels. Then she was back on the road, hurtling northwards.

'Warn Johnny! Warn Johnny!'

Benedict van der Byl sat in his father's chair, in his father's house, and he was alone. His loneliness ate deep into the fibres of his whole being. Before him on the stinkwood desk stood a crystal glass and a decanter. The brandy was no comfort, its warmth in his throat and belly seemed only to accentuate the icy cold of his loneliness. His fantasy showed him as a hollow man. He thought of himself as a husk, filled only with the cold of melancholia.

He looked about the room with its dark panelled woodwork and he smelled the musty dead smell. He wondered how many times his father had sat in this chair alone and lonely. Lonely and afraid as the cancer ate him alive.

He stood up and moved listlessly about the room, touching the furniture as if he were trying to communicate with the man who had lived and died here. He moved across and stood in front of the curtained windows. The rug was new. It replaced the other that they had been unable to clean.

'The Old Man had the right idea.' He spoke aloud, his voice sounding strange in his own ears.

Then on an impulse he crossed quickly to the cupboard that flanked the massive stone fireplace, and tried the door. It was locked.

Without passion he stood back and kicked in the panel. The wood splintered and he kicked again, smashing the door from its hinges.

The oblong leather case was on the top shelf, and he took it down and carried it to the desk. He sprang the catches and laid back the lid.

He lifted out the blue metalled double barrels of the Purdy Royal, and the gun oil was greasy on his hands.

'Jacobus Isaac van der Byl.' He read aloud the name in gold inlay set into the steel among the engraved pheasants and gundogs.

He smiled then.

'The old devil.' He shook his head smiling as though at some private joke, and began slowly to assemble the shotgun. He weighed it in his hands, feeling the sweet pure balance of the weapon.

'The old bastard made his own decisions.' And still smiling he carried the gun across to the new carpet. He placed it butt down between his feet with the barrels pointed at the ceiling and leaning slowly forward he opened his mouth and placed the muzzles between his lips, then reaching farther down he placed a thumb on each trigger and pushed them simultaneously.

Click! Click!

The firing pins fell on the empty chambers, and Benedict straightened up and wiped the taste of gun oil from his lips. He grinned again.

'That's the way he did it. Both barrels in the back of the throat. What a cure for tonsilitis!' he chuckled, and glanced across at the shattered cupboard door. The square packets of cartridges were on the second shelf.

He tucked the gun under his arm and went to the cupboard again, moving more purposefully now. He snatched down a packet of SSG and broke it open. Suddenly his hands were shaking and the fat red cartridges spilled on to the floor. He stooped and picked up two of them.

With mounting excitement and dread he broke open the shotgun and slipped the cartridges into the blank eyes of the breeches. They slid home against the seating with a solid double thunk, and he hurried back to the spot in front of the window.

His eyes were bright and his breathing quick as he pushed the safety catch on to 'Fire' and placed the butt between his feet once more.

He took the muzzles in his mouth again, in an obscene soul kiss and reached down for the triggers. They were cold and oily. He caressed them lightly, feeling the fine grooving in the curves of metal, thrilling to the touch and feel of them as he had never thrilled to the feel of a woman's body.

Then abruptly he stood up again. He was gasping for breath.

Unsteadily he carried the weapon back to the desk and laid it on the dark polished wood.

As he poured brandy into the crystal glass his eyes were fastened with perverse fascination on the beautiful glistening weapon.

The steam had fogged the mirrored walls of the bathroom, so her image was dewed and misty. Ruby Lance dried herself slowly with one of the thick fluffy towels. She was in no hurry; she wanted Tracey to have a start of at least four hours on her journey to Cartridge Bay. With a deep narcissistic pleasure she noticed in the mirrors how her whole body glowed with soft pink highlights from the hot waters of the bath.

Wrapping herself in the towel she went through into the dressing-room and picking up one of the silver-backed brushes began stroking it through her hair, moving across to the open wardrobe to select a dress for the occasion. It must be something special, perhaps the unworn full-length Louis Feraud of daffodil satin.

Still undecided she went back to seat herself at the dressing-table and began the complicated ritual of applying her make-up. She worked with meticulous care until at last she smiled at her reflection with satisfaction.

She dropped the towel, went back to the wardrobe, and stood slim and naked before it. Pouting slightly with concentration she decided against the Feraud. Then suddenly she smiled, and reached for Benedict's mink.

She wrapped herself in the pale cloud of fur, fluffing up

the collar to frame her face. It was perfect. Just the fur and a pair of golden slippers, pale gold, a perfect match for her hair.

Now suddenly she was eager to go. She ran from the house to where her car was parked in the driveway.

She switched off the headlights as she turned into the driveway that curved up to where the old house crouched on the top of Wynberg Hill. The whisper of the engine was unobtrusive and blended with the whimper of the night breeze in the chestnut trees that flanked the driveway.

She parked in the courtyard, and saw that Benedict's Rolls was still in the garage and a light burned in the window of the study, a yellow oblong behind the curtains. The front door was open. Her slippered feet made no sound along the gloomy passages, and when she tried the door to the study it swung open readily. She stepped into the room, and closed the door behind her. She stood with her back to the dark panelled wood. A single shaded lamp lit the room dimly.

Benedict sat behind the desk. The room was heavy with the smell of cigar smoke and brandy fumes. He had been drinking. His face was flushed, and the top button of his shirt was undone. On the desk in front of him lay a shotgun. Ruby was surprised at the presence of the weapon, it disconcerted her and the words she had prepared were forgotten.

Benedict looked up at her. His eyes were slightly unfocused and he blinked slowly. Then he grinned; it twisted his mouth and his voice when he spoke was slurred.

'So you've come back.'

Instantly her hatred returned in full flood. But she kept her face impassive. 'Yes,' she agreed. 'I've come back.'

'Come here.' He swivelled his chair to the side of the desk. Ruby did not move, she leaned back against the door.

'Come here.' Benedict's voice was stronger now, and suddenly Ruby smiled and obeyed.

She stood in front of him, huddled in the fur.

'Kneel down,' commanded Benedict, and she hesitated.

'Down!' his voice crackled. 'Down, damn you!'

Ruby sank to her knees in front of him, and he straightened up in the chair. She knelt in front of him in the attitude of submission, with her head forward so the golden hair hung like a curtain over her face.

'Say it,' he gloated. 'Ask me to forgive you.'

Slowly she lifted her face and looked up at him. She spoke softly.

'Tracey left for Cartridge Bay at five-thirty this evening.'

Benedict's expression changed.

'She has a start of four hours – she is half-way there already.'

He stared at her with his lips parting, soft and red and slack.

'She is going to Johnny,' Ruby went on. 'She knows about the thing in *Kingfisher*. She knows about the big blue diamond.'

He began to shake his head in disbelief.

'By dawn tomorrow Johnny will know also. So you see, my darling, you have lost again – haven't you? You can never beat him, can you, Benedict? Can you, my darling?'

Her voice was rising, ringing with triumph.

'You?' he croaked. 'You?'

And she laughed, nodding her head in agreement, unable to speak through her laughter.

Benedict lunged clumsily out of the chair, his hands going for her throat. She went over backwards with him on top of her. Her laughter died gurgling in her throat.

They rolled together on the floor. Benedict's hands locked on her neck, his voice rising in a scream of fury and despair. Her long legs kicking and thrashing, clawing at his face and hands, she fought him with the strength of a cornered animal.

They rolled back suddenly and Benedict's head struck

the solid leg of the desk with a crack that jarred his whole body. His grip on her throat loosened and she tore herself free with fresh breath hissing into her open mouth. She rolled away from him and in one fluid movement gained her feet, reeling back from him with the front of the mink torn open and her hair tangled across her face.

Benedict dragged himself up the desk on to his knees. He was still screaming, a high keening note without form or coherence, as Ruby spun away from him and stumbled to the door.

Blinded by her own hair, fighting for strangled breath, she fumbled for the door handle with her back turned to him.

Benedict reached up and lifted the shotgun off the desk. Still kneeling beside the desk he held the weapon across his hip. The recoil was a liquid pulsing jolt in his hands and the muzzle blast was thunderous in the confines of the room, the long yellow flame lighting the scene like a photographer's flash-bulb.

The heavy charge caught Ruby in the small of her back. At that range there was no spread of shot and it went through spine and pelvis in a solid shattering ball. It tore out through the front of her belly, spinning her sideways along the wall. She slid down into a sitting position, facing him with the mink flared open about her.

On his knees Benedict swung the gun to follow her fall and he fired the second barrel; again the brief thunder and flame of the muzzle blast flashed across the room.

At even closer range than the first charge it struck her full in her beautiful golden face.

B enedict stood in the garage with his forehead pressed against the cold metal of the Rolls-Royce. The shotgun was still in his hands, and his pockets were crammed with cartridges that he had picked up from the floor before leaving the study.

He was shivering violently, like a man in high fever.

'No!' he moaned to himself, repeating the single negative over and over again, leaning against the big car.

Abruptly he gagged, remembering the carnage he had created. Then he retched, still leaning against the Rolls, bringing up the brandy mingled with his horror.

It left him pale and weak, but steadier. Through the open window he threw the gun on to the back seat of the Rolls, and climbed shakily into the driver's seat.

He sat there bowed over the steering wheel, and now his instinct of self-preservation took hold of him.

It seemed to him there was but one avenue of escape still open to him. *Wild Goose* had the range to take him across an ocean – South America perhaps, and there was money in Switzerland.

He started the Rolls and reversed out of the garage, the spin of tyres against concrete burning blue smoke into the beams of the headlights.

T he Mercedes crawled through the thick sand, the headlights probing ineffectually into the bright orange fog of dust that whipped endlessly over the track ahead. The hot gritty wind buffeted the car, rocking it on its suspension.

Tracey sat forward in the driver's seat peering ahead through eyes that felt raw and swollen with fatigue and mica dust.

From the main road to the coast this Jeep track was the only land access to Cartridge Bay. It was a hundred miles of tortuous trail, made up of deep sandy ruts and broken stone where it crossed one of the many rocky ridges.

The radiator of the Mercedes was boiling furiously, over-heating in the searing wind and the slogging low-gear grind through thick sand. In places Tracey followed the track only by driving through gaps in the stunted knee-high growth of desert bush. Every few minutes a tumbleweed, driven by the wind, would bowl across the track like a frightened furry animal.

At times she was sure she had missed a turning and was now grinding aimlessly out into the desert, then reassuringly the twin ruts would show up in the lights ahead of her. Once she did drive off the road, and immediately the Mercedes came to a gentle standstill with its rear wheels spinning helplessly in the soft sand. She had to climb out of the cab and, with her bare hands, scoop away the sand from behind the wheels and stuff bundles of tumbleweed into the depressions to give the wheels purchase. She almost wept with relief when the Mercedes pulled back sluggishly on to the trail again.

The slow dawn broke through the dust clouds and Tracey switched off the headlights and drove on until suddenly, and quite unexpectedly, she reached Cartridge Bay. The depot buildings loomed suddenly before her, and she left the Mercedes and ran to the living quarters. The foreman opened the door to her insistent hammering, and stared at her in astonishment before ushering her in. Tracey cut off his questions with her own.

'Where is *Wild Goose?*'

'She took Mr Lance out to *Kingfisher*, but she's back now lying at the jetty.'

'Hugo Kramer – the Captain?'

'He's aboard, holed up in his cabin.'

'Thanks.' Tracey left him, pushed the door open against the wind and ran out into the storm.

Wild Goose lay at her moorings, secured by heavy lines

173

to the bollards, but fidgeting and fretting at the push of the wind. There was a gangplank laid to her deck, and lights showed at her portholes. Tracey went aboard.

Hugo Kramer came to the doorway of his cabin in a suit of rumpled striped pyjamas. Tracey pushed past him.

'You took Lance out to *Kingfisher*?' she accused him, her voice sharp and anxious.

'Yes.'

'You idiot, didn't you realize there was something up? Good God, why otherwise would he fly in through this weather?'

Hugo stared at her, and instinctively she knew that what Ruby had told her was true.

'I don't know what you're talking about,' he blurted.

'You'll know all right when we are all sitting behind bars – we'll have fifteen long years to think about it. Lance has tumbled to it, you fool, I've got to stop him. Take me out to *Kingfisher*.'

He was confused – and afraid.

'I know nothing about—' Hugo started again.

'You're wasting time.' Brusquely Tracey brushed his protests aside. 'Take me out to *Kingfisher*.'

'Your brother – where is he? Why didn't he come?'

Tracey had anticipated the question. 'Lance beat him up – badly. He's in hospital. He sent me.'

Suddenly Hugo was convinced.

'*Gott!*' he swore. 'What are we going to do? This storm – I may be able to get you out there, but I won't be able to leave *Wild Goose*. My crew can't handle her in this sea. What can you do on your own?'

'Get me out there,' said Tracey. 'Get me aboard *Kingfisher* and you can come back. The Italian, Caporetti, he and I will take care of Lance. In this storm a man can be washed overboard very easily.'

'*Ja.*' Hugo's face lit with relief. 'That's it. The Italian!' And he a reached for his oilskins hanging on the bulkhead.

As he pulled them on over his pyjamas he looked at Tracey with new respect.

'You,' he said. 'I didn't know you were in it.'

'Did you think my brother and I would stand by and let a stranger take our birthright from us?'

Hugo grinned. 'You're a cool one, I'll say that for you. You had me fooled.' And he went out on to the bridge.

Johnny Lance and Sergio Caporetti stood shoulder to shoulder on *Kingfisher*'s bridge. The ship was taking the big green seas over her bows, solid walls of water, and the wind whipped spray that spattered the armoured glass windows of the bridge house.

Kingfisher had slipped her moorings the previous evening, leaving the big yellow buoys floating on their anchor cables and she was working free of her fetters. She was on computer navigation, holding her position over the ground against the swells and the wind by use of her engine and rudder.

'She is no good.' Sergio spoke morosely. 'We come too close to the rocks. I get sick in my heart looking at them.'

The dust clouds did not carry this far out to sea despite the vicious screeching of the wind. The visibility was a mile or more, quite enough to show the brooding twin hulks of Thunderbolt and Suicide. The storm-crazed swells burst against them, throwing white spray two hundred feet into the gloomy sky, then surging back to expose the gleaming white rock.

'Hold her,' growled Johnny. Twice during the night they had changed position, each time edging down closer on the gap between the two islands. *Kingfisher* was battling gamely to hold her ground against the insidious sucking current that added its pull to that of the swell and the wind.

Johnny was not attempting to work any one of the gullies extensively, he wanted only to sample as much of the field

175

as possible in the time that was left to him. The storm would not stop him – for *Kingfisher* was constructed to work in worse weather than his. Her compensating hose section was keeping the dredge head on the bottom despite the lift and fall of her hull.

'Calm down, Sergio.' Johnny relented a little. 'The computer is foolproof.'

'The goddamned computer she no got eyes to see those rocks. Me, I got eyes – and it gives me a sick heart.'

Twice during the night Johnny had gone down into the control room and ordered the computer to report its recovery of diamonds. Each time the reply had been consistent – not a single stone over four carats, and a very precious few of any others.

'I'm going through to the plot. Watch her,' Johnny told Sergio, and staggering against the pitch and roll he went through the door behind the bridge.

He paused behind the repeater screen of the computer, and at a glance saw that *Kingfisher* was holding her primary operation and all departments were running normally. He passed the screen and leaned over the chart table.

The large-scale chart of the South West African coast between Luderitz and Walvis Bay was pinned down on the board. The *Wild Goose* soundings were pencilled in, and the pattern of *Kingfisher*'s sweeps were carefully plotted around the islands of Thunderbolt and Suicide.

Johnny picked up a pair of dividers and stared moodily at the chart. Suddenly a surge of anger rose in him against those two names. They had promised so much and delivered so little.

He stared at the names Thunderbolt and Suicide printed in italics among the maze of soundings, and his anger turned to blind red hatred.

With the points of the dividers he slashed at the chart, ripping the thick linen paper once, and twice, in a ragged cross-shaped tear.

This small act of violence dissipated his anger. He felt embarrassed, it had been a petty childish gesture. He tried to smooth the edges of the tear, and through the gap he felt another loose scrap of paper which someone had slipped under the chart. He probed a finger through the tear in the chart and wormed the scrap out. He glanced at the scribbled title and the lines of figures and numbers that followed.

The sheet was headed: KAMINIKOTO SECONDARY RECOVERY PROGRAMME.

He studied it, puzzled by the title but recognizing the numbers as a computer programme. The writing was in Sergio Caporetti's pointed continental style. The easiest way to resolve the mystery was to ask Sergio. Johnny started back for the bridge.

'Boss,' Sergio called anxiously, as Johnny stepped through the door. 'Look!'

He was pointing ahead into the eye of the wind. Johnny hurried to his side, the paper crumpled and forgotten in his hand.

'*Wild Goose*.' Sergio identified the small craft that was staggering and plunging towards them out of the gloom.

'What the hell is he doing here?' Johnny wondered aloud. *Wild Goose* was lost for long seconds behind the walls of green sea, then again she was lifted high into unnatural prominence, showing the red lead of her bottom as she rode the crests; water poured from her scuppers, before she shot down the steep slope of the next wave to bury her nose deep in frothing water. She came down swiftly on the wind, rounding to and beginning to edge in under *Kingfisher*'s counter.

'What the hell is he playing at?' Johnny protested, and then in disbelief he saw a slim figure dart from *Wild Goose*'s wheelhouse and run to the side nearest *Kingfisher*.

'It's Tracey,' shouted Johnny.

She reached the rail just as another swell burst over the

177

bows and smothered her. Johnny expected to see her washed away, but she was still there clinging to the rail.

Thrusting the page of paper into his pocket, Johnny went out through the wing of the bridge and swarmed down the steel ladder to the deck, jumping the last ten feet and running the instant he landed.

He reached the side and looked down on the drowned-kitten figure of Tracey.

'Go back,' he yelled. 'Go back. Don't try it.'

She shouted something that was lost in the next smother of spray, and when it cleared he saw her poising herself to jump the gap of surging water between the two vessels.

He flung himself over *Kingfisher*'s side and climbed swiftly down the steel rungs.

He was still ten feet above her as she gathered herself for the leap.

'Go back,' he shouted desperately.

She jumped, missed her hold and fell into the murderous stretch of water between the hulls. Her head bobbed below Johnny, and he was aware of the next swell bearing down on them. It would throw *Wild Goose* against the steel cliff of *Kingfisher*, crushing Tracey between them.

Johnny went down those last ten feet and hanging outwards by one arm he got his other arm around her, and with a heave that crackled in his muscles and joints he plucked her from the water just as the two vessels dashed together with a crunching impact that tore splinters from *Wild Goose*'s planking, and left a smear of alien paint on *Kingfisher*'s steel plating.

Wild Goose swung away, and with her diesels bellowing went bucking off into the wind.

With puddles of sea water forming around her feet from her sodden clothing, Tracey stood in the centre of *Kingfisher*'s guest cabin. Her dark hair was plastered down her face and neck, and she was shivering so violently from shock and the icy water that she could not talk. Her teeth chattered together, and her lips were blue with cold.

Desperately she was trying to form words, her eyes never leaving Johnny's face.

Quickly he stripped off her clothing and throwing one towel round her shoulders he began roughly to chafe warmth back into her with another.

'You little idiot,' he berated her. 'Are you stark staring bloody mad?'

'Johnny,' she gasped through her chattering teeth.

'Christ – that was so close,' he snarled at her as he knelt to rub her legs.

'Johnny, listen.'

'Shut up and dry your hair.'

Humbly she obeyed him, her shivers became controllable as he crossed to the locker and found a thick jersey which he pulled over her head. It hung almost to her knees.

'Now,' he said, taking her roughly by the shoulders. 'What the hell is this all about?'

And she told him in a rush of words that poured out like water from a broken dam. Then she burst into tears and stood there forlornly in the voluminous jersey with her damp hair dangling about her shoulders, sobbing as though her heart was breaking.

Johnny took her in his arms.

For a long minute Tracey revelled in his warmth and strength, but she was the first to pull away.

'Do something, Johnny,' she implored him, her voice still thick with tears. 'Stop them. You mustn't let them get away with it.'

He went back to the locker, and while he ransacked it

for clothing that might fit her, Johnny's mind was racing over the story she had told him.

He watched her pull on a pair of blue serge trousers and tie them at the waist with a length of cord. She folded back the cuffs and tucked them into thick woollen socks, before thrusting her feet into a pair of sea-boots that were only a few sizes too large for her.

'Where do we start?' she asked, and he remembered the sheet of paper. He fished it out of his pocket and flattened it on the table beside the bunk. Quickly he ran his eyes over the columns of figures. His first guess was right – it *was* a computer programme.

'Stay here,' he ordered Tracey.

'No.' Her response was immediate, and he grinned.

'Listen, I'm just going up on to the bridge to keep them busy there. I'll come back for you, I promise. You won't miss anything.'

'How is she, boss?' Sergio Caporetti's concern was genuine. Johnny realized that he must be worrying himself into a frenzy trying to guess the reason for Tracey's arrival.

'She is pretty shaken up,' Johnny answered.

'What she want – that was big chance she takes. Nearly fish food.'

'I don't know,' Johnny said. 'I want you to take over up here. Keep *Kingfisher* working. I'm going to get her to bed – I'll let you know what it's all about as soon as I find out.'

'Okay, boss.'

'Oh, and Sergio – keep an eye on those rocks. Don't let her drift down any closer.'

Johnny chose a powerful incentive to keep Sergio up on the bridge.

Johnny left him and went below, stopping only at the guest cabin.

'Come on.'

Tracey followed him, lurching unsteadily with *Kingfisher*'s antics in the high sea.

Two decks down they reached the computer control room and Johnny unlocked the heavy steel door, then locked it again behind them.

Tracey wedged herself against the bulkhead and watched as Johnny seated himself at the console and clipped the rumpled sheet into the board.

Reading from the sheet he typed the first line of figures on the keyboard. Immediately the computer registered a protest.

'Operator error,' it typed back. Johnny ignored its denial and typed the second line. This time it was more emphatic.

'No procedure. Operator error.'

And Johnny typed the next line of figures. He guessed that whoever had stored this programme in the computer's memory would have placed a series of blocks to prevent accidental discovery. Again the denial flashed back at him.

'Operator error.'

And Johnny muttered, 'Thrice before the cock crows,' striking an incongruously biblical note in the tense atmosphere of the control room.

He typed the last line of figures and the denial faded from the screen. The console clicked like a monstrous crab, then suddenly it started to print again.

'KAMINIKOTO SECONDARY RECOVERY PROGRAMME. INSTALLED OCTOBER 1969. AT LAS PALMAS BY HIDEKI KAMINIKOTO. DOCTOR OF SCIENCE. TOKYO UNIVERSITY.'

The little Japanese had been unable to resist autographing his masterpiece. Tracey and Johnny crouched over the screen, staring at it with awful fascination as the computer began spelling out its report. It began with the number of hours worked, and the weight of gravel processed during that time. Next it reported the weight of concentrates recovered from the cyclone and finally, in a series of columns, it printed out the weights and sizes of all the diamonds won from the sea. The big Blue showed up in the place of honour, and wordlessly Tracey touched the figure 320 with a forefinger. Johnny nodded grimly.

The computer ended by giving the grand total of carats recovered, and Johnny spoke for the first time.

'It's true,' he said softly. 'It doesn't seem possible – but it is.'

The click and hum of the computer ceased, and the screen went blank.

Johnny straightened up in the chair.

'Where would they put it?' he asked himself, as he ran quickly over the line of recovery. He stood up from the chair and peered through the leaded glass peephole into the X-ray room. 'It must be this side of the cyclone, this side of the drier – ' He was speaking aloud. ' – Between the drier and the X-ray room.'

Then there bobbed to the surface of memory the modification in design which he had meant to query, but which he had forgotten.

'The inspection plate on the conveyor tunnel!' He punched his fist into his palm. 'They moved the inspection plate! That's it! It's in the conveyor tunnel.'

His hands were frantic with haste as he unlocked the steel door of the control room.

Sergio Caporetti paced his bridge like a captive bear, puffing so furiously on his cheroot that sparks flew from its tip. The wind howled hungrily around the wheelhouse, and the swells still marched in from the north.

Suddenly he reached a decision and turned to the helmsman.

'Watch those goddamn rocks – watch them good.'

The helmsman nodded and Sergio shambled through the chartroom to his own cabin. He locked the door behind him, and crossed to his desk. Fumbling with his keys he opened the bottom drawer of his desk and reaching under the pile of cheroot packets he brought out the canvas bag.

Weighing it thoughtfully in his hand, he looked about the cabin for a more secure hiding place. Through the canvas he could feel the nutty irregular shape of the stones.

'That Johnny, he a clever bastard,' he muttered. 'It better be good place.'

Then he reached a decision. 'Best place where I can watch them all a time.'

He opened his jacket and stuffed the bag into his inside pocket. He buttoned the jacket and patted the bulge over his heart.

'Fine!' he said. 'Good!' And stood up from the desk. He hurried back, unlocking the door into the chartroom, and headed for the bridge. He stopped in the middle of the chartroom, and his head swung towards the repeater screen of the computer. The buzzer was going like a rattlesnake, and the red bulb that warned of a new procedure was blinking softly.

Fearfully Sergio approached the screen and stooped over it. A single glance was enough, and he rushed from it to the chart table. He saw the cross-shaped tear in the chart.

'Mary Mother!'

He ripped back the thick crackling paper and searched under it. He stepped back from the table and hit himself across the chest.

'Fool!' he said. 'Idiot!' He spent ten seconds in self-castigation, then he looked about for a weapon. The locking handle of the cabin was a twelve-inch steel bar with a heavy head. He pulled out the pin and worked it loose. He slipped it into the waistband of his trousers.

'I'm going below,' he told the helmsman curtly, and clambered down the companionway. Swiftly he moved through the ship, balancing easily to her roll and pitch.

When he reached the lowest deck he became more stealthy, creeping silently forward. Now he carried the steel bar in his right hand. Every few paces he stopped to listen, but *Kingfisher's* hull was groaning and popping as she worked in the swells.

He could hear no other sound. He crept up to the door of the control room and cautiously peered through the small armoured glass window. The control room was empty. He tried the handle, and found it locked.

Then he heard voices – from the open doorway of the conveyor room behind him. Quickly he crossed to it and flattened himself against the jamb.

Johnny's voice came muffled and indistinct:

'There's another hatch in here. Get me a half-inch spanner from the tool cupboard.'

'What's a half-inch spanner look like?'

'It's a big one. The size is stamped on it.'

Sergio glanced one-eyed around the door jamb. The cover was off the inspection hatch in the conveyor tunnel, and Tracey's head was thrust into the opening.

It was clear that Johnny Lance was in there, and that he had found the secret compartment.

Tracey drew her head out of the hatch, and Sergio ducked back and looked down the passageway. The tool cupboard was bolted to the bulkhead under the stairs from the deck above. He turned and darted around the corner of the passageway. Tracey came out of the conveyor room, and went to the cupboard. She opened the doors on the glittering array of tools, each clipped securely to its rack.

While she stood before the cupboard, completely absorbed in her search for a half-inch spanner, Sergio came from around the corner and crept up silently behind her.

He lifted the steel bar over his shoulder and came up on his toes, poised to strike.

Tracey was muttering softly to herself, head bowed slightly, handling the spanners – and Sergio knew the blow would crush her skull.

He closed his mind to the thought, and aimed carefully at the base of her skull. He started the blow, and then checked it. For a second that seemed to last for a long time he remained frozen. He couldn't do it.

With an exclamation of satisfaction Tracey found what she was searching for. As she turned away from the cupboard Sergio shrank back behind the angle of the bulkhead, and Tracey hurried back into the conveyor room.

'I've got it, Johnny,' she shouted into the hatch.

'Bring it to me. Hurry, Tracey. Sergio will be getting suspicious,' he shouted back, and Tracey hitched up her voluminous trousers and wriggled into the hatch.

On hands and knees she crawled up beside him. It was cramped and hot in the narrow tunnel. He took the spanner from her.

'Hold the flashlight.' She took it from him, holding the beam on the panel while he unscrewed the retaining bolts and lifted off the cover.

Lying on his side he peered into the opening.

'There's a container of sorts,' he grunted, and reached in. For a minute he struggled with the clamps, then slowly he lifted out the stainless steel cup.

At that moment *Kingfisher* reared and plunged to a freak wave and the cup slipped from Johnny's fingers, and from it spilled the diamonds. They cascaded over both of them, a glittering shower of stones of all sizes and colours. Some lodged in Tracey's damp hair, the rest rolled and bounced and scattered about them, catching the light from the torch and throwing it back in splinters of sunshine.

'Yipes!' gasped Tracey and laughed at Johnny's whoop of triumph.

Lying side by side they scrabbled and snatched at the treasure scattered around them.

'Look at this one,' exulted Tracey.

'And this.' They were crazy with excitement, hands filled with diamonds. They hugged each other and kissed ecstatically, laughing into each other's mouths.

Johnny sobered first, 'Come on. Let's get out of here.'

'What about the diamonds?'

'Leave them. There'll be plenty of time later.'

They crawled backwards down the tunnel, still laughing and exclaiming, and one after the other emerged into the conveyor room. While they straightened their clothing, and regained their breath, Tracey asked, 'What now?'

'First thing is to get young Sergio safely under lock and key, his crew also.' Johnny's face hardened. 'The bloody bastards,' he added angrily.

'Then?' Tracey asked.

'Then we'll pull up the hose, and sail *Kingfisher* back into Cartridge Bay. Then we'll call up the police on the radio. There's going to be an accounting with the whole gang of the bastards – your darling brother included.'

Johnny started for the door, asking as he crossed the deck:

'Why did you close the door, Tracey?'

'I didn't,' she replied as she hurried after him, and Johnny's expression changed. He ran to the heavy steel door and threw his weight on it. It did not move, and he swung round to face the door that led into the cyclone room.

It was closed also. He charged across the room and grabbed the handle, heaving at it with all his strength.

He stood back at last, and looked wildly about the long narrow cabin. There was no other opening, no hatch or porthole – nothing except the tiny square peephole in the centre of the steel door that led into the cyclone room beyond. The peephole was covered with three-inch armoured glass that was as strong as the steel that surrounded it. He looked through it.

The tall cyclone reached from floor to roof, dominating the room. Beyond it the steel pipe that carried the gravel from the sea bed pierced the roof from the deck above, but the cyclone room was deserted.

Johnny turned slowly back to Tracey and put an arm around her shoulders.

'We've got problems,' he said.

After closing and locking both the doors that led into the conveyor room, Sergio climbed quickly back to his bridge. The helmsman looked at him curiously.

'How's the lady?'

'Fine,' Sergio snapped at him. 'She's safe.' And then with unnecessary violence, 'Why you no mind your own business, hey? You think you Captain for this ship?'

Startled, the helmsman quickly transferred his attention back to the storm which still raged lustily about them. Sergio began to pace up and down the bridge, balancing easily and instinctively to her exaggerated motion. His smooth baby face was crumpled into a massive scowl, and he puffed on one of his cheroots. With all his soul Sergio Caporetti was lamenting his involvement in this business. He wished that he had never heard of *Kingfisher*. He would have traded his hopes of a life hereafter to be sitting on the seafront at Ostia, sipping *grappa* and watching the girls go by.

Impulsively he pulled open the storm doors at the angle of the bridge and went out on to the exposed wing. The wind buffeted him and set his soft hair dancing and flickering.

From inside his jacket he pulled the canvas bag.

'This is the trouble,' he muttered, looking at the bag in his hand. 'Bloody little stones.'

He threw back his arm like a baseball pitcher, set to hurl the bag out into that hissing green sea below him, but again he could not make the gesture. Swearing quietly to himself, he stuffed the stones back into his jacket, and went back into the wheelhouse.

'Call the radio operator,' he ordered, and the helmsman reached quickly for the voice tube.

The radio operator reached the bridge still owl-eyed with sleep and buttoning his clothing.

'Get on to *Wild Goose*,' Sergio told him.

'I won't be able to raise her in this,' the man protested, glancing out at the storm.

'Call her.' Sergio stepped towards him threateningly. 'Keep calling until you get her.'

W*ild Goose* staggered and wallowed through the turbulence at the entrance to Cartridge Bay, then fought her way into the sanctuary of the channel.

Hugo relaxed perceptibly. It had been a long hard run back from Thunderbolt and Suicide. Yet there was an uneasy feeling that still persisted. He hoped that the girl was able to handle Lance. He was a tough cookie that Lance, he wished that he had been able to go along with her and make sure of the business. Fifteen years was one hell of a long time – he would be almost fifty years old at the end of it.

Hugo followed the channel markers that appeared like milestones out of the dust clouds, until ahead he made out the loom of the jetty and the depot buildings.

There was a figure on the jetty, crouched beside the mountain of dieseline drums. With a prickle of alarm, Hugo strained his eyes in the bad visibility.

'Who the hell is it?' he puzzled aloud. The figure straightened and came forward to stand on the edge of the jetty. Bare-headed, dressed in rumpled dark business suit, the man carried a shotgun in one hand – and it was another few seconds before Hugo recognized him.

'Christ! It's the boss!' Hugo felt alarm flare in his stomach and chest, it tightened his breathing.

Benedict van der Byl jumped down on to the deck of *Wild Goose* at the moment she touched the jetty.

'What's happened?' Benedict demanded as he barged into the wheelhouse.

'I thought you were in hospital,' Hugo countered.

'Who told you that?'

'Your sister.'

'You've seen her? Where is she?'

'I took her out to *Kingfisher*. Like you said. She went out to deal with Lance.'

'Deal with Lance! She's with him, you idiot, she's not with us. She knows the whole deal. Everything!'

'She told me—' Hugo was appalled. But Benedict cut him short.

'The whole thing's blown up. We've got to clear out. Get your crew to load those drums of dieseline into the hold. How are your water tanks?'

'Full.'

'Food?'

'We are stocked up.'

189

'For how long?'

'Three weeks – at a push, four.'

'Thank God for that.' Benedict looked relieved. 'This storm will blow another three days – we'll have that much start. They'll never find us in this. By the time it clears we'll be well on our way.'

'Where to – Angola?'

'God, no! We have to get well clear. South America.'

'South America!'

'Yes – we can do it, carrying extra fuel.'

Hugo was silent a moment, becoming accustomed to the idea.

'We can do it,' Benedict repeated.

'Yes.' Hugo nodded. 'We can do it,' he agreed thoughtfully. For the first time he examined Benedict closely. He saw that he was in an emotional and physical mess, his bloodshot eyes were sunk into deep plum-coloured hollows, dark new beard covered his jowls, and there was a gaunt hunted look to him – like some fugitive animal.

He was filthy with dust, and there was a streak of something that could have been dried vomit down the front of his jacket.

'But what do we do when we get there?' For the first time since he had known Benedict he felt in control. This was the time to deal, to make bargains.

'We'll get ashore on some deserted spot, and then we split up and disappear.'

'What about money?' Hugo spoke carefully. He glanced down at the shotgun. Benedict's hands were fidgety and restless on the weapon.

'I've got money.'

'How much?' Hugo asked.

'Enough.' Benedict blinked cautiously.

'For me also?' Hugo prodded him, and Benedict nodded.

'How much for me?' Hugo went on.

'Ten thousand.'

'Pounds?'

'Pounds,' Benedict agreed.

'That's not enough.' Hugo shook his head. 'I'll need more than that.'

'Twenty.' Benedict increased his bid, but he knew he was playing from weakness into strength. Ruby was lying mutilated in his study, the net was probably being spread for him already.

'Fifty,' said Hugo decisively.

'I haven't that much.'

'Who are you kidding, Buster!' Hugo snorted. 'You've been stacking it away for years.'

Benedict let the barrels of the shotgun swing towards Hugo's belly suggestively.

'Go ahead,' Hugo grinned at him, screwing up his pale albino eyes. 'That'll leave you to paddle this canoe – you want to try it? You'd pile her up on the bar at the entrance – that's how far you'd get.'

Benedict swung the barrels aside.

'Fifty,' he agreed.

'Right!' Hugo spoke briskly. 'Let's get the hell out of here.'

*W*ild Goose was clear of the land, and of the towering blinding dust clouds. The following seas came sweeping up under her stern urging her on her westward flight, while the high-pitched shriek of the wind in her rigging cried to her to hasten.

'Why don't you get down below and grab some sleep?' Hugo said. He found Benedict's restless haunting presence in the crowded wheelhouse disconcerting.

Benedict ignored the suggestion. 'Switch on the radio,' he said.

'What for? You'll get nothing on the set.'

'We are out of the dust,' Benedict replied. 'We might pick up a police message.'

The image of Ruby was so clear in his mind. He wanted to know if they'd found her yet. He felt his gorge rising again. That head – oh God – that head! He crossed quickly to the radio set and switched it on.

'They won't be on to us yet,' said Hugo, but Benedict was manipulating the dials – searching the tortured radio waves. The static wailed and gibbered and shrieked like a maniac.

'Turn it off,' snapped Hugo, and at that moment a voice cut in on them.

' – *Wild Goose*,' said the voice from the loudspeaker quite clearly. Benedict crouched eagerly over the set, his hands busy on the dials, and Hugo came up beside him.

' – Come in, *Wild Goose*. This is *Kingfisher*. I repeat, come in *Wild Goose*—'

Benedict and Hugo looked at each other. 'Don't answer,' said Hugo, but he made no move to intervene as Benedict lifted the microphone off its hook.

'*Kingfisher*, this is *Wild Goose*.'

'Stand by, *Wild Goose*.' The answer came back immediately. 'Stand by for Captain Caporetti.'

'*Wild Goose* standing by.'

Hugo caught Benedict's shoulder and his voice was angrily uncertain.

'Leave it, don't be a fool.'

Benedict shrugged off the hand, and Sergio's voice boomed out of the speaker.

'This is Caporetti – who dat?'

'No names,' Benedict cautioned him. 'Where are your guests?'

'They safe – battened down nicely.'

'Safe? Are you certain? Both of them safe?'

'*Si*. I have them safe and sure.'

'Stand by.' Benedict crouched over the set, and his mind

192

was racing. Johnny Lance was in his power. This was the last chance he would ever have. Plans began to form, gelling quickly in his mind.

'The diamonds. Caporetti has the diamonds. That big Blue is worth a million on its own,' said Hugo. 'If Caporetti has taken care of the others – it would be worth the risk.'

'Yes.' Benedict turned to him, he had been puzzling how he could make Hugo turn back. He had forgotten the diamonds. 'It would be worth it,' he agreed.

'Just a quick pass alongside *Kingfisher* – pick up Caporetti with the diamonds and we'd be on our way.'

'I have to go aboard.' Benedict qualified the suggestion.

'Why?' Hugo asked.

'Wipe out the reel on the computer that carries the programme – it's got the Jap's name on it. They could trace him. I paid him on my Swiss bank. They'll find the account.'

Hugo hesitated. 'No killing – or anything like that. We've got enough trouble without that.'

'You think I'm crazy?' Benedict demanded.

'Okay, then,' Hugo agreed.

'*Kingfisher*,' Benedict spoke into the microphone. 'We are coming to you. I'll be coming on board to finalize matters.'

'Fine.' Through the static they could hear the relief in Sergio's voice. 'I'll be standing by.'

It took nearly two hours for *Wild Goose* to slug her way back to where *Kingfisher* lay beneath the ghostly white shapes of Thunderbolt and Suicide, and it was after midday before Hugo began manoeuvring *Wild Goose* into the big ship's lee.

'Don't waste time,' Hugo cautioned Benedict. 'The sooner we get on our way – the better for all of us.'

'I'll be about half an hour,' Benedict answered. 'You lay off and wait for us.'

'Are you taking that bloody shotgun?' Benedict nodded.

'What for?' But Benedict did not reply, he looked up at the sky. The sun was merely a luminous patch of silver light through the ceiling of sea-fret and wind-driven mist, and still the storm hunted hungrily across the sea.

'It will slow you up on the ladder.' Hugo harped on the shotgun. He wanted very much to part Benedict from it, he wanted it over the side – for its presence aboard would prejudice the plans that Hugo had been forming during the last few hours – plans that took into account the ready market for diamonds in South America, and the undesirability of sharing the proceeds with two partners.

'I'll take it.' Benedict tightened his grip on the stock of the weapon. Without it he would feel naked and vulnerable – and it was part of his own private plans for the future. Benedict's brain had also been busy during the last two hours.

'Suit yourself.' Hugo resigned himself to Benedict's refusal; there would be an opportunity later, during the long passage across the Southern Atlantic. 'You better get up for'ard.'

This time Hugo's approach was neatly executed; in a lull between the colossal swells he touched *Wild Goose*'s bows to the steel side of the factory ship. Benedict stepped across the gap and was up the landing ladder and standing at *Kingfisher*'s rail before the next wave came marching down on them.

He waved Hugo off, then hanging on to the rail, made his way aft to *Kingfisher*'s bridge works.

'Where is Lance?' he demanded of Sergio the moment he stepped on to the bridge, but Sergio glanced significantly at the inquisitively listening helmsman and led Benedict through into his cabin.

'Where is Lance?' Benedict repeated the moment the door was locked.

'He and your sister they are in the conveyor room.'

'The conveyor room?' Benedict was incredulous.

'Si. They find out about Kammy's machine. They open the hatch and go inside. I close both doors. Lock them good.'

'They are in there now?' Benedict asked to gain time to reconstruct his plans.

'Si. Still there.'

'All right.' Benedict reached his decision. 'Now listen, Caporetti, this is what we are going to do. The whole thing has blown up on us. We are going to wipe out as much of the evidence against us as possible, then we are clearing out. We are going to run for South America in *Wild Goose*. You have got the diamonds – haven't you?'

'Si.' Sergio patted the breast of his jacket.

'Give them to me.' Benedict held out his hand, and Sergio grinned.

'I tink I look after them. They keep my heart warm.'

A frown of annoyance narrowed Benedict's eyes, but he let the moment pass.

'All right.' His tone was still friendly. 'Now, what you have to do is get down to the control room and wipe out Kaminikoto's programme.' Get his name off that reel. He showed you how to do that?'

'Si.' Sergio nodded.

'How long will it take?'

'Half an hour, not longer,' Sergio answered, and Benedict checked his wrist watch, sure that this would give him time enough to do what he had to do.

'Good! Get cracking.'

'Boss.' Sergio hesitated at the cabin door. 'What about my boys, my crew? They good boys, no trouble for them?'

'They're clean,' Benedict pointed out irritably. 'I'll get

them together now, and explain that you have to go ashore. They can keep *Kingfisher* hove to waiting for you to come back. After the storm blows out they are bound to radio base and find out we have disappeared. They'll be all right.'

Sergio nodded his satisfaction.

'I'll call them all to the bridge now. You talk to them.'

The five crew members were gathered on *Kingfisher*'s bridge, and Sergio had disappeared down below.

'Any of you speak English?' Benedict demanded, and two of them affirmed that they did.

'Right,' Benedict addressed them. 'You will have been wondering about all the coming and going in this weather. I want you all to be ready to leave the ship. I want you to get all your valuables – now!'

Quickly they translated to the others, who looked apprehensively at Benedict. He was a strange wild-eyed figure with the shotgun tucked under his arm.

'Right – let's go.' And there was no dissent from any of them as they trooped to the companionway.

Benedict followed them along the passageway towards the crew quarters, and glanced quickly at his wrist watch. Seven minutes had elapsed. He looked at the men ahead of him.

The backs of their heads formed a solid target. He had shot guineafowl like that in Namaqualand when they were on the ground running away from him in a thick file, down on one knee and aim for the thicket of heads, knocking down half the flock with both barrels.

He knew he could take all five of these men with two shots. Just let them get a little further ahead so the shot could spread. But he remembered Ruby and his stomach heaved. The other way was just as sure.

'Stop!' he commanded as the five men came level with

the paint store. They obeyed and turned back to face him. Now he held the shotgun so that there was no mistaking its menace. They stared at the gun fearfully.

'Open that door.' He pointed at the paint store. Nobody moved.

'You.' Benedict picked on one of those who spoke English. Like a man in a trance he went to the steel door and spun the locking handle. He pulled the door open.

'In!' Eloquently Benedict gestured with the shotgun. Reluctantly the five of them filed into the small windowless cubicle, and Benedict slammed the door on them. He spun the lock, throwing all his weight on the handle to set it.

Now he had a clear field, and his wrist watch gave him another twenty minutes. He hurried for'ard, he wanted to keep well clear of the control room and Sergio Caporetti.

Using the forward companionway he dropped down to the working deck, fumbling out his duplicate set of keys.

WARNING. EXPLOSIVES. NO UNAUTHORIZED ENTRY.

He unlocked the door, and laying the shotgun flat on the deck he lifted a twenty-five pound drum of plastique down from its rack.

In his haste he tore a fingernail on the lid of the drum, but hardly felt the pain. He uncoiled a six-foot length of the soft dark toffee-coloured material and slung it around his neck. Next he selected a cardboard box of pencil time fuses. He read the label.

'Fourteen-minute delay. That's about right.'

Blood from his torn nail left brown blotches on the cardboard as he took four of the pencils from the box, picked up the shotgun and hurried aft. The jet engine whine of the cyclone mounted deafeningly as he came closer to it.

Tracey was curled on the bare steel plating of the deck with Johnny's jacket folded under her head. She was in a fatigue-drugged sleep, so deep as to be almost deathlike.

Every few minutes Johnny interrupted his restless patrol of the conveyor room to stand over her and look down on her unconscious form. His worried expression softened a little each time he studied her pale lovely face. Once he stooped over her and tenderly lifted a strand of dark hair from her cheek, before resuming his pacing up and down the narrow cabin.

Each time he reached the door of the conveyor room he glanced through the tiny window. The glass had resisted his attempts to smash it with one of the spanners. He had wanted to open the window to call for help, but his efforts had not marked the thick armoured glass.

There was no way out of the cabin. Johnny had tried every possible outlet. The apertures for the conveyor system were guarded at one end by the furnace, and at the other by moving machinery which would ferociously chew to tatters anyone who became entangled in it. They were caged securely, and Johnny paced his cage.

Again he stopped before the peephole, but this time he flung himself at the door with clenched fists. The steel plate smeared the skin from his knuckles as he hammered on it and the pain sobered him. He pressed his face to the glass and through it watched Benedict van der Byl enter the conveyor room and, without glancing at the window, cross to the cyclone.

Benedict laid aside the shotgun he carried and for a moment stood looking up at the thick steel pipe that carried the gravel down from the deck pumps above. As he lifted the thick rope of plastique from around his neck, Johnny knew exactly what he was going to do.

He watched in fascination as Benedict mounted the steel ladder up the side of the cyclone. Hanging with one hand to the ladder, Benedict reached out with the other and clumsily tied the rope of plastique around the gravel pipe. It hung there like a necklace about the throat of some obscene prehistoric monster.

'You bastard! You murdering bloody swine!' Johnny shouted, and again he beat on the steel door with his fists. But the thickness of the door and the whine of the cyclone drowned his voice. Benedict showed no sign of hearing him – but Tracey sat up and looked about her blearily. Then she came to her feet and staggering to the roll and pitch of the ship she went to Johnny and pressed her face to the window beside her.

Benedict was sticking the time pencils into the soft dark explosive. He used all four fuses, taking no chances on a misfire.

'What's he doing?' Tracey asked after she had recovered from the surprise of recognizing her brother.

'He's going to cut the pipe, and let *Kingfisher* pump herself full of gravel.'

'Sink her?' Tracey's voice was sharp with alarm.

'She'll pump water and gravel into herself at pressures that will tear away all the inner bulkheads.'

'This one?' Tracey patted the steel plate.

'It'll pop like a paper bag. God, you have no idea of the power in those pumps.'

'No.' Tracey shook her head. 'He's my brother. He won't do it, Johnny. He couldn't murder us.'

'By the time he's finished – ' Johnny contradicted her grimly, ' – *Kingfisher* will be lying in 200 feet of water. Her hull will be packed so tightly with gravel that it will be like a block of cement. We, and everything in her, including his little machine, will be so flattened as to be unrecognizable. It would cost millions to salvage *Kingfisher* – and no one will care that much.'

'No, not Benedict.' Tracey was almost pleading. 'He's not that bad.'

Johnny interrupted her brusquely. 'He could get away with it. It's a good try – his best chance. Encase all the evidence against him in concrete, and bury it deep.'

'No, Benedict.' Tracey was watching her brother as he climbed down the cyclone ladder and picked up the shotgun. 'Please, Benedict, don't do it.'

Almost as if he had heard her, Benedict turned suddenly and saw the two faces at the window. The shock of guilt held him rigid for a moment as he stared at them – Tracey's pale lips forming words he could not hear, Johnny's eyes burning with accusation.

Benedict dropped his eyes, he made a gesture that was indecisive, almost pathetic. He looked up at the fused and charged rope of explosive – and then he grinned. A sardonic twitching of the lips, and he stumbled out of the cyclone room and was gone.

'He'll come back,' whispered Tracey. 'He won't let it happen.'

'I wouldn't bet on that – if I were you,' said Johnny.

B enedict reached *Kingfisher's* rail and clung to it. He looked out to where *Wild Goose* bobbed and hung on the swells. He saw Hugo's face as a white blob behind the wheelhouse window, but as the little trawler began closing in for the pick-up Benedict waved it away. He glanced at his watch again, then looked back anxiously at the bridge.

The long minutes dragged by. Where the hell was the Italian? Benedict could not leave him – not while he still had that diamond; not while he could stop the dredge pumps and release the prisoners locked below.

Again Benedict checked his watch, twelve minutes since he had set the time pencils. He must go back and find Caporetti. He started back along the rail, and at that moment Sergio appeared on the wing of the bridge. He shouted a question at Benedict that was lost in the wind.

'Come on!' Frantically Benedict beckoned to him. 'Come on! Hurry!'

With another last look about the bridge, Sergio ran to the ladder and climbed down to deck level.

'Where my boys?' he shouted at Benedict. 'Why nobody at the con? What you do with them?'

'They are all right,' Benedict assured him. He had turned to the rail and was signalling *Wild Goose* to come alongside.

'Where they?' Sergio demanded. 'Where my boys?'

'I sent them to—' Benedict's reply was cut off as *Kingfisher*'s deck jarred under their feet. The explosion was a dull concussion in her belly, and Sergio's jaw hung open. Benedict backed away from him along the rail.

'Filth!' Sergio's jaw snapped closed, his whole body appeared to swell with anger.

'You kill them, dirty pig. You kill my boys. You kill Johnny – the girl.'

'Keep away from me.' Benedict braced himself against the rail, leaving both hands free to use the gun.

Not even Sergio would advance into the deadly blank eyes of those muzzles. He paused uncertainly.

'I'll blow your guts all over the deck,' Benedict warned him, and his forefinger was hooked around the trigger.

They stared at each other, and the wind fluttered their hair and tore at their clothing.

'Give me those diamonds,' Benedict commanded, and when Sergio stood unmoving, he went on urgently, 'Don't be a hero, Caporetti. I can gun you down and take them anyway. Give them to me – and our deal is still on. You'll come with us. I'll get you out of here. I swear it.'

Sergio's expression of outrage faded. A moment longer he hesitated.

'Come on, Caporetti. We haven't got much time.' It may have been his imagination, but to Benedict it seemed that

201

Kingfisher's action in the water had altered, she was sluggish to meet the swells and her roll was more pronounced.

'Okay,' said Sergio, and began unbuttoning his jacket. 'You win. I give you.'

Benedict relaxed with relief, and Sergio thrust his hand into his jacket and stepped towards him. He grasped the canvas bag by its neck, and brought it out held like a cosh.

Sergio was close to him, too close for Benedict to swing the shotgun on to him. Sergio's expression became savage, his intentions blazed in his dark eyes as he lifted the canvas bag and poised himself to deliver a blow at Benedict's head, but he had not reckoned with the extraordinary reflexes of the natural athlete he was facing.

As Sergio launched the blow, Benedict rolled his shoulders and head away from it, lifting the butt of the shotgun as a guard. Sergio's wrist struck the seasoned walnut, and he grunted with the pain. His fingers opened nervelessly and the canvas bag flew from his grip, glanced off Benedict's temple and flew on down the deck, sliding to stop against one of the compressed air tanks thirty feet away.

Benedict danced back, dropping the barrels of the shotgun until Sergio looked into the muzzles.

'Hold it, you bastard,' Benedict snarled at him. 'You've made your choice. Now let's see what your guts look like.'

Sergio was hugging his injured wrist to his belly, crouching over it. Benedict was backing away to where the bag lay against the tank. His face was flushed and hectic with anger, but he kept darting side glances at the canvas bag.

At that moment *Kingfisher* took another wave over her bows, and the water came swooshing down the deck, picking up the bag and washing it towards the scuppers.

'Look out!' Sergio shouted. 'The bag! It's going.'

Benedict lunged for it, sprawling full length. With his free hand he grabbed the sodden canvas as it was disappearing over the side. But he was thirty feet away from Sergio, and he still held the shotgun in his other fist. Sergio could not hope to reach him without getting both charges of buckshot in his belly.

Instead Sergio spun round and sprinted back along the deck towards the bridge.

Benedict was on his knees frantically stuffing the bag of diamonds into the side pocket of his jacket and shouting after Sergio.

'Stop! Stop or I'll shoot!'

Sergio did not look back nor check his run, and Benedict had the bag in his pocket and now both hands were free. He lifted the shotgun, and tried to balance himself against *Kingfisher*'s wallowing motion as he aimed.

At the shot, Sergio stumbled slightly but kept on running. He reached the ladder and went up it.

Again Benedict aimed, and the shotgun clapped dully in the wind. This time a spasm of pain shuddered through Sergio's big body, and he froze on the ladder.

Benedict fumbled in his pocket for fresh shells, but before he could reload Sergio had begun climbing again. Benedict broke the gun and thrust the shells into the breech. He snapped the gun closed and looked up just as Sergio disappeared through the storm doors – and the two shots that Benedict loosed after him merely pockmarked the paintwork and starred the glass of the wheelhouse.

'The stupid bastard.' Hugo watched from the wheelhouse of *Wild Goose*. 'He's gone berserk.'

Hugo had heard the explosion and seen the shooting.

'Fifteen years is enough – but not the rope as well.'

He swung the wheel and *Wild Goose* sheered in towards

Kingfisher's side. Peering through the spray and salt-smattered windows, he saw Benedict drag himself to his feet and start after Sergio along the deck.

Hugo snatched the electric loudhailer from its bracket and pulled open the side window of the wheelhouse, holding the hailer to his lips.

'Hey! You stupid bastard, have you gone mad? What the hell you doing?'

Benedict glanced down at the trawler, then ignored it to give all his attention to reloading the gun. He kept going back along the deck, following Sergio to finish him off.

'You'll get us all strung up, you fool,' Hugo called through the loudhailer. 'Leave him. Let's get out of here.'

Benedict kept scrambling and slipping towards *Kingfisher*'s bridge.

'I'm leaving – now! Do you hear me? You can stew in your own pot. I'm getting out.'

Benedict checked and looked down at the trawler. He shouted and pointed at the bridge. Hugo caught one word: 'Diamonds.'

'All right, friend! Do what you like – I'll see you around,' Hugo hailed, and hit the trawler's throttle wide open. The roar of the diesels and the churning of her propeller convinced Benedict.

'Hugo! Wait! Wait for me, I'm coming.' He scampered back to the ladder and started down it.

Hugo throttled back and brought *Wild Goose* in neatly under the ladder.

'Jump!' he shouted through the hailer, and obediently Benedict jumped to hit the foredeck heavily. The shotgun flew from his hands to fall into the water alongside. Benedict cast one longing glance after the gun, then crawled to his feet and limped back to the wheelhouse.

Already *Wild Goose* was plunging away into the wind, but as Benedict entered the wheelhouse Hugo turned on him with his pink albino face set in a snarl of rage.

'What the hell have you done, you bastard? You lied to me. What was that explosion?'

'Explosion – I don't know. What explosion?'

Hugo hit him a stinging open-handed blow across the cheek.

'We agreed no killing – and you put us all on the spot.' Hugo's attention was focused completely on Benedict who had backed into the furthest corner of the wheelhouse. He massaged the dark red finger marks that stained his cheek.

'You set scuttling charges in *Kingfisher* – didn't you, you dirty son of a bitch. God, I hate to think what you've done with Lance and the girl.'

Outside the storm was nearing its climax. A rain squall swept down on *Wild Goose* – a sure sign that the wind must soon drop.

Automatically Hugo switched on the rotating wipers to clear the rain from the screen, as he continued to harangue Benedict.

'I saw you trying to murder the Italian. Christ! What for? He's one of us! Am I next on your list?'

'He had the diamonds,' mumbled Benedict. 'I was trying to get them from him.'

And Hugo's expression changed; he turned away from the wheel and stared at Benedict.

'You haven't got the diamonds? Is that what you're saying?' His tone was almost hurt.

'I tried – he wouldn't—'

And Hugo left the wheel and was across the wheelhouse like a white leopard. He grabbed the front of Benedict's coat, and screamed into his face.

'You left the diamonds! You stick my head in a noose – and I get nothing out of it.'

He was trembling with rage and his pale eyes bulged from their sockets.

Looking into those eyes Benedict realized his own danger. In the time it had taken him to leave *Kingfisher*'s deck and reach the wheelhouse of the trawler he had decided to let Hugo think that Sergio still had the diamonds. Squeamish as Hugo appeared to be about drowning Johnny and Tracey, despite his repeated demands for 'No killing', Benedict knew intuitively that Hugo had no intention of splitting a million pounds' worth of diamonds with him.

Once Hugo was certain that Benedict had the stones on board, Benedict knew there was no chance that he would reach South America alive.

The crossing might take weeks, the crew of the trawler were in Hugo's pay and loyal only to him. Benedict must sleep, and they would take him in the night.

On the other hand, of course, Benedict had no intention of splitting a million pounds' worth of diamonds with Hugo Kramer. He let his voice whine as he cringed in Hugo's grip.

'I tried. Sergio had them. He wouldn't – that's why I shot him.'

Hugo drew back his hand to slap Benedict again. Benedict twisted slightly, and drove his knee into Hugo's crutch, sending him staggering back across the wheelhouse, clutching himself between the legs and whimpering with the pain.

'Right, Kramer,' Benedict spoke softly. 'That's a little lesson for you. Behave yourself, and you'll get your fifty grand on the other side of the Atlantic.'

They stared at each other. Hugo Kramer weak and pale with agony, Benedict standing tall and arrogant again.

'Treat me gently, Kramer. I'm your meal-ticket. Remember it.'

Hugo gaped at him. The positions had reversed so swiftly. He pulled himself upright and his voice was thick with agony, but humble.

'I'm sorry, Mr van der Byl, I lost my temper. It's been a hell of a—'

'Skipper! Ahead!' The warning was shouted by the coloured crewman, Hansie.

Hugo stumbled to the untended wheel, and peered out into the storm.

Wild Goose was shooting down another slope of green water, and just ahead of her bows Hugo saw one of the huge yellow buoys that *Kingfisher* had laid down and then abandoned. It was held captive in the trough of the swells by the anchor cable. The cable was drawn as tight as a rod of steel across the trawler's bows, lifted just above the surface of the water; shivering drops of water flew from it under the tension of the buoy's drag.

'Oh God!' Hugo spun the wheel and threw *Wild Goose*'s engine into reverse – but she was racing down the swell, and her speed was unchecked as the cable scraped harshly along her keel.

Then came the harsh banging and clattering of the drive shaft as the cable fouled the propeller – followed by a crack as the shaft snapped. *Wild Goose*'s engine screamed into overrev as the load was lifted from it.

Hugo shut the throttle, and there was silence in the wheelhouse. *Wild Goose* swung beam on to the seas which came boiling in over her deck. Without her propeller she was transformed from a husky little sea creature to a piece of driftwood at the mercy of each current and the whim of the wind.

Hugo's head swung slowly until he was looking down-wind to where the massive shapes of Thunderbolt and Suicide just showed through the rain squall.

'Cover your ears – tight!' Johnny Lance pressed Tracey against the bulkhead as far from the cyclone room as they could get. 'There are twenty-five pounds of plastique in there – it will blow like a volcano. He will have used short fuse, fourteen minutes. We won't have long to wait.'

Johnny set Tracey's shoulders squarely against the steel plating, and crouched over her – trying to shield her with his own body.

They stared into each other's eyes, teeth clenched, the heels of their palms jammed hard over their ears and they cowered away from the blast that must come.

The minutes passed, the longest minutes of Tracey's life. She could not have borne them without screaming hysteria except for that big hard body covering her – even with it she felt her fear mounting steadily during the molasses drip of time.

Suddenly the air lunged at her, driving the breath from her lungs. Johnny was thrown heavily against her. The blast sucked at her eardrums, and burst in her head so that bright lights flashed across her vision and she felt the steel plates heave under her shoulders.

Then her head cleared, and although her eardrums buzzed and sang, she found with a leaping relief that she was still alive.

She reached out for Johnny, but he was gone. In panic she groped, then opened her eyes. He was lurching down the long conveyor room, and when he reached the locked door at the far end he pressed his face to the peephole.

The fumes of the explosion still filled the cyclone room, a swirling bluish fog, but through them Johnny could make out the shambles that was the aftermath.

The huge cyclone had been torn from its mountings, and now sagged against the far bulkhead – crushed. It was worth only a single glance before Johnny froze into rigidity at the true horror.

The gravel pipe had been severed cleanly just below its juncture with the upper deck. It protruded for six feet, but now the force of the jet through it was flicking and whipping it about as though it were not steel but a rubber garden hose.

The jet was a solid eighteen-inch column, a pillar of brown mud and yellow gravel and sea water that beat against the steel plates of the hull with a hollow drumming roar.

In the few seconds since the explosion the cyclone room was already half-filled with a slimy shifting porridge that rushed from wall to wall with the movement of the ship. It was like some monstrous jelly fish which each second gathered weight and strength.

Tracey reached Johnny's side and he placed his arm around her shoulders. She looked through the armoured glass and he felt her body stiffen.

At that moment the yellow monster spread over the window, obscuring it completely. Johnny felt the first straining of the steel plates under his hands. They fluttered and bulged, then began to protest aloud at the intolerable pressure. A seam started, and a fine jet of filthy water hissed from the gap and soaked icily through Johnny's jersey.

'Get back.' Johnny dragged Tracey away from the squeaking, groaning bulkhead. Back along the narrow conveyor room they stumbled, moving with difficulty for the deck beneath their feet was slanting as Kingfisher began to lean under the increasing weight in her belly.

Still holding Tracey, he reached the locked door and resisted the futile desire to attack it with his bare hands. Instead he forced his brain to work, tried to anticipate the sequence of events that would lead to the final destruction of Kingfisher – and all those aboard her.

Benedict had left the other entrance to the cyclone room wide open. Already that viscous mass of mud and water must be spreading rapidly through the lower levels of the hull, following always the avenue of least resistance – finding the weak spots and bursting through them.

If the walls of the conveyor room held against the pressure, the rest of the hull would be filled and they would be enfolded in the tentacles of that great yellow monster – a small bubble of air trapped within it and taken down with it when it returned to the depths from which it had come.

Would the bulkheads of the conveyor room hold? The answer came almost immediately in the squeal of metal against metal, and the crackle of springing rivets.

The monster had found the weak spot, the aperture through the drying furnace into the conveyor, ripping away the fragile baffles, bursting through the furnace in a cloud of steam, it gushed into the conveyor room bringing with it the sewage stench of deep-sea mud.

Kingfisher made another sluggish roll, so different from her usual spry action, and the mud came racing down the tunnel in a solid knee-high wall.

It slammed both of them back against the steel door with a shocking strength, and the feel of it was cold and loathsome as something long dead and putrefied.

Kingfisher rolled back and the mud slithered away, bunched itself against the far bulkhead then charged at them again.

Waist-deep it struck them, and tried to suck them back with the next roll.

Tracey was screaming now, nerves and muscles reaching their breaking-point. She was clinging to Johnny, coated to the waist in stinking ooze, her eyes and mouth wide open in terror as she watched the mud building up for its next assault.

Johnny groped for some hold to anchor them. They must keep on their feet to survive that next rush of mud. He found the locking handle of the door and braced himself against it, holding Tracey with all his strength.

The mud came again, silently, murderously. It burst over

their heads and punched them with stunning force against the plating.

Then it sucked back once more, and left them down on their knees, anchored only by Johnny's grip on the locking handle.

Tracey was vomiting the foul mud and it filled her ears and eyes and nostrils, clogging them so that it bubbled at her breathing.

Johnny could feel her weakening in his arms, her struggles becoming more feeble as she tried to regain her feet.

His own strength was going. It needed his last reserve to drag them both upright.

The locking handle turned in his fingers, spinning open. The steel door against which he was braced fell away, so that he staggered backwards without support but still clutching Tracey.

There was just a moment to recognize the big, reassuring bulk of Sergio Caporetti beside him and feel an arm like the trunk of a pine tree steady him before the rush of mud down the conveyor room hit them and knocked all three of them down, sending them swirling and rolling end over end before its strength dissipated in the new space beyond the conveyor room door.

Johnny pulled himself up the bulkhead. He had lost Tracey. Dazed but desperate he looked for her, mumbling her name.

He found her swilling aimlessly in the waist-deep mud, floating on her face. He took a handful of muddy hair and lifted her face out, but the mud had hold of his legs, pulling him off balance as it surged back and forth.

'Sergio. Help!' he croaked. 'For God's sake, Sergio.'

And Sergio was there, lifting her like a child in his arms and wading to the ladder that led to the deck above. The mud knocked Johnny down again, and when he surfaced Sergio was climbing steadily up the ladder.

Despite the mud and water that blurred Johnny's eyesight, he could see that Sergio's wide back, from shoulders to hips, was speckled with dozens of punctures as though he had been stabbed repeatedly with a knitting needle. From each tiny wound oozed droplets of blood that spread like brown ink on the blotting-paper of his sodden jacket.

At the head of the companionway Sergio turned, still holding Tracey in his arms; he stood like a Colossus looking down at Johnny wallowing and slipping in the mud below.

'Hey, Lance – go switch off your bloody machine. She drown my ship. I sail her myself now – the right way. No bloody fancy machine.'

Johnny steadied himself against the bulkhead and called up at him:

'Sergio, what happened to Benedict van der Byl, where is he?'

'I think he go with *Wild Goose* – but first he shoot the hell out of me, not half. Fix your machine, no time for talk.'

And he was gone, still carrying Tracey.

Another rush of mud carried Johnny down the flooded passage and threw him against the door to the control room. Already his body seemed to be one aching bruise, and still the battering continued as he tried to unlock and open the control room door.

At last, using the suck of the mud to help him, he yanked it open and went in with a burst of yellow slime following him and flooding the compartment shoulder deep.

Clinging to the console of the computer he reached up and punched the master control buttons.

'Dredge Stop.'

'Dredge engines Stop.'

'Main engines manual.'

'Navigation system manual.'

'All programmes abort.'

Instantly the roar from the severed dredge pipe, which

had echoed through the ship during all their strivings, dwindled as though some vast waterfall had dried. Then there was silence. Though only comparative silence, for the hull still groaned and squeaked at the heart-breaking burden it now carried and the mud slopped and thudded against the plating.

Weak and sick, Johnny clung to the console. He was shivering with cold, and every muscle in his body felt bruised and strained.

Suddenly the ship changed her motion, heaving under his feet like a harpooned whale as she swung broadside to the storm. Johnny roused himself with alarm.

The journey back through the flooded passages to the companionway was an agony of mind and body – for *Kingfisher* was now behaving in a strange and unnatural way.

The scene that awaited Johnny as he dragged himself on to the bridge chilled his soul as the icy mud had chilled his body.

Thunderbolt and Suicide lay less than a furlong off *Kingfisher*'s starboard quarter. Both islands were wreathed in sheets of spray that fumed from the surf that was breaking like cannon-fire on the cliffs.

The maniacal flute of the wind joined with the drum of the surf to produce a symphony fit for the halls of Hell, but above this devil's music Sergio Caporetti bellowed, 'We got no power on port main engine.'

Johnny turned to him. Sergio was hunched over the wheel, and Tracey lay on the deck at his feet like a discarded doll.

'The water, she kill port main.' Sergio was pumping the engine telegraph. Then abandoning the effort, he looked over the side.

The reeking white cliffs were closer now, much closer – as though you could reach out a hand to them. The ship was drifting down rapidly on the wind.

Sergio spun the wheel to full port lock, trying to bring *Kingfisher*'s head round to meet the sea and the wind. She was rolling as no ship was ever meant to roll, hanging over at the limit of each swing, so that the wheelhouse windows seemed but a few feet from the crests of the green waves. She hung like that as though she meant never to come upright again. Then sluggishly, reluctantly, she swung back, speeding up as she reached the perpendicular and the great mass of mud and water in her hull shifted and slammed her over on her other side, pinning her like that for eternal seconds before she could struggle upright again for the cycle to be repeated.

Sergio held the wheel at full lock, but still *Kingfisher* wallowed down towards the cliffs of Thunderbolt and Suicide. The wind had her the way a dog carries a bone in its teeth. Under half power and with her decks awash *Kingfisher* could not break that grip.

Johnny was a helpless spectator, held awe-bound so he could not break away even to succour Tracey who was still lying on the deck. He saw everything with a supernatural clarity – from the dribbling little shot holes in Sergio's back, to the ponderous irresistible rush of the white water up the cliffs that loomed so close alongside.

'She no answer helm. She too sick.' Sergio spoke now in conversational tones which carried with surprising clarity through the uproar of the elements. 'All right then. We go the other way. We take the gap.'

For a moment Johnny did not understand, then he saw it. *Kingfisher*'s bows were coming up to the narrow opening between the two islands.

A passage less than a hundred yards wide at its narrowest point, where the vicious cross-currents met head-on and leapt fifty feet into the air as they collided. Here the surface was obscured by a thick froth of spindrift that heaved and humped up as though the ocean were fighting for breath under the thick cream-coloured blanket.

'No.' Johnny shook his head, staring at that hideous passage. 'We won't make it, Sergio. We won't do it.'

But already Sergio was spinning the wheel from lock to lock, and unbelievably *Kingfisher* was responding. Helped now by the wind she came around slowly, seeming to brush her bows across the white cliff of Thunderbolt, and she steadied her swing and aimed at the gap. It was then Johnny saw it for the first time.

'Christ, there's a boat dead ahead!'

The steep swells had hidden it up to that moment, but now she bobbed up on a crest. It was a tiny trawler, flying a dirty scrap of canvas as a staysail at her stubby mast, and struggling piteously in the granite jaws of Thunderbolt and Suicide.

'*Wild Goose!*' roared Sergio, and he reached for the handle of the foghorn that hung above his head.

'Now we have some fun.' And he yanked the handle. The croaking bellow of the foghorn echoed off the cliffs that were closing on either side of them.

'Kill my boys – hey? Shoot me – hey? Trick me – hey? Now I trick you – but good!' Sergio punctuated his triumphant yells with blasts on the foghorn.

'Christ, no! You can't do it!' Johnny caught urgently at the big Italian's shoulder, but Sergio struck his hand away and steered directly for the trawler as it lay full in the narrow passage.

'I give him plenty warning.' Sergio sent another blast echoing off the cliffs. 'He no give me warning when he shoot me – the bastard.'

There was a group of men on the trawler's foredeck. Johnny could see that they were manhandling an inflatable escape raft, a thick mattress of black rubber, towards the nearest side of the trawler. But now they were frozen by the bellow of *Kingfisher*'s foghorn. They stood looking up at the tall cliff of steel that bore down on them. Their faces were pale blobs in the gloom.

'Sergio. It's murder. Turn away, damn you, you can miss them. Turn away!' Again Johnny lunged across the wheel-house and grabbed at the wheel.

Sergio swung a backhanded blow that cracked against Johnny's temple and sent him reeling back half-stunned against the storm doors.

'Who Captain for this bloody ship!' There was blood on Sergio's lips, the shout had torn something inside him.

Kingfisher's bows were lifting and swinging down like an executioner's axe over the trawler. They were close enough now for Johnny to recognize the men on the trawler's deck – but only one of them held his full attention.

Benedict van der Byl cowered against the trawler's rail, gripping it with both hands. His hair fluttered, soft and dark, in the wind. His eyes were big dark holes like those of a skull in the bone-white face, and his lips a pink circle of terror.

Then suddenly the trawler disappeared under *Kingfisher*'s massive bows, and immediately after that came the splinter-ing crunching sound of her timbers shattering. *Kingfisher* bore on down the passage between the cliffs without a check in her speed.

Johnny fumbled with the catch of the storm doors, and the wind tore it open. He staggered out on to the exposed wing of the bridge and reached the rail.

He stood there with the storm clawing at his clothing and looked down at the wreckage that dragged slowly along *Kingfisher*'s hull, and then was left behind.

There were human heads bobbing among the wreckage, and the wash from *Kingfisher*'s propeller pushed them towards the cliffs of Suicide.

A wave picked up one of the men and carried him swiftly on to the cliff, sweeping him high and then swirling back to leave the body stranded on that smooth white slope of granite.

The man was still alive, Johnny saw him clawing at the

216

smooth rock with his bare fingers, trying to drag himself above the reach of the sea.

It was Hugo Kramer; even through the fog of spray there was no mistaking that head of pale hair and the lithe twisted body.

The next wave reached up and dragged him back over the rock, tearing the nails from his hooked fingers as he tried to find a hold.

He was swirled and flung about in the turbulence below the cliff before another wave lifted him and hurled him on to the granite. One of his legs was broken at the knee by the force of the impact and the lower part of the leg spun loosely like the blade of a windmill as the water tugged at it.

Once again Hugo was left stranded but now he made no movement. His arms were flung wide, and his leg stuck out at a grossly unnatural angle from the knee.

Then from among these mighty waves there rose up a mass of green water which dwarfed all the others.

It reared up with slow majesty and hung poised over the granite cliff before it fell on Hugo's broken body with a boom that seemed to shake the very rock.

When the giant wave drew back, the cliff was washed clean. Hugo was gone.

The same wave that destroyed him came down the passage between the cliffs and, in contrast to its treatment of Hugo Kramer, it was tender as a mother as it lifted *Kingfisher* and carried her out into the open sea beyond the reach of those cruel cliffs.

Looking back into the gap between the islands, the last trace that Johnny saw of the *Wild Goose* was the black rubber escape raft tossing and leaping high on the turmoil of broken water and creamy spindrift.

'They'll have no use for that,' he said aloud. He searched for a sight of any survivor, but there was none. They were chewed to pulp in the jaws of Thunderbolt and Suicide, and swallowed down into the cold green maw of the sea.

Johnny turned away and went back into the wheelhouse. He lifted Tracey from the deck and carried her through to Sergio's cabin.

As he laid her on the bunk he whispered to her, 'I'm glad. I'm glad you didn't see it, my darling.'

A t midnight the wind still howled about the ship, hurling sheets of solid rain against the windows of the bridge. Forty minutes later the wind had veered through a hundred and eighty degrees and become a light south-easterly air. The black sky opened like a theatre curtain, and the full moonlight burst through so brightly as to pale the stars. Though the tall black swells still marched in martial ranks from the north, the gentle wind was soothing and lulling them.

'Sergio, you must rest now. I will take the con. Let Tracey dress your back.'

'You take the con!' Sergio snorted scornfully. 'I save the ship – and you sink her for me. Not bloody likely.'

'Listen, Sergio. We don't know how badly you are hurt. You are killing yourself.'

The same argument spluttered and flared intermittently during the long night hours while Sergio clung stubbornly to the helm and coaxed the labouring vessel back towards Cartridge Bay. He insisted on detouring far out to sea-to avoid the islands, so that when the bright dawn broke, the land was only a low brown line on the horizon and the mountains of the interior were a distant blue.

An hour after dawn Johnny made radio contact with the very agitated operator at Cartridge Bay.

'Mr Lance, we've been trying to raise you since yesterday evening.'

'I've been busy.' Despite his fatigue Johnny grinned at his own understatement. 'Now, listen to me. We are coming into Cartridge Bay. We'll be there in a couple of hours. I want you to have a doctor, Doctor Robin Sutherland, flown up from Cape Town – also I want you to have the police standing by. I want somebody from both the Diamond police and the Robbery and Murder squad – have you got that?'

'The police are here already, Mr Lance. They are looking for Mr Benedict van der Byl. They found his car here – they have a warrant . . .' The operator's voice broke off and Johnny heard the mumble of background voices, then – 'Mr Lance, are you there? Stand by to speak to Inspector Stander of the CID.'

'Negative!' Johnny cut in on his transmission. 'I'm not talking to anybody. He can wait until we get into the Bay. Just you have Doctor Sutherland ready. I've got a badly wounded man on board.'

Johnny leaned over the radio set and shut off the main switch, then he stood and made his way slowly back to the bridge. Every muscle in his body felt stiff and bruised, and he was groggy with tiredness, but he took up the argument with Sergio where they had left off.

'Now listen to me, Sergio. You must lie down. You can take us in over the bar; but now you must get an hour or two's rest.'

Still Sergio would not relinquish the wheel, but he consented to strip to the waist and let Tracey examine his back.

In the expanse of white muscle were little black holes each set in its own purple bruise. Some of the holes had sealed themselves with black clotted blood, from others fluid still oozed – clear or pink in colour – and there was a faint sweetish smell from the wounds.

Johnny and Tracey exchanged worried looks before Tracey reached into the first aid box and set to work.

219

'How she look, Johnny?' Sergio's jovial tone was belied by his face which was a lump of bread dough touched with greenish blue hues.

'Depends if you like your meat rare.' Johnny matched his tone, and Sergio chuckled but cut it short with a wince.

Johnny put a cheroot between Sergio's lips and held a match for him. As Sergio puffed the tip into a glow, Johnny asked casually, 'What made you change your mind?' And Sergio looked up at him quickly, guiltily, through the cloud of cheroot smoke.

'You had us cold. You could have got away with it – perhaps,' Johnny persisted quietly. 'What made you come back?'

'Listen, Johnny. Me, I've done some damned awful bloody things – but I never killed a man or a woman – ever. He said no killing. Fine, I go along. Then I hear the plastique blow. I know you two in conveyor room. I think the hell with it. Now, I climb off the wagon – but she's going too fast. I get bum full of buckshot.'

They were silent for a while. Tracey was absorbed in patching the shot-wounds with adhesive tape.

Johnny broke the silence. 'Was there a big diamond, Sergio? A big blue diamond?'

'Si.' Sergio sighed. 'Such a diamond you will never see again.'

'Benedict had it?'

'Si. Benedict had it.'

'Did he have it on him?'

'In his coat. He put it in his coat pocket.'

Tracey stepped back. 'That's all we can do for now,' she murmured and caught Johnny's eye, shaking her head slightly and frowning with worry. 'The sooner we get him to a doctor the happier I'll be.'

A little before noon Sergio took *Kingfisher* in through the entrance to Cartridge Bay, handling the mud-filled ship with all the aplomb of the master mariner, but as they approached the first turning in the channel he sagged gently to the deck and the wheel spun out of his hands.

Before Johnny could reach the helm, *Kingfisher* had yawed wearily across the channel. She had so little way on her that when she went up on the sand bank there was only a small jolt and she listed over a few degrees.

Johnny pulled the engine telegraph to 'STOP'.

'Help me, Tracey.' He stooped over Sergio and took him under the armpits. Tracey grasped his ankles. Half dragging, half carrying, they got him through to his cabin and laid him on his bunk.

'Hey, Johnny. Sorry, Johnny,' Sergio was mumbling. 'First time I put ship on bank – ever! Idiot! So close – then *wap*! Sorry, hey, Johnny.'

The motor launch left the jetty and came down the channel towards the sand bank on which *Kingfisher* lay stranded. The launch was crowded, and the whine of the outboard engine raised a storm of water fowl into a whirl-wind of frightened wings.

As it drew closer Johnny recognized some of the occu-pants. Mike Shapiro and with him Robin Sutherland, but there were also two uniformed policemen and another person in civilian clothes who stood up in the launch as it came within hail and cupped his hands about his mouth.

'I am a police officer. I have a warrant for the arrest of Benedict—'

Mike Shapiro touched the man's arm, and spoke softly to him. The officer hesitated and glanced up at Johnny again, before nodding agreement and settling back on to his seat.

'Robin, get up here as quick as you can,' Johnny shouted down at the launch, and when Robin came over the side Johnny hustled him towards the bridge, but Mike Shapiro hurried after them.

'Johnny, I must talk to you.'

'It can wait.'

221

'No, it can't.' Mike Shapiro turned to Tracey. 'Won't you take care of the doctor, please? I must speak to Johnny before the police do.'

Mike led Johnny down the deck and offered him a cigarette, while the three policemen hovered at a discreet distance.

'Johnny, I have some dreadful news. I want to break it to you myself.'

Johnny visibly braced himself. 'Yes?'

'It's about Ruby—'

Johnny made his statement to the police inspector in *Kingfisher*'s guest cabin. It took two hours for him to relate the full story, and during that time one of the uniformed policemen discovered the crew locked in the paint store below decks. They were half poisoned with paint fumes but able to make their statements to the police.

The inspector kept them waiting in the next-door cabin while he finished his interrogation of Johnny.

'Two more questions for now, Mr Lance. In your opinion was the collision between the two ships accidental or deliberate?'

Johnny looked into the steel-grey eyes and lied for the first time.

'It was unavoidable.'

The inspector nodded and made a note on his pad.

'Last question. The survivors from the trawler, what were their chances?'

'In that storm they had none. There was no hope of effecting a rescue with *Kingfisher* almost disabled, and considering the condition of the surf in the passage between the islands.'

'I understand.' The inspector nodded. 'Thank you, Mr Lance. That is all for the present.'

Johnny left the cabin and went quickly to the upper deck. Tracey and Robin were still working over Sergio's bunk, but Robin looked up and came immediately to Johnny as he stood in the doorway.

'How is he, Robin?'

'He hasn't a chance,' Robin replied, keeping his voice low. 'One lung has collapsed, and there appear to be perforations of the bowel and intestine. I suspect a massive peritonitis. I can't move him without risking a secondary haemorrhage.'

'Is he conscious?'

Robin shook his head. 'He's going fast. God knows how he has lasted this long.'

Johnny moved across to the bunk and placed his arm about Tracey's shoulders. She moved closer to him and they stood looking down at Sergio.

His eyes were closed, and a dark pelt of new beard covered the lower part of his face. His breathing sawed and hissed loudly in the quiet cabin, and the fever lit bright spots of colour in his cheeks.

'You magnificent old rogue.' Johnny spoke softly, and Sergio's eyes blinked open.

Quickly Johnny stooped to him.

'Sergio. Your crew – your boys are safe.'

Sergio smiled. He closed those dark gazelle eyes, then opened them again and whispered painfully, 'Johnny, you give me job when I come out of prison?'

'They won't have you in prison – you'd lower the tone of the place.'

Sergio tried to laugh. He managed one strangled chuckle, then he came up on his elbows in the bunk with his eyes bulging, his mouth gaping for breath. He coughed once, a harsh tearing sound, and the blood burst from his lips in thick black clots and a bright red spray of droplets.

He fell back on the pillows, and was dead before Robin reached his side.

Tracey was asleep in the bedroom next door. Robin had sedated her heavily enough to keep her that way for the next twelve hours.

Johnny lay naked on the narrow bunk in the second guest room of the Cartridge Bay depot, and when he switched on the beside lamp his wrist watch showed the time as 2.46 in the morning.

He looked down at his own body. The bruises were dark purple and hot angry red across his ribs and flanks from where the mud had battered him against rough steel plating. He wished now that he had accepted the sleeping pills Robin had offered him, for the ache of his body and the whirl of his thoughts had kept him from sleep all that night.

His mind was trapped on a nightmare roundabout, revolving endlessly the two deaths which Benedict van der Byl must answer for in the dark places to which he had surely gone.

Ruby and Sergio. Ruby and Sergio. One he had seen die, the other he could imagine in all its gruesome detail.

Johnny sat up and lit a cigarette, seeking a distraction from the tortured images with which his overexcited brain bombarded him.

He tried to concentrate on reviewing the practical steps that would be necessary to clear up the aftermath of these last disastrous days.

He had spoken that evening by radio to Larsen, and received from him a promise of complete financial support during the time it would take to clear the mud from *Kingfisher*'s hull and recover the diamonds in the conveyor tunnel, and to tide over the period of salvage and repair before the dredger was ready to begin once more harvesting the rich fields of Thunderbolt and Suicide.

A salvage team would fly in tomorrow to begin the work on *Kingfisher*. He had cabled IBM requesting engineers to check out the computer for water damage.

224

Six weeks, Johnny estimated, before *Kingfisher* was ready for sea.

Then his unruly imagination leapt suddenly ahead to Ruby's funeral. It was set for Tuesday next week. Johnny rolled restlessly on his bunk, trying to shut his mind against the thoughts that assaulted it – but they crowded forward in a dark host.

Ruby, Benedict, Sergio, the big blue diamond.

He sat up again, stubbed out his cigarette and reached across to switch out the bedside lamp.

He froze like that, as a new thought pressed in on him. He heard Sergio's voice in his memory.

'Such a diamond as you will never see again.'

Now he felt the idea come ghosting along his spine so that the hair at the nape of his neck and on his forearms prickled with excitement.

'The Red Gods!' he exclaimed, almost shouting the name. And again Sergio's voice spoke.

'In his coat. He put it in his coat pocket.'

Johnny swung his legs off the bunk, and reached for his clothes. He felt the pounding of his heart beneath his fingers as he buttoned his shirt. He pulled on slacks and sweater, tied the laces of his shoes and snatched up a sheepskin jacket as he ran from the room.

He was shrugging on the jacket as he entered the deserted radio room and switched on the lights. He crossed quickly to the chart table and pored over it.

He found the name on the map, and repeated it aloud.

'The Red Gods.'

North of Cartridge Bay the coast ran straight and featureless for thirty miles, then abruptly the line of it was broken by the out-thrust of red rock, poking into the sea like an accuser's finger.

Johnny knew it well. It was his job to find and examine any such natural feature that might act as a barrier to the

225

prevailing inshore currents. At such a place diamonds and other seaborne objects would be thrown ashore.

He remembered the red rock cliffs carved by wind and sea into the grotesque natural statues which gave the place its name, but more important he remembered the litter of ocean debris on the beaches beneath the cliff. Driftwood, waterlogged planking, empty bottles, plastic containers, scraps of nylon fishing-net and corks – all of it cast overboard and carried up by the current to be deposited on this promontory.

He ran his finger down the chart and held it on the dots of Thunderbolt and Suicide. He read the laconic notation over the tiny arrows that flew from the islands towards the stark outline of the Red Gods.

'Current sets South South-West. 5 knots.'

Above the chart table the depot keys hung on their little cuphooks, each labelled and numbered.

Johnny selected the two of them marked 'GARAGE' and 'LAND-ROVER'.

The moon was full and high. The night was still and without a trace of wind. Johnny swung the double doors of the garage open and switched on the parking lights of the Land-Rover. By their glow he checked out the vehicle; petrol tank full, the spare five-gallon cans in their brackets full, the can of drinking-water full. He dipped his finger into the neck of the water container and tasted it. It was clean and sweet. He lifted the passenger seat and checked the compartment beneath it. Jack and tyre spanner, first aid kit, flashlight, signal rockets and smoke flares, water bottle, canvas groundsheet, two cans of survival rations, towrope, tool kit, knapsack, knife and compass. The Land-Rover was equipped to meet any of the emergencies of desert travel.

Johnny climbed behind the wheel and started the engine. He drove quietly and slowly past the depot buildings, not wanting to awaken those sleeping inside, but when he hit the firm sand at the edge of the lagoon he switched on the headlights and gunned the engine.

He cut across the sand dunes at the entrance to the bay, and swung northwards on to the beach. The headlights threw solid white beams into the sea mist, and startled sea-birds rose on flapping ghost wings before the rush of the Land-Rover.

The tide was out and the exposed beach was hard and shiny wet, smooth as a tarmac road. He drove fast, and the white beach crabs were blinded by the headlights and crunched crisply beneath the tyres.

The dawn came early, silhouetting the mystic shapes of the dunes against the red sky.

Once he startled a strand wolf, one of the brown hyenas which scavenged this bleak littoral. It galloped, hunch-shouldered, in hideous panic for the safety of the dunes. Even in his urgency Johnny felt a stir of revulsion for the loathsome creature.

The cold damp rush of the wind into his face refreshed Johnny. It cooled the gritty feeling of his eyes, and eased the throb of sleeplessness in his temples.

The sun burst over the horizon, and lit the Red Gods five miles ahead with all the drama of stage lighting. They glowed golden red in the dawn, a procession of huge half-human shapes that marched into the sea.

As Johnny drove towards them the light and shadow played over the cliffs and he saw a hundred-foot tall figure of Neptune stooping to dip his flowing red beard into the sea, while a monstrous hunchback with the head of a wolf pranced beside him. Ranks of Vestal Virgins in long robes of red rock jostled with the throng of weird and fantastic shapes. It was eerie and disquieting. Johnny curbed his fancy and turned his attention to the beaches at the foot of the cliffs.

What he saw started his skin tingling again, and he

227

pressed the accelerator flat against the floorboards, racing across the wet sand to where a white cloud of seabirds circled and dived and hopped about something that lay at the water's edge.

As he drove towards them a gull flew across the front of the Land-Rover. A long ribbon of something wet and fleshy dangled from its beak, and the gull gulped at it greedily in flight. Its crop was distended and engorged with food.

The seabirds scattered raucously and indignantly as the Land-Rover approached, leaving a human body lying in the centre of an area of sand that was dappled by the prints of their webbed feet, and fouled with dropped feathers and excreta.

Johnny braked the Land-Rover and jumped out. He took one long look at the body, then turned quickly away and braced himself against the side of the vehicle.

His gorge rose in a hot flood of nausea, and he gagged it back.

The body was nude but for a few sodden tatters of clothing and a sea boot still laced on to one foot. The birds had attacked every inch of exposed flesh – except for the scalp. The face was unrecognizable. The nose was gone, the eye sockets were empty black holes. There were no lips to cover the grinning teeth.

Above this ruined face the shock of colourless albino hair looked like a wig placed there as an obscene and tasteless joke.

Hugo Kramer had made the long voyage from Thunderbolt and Suicide to the Red Gods.

Johnny took the canvas groundsheet from under the passenger seat of the Land-Rover. Averting his eyes from the task, he wrapped the corpse carefully, tied the whole bundle with lengths of rope cut from the tow line, then laboriously dragged it up the beach well above the high-water mark.

The thick canvas would keep off the birds, but to make doubly certain Johnny collected the driftwood and planking that was scattered thickly along the high-water line and piled it over the corpse.

Some of the planking was freshly broken and the paint on it was still bright and new. Johnny guessed this was part of the wreckage of *Wild Goose*.

He went back to the Land-Rover, and drove on towards the Red Gods which lay only a mile ahead.

The sun was well up by now, and already its heat was uncomfortable. As he drove he struggled out of the sheepskin jacket without interrupting his search of the beach ahead.

He was looking for another gathering of seagulls, but instead he saw a large black object stranded in the angle formed by the red stone cliffs.

He was fifty yards from it before he realized what it was.

He felt his stomach jar violently and then clench at the shock.

It was a black rubber inflatable life raft – and it had been dragged up the beach *above the high-water line*.

As he climbed out of the Land-Rover Johnny felt his legs trembling beneath him, as though he had just climbed a mountain. The hard knotted sensation in his chest shortened his breathing.

He went slowly towards the raft, and there was a story to read in the soft sand.

The smooth drag mark of the raft, and the two sets of footprints. One set made by bare feet; broad, stubby-toed and with flattened arches, the prints of a man who habitually went barefooted.

These tracks had been made by one of the coloured crew of *Wild Goose*, Johnny decided, dismissed them and turned his whole attention to the other set of footprints.

Shod feet, long and narrow, smooth leather soles; the

imprints were sharp-edged suggesting new shoes little worn, the length of the stride and the depth of prints were those of a tall heavily built man.

Johnny realized with mild surprise that his hands were shaking now, and even his lips quivered. He was like a man in high fever; light-headed, weak and shaking. It was Benedict van der Byl. He knew it with complete and utter certainty. Benedict had survived the maelstrom of Thunderbolt and Suicide.

Johnny balled his fists, squeezing hard and he thrust out his jaw, tightening his lips. Still the hatred washed over his mind in dark hot waves.

'Thank God,' he whispered. 'Thank God. Now I can kill him myself.'

The footprints had churned the sand all about the raft. Beside them lay a thick piece of planking which had been used as a lever to rip the emergency water container and the food locker from the floor-boards of the raft.

The food locker had been ransacked and abandoned. They would be carrying the packets of iron rations in their pockets to save weight, but the water container was gone.

The two sets of prints struck out straight for the dunes. Johnny followed them at a run and lost them immediately in the shifting wind-blown sands of the first dune.

Johnny was undismayed. The dunes persisted for only a thousand yards or so, then gave way inland to the plains and salt flats of the interior.

He ran back to the Land-Rover. He had his emotions under control again. His hatred was reduced to a hard indigestible lump below his ribs, and he contemplated for a few seconds lifting the microphone of the Land-Rover's R/T set and calling Cartridge Bay.

Inspector Stander had the police helicopter parked on the landing-strip behind the depot buildings. He could be here in thirty minutes. An hour later they would have Benedict van der Byl.

Johnny dismissed the idea. Officially Benedict was dead, drowned. No one would look for him in a shallow grave in the wastes of the Namib desert.

The crewman with him would be a complication; but he could be bribed and frightened or threatened. Nothing must stand in the path of his vengeance. Nothing.

Johnny opened the Land-Rover's locker and found the knife. He went to the raft and stabbed the blade through the thick material at a dozen places. The air hissed from the holes, and the raft collapsed slowly.

Johnny bundled it into the back of the Land-Rover. He would bury it in the desert; there must be no evidence that Benedict had come ashore.

He started the engine, engaged the four-wheel drive, and followed the spoor to the foot of the dunes.

He picked his way through the valleys and across the knife-backed ridges of sand.

As he descended the last slope of the dunes he felt the oppressive silence and immensity of the land enfold him. Here, only a mile from the sea, the moderating influence of the cold Benguela current did not reach.

The heat was appalling. Johnny felt the sweat prickling from the pores of his skin and drying instantly in the lethal desiccating air.

He swung the Land-Rover parallel to the line of the dunes and crawled along at walking speed, hanging over the side of the vehicle and searching the ground. The bright specks of mica in the sand bounced the heat of the sun into his face.

He cut the spoor again where it came down off the dunes and went away on it, headed arrow straight at the far line of mountains which were already receding into the blue haze as the heat built up towards noon.

Johnny's progress was a series of rushes where the spoor ran true, broken by halts and painstaking casts on the rocky ridges and areas of broken ground. Twice he left the Land-

Rover to work the spoor through difficult terrain, but across one of the flat white salt pans he covered four miles in as many minutes. The prints were strung like the beads of a necklace, cut clearly through the glistening crust of salt.

Beyond the pan they ran into a maze of black rocks, riven by gullies, and guarded by the tall misshapen monoliths.

In one of the gullies he found Hansie, the little old coloured crewman from *Wild Goose*. His skull had been battered in with the blood-caked rock that lay beside him. The blood had dried slick and shiny, and Hansie stared with dry eyeballs at the merciless sky. His expression was of mild surprise.

The story of this new tragedy was written in the sandy bottom of the gully. In an area of milling, confused prints the two men had argued. Johnny could guess that Hansie had wanted to turn back for the coast. He must have known that the road lay beyond the mountains, a hundred miles away. He wanted to abandon the attempt, try for the coast and Cartridge Bay.

The argument ended when he turned his back on Benedict, and returned on his old tracks.

There was a depression in the sand from which Benedict had picked up the rock and followed him.

Standing over Hansie, and looking down at that pathetic crushed head, Johnny realized for the first time that he was following a maniac.

Benedict van der Byl was insane. He was no longer a man, but a raging demented animal.

'I will kill him,' Johnny promised the old white woolly head at his feet. There was no need for subterfuge now.

If he caught up with Benedict and did it, no court in the world would question but that it was self-defence. Benedict had placed himself beyond the laws of man.

Johnny took the deflated rubber raft and spread it over

Hansie. He anchored the edges of the rubber sheet with rocks.

He drove on into the dancing, shimmering walls of heat with a new mood on him; murderous, elated expectation. He knew that at this moment in time he was part animal also, corrupted by the savagery of the man he was hunting. He wanted payment in full from Benedict van der Byl in his own coin. Life for life, and blood for blood.

A mile farther on he found the water container. It had been flung aside violently, skidding across the sand with the force of its rejection; the water had poured from its open mouth, leaving a dried hollow in the thirsty earth.

Johnny stared at it in disbelief. Not even a maniac would condemn himself to such a horrible ending.

Johnny went across to where the five-gallon brass drum lay on its side. He picked it up and shook it, there was the sloshy sound of a pint or so of liquid in it.

'God!' he whispered, awed and feeling a twinge of pity despite himself. 'He won't last long now.'

He lifted the container to his lips and sucked a mouthful. Immediately his nostrils flared with disgust, and he spat violently, dropping the can and wiping at his lips with the back of his hand.

'Sea water!' he mumbled. He hurried to the Land-Rover and washed out his mouth with sweet water.

How the contamination had occurred he would never know. The raft might have lain for years in *Wild Goose* without its stores being checked or renewed.

From that point onwards Benedict must have known he was doomed. His despair was easy to read in the blundering footsteps. He had started running, with panic driving him. Five hundred yards further on he had fallen heavily into the bed of a dry ravine, and lain for a while before dragging himself up the bank.

Now he had lost direction. The spoor began a long curve

to the northwards, running again. It came round full circle, and where it crossed itself, Benedict had sat down. The marks of his buttocks were unmistakable. He must have controlled his panic here because once more the spoor struck out with determination towards the mountains.

However, within half a mile he had tripped and fallen. Now he was staggering off course again, drifting southwards. Once more he had fallen, but here he had lost a shoe.

Johnny picked it up and read the printed gold lettering on the inner sole. 'BALLY OF SWITZERLAND, SPECIALLY MADE FOR HARRODS. That's our boy Benedict, all right. Forty-guinea black kid,' he muttered grimly, and climbed back into the Land-Rover. His excitement was climaxing now. It would be soon, very soon.

Farther on Benedict had wandered down into the bed of an ancient watercourse, and turned to follow it. His right foot was lacerated by the razor flints in the river bed, and at each pace he had left a little dab of brown crumbly blood. He was staggering like a drunkard.

Johnny zigzagged the Land-Rover through the boulders that choked the watercourse. The gully deepened, and spiky cockscomb ridges of black rock hedged it in on either hand. The air in the watercourse was a heavy blanket of heat. It seared the throat, and dried the mucus in Johnny's nostrils brick hard. A small noon breeze came off the mountains, a sluggish stirring of the heavy air, that provided no relief but seemed only to heighten the bite of the sun and the suffocating oppression of the air.

Scattered along the river bed were bushes of stunted scrub. Grotesque little plants, crippled and malformed by the drought of years.

From one of the bushes ahead of the Land-Rover a monstrous black bird flapped its wings lethargically. Johnny screwed up his eyes, uncertain if it was reality or a mirage of the heat and the tortured air.

Suddenly the bird resolved itself into the jacket of a dark

blue suit. It hung in the thorny branches, the breeze stirring the folds of expensive cloth.

'In his coat. He put it in his coat pocket.'

With eyes only for the jacket, recklessly he pressed down the accelerator and the Land-Rover surged forward. Johnny did not see the knee-high boulder of ironstone in his path. He hit it at twenty miles an hour, and the Land-Rover stopped dead with the squeal of tearing metal. Johnny was flung forward against the steering-wheel, the impact driving the breath from his lungs.

He was still doubled up with the pain of it, wheezing for breath, as he hobbled to the jacket and snatched it out of the bush.

He felt the heavy drag of the weighted pocket.

Then the fat canvas bag was in his hands, the contents crunched nuttily as he tore at the drawstring. Nothing else in the world felt like that.

'Such a diamond as you will never see again.'

The drawstring was knotted tightly. Johnny ran back to the Land-Rover. Frantically he scrabbled in the seat locker and found the knife. He cut the drawstring and dumped the contents of the bag on to the bonnet of the Land-Rover.

'Oh God! Oh sweet God!' he whispered through cracked lips. His eyesight blurred, and the big blue diamond glowed mistily, distorted by the tears that flooded his vision.

It was a full minute before he could bring himself to touch it. Then he did so reverently – as though it were a sacred relic.

Johnny Lance had worked all his life to take a stone such as this.

He held it in both hands and sank down into the scrap of shade beside the body of the Land-Rover.

It was another five minutes before the hot cloying smell of engine oil reached the conscious level of his mind.

He turned his head and saw the slowly spreading pool of it beneath the Land-Rover chassis. Quickly he rolled on to his stomach and, still clutching the diamond, crawled under the vehicle. The ironstone boulder had shattered the engine sump. The Land-Rover had bled its lifeblood into the hot sand of the river bed.

He wriggled out from under the body of the Land-Rover and leaned against the front tyre. He looked at his wrist watch and was surprised to see it was already a few minutes after two o'clock in the afternoon.

He was surprised also at the conscious effort it required to focus his eyes on the dial of the watch. Two days and two nights without sleep, the unremitting emotional strain of those days and nights, the battering his body had taken, the long hours in the heat and the soul-corroding desolation of this lunar landscape – all these had taken their toll. He knew he was as light-headed as in the first stages of inebriation, he was beginning to act irrationally. That sudden reckless charge down the boulder-strewn river bed, which had wrecked the Land-Rover, was a symptom of his present instability.

He fondled the great diamond, touching the warm smooth surface to his lips, rubbing it softly between thumb and forefinger, changing it from hand to hand, while every fibre of his muscles and the very marrow of his bones cried out for rest.

A soft and treacherous lethargy spread through his body and reached out to numb his brain. He closed his eyes for a moment to shut out the flare, and when he opened them again with an effort the time was four o'clock. He scrambled to his feet. The shadows in the gully were longer, the breeze had dropped.

Although he moved with the stiffness of an old man, the sleep had cleared his mind and while he wolfed a packet of biscuits spread with meat paste and washed it down with a mugful of lukewarm water he made his decision.

He buried the canvas bag of rough diamonds in the sand

beneath the Land-Rover, but he could not bring himself to part with the big blue. He buttoned it securely into the back pocket of his slacks. Into the light knapsack from the seat locker he packed the two-pint water bottle, the first aid kit, a small hand-bearing compass, two of the smoke flares and the knife. He checked his pockets for his cigarette lighter and case.

Then without another glance at the radio set on the dashboard of the Land-Rover he turned away and hobbled up the gully on the spoor of Benedict van der Byl.

Within half a mile he had walked the stiffness out of his body, and he lengthened his stride, going well now. The hatred and hunger for vengeance which had died to smouldering ash since he had found the diamonds now flared up again strongly. It gave power to his legs and sharpened his senses.

The spoor turned abruptly up the side of the gully and he lost it on the black rock of the ridge, but found it again on his first cast.

He was closing fast now. The spoor was running across the grain of the land, and Benedict was clearly weakening rapidly. He had fallen repeatedly, crawled on bloody knees over cruel gravel and rock, he had blundered into the scrub bushes and left threads of his clothing on the hooked red-tipped thorns.

Then the spoor led out of the ridges and scrub into another area of low orange-coloured sandhills and Johnny broke into a jog trot. The sun was sliding down the sky, throwing blue shades in the hollows of the dunes and the heat abated so that Johnny's sweat was able to cool him before drying.

Johnny was intent on the staggering footprints, beginning to worry now that he would find Benedict already dead. The signs were those of a man in extreme distress, and still he was driving himself on.

Johnny did not notice the other prints that angled in from the dunes and ran parallel to those of Benedict, until they closed in again and began overlaying the human prints.

Johnny stopped and went down on one knee to examine the broad dog-like pug marks.

'Hyena!' He felt the sick little flutter of revulsion in his stomach as he spoke. He glanced around quickly and saw the other set of prints out on the left.

'A pair of them! They've smelt the blood.'

Johnny began to run on the spoor now. His skin crawled with what he knew could happen when they caught up with a helpless man. The filthiest and most cowardly animals in Africa, but with jaws that could crunch to splinters the thigh bone of a full-grown buffalo, and their thick stubby fangs were coated with such a slime of bacteria from a diet of putrid carrion that their bite was as deadly as that of a black mamba.

'Let me be in time; please God, let me find him in time.'

He heard it then. From beyond the crest of the next dune. The horror of the sound stopped him in mid-stride. It was a shrill giggling gibbering cry that sobbed into silence.

Johnny stood listening, panting wildly from his run.

It came again. The laughter of demons, excited, blood-crazy.

'They've got him.'

Johnny flung himself at the soft slope of sand. He reached the crest and looked down into the saucer-shaped arena formed by the crescent of the dune.

Benedict lay on his back. His white shirt was open to the waist. The blue trousers of his suit were ripped and shredded, exposing his knees. One foot was a bloody lump of sock and congealed dirt.

The pair of hyenas had trampled a path in the sand around his body. They had been circling him for hours, while greed overcame their cowardice.

One hyena sat ten feet from him, squatting obscenely

with its flat snakelike head lowered between humped shoulders. Brown and shaggy, spotted with darker brown, its round ears pricked forward, its black eyes sparkling with greed and excitement as it watched its mate.

The other hyena stood with its front paws on Benedict's chest. Its head was lowered, and its jaws were locked into Benedict's face. It was leaning back, bracing its paws on his chest, tugging viciously as it sought to tear off a mouthful of flesh. Benedict's head was jerking and twitching as the hyena worried it. His legs were kicking weakly, and his hands fluttered on the sand like maimed white birds.

The flesh of his face tore. Johnny heard it distinctly in the utter silence of the desert evening. It tore with the soft sound of silk – and Johnny screamed.

Both hyenas bolted at the scream, scrambling over the far crest of the dune in horrible clownish panic, leaving Benedict lying with a bloody mask for a face.

Looking down at that face Johnny knew he could not kill him now, perhaps could never have killed him. He could not revenge himself on this broken thing with its ruined face and twisted mind.

He dropped on to his knees beside him, and loosened the flap of the knapsack with clumsy fingers.

Benedict's one ear and cheek were hanging over his mouth in a thick flap of torn flesh. The teeth in the side of his jaw were exposed and the blood dribbled and spurted in fine needle jets.

Johnny tore the paper packaging off an absorbent dressing and with it pressed the flap back into place. Holding it there with the full pressure of his spread fingers. The blood soaked through the dressing, but it was slowing at the pressure.

'It's all right, Benedict. I'm here now. You'll be all right,' he whispered hoarsely as he worked. With his free hand he stripped the packaging off another dressing, and substituted it neatly for the sodden one. He maintained the pressure on the clean dressing while he lifted Benedict's head and cradled it in his lap.

'We'll just dry this bleeding up, then we'll give you a drink.' He reached into the first aid kit for a piece of cotton wool and tenderly began to clean the blood and sand from Benedict's nostrils and lips. Benedict's strangled breathing eased a little but still whistled through the black lips. His tongue was swollen, filling his mouth like a fat purple sponge.

'That's better,' Johnny muttered. Still without relaxing pressure on the compress dressing, he got the screw top off the water bottle. Holding his thumb over the opening to regulate the flow, he let a drop of water fall into the dark dry pit of a mouth.

After another ten drops he propped the water bottle in the sand, and massaged Benedict's throat gently to stimulate the swallowing reflex. The unconscious man gulped painfully.

'That's my boy,' Johnny encouraged him, and began again feeding him a drop at a time, crooning softly as he did it.

'You're going to be all right. That's it, swallow it down.'

It took him twenty minutes to administer half a pint of the warm sweet water, and by then the bleeding was negligible. Johnny reached into the kit again and selected two salt and two glucose tablets. He placed them in his own mouth and chewed them to a smooth thin paste then he bent over the mutilated face of the man he had sworn to kill and pressed his own lips against Benedict's swollen dry lips. He injected the solution of salt and glucose into Benedict's mouth, then straightened up and began again dripping the water.

When he had given Benedict another four tablets and half the contents of the water bottle, he stoppered it and returned it to the knapsack. He soaked the compress with bright yellow acriflavine solution, and bandaged it firmly into place. This was a more difficult task than he had anticipated and after a few abortive attempts he passed the bandage under the jaw and over the eyes, swathing Benedict's head completely except for the nose and mouth.

By this time the sun was on the horizon. Johnny stood up and stretched his back and shoulders as he watched the splendid gold and red death of another desert day.

He knew he was delaying his next decision. He reckoned it was five miles to where he had abandoned the Land-Rover in the gully. Five miles of hard going, a round trip of four hours – probably five in the dark. Could he leave Benedict here, get back to the vehicle, radio Cartridge Bay, and return to him?

Johnny swung round and looked up at the dunes. There was his answer. One of the hyenas was squatting on the top of a dune watching him intently. Hunger and the approach of night had made it unnaturally bold.

Johnny shouted an obscenity and made a threatening gesture towards it. The hyena jumped up and loped over the back of the ridge.

'Moon rise at eight tonight. I'll rest until then – and we'll go in the cool,' he decided and lay down on the sand beside Benedict. The lump in his back pocket prodded him, and he took the diamond out and held it in his hand.

In the darkness the hyenas began to cackle and shriek, and when the moon rose it silhouetted their evil shapes on the ridge above the saucer.

'Come on, Benedict. We're going home. There are a couple of nice policemen who want to talk to you.' Johnny lifted him into a sitting position, draped Benedict's arm over his shoulder and came up under him in a fireman's lift.

Johnny stood like that a moment, sinking ankle deep into the soft sand, dismayed at the dead weight of his burden.

'We'll rest every thousand paces,' he promised himself, and began plodding up the dune, counting softly to himself, but knowing that he would not be able to perform that lift again without a rock shelf or some support, against which to brace himself. He had to make it out of the sandhills in one go.

' – Nine hundred and ninety nine. One thousand.' He was counting in his mind only. Husbanding his strength, bowed under the weight, his shoulders and back locked in straining agony, the sand hampering each pace. 'Another five hundred. We'll go another five hundred.'

Behind him padded the two hyenas. They had gobbled the bloody dressings that Johnny had left in the saucer, and the taste of blood was driving them hysterical.

'Right. Just another five hundred.' And Johnny began the third count, and then the fourth, and the fifth.

Johnny felt the drip, drip on the back of his legs. Benedict's head-down position had restarted the bleeding, and the hyenas warbled and wailed at the smell.

'Nearly there, Benedict. Stick it out. Nearly there.'

The first cluster of moon-silver rocks floated towards them and Johnny reeled in amongst them and collapsed face forward. It was a long time before he had regained enough strength to shift Benedict's weight off his shoulders.

He readjusted Benedict's bandages, and fed him a mouthful of water which he swallowed readily. Then Johnny washed down a handful of salt and glucose tablets with two carefully rationed swallows from the water bottle. He rested for twenty minutes by his watch, then using one of the rocks as an anchor he got Benedict across his shoulder again and they went on.

Johnny rested every hour for ten minutes. At one o'clock in the morning they finished the last of the water, and at two o'clock Johnny knew beyond all possibility of doubt that he had missed the watercourse and that he was lost.

He lay against a slab of ironstone, numb with fatigue and despair, and listened to the cackling chorus of death among the rocks nearby. He tried to decide where he had gone wrong. Perhaps the watercourse curved away and he was now moving parallel to it, perhaps he had already crossed it without having recognized it. That was possible, he had heard of others stumbling blindly across a tarmac road without realizing it.

How many ridges had they climbed and descended? He could not remember. There was a place where he had stumbled into a scrub thorn and ripped his legs. Perhaps that was the watercourse.

He crawled across to Benedict.

'Brace up, bucko. We're going back.'

Johnny fell for the last time a little before dawn. When he rolled his head and squinted sideways at his wrist watch it was light enough to read the dial. The time was five o'clock.

He closed his eyes and lay for a long time, he had given up. It had been a good try – but it hadn't worked. In an hour the sun would be up. Then it was finished.

Something was moving near him, soft and stealthy-footed. It was of no interest, he decided. He just wanted to lie here quietly, now that it was finished.

Then he heard the sniffing, the harsh sniffing of a hungry dog. He opened his eyes. The hyena was ten feet away, watching him. Its bottom jaw hung open, and the pink tongue lolled loosely from the side of its mouth. He could smell it, a stink like an animal cage at the zoo, dung and offal and rotting carrion.

Johnny tried to scream, but no sound came from his mouth. His throat was closed, and his tongue filled his mouth. He struggled on to his elbows. The hyena drew back, but without the ludicrous panic of before.

Leisurely it trotted away, and then turned to face him again from a distance of twenty yards. It grinned at him, slurping the pink tongue into its mouth as it gulped saliva.

Johnny dragged himself to where Benedict lay, and looked down at him.

Slowly the blind bandaged head turned towards him, the black lips moved.

'Who's there?' A dry husky whisper. Johnny tried to answer but his voice failed him again. He hawked and chewed painfully, working a trace of moisture into his mouth. Now that Benedict was conscious Johnny's hatred flared again.

'Johnny,' he croaked. 'It's Johnny.'

'Johnny?' Benedict's hand came up and he touched the bandages over his eyes.

'What?'

Johnny reached across, lying on his side, and untied the knot at Benedict's temple. He peeled the bandages from his eyes, and Benedict blinked at him. The light of dawn was stronger now.

'Water?' Benedict asked.

Johnny shook his head.

'Please.'

'None.'

Benedict closed his eyes and then opened them, staring in terror at Johnny.

'Ruby!' Johnny whispered. 'Sergio! Hansie!'

A spasm of guilt twisted Benedict's face, and Johnny leaned closer to him to hiss a single word into his ear.

'Bastard!'

Johnny rested on his elbows, swallowing thickly, then he spoke again.

'Up!' He crawled behind Benedict and pushed and dragged him into a sitting position.

'Look.'

Twenty yards away the two hyenas sat expectantly, leering idiotically and bright-eyed with impatience.

Benedict began to tremble. He made a mewing whimpering sound. Johnny worked him slowly backwards until he had him propped against a rock.

He rested again, leaning on the rock beside Benedict.

'I'm going,' he whispered. 'You stay.'

Benedict made that mewing sound again, shaking his head weakly, staring at the two slobbering animals ahead of him.

Johnny slung the knapsack about his neck. He closed his eyes and called upon the last reserves of his strength. With a heave he got to his knees. Darkness and bright lights obscured his vision. They cleared and he heaved again and he was on his feet. His knees buckled and he grabbed at the rock to steady himself.

'Cheerio!' he whispered. 'Have fun!' And he went lurching and staggering away into the wilderness of black rock.

Behind him the mewing whimper rose to a bubbling scream.

'Johnny. Please, Johnny.'

Johnny closed his mind to that cry, and staggered on.

'Murderer!' screamed Benedict. The accusation checked Johnny. He leaned against another rock for support, and looked back.

Benedict's face was convulsed, and a thin line of bloody froth rimmed his lips. The tears were pouring unashamedly down his cheeks to soak into the blood and antiseptic stained bandages.

'Johnny. My brother. Don't leave me.'

Johnny pushed himself away from the rock. He swayed and almost fell. Then he staggered back to Benedict and slipped down into a sitting position beside him.

From the knapsack he took out the knife and laid it on his lap. Benedict was sobbing and moaning.

'Shut up. Damn you!' whispered Johnny.

245

The sun was well up now. It was burning directly into Johnny's face. He could feel the skin of his cheeks stretching to bursting-point. The veils of darkness kept passing over his vision, but he blinked them away. The flutter of his eyelids was the only movement he had made in the last hour.

The hyenas had closed in. They were pacing nervously back and forth in front of where Johnny and Benedict sat. Now one of them stopped and stretched its neck out, sniffing eagerly at Benedict's blood-clotted foot, creeping inch by inch closer.

Johnny stirred and the creature jumped back, bobbing its head ingratiatingly, grinning as if in apology.

The time had come to fall back on their last line of defence. Johnny hoped he had not left it too late. He was very weak. His eyes and ears were tricking him, his vision jumped and blurred and there was a humming sound in the silence as though the desert was an orchard filled with bees. He spun the cog-wheel of his cigarette lighter and the flame lit. Carefully he applied it to the fuse of the smoke flare, and it spluttered and caught.

Johnny lobbed the flare towards the hyenas, and as the clouds of pink smoke spewed out, they fled in shrieking terror.

An hour later they were back. Slinking out of the rocks, cautious again. Johnny saw them only in flashes, between the bursts of darkness in his head. The insect drone in his ears was louder, it was confusing, making it difficult for him to think clearly.

It took him ten minutes to light the second flare. His throw was so weak that the flare pitched only a few inches beyond his own feet. The pink smoke spread over them.

Johnny felt the blood humming in his ears as the swirling pink clouds engulfed him. The sulphurous bite of the smoke in his throat choked him. The sound in his ears became a drumming roar, a rushing clattering hissing bellow. Then there was a wild wind in the stillness of the desert. Miraculously the smoke cloud was ripped away by the wind.

Johnny looked up into the sky from which the great wind came. Twenty feet above him, hanging on the glistening dragon-fly wing of its rotor, was the police helicopter.

Tracey's face was framed in the cabin window of the helicopter. He saw her lips form his name before he fainted.